D1084625

MASTERS OF SUSPENSE

MASTERS OF SUSPENSE

EDITED BY ELLERY QUEEN
& ELEANOR SULLIVAN

GALAHAD BOOKS

NEW YORK

Published in 1992 by

Galahad Books
A division of LDAP, Inc.
386 Park Avenue South
New York, NY 10016

Galahad Books is a registered trademark of LDAP, Inc.

Published by arrangement with Davis Publications.
Library of Congress Catalog Card Number: 92-70619
ISBN: 0-88365-787-2

Printed in the United States of America.

ACKNOWLEDGMENTS

The editor hereby makes grateful acknowledgment to the following authors and authors' representatives for giving permission to reprint the material in this volume.

Jean L. Backus for *Last Rendezvous*, © 1977 by Jean L. Backus.

Barrie & Jenkins, Ltd. for *This Is Death* by Donald E. Westlake, © 1978 by Barrie & Jenkins, Ltd.

L. E. Behney for *The Man Who Kept His Promise*, © 1966 by Davis Publications, Inc.; and for *Why Don't You Like Me!*, © 1966 by Davis Publications, Inc.

Lloyd Biggle, Jr. for *Have You a Fortune in Your Attic!*, © 1963 by Davis Publications, Inc.

Georges Borchardt, Inc. for *A Drop Too Much* by Ruth Rendell, © 1975 by Ruth Rendell.

Brandt & Brandt Literary Agents, Inc. for *Jericho and the Deadly Errand* by Hugh Pentecost, © 1972 by Hugh Pentecost; for *Jericho and the Studio Murders* by Hugh Pentecost, © 1975 by Hugh Pentecost; for *One for Virgin Tibbs* by John Ball, © 1975 by John Ball; for *The Pool Sharks* by Ursula Curtiss, © 1976 by Ursula Curtiss; and fir *Virgil Tibbs and the Cocktail Napkin* by John Ball, © 1977 by John Ball.

Curtis Brown, Ltd. for *The Killer with No Fingerprints* by Lawrence G. Blochman, © 1964 by Lawrence G. Blochman; for *Nothing But the Truth* by Patricia McGerr, © 1973 by Patricia McGerr; for *The Pencil* by Edmund Crispin, © 1953, renewed by Edmund Crispin; for *A Stroke of Genius* by Victor Canning, © 1964 by Victor Canning. Curtis Brown Associates, Ltd. for *The Happy Brotherhood* by Michael Gilbert, © 1977 by Michael Gilbert.

Curtis Brown Associates, Ltd. for *The Merry Band* by Michael Gilbert, © 1957 by Michael Gilbert.

Barbara Callahan for *The Pinwheel Dream*, © 1977 by Barbara Callahan.

Celia Fremlin for *A Case of Maximum Need*, © 1977 by Celia Fremlin; for *Dangerous Sport*, © 1976 by Celia Fremlin; for *Etiquette for Dying*, © 1976 by Celia Fremlin; and for *Waiting for the Police*, © 1972 by Celia Fremlin.

Brian Garfield for *Charlie's Shell Game*, © 1977 by Brian Garfield; and for *Hunting Accident*, © 1977 by Brian Garfield.

Kathryn Gottlieb for *Dream House*, © 1977 by Kathryn Gottlieb.

Joyce Harrington for *Blue Monday*, © 1976 by Joyce Harrington; and for *The Plastic Jungle*, © 1972 by Joyce Harrington.

Edward D. Hoch for *Captain Leopold Plays a Hunch*, © 1973 by Edward D. Hoch; and for *The Theft of Nick Velvet*, © 1973 by Edward D. Hoch.

International Creative Management for The Men in Black Raincoats by Pete Hamill, © 1977 by Pete Hamill.

Richard Laymon for *Paying Joe Back*, © 1975 by Richard Laymon.

Ann Mackenzie for *I Can't Help Saying Goodbye*, © 1978 by Ann Mackenzie.

Harold Q. Masur for *Murder Never Solves Anything*, © 1976 by Harold Q. Masur; and for *One Thing Leads to Another*, © 1978 by Harold Q. Masur.

Harold Matson Co., Inc. for *Cry Havoc* by Davis Grubb, © 1976 by Davis Grubb.

Florence V. Mayberry for *The Grass Widow*, © 1977 by Florence V. Mayberry.

Vincent McConnor for *Just Like Inspector Maigret*, © 1964 by Davis Publications, Inc.

McIntosh & Otis, Inc. for *When in Rome* by Patricia Highsmith, © 1978 by Patricia Highsmith.

Scott Meredith Literary Agency, Inc. for *Locks Won't Keep You Out* by Nedra Tyre, © 1972 by Nedra Tyre; and for *Still a Cop* by James Holding, © 1975 by James Holding.

Henry T. Parry for *Homage to John Keats*, © 1973 by Henry T. Parry.

Barry Perowne for *Raffles and the Dangerous Game*, © 1976 by Barry Perowne.

Bill Pronzini for *Under the Skin*, © 1977 by Bill Pronzini.

Ellery Queen for *Dead Ringer*, © 1965 by 1968 by Ellery Queen; and for *The Odd Man*, originally appeared in Playboy Magazine, © 1971 by Ellery Queen.

Ernest Savage for *Doc Wharton's Legacy*, © 1977 by Ernest Savage.

Douglas Shea for *Advice, Unlimited*, © 1976 by Douglas Shea.

Larry Sternig Literary Agency for *Nobody Tells Me Anything* by Jack Ritchie, © 1976 by Jack Ritchie; and for *The Seed Caper* by Jack Ritchie, © 1977 by Jack Ritchie.

Thayer Hobson & Company for *The Clue of the Screaming Woman* by Erle Stanley Gardner, © 1948, 1949 by The Curtis Publishing Company, copyright renewed by Jean Bethell Gardner.

Lawrence Treat for *A As in Alibi*, © 1965 by Davis Publications, Inc.

Robert Twohy for *Installment Past Due*, © 1978 by Robert Twohy.

Penelope Wallace and A. P. Watt, Ltd. for *Warm and Dry* by Edgar Wallace, © 1975 by Penelope Wallace.

Thomas Walsh for *The Sacrificial Goat*, © 1977 by Thomas Walsh.

CONTENTS

Still a Cop

Detective:
HAL JOHNSON

Lieutenant Randall telephoned me on Tuesday, catching me in my cell-sized office at the public library just after I'd finished lunch.

"Hal?" he said. "How come you're not out playing patty-cake with the book borrowers?" Randall still resents my leaving the police department to become a library detective—what he calls a "sissy cop." Nowadays my assignments involve nothing more dangerous than tracing stolen and overdue books for the public library.

I said, "Even a library cop has to eat, Lieutenant. What's on your mind?"

"Same old thing. Murder."

"I haven't killed anyone for over a week," I said.

His voice took on a definite chill. "Somebody killed a young fellow we took out of the river this morning. Shot him through the head. And tortured him beforehand."

"Sorry," I said. I'd forgotten how grim it was to be a Homicide cop. "Tortured, did you say?"

"Yeah. Cigar burns all over him. I need information, Hal."

"About what?"

"You ever heard of *The Damion Complex*?"

"Sure. It's the title of a spy novel published last year."

"I thought it might be a book." There was satisfaction in Randall's voice now. "Next question: you have that book in the public library?"

"Of course. Couple of copies probably."

"Do they have different numbers or something to tell them apart?"

"Yes, they do. Why?"

"Find out for me if one of your library copies of *The Damion Complex* has this number on it, will you?" He paused and I could hear paper rustling. "ES4187."

"Right," I said. "I'll get back to you in ten minutes." Then, struck by something familiar about the number, I said, "No, wait, hold it a minute, Lieutenant."

I pulled out of my desk drawer the list of overdue library books I'd received the previous morning and checked it hurriedly. "Bingo," I said into the phone, "I picked up that book with that very number yesterday morning. How about that? Do you want it?"

"I want it."

"For what?"

"Evidence, maybe."

"In your torture-murder case?"

He lost patience. "Look, just get hold of the book for me, Hal. I'll tell you about it when I pick it up, okay?"

"Okay, Lieutenant. When?"

"Ten minutes." He sounded eager.

I hung up and called Ellen on the checkout desk. "Listen, sweetheart," I said to her because it makes her mad to be called sweetheart and she's extremely attractive when she's mad, "can you find me *The Damion Complex,* copy number ES4187? I brought it in yesterday among the overdues."

"The Damion Complex?" She took down the number. "I'll call you back, Hal." She didn't sound a bit mad. Maybe she was softening up at last. I'd asked her to marry me seventeen times in the last six months, but she was still making up her mind.

In two minutes she called me back. "It's out again," she reported. "It went out on card number 3888 yesterday after you brought it in."

Lieutenant Randall was going to love that. "Who is card number 3888?"

"A Miss Oradell Murphy."

"Address?"

She gave it to me, an apartment on Leigh Street.

"Telephone number?"

"I thought you might be able to look that up yourself." She was tart. "I'm busy out here."

"Thank you, sweetheart," I said. "Will you marry me?"

"Not now. I told you I'm busy." She hung up. But she did it more gently than usual, it seemed to me. She *was* softening up. My spirits lifted.

Lieutenant Randall arrived in less than the promised ten minutes. "Where is it?" he asked, fixing me with his cat stare. He seemed too big to fit into my office. "You got it for me?"

I shook my head. "It went out again yesterday. Sorry."

He grunted in disappointment, took a look at my spindly visitor's chair, and decided to remain standing. "Who borrowed it?"

I told him Miss Oradell Murphy, Apartment 3A at the Harrington Arms on Leigh Street.

"Thanks." He tipped a hand and turned to leave.

"Wait a minute. Where you going, Lieutenant?"

"To get the book."

"Those apartments at Harrington Arms are efficiencies," I said. "Mostly occupied by single working women. So maybe Miss Murphy won't be home right now. Why not call first?"

He nodded. I picked up my phone and gave our switchboard girl Miss Murphy's telephone number. Randall fidgeted nervously.

"No answer," the switchboard reported.

I grinned at Randall. "See? Nobody home."

"I need that book." Randall sank into the spindly visitor's chair and sighed in frustration.

"You were going to tell me why."

"Here's why." He fished a damp crumpled bit of paper out of an envelope he took from his pocket. I reached for it. He held it away. "Don't touch it," he said. "We found it on the kid we pulled from the river this morning. It's the only damn thing we *did* find on him. No wallet, no money, no identification, no clothing labels, no nothing. Except for this he was plucked as clean as a chicken. We figure it was overlooked. It was in the bottom of his shirt pocket."

"What's it say?" I could see water-smeared writing.

He grinned unexpectedly, although his yellow eyes didn't seem to realize that the rest of his face was smiling. "It says: *PL Damion Complex ES4187.*"

"That's all?"

"That's all."

"Great bit of deduction, Lieutenant," I said. "You figured the *PL* for Public Library?"

"All by myself."

"So what's it mean?"

"How do I know till I get the damn book?" He sat erect and went on briskly, "Who had the book before Miss Murphy?"

I consulted my overdue list from the day before. "Gregory Hazzard. Desk clerk at the Starlight Motel on City Line. I picked up seven books and fines from him yesterday."

The Lieutenant was silent for a moment. Then, "Give Miss Murphy another try, will you?"

She still didn't answer her phone.

Randall stood up. My chair creaked when he removed his weight. "Let's go see this guy Hazzard."

"Me, too?"

"You, too." He gave me the fleeting grin again. "You're mixed up in this, son."

"I don't see how."

"Your library owns the book. And you belong to the library. So move your tail."

Gregory Hazzard was surprised to see me again so soon. He was a middle-aged skeleton, with a couple of pounds of skin and gristle fitted over his bones so tightly that he looked like the object of an anatomy lesson. His clothes hung on him—snappy men's wear on a scarecrow. "You got all my overdue books yesterday," he greeted me.

"I know, Mr. Hazzard. But my friend here wants to ask you about one of them."

"Who's your friend?" He squinted at Randall.

"Lieutenant Randall, City Police."

Hazzard blinked. "Another cop? We went all through that with the boys from your robbery detail day before yesterday."

Randall's eyes flickered. Otherwise he didn't change expression. "I'm not here about that. I'm interested in one of your library books."

"Which one?"

"The Damion Complex."

Hazzard bobbed his skull on his pipestem neck. "That one. Just a so-so yarn. You can find better spy stories in your newspaper."

Randall ignored that. "You live here in the motel, Mr. Hazzard?"

"No. With my sister down the street a ways, in a duplex."

"This is your address on the library records," I broke in. "The Starlight Motel."

"Sure. Because this is where I read all the books I borrow. And where I work."

"Don't you ever take library books home?" Randall asked.

"No. I leave 'em here, right at this end of the desk, out of the way. I read 'em during slack times, you know? When I finish them I take 'em back to the library and get another batch. I'm a fast reader."

"But your library books were overdue. If you're such a fast reader, how come?"

"He was sick for three weeks," I told Randall. "Only got back to work Saturday."

The Lieutenant's lips tightened and I knew from old experience that he wanted me to shut up. "That right?" he asked Hazzard. "You were sick?"

"As a dog. Thought I was dying. So'd my sister. That's why my books were overdue."

"They were here on the desk all the time you were sick?"

"Right. Cost me a pretty penny in fines, too, I must say. Hey, Mr. Johnson?"

I laughed. "Big deal. Two ninety-four, wasn't it?"

He chuckled so hard I thought I could hear his bones rattle. "Cheapest pleasure we got left, free books from the public library." He sobered suddenly. "What's so important about *The Damion Complex,* Lieutenant?"

"Wish I knew." Randall signaled me with his eyes. "Thanks, Mr. Hazzard, you've been helpful. We'll be in touch." He led the way out to the police car.

On the way back to town he turned aside ten blocks and drove to the Harrington Arms Apartments on Leigh Street. "Maybe we'll get lucky," he said as he pulled up at the curb. "If Murphy's home, get the book from her, Hal, okay? No need to mention the police."

A comely young lady, half out of a nurse's white uniform and evidently just home from work, answered my ring at Apartment 3A. "Yes?" she said, hiding her dishabille by standing behind the door and peering around its edge.

"Miss Oradell Murphy?"

"Yes." She had a fetching way of raising her eyebrows.

I showed her my ID card and gave her a cock-and-bull story about *The Damion Complex* having been issued to her yesterday by mistake. "The book should have been destroyed," I said, "because the previous borrower read it while she was ill with an infectious disease."

"Oh," Miss Murphy said. She gave me the book without further questions.

When I returned to the police car Lieutenant Randall said, "Gimme," and took the book from me, handling it with a finicky delicacy that seemed odd in such a big man. By his tightening lips I could follow his growing frustration as he examined *The Damion Complex*. For it certainly seemed to be just an ordinary copy of another ordinary book from the public library. The library name was stamped on it in the proper places. Identification number ES4187. Card pocket, with regulation date card, inside the front cover. Nothing concealed between its pages, not even a pressed forget-me-not.

"What the hell?" the Lieutenant grunted.

"Code message?" I suggested.

He was contemptuous. "Code message? You mean certain words off certain pages? In that case why was this particular copy specified—number ES4187? Any copy would do."

"Unless the message is in the book itself. In invisible ink? Or indicated by pin pricks over certain words?" I showed my teeth at him. "After all, it's a spy novel."

We went over the book carefully twice before we found the negative. And no wonder. It was very small—no more than half an inch or maybe five-eighths— and shoved deep in the pocket inside the front cover, behind the date card.

Randall held it up to the light. "Too small to make out what it is," I said. "We need a magnifying glass."

"Hell with that." Randall threw his car into gear. "I'll get Jerry to make me a blowup." Jerry is the police photographer. "I'll drop you off at the library."

"Oh, no, Lieutenant, I'm mixed up in this. You said so yourself. I'm sticking until I see what's on that negative." He grunted.

Half an hour later I was in Randall's office at headquarters when the police photographer came in and threw a black-and-white $3^1/_2$-inch by $4^1/_2$-inch print on the Lieutenant's desk. Randall allowed me to look over his shoulder as he examined it.

Its quality was poor. It was grainy from enlargement, and the images were slightly blurred, as though the camera had been moved just as the picture was snapped. But it was plain enough so that you could make out two men sitting facing each other across a desk. One was facing the camera directly; the other showed only as part of a rear-view silhouette—head, right shoulder, right arm.

The right arm, however, extended into the light on the desk top and could be seen quite clearly. It was lifting from an open briefcase on the desk a transparent bag of white powder, about the size of a pound of sugar. The briefcase contained three more similar bags. The man who was full face to the camera was reaching out a hand to accept the bag of white powder.

Lieutenant Randall said nothing for what seemed a long time. Then all he did was grunt noncommittally.

I said, "Heroin, Lieutenant?"

"Could be."

"Big delivery. Who's the guy making the buy? Do you know?"

He shrugged. "We'll find out."

"When you make him, you'll have your murderer.   Isn't that what you're thinking?"

He shrugged again.   "How do you read it, Hal?"

"Easy.   The kid you pulled from the river got this picture somehow, decided to cut himself in by a little blackmail, and got killed for his pains."

"And tortured.   Why tortured?"   Randall was just using me as a sounding board.

"To force him to tell where the negative was hidden?   He wouldn't have taken the negative with him when he braced the dope peddler."

"Hell of a funny place to hide a negative," Randall said.   "You got any ideas about that?"

I went around Randall's desk and sat down.   "I can guess.   The kid sets up his blackmail meeting with the dope peddler, starts out with both the negative and a print of it, like this one, to keep his date.   At the last minute he has second thoughts about carrying the negative with him."

"Where's he starting out from?"   Randall squeezed his hands together.

"The Starlight Motel.   Where else?"

"Go on."

"So maybe he decides to leave the negative in the motel safe and stops at the desk in the lobby to do so.   But Hazzard is in the can, maybe.   Or has stepped out to the restaurant for coffee.   The kid has no time to waste.   So he shoves the little negative into one of Hazzard's library books temporarily, making a quick note of the book title and library number so he can find it again.   You found the note in his shirt pocket.   How's that sound?"

Randall gave me his half grin and said, "So long, Hal.   Thanks for helping."

I stood up.   "I need a ride to the library.   You've wasted my whole afternoon. You going to keep my library book?"

"For a while.   But I'll be in touch."

"You'd better be.   Unless you want to pay a big overdue fine."

It was the following evening before I heard any more from Lieutenant Randall. He telephoned me at home.   "Catch any big bad book thieves today, Hal?" he began in a friendly voice.

"No.   You catch any murderers?"

"Not yet.   But I'm working on it."

I laughed.   "You're calling to report progress, is that it?"

"That's it."   He was as bland as milk.

"Proceed," I said.

"We found out who the murdered kid was."

"Who?"

"A reporter named Joel Homer from Cedar Falls.   Worked for the *Cedar Falls Herald*. The editor tells me Homer was working on a special assignment the last few weeks.   Trying to crack open a story on dope in the Tri-Cities."

"Oho.   Then it *is* dope in the picture?"

"Reasonable to think so, anyway."

"How'd you find out about the kid?   The Starlight Motel?"

"Yeah.   Your friend Hazzard, the desk clerk, identified him for us.   Remembered checking him into Room 18 on Saturday morning.   His overnight bag was still in the room and his car in the parking lot."

"Well, it's nice to know who got killed," I said, "but you always told me you'd rather know who did the killing.   Find out who the guy in the picture is?"

"He runs a ratty café on the river in Overbrook, just out of town.   Name of Williams."

"Did you tie up the robbery squeal Hazzard mentioned when we were out there yesterday?"

"Could be.   One man, masked, held up the night clerk, got him to open the office safe, and cleaned it out.   Nothing much in it, matter of fact—hundred bucks or so."

"Looking for that little negative, you think?"

"Possibly, yeah."

"Why don't you nail this Williams and find out?"

"On the strength of that picture?" Randall said.   "Uh, uh.   That was enough to put him in a killing mood, maybe, but it's certainly not enough to convict him of murder.   He could be buying a pound of sugar.   No, I'm going to be sure of him before I take him."

"How do you figure to make sure of him, for God's sake?"

I shouldn't have asked that, because as a result I found myself, two hours later, sitting across that same desk—the one in the snapshot—from Mr. Williams, suspected murderer.   We were in a sizable back room in Williams' café in Overbrook. A window at the side of the room was open, but the cool weed-scented breeze off the river didn't keep me from sweating.

"You said on the phone you thought I might be interested in a snapshot you found," Williams said.   He was partially bald.   Heavy black eyebrows met over his nose.   The eyes under them looked like brown agate marbles in milk.   He was smoking a fat cigar.

"That's right," I said.

"Why?"

"I figured it could get you in trouble in certain quarters, that's all."

He blew smoke.   "What do you mean by that?"

"It's actually a picture of you buying heroin across this desk right here.   Or maybe selling it."

"Well, well," he said, "that's interesting all right.   If true."   He was either calm and cool or trying hard to appear so.

"It's true," I said.   "You're very plain in the picture.   So's the heroin."   I gave him the tentative smile of a timid, frightened man.   It wasn't hard to do, because I felt both timid and frightened.

"Where is this picture of yours?" Williams asked.

"Right here."   I handed him the print Lieutenant Randall had given me.

He looked at it without any change of expression I could see. Finally he took another drag on his cigar. "This guy does resemble me a little. But how did *you* happen to know that?"

I jerked a thumb over my shoulder. "I been in your café lots of times. I recognized you."

He studied the print. "You're right about one thing. This picture might be misunderstood. So maybe we can deal. What I can't understand is where you found the damn thing."

"In a book I borrowed from the public library."

"A book?" He halted his cigar in midair, startled.

"Yes. A spy novel. I dropped the book accidentally and this picture fell out of the inside card pocket." I put my hand into my jacket pocket and touched the butt of the pistol that Randall had issued me for the occasion. I needed comfort.

"You found this print in a book?"

"Not this print, no. I made it myself out of curiosity. I'm kind of an amateur photographer, see? When I found what I had, I thought maybe you might be interested, that's all. Are you?"

"How many prints did you make?"

"Just the one."

"And where's the negative?"

"I've got it, don't worry."

"With you?"

"You think I'm nuts?" I said defensively. I started a hand toward my hip pocket, then jerked it back nervously.

Mr. Williams smiled and blew cigar smoke. "What do you think might be a fair price?" he asked.

I swallowed. "Would twenty thousand dollars be too much?"

His eyes changed from brown marbles to white slits. "That's pretty steep."

"But you'll pay it?" I tried to put a touch of triumph into my expression.

"Fifteen. When you turn over the negative to me."

"Okay," I said, sighing with relief. "How long will it take you to get the money?"

"No problem. I've got it right here when you're ready to deal." His eyes went to a small safe in a corner of the room. Maybe the heroin was there, too, I thought.

"Hey!" I said. "That's great, Mr. Williams! Because I've got the negative here, too. I was only kidding before." I fitted my right hand around the gun butt in my pocket. With my left I pulled out my wallet and threw it on the desk between us.

"In here?" Williams said, opening the wallet.

"In the little pocket."

He found the tiny negative at once.

He took a magnifying glass from his desk drawer and used it to look at the negative against the ceiling light. Then he nodded, satisfied. He raised his voice a little and said, "Okay, Otto."

Otto? I heard a door behind me scrape over the rug as it was thrust open. Turning in my chair, I saw a big man emerge from a closet and step toward me. My eyes went instantly to the gun in his hand. It was fitted with a silencer, and oddly, the man's right middle finger was curled around the trigger. Then I saw why. The tip of his right index finger was missing. The muzzle of the gun looked as big and dark as Mammoth Cave to me.

"He's all yours, Otto," Williams said. "I've got the negative. No wonder you couldn't find it in the motel safe. The crazy kid hid it in a library book."

"I heard," Otto said flatly.

I still had my hand in my pocket touching the pistol, but I realized I didn't have a chance of beating Otto to a shot, even if I shot through my pocket. I stood up very slowly and faced Otto. He stopped far enough away from me to be just out of reach.

Williams said, "No blood in here this time, Otto. Take him out back. Don't forget his wallet and labels. And it won't hurt to spoil his face a little before you put him in the river. He's local."

Otto kept his eyes on me. They were paler than his skin. He nodded. "I'll handle it."

"Right." Williams started for the door that led to his café kitchen, giving me an utterly indifferent look as he went by. "So long, smart boy," he said. He went through the door and closed it behind him.

Otto cut his eyes to the left to make sure Williams had closed the door tight. I used that split second to dive headfirst over Williams' desk, my hand still in my pocket on my gun. I lit on the floor behind the desk with a painful thump and Williams' desk chair, which I'd overturned in my plunge, came crashing down on top of me.

From the open window at the side of the room a new voice said conversationally, "Drop the gun, Otto."

Apparently Otto didn't drop it fast enough because Lieutenant Randall shot it out of his hand before climbing through the window into the room. Two uniformed cops followed him.

Later, over a pizza and beer in the Trocadero All-Night Diner, Randall said, "We could have taken Williams before. The Narc Squad has known for some time he's a peddler. But we didn't know who was supplying him."

I said stiffly, "I thought I was supposed to be trying to hang a murder on him. How did that Otto character get into the act?"

"After we set up your meeting with Williams, he phoned Otto to come over to his café and take care of another would-be blackmailer."

"Are you telling me you didn't think Williams was the killer?"

Randall shook his head, looking slightly sheepish. "I was pretty sure Williams wouldn't risk Murder One. Not when he had a headlock on somebody who'd do it for him."

"Like Otto?"

"Like Otto."

"Well, just who the hell *is* Otto?"

"He's the other man in the snapshot with Williams."

Something in the way he said it made me ask him, "You mean you knew who he was *before* you asked me to go through that charade tonight?"

"Sure. I recognized him in the picture."

I stopped chewing my pizza and stared at him. I was dumfounded, as they say. "Are you nuts?" I said with my mouth full. "The picture just showed part of a silhouette. From behind, at that. Unrecognizable."

"You didn't look close enough." Randall gulped beer. "His right hand showed in the picture plain. With the end of his right index finger gone."

"But how could you recognize a man from that?"

"Easy. Otto Schmidt of our Narcotics Squad is missing the end of his right index finger. Had it shot off by a junkie in a raid."

"There are maybe a hundred guys around with fingers like that. You must have had more to go on than that, Lieutenant."

"I did. The heroin."

"You recognized that, too?" I was sarcastic.

"Sure. It was the talk of the department a week ago, Hal."

"What was?"

"The heroin. Somebody stole it right out of the Narc Squad's own safe at headquarters." He laughed aloud. "Can you believe it? Two kilos, packaged in four bags, just like in the picture."

I said, "How come it wasn't in the news?"

"You know why. It would make us look like fools."

"Anyway, one bag of heroin looks just like every other," I said, unconvinced.

"You didn't see the *big* blowup I had made of that picture," the lieutenant said. "A little tag on one of the bags came out real clear. You could read it."

All at once I felt very tired. "Don't tell me," I said.

He told me anyway, smiling. "It said: Confiscated, such and such a date, such and such a raid, by the Grandhaven Police Department. That's us, Hal. Remember?"

I sighed. "So you've turned up another crooked cop," I said. "Believe me, I'm glad I'm out of the business, Lieutenant."

"You're *not* out of it." Randall's voice roughened with some emotion I couldn't put a name to. "You're still a cop, Hal."

"I'm an employee of the Grandhaven Public Library."

"Library fuzz. But still a cop."

I shook my head.

"You helped me take a killer tonight, didn't you?"

"Yeah. Because you fed me a lot of jazz about needing somebody who didn't *smell* of cop. Somebody who knew the score but could act the part of a timid greedy citizen trying his hand at blackmail for the first time."

"Otto Schmidt's a city cop. If I'd sent another city cop in there tonight, Otto would have recognized him immediately. That's why I asked you to go."

"You could have told me the facts."

He shook his head. "Why? I thought you'd do better without knowing. And you did. The point is, though, that you *did* it. Helped me nail a killer at considerable risk to yourself. Even if the killer wasn't the one you thought. You didn't do it just for kicks, did you? Or because we found the negative in your library book, for God's sake?"

I shrugged and stood up to leave.

"So you see what I mean?" Lieutenant Randall said. "You're still a cop." He grinned at me. "I'll get the check, Hal. And thanks for the help."

I left without even saying good night. I could feel his yellow eyes on my back all the way out of the diner.

JOYCE HARRINGTON

Blue Monday

She was dressed all in pink. As I boarded the bus behind her, I couldn't stop looking at her pink shoes. Up the high grimy steps they went. Cheap shoes. Flimsy sandals made to last for one summer, if that long. The feet inside them were long and lumpy, as if too many years of ill-fitting shoes had caused them to break out in bumps of protest.

I followed her into the bus, dropped my fare into the change box, and watched her walk up the aisle. The skirt of her pink dress was wrinkled. I tried to imagine where she had spent her day, all her days, the kind of office she worked in, the chair she sat in that had pressed wrinkles into the skirts of all her dresses.

Yesterday she had been all in lavender.

She sat in a window seat in the middle of the bus. As she slid into the seat her pink handbag, a long pouchy thing, swung and thumped against her hip. I walked past her, carefully averting my eyes so that she wouldn't notice that I had been watching her, and chose a seat two rows behind her. From there I could see her shoulders, her neck and the back of her head. I opened my newspaper and settled down for the ride.

On her head she wore a scarf of some filmy material, probably nylon. It was folded into a triangle and tied under her chin. Pink. Through it her hair, arranged in some intricate and unfashionable manner, was visible as a series of knobby clusters of curls. The scarf was evidently intended to keep the knobs in place.

The bus started on its long haul to the suburbs. Normally I read the paper a little, doze a little, look out the window and take note of the small changes that occur along the familiar route and the things that remain the same.

But lately I find my eyes drifting away from the newspaper and from the window and fastening on the back of her head. I no longer doze. Each day the scarf is a different color.

She was talking to her seat companion. I couldn't hear what she was saying. Her head was turned slightly so I could see her lips moving. She wore a pink lipstick and her teeth protruded just enough to give her mouth a somewhat pouting appearance. Against her sallow skin, her mouth seemed to be a separate living organism. She spoke rapidly, interspersing her words with quick half-hearted smiles. When she did this, the side of her face creased into concentric curved lines which would one day be permanent wrinkles. I guessed her age to be about forty.

The bus rattled on through the outlying part of town where ramshackle frame houses lean discouraged against each other down the slope toward the river. Normally I like to look out the window along this stretch of the ride. I was born in this part of town, although the house I grew up in was torn down long ago to make room for a new section of highway. If I feel a bit self-congratulatory as the bus carries me by this decayed remnant of my childhood, I feel I've earned it. I've worked long and hard to give my family a decent place to live.

Lately I have been distracted from even this pleasant satisfaction. I don't quite understand why it should be so, but somehow her presence on the bus produces in me a vague irritability. She is a source of discomfort, and I wish she would take a different bus. I find myself watching for her at the bus stop each evening, waiting to see what her day's color will be, and then, unconsciously at first, but quite deliberately now, taking a seat somewhere behind her so that she is never out of sight.

Let me explain that in twenty-five years of marriage I have never looked at another woman. My wife is small, quiet, and kind. She has never demanded more of me than I could give. I have worked for the same company all my life. I started as a messenger boy and now I am a division manager. A few years ago I realized that I would rise no higher in the company. But I am content.

My division runs smoothly. The typists come to me with their problems and my wife and I attend their weddings. The young men regard me as an old fogey, but they are eager to take advantage of my long experience. Some of them will rise above me in the company; others will leave. It no longer matters. In due time I will retire on full pension.

My life, like my division, has also run smoothly. My children, a boy and a girl, grew up respectful and well-mannered. My son is a science teacher in a high school on the other side of town, and my daughter is married and lives nearby. She is expecting her second child. My wife makes dresses for our three-year-old granddaughter. We have never been plagued with accident or illness, although my wife occasionally suffers from arthritis when the weather is damp.

Why, then, should I be irritated by this woman on the bus? She is nothing to me. If she chooses to dress one day entirely in pink and the next entirely in orange, and so on through the rainbow, surely that's her affair. It needn't concern me. Why do my thoughts persist in speculating on the probable contents of her closet? Particularly on the rows of shoes it must contain, neatly ranked in pairs of every conceivable color. I wonder if she's married, and what her husband thinks of this color mania of hers.

The bus rolled through the belt of light industry that serves as a boundary between town and suburb. My newspaper lay forgotten in my lap. Soon she would be getting off. My own stop lay a half mile farther on. In a way we were neighbors, although I had never seen her anywhere but on the bus.

Suddenly I yearned to know where she lived. I folded my newspaper—my wife likes to read it in the evening after dinner—and felt an unaccustomed quickening of my heartbeat.

She always pulled the signal cord for the bus to stop—even if someone else had pulled it before her, even though the bus always stopped at her corner.   Perhaps she was afraid that if she personally did not pull the cord, the bus would go on and on forever and she would never be able to change into her next day's outfit, red or gray or purple, whatever it might be.   Five or six people stood and lurched down the aisle while the bus was still moving.   I was among them.

On the corner the people fanned out in all directions.   She crossed the main road in front of the bus and headed north.   I stood on the corner feeling slightly displaced and watched the bus drive away.   I instantly regretted having gotten off.   There was nothing for me to do but walk.   I could follow the bus down the road to my usual stop.   Or I could follow her.

At the first gap in the stream of traffic I hurried across the road.   She was about half a long block ahead of me.   She walked with a stiff-legged jouncy stride and the pink handbag swung rhythmically from her arm.   Her pink dress had some kind of ruffled collar and this flapped up and down as she walked.   The tail of the pink scarf fluttered and at one point flew up, exposing the back of her head. I could not distinguish the exact color of her hair, although it seemed to be dark, a kind of dusty brown.

She turned the corner and I hurried to catch up.   My heart pounded and I was having trouble drawing breath.   My legs were trembling from the effort not to run.   When I reached the corner, she was nowhere in sight but the door of the third house from the corner was just closing.   There was no one else on the street.

I walked on casually, taking in as much of the house as I could without stopping. It was a small house, as most of the houses were in this area, and it sat back from the street on a small plot of lawn.   It was painted pale green with darker green trim.   There was a wide front window with green drapes hanging open at the sides, and in the middle a green ceramic lamp with a green shade.   I could see no more without stopping to stare.   It was a house like all the others on the block, unrelenting in its greenness, but in no way out of the ordinary.   With one exception.

The house was surrounded with flower beds.   The flowers tumbled against each other with no regard for order: orange marigolds, purple petunias, stiff zinnias of many colors, daisies and delphinium, nasturtium and portulaca, all thrown in together in heaps and huddles of every kind and color.   It was a surprise.

I walked on down the block.   My eyes still tingled with the shock of those tumultuous flower beds.   My heart slowed to its normal steady pace and I breathed more freely.   My legs, however, were extremely tired and I longed for a place to sit down and rest.

Could she be the gardener?   The creator of that flamboyant atrocity?   Indeed, I suppose she could, although I would have expected something else.   A garden of many kinds of flowers all chosen for a uniformity of color would have been my guess.

It became more and more necessary for me to sit down and pull myself together before going home.   My way took me through the small shopping area of the village: a few shops, a beauty salon, the post office, and a small cocktail lounge. I had never been inside the cocktail lounge.   I knew that some of the bus riders stopped off there occasionally before going home.   I hoped that none would be there to see me—or at least none with whom I had a nodding acquaintance.   I was not in the mood for conversation.

I found myself standing at the bar before my eyes had accustomed themselves to the gloom.   The bartender was attentive.   I have never been much of a drinker and ordered the first thing that came into my head.

"A whiskey sour, please."

I laid my newspaper on the bar and noticed that my hands were stained with ink. The paper was damp where I had clutched it.

"The men's room?" I murmured.

The bartender pointed to a glowing sign at the rear of the long room.

As I made my way down the room I became aware that my hands were not the only part of me that had been sweating.   My clothes felt limp and sodden, and in the air-conditioned chill I began to shiver uncontrollably.   It had been warm outdoors, but not uncomfortably hot.   I wondered if I were coming down with something, a summer cold or a touch of the flu.

I let the hot water run over my hands until the shivering stopped, then washed with the gritty powdered soap from the dispenser.   As the ink ran away down the drain, I glanced into the mirror.   I was shocked by what I saw.

Instantly I blamed it on the distortion of the glass, the fact that the mirror was old and flaked.   But for a split second the face I saw was not my own—or rather it was my own, but with a subtle difference.   The features were those I'd known for many years, the face I shaved each morning, the face whose lines and pouches and discolorations I'd accepted as badges of respectable seniority.   But the mouth had an unpleasant downward quirk, the nose was pinched, and the eyes—the eyes were worst of all.

I dried my hands on the roller towel.   Imagination, I thought.   No sense in feeling guilty over stopping for a quick drink, even though I'd never done it before. Nothing wrong in taking a walk through the quiet suburban streets.   I would have to come up with some reason for getting home late, but there would be no need to lie.   I had never lied to my wife.

"It was such a nice evening, I took a walk and then stopped off for a drink."

Back at the bar my whiskey sour was sitting in a circle of wetness.   I sat on the barstool and glanced around the room.   It was a pleasant enough place, running heavily to wood paneling and beamed ceiling.   There were perhaps five or six other customers.   A man and a woman sat at a table lost in an earnest whispered conversation.   The others were congregated at the end of the bar chatting raucously with the bartender.   Politics or baseball, most likely.   I sipped my drink.   Oh, it tasted good.   It was just what I needed.   Strength flowed back into my legs, and the evil vision in the men's-room mirror faded from my mind.

My wife accepted my explanation without question, but she was a little disappointed that I had forgotten to bring her the newspaper.   I had left it on the bar. I offered to walk down to the stationery store after dinner to get her one.   I detoured past the green house with the flower beds, but saw no one.

The next evening I left the office a few minutes early and hurried to the bus stop.   I wanted to get there before she did, so that I could determine from which direction she came.   Things had gone badly in my division.   A report that was due in the president's office the following morning had been badly botched by a new typist.   She came to me in tears, claiming she had not been given adequate instructions and she couldn't read Mr. Pfister's handwriting anyway and there was no need for him to be insulting.

"He called me a dumb little idiot," she sobbed.

Normally I can settle these upheavals with a few words.   Mr. Pfister was ambitious, ingratiating with those above him and overbearing with those below. The girl probably had some justification.   But as she poured out her woes, I found my eyes wandering to her thin summer blouse.   It had no sleeves and its round neck was cut low.   It quivered with her sobs.   As she bent into her handkerchief I could see that she wore no brassiere.

My thighs trembled in the kneehole of my desk.   Beneath my jacket my shirt grew suddenly clammy.   I wondered if my face had changed into the face I had seen in the men's-room mirror the night before.   I swung my chair around to face the window.

"Go back to your desk," I said.   "Do the report over and see that you get it right, even if it takes you all night."

I heard her gasp and mumble, "Yes, sir."   Her soft footsteps receded.   Before she reached the door, I said, "Miss—um," I couldn't remember her name.   "In the future see that you dress more suitably."

She ran down the hall.   A few minutes later I left and went to the bus stop.

The sky was the color of tarnished brass.   The air was hot and heavy, and little whirlpools of wind lifted bits of scrap paper from the gutter, flapped them about, and dropped them abruptly.   We would have rain.   I stood on the corner and tried to look in all directions at once.   I wanted to see where she came from, to find out, if I could, which building she worked in.   There was still five minutes before the bus was due.

I was watching the entrance to the new glass-fronted office building across the street and might have missed her had not a screaming siren called my attention back down the street to the entrance of my own building.   The police car sped past me bound for some emergency or other, but my eyes remained riveted on the high arched doorway of the building where I had invested all the working years of my life.   She stood just outside the revolving doors, scanning the livid skies. Then she turned and walked with her stiff jouncing stride toward the bus stop.

I faded back into the doorway of a shop.   Could it be possible she worked for my company?   I had never seen her in the elevators or in the lobby.   The company employed hundreds of people.   It occupied the entire building.   There were many divisions and sections.   I suppose there were many people working there whom I didn't know.   That she should be one of them seemed a bad joke on me.

As she neared the bus stop, I saw that she carried a red umbrella.   Had she worn red today because she knew it would rain and she wanted her costume to match her umbrella?   Or had she an umbrella as well as scarf, shoes, and handbag to match every dress in her wardrobe?

Today's red dress was tightly cinched with a red plastic belt.   I had not noticed before how small her waist was, nor that she was very tall.   Below the gleaming belt her haunches flared and filled the red cloth.   The red shoes seemed even more hurtful than yesterday's pink ones.   I was impatient for the bus to appear.

At last it came, and she was among the first to get on.   Have I said that the riders of this bus are extremely well-mannered?   That among this small crowd of homeward-bound suburbanites, it is customary for the gentlemen to stand back and allow the ladies to board first?   I consciously violated that rule.   Pretending absorption in some deep mental problem, I elbowed my way to the door of the bus and chose a seat immediately behind her.   There were a few shocked murmurs, but I ignored them.   She was joined by the same woman who had shared her seat before.

It is truly amazing how much you can learn about a person simply by listening in on fragments of conversation.   For instance, I learned that she was a widow.

". . . when poor Raymond was alive . . ."

That she didn't sleep well.

". . . and those pills didn't help a bit . . ."

That she lived with her invalid sister.

". . . so I said, my sister needs that ramp for her wheel chair, so it'll just have to stay . . ."

That she didn't have a dog.

". . . I'd like to, but she's allergic to animal dander . . ."

And that she would be alone in the house over the weekend.

". . . I have to take her back to the hospital on Saturday for another series of tests.   It may take a week . . ."

And all the while I watched her red mouth swimming in the placid pudding of her face.   Yes, she had changed her lipstick from pink to red.   I noticed, too, that at close range her cheeks were covered with a fine down and there were patches of skin where the pores had coarsened.   I wondered how she failed to notice my scrutiny, but she seemed oblivious.

About halfway home the rain started.   It fell straight down at first, heavy blinding sheets of water.   Lightning flickered on the hilltops and the streets were quickly swamped.   The bus ground slowly on, its windshield wipers barely able to cope with the deluge.   She scarcely noticed the storm, but continued chatting with her neighbor.   Her voice, now that I was close enough to hear it, was jarring and nasal.   She was so very different from my wife.

The rain had slackened off before we reached her stop, but it was still coming down in a fine slanting spray when we got off.   She was safe beneath her red umbrella.   I had no protection but my newspaper.   It seemed ridiculous to hold it over my head.   However I held it, the paper would be soaked before I got home.   I tossed it into a trash can and followed her from the bus stop.

This time I followed quite close behind her. She was engrossed in managing her umbrella, her large red handbag, and a shopping bag from a downtown department store. (Had she shopped in that store today because its shopping bags were red?) Besides, it seemed to me that she was one of those semiconscious people, only becoming aware of others when they had a direct effect on herself. I had no meaning in her life.

I saw her go to the door of the green house, search in her red bag for a key. I passed by as she was struggling to close her umbrella, then heard the door slam shut as I walked on. By the time I reached the cocktail lounge I was drenched and shivering.

"Whiskey," I said to the bartender and went straight to the men's room. I toweled my head on the roller towel and then quite deliberately stood before the mirror. This time I did not look away, but examined my reflection closely as if by doing so I could force my features back into their usual aspect of gentleness and benevolence. I was able to manage a compromise—a mask of bland indifference.

A shot glass was waiting for me on the bar, with a water chaser. I drained it and gestured for another. Tonight I would not have the excuse of taking a walk on a fine evening.

"The bus was delayed. I got soaked, so I stopped for a drink."

No use lying. My wife would smell the whiskey on my breath. When I left the cocktail lounge, I remembered to stop at the stationery store to buy another paper. The rain was only a fine mist now, but I tucked the paper under my jacket and went home.

After dinner, while my wife read the newspaper and I pretended to watch television, I thought about the woman on the bus. Why was it I never saw her in the mornings? Perhaps she took an earlier bus and had breakfast in a coffee shop downtown. Or maybe she took as late a bus as she could so as to spend more time with her invalid sister. How long had she been widowed? Did she have men friends? Did she perhaps go off on weekends with them? Did she have drawers full of underwear of many colors to match her dresses?

"Don't you feel well? You look a bit off-color."

"No, fine. I'm fine. I think I'll go to bed."

My wife had accepted my excuse, only frowned a little over my drinking, and had made me change out of my wet clothes.

"Would you like some hot tea with lemon?"

"Nothing. I'm just tired."

The next evening was Friday. She wore brown, a sad color and one that made her look unhealthy. I'd had a bad day. The vice-president in charge of marketing had named my division as one suffering from antiquated methods, and I had been called on to justify my procedures. Business was bad all over and my results did not look good. Rumors flew in and out of cubicles all afternoon.

I still had not been able to find out where in the company she worked. I didn't even know her name. When I followed her from the bus stop it was without the usual excitement, and my two drinks at the cocktail lounge seemed more a matter of habit than of need. I didn't go into the men's room. As I sat at the bar I thought about my retirement plans.

Years ago I had bought an old farmhouse on an isolated lake in the southeastern part of the state. We always spent our vacations there and many weekends, and I had tinkered it into passably modern condition. When I thought about the time when I would finally leave the company, it was always with the farmhouse in mind. There would be time to read—I had always promised myself that I would one day make up for my lack of a college education by reading all the world's great literature. The fishing was good, and my wife could grow a vegetable garden.

When I got home I didn't bother to make an excuse for my lateness. My wife didn't demand any.

"Would you like to go to the farm this weekend?" she asked.

"No, I don't think so. Maybe next week."

On Saturday I took a walk. There didn't seem to be anyone at home in the green house. No doubt she was with her sister at the hospital.

On Sunday I took the car. I drove past the house twice in the early afternoon. On my third circuit of the block I saw her coming down the drive with her hands full of gardening tools. She wore faded green slacks and a green smock. Her gardening gloves were green and her head was covered with a green scarf. I couldn't see her shoes.

I parked the car around the corner and walked back. The street was deserted except for the two of us.

"What a lovely garden," I called out, hovering on the sidewalk and hoping that my face was safely keeping to its usual unremarkable lines.

"Oh," she said. "Why, thank you. It's a lot of hard work."

"Must be. I never have much luck with flowers. I guess I must be lazy."

"Oh, now," she tittered. "It's not *that* difficult. But people do say I have a green thumb."

"Now, tell me," I said, taking the liberty of crossing the lawn to where she stood. "How do you get such good results with carnations? Mine are always so spindly and have hardly any blooms at all."

I listened to a long harangue on fertilizers, bone meal, and the efficacy of good drainage, nodding wisely all the while, my eyes fixed on her green sneakers. At the conclusion she giggled girlishly and said, "Well, I've talked your ear off and myself into a fine thirst. Would you care for a glass of iced tea?"

"That's very kind of you. It's pretty hot out here in the sun."

"Well, come on inside. It's always nice to meet a fellow gardener. Someone who understands."

I understood. I'd seen her sharp glance at the third finger of my left hand. I've never worn a wedding band.

We went round to the back door. Across half of the back steps lay a sturdily braced wooden ramp.

"My sister," she explained. "She's confined to a wheel chair. She'd be much happier in a nursing home, but after my husband died she insisted on living with me. To keep me company, she says. To keep an eye on me, I say. But don't worry. She's not here today."

We entered the kitchen. It was yellow. Yellow wallpaper, yellow cabinets, yellow cloth on the table. Even a yellow refrigerator. She poured tea into tall yellow glasses.

"Do you live around here?" she asked.

"Not far. I have to confess, I saw your flowers a few days ago and came back in the hope of meeting the person responsible."

"You must be married." She certainly believed in coming to the point.

"I have been." Sometimes a little lie is unavoidable.

"Come into the living room. We can be comfortable there."

The house was small. I stood in the kitchen doorway and looked into the green living room, the magenta dining room, a rose-colored bedroom. On the open door of a closet in the bedroom hung a blue dress. On the floor a pair of blue shoes stood ready. Tomorrow was Monday.

"May I trouble you for another napkin? I've slopped my tea a little."

She obligingly went across the kitchen to a cupboard. I picked up her green gardening gloves. She had large hands. I picked up the knife with which she had sliced a lemon for the tea . . .

Afterward I was really thirsty. I drank the tea. It was slightly warm. My clothes were damp. I left the green gardening gloves on the yellow counter. I went out by the back door and drove home.

On Monday morning the office was agog. One of the telephone operators had been brutally murdered in her home. The police came and interviewed everyone who had known her. They ignored my division. The rumor that went the rounds had it that she had been stabbed twenty-seven times. It seemed a bit exaggerated to me. My division ran smoothly that day.

In the evening I went to the bus stop. I looked for her in her blue dress, but she didn't come. Maybe she had taken an earlier bus. Or perhaps she was working late. She could even be on vacation.

I settled down on the bus and opened my newspaper. The woman sitting in front of me had the most irritating way of shaking her head as she talked to her seat companion. She wore long dangling earrings and they distracted me from my newspaper, from the view out the bus window.

Perhaps I'll take the early retirement option.

ROBERT TWOHY

Installment Past Due

The phone rang. Moorman was lying on his back, on the couch. He was a large man, pushing forty, tousled and unshaved this morning in October. He wore a T-shirt, old slacks, no shoes. A glass of white wine was balanced on his stomach; a bottle of it stood on the floor. It was about eleven o'clock.

Moorman set the glass carefully on the floor, reached back over his head, and groped until his hand connected with the phone on the end table. He put it to his head and said in deep gentle tones, "I'm terribly sorry, but your application is rejected."

A moment of silence. Then, "What?"

"You heard me, Kleistershtroven."

"Klei . . . what is this?"

"You *are* Kleistershtroven, aren't you?"

"No."

"I didn't say you were. Who'd want a name like that? Is it a Welsh name?"

"Listen, is this Mr. Moorman?"

"That doesn't matter. The fact is that no more entries for the quadrennial bobsled steeplechase are being accepted. That's on orders from my psychoanalyst. Would you care for his address?"

"This is Mr. Dooney." The voice was suddenly sepulchral.

Moorman said eagerly, "Dooney? Mr. Dooney? *The* Mr. Dooney? Calling *me*? At this hour?"

"Is this Mr. Moorman?"

"It certainly is. Are you really Mr. Dooney? Well, how in the world are you? How's the wife and all the brood? How's Miss LaTorche?"

"Miss LaTorche?"

Moorman emitted rich laughter. "Come on, Dooley, you old lecher, who do you think you're talking to? Everybody knows about you and Fifi LaTorche!"

"Who is this? Is this Jack Moorman?"

"Wait a minute, I'll find out."

Moorman put his hand lightly over the mouthpiece, and made loud braying noises. Then he said into the phone, "Yeah, Dr. Kleistershtroven says there's no question about it—I've been Moorman for years. Days, even."

"This is Mr. Dooney of Affiliated Finance.   I talked to Mrs. Moorman on Friday—is she there?"

"Is she where?"

"Is she home?"

"Hold on."   He took the mouthpiece from his mouth, turned his head, and called, "Lisa, some character named Dooley wonders if you're home . . . Where? I don't know where.   I'll ask him."

He said into the phone, "She wants to know where you want to go, and if she should wear anything."

There was deep breathing.   Moorman said admiringly, "You're a terrific deep breather!"

The voice was low and deadly: "I don't know what you're trying to pull here, Mr. Moorman.   You've made a loan through us, and I talked to Mrs. Moorman on Friday and she said the payment would be in the mail.   And this is Monday, and—"

"Don't tell me—let me guess.   There's nothing in the mail, right?"

"I want to know why not."

"I can explain that.   I put the check in one of those new self-destructing envelopes and must have miscalculated the time it would take to reach you.   It must have blown up in the mailbox."

"That's very funny," said Mr. Dooney, after a long silence.   "Your wife promised Friday that the payment would be in the mail."

"Well, that's Lisa—always the cheerful word.   You can't blame her for that. A recent Harris survey indicates that too much bad news is given over the telephone."

"You're very funny, Mr. Moorman.   But this isn't funny—this is serious.   You have an account with us for $784.47.   Your September payment of $71.88 was due two weeks ago, and we haven't received it.   We have a chattel mortgage on your furniture . . . I'm on the verge of going to the sheriff.   But on the way I'm willing to stop by your place."

"Well, Lisa's not here.   And things are kind of a mess."

"I'm leaving my office right now.   When I get there I expect a check."

"When you get here I expect a disappointed man.   But come anyway.   I have some white wine and salami."

"I'm bringing Mr. Hector with me."

"That's okay.   I have plenty of salami . . . Hector, eh?   Do I know him?"

"No, you don't.   I bring Mr. Hector when I want to convince someone that paying legitimate bills isn't a matter for joking.   Do you understand?"

"Not really.   But he sounds like an interesting guy . . . Does he like salami and white wine?"

"We'll be there in twenty minutes."

"Good.   Be nice to see you both."

He hung up, and sipped wine, then lay back, placing the glass on his stomach. There was a pleasant smile on his face.

*   *   *

Inside twenty minutes the door chime sounded.   Moorman set the glass on the floor, bounced from the couch, ran to the door, and threw it open, calling, "So good of you to come!   How are you?   It's Colonel Kleistershtroven, isn't it, formerly with the S.S.?   How I remember those wonderful seminars of yours! . . . Ah, you brought a friend with you . . . don't I know him from somewhere?"

He had grasped the nearer man's hand, pumped it, and still held it as he peered in a benevolent manner at the other man.   The man whose hand he held wore a neat tan suit, and had a pallid, tense young face with harried eyes.   The other man was small, narrow-shouldered, balding, dressed in a dark suit; he had tight lips and cold eyes enlarged by thick-lensed glasses.

The first man, grimacing angrily, pulled his hand free.   "I'm Mr. Dooney. This is Mr. Hector."

"Don't I know you, Mr. Hector?"

Mr. Hector's lips went tighter, and he shook his head.

"Sure I do!   I've seen you plenty, out at the track."

Mr. Hector's enlarged eyes became more so.   He shook his head harder.

"Sure, you're the guy."   Moorman laughed in a friendly fashion.   "You're pretty well-known out there.   Everybody calls you 'The Stooper.' "

Mr. Hector said, in a strained voice, "What are you talking about?"

"He's being funny," said Mr. Dooney.   "He thinks he's a comedian.   He thinks this is all a joke."

"It isn't a joke," said Mr. Hector, and hefted his briefcase.

"Sure, the old Stooper—goes around picking up discarded mutuel tickets, looking for a winner somebody missed.   You get many of those, Stoop?   Is it a living?" He made to pat Mr. Hector in a comradely way on the shoulder; Mr. Hector twisted his narrow shoulder away from Moorman.

Dooney said, "The joke's just about over, Moorman."

"Oh.   Well, why don't you come in?"   His broad frame filled the doorway. "Why are you standing around in the hot sun?   Come in, come in . . . How're the wife and all the brood?   How's Miss LaTorche?"

He stepped back.   Dooney proceeded in, his face stony.   Mr. Hector followed.

"Sit down," said Moorman.   "Sit down anywhere.   Take that chair there, Stoop.   Just throw the clothes on the floor.   They're fresh ironed, but what's that to you?   Like you say—*you* don't have to wear 'em.   Just pitch 'em in the corner . . . right?"

Mr. Hector stared at him, then walked away across the room.   There was a folding chair near the dining table.   He sat down on it, with his briefcase on his knees, and looked at Moorman, his narrow face lowered and his lips drawn in.

Moorman dropped on the couch, crossing his legs.   "Where are *you* going to sit, Dooley?"

"Dooney."

"Right, Dooney.   Where are *you* going to sit?"

"I'll sit in this chair here."

"There's an applecore on it."

"I can see the applecore. I'll remove it."

"Good thinking." Moorman nodded approvingly as Dooney picked up the applecore by the stem and dropped it in the near fireplace. "That's a good place for it. You must have been raised in the country. Nothing like a frosty night with the wind howling, and the sweet smell of roasting applecores . . . remember those nights, Dooley?" He blinked, and nodded, smiling reminiscently.

Dooney sat down. He said, his voice flat, "This has been very amusing, Moorman. You're a very funny fellow. Now it's time to face some realities that are going to be a little bit harsher. Do you know what failure to meet the terms of a contract means?"

"Not really, no. Do *you* know, Stoop?"

"Stop calling him Stoop!"

"He doesn't mind, he's used to it. Everybody at the track calls him that." He smiled genially at Mr. Hector, whose thin lips became thinner. "Well, Dooley, what's on your mind? What can I do for you?"

"You can write me a check for $71.88. That's what you can do."

"Sure, I can do that easy enough. Is that all you want?" He slapped various pockets. "I don't seem to have my checkbook. Maybe Lisa's got it. Sorry. Well, I'll get it in the mail tonight—okay? As you know, my word is my bond." He smiled widely.

Dooney said, "You think you're such a comedian. Well, here are some facts." His forefinger picked out various articles in the room. "That color TV there, that dining table, those bookcases, the rug, the drapes—they're all going out of here. All of them. Today, this afternoon. And the beds in the bedroom, and the washing machine in the kitchen. When we leave here, we're going directly to the sheriff. We're going to get an order, Mr. Moorman—Mr. Hector is our company lawyer. He has the contract there in his briefcase—the contract you and Mrs. Moorman signed in our office. You're delinquent. You think it's all a big joke don't you? Tell him, Mr. Hector."

Mr. Hector nodded, fished in his briefcase, and pulled out a document. "This is the contract. It's all here, all signed and witnessed. There's no legal way to block appropriation. The furniture and appliances are all covered by the chattel mortgage—and as of now, it all belongs to Affiliated Finance."

"Oh." Moorman rubbed his jaw and looked solemn. "Well, all right. But I should tell you that the TV doesn't work too good. You got to keep kicking it to hold the picture. When you want to watch it, get some guy to stand by it and boot it every ten seconds. Otherwise, you have to keep throwing things at it."

Mr. Hector looked at him with huge glazed eyes. Moorman said, "Before you escalate your terror tactics . . . you claim to be a lawyer?"

"I am a lawyer."

"Anybody can say that. Do you have a badge?"

"A badge?"

"I didn't think so. Also, a real lawyer always carries a diploma."

"I have a diploma in my office."

"And I have a Thompson submachine gun in *my* office.   That makes me the neighborhood hit man."

Dooney said, "This is one of his jokes, Morris—don't pay any attention."

"You say it's a joke?"   Moorman sat forward, large hands clasped, face intent, brows drawn down.   "Is that what I am to you?   Is that what all of us are, all us little people who grub in the grime for our washing machines and color TVs, who sweat and strain to make our monthly payments so you and your flunky here can spend the day joy-riding around in your swanky Mercedes-Benz—"

"I have a Pontiac—'72 Pontiac."

"Whatever.   Is that what we are to you—just a contemptible joke?"

He whipped his anguished face to Mr. Hector and jabbed a finger at him, his face gone suddenly hard and grim.   "I want the simple truth, fellow—that's all I'm asking.   You're The Stooper, and I know it and you know it.   Your boss here doesn't know it, but—"

"He's not my boss."

"Well, whatever he is to you . . . that's none of my affair, I'm not going to open *that* can of worms.   But the point is, you claim to know something about the law—"

"I'm a lawyer!"

"Yeah.   You bragged about your famous diploma.   Where'd you get it, some correspondence course advertised on a book of matches?   Even from there you should have learned one thing—that if you can't prove the signatures on a contract are valid, that contract isn't worth the paper it's printed on."

Mr. Hector said, "Are you saying that these are not valid signatures?"

"Of course they're valid.   Who says they're not?   Are you implying that there's been a detent to infraud?"

"This is ridiculous," said Dooney.   "Stop it, Moorman—we're busy men."

"Yeah.   It's almost noon.   You're probably hungry . . . Want some salami?"

"No."

"Bet Stoop does.   He looks like he could use a good meal."

He went into the kitchen.   They heard him whistling.

Mr. Hector muttered, "I've got a headache.   This guy is crazy."

Dooney nodded glumly.

Moorman called, "How do you want your salami?"

"We don't.   We're going, but we'll be back.   With the sheriff."

Moorman came in.   He bore in his right hand a four-foot salami.   "Stick around, there's plenty.   Stoop really looks hungry.   Look at his eyes bug out at the sight of this!"   He beamed at Mr. Hector.   "Really go for salami, eh, Stoop?   You want to wait for a knife, or you just want to start chewing?"

Mr. Hector was tucking the contract in his briefcase.   Moorman tossed the salami gently so that it landed across Mr. Hector's knees.   The lawyer stared at it in wonderment.

"You want one, Rooney?   I got a couple more . . . If you don't want to eat it now, Stoop, shove it in your briefcase."

Dooney was on his feet.   Mr. Hector stood up too, the salami rolling off his lap to the rug.

Dooney said, "Enjoy your joke.   It'll be a lot of fun when Mrs. Moorman comes home and you tell her that all the furniture and the color TV and the beds and the washing machine are gone."

Moorman was quiet.   His face looked suddenly strange and still.

He murmured, "I wish I could."

He had turned and was gazing out the wide sliding window at the back lawn.

At the far end, near the redwood fence, was a patch of raw earth, recently spaded.

Dooney said, "What did you say?"

Moorman gazed out the window.   The two men stared at him.

Dooney said sharply, "Are you all right, Moorman?"

"What?"   Moorman turned quickly.   "Of course, of course!   Why shouldn't I be?"   He shook his head and laughed, a low forced note.   "Thinking of something, that's all . . . just thinking of something."

Mr. Hector and Dooney looked at each other.   Dooney said, "What's going on, Moorman?"

"Nothing."   Moorman's smile looked set; he rapidly blinked his eyes.   "Look, uh . . . all right, I did make some jokes.   It was because I—well, all right, I wanted to take my mind off . . . listen, we all got problems, is that right?   They're not all money problems.   There's other things, too.   I—I'm sorry if anything I said sounded insulting.   It wasn't meant to be, it was just for fun—you seemed like good guys.   There's nothing, nothing."   He shook his head quickly and his stiff smile widened.   "It was all just fooling around.   Look, how much was that?   Seventy-what?"

Dooney said, "$71.88."

"Okay.   I got it right here, in my pocket. $71.88, eh?   I was going to give it to you . . ."   He pulled out bills, and counted them off: "Twenty, forty, fifty, sixty, sixty-five, seventy, seventy-one . . . I got no change.   Call it $72.00."

Dooney took the money.   He said, "Do you have twelve cents, Morris?"

"I've got nine cents.   That's all I have."   The lawyer was going through his pockets.

Moorman said, "That's okay.   That's fine."   He pocketed the coins Mr. Hector held out.   "That takes care of it, huh?"

"I'll write you a receipt for $71.91."   Dooney had sat down again and taken a receipt book and pen from his pocket.

Mr. Hector was watching Moorman.   He said quietly, "I suppose your wife will be pleased when you tell her the bill is paid."

"Yeah.   She will."   His quick responding smile was only a stretching of his lips.   It did not touch his shadowed eyes.

"Is she away on a little trip?"

"What?   Yeah.   Right.   She's visiting some relatives."   He glanced out the window, across the lawn, then his glance shot back.   "Yeah, she'll be pleased. Look, I'm sorry if I said some silly things, but that's the way the mind works sometimes."   He walked them to the door.   "Everything okay now?"

Dooney said, "All right, Mr. Moorman.   Another payment is due in a couple of weeks."

"I know.   It'll be there.   You can count on it."

They walked down the drive.   He watched them.

Mr. Hector looked back, as he got in the car.   He saw Moorman watching, his face set, his eyes still.

He said, as Dooney started the car, "Drive to the police station."

"What?"

"He's crazy.   That was plain from the beginning . . . That patch of earth was almost raw."

Dooney stared ahead, as he drove through the tract.

"You saw what happened right after he first glanced out there.   How he changed."

Dooney nodded.

"And right after that, so anxious to get things straightened out with us.   To know that everything was all right—and that we weren't going to the sheriff."

Dooney said, "We got the payment."

"Yes, but . . . the way he changed, what he said, his craziness, his wife not being there . . . and the look of that spaded earth.   This was no joke, Ron.   Not that look in his eyes.   There was a look of . . . I don't know—something horrible, something recent."

His thin lips tightened into a hint of a smile, and his large eyes glittered behind the thick glasses.

He said softly, "The next joke for Mr. Moorman may be a long time coming."

Moorman cut off a chunk of salami, which he ate as he finished the bottle of wine.   Then he lay down on the couch.

The phone rang.

He picked it up, gave a deep vocal yawn, and sighed wearily, "Cannonball Express."

"Honey, how are you doing?"

"Good.   Fine."

"How's the day off?"

"Terrific.   How's your Aunt Letitia?"

"You mean Aunt Charlotte.   She's fine.   I'll stay a couple more days, I think."

"Okay."

"Good weather here . . . Love you, honey.   Say, did you get hold of Affiliated Finance?"

"They got hold of me.   Mr. Dooney called."

"You told him I just plain forgot to send the check, what with hurrying to catch the plane and all?"

"Well, not quite.   But he got his money.   He came out here with a lawyer. They were going to hijack the furniture."

"Good Lord!   Is everything okay?"

"Oh, it's great.   They think I've murdered you and buried you in the back yard."

"What!   What did you tell them?"

"Nothing.   I just looked out at the place I'd dug up Saturday to put in some tomato plants.   And they got this weird notion."

"I wonder why."

"Well, you know . . . I have a few days off, and don't want to hang around the bars.   I'm drinking a little white wine and missing you, and just hatching up a few things to pass the time . . . I expect the cops here shortly."

"Oh, Jack!"   He could picture her shaking her head, and her eyes warm and loving and bewildered and at the same time not unhappy, and accepting the fact that he wasn't quite the standard suburban husband.   "So you've been playing your games!   When are you going to grow up?"

"Never, I hope.   Sounds like no fun at all."

"You're almost forty!"

"That's a *canard*.   I'm just sexually precocious.   I'm really fourteen."

"Six, more likely."

"You could be right.   Six is a good age for games."

"What are the cops going to do?"

"Belabor me with cacklebladders and boil me in midnight oil.   Then they'll dig up the tomato plot again."

"You could be in trouble."

"Yeah, if you should get clumsy up there and fall into some bottomless pit.   So don't disappear.   Come home radiant and rambunctious, and we'll have a lot of fun."

"We always do . . . . what'll come of it all?"

"What, game playing?   Well, in the end you stop breathing, however you've lived—so why not have some fun while you still see the colors and hear the music?"

"Why not indeed?" she said softly.   Then, briskly, "All right, Scarlet Pimpernel—what's the scenario, when I get back?"

"You go to the D.A. and do your damnedest to convince him that you're not dead and buried somewhere, and spring me.   Then we sue Affiliated Finance for four hundred and eighty million dollars, for false arrest, slander, and general terpsichore . . . Oh, sweetheart, you know something?   You won't believe it!"

"I know I won't.   Tell me anyway."

"You know that little creep we've seen at the track a couple of times—long-nosed, ghoulish-eyed, sneaky-looking?   Picks up the used tickets and looks them over?"

"The Stooper?"

"Yeah.   Well, he's Affiliated Finance's lawyer."

"No!"

"You're right—not really.   But I think I've got Mr. Dooney thinking he might be."

"That's terrible."

"I know.   But I didn't play favorites.   I tried to plant the idea in the lawyer's head that Mr. Dooney has a kept woman on the side—Fifi LaTorche."

"You ought to be ashamed of yourself!"

"I know.   Why aren't I?"

"Goodbye, Jack.   I love you."

"I love you too.   Stay out of drafts and don't let Aunt Mehitabel push you off a cliff."

"I'll be home Wednesday."

"I'll be looking forward.   Pick me up at the jailhouse."

He hung up, then snapped his fingers.   A new thought had come to him.

He'd better hurry—the cops should be here in a few minutes.   He went to her bedroom, grabbed a bra and a pair of stockings from the bureau; slid the rear glass door open, ran in the back door of the garage; got his shovel, ran to the patch of earth, dug quickly, shoved the bra and stockings into the hole, and covered them up.   He ran back to the garage with the shovel.   Then he sauntered into the kitchen, washed his hands, and hummed in a satisfied way.

They would dig up the items, and their interment wouldn't make any sense, but that was all right; the men wouldn't want to have wasted their time in fruitless digging, so they would attach some kind of sinister significance to what they had uncovered.   Bras and stockings always convey a message, and are nice to come upon unexpectedly.   So everybody would have a good time.   And wasn't that what life was all about?

The door chime rang.   He ran to open the door.   Standing outside were Dooney, Mr. Hector, and two other men; one of the two was a uniformed policeman, the other looked like a plainclothesman.

Dooney looked firm but a little apprehensive.   Mr. Hector looked righteous and retributive.   The other two looked like men on a job.

Moorman cried heartily, "Hey!   You came back!"   He swung a jovial hand, to hammer Mr. Hector's shoulder affectionately; Mr. Hector twisted away.   "Hey, all right!   How are you, Chief?"   He was beaming at the policeman.   "Y'all come in, heah?   I got plenty of salami—no wine left, though.   Stoop, do us a favor, will you?"   He thrust bills at Mr. Hector, who drew back.   "Run down to the store and pick us up a couple jugs of wine . . . No?   Okay, we'll have to do without.   Come in, guys . . . Lisa," he called, "some guys have stopped by . . . No, I forgot.   She's asleep."

Mr. Hector glanced at the plainclothesman.   He and the policeman were gazing fixedly at Moorman.

Mr. Hector said, "You told us she was visiting some relatives."

"What?   Yeah, sure.   Of course I did.   I forgot for a moment.   Yeah, that's where she is.   She's away.   Visiting some relatives."

His face seemed suddenly ashen.   They were all looking at him.

His eyes slid away from them and looked out the window.

Their gaze followed his.   They all stared out the window, at the patch of fresh-spaded earth at the end of the lawn.

ERLE STANLEY GARDNER

The Clue of the Screaming Woman

Detective:
SHERIFF BILL ELDON

Frank Ames surveyed the tumbling mountain torrent and selected the rock he wanted with great care.

It was on the edge of the deep water, a third of the way across the stream, about sixty feet below the little waterfall and the big eddy. Picking his way over half-submerged stepping stones, then across the fallen log to the rounded rock, he made a few whipping motions with his fishing rod to get plenty of free line. He knew only too well how much that first cast counted.

Up here in the high mountains the sky was black behind the deep blue of interstellar space. The big granite rocks reflected light with dazzling brilliance, while the shadows seemed deep and impenetrable. Standing down near the stream, the roar of the water kept Frank Ames' ears from accurately appraising other sounds, distorting them out of all semblance to reality.

The raucous abuse of a mountain jay sounded remarkably like the noise made by a buzz saw ripping through a pine board, and some peculiar vagary of the stream noises made Frank Ames feel he could hear a woman screaming.

Ames made his cast. The line twisted through the air, straightened at just the right distance above the water and settled. The Royal Coachman came to rest gently, seductively, on the far edge of the little whirlpool just below the waterfall.

For a moment the fly reposed on the water with calm tranquillity, drifting with the current. Then there was a shadowy dark streak of submerged motion. A big trout raised his head and part of his body up out of the water.

The noise made by the fish as it came down hard on the fly was a soul-gratifying "*chooonk*." It seemed the fish had pushed its shoulders into a downward strike as it started back to the dark depths of the clear stream, the Royal Coachman in its mouth.

Ames set the hook and firmed his feet on the rock. The reel sounded like an angry rattlesnake. The line suddenly stretched taut. Even above the sound of the mountain stream, the hissing of the wire-tight line as it cut through the water was plainly audible.

The sound of a woman's scream again mingled with the stream noises. This time the scream was louder and nearer.

The sound knifed through to Frank Ames' consciousness. It was as annoying, as much out of place, as the ringing of a telephone bell at four o'clock in the morning.   Frank desperately wanted that trout.   It was a fine, big trout with a dark back, beautiful red sides, firm-fleshed from ice-cold, swift waters, and it was putting up a terrific fight.

That first time there had been some doubt as to the sound Ames had heard.   It might have been the stream-distorted echo of a hawk crying out as it circled high in the heavens.   But as to this second noise there could be no doubt.   It was the scream of a woman, and it sounded from the trail along the east bank of the stream.

Ames turned to look over his shoulder, a hurried glance of apprehensive annoyance.

That one moment's advantage was all the trout needed.   With the vigilance of the fisherman relaxed for the flicker of an eyelash, the trout made a swift rush for the tangled limbs of the submerged tree trunk on the far end of the pool, timing his maneuver as though he had known the exact instant the fisherman had turned.

Almost automatically Ames tightened on the rod and started reeling in, but he was too late.   He felt the sudden cessation of the surging tugs which come up the line through the wrist and into the arm in a series of impulses too rapid to count, but which are the very breath of life to the skilled fisherman.   Instead, the tension of the line was firm, steady and dead.

Knowing that his leader was wrapped around a submerged branch, Ames pointed the rod directly at the taut line, applied sufficient pressure to break the slender leader, and then reeled in the line.

He turned toward the place from which the scream had sounded.

There was no sign of animation in the scenery.   The high mountain crags brooded over the scene.   A few fleecy clouds forming over the east were the only break in the tranquil blue of the sky.   Long sweeps of majestic pines stretched in a serried sequence up the canyons, their needles oozing scent into the pure, dry air.

Ames, slender-waisted, long-legged, graceful in his motions, was like a deer bounding across the fallen log, jumping lightly to the water-splashed stepping stones.

He paused at the thin fringe of scrub pine which grew between the rocky approach to the stream and the winding trail long enough to divest himself of his fishing creel and rod.   Then he moved swiftly through the small pines to where the trail ran in a north and south direction, roughly paralleling that of the stream.

The decomposed granite dust of the trail held tracks with remarkable fidelity.   Superimposed over the older horse and deer tracks that were in the trail were the tracks made by a woman who had been running as fast as she could go.

At this elevation of more than seven thousand feet above sea level, where even ordinary exertion left a person breathless, it was evident either that the woman could not have been running far, or that she had lived long enough in this country to be acclimated to the altitude.

The shoes she was wearing, however, were apparently new cowboy boots, completely equipped with rubber heels, so new that even the pattern of the heel showed in the downhill portion of the trail.

For the most part, the woman had been running with her weight on her toes.   When she came to the steep downhill pitch, however, her weight was back more on her heels, and the rubber heel caps made distinct imprints.   After fifty yards,

Ames saw that the tracks faltered.   The strides grew shorter.   Slowly, she had settled down to a rapid, breathless walk.

With the unerring instinct of a trained hunter, Ames followed those tracks, keeping to one side of the trail so that his tracks did not obliterate those of the hurrying woman.   He saw where she had paused and turned, the prints of her feet at right angles to the trail as she looked back over her shoulder.   Then, apparently more reassured, she had resumed her course, walking now at a less rapid rate.

Moving with a long, lithe stride which made him glide noiselessly, Frank Ames topped a rise, went down another short, steep pitch, rounded a turn in the pine trees and came unexpectedly on the woman, standing poised like some wild thing. She had stopped and was looking back, her startled face showing as a white oval.

She started to run, then paused, looked back again, stopped, and, as Ames came up, managed a dubious and somewhat breathless smile.

"Hello," Ames said with the casual simplicity of a man who has the assurance of complete sincerity.

"Good afternoon," she answered, then laughed, a short, oxygen-starved laugh. "I was taking—a quick walk."   She paused to get her breath, said, "Trying to give my figure some much-needed discipline."

Another pause for breath.   "When you rounded the bend in the trail, you—you startled me."

Ames' eyes said there was nothing wrong with her figure, but his lips merely twisted in a slow grin.

She was somewhere in the middle twenties.   The frontier riding breeches, short leather jacket, shirt open at the front, the bandanna around her neck, held in place with a leather loop studded with brilliants, showed that she was a "dude" from the city.   The breeches emphasized the slenderness of her waist, the smooth, graceful contours of her hips and legs.   The face was still pale, but the deep red of sunburn around the open line of the throat above the protection of the bandanna was as eloquent as a complete calendar to Frank's trained eyes.

The sunburned skin told the story of a girl who had ridden in on a horseback pack trip, who had underestimated the powerful actinic rays of the mountain sun, who had tried too late to cover the sunburned V-shaped area with a scarf.   A couple of days in the mountains and some soothing cream had taken some of the angry redness out of the skin, but that was all.

He waited to see if there would be some explanation of her scream or her flight. Not for worlds would he have violated the code of the mountains by trying to pry into something that was none of his business.   When he saw she had no intention of making any further explanation, he said casually, "Guess you must have come up the trail from Granite Flats about Sunday.   Didn't you, ma'am?"

She looked at him with sudden apprehension.   "How did *you* know?"

"I had an idea you might have been in the mountains just about that long, and I knew you didn't come up from this end because I didn't see the tracks of a pack train in the trail."

"Can you follow tracks?" she asked.

"Why, of course." He paused and then added casually, "I'm headed down toward where your camp must be. Perhaps you'd let me walk along with you for a piece."

"I'd love it!" she exclaimed, and then with quick suspicion, "How do *you* know where our camp is?"

His slight drawl was emphasized as he thought the thing into words. "If you'd been camped at Coyote Springs, you'd need to have walked three miles to get here. You don't look as though you'd gone that far. Down at Deerlick Springs, there's a meadow with good grass for the horses, a nice camping place and it's only about three quarters of a mile from here, so I—"

She interrupted with a laugh which now carried much more assurance. "I see that there's no chance for me to have *any* secrets. Do you live up here?"

Frank wanted to tell her of the two years in the Japanese prison camp, of the necessity of living close to nature to get his health and strength back, of the trap line which he ran through the winter, of the new-found strength and vitality that were erasing the disabilities caused by months of malnutrition. But when it came to talking about himself, the words dried up. All he could say was, "Yes, I live up here."

She fell into step at his side. "You must find it isolated."

"I don't see many people," he admitted, "but there are other things to make up for it—no telephones, no standing in line, no exhaust fumes."

"And you're content to be here always?"

"Not always. I want a ranch down in the valley. I'm completing arrangements for one now. A friend of mine is giving me a lease with a contract to purchase. I think I can pay out on it with luck and hard work."

Her eyes were thoughtful as she walked along the trail, stepping awkwardly in her high-heeled cowboy riding boots. "I suppose really you can't ask for much more than that—luck and hard work."

"It's all *I* want," Frank told her.

They walked for some minutes in the silence of mutual appraisal, then rounded a turn in the trail, and Deerlick Meadows stretched out in front of them. And as soon as Frank Ames saw the elaborate nature of the camp, he knew these people were wealthy sportsmen who were on a de luxe trip. Suddenly awkward, he said, "Well, I guess I'd better turn—" And then stopped abruptly as he realized that it would never do to let this young woman know he had been merely escorting her along the trail. He had told her he was going in her direction. He'd have to keep on walking past the camp.

"What's your name?" she asked suddenly, and then added laughingly, "Mine's Roberta Coe."

"Frank Ames," he said uncomfortably, knowing she had asked him his name so abruptly because she intended to introduce him to her companions.

"Well, you must come in and have a cup of coffee before you go on," she said. "You'd like to meet my friends and they'd like to meet you."

They had been seen now and Ames was aware of curious glances from people who were seated in folding canvas chairs, items of luxury which he knew could have been brought in only at much cost to the tourist and at much trouble to both packer and pack horse.

He tried to demur, but somehow the right words wouldn't come, and he couldn't let himself seem to run away. Even while he hesitated, they entered the camp, and he found himself meeting people with whom he felt awkwardly ill at ease.

Harvey W. Dowling was evidently the business executive who was footing the bills. He, it seemed, was in his tent, taking a siesta and the hushed voices of the others showed the fawning deference with which they regarded the man who was paying the bills. His tent, a pretentious affair with heating stove and shaded entrance, occupied a choice position, away from the rest of the camp, a small tributary stream winding in front, and the shady pine thicket immediately in the back.

The people to whom Ames was introduced were the type a rich man gathers around him, people who were careful to cultivate the manners of the rich, who clung tenaciously to their contacts with the wealthy.

Now these people, carefully subdued in voice and manner, so as not to disturb the man in the big tent, had that amused, patronizing tolerance of manner which showed they regarded Frank Ames merely as a novel interlude rather than as a human being.

Dick Nottingham had a well-nourished, athletic ease of manner, a smoothly muscled body and the calm assurance of one who is fully conscious of his eligibility. Two other men, Alexander Cameron and Sam Fremont, whose names Ames heard mentioned, were evidently downstream fishing.

The women were young, well-groomed and far more personal in their curiosity. Eleanor Dowling relied on her own beauty and her father's wealth to display a certain arrogance. Sylvia Jessup had mocking eyes which displayed challenging invitation as she sized up Frank's long, rangy build.

Conscious of his faded blue shirt and overalls with the patched knees, Frank felt distinctly ill at ease, and angry at himself because he did. He would have given much to have been articulate enough to express himself, to have joined in casual small talk; but the longer he stayed the more awkward and tongue-tied he felt, and that in turn made him feel more and more conspicuous.

There was good-natured banter. Sylvia Jessup announced that after this *she* was going to walk in the afternoons and see if *she* couldn't bag a little game, veiled references to open season and bag limit; then light laughter. And there were casually personal questions that Ames answered as best he could.

Whenever they would cease their light banter, and in the brief period of silence wait for Frank Ames to make some comment, Frank angrily realized his tongue-tied impotence, realized from the sudden way in which they would all start talking at once that they were trying to cover his conversational inadequacy.

Sam Fremont, camera in hand, came into camp almost unnoticed. He had, he explained, been hunting wildlife with his camera, and he grinningly admitted approaching camp quietly so he could get a couple of "candid camera" shots of the "sudden animation."

He was a quick-eyed opportunist with a quick wit and fast tongue, and some of his quips brought forth spontaneous laughter.   After one particularly loud burst of merriment, the flap of the big tent parted and Harvey W. Dowling, scowling sleepily at the group, silenced them as effectively as would have been the case if some grim apparition had suddenly appeared.

But he came down to join them, a figure of heavy power, conscious of the deference due him, boomingly cordial to Frank, and with regal magnanimity saying nothing of the loud conversation which had wakened him.

A few moments later Alexander Cameron came stumbling up the trail, seeming to fall all over his heavy leather boots, boots that were stiff with newness.   He seemed the most inexperienced of them all, and yet the most human, the one man who seemed to have no fear of Dowling.

There were more introductions, an abrupt cessation of the banter, and a few minutes later Ames found himself trudging angrily away from the camp, having offered the first excuse which came to his tortured mind, that he must inspect a site for a string of traps, knowing in his own mind how utterly inane the reason sounded, despite the fact that these people from the city would see nothing wrong with it.

Once clear of the camp, Frank circled up Deerlick Creek and cut back toward the main trail of the North Fork, so that he could retrieve his rod and creel.

He knew that it was too late now to try any more fishing.   The white, woolly clouds had grown into great billowing mushrooms.   Already there was the reverberation of distant thunder echoing from the high crags up at the divide and ominous black clouds were expanding out from the bases of the cloud mushrooms.

The thunderstorm struck just as Ames was crossing the top of the ridge which led down to the main trail.

The first patter of heavy raindrops gave a scant warning.   A snake's tongue of ripping lightning dissolved a dead pine tree across the valley into a shower of yellow splinters.   The clap of thunder was almost instantaneous, and, as though it had torn loose the inner lining of the cloud, rain deluged down in torrents until the sluicing streams forging their way down the slope were heavy with mud.

Knowing better than to seek shelter under a pine tree, Ames ran along the base of a granite ridge until he found the place where an overhanging rock, sandblasted by winds and worn by the elements, offered a place where he could crawl in and stretch out.

The lightning glittered with greenish intensity.   The thunder bombarded the echoing crags and rain poured in cascades from the lip of the rock under which Ames had taken shelter.

Within ten minutes the heaviest part of the rain had ceased.   The thunder began to drift sullenly to the south, but the rain continued steadily, then intensified into a clearing-up shower of cloudburst proportions and ceased abruptly.   Half a minute later a venturesome shaft of afternoon sunlight explored its way into the glistening pines.

Ames crawled from under his protecting rock and resumed his way down the slippery slope to the main trail.

The soaking rain had obliterated the tracks in the trail.   In fact, the ditchlike depression in the center of the trail still held puddles of water, so Ames, so far as he was able, kept to one side, working his way between rocks, conscious of the sudden chill in the atmosphere, conscious also of the fact that the clouds were gathering for another downpour, one that could well last all night.

Ames found his fishing rod and creel where he had left them.   He slipped the soggy strap of the creel over his shoulder, started to pick up the rod, then stopped. His woodsman's eyes told him that the position of the rod had been changed since he had left it.   Had it perhaps been the wind which accompanied the storm?   He had no time to debate the matter, for once more raindrops began to patter ominously.

Picking up his rod, he swung into a long, rapid stride, the rain whipping against his back as he walked.   He knew that there was no use trying to wait out this show. This would be a steady, sodden rain.

By the time Frank Ames reached his cabin he was wet to the skin.

He put pine-pitch kindling and dry wood into the stove, and soon had a roaring fire.   He lit the gasoline lantern, divested himself of his wet clothes, took the two medium-sized fish from the creel and fried them for supper.   He read a magazine, noticed casually that the rain on the cabin roof stopped about nine-thirty, listened to the news on the radio and went to bed.   His sleep was punctuated with dreams of women who screamed and ran aimlessly through the forest, of shrewd-eyed city men who regarded him with patronizing cordiality, of snub-nosed, laughing-eyed women who pursued him with pronged spears, their mouths giving vent to sardonic laughter.

Ames was up with the first grayness of morning.   The woodshed yielded dry wood, and, as the aroma of coffee filled the little cabin, Ames poured water into the jar of sour dough, thickened the water with flour, beat it to just the right consistency and poured out sour-dough hot cakes.

He had finished with the breakfast dishes and the chores, and was contemplating the stream which danced by in the sunlight just beyond the long shadows of the pine trees, when his eyes suddenly rested with startled disbelief on the two rounded manzanita pegs which had been driven into holes drilled in the wall of the log cabin.

The .22 rifle, with its telescopic sight, was missing.

The space immediately below, where his .30-.30 rifle hung suspended from pegs, was as usual, and the .30-.30 was in place.   Only the place where the .22 should have been was vacant.

Ames heard steps outside the door.   A masculine voice called, "Hello!   Anyone home?"

"Who is it?" Ames called, whirling.

The form of Sheriff Bill Eldon was framed in the doorway.

"Howdy," he said.   "Guess I should drop in and introduce myself.   I'm Bill Eldon, sheriff of the county."

Ames took in the spare figure, tough as gristle, straight as a lodgepole pine, a man who was well past middle age, but who moved with the easy, lithe grace of a man in his thirties, a man who carried not so much as an ounce of unnecessary weight, whose eyes, peering out from under shaggy eyebrows, had the same quality of fierce penetration which is so characteristic of the hawks and eagles, yet his manner and voice were mild.

"I'm camped up the stream a piece with a couple of head of pack stock," the sheriff said, "just riding through.   This country up here is in my county and I sort of make a swing around through it during the fishing season.   I was up here last year, but missed you.   They said you were in town."

Ames stretched out his hand.   "Come right in, sheriff, and sit down.   Ames is my name.   I'm mighty glad to know you.   I've heard about you."

Bill Eldon thanked him, walked over to one of the homemade chairs built from pine slabs and baling wire, settled himself comfortably, rolled a cigarette.   "Been up here long?"

"Couple of years.   I run a trap line in the winters.   I have a small allowance and I'm trying to stretch it as far as possible so I can build up health and a bank account at the same time—just enough for operating capital."

Eldon crossed his legs, said, "Do you get around the country much?"

"Some."

"Seen the folks camped down below?"

"Yes.   I met some of them yesterday.   I guess they came in the other way."

"That's right.   Quite an outfit.   Know any of the people camped up above?"

"I didn't know there were any."

"I didn't know there were either," the sheriff said, and then was quiet.

Ames cocked an eyebrow in quizzical interrogation.

"Seen anybody up that way?" Eldon asked.

"There are some folks camped up on Squaw Creek, but that's six miles away. A man and his wife."

"I know all about them," the sheriff said.   "I met them on the trail.   Haven't seen anything of a man about thirty-five, dark hair, stubby, close-cut mustache, gray eyes, about a hundred and sixty pounds, five feet, eight or nine inches tall, wearing big hobnail boots with wool socks rolled down over the tops of the boots—*new* boots?"

Ames shook his head.

"Seems as though he must have been camped up around here somewhere," the sheriff said.

"I haven't seen him."

"Mind taking a little walk with me?" the sheriff asked.

Ames, suddenly suspicious, said, "I have a few chores to do.   I—"

"This is along the line of business," the sheriff answered, getting up out of the chair with the casual, easy grace of a wild animal getting to its feet.

"If you put it that way, I guess we'll let the chores go," Ames said.

They left the cabin and swung up the trail.   Ames' long legs moved in the steady rhythm of space-devouring strides.   The sheriff kept pace with him, although his shorter legs made him take five strides to the other man's four.

For some five minutes they walked silently, walking abreast where the trail was wide; then as the trail narrowed, the sheriff took the lead, setting a steady, un-wavering pace.

Abruptly Bill Eldon held up his hand as a signal to halt. "Now from this point on," he said, "I'd like you to be kind of careful about not touching things. Just follow me."

He swung from the side of the trail, came to a little patch of quaking asp and a spring.

A man was stretched on the ground by the spring, lying rigid and inert.

Eldon circled the body. "I've already gone over the tracks," he said. And then added dryly, "There ain't any, except the ones made by his own boots, and they're pretty faint."

"What killed him?" Ames asked.

"Small-caliber bullet, right in the side of the head," the sheriff said.

Ames stood silently looking at the features discolored by death, the stubby mustache, the dark hair, the new hobnail boots with the wool socks turned down over the tops.

"When—when did it happen?"

"Don't rightly know," the sheriff said. "Apparently it happened before the thunderstorm yesterday. Tracks are pretty well washed out. You can see where he came running down this little slope. Then he jumped to one side and then to the other. Didn't do him no good. He fell right here. But the point is, his tracks are pretty indistinct, almost washed out by that rainstorm. If it hadn't been for the hobnails on his new boots, I doubt if we'd have noticed his tracks at all.

"Funny thing is," the sheriff went on, "you don't see any stock. He must have packed in his little camp stuff on his back. Pretty husky chap but he doesn't look like a woodsman."

Ames nodded.

"Wouldn't know anything about it, would you?" the sheriff asked.

Ames shook his head.

"Happened to be walking down the stream yesterday afternoon just a little bit before the rain came up," the sheriff said. "Didn't see this fellow's tracks any-where in the trail and didn't see any smoke. Wouldn't have known he had a camp here if it hadn't been for—"

Abruptly the sheriff ceased speaking.

"I was fishing yesterday," Ames said.

"I noticed it," the sheriff said. "Walked by your cabin but you weren't there. Then I walked on down the trail, caught the glint of sunlight from the reel on your fishing rod."

Eldon's silence was an invitation.

Ames laughed nervously and said, "Yes, I took a hike down the trail and didn't want to be burdened with the rod and the creel."

"Saw the leader was broken on the fishing rod," the sheriff commented. "Looked as though maybe you'd tangled up with a big one and he'd got away—leader twisted around a bit and frayed. Thought maybe you'd hooked on to a big one over in that pool and he might have wrapped the leader around some of the branches on that fallen tree over at the far end.''

"He did, for a fact," Ames admitted ruefully.

"That puzzled me," the sheriff said. "You quit right there and then, without even taking off the broken leader. You just propped your fishin' rod up against the tree and hung your creel on a forked limb, fish and all. Tracks showed you'd been going pretty fast."

"I'm a fast walker."

"Uh-huh," Eldon said. "Then you hit the trail. There was tracks made by a woman in the trail. She was running. I saw your tracks following."

"I can assure you," Ames said, trying to make a joke of it, "that I wasn't chasing any woman down the trail."

"I know you weren't," Eldon said. "You were studying those tracks, kind of curious about them, so you kept to one side of the trail where you could move along and study them. You'd get back in the trail once or twice where you had to and then your tracks would be over those of the woman, but for the most part you were sort of trailing her."

"Naturally," Ames said. "I was curious."

"I didn't follow far enough to see whether you caught up with her," the sheriff said. "I saw the rain clouds piling up pretty fast and I hightailed it back to my camp and got things lashed down around the tent. Of course," the sheriff went on, "I don't suppose you know how close you were to that running woman?"

"The tracks looked fresh," Ames said.

"Thought you might have seen her as she went by," the sheriff said. "Thought that might have accounted for the way you went over to the trail in such a hurry. You were walking pretty fast. Then I went back to the place where you must have been standing on that rock where you could get a good cast, up by the eddy below the waterfall, and darned if you could see the trail from there! It runs within about fifty yards, but there's a growth of scrub pine that would keep you from seeing anyone."

Ames was uncomfortable. Why should he protect Roberta Coe? Why not tell the sheriff frankly what he had heard? He realized he was playing with fire in withholding this information, and yet he couldn't bring himself to come right out and say what he knew he should be saying.

"So," the sheriff said, "I sort of wondered what made you drop everything in such a hurry and go over to the trail and start taking up the tracks of this woman. Just a lot of curiosity. Sort of felt I was snooping, but, after all, snooping is my business."

Once more the sheriff's silence invited confidence from Frank Ames.

"Well," the sheriff went on after a few moments, "I got up this morning and thought I'd stop down and pay you a visit, and then coming down the trail I saw a long streak down the side of the hill. It had been rained on but you could see it was a fresh track where someone had dragged something. I looked over here and found this camp. He'd dragged in a big dead log that he was aiming to chop up for firewood.   Thought at first it might have been a sort of a tenderfoot trick because he only had a little hand ax, but after looking the camp over, I figured he might not have been quite so green as those new boots would make you think.   Evidently he intended to build a fire under the middle of this log and as the two ends burned apart he'd shove the logs up together—make a little fire that way that would keep all night.   He didn't have any tent, just a bedroll with a good big tarp.   It's pretty light weight but it would turn water if you made a lean-to and was careful not to touch it anyplace while it was raining.''

"You—you know who he is?" Ames asked.

"Not yet, I don't," the sheriff admitted.   "So far I've just looked around a bit. I don't want to do any monkeying with the things in his pockets until I get hold of the coroner.   Too bad that rain came down just when it did.   I haven't been able yet to find where the man stood that did the shooting."

"How long ago did you find him?"

"Oh, an hour or two, maybe a little longer.   I've got to ride over to the forest service telephone and I thought I'd go call on you.   Now that you're here, I guess the best thing to do is to leave you in charge while I go telephone.   You can look around some if you want to, because I've already covered the ground, looking for tracks, but don't touch the body and don't let anyone else touch it."

Ames said, "I suppose I can do it if—if I have to."

"Isn't a very nice sort of a job to wish off on a man," the sheriff admitted, "but at a time like this we all of us have to pull together.   I've got to go three, four miles to get to that ranger station and put a call in.   My camp's up here about three quarters of a mile.   I've got a pretty good saddle horse and it shouldn't take long to get up there and back."

"I'll wait," Ames said.

"Thanks," the sheriff told him, and without another word turned and swung silently down the slope to the trail and vanished . . .

Ames, his mind in a turmoil, stood silently contemplating the scenery with troubled eyes that were unable to appreciate the green pines silhouetted against the deep blue of the sky, the patches of brilliant sunlight, the dark, somber segments of deep shadow.

A mountain jay squawked raucously from the top of a pine, teetering back and forth as though by the very impetus of his body muscles he could project his voice with greater force.

The corpse lay stiff and still, wrapped in the quiet dignity of death.   The shadow of a nearby pine marched slowly along until it rested on the dead man's face, a peaceful benediction.

Ames moved restlessly, at first aimlessly, then more deliberately, looking for tracks.

His search was fruitless.   There were only the tracks of the sheriff's distinctive, high-heeled cowboy boots, tracks which zigzagged patiently around a complete circle.   Whatever previous tracks had been on the ground had been washed out by the rain.   Had the murderer counted on that?   Had the crime been committed when the thunderheads were piled up so ominously that he knew a deluge was impending?

Ames widened his circle still more, suddenly came to a halt as sunlight glinted on blued steel. He hurriedly surveyed the spot where the gun was lying.

This was quite evidently the place where the murderer had lain in ambush, behind a fallen pine.

Here again there were no tracks because the rain had washed them away, but the .22 caliber rifle lay in plain sight. Apparently the sheriff had overlooked it. He doubted that he himself would have seen the gun had it not been for that reflecting glint cast by the sunlight.

The fallen log offered an excellent means of approach without leaving tracks.

Ames stepped carefully on the dead roots which had been pulled up when the tree was blown over, worked his way to the top of the log, then moved silently along the rough bark.

The gun was a .22 automatic with a telescopic sight, and the single empty shell which had been ejected by the automatic mechanism glinted in the sunlight a few feet beyond the place where the gun was lying.

Ames lay at length on the log so he could look down at the gun.

There was a scratch on the stock, a peculiar indentation on the lock where it had at one time been dropped against a rock. The laws of probability would not admit of two weapons marked exactly like that.

For as much as five minutes Ames lay there pondering the question as to what he should do next. Apparently the sheriff had not as yet discovered the gun. It would be a simple matter to hook a forked stick under the trigger guard, pick the gun up without leaving any trace, put it in some safe place of concealment, then clean the barrel and quietly return it to the wall of his own cabin.

Ames pondered the matter for several minutes, then pushed himself up to his hands and knees, then back to his feet and ran back down the log, afraid that the temptation might prove too great for him. He retraced his steps back to a position where he could watch both the main trail and the spot where the body lay.

Some thirty minutes later Ames heard the sound of voices, a carefree, chattering babble which seemed oddly out of place with the tragic events which had taken place in the little sun-swept valley.

Ames moved farther back into the shadows so as to avoid the newcomers.

Ames could hear a voice which he thought was that of Dick Nottingham saying quite matter-of-factly, "I notice a couple of people are ahead of us on the trail. See the tracks? Let's wait a minute. They turn off right here. They look like fresh tracks—made since the rain. Hello, there!"

One of the girls laughed nervously. "Do you want reinforcements, Dick?"

"Just good woodcraft," Nottingham said in a tone of light banter. "Old Eagle Scout Nottingham on the job. Can't afford to lead you into an ambush. Hello, anyone home?"

Ames heard him coming forward, the steps alternately crunching on the patches of open decomposed granite and then fading into nothing on the carpeted pine needles. "I say," Nottingham called, "is anyone in here?"

Ames strove to make his voice sound casual. "I wouldn't come any farther."

The steps stopped, then Nottingham's cautious voice, "Who's there?"

"Frank Ames. I wouldn't come any farther."

"Why not?"

"There's been a little trouble here. I'm watching the place for the sheriff."

Nottingham hesitated a moment. Then his steps came forward again so that he was in full view.

"What happened?" he asked.

"A man was shot," Ames said in a low voice. "I don't think it's a good place for the women and I think your party had better stay on the trail."

"What is it, Dick?" someone called softly, and Ames felt a sudden thrill as he identified Roberta Coe's voice.

"Apparently there's some trouble in here. I guess we'd better get back to the trail," Nottingham called out. "A man's been shot."

Eleanor Dowling said, "Nonsense. We're not babies. The woman who needed her smelling salts went out of fashion years ago. What is it?"

Ames walked over to the trail. "Hello," he said self-consciously.

They acknowledged his salutation. There was a certain tension of awkward restraint, and Ames briefly explained what had happened.

"We were just taking a walk up the trail," Nottingham said. "We saw your tracks and then they turned off. There was someone with you?"

"The sheriff," Ames said.

Nottingham said, "Look here, old man, I'm sorry, but I think you owe us a little more explanation than that. We see the tracks of two men up the trail. Then we find one man standing alone and one man dead. You tell us that the sheriff has been with you, but we should have a little more than your word for it."

"Take a look for yourself," Ames said, "but don't try to touch the body. You can look at the dead man's shoes. They're full of hobnails."

Roberta Coe held back, but Nottingham, Eleanor Dowling and Sylvia Jessup pushed forward curiously.

"No closer than that!" Ames said.

"Who are you to give *us* orders?" Nottingham flared, circling the body.

"The sheriff left me in charge."

"Well, I don't see any badge, and as far as I'm concerned, I—"

He stepped forward.

Ames interposed himself between Nottingham and the inert figure. "I said to keep back."

Nottingham straightened, anger in his eyes. "Don't talk to me in that tone of voice, you damned lout!"

"Just keep back," Ames said quietly.

"Why, you poor fool," Nottingham blazed. "I used to be on the boxing team in college. I could—"

"You just keep back," Ames interrupted quietly, ominously.

Sylvia Jessup, acting as peacemaker, said, "I'm sure you'll understand Mr. Ames' position, Dick. He was left here by the sheriff."

"He *says* he was. I'm just making certain. Where did the sheriff go?"

Ames remained silent.

Sylvia pushed Nottingham to one side. "Where did the sheriff go, Mr. Ames?"

"He went to phone the coroner."

"Were you with him when the body was discovered?"

"No, the sheriff found the body, then came and got me, and then went to the ranger station to telephone."

Nottingham's voice and manner showed his skepticism. "You mean the sheriff discovered the body, then he walked away and left the body all alone to go down and get you at your cabin, and then after all that, went to notify the coroner?"

"Well, what's wrong with that?" Ames asked.

"Everything," Nottingham said, and then added, "Frankly, I'm skeptical. While I'm on vacation right now, I'm a lawyer by profession, and your story doesn't make sense to me."

Ames said quietly, "I don't give a damn whether it makes sense to you or not. If you don't think the sheriff's actions were logical, take it up with the sheriff, but don't try to argue with me about it because in just about a minute you're going to have to do a lot of backing up."

Nottingham said, "I don't back up for anyone," but his eyes were cautious as he sized up Frank Ames as a boxer sizes up an opponent in the ring.

There was contrast in the two types; Nottingham well-fed, heavily muscled, broad of shoulder; Frank Ames slender, lithe with stringy muscles. Nottingham had well-muscled weight; Ames had rawhide endurance.

Abruptly the tension was broken by steps and H. W. Dowling called out from the trail, "What's everyone doing over there?"

"There's been a murder, father," Eleanor said.

Dowling pushed his way through the scrub pines. "This damned altitude gets me. What's the trouble?"

Eleanor explained the situation.

"All right," Dowling said, "let's keep away from the place." He paused to catch his breath. "We don't want to get mixed up in any of this stuff." Again he paused for breath. "Who's the sheriff?"

"Bill Eldon," Ames said. "I think he visited your camp."

"Oh, yes," Dowling said, and his patronizing smile was as eloquent as words. "Dehydrated old coot. Where's he gone?"

"To notify the coroner."

"Well, I want everyone in my party to keep away from that body. That includes you, Dick. Understand?"

"Yes, H. W.," Nottingham said, suddenly meek.

"And," Dowling went on, "under the circumstances, I think we'll wait." He paused for two or three breaths, then added, "Until the sheriff gets back." His eyes swiveled to glower at Ames. "Any objection, young man?"

"Not in the least," Ames said. "Just so you don't mess up the evidence."

"Humph," Dowling said, and sat down, breathing heavily.

More voices sounded on the trail. A carefree, casual, man's laugh sounded garishly incongruous.

Dowling raised his voice and called out, "We're in here, Sam."

Crunching steps sounded on the decomposed granite, and Alexander Cameron and Sam Fremont came to join the party.

The abrupt cessation of their conversation, the startled consternation on their faces as they saw the body seemed to revive the shock of the others. A period of uncomfortable silence spread over the group.

Alexander Cameron, his equipment stiff and new, from the high-topped boots to the big sheath knife strapped to his belt, seemed about to become ill. Sam Fremont, quickly adjusting himself to the situation, let his restless eyes move in a quick survey from face to face, as though trying to ferret out the secret thoughts of the others.

Roberta Coe moved over to Frank Ames' side, drew him slightly away, said in a whisper, "I suppose it's too much to ask, but—could you—well—give me a break about what happened yesterday?"

"I've already covered for you," Frank Ames said, a note of anger showing in his voice, despite the fact that it was carefully lowered so the others could not hear. "I don't know why I did it, but I did. I stuck my neck out and—"

"Roberta!" Dowling said peremptorily. "Come over here!"

"Yes, H. W. Just a moment."

Dowlings eyes were narrowed. "Now!" he snapped. "I want you."

The tension was for a moment definitely noticeable to all. Roberta Coe's hesitancy, Dowling's steady, imperative eyes boring into hers, holding her in the inflexible grip of his will.

"Now," Dowling repeated.

"Yes, H. W.," Roberta Coe said, and moved away from Frank Ames.

Sheriff Bill Eldon, squatting on his heels cowboy fashion on the side of the ridge, kept to the concealing shadows of the pine fringe just in front of the jagged rock backbone. John Olney, the ranger, sat beside him.

Here the slope was carpeted by pine needles and deeply shaded. Fifty yards back the towering granite ridge reflected the sunlight with such blinding brilliance that anyone looking up from below would see only the glaring white, and unless he happened to be a trained hunter, could never force his eyes to penetrate into the shadows.

The sheriff slowly lowered his binoculars.

"What do you see?" Olney asked.

Bill Eldon said, "Well, he ain't going to walk into our trap. He found the gun all right, looked it over and then let it lay there. Now all these other folks have come up and it looks like they aim to stick around."

"It's his gun?"

"I figure it that way—sort of figured that if he *had* been mixed up in it, he'd try to hide the gun. He wouldn't know we'd found it and he'd figure the safest thing to do would be to hide it."

"I still think he'll do just that," Olney said.

The sheriff said, "Nope, he's lost his chance now. Somehow I just can't get that gun business straight. If Ames had done the killing and it's his gun, you'd think he'd either have hidden it or taken it back home.   The way it is now, somebody must have wiped it clean of fingerprints, then dropped it, walked off and left it. That someone had to be either pretty lucky or a pretty fair woodsman; knew that a storm was coming up and knew a heavy rain would wash out all the tracks. Hang it, I thought Ames would give us a lead when he found that gun.   Guess we've got to figure out a new approach.   Well, let's go on back and tell him we've phoned the coroner."

"When do you reckon Coroner Logan will get here?"

"Going to take him a while," the sheriff said.   "Even if he gets a plane, he's got a long ride."

"We just going to wait?"

"Not by a damn sight," Eldon said cheerfully.   "We ain't supposed to move the body or take anything out of the pockets until the coroner gets here, but I'm not going to sit on my haunches just waiting around.   Let's be kind of careful sneaking back to our horses.   We wouldn't want 'em to know we'd been watching! There's a lot more people down there now."

"City guys," Olney said, snorting.

"I know, but they all have eyes, and the more pairs of eyes there are, the more chance there is of seeing motion.   Just take it easy now.   Keep in the shadows and back of the trees."

They worked their way back around the slope carefully.

Bill Eldon led the way to the place where their horses had been tied.   The men tightened the cinches and swung into their saddles.   "We don't want to hit that trail too soon," Sheriff Eldon announced.   "Some of those people might be smart enough to follow our tracks back a ways."

"Not those city folks," Olney said, and laughed.

"Might not be deliberately backtracking us," Bill Eldon said, "but they might hike back up the trail.   If they do, and should find they ran out of horse tracks before they got very far, even a city dude might get suspicious.   Remember when they came walking up the trail, that chap in the sweater stopped when he came to the point where the tracks led up to the place we found the body.   He's probably been around the hills some."

"Been around as a dude," Olney said scornfully, "but perhaps we'd better ride up a mile or so before we hit the trail."

"How do you figure this Ames out?" asked the sheriff.

Olney put his horse into a jog trot behind the sheriff's fast-stepping mount. "There's something wrong with him.   He broods too much.   He's out there alone and—Well, I always did think he was running away from someone.   I think maybe he's on the lam.   I've stopped in on him a few times.   He's never opened up. That ain't right.   When a man's out here in the hills all alone he gets lonesome, and he should talk his head off when he gets a chance to visit with someone."

Sheriff Eldon merely grunted.

"I think he's running away," Olney insisted.

The ridge widened and the ranger put his horse alongside the sheriff.

"Sometimes people try running away from themselves," the sheriff said.   "They go hide out someplace, thinking they're running away. Then they find—themselves.''

"Well, this man, Ames, hasn't found anything yet.''

"You can't ever tell,'' Bill Eldon rejoined. "When a man gets out with just himself and the stars, the mountains, the streams and the trees, he sort of soaks up something of the eternal bigness of things. I like the way he looks you in the eye.

"When you're figurin' on clues you don't just figure on the things that exist. You figure on the people who caused 'em to exist.'' And Bill Eldon, keeping well to one side of the trail, gently touched the spurs to the flanks of his spirited horse and thereby terminated all further conversation.

The sheriff reined the horse to a stop, swung from the saddle with loose-hipped ease, dropped the reins to the ground and said easily, "Morning, folks.''

He was wearing leather chaps now, and the jangling spurs and broad-brimmed, high-crown hat seemed to add to his weight and stature.

"This is John Olney, the ranger up here,'' he said by way of blanket introduction. "I guess I know all you folks and you know me. We ain't going to move the body, but we're going to look things over a little bit. Coroner's not due here for a while and we don't want to lose any more evidence.''

The spectators made a tight little circle as they gathered around the two men. Sheriff Eldon, crouching beside the corpse, spoke with brisk authority to the ranger.

"I'm going to take a look through his pockets, John. I want to find out who he was. You take your pencil and paper and inventory every single thing as I take it out.''

Olney nodded. In his official olive-green, he stood quietly efficient, notebook in hand.

But there was nothing for the ranger to write down.

One by one the pockets in the clothes of the dead man were explored by the sheriff's fingers. In each instance the pocket was empty.

The sheriff straightened and regarded the body with a puzzled frown.

The little circle stood watching him, wondering what he would do next. Overhead an occasional wisp of fleecy white cloud drifted slowly across the sky. The faint beginnings of a breeze stirred rustling whispers from the pine trees. Off to the west could be heard, faintly but distinctly, the sounds of the restless water in the North Fork, tumbling over smooth-washed granite boulders into deep pools rippling across gravel bars, plunging down short foam-flecked stretches of swift rapids.

"Maybe he just didn't have anything in his pockets,'' Nottingham suggested.

The sheriff regarded Nottingham with calmly thoughtful eyes. His voice when he spoke withered the young lawyer with remorseless logic. "He probably wouldn't have carried any keys with him unless he'd taken out the keys to an automobile he'd left somewhere at the foot of the trail. He *might* not have had a handkerchief. He could have been dumb enough to have come out without a knife, and it's conceivable he didn't have a pen or pencil. Perhaps he didn't care what time it was, so he didn't carry a watch. But he knew he was going to camp out here in the hills. He was carrying a shoulder pack to travel light. The man would have had matches in his pocket. What's more, you'll notice the stain on the inside of the first and second fingers of his left hand. The man was a cigarette smoker. Where are his matches? Where are his cigarettes? Not that I want to wish my problems off on you, young man. But since you've volunteered to help, I thought I'd point out the things I'd like to have you think about."

Nottingham flushed.

Dowling laughed a deep booming laugh, then he said, "Don't blame him, sheriff. He's a lawyer."

The sheriff bent once more, to run his hands along the man's waist, exploring in vain for a money belt. He ran his fingers along the lining of the coat, said suddenly to the ranger, "Wait a minute, John. We've got something here."

"What?" the ranger asked.

"Something concealed in the lining of his coat," the sheriff answered.

"Perhaps it slipped down through a hole in the inside pocket," Nottingham suggested.

"Isn't any hole in the pocket," Eldon announced. "Think I'm going to have to cut the lining, John."

The sheriff's sharp knife cut through the stitches in the lining with the deft skill of a seamstress. His fingers explored through the opening, brought out a Manila envelope darkened and polished from the friction of long wear.

The sheriff looked at the circled faces. "Got your pencil ready, John?"

The ranger nodded.

The sheriff opened the flap of the envelope and brought out a photograph frayed at the corners.

"Now, what do you make of that?" he asked.

"I don't make anything of it," Olney said, studying the photograph. "It's a good-looking young fellow standing up, having his picture taken."

"This is a profile view of the same man," the sheriff said, taking out another photograph.

"Just those two pictures?" Olney asked.

"That's all. The man's body kept 'em from getting wet."

Ames, looking over the sheriff's shoulder, saw very clear snapshots of a young man whom he judged to be about twenty-six or twenty-seven, with a shock of wavy dark hair, widespread intelligent eyes, a somewhat weak vacillating mouth, and clothes which even in the photograph indicated expensive tailoring.

Quite evidently here was a young man who was vain, good-looking and who knew he was good-looking, a man who had been able to get what he wanted at the very outset of life and had then started coasting along, resting on his oars at an age when most men were buckling down to the grim realities of a competitive existence.

The picture had been cut off on the left, evidently so as to exclude some woman who was standing on the man's right, but her left hand rested across his shoulder, and, seeing that hand, Ames suddenly noticed a vague familiarity about it. It was a shapely, delicate hand with a gold signet ring on the third finger.

Ames couldn't be absolutely certain in the brief glimpse he had, but he *thought* he had seen that ring before.

Yesterday, Roberta Coe had been wearing a ring which was startlingly like that.

Ames turned to look at Roberta.   He couldn't catch her eye immediately, but Sylvia Jessup, deftly maneuvering herself into a position so she could glance at the photographs, caught the attention of everyone present by a quick, sharp gasp.

"What is it?" the sheriff asked.   "Know this man?"

"Who?" she asked, looking down at the corpse.

"The one in the picture."

"Heavens no.   I was just struck by the fact that he's—well, so good-looking. You wonder why a dead man would be carrying his photograph."

Sheriff Eldon studied her keenly.   "That the only reason?"

"Why, yes, of course."

"Humph!" Bill Eldon said.

The others crowded forward.   Eldon hesitated a moment, then slipped the photographs back into the envelope.

"We'll wait until the coroner gets here," he said.

Frank Ames caught Roberta Coe's eye and saw the strained agony of her face. He knew she had had a brief glimpse of those photographs, and he knew that unless he created some diversion her white-faced dismay would attract the attention of everyone.

He stepped forward calmly.   "May I see those photographs?" he asked.

The sheriff turned to look at him, slipped the Manila envelope down inside his jacket pocket.

"Why?" he asked.

"I want to see if I know the man.   He looked like a man who was a buddy of mine."

"What name?" Bill Eldon asked.

Frank Ames could see that his ruse was working.   No one was looking at Roberta Coe now.   All eyes were fastened on him.

"What name?" the sheriff repeated.

Ames searched the files of his memory with frantic haste.   "Pete Ingle," he blurted, giving the name of the first man whom he had ever seen killed; and because it was the first time he had seen a buddy shot down, it had left an indelible impression on Frank's mind.

Sheriff Eldon started to remove the envelope from his jacket pocket, then thought better of it.   His eyes made shrewd appraisal of Frank Ames' countenance, said, "Where is this Pete Ingle now?"

"Dead."

"Where did he die?"

"Guadalcanal."

"How tall?"

"Five feet, ten inches."

"What did he weigh?"

"I guess a hundred and fifty-five or sixty."

"Blond or brunette?"

"Brunette."

"I'm going to check up on this, you know," Bill Eldon said, his voice kindly. "What color eyes?"

"Blue."

Eldon put the picture back in his pocket. "I don't think we'll do anything more about these pictures until after the coroner comes."

Ames flashed a glance toward Roberta, saw that she had, in some measure, recovered her composure. It was only a quick fleeting glance. He didn't dare attract attention to her by looking directly at her.

It was as he turned away that he saw Sylvia Jessup watching him with eyes that had lost their mocking humor and were engaged in respectful appraisal, as though she were sizing up a potential antagonist, suddenly conscious of his strong points, but probing for his weak points.

By using the Forest Service telephone to arrange for horses, a plane, and one of the landing fields maintained by the fire-fighting service, the official party managed to arrive at the scene of the crime shortly before noon.

Leonard Keating, the young, ruthlessly ambitious deputy district attorney, accompanied James Logan, the coroner.

Sheriff Bill Eldon, John Olney the ranger, Logan the coroner, and Keating the deputy district attorney, launched an official investigation, and from the start Keating's attitude was hostile. He felt all of the arrogant impatience of youth for anyone older than forty, and Bill Eldon's conservative caution was to Keating's mind evidence of doddering senility.

"You say that this is Frank Ames' rifle?" Keating asked, indicating the .22 rifle with the telescopic sight.

"That's right," Bill Eldon said, his slow drawl more pronounced than ever. "After the other folks had left, Ames took me over here, showed me the rifle, and—"

"*Showed* you the rifle!" Keating interrupted.

"Now don't get excited," Eldon said. "We'd found it before, but we left it right where it was, just to see what he'd do when he found it. We staked out where we could watch."

"What did he do?"

"Nothing. Later on he showed it to me after the others had left."

"Who were the others?"

"This party that's camped down here a mile or so at the Springs."

"Oh, yes. You told me about them. Vacationists. I know Harvey W. Dowling, the big-time insurance man. You say there's a Richard Nottingham with him. That wouldn't be Dick Nottingham who was on the intercollegiate boxing team?"

"I believe that's right," the sheriff said. "He's a lawyer."

"Yes, yes, a good one too. I was a freshman in college when he was in his senior year. Really a first-class boxer, quicker than a streak of greased lightning and with a punch in either hand. I want to meet him."

"Well, we'll go down there and talk with them. I thought you'd want to look around here. There was nothing in his pockets," the sheriff said. "But when we got to the lining of the coat—"

"Wait a minute," Keating interrupted. "*You're* not supposed to look in the pockets. You're not supposed to touch the body. No one's supposed to move it until the coroner can get here."

"When those folks wrote the lawbooks," the sheriff interrupted, "they didn't have in mind a case where it would take hours for a coroner to arrive and where it might be necessary to get some fast action."

"The law is the law," Keating announced, "and it's not for us to take into consideration what was in the minds of the lawmakers. We read the statutes and have no need to interpret them unless there should be some latent ambiguity, and no such latent ambiguity seems to exist in this case. However, what's done now is done. Let's look around here."

"I've already looked around," the sheriff said.

"I know," Keating snapped, "but we'll take *another* look around the place. You say it rained here yesterday afternoon?"

"A little before sundown it started raining steady. Before then we'd had a thunderstorm. The rain kept up until around ten o'clock. The man was killed before the first rain. I figure he was killed early in the afternoon."

Keating looked at him.

"What makes you think so?"

"Well, he'd been hiking, and he was trying to establish an overnight camp here. Now, I've got a hunch he came in the same way you did—by airplane, only he didn't have any horses to meet him."

"What makes you think that?"

"Well," the sheriff said, "he brought in what stuff he brought in on his back. There's a pack board over there with a tumpline, and his roll of blankets is under that tree. His whole camp is just the way he'd dropped it. Then he'd gone up to get some wood, and the way I figure it, he'd wanted to get that big log so he could keep pushing the ends together and keep a small fire going all night. He didn't have a tent. His bedroll is a light down sleeping bag, the whole thing weighing about eight pounds. But he had quite a bit of camp stuff, maybe a thirty-five pound pack."

"What does all that have to do with the airplane?" Keating asked impatiently.

"Well, now," Eldon said, "I was just explaining. He carried this stuff in on his back, but you look at the leather straps on that pack board and you see that they're new. The whole outfit is new. Now, those leather straps are stained a little bit. If he'd had to bring that stuff in from up the valley, he'd have done a *lot* of sweating."

"Humph," Keating said. "I don't see that necessarily follows. Are there no roads into this back country?"

The sheriff shook his head. "This is a primitive area. You get into it by trails. There aren't any roads closer than twenty miles. I don't think that man carried that camp outfit on his back for twenty miles uphill. I think he walked not more than three or four miles, and I think it was on the level. I've already used Olney's telephone at the ranger station to get my under-sheriff on the job, checking with all charter airplanes to see if they brought a man like this into the country."

Keating said, "Well, I'll look around while the coroner goes over the body. There's a chance you fellows may have overlooked some clues that sharper—and younger—eyes will pick up."

Logan bent over the body. Keating skirmished around through the underbrush, his lean, youthful figure doubled over, moving rapidly as though he were a terrier prowling on a scent. He soon called out.

"Look over here, gentlemen. And be careful how you walk. The place is all messed up with tracks already, but try not to obliterate *this* piece of evidence."

"What have you got?" Olney asked.

"Something that has hitherto been overlooked," Keating announced importantly.

They bent over to look, and Keating pointed to a crumpled cloth tobacco sack which had evidently been about a quarter full of tobacco when the drenching rain had soaked through to the tobacco, stiffening the sack and staining it all to a dark brown which made it difficult to see against the ground.

"And over here," Keating went on, "just six or eight inches from this tobacco sack you'll find the burnt ends of two cigarettes rolled with brown rice paper, smoked down to within about an inch of the end and then left here. Now *I'm* no ex-cattleman," and he glanced meaningly at Bill Eldon, "but *I* would say there's something distinctive about the way these cigarettes are rolled."

"There sure is," Bill Eldon admitted ruefully.

"Well," Keating said, "that's my idea of a clue. It's just about the same as though the fellow had left his calling card. Here are those cigarettes, the stubs showing very plainly how they're rolled and folded. As I understand it, it's quite a job to roll a cigarette, isn't it, sheriff, that is, to do a good job?"

"Sure is," Bill Eldon observed, "and these were rolled by a man who knew his business."

"Don't touch them now," Keating warned. "I want to get a photograph of them just the way they were found, but you can see from just looking at this end that the paper has been rolled over and then there's been a trick fold, something that makes it hold its shape when it's rolled."

"That's right," Olney said—there was a new-found respect in his voice.

"Let's get that camera, coroner," Keating announced, "and take some pictures of these cigarettes. Then we'll carefully pick this evidence up so as not to disturb it. Then I think we'd better go check on the telephone and see if there are any leads to the inquiries Sheriff Eldon put out about someone bringing this chap in by airplane. I have an idea that's where we are going to get a line on him."

"What do you make of this evidence, Bill?" the ranger asked Eldon.

It was Keating who answered the question. "There's no doubt about it. The whole crime was deliberately premeditated. This is the thing that the layman might overlook. It's something that shows its true significance only to the legal mind. It establishes the premeditation which makes for first-degree murder. The murderer lay here waiting for his man. He waited while he smoked two cigarettes."

"How do you suppose the murderer knew the man was going to camp right here?" Bill Eldon asked.

"That's a minor matter," Keating said. "The point is, he did know. He was lying here waiting. He smoked two cigarettes. Probably the man had already made his camp here and then gone up the hill for firewood, dragging that log down the hill along the trail that you pointed out."

Eldon's nod was dubious.

"Don't you agree with that?" Keating demanded truculently.

"I was just wondering if the fellow that was killed wasn't pretty tired from his walk," Eldon said.

"Why? You said he only had to walk three or four miles from an airfield and it was pretty level ground all the way."

"I know," Eldon said, "but if he'd already established his camp here and then gone up the hill to get that firewood and dragged it down, the murderer must have moved into ambush *after* the man went up to get that log."

"Well?"

"The victim certainly must have been awfully tired if it took long enough getting that log for the murderer to smoke two cigarettes."

"Well, perhaps the murderer smoked them after the crime, or he may have been waiting for his man to get in just the right position. There's no use trying to account for all these little things."

"That's right," Eldon said.

"This evidence," Keating went on significantly, "would have been overlooked if I hadn't been prowling around, crawling on my hands and knees looking for any little thing that might have escaped observation."

"Just like a danged bloodhound," Olney said admiringly.

"That's right," Bill Eldon admitted. "Just like a bloodhound. Don't see anything else there, do you, son?"

"How much else do you want?" Keating flared impatiently. "And let's try and retain something of the dignity of our positions, sheriff. Now, if you've no objection, we'll go to the telephone and see what we can discover."

"No objection at all," Eldon said. "I'm here to do everything I can."

Information was waiting for them at the Forest Service telephone office.

The operator said, "Your office left a message to be forwarded to you, sheriff. A private charter plane took a man by the name of George Bay, who answers the description you gave over the telephone, into forest landing field number thirty-six, landing about ten o'clock yesterday morning. The man had a pack and took off into the woods. He said he was on a hiking trip and wanted to get some pictures. He told a couple of stories which didn't exactly hang together and the pilot finally became suspicious. He thought his passenger was a fugitive and threatened to turn the plane around and fly to the nearest city to report to the police. When George Bay realized the pilot meant business, he told him he was a detective employed to trace some very valuable jewels which had been stolen by a member of the military forces while he was in Japan. He showed the pilot his credentials as a detective and said he was on a hot lead, that the jewels had been hidden for over a year, but the detective felt he was going to find them. He warned the aviator to say nothing to anyone.''

Bill Eldon thanked the operator, relayed the information to the others.

''Well,'' Keating said, ''I guess that does it.''

''Does what?'' the sheriff asked.

''Gives us our murderer,'' Keating said. ''It has to be someone who was in the Army during the war, someone who was in Japan. How about this man Ames? Isn't he a veteran?''

''That's right. I think he was a prisoner in Japan.''

''Well, we'll go talk with him,'' Keating said. ''He's our man.''

''Of course,'' Eldon pointed out, ''if this dead man was *really* a detective, it ain't hardly likely he'd tell the airplane pilot what he was after. If he said he was after Japanese gems, he's like as not looking for stolen nylons.''

''You forget that the pilot was calling for a showdown,'' Keating said. ''He forced this man's hand.''

''Maybe. It'd take more force than that to get *me* to show *my* hand on a case.''

''Well, I'm going to act on the assumption this report is true until it's proven otherwise,'' Keating said.

Sheriff Bill Eldon said, ''Okay, that's up to you. Now my idea of the way to really solve this murder is to sort of take it easy and . . .''

''And *my* idea of the way to solve it,'' Keating interrupted impatiently, ''is to lose no more time getting evidence and lose no time at all getting the murderer. It's the responsibility of your office to get the murderer; the responsibility of my office to prosecute him. Therefore,'' he added significantly, ''I think it will pay you to let me take the initiative from this point on. I think we should work together, sir!''

''Well, we're together,'' Bill Eldon observed cheerfully. ''Let's work.''

Roberta Coe surveyed the little cabin, the grassy meadow, the graveled bar in the winding stream, the long finger of pine trees which stretched down the slope.

''So *this* is where you live?''

Frank Ames nodded.

''Don't you get terribly lonely?''

''I did at first.''

''You don't now?''

''No.''

He felt at a loss for words and even recognized an adolescent desire to kick at the soil in order to furnish some outlet for his nervous tension.

''I should think you'd be lonesome *all* the time.''

''At first,'' he said, ''I didn't have any choice in the matter. I wasn't physically able to meet people or talk with them. They exhausted me. I came up here and lived alone because I *had* to come up here and live alone. And then I found that I enjoyed it. Gradually I came to learn something about the woods, about the deer, the trout, the birds, the weather. I studied the different types of clouds, habits of game. I had some books and some old magazines sent me and I started to read, and enjoyed the reading. The days began to pass rapidly and then a tranquil peace came to my mind." He stopped, surprised at his own eloquence.

He saw her eyes light with interest. "Could you tell me more about that, and aren't you going to invite me in?"

He seemed embarrassed. "Well, it's just a bachelor's cabin, and, of course, I'm alone here and—"

She raised her eyebrows. Her eyes were mocking. "The conventions?"

He would have given much to have been able to meet the challenge of her light, bantering mood, but to his own ears the words seemed to fairly blurt from his mouth as he said, "People up here are different. They wouldn't understand, in case anyone should—"

"I don't care whether they understand or not," she said. "You were talking about mental tranquillity. I could use quite an order of that."

He said nothing.

"I suppose you have visitors about once a month?"

"Oh, once every so often. Mr. Olney, the ranger, rides by."

She said, "And I presume you feel that your cabin is a mess because you've been living here by yourself and that, as a woman, I'd look around disapprovingly and sniff. Come on, let's go in. I want to talk with you and I'm not going to stand out here."

Silently he opened the door.

"You don't even keep it locked?"

He shook his head. "Out here I never think of it. If Olney, for instance, found himself near this cabin and a shower was coming up, he'd go in, make himself at home, cook up a pot of tea, help himself to anything he wanted to eat, and neither of us would think anything of it. The only rule is that a man's supposed to leave enough dry wood to start a fire."

"What a cute little place! How snug and cozy!"

"You think so?" he asked, his face showing surprised relief.

"Heavens, yes. It's just as neat and spick-and-span as—as a yacht."

"I'm afraid I don't know much about yachts."

"Well, what I meant was that—well, you know, everything shipshape. You have a radio?"

"Yes, a battery set."

"And a gasoline reading lamp and a cute little stove and bookshelves. How wonderful!"

He suddenly found himself thoroughly at ease.

Abruptly she said, "Tell me more about this mental tranquillity. I want some of that."

"You can't saw it off in chunks, wrap it up in packages and sell it by the pound."

"So I gathered. But would you mind telling me how one goes about finding it? Do you find it at outcroppings and dig it up, or do you sink shafts, or . . .?"

"I guess it's something that's within you all the time. All you do is relax and let it come to the surface. The trouble is," he said, suddenly earnest, "that it's hard to understand it because it's all around you.   It's a part of man's heritage, but he ignores it, shuts it out.

"Look at the view through the window.   There's the mountain framed against the blue sky.   The sunlight is casting silver reflections on the ripples in the water where it runs over the rapids by the gravel bar.   There's a trout jumping in the pool just below the bar.   The bird perched on the little pine with that air of impudent expectancy is a Clark jay, sometimes called a camp robber.   I love him for his alert impudence, his fearless assurance.   Everything's tranquil and restful and there's no reason for inner turmoil."

Her eyes widened.   "Say, when you warm up to something, you *really* talk, don't you?"

He said, "I love these mountains and I can talk when I'm telling people about them.   You see, lots of people don't really appreciate them.   During hunting season, people come pouring in.   They come to kill things.   If they don't get a deer, they think the trip has been a failure.   What they see of the mountains is more or less incidental to killing.

"Same way with the fishing season crowd.   But when you come to *live* in the mountains, you learn to get in time with the bigness of it all.   There's an underlying tranquillity that finally penetrates to your consciousness and relaxes the nerve tension.   You sort of quiet down.   And then you realize how much real strength and dignity there is in the calm certainty of your own part in the eternal universe.

"These mountains are a soul tonic.   They soothe the tension out of your nerves and take away the hurt in one's soul.   They give strength.   You can just *feel* them in their majestic stability.   Oh, hang it, you can't put it in words, and here I am trying!"

The interest in her eyes, the realization of his own eloquence made him suddenly self-conscious once more.

"Mind if I smoke?" she asked.

"Certainly not.   I'll roll one myself."

He took the cloth tobacco sack from his pocket, opened a package of cigarette papers.

She said, "Won't you try one of mine?"

"No thanks.   I like to roll my own.   I—" He broke off and said, "Something frightened those mountain quail."

He held a match for her cigarette, rolled his own cigarette and had just pinched the end into shape when he said, "I knew something frightened them.   Hear the horses?"

She cocked her head to one side, listening, then nodded, caught the expression on Frank Ames' face and suddenly laughed.   "And you're afraid I've compromised your good name."

"No.   But suppose it should be *your* companions looking for you and . . ."

"Don't be silly," she said easily.   "I'm free to do as I please.   I came up here to explain to you about yesterday.   I—I'm sorry."

The riders came up fast at a brisk trot.   Then the tempo of hoofbeats changed from a steady rhythm to the disorganized tramping of horses being pulled up and circling, as riders dismounted and tied up.   Ames, at the door, said, "It's the sheriff, the ranger, and a couple of other people.

"Hello, folks," he called out.   "Won't you come in?"

"We're coming," Bill Eldon said.

Frank Ames' attitude was stiffly embarrassed as he said, "I have company. Miss Coe was looking over my bookshelf."

"Oh, yes," the sheriff said quite casually.   "This is James Logan, the coroner, and Leonard Keating, the deputy district attorney.   They wanted to ask you a few questions."

Keating was patronizingly contemptuous as he looked around the interior of the neat little cabin, found that the only comfortable chair was that occupied by Roberta Coe, that the others were homemade stools and boxes which had been improvised into furniture.   "Well," he said, "we won't be long.   We wanted to get all the details, everything that you know about that murder, Ames."

"I told the sheriff everything I know about it."

"You didn't see anything or hear anything out of the ordinary yesterday afternoon?"

"No.   That is, I—"

"Yes, go ahead," Keating said.

"Nothing," Ames said.

Keating's eyes narrowed.   "You weren't up around that locality?"

"I was fishing downstream."

"How far below here?"

"Quarter of a mile, I guess."

"And the murder was committed half a mile upstream?"

"I guess that distance is about right."

"You weren't fishing upstream at all?"

"No.   I fished downstream."

Keating's eyes showed a certain sneering disbelief.   "What are you doing up here, anyway?"

"I'm—Well, I'm just living up here."

"Were you in the Army?"

"Yes."

"In Japan?"

"Yes."

"How long?"

"I was a prisoner of war for a while and then I was held there a while before I was sent home."

"Picked up some gems while you were there, didn't you?"

"I had a pearl and—What do you mean I *picked up* gems?"

Keating's eyes were insolent in their contemptuous hostility.   "I mean you stole them," he said, "and you came up here to lie low and wait until things blew over. Isn't that about it?"

"That's definitely not true."

"And," Keating went on, "this man who was killed was a detective who was looking for some gems that had been stolen from Japan. He looked you up yesterday afternoon and started questioning you, didn't he?''

"No!''

"Don't lie to me.''

Ames was suddenly on his feet. "Damn you!" he said. "I'm not lying to you and I don't have to put up with this stuff. Now, get out of here!''

Keating remained seated, said, "Sheriff, will you maintain order?''

Bill Eldon grinned. "You're doing the talking, Keating.''

"I'm questioning this man. He's suspect in a murder case.''

"*I'm* suspect?'' Ames exclaimed.

"You said it," Keating announced curtly.

"You're crazy, in addition to the other things that are wrong with you," Ames told him. "I don't have to put up with talk like that from you or from anyone else.''

Keating said, "We're going to look around here. Any objection?''

Ames turned to Bill Eldon. "Do I have to—''

Roberta Coe said very firmly and definitely, "Not unless you want him to, Frank; not unless he has a search warrant. Don't let them pull that kind of stuff. Dick Nottingham is an attorney. If you want, I'll get him and—''

"I don't want a lawyer," Ames said. "I haven't any money to pay a lawyer.''

"Go ahead. Get a lawyer if you want," Keating said, "but I think I have enough evidence right now to warrant this man's arrest. Would you mind letting me see that cigarette, Mr. Ames.''

"What cigarette?''

"The one you just put in the ash tray. Thank you.''

Keating inspected the cigarette, passed the tray silently to the sheriff.

"What's strange about the cigarette?'' Ames asked.

"The cigarette," Keating said, "is rolled in a peculiarly distinctive manner. Do you always roll your cigarettes that way?''

"Yes. That is, I have for years. I pull one edge of the paper over and then make a little crimp and fold it back before I start rolling. That helps hold the cigarette in shape.''

Keating took a small pasteboard box from his pocket. This box was lined with soft moss and on the moss were two cigarette stubs. "Would you say these were rolled by you?''

Ames leaned forward.

"Don't touch them," Keating warned. "Just look at the ends.''

"I don't think you'd better answer that, Frank," Roberta Coe said.

"I have nothing to conceal," Ames said. "Certainly those are my cigarettes. Where did you find them?''

"You rolled those?''

"Yes.''

Keating stood up and dramatically pointed his finger at Frank Ames. "I accuse you of the murder of George Bay, a private detective.''

Ames' face flushed.

"Will you take him into custody, sheriff? I order you to."

"Well, now," the sheriff said in a drawl, "I don't know as I have to take anybody into custody on the strength of your say-so."

"This man is to be arrested and charged with murder," Keating said. "A felony has been committed. There is reasonable ground to believe this man guilty. It is not necessary to have a warrant of arrest under those circumstances, and, as a member of the district attorney's office, I call on you as the sheriff of this county to take that man into custody. If you fail to do so, the responsibility will be entirely on your shoulders."

"Okay," Bill Eldon said cheerfully, "the responsibility is on my shoulders."

"And I want to look around here," Keating said.

"As long as you're halfway decent, I'm willing to do anything I can to cooperate," Ames told him, "but you're completely crazy if you accuse me of having anything to do with that murder."

"It was your gun that killed him, wasn't it?"

"My gun was at the scene of the crime—near the scene of the crime."

"And you don't know how it got there?"

Ames said, "Of course I don't. Do you think I'd be silly enough to go out and kill a man and then leave my rifle lying on the ground? If I'd killed him, I'd have taken my gun to the cabin, cleaned it, and hung it up on those pegs where it belongs."

"If you were smart, you wouldn't," Keating sneered. "You'd know that the officers would recover the fatal bullet and shoot test bullets from all the .22 rifles owned by anyone in these parts. Sooner or later you would have to face the fact that the man was killed with a bullet from your gun. You were smart enough to realize it would be a lot better to have the gun found at the scene of the murder and claim it had been stolen."

"I wouldn't let them search this cabin, Frank," Roberta Coe said in a low voice. "I'd put them all out of here and lock the cabin up and make certain that no one got in until they returned with a search warrant, and then you could have your attorney present when the search was made. How do you know they aren't going to plant something?"

Keating turned to regard her with hostile eyes. "You're doing a lot of talking," he said. "Where were *you* when the murder was committed?"

Her face suddenly drained of color.

"Were you up here yesterday in this cabin?"

"No."

"Anywhere near it?"

"No."

"Go past here on the trail?"

"I—I took a walk."

"Where did you walk?"

"Up the trail."

"Up to the point where the murder was committed?"

"No, not that far. I turned back. I don't know. Quite a bit downstream from here."

"See this man yesterday?"

Roberta tightened her lips. "Yes."

"Where?"

"I met him on the trail. He was walking down toward the place where I was camped."

"Why was he walking down there?"

"I didn't ask him. He overtook me on the trail, and we exchanged greetings and then walked together down the trail to the place where I'm camped, and I introduced him to the others."

"And then he turned back?"

"No. He said he was going on."

"Well, now isn't that interesting! I thought you said he was fishing yesterday afternoon, sheriff."

"He'd been fishing. I found his rod and creel where he'd left it, apparently when he walked down the trail."

"Well, well, well, isn't *that* interesting," Keating sneered. "So he went fishing and then left his rod and creel by the water. Just laid them down, I presume, and walked away."

"No, he propped the rod up against the tree and hung the creel over a forked limb."

"And then what?"

"Apparently he walked on down the trail."

"What was the idea, Ames?" Keating asked.

Frank said, "I wanted to look over some of the country. I—I walked on down the trail and met Miss Coe."

"I see. Went as far as her camp with her?"

"Well, I walked on a ways below camp."

"How far?"

"Oh, perhaps two hundred yards."

"Then what?"

"Then I turned back."

"Back up the trail?"

"No, I didn't. I made a swing."

Roberta Coe, rushing to his assistance, said, "He was looking over the country in order to find a site for some traps this winter."

"Oh, looking for traps, eh?"

"A place to put traps," Roberta Coe said acidly.

"Which way did you turn, Ames? Remember now, we can check on some of this."

Ames said, "I turned up the draw, crossed over the divide and then the rainstorm overtook me, and I lay in a cave up there by the ridge."

"You turned east?" the ranger asked, suddenly interested, and injecting himself into the conversation.

"Yes."

"Looking for a trap-line site?" Olney asked, incredulously.

"Well, I was looking the country over.   I had intended to look for a trap-line site and then—"

"What are you talking about?" Olney said.   "You know this country as well as you know the palm of your hand.   Anyhow, you wouldn't be trapping up there. You'd be trapping down on the stream."

Ames said, "Well, I told Miss Coe that I—Well, I was a little embarrassed. I wanted to walk with her but I didn't want her to think I—It was just one of those things."

"You mean you *weren't* looking for a trap site?" Keating asked.

"No.   I wanted to walk with her."

"In other words, you lied to her.   Is that right?"

Ames, who had seated himself once more on a box, was up with cold fury. "Get out of here," he said.

"And don't answer any more questions, Frank," Roberta Coe pleaded.   "You don't have to talk to people when they are that insulting."

Keating said, "And I'm going to give you the benefit of a little investigation too, Miss Coe."

Ames, his face white with fury, said, "Get out!   Damn you, get out of my cabin!"

Bill Eldon grinned.   "Well, Keating, you wanted to do the questioning.   I guess you've done it."

"That's it," Keating said grimly.   "I've done it, and I've solved your murder case for you."

"Thanks," Bill Eldon said dryly.

They filed out of the cabin.

Once more Keating said, "I order you to put that man under arrest."

"I heard you," Bill Eldon said.

Keating turned to Olney.   "What sort of title does this man have to this property?"

"Well, he's built this cabin under lease from the Forestry Service—"

"And the Forestry Service retains the right to inspect the premises?"

"I guess so, yes."

. "All right," Keating said, "let's do some inspecting."

Frank Ames stood in the doorway, his heart pounding with anger, and the old nervous weakness was back, making the muscles of his legs quiver.   He watched the men moving around in front of the cabin, saw the ranger suddenly pause. "This chopping block has been moved," Olney said.   "It was over there for quite a while.   You can see the depression in the ground.   Why did you move it, Ames?"

Ames, suddenly surprised, said, "I didn't move it.   Someone else must have moved it."

Olney tilted the chopping block on edge, rolled it back to one side.   Keating said, "Someone has disturbed this earth.   Is there a spade here?"

Olney said, "Here's one," and reached for the shovel which was standing propped against the cabin.

Keating started digging under the place where the chopping block had been.

Ames pushed forward to peer curiously over Bill Eldon's shoulder.

Roberta Coe, standing close to him, slipped her hand into his, giving it a reassuring squeeze.

"What's this?" Keating asked.

The spade had caught on a piece of red cloth.

Keating dropped to his knees, pulled away the rest of the loose soil with his fingers, brought out a knotted red bandanna, untied the knots and spread on the ground the assortment of things that were rolled up in it.

Ames, looking with incredulous eyes, saw a leather billfold, a card case distended from cards and documents, a fountain pen, a pencil, a notebook, a knife, some loose silver, a white handkerchief, a package of cigarettes, a folder of matches and a small, round waterproof match case.

Keating picked up the card case, opened it to show the cards of identification, neatly arranged in hinged cellophane pockets.

The first card showed a picture of a man with thick hair, a close-clipped dark mustache, and, even in the glimpse he had of it, Frank Ames could see it was the photograph of the murdered man.

"Deputy license of George Bay," Keating announced.   "Here's another one. Identification showing George Bay licensed as a private detective.   Here's a credit card, Standard Oil Company, made out to George Bay.   Some stuff that's been in here is missing.   You can see this card case has been distended with cards that were in the pockets.   They're gone now.   What did you do with them, Ames?"

Ames could only shake his head.

"You see," Keating said triumphantly, turning to Eldon.   "He thought he could keep anyone from finding out the identity of the murdered man, so he removed everything that could have been a means of identification."

The sheriff shook his head sadly.   "This murderer is making me plumb mad."

"You don't act like it," Keating said.

"Thinking we'd be so dumb we couldn't find all the clues he planted unless he was so darned obvious about it," the sheriff went on sadly.   "It's just plumb insultin' to our intelligence.   He was so darned afraid we wouldn't find all that stuff he even moved the choppin' block.   I'd say that man just don't think we've got good sense."

"You mean you're going to try to explain away *this* evidence?" Keating asked.

Bill Eldon shook his head.   "I'm not explaining a thing.   It's just plumb insultin', that's all."

Roberta Coe, her mind in a turmoil, followed a tributary of the main stream, walking along a game trail, hardly conscious of where she was going or of her surroundings, wanting only to get entirely away from everyone.

She could keep silent, protect her secret and retain her position in her circle of friends, or she could tell what she knew, help save an innocent man—and bring the security of her life, with all of its pleasant associations, tumbling down in ruins. After all, the sheriff had not specifically asked her to identify those photographs.

It was not an easy decision.

Yet she knew in advance what her answer was to be. She had sought the vast, rugged majesty of the mountains, the winding trail along the talkative stream, to give her strength.

If she had been going to take refuge in weakness, she would have been in camp with her companions, a highball glass in her hand, talking, joking, using the quick-witted repartee of her set to shield her mind from the pressure of her conscience.

But she needed strength, needed it desperately. Frank Ames had managed to get spiritual solace from these mountains. If she could only let some of their sublime indifference to the minor vicissitudes of life flow into her own soul.

Then it would be easy. Now it was—

Suddenly Roberta sensed something wrong with a patch of deep shadow to the left of the trail. There was the semblance of solidity about that shadow, and then, even as her eyes tried to interpret what she saw, the figure that was almost hidden in the shadow moved.

Roberta screamed.

Bill Eldon, who had been sitting motionless, squatting on his heels cowboy-fashion, straightened himself with sinewy ease.

"Now, don't be frightened, ma'am," he said. "I just wanted to talk with you."

"You—You—How did you—find me here?"

"Now, take it easy," Bill Eldon said, his eyes smiling. "I just thought you and I should have a little talk."

"But how did you know where I was—where you could find me—where I was going to be? Why, even I didn't know where I was going."

Eldon said, "Figure it out, ma'am. This game trail follows the stream. The stream follows the canyon, and the canyon winds around. When I cut your tracks back there in the trail, I knew I only had to walk up over that saddle and come down here to gain half a mile on you. Now, suppose you sit down on that rock there and we just get sociable-like for a little while."

"I'm sorry, sheriff, but I don't feel like—"

"You've got to tell me what frightened you yesterday," the sheriff insisted, kindly but doggedly.

"But I wasn't frightened."

Bill Eldon settled back on his heels once more. Apparently he was completely at ease, thoroughly relaxed.

With the peculiar feeling that she was doing something entirely against her own volition, Roberta sat down.

Bill Eldon said, "Lots of people make a mistake about the mountains. When they're out in the wilds with no one around they feel they're hidden. They're wrong. Wherever they go, they leave tracks."

Roberta Coe said nothing.

When Bill Eldon saw she was not going to speak, he went on. "Now, you take that trail yesterday, for instance. It carried tracks just like a printed page. I came along that trail and saw where you'd been running. I saw where Frank Ames had put down his fishing rod and his creel and hurried after you. The way

I figure it, you must have screamed and run past the hole where he was fishing just about the time he had a big one on.

"By getting up on the bank, looking down in the pool, I could see the submerged branches of that dead tree.   Sure enough, on one of those branches was part of a leader, just wrapped around the snag, and a hook was on the end of the leader. Because I was curious, I took off my clothes, worked my way down into the water and got that fly out.   Gosh, it was cold."

The sheriff reached in his pocket, took out a little fly book, opened it, and showed a section of leader and a Royal Coachman fly.

"Same kind Frank Ames uses," he said.   "You can see a little piece of the fish's lip still stuck on the hook.   The way I figure it, Ames hadn't hooked him too solid, but he had him hooked well enough to land, but as soon as the fish got in that submerged tangle of branches and wrapped the line around a branch, he only had to give one jerk to tear the hook loose.   Now, Ames wouldn't have let that fish get over in the submerged branches unless something had distracted his attention.   That something must have been something he heard, because his eyes were busy looking at the water."

Abruptly Bill Eldon turned to look at her.   "What made you scream?"

She pressed white knuckles against her lips.   "I'm going to tell you," she said.

"I've known that, ever since I—ever since I left Frank Ames.   I was just walking to—well, the mountains seem to do so much for him—I wish I could feel about them the way he does.   Sometimes I think I'm beginning to.

"I was just out of college," she continued, "a naive little heiress.   This man was working for Harvey Dowling.   He was both a secretary and general assistant. His name was Howard Maben.   He was fascinating, dashing.   Women simply went wild over him.   And I fell in love with him."

"What happened?"

"We were secretly married."

"Why the secrecy?"

"It was his idea.   We ran away across the state line to Yuma, Arizona.   Howard said he had to keep it secret."

"Did you know Harvey Dowling then?"

"Yes.   Harvey, and Martha, his wife.   It was her death that caused the scandal."

"What scandal?"

She said, "I don't know if I can explain Howard to you so you'll understand him.   He's a dashing, high-pressure type of man who was a great favorite with women.   He loved to sell things, himself included.   I mean by that he liked to make a sale of his personality.   I don't think there's any question but what he'd get tired of home life within the first thirty days.

"Well, anyway, I guess—it's something I don't like to talk about, but—well, I guess Howard had been—Well, Martha Dowling was attractive.   She was an older woman.   Harvey was always busy at the office, terribly intent on the deals he was putting across, and—Well, they fooled H. W. and they fooled me.

"Apparently Howard started going with Martha Dowling.   They were very discreet about it, pretty cunning, as a matter of fact.   They'd never go except when Harvey Dowling was out of town, and—well, I guess they stayed at motor courts. It was a mess.''

"Go ahead," Bill Eldon said.

"Harvey Dowling was on a two weeks' trip.   He was in Chicago, and Howard made certain he was in Chicago, because he'd talked with him that morning on long-distance telephone.   Then he and Martha went out.   They looked over some property that Harvey Dowling wanted a report on, and then—well, they went to an auto camp.   They didn't like to be seen in restaurants.   Howard had brought a little camp kit of dishes and cooking utensils, one of those outfits that folds up to fit into a suitcase.''

"Go ahead."

"Martha Dowling got sick, some form of an acute gastroenteric disturbance. Well, naturally, they didn't want to call a doctor until after she got home.   She died in Howard's car on the road home.   Of course, Howard tried to fix up a story, but the police began to investigate and put two and two together.   Harvey was called from Chicago by his wife's death and talked with the servants and—well, you can see what happened.''

"What did happen?"

"Howard knew the jig was up.   It seems he'd been left in charge of Dowling's business.   He was already short in his accounts.   So he embezzled everything he could get his hands on and skipped out.

"Dowling left no stone unturned to get him.   He spent thousands of dollars. The police finally caught Howard and sent him to prison.   No one knows that I was married to him.   I was able to get the marriage annulled.   I was able to prove fraud, and—well, of course, I'd been married in Arizona, so I went there and I had a friendly judge and a good lawyer and—there you are.   There's the skeleton in my closet.''

"I still don't know what made you scream," the sheriff said.

"I saw Howard.   You see, his sentence has expired.   He's out.''

"Now, then," Bill Eldon remarked, "we're getting somewhere.   Where was he when you saw him?"

"In the deep shadows of a clump of pines, well off the trail.   I saw just his head and shoulders.   He turned.   Then he whistled.''

"Whistled?"

"That's right.   Howard had a peculiar shrill whistle we used to have as a signal when he wanted me to know he was near the house where I stayed.   I'd let him in by the side door.   It was a peculiar whistle that set my teeth on edge.   It affected me just like the sound of someone scraping his nails along rough cloth. I *hated* it.   I asked him to use some other signal, but he only laughed and said someone else might imitate any other call, but that whistle was distinctively his. It was harsh, strident, metallic.   When he whistled yesterday, I felt positively sick at my stomach—and then I turned and ran just as fast as I could go.''

"You aren't mistaken?"

"In that whistle?   Never!''

"See his face?"

"Not clearly.   The man was standing in the deep shadows.   It was Howard. He had a rifle."

"Who else knows Howard Maben—that is, in your party?"

"Mr. Dowling is the only one; but that girl, Sylvia—I *think* she went back to dig up some of the old newspaper files.   She's made remarks about Mrs. Dowling's death—well, questions.   You understand, it's a subject that's taboo in Dowling's crowd."

"How was your ex-husband dressed when you saw him?"

"I only had a quick glimpse.   I couldn't say."

"Wearing a hat?"

"Yes, a big Western hat."

"Now, then, try and get this one right," the sheriff said.   "Had he been shaved lately?"

"Heavens, I couldn't tell that.   He was in the shadows, but he could see me plainly and that's why he whistled for me to come to him."

"I'm wondering whether he'd been sort of hanging around for a while, watching your camp, or whether he just came in yesterday.   I'd certainly like to know if he was shaved."

"I really couldn't see."

"And you didn't tell anyone about this?"

"No."

"Now, how much did Dowling know about you and Maben?"

"He knew that we were going together.   I guess that's one of the reasons Harvey Dowling didn't suspect his wife.   It was a nasty mess—well, you know how Dowling would feel.   We've never talked much about it."

"I know," Bill Eldon said, his eyes looking off into space, "but there's still something I don't get about it."

She said, "All right, I suppose I've been a sneak.   I suppose I'm living a lie; but I didn't want anyone to know about my marriage."

"On account of Dick Nottingham?"

Her eyes snapped around in startled appraisal.   "How did you—?"

"Sort of guessed from what I saw the other day.   Having a little trouble?"

"You mean Sylvia?"

"Yes."

"Well, you guessed that too."

"How do you feel about Sylvia?"

"I'd like to cut her heart out.   Not that I care about Dick anymore.   He's shown what a conceited boor *he* is.   I'd like to have him at my feet just long enough to walk on him, though."

"Just to show Sylvia?"

"And to show Dick.   Sylvia doesn't care about Dick.   She's a love pirate, one of the girls who have to satisfy their ego by stealing some man.   And I'm—well, I'm living a lie.   I wish now I'd played my cards differently, but I can't do it now.   I've made my choice.   To tell anyone now would make me out a miserable little liar. I don't want to be 'exposed,' particularly with Sylvia to rub it in, and I think Sylvia suspects."

"Never told Nottingham anything about this?"

"Nothing. Should I have done so?" she asked.

"I don't think so," Eldon answered.

The defiance melted from her face. "I was afraid you were going to be self-righteous," she said.

Bill Eldon said nothing.

"The marriage was annulled," she said. "I'm living for the future. Suppose Dick Nottingham and I had married? Suppose I had told him? He'd have been magnanimous about it and all of that, but the thing would have been buried in his mind. Sometime, four or five years later, when I burned the biscuits or was slow in getting dressed to go to a bridge party, he'd flare up with some nasty remark about the grass widow of a jailbird. He'd be sorry the next day, but it would leave a scar."

She paused. "I suppose I'll have to repeat this to that deputy district attorney?"

"I don't think so," Eldon said. "He'd do a little talking and the first thing you know, you'd be reading all about yourself in the newspapers. What is now just a plain murder would suddenly get a sex angle, and the big city papers would send reporters up to get pictures of you and write up a bunch of tripe. You'd have your past 'exposed.' You'd better go right ahead just the way you're doing."

"You mean you're going to keep my secret?"

"I'm going to let you keep it."

She remained silent.

The sheriff pulled an envelope from his pocket, took out the pictures he had removed from inside the lining of the coat of the murdered man.

"These pictures are of Howard—the man you married?"

She barely glanced at them, nodded.

"You recognized them when I first found them?"

"Yes, and that's my hand on his shoulder. That ring is a signet ring my father gave me."

"Any idea what this detective was doing with those pictures?"

"Howard's sentence expired about two months ago. He's after Dowling—or me. And the detective somehow got on Howard's trail. And Howard, with all that fiendish cunning of his—well, he got the detective."

The sheriff got to his feet, moving with a smooth ease. "Well, I've got work to do."

Roberta Coe moved impulsively forward, said, "I don't suppose you'd have any way of knowing that you're a dear!" and kissed him.

"Oh," she said in dismay, "I've ruined your face! Here, let me get that off."

She took a handkerchief from her pocket. The sheriff grinned as she removed the lipstick. "Good idea," he said. "That young deputy district attorney would think I'd been bribed. Hell, you can't tell, maybe I have!"

Bill Eldon reined his horse to a stop, swung his left leg over the horse's neck and sat with it crooked around the saddle horn.

"How are things coming?" he asked.

"As far as I'm concerned," Leonard Keating said, "it's an open-and-shut case. I'm ready to go back any time you're ready to pick up the prisoner."

Eldon said, "I want to look around the country a little bit before I start back. Got to check up on some of the homesteaders up here."

"What are we going to do with Ames?" Keating demanded. "Let him run away?"

"He won't get away."

Keating said indignantly, "Well, I'll tell you one thing, he isn't *my* responsibility."

"That's right," Eldon said. "He's mine."

John Olney, the ranger, looked at the sheriff questioningly.

"Now then," Bill Eldon went on, "we, all of us, have our responsibilities. Now, Keating, here, has got to prosecute the man."

"There's plenty of evidence to get a conviction of first-degree murder," Keating said.

"And," Bill Eldon went on, "part of the evidence you're going to present to the jury is the evidence of those two cigarette stubs. That's right, eh?"

"Those cigarette stubs are the most damning piece of evidence in the whole case. They show premeditation."

"Nicely preserved, aren't they?"

"They're sufficiently preserved so I can identify them to a jury and get a jury to notice their distinctive peculiarities."

"All right," Eldon said cheerfully, and then added, "Of course, that murder was committed either during the rainstorm or just before the rainstorm. The evidence shows that."

"Of course it does," Keating said. "That cloth tobacco sack which was left on the ground had been soaked with rain. The tobacco had been moistened enough so that the stain from it oozed out into the cloth."

"Sure did," the sheriff said. "Now then, young man, when you get up in front of a jury with this ironclad, open-and-shut case of yours, maybe some smart lawyer on the other side is going to ask you how it happened that the tobacco got all wet, while those cigarette ends made out of delicate rice paper are just as dry and perfectly formed as the minute the smoker took them out of his mouth."

The sheriff watched the expression on the deputy district attorney's face. Then his lips twisted in a grin. "Well, now, son," he said, "I've got a little riding to do. How about it, John? Think you got a little free time on your hands?"

"Sure," the ranger said.

"What?" the deputy district attorney exclaimed. "Do you mean—?"

"Sure," the sheriff said. "Don't worry, buddy. Ames is *my* prisoner. I'm responsible for him. You just think out the answer to that question about the cigarette ends, because somebody's going to ask it of you when you get in court."

"There's no reason why the murderer couldn't have returned to the scene of the crime."

"Sure, sure," Eldon said soothingly. "Then he rolled cigarettes out of soggy, wet tobacco, and smoked 'em right down to the end. But somehow, I reckon, you've got to do better than that, young fellow."

Bill Eldon nodded to the ranger. "Come on, John, you can do more good riding with me than—"

"But this is an outrage!" Keating stormed. "I protest against it. This man, Ames, was arrested for murder!"

"Who arrested him?" the sheriff asked.

"If you want to put it that way, *I* did," Keating said. "As a deputy district attorney and as a private citizen, I have a right to take this man in custody for first-degree murder."

"Go ahead and take him in custody then," the sheriff grinned. "Then he'll be your responsibility. Come on, John, let's go riding."

The sheriff swung his leg back over the horse's neck and straightened himself in the saddle.

"You'll have to answer for this," Leonard Keating said, his voice quivering with rage.

"That's right," Eldon assured him cheerfully, "I expect to," and rode off.

Bill Eldon and the ranger found a live lead at the second cabin at which they stopped.

Carl Raymond, a tall, drawling, tobacco-chewing trapper in his late fifties, came to the door of his cabin as soon as his barking dog had advised him of the approaching horsemen.

His eye was cold, appraising and uncordial.

"So, you folks are working together now," he said scornfully. "I haven't any venison hanging up, and I have less than half the limit of fish. As far as I'm concerned—"

Bill Eldon interrupted. "Now, Carl, I've never asked any man who lives in the mountains where he got his meat. You know that."

Raymond swung his eyes to the ranger. "You ain't riding alone," he said to the sheriff.

"This is other business," the sheriff said. "The ranger is with me. I'm not with him."

"What's on your mind?"

"A man's been murdered down here, five or six miles over on the Middle Fork."

Raymond twisted the wad of tobacco with his tongue, glanced once more at both men, then expectorated between tightly clenched lips. "What do you want?"

"A little assistance. Thought maybe you might have crossed some tracks of a man I might be looking for."

"The mountains are full of tracks these days," Raymond said bitterly. "You can't get a hundred yards from your cabin without running across dude tracks."

"These would be the tracks of someone that was living in the mountains, playing a lone hand," the sheriff said.

"Can't help you a bit," Raymond told him.   "Sorry."

The sheriff said, "I'm interested in any unusually big fires, particularly any double fires."

Raymond started to shake his head, then paused.   "How's that?"

The sheriff repeated his statement.

Raymond hesitated, seemed about to say something, then became silent.

At the end of several seconds Olney glanced questioningly at the sheriff, and Eldon motioned him to silence.

Raymond silently chewed his tobacco.   At length he moved out from the long shadows of the pines, pointed toward a saddle in the hills to the west.   "There's a little game trail, works up that draw," he said, "and goes right through that saddle.   Fifty yards on the other side it comes to a little flat against a rocky ledge. There was a double fire built there last night."

"Know who did it?"

"Nope.   I just saw the ashes of the fire this morning."

"What time?" asked the sheriff.

"A little after daylight."

"Carl," the sheriff said, "I think that's the break we've been looking for. You've really been a help."

"Don't mention it," Raymond said, turned on his heel, whistled to his dog, and strode into his cabin.

"Come on," Bill Eldon said to Olney.   "I think we've got something!"

"I don't get it," Olney said.   "What's the idea of the double fire?"

Eldon swung his horse into a rapid walk.   "It rained last night.   The ground was wet.   A man who was camping out without blankets would build a big, long fire.   The ground underneath the fire would get hot and be completely dry.   Then when the rain let up and it turned cold, the man only needed to rake the coals of that fire into two piles, chop some fir boughs, and put them on the hot ground. In that way he'd have dry, warm ground underneath him, sending heat up through the fir boughs, and the piles of embers on each side would keep his sides warm. Then about daylight, when he got up, he could throw the fir boughs on the embers and burn them up.   He'd put out the fire, after he'd cooked breakfast, by pouring water from the stream on the coals."

"A man sleeping out without blankets," Olney said musingly.   "There's *just* a chance," he added, "that you know something I don't."

Bill Eldon grinned.   "There's just a chance," he admitted, "that I do."

Roberta Coe found Frank Ames in his cabin, pouring flour and water into the crusted crock in which he kept his sour dough.   The door was ajar and from the outer twilight the illumination of the gasoline lantern seemed incandescent in its brilliance.

"Hello," she called, "may I come in?   I heard you were released on your own recognizance."

"The sheriff," Ames said, "has some sense. Come on in. Are you alone?"

"Yes. Why?"

"But you can't be going around these trails at night. It'll be dark before you can possibly get back, even if you start right now."

"I brought a flashlight with me, and I'm not starting back right now. I just got here!"

"But, gosh, I—"

She crossed the floor of the cabin, to sit on one of the homemade stools, her elbows propped on the rustic table. "Know something?" she asked.

"What?"

"I told the sheriff about screaming and about how you came after me and all that. I realized I'd have to tell him sooner or later, but—well, thanks for protecting me—for covering up."

"You didn't need to tell them. They've got no case against me, anyway."

She felt that his tone lacked the assurance it should have.

"I told them anyway. What are you making?"

"Sour-dough biscuit."

"Smells—terrible."

"Tastes fine," he said, grinning. "A man must eat even if the state *is* trying to hang him."

"Oh, it's not that bad."

"It is, as far as that deputy district attorney is concerned."

"I hate him!" she said. "He's intolerant, officious and egotistical. But—well, I wanted you to know I'd told the sheriff and there's no reason why you should try to—to cover up for me anymore."

"How much did you tell him?"

"Everything."

For a moment his look was quizzical.

"You don't seem to show much curiosity," she said.

"Out here we don't show curiosity about other people's business."

She said rather gaily, "I think I'm going to stay to supper—if I'm invited."

"You'd better get back to your folks," he said. "They'll be worried about you."

"Oh, no they won't. I explained to them that I'm going to be out late. I told them I was conferring with the sheriff."

"Look here," he said, "you *can't* do things like that."

"Why can't I?"

"Because, for one thing, I'm here alone—and for another thing, you can't wander around the mountains at night."

"Are you going to invite me to supper?"

"No."

"That's fine," she said. "I'll stay anyway. What else are *we* going to have besides sour-dough biscuit?"

Watching her slip off her jacket and roll up her sleeves, he surrendered with a grin. *"We're* going to have some jerked venison, stewed up with onions and canned tomatoes.   You wouldn't have the faintest idea how to cook it, so go over there and sit down and watch.''

Two hours later, when they had eaten and the dishes had been cleaned up and when they had talked themselves into a better understanding, Roberta Coe announced that she was starting back down the trail.   She knew, of course, that Ames would go with her.

"Do you have a flashlight,'' she asked, "so that you can see the trail when you come back?''

"I don't need a flashlight.''

He walked over to the wall, took down the .30-.30 rifle, pushed shells into the magazine.

"What's that for?'' she asked.

"Oh,'' he said, "sometimes we see deer, and fresh meat is—''

She laughed and said, "It's illegal to shoot after sundown.   The deer season is closed, and the hills are simply crawling with game wardens and deputy sheriffs. You must think I'm terribly dumb.   However, I'm glad you have the rifle.   Come on.''

They left the cabin, to stand for a moment in the bracing night air, before starting down the trail.

"You're not locking the door?'' she asked.

"No need to lock the barn door after the horse has been stolen.''

"Somehow I wish you would.   You might—have a visitor.''

"I think I'd be glad to see him,'' he said, swinging the rifle slightly so that it glinted in the moonlight.

"Do you want me to lead the way with the flashlight or to come behind?''

"I'll go ahead,'' he said, "and please don't use the flashlight.''

"But we'll need it.''

"No we won't.   There's a moon that will give us plenty of light for more than an hour.   It's better to adjust your eyes to the darkness, rather than continually flashing a light on and off.''

He started off down the trail, walking with his long, easy stride.

The moon, not yet quite half full, was in the west, close to Venus, which shone as a shining beacon.   It was calm and still, and the night noises seemed magnified. The purling of the stream became the sound of a rushing cascade.

The day had been warm, but now in the silence of the night the air had taken on the chill that comes from the high places, a windless, penetrating chill which makes for appreciation of the soft warmth of down-filled sleeping bags.   The moon-cast shadows of the silhouetted pine trees lay across the trail like tangible barriers, and the silent, brooding strangeness of the mountains dwarfed Roberta Coe's consciousness until her personality seemed to her disturbed mind to be as puny as her light footfalls on the everlasting granite.

There was a solemn strangeness about the occasion which she wished to perpetuate, something that she knew she would want to remember as long as she lived;

so when they were a few hundred yards from camp, she said, "Frank, I'm tired. Can't we rest a little while? You don't realize what a space-devouring stride you have."

"Your camp's only around that spur," he said. "They'll be worrying about you and—"

"Oh, bother!" she said. "Let them worry. I want to rest."

There was the trunk of a fallen pine by the side of the trail, and she seated herself on it. He came back to stand uncomfortably at her side, then, propping the gun against the log, seated himself beside her.

The moon was sliding down toward the mountains now, and the stars were beginning to come out in unwinking splendor. She knew that she would be cold as soon as the warmth of the exercise left her blood, but knew also that Frank Ames was under a tension, experiencing a struggle with himself.

She moved slightly, her shoulder brushed against his, her hair touched his cheek, and the contact set off an emotional explosion. His arms were about her, his mouth strained to hers. She knew this was what she had been wanting for what had seemed ages.

She relaxed in the strength of his sinewy arms, her head tilting back so he could find her lips. Sudden pulses pounded in her temples. Then suddenly he had pushed her away, was saying contritely, "I'm sorry."

She waited for breath and returning self-assurance. Glancing at him from under her eyelashes, she decided on the casual approach. She laughed and said, "Why be sorry? It's a perfect night, and, after all, we're human." She hoped he wouldn't notice the catch in her voice, a very unsophisticated catch which belied the casual manner she was trying to assume.

"You're out of my set," he said. "You're—you're as far above me as that star."

"I wasn't very far above you just then. I seemed to be—quite close."

"You know what I mean. I'm a hillbilly, a piece of human flotsam cast up on the beach by the tides of war. Damn it, I don't mean to be poetic about it and I'm not going to be apologetic. I'm—"

"You're sweet," she interrupted.

"You have everything; all the surroundings of wealth. You're camped up here in the mountains with wranglers to wait on you. I'm a mountain man."

"Well, good Lord," she laughed, a catch in her throat, "you don't need to plan marriage just because you kissed me."

And in the constricted silence which followed, she knew that was exactly what he had been planning.

Suddenly, she turned and put her hand over his. "Frank," she said, "I want to tell you something—something I want you to keep in confidence. Will you?"

"Yes." His voice sounded strained.

She laughed. "I just finished promising the sheriff I'd never tell this to anyone." And then, without further preliminaries, she told him about her marriage, about the scandal, the annulment of her marriage.

When she had finished, there was a long silence. Abruptly she felt a nervous reaction.   The cold, still air of the mountains seemed unfriendly.   She felt terribly alien, a hopelessly vulnerable morsel of humanity in a cold, granite world which gave no quarter to vulnerability.

"I'm glad you told me," Frank Ames said simply, then jackknifed himself up from the log.   "You'll catch cold sitting here.   Let's move on."

Angry and hurt, she fought back the tears until the lighted tents of her camp were visible.

"I'm all right now," she said hastily.   "Good-by—thanks for the dinner."

She saw that he wanted to say something, but she was angry both at him and at herself, thoroughly resentful that she had confided in this man.   She wanted to rush headlong into the haven of her lighted camp, escaping the glow of the campfire, but she knew he was watching, so she tried to walk with dignity, leaving him standing there, vaguely aware that there was something symbolic in the fact that she had left him just outside the circle of firelight.

She would have liked to reach her tent undiscovered, but she knew that the others were wondering about her.   She heard Dick Nottingham's voice saying, "Someone's coming," then Sylvia Jessup calling, "Is that you, Roberta?"

"In person," she said, trying to make her voice sound gay.

"Well, you certainly took long enough.   What happened?"

"I'll tell you about it tomorrow," she said.   "I'm headed for my sleeping bag. I'm chilled."

Eleanor Dowling said, "I'll bring you a hot toddy when you get in bed, honey."

She knew they wanted to pump her, knew they wanted to ask questions about the sheriff, about her supposed conference.   And she knew that she couldn't face them—not then.

"Please don't," she said.   "I'm all in.   I have a beastly headache and I took two aspirin tablets coming down the trail.   Let me sleep."

She entered the tent, conscious as she did so of Frank Ames' words about how she was waited on hand and foot.   They had kept a fire going in the little sheet-metal stove.   The tent was warm as toast.   A lantern was furnishing mellow light. The down interior of her sleeping bag was inviting.   Not only did she have an air mattress, but there was a cot as well.

"Oh, what a fool I was!" she said.   "Why did I have to go baring my soul. The big ignoramus!   He's out of my world.   He—he thinks I'm second-hand merchandise!"

Roberta Coe's throat choked up with emotion.   She sat on the edge of the cot there in her little tent, her head on her hands.   Hot tears trickled between her fingers.

She realized with a pang how much that moment had meant to her, how much it had meant when Frank Ames' arms were around her, straining, eager and strong.

Sylvia Jessup's voice sounded startlingly close.   "What's the matter, darling?" she asked.   "Has something happened—"

Roberta looked up quickly, realizing now that the damage had been done, that the lantern was in such a position that her shadow was being thrown on the end of the tent.   Sylvia, sitting by the campfire, had been able to see silhouetted dejection, to see the shadow of Roberta seated on the cot, elbows on her knees, face in her hands.

"No thanks, it's all right," Roberta said, jumping up and bustling about. "I just got a little over-tired coming down the trail. I think it's the elevation."

"You don't want me—"

"No, thank you," Roberta said with a tone of finality which meant that the conversation was terminated.

Roberta crossed over to the lantern, turned it out, and the tent was in warm darkness, save for little ruddy spots which glowed on the canvas where small holes in the wood stove gave shafts of red light from the glowing embers.

Sylvia hesitated a moment, then Roberta could hear her steps going back toward the campfire. Sylvia undoubtedly was bursting with curiosity. She realized that Roberta would hardly have walked back alone over the mountain trail at night, and Sylvia was a prying little sneak as far as Roberta was concerned.

But somehow that momentary interlude, that flare of feeling against Sylvia Jessup, made Roberta Coe reappraise herself and the situation.

She knew instinctively that Frank Ames would not be back. Perhaps his coolness had not been because he had learned of her prior marriage. Perhaps—it could have been that it had made no difference to him. His constrained attitude, his abrupt departure might have been merely the result of what he had said previously—that they were worlds apart.

The doubt, the reaction, left her with the most devastating loneliness she had ever experienced.

Almost without thinking, she put her coat back on, quickly glanced around the tent to see that she was leaving no telltale shadow, then she slipped to the flap and out into the night, detouring so that she kept the tent between her and the campfire until she had reached the circle of scrub pine which surrounded the camp.

Once or twice she stumbled in the shadows. There was no moonlight here in this little valley, and the light from the campfire served only to make the terrain more deceiving, but Roberta kept moving rapidly, heedless of the natural obstacles, stumbling over roots and little hummocks until she was able to skirt the sheltering rim of pines and come to the main trail.

The cold, crisp air of the mountain night seemed like a stimulus which enabled her to rush along the trail. In the starlight, the trail showed as a faint gray thread, and Roberta, feeling as weightless as some gliding creature of the woods, buoyed up by surging hope, moved rapidly along this faint thread.

But after a few minutes the strange exhilaration left her. All at once her body mechanism asserted itself, and her laboring lungs told her all too plainly that she needed air. The unaccustomed effort of running, the steady upgrade, the elevation, all contributed to a breathlessness which made the strength drain out of her legs.

She knew she couldn't make it. Frank Ames had had too much of a headstart on her, and his own hurt pride would make for an emotional unrest which would demand some physical outlet. He would be swinging along up the trail, with his long legs devouring the space.

"Frank!" she called, and there was desperate pleading in her voice.

She had not brought her flashlight.   The moon had now settled almost to the mountains.   Only occasionally, where there was a break in the pines, was there a field of weak illumination over the trail.

She could hear steps ahead of her.   She wanted to call out again, but her laboring lungs had barely enough air for breath.   Her pounding heart threatened to push itself out of her chest.

"Frank!" she called with the very last bit of breath that she could muster. And then her laboring heart gave a wild surge as she saw motion in the shadow ahead.

But the figure that stepped out to meet her was not that of Frank Ames.   A shrill, metallic whistle, harsh as the strum of an overtaxed taut wire, knifed her eardrums.   Cold horror gripped her.

"No—No!" she half sobbed.

She turned, but there was no more strength left for flight.   Her feet were like heavy rocks, the legs limber.

The figure moved swiftly.

Sheriff Bill Eldon, down on hands and knees, poked slowly around the two parallel piles of ashes.   Undoubtedly these two campfires marked the spot where some man had been camping the night before, a man who was a seasoned veteran of the woods, who had spent a cold night without blankets, yet without inconvenience.

John Olney, standing a little to one side, watching with keen interest, was careful not to disturb the ground so that any remaining tracks would be obscured.   The long western slant of the sunlight built up shadows, gave a transverse lighting which made tracks far more easy to see than would have been the case during the middle of the day.

The sheriff's forefinger pointed to slight disturbances in the ground that would have escaped the attention of any except the most skilled tracker.   "Now here," he said, "is where Carl Raymond came along.   Raymond was hunting deer.   You can see that he skirted the edge of the plateau, keeping in the shadows, hoping he'd catch something still feeding in this little meadow.

"Anything out there would have been most apt to be a doe with a fawn, a spike buck, or perhaps a good fat barren doe.   So you can figure Raymond was hunting for meat.

"Now, he got to this place right here and then could see where the campfire had been, so he moved over to investigate.   Now that accounts for Raymond's tracks."

Olney nodded.   The ground to that point was to him as plain as a blueprint to an architect.

"Now then, these two fires," the sheriff went on, "tell quite a story.   The man used wood from that dead pine over there.   Then he cut fir boughs, raked the coals to one side, slept on the warm ground with a fire on each side of him, and early in the morning threw the fir boughs on the flames.   You can see where the stuff caught into instant flame and burnt up until it left only the naked branches.   Those were still green and didn't burn easily.   The man didn't try to burn them at all. He simply brought water over here from that little spring and doused the fire and covered it up, so as to eliminate that much of the fire hazard.   He certainly didn't want the faintest wisp of smoke to show when it came daylight.''

Again Olney nodded.

"So the fir boughs must have been burned up pretty early, probably just as it started to turn daylight.   Now, notice the way these boughs are cut.   They're not cut through with a single clean stroke.   Every one of them has taken two or three cuts, but the cuts are clean.

"Our man wasn't carrying a hatchet, but he was carrying a big knife and it was razor-sharp.''

Again Olney nodded.

"You can see his tracks around here," the sheriff went on.   "He's wearing a good sensible boot, a wide last, with a composition cord sole and heel.   That man could move through the forest without making any noise at all.   He could be as quiet as a panther.   Now then, he had to have something to carry the water from the spring to put out this fire.   What do you suppose it was?''

"His hat?'' Olney asked.

"Could have been," the sheriff said, "but somehow I doubt it.   Notice the number of trips he made here to the spring.   He's worn a regular trail up there, and the place where the little trickle of water has carried the charcoal down from the fire shows that he was using something that didn't hold much water.   Let's sort of look around over here in the brush.   Wait a minute!''

The sheriff stood up by the edge of the blackened space, made throwing motions in several different directions, said, "Over here is the best place to look.   There's no high ground here.   He could have thrown a can farther this way than in any other direction.''

The sheriff and the ranger moved over to a place where the brush was lower and the ground sloped away from the fire.

"Getting dark," the sheriff said.   "We're going to have to move along fast if we're going to find what we—Here it is.''

With the deft swiftness of a cat pouncing on a gopher, the sheriff dove into a little clump of mountain manzanita and came out triumphantly bearing a soot-covered can.   The top of the can showed an irregular, jagged crosscut, indicating that it had been opened by a few thrusts with a wide-bladed knife.

"Well," the sheriff said, "we're begnning to find out something about him. He has a knife with a blade a little over an inch wide.   It's razor-sharp, but he's using it for opening cans as well as cutting brush.   Therefore, he must have some pocket whetstone that he's using to keep the edge in shape.

"Now this can has been on the fire.   The label is all burned off, but from what you can see on the inside, it must have been a can of baked pork and beans.   It doesn't look as though he had a spoon to eat it with but whittled himself out a flat piece of wood that he used for a spoon.   I s'pose we'd better hold that can for fingerprints, but it tells me a story without using any magnifying glass.   He didn't carry that can of beans in here with him, John.   He must have stolen it someplace.''

The ranger nodded.

"He's traveling light and fast, and he knows the mountains," the sheriff went on.   "He can move as silent as a cat, and he's broken into a cabin and stolen a few provisions and a rifle."

"A rifle?" Olney asked.

"Sure," the sheriff told him.   "Come on over here and I'll show you."

In the fading light, the sheriff took the ranger back to the place where a pine tree was growing straight and slim within some twenty feet of the place where the fire had been made.

"He put the rifle down here," Bill Eldon said, "while he was cutting the branches for his bed.   You can see where the butt of the rifle rested in the ground.   Now, John, just as sure as shooting that was *after* it had quit raining.   You can still see the little cross-checks from the shoulder plate on the stock.   The ground was soft and—well, that's the way it is."

"You don't suppose he could have made camp *before* it started to rain and then put the rifle here while he was getting breakfast, do you?"

"I don't think so," Eldon said.   "This is the place where he would naturally have propped the rifle while he was getting those fir boughs.   It's just about the right distance from the fire and a nice place to stand the rifle.   When he was getting breakfast he'd let the fire get down to coals—of course, he could have had the canned beans for supper instead of breakfast.   Anyhow, it was after it'd quit raining. I've had a hunch he made this camp after the rain had quit.

"Now, the rain didn't quit until after dark.   A man wouldn't have blundered onto this little spring here in the dark, particularly on a rainy night.   No, John, this is some fellow that not only knows the mountains, but he knows this particular section of the country.   He's able to move around pretty well at night and when he left here early this morning he was smart enough to try and cover his tracks as much as possible.   You see, he took off up that rocky ridge.   My best guess is he kept to the rocks and the timber all day and kept holed up where he could watch, while he was waiting for dark."

The sheriff pursed his lips thoughtfully, looked at the streak of fading daylight over the Western mountains, said, "He's probably trying to get out of the mountains. But there just ain't any telling just what he has in mind.   If he's the one that killed the detective, he planted that evidence by Ames' cabin.   He might be intending to do another job or two before he gets out of the mountains—and he may be sort of hard to stop.   Let's see if we can look around a bit before it gets slap dark."

The men reined their horses down the trail.   Suddenly, Bill Eldon pulled up and urged his horse into the fringe of light brush.   "Take a look at that, John."

The ranger peered down at a light-brown pile on the ground.   "That's the beans," he said in astonishment.

Eldon nodded.

"Why did he open a can of beans, cook 'em over a campfire and then dump 'em all out?"   the ranger asked.

Bill Eldon considered that question for a space of seconds, then said, "There has to be only one answer, John.   He didn't want to eat 'em."

"But why?"

Bill Eldon touched the reins.   "Now," the sheriff said, "we know where we're going. But we're going to have to sort of wait around after we get there, until this man we want makes the first move. Come on, John.''

Trying her best to make time, Roberta fled down the trail. Her lungs were laboring, her heart pounding, and the trail pulled at her feet, making each step an individual effort.

She realized this man behind her was not trying to catch her. He was running slowly, methodically, as though following some preconceived plan.

Roberta tried once more to scream, but her call for help sounded faint and puny, even to her own ears.

Her heavy feet failed to clear an outcropping of rock. She stumbled, tried in vain to catch herself, threw out her arms and at exactly that moment heard behind her the vicious crack of a rifle.

The wind made by the bullet fanned her hair as she went down in a huddled heap on the trail. Lying prone, she simply lacked the strength to struggle back to her feet. She knew that the man behind her could reach her long before she could get up, and this dispiriting knowledge drained the last of her strength.

She heard Frank Ames' voice saying, ''Drop that gun,'' then the sound of another rifle crack arousing echoes through the mountain canyon.

Roberta got to her hands and knees, and seemed unable to get the strength to rise to her feet.

She heard Frank Ames saying, ''Darling, are you all right? You're not hurt? He didn't get you?''

She heard voices from the direction of the camp, saw flashlights sending beams which crisscrossed in confusion, making lighted patches on the boulders and the pine trees.

She turned from her knees to a sitting position, laughed nervously, and felt a touch of hysteria in the laugh. She tried to talk, but was only able to say gaspingly, ''I'm—all right.''

She saw Frank Ames standing rigid, watchful, dimly silhouetted against a patch of starlit forest, then off to the left she saw an orange-red spit of flame, and another shot aroused reverberating echoes from the peaks. The bullet struck a tree within inches of Frank Ames' head, and even in the dim gray of starlight, Roberta could see the swift streak on the trunk of the pine tree where the bullet ripped aside the bark.

Ames merely stood more closely behind the tree, his rifle at ready.

''Keep down, Roberta,'' he warned, without even turning to look at her.

Roberta remained seated, her head slightly back so that she could get more oxygen into her starved lungs.

Lights were coming up the trail now, a procession of winding, jiggling fireflies, blazing momentarily into brilliance as the beam of some flashlight would strike her fairly in the eyes.

Frank Ames called, ''Put out the lights, folks. He'll shoot at them.''

The rifle barked again, twice, one bullet directed at the place where Frank Ames was standing, the other at Roberta Coe, crouched on the trail.   Both bullets were wide of the mark, yet close enough so the cracking pathway of the high-power bullet held vicious menace.

Roberta heard the sound of galloping horses, realized suddenly the precariousness of her position on the trail, and scrambled slightly to one side.   She saw Frank Ames move, a silent, shadowy figure gliding through the trees, noticed, also, that the procession of flashlights had ceased.

The sheriff's horse, which was in the lead, shied violently, as it saw Roberta Coe crouched by the trail.   Roberta saw the swift glint of starlight from metal, heard the sheriff's voice, hard as a whiplash, saying, "Get 'em up!"

"No, no!" Roberta gasped.   "He's back there, over to the left.   He—"

The man betrayed his location by another shot, the bullet going high through the trees, the roar of the gun for a moment drowning out all other sounds.   Then, while the gun echoes were still reverberating from the crags, the dropping of small branches and pine needles dislodged by the bullet sounded startlingly clear.

"What the heck's he shooting at?" the sheriff asked.

Frank Ames said cautiously, "I'm over here, sheriff, behind this tree."

"Swing around, Olney," the sheriff said.   "Cut off his escape.   He's up against a sheer cliff in back.   We can trap him in here."

By this time the others were trooping up from camp, and the sheriff stationed them along the trail.   "I'm closing a circle around this place," the sheriff said. "Just yell if you see him, that's all."

Bill Eldon became coldly efficient.   "Where are you, Ames?"

"Over here."

Eldon raised his voice.   "Any of you from the camp got a gun on you?"

"I have," one of the wranglers said.

"All right," the sheriff announced.   "That's four of us.   If we go in after that man, he can't escape.   He could make his way up that high cliff if he had time, but he'll make a lot of noise doing it and expose himself to our fire.   He's only safe as long as he stays in this clump of trees.   We have men stationed along the trail who can let us know if he breaks cover in that direction.   The four of us can flush him out.   Anyone have any objections?   You don't *have* to go, you know."

"Not me," the wrangler said.   "I'll ride along with you."

The silence of the others indicated that the sheriff's question could have had significance for only the wrangler.

"Let's go," Bill Eldon said.   "Keep in touch with each other.   Walk abreast. We'll force him to surrender, to stand and fight it out, or to try climbing that steep cliff.   When you see him, if he hasn't got his hands up, shoot to kill."

The sheriff raised his voice, said, "We're coming in.   Drop your gun, get your hands up and surrender!"

There was no sound from the oval-shaped thicket at the base of the big cliff which walled it in as something of an amphitheater.

Bill Eldon said to the ranger, "We're dealing with a man who's a tricky woodsman.   Be on your toes; let's go!"

A tense silence fell upon the mountain amphitheater where the grim drama was being played.   Overhead the stars shone silent and steady, but within the thicket of pines was an inky darkness.

The men advanced for a few feet.   Then Bill Eldon said, "We're going to need a flashlight, folks."

"Don't try it.   It'll be suicide," Ames said.   "He'll shoot at the flashlight and—"

"Just hold everything," the sheriff said.   "Hold this line right here."

Eldon walked back to his saddlebags, took out a powerful flashlight which fastened on his forehead.   A square battery hung over his back, held in place by a harness, leaving his hands free to work his rifle.

The sheriff said reassuringly, "If he starts shooting, I can switch this off."

"Not after you're dead, you can't," Frank Ames said.

"It's a chance I have to take," Eldon said.   "That's a part of my job.   You folks keep back to one side."

Eldon switched on the flashlight.   The beam cut through the darkness into the pine trees a pencil of light, terminating in a splash of brilliance.

The sheriff kept slightly forward, away from the others, his rifle ready.   He kept turning his head slowly, searching the long lanes of pine trees until at length he suddenly snapped the gun forward and held it steady.

The beam of the flashlight showed a gun, neatly propped against a tree.

"Now, what the heck do you make of that?" Olney asked.

"Reckon he's going to give himself up," the wrangler from the dude camp said, and called out, "Get your hands up or we'll shoot!"

There was no answer.

They advanced to where the gun was leaning against the tree.

"Don't touch it!" the sheriff said.   "We'll look it over for fingerprints.   He must have been standing right behind that rock.   You can see the empty shells around on the ground."

"Have you got him?" a voice called from the trail.

"Not yet," Eldon said.

"What the devil's all this about?" stormed H. W. Dowling, crashing in behind the searching party.   "I demand to know the reason for all these—"

"Get back out of the way!" Eldon said.   "There's a desperate man in here. You'll be shot."

"A sweet howdy-do," Dowling said.   "What the devil's the matter with the law-enforcement officers in this county?   Can't I organize a camping trip into the mountains without having someone turn it into a Wild West show?   My sleep's gone for the night now.   I—The whole camp pulled out on me.   I had to run—"

Sheriff Eldon said grimly, "We can't pick the places where murderers are going to strike.   All we can do is try and capture the criminals so men like you will be safe.   Okay, boys, let's go.   I think he's out of shells.   Do you remember, that last shot went high through the trees?"

"I'd been wondering about that," Ames said.   "What was he shooting at?"

"We'll find out," the sheriff said, "when we get him."

They moved forward.   Then, as the thicket of trees narrowed against the per-
pendicular cliff, they closed in compact formation until finally they had covered
the entire ground.

"Well, I'll be darned!" Olney said.   "He's managed to get up those cliffs."

"Or out to the trail," Eldon said.

He moved out from the protection of the trees, moved his head slowly so that
his beam covered the precipitous mountainside.   "Don't see anything of him up
there.   Don't hear anything," he said.   "I told you he was a clever woodsman.
Let's get over and see if anyone saw him cut across the trail."

They moved back to the trail where the shivering dudes, the cook and the outfitter
were spaced at regular intervals.   "Anybody come through here?" the sheriff
asked.

"No one," they said.   "We could see well enough—"

"He might have been pretty clever," the sheriff said, "might have worked into
the shadows."

He moved slowly along, looking for tracks on the trail.

"What this country needs is more efficiency!" Dowling growled sullenly.

"Well, I missed him," Eldon said resignedly.   "Let's go on back to camp.
If he got through our lines, and abandoned an empty gun, it's possible he's planning
to go down and raid your camp for another gun."

Eldon untied his horse, swung into the saddle, said, "I'll go on ahead on a gallop
so as to beat him to it."

Olney mounted his own horse, followed the sheriff.

"You folks come on," Bill Eldon called over his shoulder.

The huddled group watched the shadowy figures gallop on down the trail.

Dowling said, "I want you boys to organize a guard for our camp tonight.   I
don't like the idea of a murderer being loose.   Come on, let's get out of here."

Roberta and Frank managed by some unspoken understanding to wait behind
until the others had gone.

"You're not hurt?" Frank asked.

"No."

"What happened?   How did you run onto him?"

"He was—I don't know, he was just loitering there in the shadows.   I got a
vague, indistinct glimpse of head and shoulders and—"

"I know," Ames said.   "I heard that peculiar whistle you were telling about,
so I turned and came back.   He shot and I saw you fall—"

"I fell just before he shot," Roberta said.   "I stumbled.   The bullet grazed
my hair."

"What I don't understand is how you happened to be out on the trail.   You'd
gone into your tent and blown out the candle," Ames said.

"You were watching?" she asked, almost before she thought.

He waited for some five seconds before he answered.   "Yes," he said.

She said, "Frank, let's not let foolish pride come between us.   I thought—I thought you were going away—out of my life—because of my prior marriage—I started up the trail after you.   I had to find out—I—"

"I was leaving because I knew you were too far above me.   For a minute I thought—well, you acted as though—Oh, shucks, I love you!   I love you!"

Bill Eldon sat by the big campfire, drinking coffee.

"If you ask me," Nottingham protested, "this is about the fourth fool thing that's been done tonight."

"What?" Bill Eldon asked.

"Having us all gather around a campfire while we know there's a desperate killer out in the hills.   He can see our figures silhouetted against the blaze and—"

"I know," the sheriff said, "but it takes a good man to shoot at night."

"Well, I think this murderer is what you'd call a 'good man.' Good enough to do just about as he pleases."

The sheriff ignored the insult.   "Funny thing about that murderer, now," he said.   "I've been sort of checking up with people about where everyone was when Frank Ames first came into this camp.   It seems like there were two people missing, Alexander Cameron and Sam Fremont.   Now, were you two boys together?"

"No, we weren't," Cameron said.   "I went on downstream, fishing."

"*Down*stream?"

"That's right."

"And you?" the sheriff asked Fremont.

"I went downstream a ways with Cameron and then I left him and started hunting for pictures of wildlife," Fremont said.   "I suppose you have the right to ask."

"You got those pictures?" the sheriff asked.

"Certainly.   They aren't developed.   I have two rolls of film."

"Of course," Nottingham pointed out, "those pictures wouldn't prove a thing, because he could have gone downstream *any* time and taken a couple of rolls of film."

"Don't be so officious," Fremont said, grinning.   "When I came back the girls were all strutting sex appeal for the benefit of a newcomer.   I stole a couple of pictures showing 'em all grouped around Ames.   Those will be the last two pictures on the last roll."

"How about the guides?" Sylvia asked.   "They weren't here.   At least one of them was out—"

"Rounding up the horses," the wrangler cut in.   "And unless horses can talk, I haven't any witnesses."

"I was in my tent taking a siesta," Dowling said.   "The unusual chatter finally wakened me."

"Well, I was just checking up," the sheriff said.   "Were you in bed tonight when the shooting started, Dowling?"

"Yes.   I dressed and came barging up the trail as fast as I could.   The others hadn't turned in; they got up there well ahead of me."

"You hurried right along?"

"Naturally.   I was as afraid to stay in camp alone as I was to go up there where the shooting was taking place."

The sheriff regarded his toes with a puzzled frown.

"You folks do whatever you want," Dowling said indignantly, "but I'm going to get away from this fire."

"I don't think there's the slightest danger," the sheriff said.

"Well, I'm quite able to think for myself, thank you.   I'm not accustomed to letting others do my thinking for me.   You evidently didn't think fast enough to keep him from shooting at Roberta."

"That's right," Bill Eldon admitted.   "I didn't.   Of course, I didn't have quite as much to go on as I have now."

"Well, as far as I'm concerned," Dowling said, "*I'm* going to get away from this campfire."

"You seem to be pretty much of a woodsman," the sheriff said.

"I did a little trapping in my younger days," Dowling admitted.

"You know," the sheriff drawled, "I think I know how that murderer got through our cordon.   I think he climbed a tree until we went past.

"And," the sheriff went on, "after we'd passed that tree a few steps, he dropped back down to the ground."

"And ran away?" Nottingham asked.

"No, just mingled with us," Eldon said.   "You see, he was well known, so he only had to get through the line.   I had that all figured out as soon as we came on the empty gun propped against the tree.   That's why I brought you all down here and built up a bright campfire.   I wanted to see which one of you *had pitch on his hands*!"

In the second or two of amazed silence which followed, one or two of the men looked at their hands.

The others looked at the sheriff.

"The man who did the killing," the sheriff went on, "went to a lot of trouble to make it appear that there was someone else running around the hills.   He had practiced the whistle that was used by a certain man whose name we won't mention at the moment.   He went to a lot of trouble to make a bed of fir boughs that hadn't been slept in, to open a can of beans that wasn't eaten.   He tried to kill Roberta Coe, but Ames showed up and spoiled his aim.   Then he jumped into the thicket of pine trees, did a lot of shooting, dropped the gun, climbed a tree, waited for us to enter the brush, then came threshing around, indignantly demanding an explanation."

"Indeed!" Dowling sneered.   "I wonder if you're asinine enough to be trying to implicate me."

"Well," the sheriff said, "there are some things that look a little queer.   You were in your tent when the shooting started?"

"Fast asleep.   I jumped up, dressed, grabbed my six-shooter and ran up the trail to join the others.   Here's my gun.   Want to look at it?"

"Not right now," Eldon said, casually taking his cloth tobacco sack from his pocket and starting to roll a cigarette.   "But if you'd run all the way up the trail, you'd have been out of breath. Instead of which, you took time to curse my bucolic stupidity and you weren't out of breath in the least. In fact, you strung quite a few words together.''

The sheriff used both hands to roll the cigarette. ''And you have pitch on your hands and on your clothes, and somewhere in your tent I think we'll find a pair of cord-soled shoes that will fit the tracks of—''

''Take a look at this gun now,'' Dowling said, moving swiftly. ''And take a look at the *front* end.''

The sheriff was motionless for a moment, then went on rolling his cigarette.

''I don't want anyone to move,'' Dowling said. ''Keep right here in plain sight by this campfire and—''

Suddenly from the other side of the campfire came the swift flash of an explosion, the roar of a gun, and Dowling stood dazed, glancing incredulously at his bloody right hand from which the gun had disappeared.

The sheriff put the cigarette to his lips to moisten the paper, drew his tongue along the crease in the rice paper, and said in a low drawl, ''Thanks for that, Ames, I sort of figured you'd know what to do in case I could talk him into making a break.''

The eastern sun had long since turned the crags of the big granite mountains into rosy gold. The shadows were still long, however, and the freshness of dawn lingered in the air.

Frank looked up as he heard the sound of the horse's hoofs trampling the ground. Then Roberta's voice called, ''Ahoy, how are the hot cakes?''

''All eaten up,'' Ames said, ''and the dishes washed. Why don't you city slickers get up before lunch?''

She laughed. ''We did,'' she said. ''In fact, no one went to bed at all. The packers broke camp with daylight, and the sheriff has already taken Dowling out to stand trial. I thought you'd want to know all the latest. Bill Eldon certainly isn't the slow-thinking hick he might seem. Howard Maben was released from the penitentiary two months ago, but he got in trouble again over some forged papers and is awaiting trial in Kansas right now. The sheriff got all that information over the phone.

''George Bay was free-lancing to see if he couldn't clear up Mrs. Dowling's death. He had an idea he could collect a reward from the insurance company if he showed it was murder.

''Bay didn't have much to go on. But Bill Eldon has just about solved *that* case too. He found out that Howard and Mrs. Dowling had a picnic outfit in a suitcase. They carried powdered milk. She was the only one who took cream in her coffee.

''Dowling only had to put poison in the powdered milk and then leave on a business trip, where he'd have an alibi for every minute of the time. The picnic case, you see, was never used except when he was gone, and only his wife used the powdered milk.

"You should have heard Sheriff Eldon questioning Dowling.   He soon had him floundering around in a mass of contradictory stories.

"He'd learned Bay was on his trail and decided to kill Bay so it would look as though Howard had done it.   He knew Howard's term had expired but didn't know Howard had been rearrested and was in jail.   Dowling had had his tent placed so the back was right up against that pine thicket.   He'd pretend to be asleep, but he'd taken the pegs out of the back and he'd carry a change of shoes and prowl along the mountain trails.   I guess he was pretty desperate, after getting all that wealth together, to be trapped by an old crime.   He tried to frame it on you, of course, stealing your gun, then later even planting some of your cigarette stubs. He buried the things from his victim's pockets at your place where officers would be sure to find them.   But because he thought Sheriff Eldon was a doddering old man, he overdid everything.

"Well, that's all the news, and I must skip.   I'm supposed to be back in the main trail in ten minutes.   The others are going to pick me up on the way out. I thought I'd just stop by and—leave you my address.   I suddenly realized I hadn't told you where you could reach me."

She was standing in the door of the cabin, smiling, looking trim and neat in her leather riding skirt, cowboy boots and soft green silk blouse.

Frank Ames strode toward her, kicking a chair out of his way.   "I know where to reach you," he said.

Five minutes later she pushed herself gently back from his arms and said, "Heavens, I'll be late!   I won't know how to catch up with them.   I don't know the trails."

Ames' circling arms held her to him.

"Don't worry," he said.   "You have just left lipstick smears all over one of the best guides in the mountains."

"You mean we can catch up with the others?" she asked.

"Eventually," Frank Ames said.   "You probably don't know it, however, but you're headed for the County Clerk's office."

"The County Clerk's office?   Surely you don't mean—?"

"I'm leaving just as soon as I can get a few things together," he said.   "You see, I want to record a claim.   Up here in the mountains when we find something good, we file on it."

"You—you'd better have it assayed first, Frank."

"I've assayed 'it,' " he said.   "Underneath that raspberry lipstick there's pure gold, and I don't want anyone to jump my claim."

"They won't," she assured him softly.

BARBARA CALLAHAN

The Pinwheel Dream

Sometimes I wish I could trade my recurring dream with someone.
My dream is like a kaleidoscope, very colorful, almost pretty. I would be glad
to accept a black and white dream in return for my living-color one. I would even
accept a horror dream, a terrible one in which the sleeper is chased up and down
cliffs, by a mad dog. Any dream would be better than mine. My dream focuses
on a pinwheel, a child's toy, a stick on which bits of plastic are pinned to be set
into motion by the wind.

My pinwheel is red, white, and blue. In my dream I spin it with my finger.
As soon as my finger touches it, the colors change into black and white polka dots.
Then the polka dots dissolve into a solid purple. Then the purple turns to red.
After redness floods the dream I wake up.

It's such an innocent-looking dream but after I've dreamed it a few nights, I
make those awful phone calls. I don't pick names randomly from the phone book.
I call the relatives or friends of people who work in the same office I do.

When Ellen, the stenographer, stopped after work at the bar on the first floor of
our building with John, the engineer, I was compelled to call her husband. I had
overheard Ellen telling her husband on the phone that she had to work late. I
knew she was lying. After John and Ellen left the office, I took the next elevator
downstairs and saw them through the open door of the bar. They were sitting
close together in a booth.

I hurried to a pay phone in the drug store, pulled out my address book, and
called Ellen's husband.

"I think you should know," I told him, "that your wife is having a drink in
Richard's Bar with a man she works with. They're there right now."

I hung up before he could say anything.

Ellen's eyes looked terribly red the following morning. She told everyone that
her allergies were acting up. I knew differently. I knew she must have spent
the entire evening in tears because after my call to her husband I went back to the
lobby of our building and sat in a chair with a newspaper opened out to conceal
my face. I lowered it to see Ellen pulled roughly out of the bar by her husband.

She looked so pathetic that I felt a little guilty. I brought coffee to her desk.
She thanked me before pouring out the story of her humiliating exit from the bar.

"I have to tell someone, Lorna," she sobbed, "and you're so good, such a good person, I hope you don't mind."

"Not at all, Ellen," I replied.

"I don't know how he found out. He must have been suspicious about all the overtime that didn't appear on my paycheck."

"You won't do it again, dear? Promise Lorna."

"I promise," she said like a repentant child.

I went back to my desk and opened my ledgers. I'm a bookkeeper and my books are a work of art. They are neat and orderly, just as life should be but isn't, unless a person steps in at the right moment to see that life balances out properly. I smiled down at the figures in the books. Ellen's life was balanced. She had erred and been punished for it.

A simple phone call from Lorna, good old Lorna, the office's maiden aunt, everybody's friend and confidante, had straightened her out. And good old Lorna could continue her behind-the-scenes accounting like an invisible but efficient guardian angel. Ellen's husband had not mentioned the phone call to her. Telling her would have destroyed the image of omniscience he needed to keep Ellen in line in the future.

After the incident with Ellen, I looked forward to my pinwheel dream. I seemed to derive courage from it, the courage to do the necessary calling. So much time and energy in our office seemed to be devoted to perpetrating deceptions that I felt our business motto should be "Deception is our most important product."

After dreaming the pinwheel dream for five nights, I called Harry's wife to tell her that Harry had gone to the race track one afternoon. Harry belongs to Gamblers Anonymous and he shouldn't go to the track. I had heard Harry telling his wife on the phone that he had to meet a client in the afternoon, but I saw the racing forms on his desk when I brought him a doughnut and coffee. Deception, deception!

Harry was red-faced when he asked Payroll to mail his check home each week instead of giving it to him. Like Ellen's husband, his wife must not have told him about the anonymous call.

The pinwheel dream receded from the proscenium of my sleep for nearly a month after my call to Harry's wife. I was grateful. The forces set into motion by the dream caused me elation, I do admit that, but they also caused me some anxiety. If I were discovered, I would no longer be "good old Lorna" to my associates. Stripped of that title, I would have lost access to the deceptions that proliferated in our office like fruit flies.

The new employee, Paul Mason, forced me to summon the dream from the wings where it always lurked. At first Paul puzzled me; then he angered me. He not only refused to confide in me but he refused to make self-incriminating phone calls in my hearing. Yet I knew his poker face and formal mannerisms masked a deception more evil than anyone's. Paul became my greatest challenge. I brought coffee and discussed the weather more times with him than I had ever done with a new employee. My efforts at conversations yielded only polite responses.

After dreaming the dream, I knew what I had to do.   Under the pretext of working late I stole through the empty offices to Personnel.   In the filing cabinet I found his personnel folder.   It revealed a deception more vile than I had expected. True, he had not deceived Personnel but he had deceived me and the others in the office who had a right to know about him.   After all, sharing deceptions was part of our office mystique.   Even I had contributed a deception to the office gossip— a false deception if that's not a redundancy.   I had invented an affair I supposedly had years ago with a married man.   I shared this imaginary escapade with everyone so I'd appear more human.

My excitement at the discovery in Paul's folder left me breathless.   I slipped the folder back into the cabinet and sank into the Personnel Director's chair.   If I might resort to a bit of humor, Paul Mason's case was to be my greatest balancing act.

But excitement, such a fickle sensation, ebbed almost immediately.   Whom could I call?   His wife?   Hardly.   She had to know the contents of his folder. My co-workers?   Impossible.   If I passed Paul's data along, Sue Nelson, the Personnel Director, would know someone had peeked into the files, and she might remember I had worked late.   I could not afford to lose my job.   At fifty it's not easy to get another one.

Then whom to call?   I picked up a small flag that stood on Sue's desk.   I twirled it around and around like the pinwheel in my dream.   Invoking the power of the dream, I sat back and waited.   In minutes I knew whom to call.

But first I had to take a short ride.   I drove to Paul's street.   Pretending the car had stalled, I glanced at the house next to his.   In the middle of the grille-work on the storm door I read the name *Barrett*.   My excitement returned.   I drove home, sailing through yellow lights which I don't ordinarily do.   My hands shook as I picked up the telephone directory.   Yes, yes, it was there—Paul's neighbor's listing: J. B. Barrett, 45 Dover Drive, 867–4259.

A child answered the phone.   "Get your mother," I ordered.   After his mother said hello, I said, "Your next-door neighbor, Paul Mason, is a child molester who spent five years in Rutherford Prison."

I hung up in the middle of a gasp at the other end.

A week after the phone call I met Paul's wife.   She came into the office to pick up his belongings, the photographs and other things from his desk that were of no value to anyone else.   With the usual solicitude of good old Lorna, I helped her put them into a cardboard box.   Collecting his office mementos proved to be too much for her.   She slumped into his chair and cried, "Why did he have to slash his wrists?   Things were going so well for us until the neighbors refused to let their children play with ours.   They told their kids Paul was a bad man.   And that he was cured."

I gave her two aspirins and helped her to the elevator.   I winced when she smiled through quivering lips to tell me what a good person I was.   That night I stayed late at the office, but not to prowl through filing cabinets.   I stayed to do some prowling through my mind.

The exultation I usually experienced for weeks after a phone call had disappeared.

I realized I had gone too far. Rather than balancing Paul's accounts, I had placed his liabilities on the first page of the ledger where they had overwhelmed him. That wasn't good bookkeeping. And the anxiety that I might someday be caught had almost overwhelmed me. I had to stop making those calls.

From the office I called Dr. Kevin Adams, the first psychologist listed in the phonebook. I hoped he could help me to stop. But on my first visit I detested him and sustained the emotion throughout all my visits. He sat behind a desk, puffing on a pipe, a thirtyish sandy-haired man with a studied poker face that reminded me of Paul Mason.

"Just tell me who you are," he said on the first visit. "That's always good for starters."

"I'm Lorna Tyson," I answered.

He puffed on his pipe for fifteen minutes, saying nothing. The clock on his desk ticked away my time and my money.

Finally he said, "Just who is Lorna Tyson?"

Unable to decide if he wanted a philosophical discourse on the concept of "person," or if he simply wanted some background information on me, I sat silently for almost fifteen minutes. I finally settled on: "She's a bookkeeper."

"A bookkeeper." He scribbled some words on a pad before telling me my time was up. I had spent $30.00 for the privilege of telling him my name and occupation.

During the next three sessions I told him about good old Lorna, everybody's friend and confidante. He nodded once or twice before saying "umph" and telling me my time was up. Seething, I left his office. I was so upset I forgot my gloves. When I went back to get them, I saw Dr. Adams locked in a passionate embrace with his receptionist. I quickly closed the door. The next morning I called the Psychological Association and reported his unprofessional behavior. For the first time since Paul committed suicide, I felt relaxed.

Dr. Adams shattered that good feeling on my next visit.

"Tell me, Lorna," he said, "about your compulsion to report people's transgressions."

"I don't know what you mean," I stammered.

"Oh, come now, Lorna, let's not play any more games. We've had four sessions together and not once have you indicated what's bothering you. I saw your gloves on the table in the waiting room and knew you'd come back. I deliberately kissed my receptionist to see what your reaction would be. You called the Psychological Association to report me. That didn't upset me or the Association. The receptionist is my wife. As a new patient, you wouldn't have known that."

Along with some other epithets that I didn't know spiced my vocabulary, I called him Dr. God.

"You're quite unprincipled, Dr. God," I shouted. "You manipulate behind the scenes like some superior being so you can make lesser creatures squirm!"

"Then we're very much alike, aren't we, Lorna?" he said.

I was too stunned to answer. I dropped into the leather armchair across from his desk and watched as he emptied the ashes from his pipe into a large ashtray.

He was waiting for me to speak. All my defenses had toppled, so I told him about the phone calls to Ellen's husband and to Harry's wife. He said nothing, but he knocked his pipe against his desk as if it were a judge's gavel. On the following visit I told him about my call to Paul's neighbor. The pipe hit the desk with metronomic frequency.

"Stop that, Dr. God," I said.

"Stop what?" he asked.

"Stop passing judgment on me with your pipe."

"Sorry, I didn't realize what I was doing. You're quite astute."

"Quite," I answered.

When I returned to my office, I doodled the number seven all over a memo pad. The next visit with Dr. God would be my last. I had seen him six times and poured all my deceptions into his gossip-pot. He had a great racket going. He sat on his chair, a dead-pan Father Confessor, consuming all the meat from the patient's pitiful emotional stew as well as chomping on all the money in the patient's pitiful wallet, and he offered nothing in return. My bookkeeper's mind rebelled against the imbalance of it.

On the seventh visit, before I could say a word, he opened with, "Tell me about your dreams."

I almost slipped off my chair. I had said nothing to him about my dream. Dr. God could read minds!

"How did you know about my dream?" I choked.

"Ah," he said, "now we're getting somewhere. I didn't say, 'Tell me about your dream!' I said, 'Tell me about your dreams.' You heard the singular of the word, therefore I must conclude you have a recurring dream."

Trapped, I told him the dream.

"I dream I have a red, white, and blue pinwheel. Since there is no wind to move it, I must turn it with my finger. After I touch the pinwheel it disintegrates into spinning black and white polka dots. The polka dots stop moving and are replaced by purple. Then the purple dissolves into red and the red fills up the dream."

Dr. God put his pipe down because he had no verdict to tap out on the dream. He looked baffled. I rejoiced. He stood up and began to pace behind his desk. For five beautiful minutes I reveled in his bewilderment.

"I admit the dream puzzles me, but I do see one clue. Since the pinwheel is a child's toy, I assume the dream relates to an incident in your childhood."

"Bravo, Dr. God. You've hit on the old psychological standby—childhood. I was wondering when you'd get to that."

He ignored my jibe and sat down. He led me into a game. Free association, he called it. I had to sit like an obedient child and tell him all the words that came to my mind when I thought of a pinwheel.

"Flag," I told him because of the pinwheel's red, white, and blue colors. Windmill, bicycle wheel, I told him—spinning wheel, roulette wheel, wagon wheel.

He eyed me like a teacher about to fail a student. "Think harder," he urged, "harder! What else is round like a pinwheel and needs an outside force to move it?"

I glanced around the room. Nothing came to my mind until I looked at the phone on his desk. "A telephone dial," I said softly.

"Eureka!" he shouted. "As a child, the pinwheel reminded you of a telephone dial, something else that you had to turn with your finger. And the black and white polka dots spinning in your dream are the letters and numbers on a black instrument. When you were a child, telephones were only black with white letters and numbers. We are decoding the dream, Lorna," he said.

I ignored his use of the word "we." *I* was decoding the dream. I began to cry. He came to me and patted me on the shoulder, a gesture that made me cry harder. It reminded me of the day the policeman patted eight-year-old Lorna on the shoulder as she sat on the front steps watching the three stretchers being lifted into ambulances.

"One of the stretchers," I heard myself telling him, "held my mother, the other, her lover, and the other, my father. My father came home from work and found my mother upstairs with another man. My father shot both of them, and then himself."

He handed me his handkerchief. "And all that happened on a day when you were playing happily with a pinwheel. Then you heard shots, ran into the house, and dialed the police. They probably told you to wait outside, but you went upstairs—were you wearing a purple dress?—and saw all the redness from the blood of the three bodies.

"Now we understand the meanings of the pinwheel, the polka dots, the purple, and the red. And now we understand why you made those calls to damn your co-workers. You wanted to punish them. You transferred your rage at being deceived by your mother to your co-workers who, in your mind, were deceiving others."

"Yes, Dr. God," I admitted. I said yes to his interpretation so I could leave. I had to think. I had to plan.

"May I use your phone, Doctor, my car is in the shop. I must call a cab."

"Of course."

He watched me dial the phone. I put through my request for a cab in a shaky voice. Then I hung up.

"Do you always do that?" he asked.

"Do what?"

"Hang up the phone by tapping the listening end of the receiver on the table before putting the receiver back in its cradle."

"I guess so. Why?"

"Because tapping the phone on the table reminds me of a judge tapping his gavel at a trial."

"Then we have something in common, Doctor," I said casually. "You tap your pipe when you deliver a verdict. I tap the phone."

His face became dead-pan again. "Now that you understand your dream you've probably delivered your last verdict via the telephone."

"But you have more verdicts to tap out, don't you, Dr. God?"

"If you say so," he responded.

He was wrong about my delivering my last verdict on the phone. I had another one to deliver.   He was correct about some of my dream, but not all of it.   In his egotism he missed the more complex points.   I had to see to it that he never discovered the truth when he had a chance to think it over.

The truth was mine alone.   The dream did unravel its meaning to me in Dr. God's office.   On that summer day when I was eight years old, I walked two blocks to wait for the bus that was to take me on a day trip with my Brownie troop.   My mother waved to me from the door.   She seemed happy that I would be gone all day.

But the bus didn't come.   It had broken down.   Our Scout Leader knew we were disappointed so she gave us each a pinwheel to take home.   The pinwheel didn't move because there was no wind.   I took it in the house so that the fan in the living room would make it spin.   I heard them, my mother and him, laughing upstairs.   I turned the pinwheel round and round with my finger.

The spinning pinwheel made me think of the telephone dial.   I called my father at work and told him about my mother and the man upstairs.   As I waited for him to come home, I colored a picture of a queen in my fairy-tale coloring book.   I used purple for her dress.   My father had told me that purple was a royal color, the color of kings and queens.   I felt like a queen sitting there.   I felt powerful. I felt royal.   I felt purple.   And purple was exciting.   I always felt purple when I made the calls about my co-workers.

Dr. God was right about the red in the dream.   It was blood, the blood all over my mother and that man.   I didn't look at my father.   Red is a good color too. It's the color of satisfaction, of a verdict delivered, of sentencing received.   Harry— his gambler's face was red from embarrassment when he asked to have his paycheck mailed home.   Ellen's eyes were red after a night's crying.   Paul's wrists were red after he slashed them.

And Dr. God's pipe will glow red when he puffs and puffs on it as he desperately tries to extricate himself from the situation I am planning for him.   I feel no pity for him.   He too was feeling purple in that office when he thought he had interpreted my dream.   I can't have that—purple belongs to me.   And so does red.

I looked at my mussed hair and my scratched face and my ripped dress in the mirror of my apartment.   I had had time to do those things to myself in the ladies room before the cab came.   The cab driver noticed and asked if I was all right. I acted too distraught to answer him.   I smiled at my cleverness.   My car isn't in the shop.   I just needed a witness to my disheveled state.   And luckily Dr. God's wife hadn't come to work today.

I dialed my beige phone, regretting that it wasn't an old black one.   When a voice said, "Jones, Twenty-second Precinct," I began to sob.   I was quite good at it.   "Dr. Adams of the Baker Building tried to attack me in his office this afternoon.   Please come, please!"

It was the best acting job of my life.   It's hard to feign tears when one is feeling so purple.   The police promised to come at once.   Before I hung up the phone, I carefully tapped the listening part of the receiver on the table.

DONALD E. WESTLAKE

This Is Death

I t's hard not to believe in ghosts when you are one. I hanged myself in a fit of truculence—stronger than pique, but not so dignified as despair—and regretted it before the thing was well begun. The instant I kicked the chair away I wanted it back, but gravity was turning my former wish to its present command; the chair would not right itself from where it lay on the floor, and my 193 pounds would not cease to urge downward from the rope thick around my neck.

There was pain, of course, quite horrible pain centered in my throat, but the most astounding thing was the way my cheeks seemed to swell. I could barely see over their round red hills, my eyes staring in agony at the door, *willing* someone to come in and rescue me, though I knew there was no one in the house, and in any event the door was carefully locked. My kicking legs caused me to twist and turn, so that sometimes I faced the door and sometimes the window, and my shivering hands struggled with the rope so deep in my flesh I could barely find it and most certainly could not pull it loose.

I was frantic and terrified, yet at the same time my brain possessed a cold corner of aloof observation. I seemed now to be everywhere in the room at once, within my writhing body but also without, seeing my frenzied spasms, the thick rope, the heavy beam, the mismatched pair of lit bedside lamps throwing my convulsive double shadow on the walls, the closed locked door, the white-curtained window with its shade drawn all the way down. *This is death,* I thought, and I no longer wanted it, now that the choice was gone forever.

My name is—was—Edward Thornburn, and my dates are 1938–1977. I killed myself just a month before my fortieth birthday, though I don't believe the well-known pangs of that milestone had much if anything to do with my action. I blame it all (as I blamed most of the errors and failures of my life) on my sterility. Had I been able to father children my marriage would have remained strong, Emily would not have been unfaithful to me, and I would not have taken my own life in a final fit of truculence.

The setting was the guestroom in our house in Barnstaple, Connecticut, and the time was just after seven P.M.; deep twilight, at this time of year. I had come home from the office—I was a realtor, a fairly lucrative occupation in Connecticut, though my income had been falling off recently—shortly before six, to find the note on the kitchen table: "Antiquing with Greg.   Afraid you'll have to make your own dinner.   Sorry.   Love, Emily."

Greg was the one; Emily's lover.   He owned an antique shop out on the main road toward New York, and Emily filled a part of her days as his ill-paid assistant. I knew what they did together in the back of the shop on those long midweek afternoons when there were no tourists, no antique collectors to disturb them.   I knew, and I'd known for more than three years, but I had never decided how to deal with my knowledge.   The fact was, I blamed myself, and therefore I had no way to *behave* if the ugly subject were ever to come into the open.

So I remained silent, but not content.   I was discontent, unhappy, angry, resentful—truculent.

I'd tried to kill myself before.   At first with the car, by steering it into an oncoming truck (I swerved at the last second, amid howling horns) and by driving it off a cliff into the Connecticut River (I slammed on the brakes at the very brink, and sat covered in perspiration for half an hour before backing away) and finally by stopping athwart one of the few level crossings left in this neighborhood.   But no train came for twenty minutes, and my truculence wore off, and I drove home.

Later I tried to slit my wrists, but found it impossible to push sharp metal into my own skin.   Impossible.   The vision of my naked wrist and that shining steel so close together washed my truculence completely out of my mind.   Until the next time.

With the rope; and then I succeeded.   Oh, totally, oh, fully I succeeded.   My legs kicked at air, my fingernails clawed at my throat, my bulging eyes stared out over my swollen purple cheeks, my tongue thickened and grew bulbous in my mouth, my body jigged and jangled like a toy at the end of a string, and the pain was excruciating, horrible, not to be endured.   I can't endure it, I thought, it can't be endured.   Much worse than knife slashings was the knotted strangled pain in my throat, and my head ballooned with pain, pressure outward, my face turning black, my eyes no longer human, the pressure in my head building and building as though I would explode.   Endless horrible pain, not to be endured, but going on and on.

My legs kicked more feebly.   My arms sagged, my hands dropped to my sides, my fingers twitched uselessly against my sopping trouser legs, my head hung at an angle from the rope, I turned more slowly in the air, like a broken windchime on a breezeless day.   The pains lessened, in my throat and head, but never entirely stopped.

And now I saw that my distended eyes had become lusterless, gray.   The moisture had dried on the eyeballs, they were as dead as stones.   And yet I could see them, my own eyes, and when I widened my vision I could see my entire body, turning, hanging, no longer twitching, and with horror I realized I was dead.

But *present*.   Dead, but still present, with the scraping ache still in my throat and the bulging pressure still in my head.   Present, but no longer in that used-up clay, that hanging meat; I was suffused through the room, like indirect lighting, everywhere present but without a source.   What happens now?   I wondered, dulled by fear and strangeness and the continuing pains, and I waited, like a hovering mist, for whatever would happen next.

But nothing happened.   I waited; the body became utterly still; the double shadow on the wall showed no vibration; the bedside lamps continued to burn; the door remained shut and the window shade drawn; and nothing happened.

What *now*?   I craved to scream the question aloud, but I could not.   My throat ached, but I had no throat.   My mouth burned, but I had no mouth.   Every final strain and struggle of my body remained imprinted in my mind, but I had no body and no brain and no *self*, no substance.   No power to speak, no power to move myself, no power to *re*move myself from this room and this suspended corpse. I could only wait here, and wonder, and go on waiting.

There was a digital clock on the dresser opposite the bed, and when it first occurred to me to look at it the numbers were 7:21—perhaps twenty minutes after I'd kicked the chair away, perhaps fifteen minutes since I'd died.   Shouldn't something happen, shouldn't some *change* take place?

The clock read 9:11 when I heard Emily's Volkswagen drive around to the back of the house.   I had left no note, having nothing I wanted to say to anyone and in any event believing my own dead body would be eloquent enough, but I hadn't thought I would be *present* when Emily found me.   I was justified in my action, however much I now regretted having taken it, I was justified, I knew I was justified, but I didn't want to see her face when she came through that door.   She had wronged me, she was the cause of it, she would have to know that as well as I, but I didn't want to see her face.

The pains increased, in what had been my throat, in what had been my head. I heard the back door slam, far away downstairs, and I stirred like air currents in the room, but I didn't leave.   I couldn't leave.

"Ed?   Ed?   It's me, hon!"

I know it's you.   I must go away now, I can't stay here, I must go away.   Is there a God?   Is this my soul, this hovering presence?   *Hell* would be better than this, take me away to Hell or wherever I'm to go, don't leave me here!

She came up the stairs, calling again, walking past the closed guestroom door. I heard her go into our bedroom, heard her call my name, heard the beginnings of apprehension in her voice.   She went by again, out there in the hall, went downstairs, became quiet.

What was she doing?   Searching for a note perhaps, some message from me. Looking out the window, seeing again my Chevrolet, knowing I must be home. Moving through the rooms of this old house, the original structure a barn nearly 200 years old, converted by some previous owner just after the Second World War, bought by me twelve years ago, furnished by Emily—and Greg—from their interminable, damnable, awful antiques.   Shaker furniture, Colonial furniture, hooked rugs and quilts, the old yellow pine tables, the faint sense always of being in some slightly shabby minor museum, this house that I had bought but never loved.   I'd bought it for Emily, I did everything for Emily, because I knew I could never do the one thing for Emily that mattered.   I could never give her a child.

She was good about it, of course.   Emily *is* good, I never blamed her, never completely blamed *her* instead of myself.   In the early days of our marriage she made a few wistful references, but I suppose she saw the effect they had on me, and for a long time she has said nothing.   But I have known.

The beam from which I had hanged myself was a part of the original building, a thick hand-hewed length of aged timber eleven inches square, chevroned with the marks of the hatchet that had shaped it.   A strong beam, it would support my weight forever.   It would support my weight until I was found and cut down. Until I was found.

The clock read 9:23 and Emily had been in the house twelve minutes when she came upstairs again, her steps quick and light on the old wood, approaching, pausing, stopping.   "Ed?"

The doorknob turned.

The door was locked, of course, with the key on the inside.   She'd have to break it down, have to call someone else to break it down, perhaps she wouldn't be the one to find me after all.   Hope rose in me, and the pains receded.

"Ed?   Are you in there?"   She knocked at the door, rattled the knob, called my name several times more, then abruptly turned and ran away downstairs again, and after a moment I heard her voice, murmuring and unclear.   She had called someone, on the phone.

Greg, I thought, and the throat-rasp filled me, and I wanted this to be the end. I wanted to be taken away, dead body and living soul, taken away.   I wanted everything to be finished.

She stayed downstairs, waiting for him, and I stayed upstairs, waiting for them both.   Perhaps she already knew what she'd find up here, and that's why she waited below.

I didn't mind about Greg, about being present when he came in.   I didn't mind about *him*.   It was Emily I minded.

The clock read 9:44 when I heard tires on the gravel at the side of the house. He entered, I heard them talking down there, the deeper male voice slow and reassuring, the lighter female voice quick and frightened, and then they came up together, neither speaking.   The doorknob turned, jiggled, rattled, and Greg's voice called, "Ed?"

After a little silence Emily said, "He wouldn't—he wouldn't *do* anything, would he?"

"Do anything?"   Greg sounded almost annoyed at the question.   "What do you mean, do anything?"

"He's been so depressed, he's—Ed!"   And forcibly the door was rattled, the door was shaken in its frame.

"Emily, don't.   Take it easy."

"I shouldn't have called you," she said.   "Ed, *please!*"

"Why not?   For heaven's sake, Emily—"

"Ed, *please* come out, don't scare me like this!"

"Why *shouldn't* you call me, Emily?"

"Ed isn't stupid, Greg.   He's—"

There was then a brief silence, pregnant with the hint of murmuring. They thought me still alive in here, they didn't want me to hear Emily say, "He *knows*, Greg, he knows about us."

The murmurings sifted and shifted, and then Greg spoke loudly, "That's ridiculous. Ed? Come out, Ed, let's talk this over." And the doorknob rattled and clattered, and he sounded annoyed when he said, "We must get in, that's all. Is there another key?"

"I think all the locks up here are the same. Just a minute."

They were. A simple skeleton key would open any interior door in the house. I waited, listening, knowing Emily had gone off to find another key, knowing they would soon come in together, and I felt such terror and revulsion for Emily's entrance that I could feel myself shimmer in the room, like a reflection in a warped mirror. Oh, can I at least stop seeing? In life I had eyes, but also eyelids, I could shut out the intolerable, but now I was only a presence, a total presence, I *could not* stop my awareness.

The rasp of key in lock was like rough metal edges in my throat; my memory of a throat. The pain flared in me, and through it I heard Emily asking what was wrong, and Greg answering, "The key's in it, on the other side."

"Oh, dear God! Oh, Greg, what has he done?"

"We'll have to take the door off its hinges," he told her. "Call Tony. Tell him to bring the toolbox."

"Can't you push the key through?"

Of course he could, but he said, quite determinedly, "Go *on*, Emily," and I realized then he had no intention of taking the door down. He simply wanted her away when the door was first opened. Oh, very good, *very* good!

"All right," she said doubtfully, and I heard her go away to phone Tony. A beetle-browed young man with great masses of black hair and an olive complexion, Tony lived in Greg's house and was a kind of handyman. He did work around the house and was also (according to Emily) very good at restoration of antique furniture; stripping paint, re-assembling broken parts, that sort of thing.

There was now a renewed scraping and rasping at the lock, as Greg struggled to get the door open before Emily's return. I found myself feeling unexpected warmth and liking toward Greg. He wasn't a bad person; an opportunist with my wife, but not in general a bad person. Would he marry her now? They could live in this house, he'd had more to do with its furnishing than I. Or would this room hold too grim a memory, would Emily have to sell the house, live elsewhere? She might have to sell at a low price; as a realtor, I knew the difficulty in selling a house where a suicide has taken place. No matter how much they may joke about it, people are still afraid of the supernatural. Many of them would believe this room was haunted.

It was then I finally realized the room *was* haunted. With me! *I'm a ghost*, I thought, thinking the word for the first time, in utter blank astonishment. I'm a ghost.

Oh, how dismal! To hover here, to be a boneless fleshless aching *presence* here, to be a kind of ectoplasmic mildew seeping through the days and nights, alone, unending, a stupid pain-racked misery-filled observer of the comings and goings of strangers—she *would* sell the house, she'd have to, I was sure of that. Was this my punishment?   The punishment of the suicide, the solitary hell of him who takes his own life.   To remain forever a sentient nothing, bound by a force greater than gravity itself to the place of one's finish.

I was distracted from this misery by a sudden agitation in the key on this side of the lock.   I saw it quiver and jiggle like something alive, and then it popped out—it seemed to *leap* out, itself a suicide leaping from a cliff—and clattered to the floor, and an instant later the door was pushed open and Greg's ashen face stared at my own purple face, and after the astonishment and horror, his expression shifted to revulsion—and contempt?—and he backed out, slamming the door.   Once more the key turned in the lock, and I heard him hurry away downstairs.

The clock read 9:58.   *Now* he was telling her.   *Now* he was giving her a drink to calm her.   *Now* he was phoning the police.   *Now* he was talking to her about whether or not to admit their affair to the police; what would they decide?

"Noooooooooo!"

The clock read 10:07.   What had taken so long?   Hadn't he even called the police yet?

She was coming up the stairs, stumbling and rushing, she was pounding on the door, screaming my name.   I shrank into the corners of the room, I *felt* the thuds of her fists against the door, I cowered from her.   She can't come in, dear God don't let her in!   I don't care what she's done, I don't care about anything, just don't let her see me!   *Don't let me see her!*

Greg joined her.   She screamed at him, he persuaded her, she raved, he argued, she demanded, he denied.   "Give me the key!   Give me the key!"

Surely he'll hold out, surely he'll take her away, surely he's stronger, more forceful.

He gave her the key.

No.   *This* cannot be endured.   *This* is the horror beyond all else.   She came in, she walked into the room, and the sound she made will always live inside me. That cry wasn't human; it was the howl of every creature that has ever despaired. *Now* I know what despair is, and why I called my own state mere truculence.

Now that it was too late, Greg tried to restrain her, tried to hold her shoulders and draw her from the room, but she pulled away and crossed the room toward . . . not toward *me*.   I was everywhere in the room, driven by pain and remorse, and Emily walked toward the carcass.   She looked at it almost tenderly, she even reached up and touched its swollen cheek.

"Oh, Ed," she murmured.

The pains were as violent now as in the moments before my death.   The slashing torment in my throat, the awful distension in my head, they made me squirm in agony all over again; but I *could not* feel her hand on my cheek.

Greg followed her, touched her shoulder again, spoke her name, and immediately her face dissolved, she cried out once more and wrapped her arms around the corpse's legs and clung to it, weeping and gasping and uttering words too quick and broken to understand. Thank *God* they were too quick and broken to understand!

Greg, that fool, did finally force her away, though he had great trouble breaking her clasp on the body. But he succeeded, and pulled her out of the room, and slammed the door, and for a little while the body swayed and turned, until it became still once more.

That was the worst. Nothing could be worse than that. The long days and nights here—how long must a stupid creature like myself *haunt* his death-place before release?—would be horrible, I knew that, but not so bad as this. Emily would survive, would sell the house, would slowly forget. (Even I would slowly forget.) She and Greg could marry. She was only 36, she could still be mother.

For the rest of the night I heard her wailing, elsewhere in the house. The police did come at last, and a pair of grim silent white-coated men from the morgue entered the room to cut me—it—down. They bundled it like a broken toy into a large oval wicker basket with long wooden handles, and they carried it away.

I had thought I might be forced to stay with the body, I had feared the possibility of being buried with it, of spending eternity as a thinking nothingness in the black dark of a casket, but the body left the room and I remained behind.

A doctor was called. When the body was carried away the room door was left open, and now I could plainly hear the voices from downstairs. Tony was among them now, his characteristic surly monosyllable occasionally rumbling, but the main thing for a while was the doctor. He was trying to give Emily a sedative, but she kept wailing, she kept speaking high hurried frantic sentences as though she had too little time to say it all. "I did it!" she cried, over and over. "I did it! I'm to blame!"

Yes. That was the reaction I'd wanted, and expected, and here it was, and it was horrible. Everything I had desired in the last moments of my life had been granted to me, and they were all ghastly beyond belief. I *didn't* want to die! I *didn't* want to give Emily such misery! And more than all the rest I didn't want to be here, seeing and hearing it all.

They did quiet her at last, and then a policeman in a rumpled blue suit came into the room with Greg, and listened while Greg described everything that had happened. While Greg talked, the policeman rather grumpily stared at the remaining length of rope still knotted around the beam, and when Greg had finished the policeman said, "You're a close friend of his?"

"More of his wife. She works for me. I own The Bibelot, an antique shop out on the New York road."

"Mm. Why on earth did you let her in here?"

Greg smiled; a sheepish embarrassed expression. "She's stronger than I am," he said. "A more forceful personality. That's always been true."

It was with some surprise I realized it *was* true. Greg was something of a weakling, and Emily was very strong. *(I* had been something of a weakling, hadn't I? Emily was the strongest of us all.)

The policeman was saying, "Any idea why he'd do it?"

"I think he suspected his wife was having an affair with me."   Clearly Greg had rehearsed this sentence, he'd much earlier come to the decision to say it and had braced himself for the moment.   He blinked all the way through the statement, as though standing in a harsh glare.

The policeman gave him a quick shrewd look.   "Were you?"

"Yes."

"She was getting a divorce?"

"No.   She doesn't love me, she loved her husband."

"Then why sleep around?"

"Emily wasn't sleeping *around*," Greg said, showing offense only with the emphasized word.   "From time to time, and not very often, she was sleeping with me."

"Why?"

"For comfort."   Greg too looked at the rope around the beam, as though it had become me and he was awkward speaking in its presence.   "Ed wasn't an easy man to get along with," he said carefully.   "He was moody.   It was getting worse."

"Cheerful people don't kill themselves," the policeman said.

"Exactly.   Ed was depressed most of the time, obscurely angry now and then. It was affecting his business, costing him clients.   He made Emily miserable but she wouldn't leave him, she loved him.   I don't know what she'll do now."

"You two won't marry?"

"Oh, no."   Greg smiled, a bit sadly.   "Do you think we murdered him, made it look like suicide so we could marry?"

"Not at all," the policeman said.   "But what's the problem?   You already married?"

"I am homosexual."

The policeman was no more astonished than I.   He said, "I don't get it."

"I live with my friend; that young man downstairs.   I am—capable—of a wider range, but my preferences are set.   I am very fond of Emily, I felt sorry for her, the life she had with Ed.   I told you our physical relationship was infrequent. And often not very successful."

Oh, Emily.   Oh, poor Emily.

The policeman said, "Did Thornburn know you were, uh, that way?"

"I have no idea.   I don't make a public point of it."

"All right."   The policeman gave one more half-angry look around the room, then said, "Let's go."

They left.   The door remained open, and I heard them continue to talk as they went downstairs, first the policeman asking, "Is there somebody to stay the night? Mrs. Thornburn shouldn't be alone."

"She has relatives in Great Barrington.   I phoned them earlier.   Somebody should be arriving within the hour."

"You'll stay until then?   The doctor says she'll probably sleep, but just in case—"

"Of course."

That was all I heard.   Male voices murmured awhile longer from below, and then stopped.   I heard cars drive away.

How complicated men and women are.   How stupid are simple actions.   I had never understood anyone, least of all myself.

The room was visited once more that night, by Greg, shortly after the police left.   He entered, looking as offended and repelled as though the body were still here, stood the chair up on its legs, climbed on it, and with some difficulty untied the remnant of rope.   This he stuffed partway into his pocket as he stepped down again to the floor, then returned the chair to its usual spot in the corner of the room, picked the key off the floor and put it in the lock, switched off both bedside lamps and left the room, shutting the door behind him.

Now I was in darkness, except for the faint line of light under the door, and the illuminated numerals of the clock.   How long one minute is!   That clock was my enemy, it dragged out every minute, it paused and waited and paused and waited till I could stand it no more, and then it waited longer, and *then* the next number dropped into place.   Sixty times an hour, hour after hour, all night long.   I couldn't stand one night of this, how could I stand eternity?

And how could I stand the torment and torture inside my brain?   That was much worse now than the physical pain, which never entirely left me.   I had been right about Emily and Greg, but at the same time I had been hopelessly brainlessly wrong.   I had been right about my life, but wrong; right about my death, but wrong.   How *much* I wanted to make amends, and how impossible it was to do anything anymore, anything at all.   My actions had all tended to this, and ended with this: black remorse, the most dreadful pain of all.

I had all night to think, and to feel the pains, and to wait without knowing what I was waiting for or when—or if—my waiting would ever end.   Faintly I heard the arrival of Emily's sister and brother-in-law, the murmured conversation, then the departure of Tony and Greg.   Not long afterward the guestroom door opened, but almost immediately closed again, no one having entered, and a bit after that the hall hight went out, and now only the illuminated clock broke the darkness.

When next would I see Emily?   Would she ever enter this room again?   It wouldn't be as horrible as the first time, but it would surely be horror enough.

Dawn grayed the window shade, and gradually the room appeared out of the darkness, dim and silent and morose.   Apparently it was a sunless day, which never got very bright.   The day went on and on, featureless, each protracted minute marked by the clock.   At times I dreaded someone's entering this room, at other times I prayed for something, anything—even the presence of Emily herself—to break this unending boring *absence*. But the day went on with no event, no sound, no activity anywhere—they must be keeping Emily sedated through this first day— and it wasn't until twilight, with the digital clock reading 6:52, that the door again opened and a person entered.

At first I didn't recognize him.   An angry-looking man, blunt and determined, he came in with quick ragged steps, switched on both bedside lamps, then shut the door with rather more force than necessary, and turned the key in the lock.   Truculent, his manner was, and when he turned from the door I saw with incredulity that he was *me*.   Me!   I wasn't dead, I was alive!   But how could that be?

And what was that he was carrying?   He picked up the chair from the corner, carried it to the middle of the room, stood on it—

No!   No!

He tied the rope around the beam.   The noose was already in the other end, which he slipped over his head and tightened around his neck.

Good God, *don't!*

He kicked the chair away.

The instant I kicked the chair away I wanted it back, but gravity was turning my former wish to its present command; the chair would not right itself from where it lay on the floor, and my 193 pounds would not cease to urge downward from the rope thick around my neck.

There was pain, of course, quite horrible pain centered in my throat, but the most astounding thing was the way my cheeks seemed to swell.   I could barely see over their round red hills, my eyes staring in agony at the door, *willing* someone to come in and rescue me, though I knew there was no one in the house, and in any event the door was carefully locked.   My kicking legs caused me to twist and turn, so that sometimes I faced the door and sometimes the window, and my shivering hands struggled with the rope so deep in my flesh I could barely find it and most certainly could not pull it loose.

I was frantic and terrified, yet at the same time my brain possessed a cold corner of aloof observation.   I seemed now to be everywhere in the room at once, within my writhing body but also without, seeing my frenzied spasms, the thick rope, the heavy beam, the mismatched pair of lit bedside lamps throwing my convulsive double shadow on the walls, the closed locked door, the white-curtained window with its shade drawn all the way down.   *This is death*

EDITORIAL POSTSCRIPT

The story you have just read was nominated by MWA (Mystery Writers of America) as one of the five best new mystery short stories published in American magazines and books during 1978.

HUGH PENTECOST

Jericho and the Deadly Errand

Detective:
JOHN JERICHO

It was a chance meeting with an old love, almost forgotten with the passage of years, that brought John Jericho face to face with a violent murder. Words spoken to him in the strictest confidence set him on a path totally different from the ones taken by the police and the District Attorney's staff. That he walked that path at all was due to a blazing anger that made it imperative for him, personally, to see to it that Justice was not blind.

What developed into a bloody horror began in the most pleasant of ways. It was a summer day in New York City, one of those rare blue-sky days without smog or unbearable humidity. The sky was cloudless. Jericho, walking uptown on Fifth Avenue, felt younger than he was and carefree. This was a coincidence because, unsuspecting, he was about to encounter his youth again. He found himself thinking of a day like this in Paris, ten years or more ago, when he had been sitting at an outdoor café with friends, drinking a particularly good wine, watching the world go by, and thinking how marvelous it was just to be alive. He had been a young artist in those days, just launching a career that was to make him world-famous. The future hadn't seemed too important that day in Paris—just the present, the joy of being alive and doing what he wanted to do, of being mildly in love.

Remembering that, Jericho now paused at a crossing and looking east saw a sign outside a building: *WILLARD'S BACK YARD.* This was an expensive little restaurant he could afford to patronize in these days of success, and in the summer months there was a charming outdoor garden, shaded by awnings and potted trees. It would be pleasant to sit there and drink a glass of wine and remember Paris. So he turned east and went into Willard's.

Coincidences are the enemies of fiction writers, but life is full of them. Willard's was filling up for luncheon, but Willard, an old friend, found Jericho a table in the garden. People turned to look at him as he was led to his place. He was eye-catching: six feet four inches tall, 240 pounds of solid muscle, with flaming red hair and a blazing red beard.

He sat down, ordered a split of champagne, filled and lit a black curve-stemmed pipe, and leaned back to watch the world go by, just as he had years ago in Paris.

A woman was led to a table a few yards away from Jericho and he looked at her, enjoying her as he always enjoyed looking at beautiful women. She was, he guessed, in her very early thirties, expensively dressed, with an unusual personal electricity.   There was something familiar about her, he thought—the familiar charm of a woman of taste and experience, without a veneer of toughness.   This kind was rare—familiar but rare.

The woman looked at him, her dark violet eyes widening.   "Johnny?" she said. It was a question.

She was no stranger.   The absurd thing was that he had been thinking about her as he walked up Fifth Avenue, thinking of her as she had been ten or more years ago, thinking of her as she had been in Paris when he was mildly in love with her.

"Fay!"

He went over to her table and her small cool hands were in his.

"The beard," she said.   "I wasn't sure for a moment."

He had been a smooth-faced young man in Paris.   "May I join you?   Are you expecting someone?"

"Please.   No," she said.

He beckoned to the waiter to bring his wine.

"It's wild," she said.   "I came in here because I was thinking of you and the old days."

"ESP," he said.   "That's exactly what happened to me."

"Oh, Johnny!"

He ordered a stinger for her.   Her taste couldn't have changed.   Nothing had changed.   He said something to that effect.

"I wear a size twelve dress today," she said.   "It was an eight back in those days.   That much has changed."

She had been a model in those Paris times.   She had also been a member of a young group of Revolutionaries bent on destroying the establishment in general and General de Gaulle in particular.   Jericho had thought of them as crackbrained and lovable, particularly Fay.   She had posed for him and they had made love and she had forgotten about the Revolution.   There had been no anxieties, no guilts, no regrets when they came to the inevitable parting.

"Of course I've kept track of you, Johnny.   You're famous now.   I've gone to all your exhibitions, including your one-man show at the Mullins Gallery last month."

"You're living in New York?" he asked.

"Yes."

"And you never tried to get in touch with me?   I'm in the phone book."

"So am I.   You've forgotten, Johnny, that it was you who walked out.   You would have to do the getting in touch—if you wanted to."

"I was young and stupid," he said.   "I always thought of you as still being back in that other world, taking pot shots at General de Gaulle."

She laughed.   "We were pretty crazy kids, weren't we?   No, I came back here right after we broke up.   I am a respectable secretary now, for a man in the brokerage business.   You may have heard of him.   He's in the news these days. Lloyd Parker."

"He's running for the United States Senate.   That your man?"

She nodded. A tiny frown edged lines in her forehead. "A fine man," she said. "A good warm idealistic man."

Her man? Jericho wondered. Something in her voice—

"I don't have very good luck with men, Johnny," she said, reading his mind. She'd been like that in the old days. "First it was you who mattered. You walked out. Then there was—is—Lloyd Parker. I am his efficient, loyal, ever-ready office machine. He couldn't get along without me—in the office. Out of the office he is married to a beautiful, exotic, fabulously rich gal. Crandall Steel— she was Ellen Crandall. I am the classic figure of the secretary hopelessly in love with her boss, preferring to work with him every day and not have him rather than drop him and find someone who might want me as a woman."

"There are probably a hundred such someones," Jericho said.

She seemed not to hear that. "I was thinking of you when I came in here, Johnny, because I need help."

"Oh?"

"I need advice from someone who understands how complex people are, who wouldn't make judgments by hard and fast rules. I thought that of all the people I'd ever known you never prejudged, never insisted that all people follow black-and-white formulas." She tried a smile. "I thought that if I could only get advice from you—and presto, here you are."

"Try me, before I make improper advances," he said, answering her smile.

Her frown returned and stayed fixed. "Lloyd is running against a man named Molloy—Mike Molloy to his friends. Molloy is a machine politician, supported by the big-city moguls, the hardhats, the labor bosses. Perhaps not a bad man, Johnny, but not a man of Lloyd's caliber, not a potential statesman, not in any way an idealist. Lloyd could be Presidential material in the future. Molloy belongs to other men. Lloyd belongs to himself and his country."

"He can have my vote."

"Lloyd is about forty-five. He has always had a little money. His family was Plymouth Rock-Mayflower stuff. I say 'a little money' in comparison to his wife's fortune. He was graduated from Harvard in the late forties, having missed the War. He knew that sooner or later he would be faced with the Army, and he didn't know what he wanted to do, really. A college friend persuaded him to put some money into a business, one of the first computer-dating services. Lloyd had nothing to do with the operation of the business; he was just a part owner. Someone blew the whistle on them. Lloyd's partner was using information they gathered to blackmail clients. He was indicted, convicted, and sent to prison. Lloyd was cleared."

"So?"

"After that came the Army in Korea. One day Lloyd's top sergeant asked him to mail a package for him. On the way to the post office Lloyd was stopped by M.P.s and it was discovered that the package contained about thirty thousand dollars in cash. The sergeant, it turned out, had been stealing the P.X. blind. There was a court-martial. The sergeant went to Leavenworth. Lloyd was cleared. He had simply been an innocent messenger boy."

"But not lucky with his friends or connections," Jericho said.

"Neither of these things was a great scandal at the time," Fay said. "They've been long forgotten. But suddenly they've reappeared in Wardell Lewis' political column. Lewis is supporting Molloy. Someone has fed him these two old stories, along with some malicious gossip about a love affair which Lloyd is supposed to have broken off in order to marry the Crandall money."

"A love affair with you, Fay?"

"No," she said sharply. "There is some truth in it, though. He did have an affair with a girl, he did break it off, he did marry Ellen Crandall five years ago. Lewis is using all this and I've been trying to find out who's been feeding Lewis this information."

"Any luck? The partner, the sergeant, the dropped girl?"

Fay shook her head. She looked at Jericho, her eyes wide. "Ellen, Lloyd's wife, is having an affair with Wardell Lewis."

"Wow!" Jericho said.

"Of course Lloyd has no knowledge of it," Fay said. "That's what creates my problem. He loves his wife deeply. If he learns the truth, I think it will destroy him. What do I do? Do I go to Lloyd and wreck his life with the truth? Do I go to her and Lewis and threaten them with exposure? They would laugh at me. Exposure, beyond what it might do to Lloyd personally, would ruin his political future. A cuckolded candidate for the Senate becomes a national joke." Fay brought her closed fist down on the table. "What do I do, Johnny?"

"Have another stinger," he said, wondering just what she should do. She obviously was in love with the man.

Jericho didn't come up with an immediate answer for Fay Martin. Parker, his wife, and Wardell Lewis were not real people to him. They were X, Y, and Z in a problem. Fay was real, very real. She had set out to help a man she loved and she could only help him, it developed, by hurting him terribly. It mattered to her whether or not Lloyd Parker won an election; but it mattered even more that he not be hurt.

The only thing that occurred to Jericho was that there might be a way to silence Wardell Lewis without using Ellen Parker's adultery as the weapon. Lewis' kind of muckraking journalism suggested the kind of man who might well have skeletons in his own closet. Jericho had friends. He would, he promised Fay, put something in motion.

Would she have dinner with him? That was impossible. She had to go to a public debate that was being held up in Westchester between Parker and Molloy. She would, however, join him for lunch again tomorrow. By then he might have dug up something that could be used as leverage against Lewis. A newspaperman and a friend in the District Attorney's office would nose around for Jericho. But Jericho promised he would not tell either of them about the triangle.

The next morning Jericho woke early as usual. He was in his apartment on Jefferson Mews in Greenwich Village. When he came out of the shower he switched on the radio to hear the eight o'clock news.   What he heard turned him to stone.

Fay Martin was dead.

The facts, put together from the radio account and from the morning papers, were as follows: the debate between Lloyd Parker and Mike Molloy was to be held in the auditorium of the Community Center Building in White Hills.   Parker and his wife had driven out there in his Cadillac and left the car, locked, in the parking area.   Shortly before the debate was to begin, Parker's secretary, Fay Martin, had come out to the parking area, and asked the attendant where the Parker Cadillac had been left.   She identified herself and showed the man keys.   Parker, she said, had left something he needed in the Cadillac's glove compartment.

The attendant pointed out where the car was and watched her go to it.   She unlocked the door, got in, and leaned forward to open the glove compartment.   An explosion blew the car and Fay to bits, started a raging fire, and severely damaged a half dozen other cars parked nearby.

The debate was never held.   Some odd facts were turned up by the police. Parker, in a state of shock, denied that he had sent Fay to the car to get anything for him.   She had, he told police, come to White Hills in her own car to make sure everything was in order for the debate.   He hadn't sent her out to his car for anything.   There wasn't anything he needed.   Furthermore, he insisted that she didn't have a set of keys for the car, which he had locked himself.   There was only one set of keys, his own, and he had them in his pocket.   There was no other set!   Why Fay had gone to the car and where she had got a set of keys was completely inexplicable to Parker.

The police were certain the bomb had been planted in the glove compartment and rigged so that when the compartment door was opened, the bomb would go off.   The bomb had obviously been meant to kill Parker, the police said, since he was the only person who drove the Cadillac and the only person who had keys to it.

Except that there must have been a second set of keys.

Mrs. Ellen Parker confirmed her husband's statement.   There was no second set of keys that she knew of.   She had her own car—she never drove her husband's Cadillac.

Public outrage was high.   People were sick of bombings and assassinations. A political analyst expressed the opinion that Parker, who had been running behind Molloy in the polls, would now be an odds-on favorite to win the election.   Sympathy would push him into the head.   The Molloy forces would be high on the suspect list.   Innocent as it might be, the Molloy machine had been put behind the eight-ball.

Jericho, his muscles aching from tension, didn't give a damn about the election.

Fay was dead—loyal, dedicated Fay, in love with a man who had passed her by for ten years, and for whom she had been murdered.

Someone must have handed Fay a set of keys, probably saying they were Parker's.

"He wants you to get an envelope he left in the glove compartment of his car." Of course she had gone, cheerfully.   She would have done anything in the world for Parker without question.   Whoever gave her the keys, not Parker's, had to know what would happen when the glove compartment door was opened.   The bomb hadn't been meant for Parker, not ever.

Fay was dead, and it had been meant that she should die.

Do you set an elaborate and dangerous trap to kill a girl simply because she has found out about a case of adultery?   What did Ellen Parker have to lose if her affair with Lewis became public?   She had all the money in the world; she was tired of her husband.

What did Lewis have to lose?   His man-about-town reputation would only be enhanced by the news that Ellen Parker was his latest conquest.   This was 1972, not 1872.   Infidelity was no longer a "curiosity."   Fay had wanted to keep Parker from learning the truth about his wife.   To kill her to keep her silent made no sense, not when she would have kept silent under any circumstances.

But she had known something, or had done something, that called for violence— something, Jericho concluded, that she hadn't mentioned to him during their brief reunion.

The police, Jericho learned from his friend in the D.A.'s office, were still working on the theory that the bomb had been meant for Parker.   Experts had put together small pieces.   The bomb had evidently been a simple device—sticks of dynamite tied together, set off by a Fourth of July cap and triggered when the glove compartment door was opened.   The killer didn't have to be an explosives expert.

There was simply no way to guess who had sent Fay on her deadly errand.   She had died with that information unrevealed.   The unexplained set of keys to the car was a puzzle.   Parker, under persistent questioning, remembered that when he'd bought the Cadillac a year ago there had been a duplicate set of keys.   He'd put them "in a safe place" and now hadn't the faintest recollection where that had been.   Ellen Parker denied all knowledge of them.   Fay might have known, but Fay was dead.   The dead kept their secrets and the living would lie to suit their own purposes.

Jericho, convinced that the bomb had not been meant for Parker, was inclined to bypass the Molloy forces.   Parker, dead by violence, could do nothing but harm them.   Parker's forces could run Mickey Mouse and win.   Molloy could only be involved if Fay had discovered something criminal about him and had kept it to herself long enough for Molloy's men to rig her death.   But it didn't make sense. If she was a danger to Molloy he would have struck swiftly and less obviously, and would have made sure that it didn't appear to have been aimed at Parker.

Yesterday had been a blue-sky day, a day for reunions, a day to remember a carefree time, a day to promise help.   Today the skies were dark and the rain, wind-swept, was swirling in the gutters.   Too late for promises, but not too late to demand payment in full.

A man wearing a slicker and a brown rain hat stood in the foyer of a remodeled brownstone on the east side.   He had a bright red beard and his eyes were pale blue, and cold as two newly minted dimes.   He had stood there while half a dozen people left the building to go to work, and two or three tradesmen arrived to deliver orders.   The buildings custodian had approached him on the subject of loitering, and a crisp ten-dollar bill had changed hands.

At about eleven o'clock a taxi stopped outside the building.   A woman got out and ran across the sidewalk to the sanctuary of the foyer.   She was a tall, very beautiful, very chic blonde.   She looked at Jericho with a kind of detached curiosity as she pressed one of the doorbells in the brass nameplate board.   The ring was a signal—one short, one long, two shorts.   The woman's picture had been in the paper that morning, so Jericho had no doubts about her.   "The Beautiful Mrs. Lloyd Parker" had been the newspaper caption.

The front door made a clicking sound and Ellen Parker opened it.   Jericho was directly behind her, then inside before the door could close in his face.   She gave him a startled look and hurried up the stairway to the second floor.   Jericho was behind her and he could sense her sudden panic.   She almost ran along the second-floor hallway to the apartment in the rear.   The door was opening and a man in a seersucker robe was smiling at her—and the man with the red beard was directly behind her.

There was a moment of confusion.

"Ward!" Ellen Parker cried out.

She was pushed hard from behind, then she and Wardell Lewis and Jericho all wound up inside the apartment.   The door was closed and Jericho was leaning against it.   Lewis, tall, with longish dark hair and a mod mustache, was naked under the seersucker robe.   He looked around, obviously frightened, for a weapon.

"He followed me in," Ellen Parker said in a husky voice.

The world is full of black tales about the city and its violences.   Women are attacked and robbed in the hallways of their apartment houses; drug addicts steal, even kill, for the price of a fix.   It would come like this, they were thinking—unexpected, catching them totally unprepared.

Jericho took off his rain hat and shook the water out of it.   He tossed it onto a chair near the door.

Lewis' eyes widened.   He was the man-about-town, the gossip hunter, the man who knew everyone.   "You're John Jericho, the painter!" he said.

"I'm John Jericho, friend of Fay Martin's," Jericho said.   "We'll have a talk and I hope for your sake you'll answer questions."

"What do you mean by breaking in this way?" Lewis demanded.

"I wanted to catch you two together," Jericho said.   "Fay told me about you. I wanted to make sure for myself.   Now I'm going to get the truth about last night if I have to scrape you out of your shells."

Lewis walked over to a table in the center of the room and took a cigarette from a lacquered box.   It was a cluttered room, every inch of the wall space covered with photographs of celebrated people in society, politics, and show business, all autographed to Wardell Lewis.   Lewis held a table lighter to his cigarette with an unsteady hand.

"If you were a friend of Parker's secretary," he said, "I can understand why you're so steamed up.   But so help me, I'm going to have you arrested for breaking and entering, and for threatening us with violence.''

Jericho's pale eyes were fixed on the woman who was standing behind a chair, gripping it to support herself.   He appeared not to have heard Lewis.   Fay had been right—she was beautiful.   What, he wondered, did she see in a creep like Lewis?

"Fay had found out about you and Lewis," Jericho said to her.   "But she was willing to do anything to keep your husband from finding out that you were having an affair with this clown and feeding him information that could hurt your husband. You didn't need to kill Fay.''

Ellen Parker's eyes were wide with fright.   "That bomb wasn't meant for Fay, God help her," she said.   "It was meant for me!''

"Keep still, Ellen," Lewis said.   "This man is your enemy.''

"What makes you think the bomb was meant for you, Mrs. Parker?" Jericho asked.

"Because I was meant to go to the car," she said.   She looked as if her legs were about to fold under her.   She clung to the chair.

"Take it slowly from the beginning," Jericho said.   He told himself he had an ear for the truth.   Lewis was the kind of man who'd grown up saying, "I didn't do it!"—but Ellen Parker was something else again.   She was two-timing her husband, betraying his secrets, but she obviously believed what she had just said. She believed the bomb had been meant for her.

"It was at the White Hills Community Center, just before last night's debate was about to begin," Ellen Parker said.   "I had left my seat to go to the powder room. When I came back there was an envelope on my seat.   In it was a set of car keys and a scribbled note saying my husband wanted me to get an envelope he'd left in the glove compartment of his car.   He was up on the speaker's stand on the stage. He smiled and waved at me.   I waved back, indicating I'd do what he asked— waved back with the note.''

"Was the note in your husband's handwriting?''

"No.   I thought one of his staff had written it.   I was just starting to edge my way out of the row of seats when Fay appeared.   She asked me if anything was wrong, because they were just about to start.   I told her Lloyd needed something from the car and she said she'd get it.   I—I was glad not to have to go, so I gave her the keys and the note.''

"Which were blown up in the car with her," Lewis said.   "Ellen can't prove a word of what she's saying and he denied he asked anyone to get anything.''

"He?''

"Parker, for God's sake.   Who else?   Of course he denies it—he meant to kill Ellen!''

"Why?''

"Because he'd found out about us, why else?''

"I don't dare go home," Ellen Parker said, her voice shaking.   "The police were there all last night—to protect him.   But once they're gone he may try again.''

"The man's turned into a homicidal maniac," Lewis said. "Ellen and I are going to have to get protection from the police."

"Were you at the Community Center in White Hills last night, Lewis?" Jericho asked.

"Of course I was there," Lewis said. "I'm covering the campaign, as you know if you read the papers."

Jericho glanced at Ellen Parker. "And how you're covering the campaign!" he said. "A man who goes berserk and tries to kill his wife for an infidelity doesn't usually leave out the wife's lover. Well, maybe Parker's saving you for dessert."

"You think it's something to joke about?" Lewis said. "I've had about enough of this." He bent down and opened the drawer of the table behind which he was standing. His hand didn't get out of the drawer with the revolver—Jericho moved too fast. His left hand grabbed Lewis' right wrist and brought it down on the edge of the table. The gun fell noiselessly to the rug. Jericho's right hand swung to Lewis' jaw. The columnist's head snapped back and he collapsed on the rug without a sound.

Ellen Parker didn't move from her place behind the chair, still clutching it for support. Her eyes, wide with fear, were fixed on Jericho, as if she expected to be next. He was moving toward her and she obviously wanted to scream, but couldn't. He took her arm gently.

"There are things I need to know about your husband," he said. "Could we go somewhere else to talk—somewhere that smells less of treachery?"

She made no move to go to Lewis, but asked, "Is he hurt?"

"He will have a severe headache—I hope," Jericho said.

They sat together in a corner booth in a little restaurant a couple of blocks from Lewis' apartment. The rain had let up and they had walked there, Ellen Parker in a kind of trance. Jericho ordered coffee, with brandy to lace it. He leaned back in the booth, watching her, waiting for her to speak. There was something unexpectedly vulnerable about her. She wasn't the kind of woman he had expected.

"I've destroyed myself," she said finally, not looking at Jericho. "It's always been that way. I have always destroyed everything that has been good in my life."

"Your marriage?" he asked quietly.

"Since I was a little girl I've always been afraid that people only liked me because I was so rich. I never believed that any man really wanted me for myself. I always tested them and tested them until I drove them away. Then Lloyd Parker came into my life and for the first time I really believed I was loved and wanted for myself, that my money didn't have anything to do with how he felt about me. For the first time in my life I was happy, without doubts, without fears."

"What changed it?"

"This venture into politics," she said, drawing a deep breath. "You can't get elected dog catcher these days, Mr. Jericho, without spending a great deal of money.

Lloyd asked me for a great deal of money and I gave it to him gladly, happily.
Then, as soon as I did, he seemed to lose interest in me.   Our love life came to
an end.   I told myself it was because he was working fourteen-eighteen hours a
day.   But the old doubts, the bitter certainty that it was only my money he wanted,
took charge again.   I guess I went a little crazy.   I went out on the town looking
for a man, any man, who'd find me attractive without knowing I was rich, rich,
rich.   It was Ward Lewis who picked me up and restored my ego.''

"Lewis, who knew who you were from the first moment he laid eyes on you,
knew you were rich, rich, rich, and who planned to use you to help the Molloy
crowd.''

"I wanted to hurt Lloyd,'' she said, her lips trembling.   "I wanted revenge.
And—and I hated myself.''

"Good for you,'' Jericho said.

"Last night, when Lloyd told me that he knew about Ward and me, I—''

"He *knew?*''   Jericho sat up straight.

"He told me while we were driving out to White Hills.   There'd been an
anonymous letter.   He'd checked on me and found out it was true.   I knew how
much it hurt him and I was glad for a moment.   But he was wonderful about it.
He took the blame, admitted he'd neglected me, begged me to give him another
chance.   I almost began to believe in him again.''

"Why do you suppose he told you he knew if he was planning to kill you?''
Jericho asked.

She looked at him, her eyes wide.   "So I'd know, at the last moment when the
bomb went off, why I was dying.''

"That makes him into some kind of monster,'' Jericho said.

Ellen Parker closed her eyes.   "God help me,'' she said.

The receptionist in the brokerage offices of Sheftel & Parker was not cordial.

"I'm afraid Mr. Parker can't see you today, Mr. Jericho.   If you've heard the
news—''

"Give him this note,'' Jericho said.   "I think he'll see me.''

Jericho felt out of place in the paneled waiting room with its rich green-leather
furnishings.   His corduroy jacket and turtlenecked shirt were altogether too casual
for this palace of wealth.   There was another out-of-place man sitting in one of
the big chairs across the room.   Jericho's artist's eyes picked up details that might
have escaped others.   A slight bulge at the other man's waistline spelled gun.
Cop, Jericho thought.   The police weren't risking another attempt on Parker's life.

The receptionist, looking mildly surprised, reappeared.   "Mr. Parker will see
you,'' she said.

She led Jericho into an inner room.   He was aware that the waiting man had
risen and was following him.   In the inner room another out-of-place man faced
him.   He showed a police shield.

"Mr. Parker doesn't know you, Mr. Jericho.   Under the circumstances you'll
understand why we must make sure you're not armed.''

Jericho raised his arms languidly.   The man behind tapped Jericho over.   There was a moment of tension when he felt a bulge in the pocket of the corduroy coat. It turned out to be Jericho's pipe.

Lloyd Parker was about six feet tall, with soft, curly brown hair. He had a square jaw, and the crow's-feet at the corners of his brown eyes suggested a man of good humor. But those eyes were red-rimmed, probably from lack of sleep. He looked like a man fighting exhaustion. This had been Fay's kind of man, Jericho thought: gentle, undemanding, considerate. Most people would instinctively like Lloyd Parker under normal circumstances. Now he was undermined by tensions and anxiety. He stood in front of his big flat-topped desk, leaning against it.

"Your note, Mr. Jericho, tells me that you were a friend of Fay's, which is why I agreed to see you. It also says that you know where my wife is. Why should you think that would interest me?"

"Aren't you wondering if she's gone back to Wardell Lewis?"

A muscle rippled along Parker's jawline. "Just what, exactly, do you mean by that?"

"Oh, come, Mr. Parker, let's not waste time with games. I've just been talking to your wife. I knew about the affair from Fay."

"Fay? Fay knew?"

"Fay knew and was prepared to do anything to keep you from finding out about it. But you did find out."

Parker's face hardened. "What do you want of me, Mr. Jericho?"

"I want to ask you a question before I call in those cops out there and charge you with the murder of Fay Martin and the intention to murder your wife."

Parker's mouth dropped and he gasped for air like a landed fish. "You're out of your mind!" he whispered.

"I think not." Jericho's voice was matter-of-fact. "Your wife got your instructions to go to the car, where a bomb was waiting for her. By mischance Fay offered to do the errand for her. I said in my note that I know where your wife is. I do. She's not with Lewis, if that matters to you. But it must be obvious to you that she won't see you or go back home with you. She's afraid you might try again."

"This is sheer madness!" Parker said. "I don't want my wife dead. I love her. There's nothing in the world that matters to me without her. I had nothing to do with the bomb, I sent no message asking her to go to the car, I had just been pleading with her to give our marriage a second chance."

"When did you tell Fay she could stop looking for the person who was feeding Wardell Lewis with information about you?"

"Last night, just a little while before the debate was to begin. I told her the truth—that I'd found out Ellen was having an affair with Lewis, which explained his source of information."

"She wasn't shocked, Parker. She had told me earlier in the day about the affair. She was, as I told you, prepared to do anything to keep you from knowing."

"She told me that. I was grateful, but I explained to her that Ellen was all that mattered to me, that I'd do anything to get her back."

Jericho's eyes wandered toward a small bar in the corner of the office. "Do you mind if I pour myself a drink?"

"Yes, I mind!" Parker said. "Does Ellen really think I tried to kill her?"

"She's sure of it," Jericho said. He went over to the bar and poured himself a bourbon. He looked at Parker and raised his glass. "Maybe I can persuade her that she's wrong."

"But you just threatened to—"

"I know," Jericho said. "You have an extraordinary effect on women, Parker. One of them runs away from you and into the arms of a heel because she thinks you don't love her enough. Another gives up being a woman for ten years just to breathe the same air that you do. But I don't suppose Fay ever gave up hope that some day, somehow, you might be more than that to her."

"Poor Fay."

"Yes, poor Fay," Jericho said. "It could have been this way, Parker. When she found out about your wife's affair with Lewis she wanted to save you the hurt. Your wife's death might be a terrible blow to you, but having your male ego shattered would be even worse. I think she had already planned a way when she talked to me at lunch yesterday. Maybe she hoped I'd come up with a better answer, but unfortunately I didn't.

"So it was she, it was Fay who rigged the bomb in your car. Keys? There was a spare set which you'd put 'in a safe place' that you no longer could remember. Fay knew. Your secretary, Parker, your devoted, loving secretary knew. Your wife might not know your 'safe place,' or the size of your collar, or how you liked your eggs, but Fay knew; she knew everything there was to know about you and she cherished the knowledge."

"It doesn't make sense," Parker said, his voice shaken. "How would *she* know how to rig a bomb? Fay? Impossible!"

"Quite possible," Jericho said. "There's an odd fact I know about her that you'd have no reason to know. When I first met Fay in Paris ten or twelve years ago she was a model. I am a painter. She was also a member of a wild young revolutionary group that was constantly demonstrating, bombing, and burning. Their aim was to get rid of General de Gaulle. They were trained by experienced people. She would know how to make a simple bomb.

"I met her, she modeled for me, we fell in love in a sort of way, and for a good many months she forgot about being a Mata Hari. When we parted she came back here and went to work for you. But she had the knowledge about explosives."

"And you say she meant to kill Ellen?"

"I think so. She would kill Ellen and at the same time improve your election prospects, because Molloy and his crowd would be suspected. She prepared the note that would send your wife out to the car and left it on her seat. It must have been after she'd done that you told her you knew. More important—more devastating to Fay—you made it clear that Ellen was still all that mattered to you. That there'd be no future for Fay even if Ellen died. If Ellen was the only one you wanted, poor defeated Fay would make certain you had her. She must have hurried to retrieve the note and the keys. But Ellen already had them."

"Good God."

Jericho looked at his empty glass. "So she volunteered to run the errand for Ellen."

"Knowing the bomb was in the car?"

"Maybe she thought she could deactivate it. Maybe, in that brief trip to the parking lot she decided to take it as a way out. Perhaps she thought she would be doing you a last service. The bomb would at least end Molloy's chances of defeating you in the election."

"Can you prove this?"

"Not one word of it," Jericho said. He turned back to the bar and poured himself another drink. "But I might persuade your wife that it's true. Care to come with me and help me try?"

EDWARD D. HOCH

The Theft of Nick Velvet

Criminal-Detective:
NICK VELVET

"It's for you, Nicky," Gloria yelled from the telephone, and Nick Velvet put down the beer he'd been savoring.   It was a lazy Sunday afternoon in late winter, when the snow had retreated to little lumps beneath the shady bushes and a certain freshness was already apparent in the air.   It was a time of year that Nick especially liked, and he was sorry to have his reverie broken.

"Yes?" he spoke into the phone, after taking it from Gloria's hand.

"Nick Velvet?"   The voice was deep and a bit harsh, but that didn't surprise him.   He'd been hearing that sort of voice on telephones for years.

"Speaking."

"You do jobs.   You steal things."   A statement, not a question.

"I never discuss my business on the telephone.   I could meet you somewhere tomorrow."

"It has to be tonight."

"Very well, tonight."

"I'll be in the parking lot at the Cross-County Mall.   Eight o'clock."

"How will I know your car?"

"The place is empty on a Sunday night.   We'll find each other."

"Could I have your name?"

The voice hesitated, then replied.   "Solar.   Max Solar.   Didn't you receive my letter?"

"No," Nick answered.   "Your letter about what?"

"I'll see you at eight."

The line went dead and Nick hung up the phone.   He'd heard the name Max Solar before, or seen it in the newspapers, but he couldn't remember in what context.

"Who was that, Nicky?"   Gloria appeared in the doorway, holding a beer.

"A land developer.   He wants to see me tonight."

"On Sunday?"

Nick nodded.   "He needs my opinion on some land he's buying near here.   I shouldn't be gone more than an hour."   The excuses and evasions came easily to Nick's lips, and sometimes he half suspected that Gloria knew them for what they were.   Certainly she rarely questioned his sudden absences, even for days at a time.

He left the house a little after 7:30 and drove the five miles to the Cross-County

Mall in less than fifteen minutes.   There was little traffic and when he reached
the Mall ahead of schedule he was surprised to see a single car already parked
there, near the drive-in bank.   He drove up beside it and parked.   A man in the
front seat nodded and motioned to him.

Nick left his car and opened the door of the other vehicle.   "You're early,"
the man said.

"Better than late.   Are you Max Solar?"

"Yes.   Get in."

Nick slid into the front seat and closed the door.   The man next to him was
bulky in a tweed topcoat, and he seemed nervous.

"What do you want stolen?" Nick asked.   "I don't touch money or jewelry or
anything of value, and my fee is—"

He never finished.   There was a movement behind him, in the back seat, and
something hit him across the side of the head.   That was the last Nick knew for
some time.

When he opened his eyes he realized he was lying on a bed somewhere.   The
ceiling was crisscrossed with cracks and there was a cobweb visible in one corner.
He thought about that, knowing Gloria's trim housekeeping would never allow such
a thing, and realized he was not at home.   His head ached and his body was
uncomfortably stretched.   He tried to turn over and discovered that his left wrist
was handcuffed to a brass bedstead.

Not the police.

But who, then?   And why?

He tried to focus his mind.   It seemed to be morning, with light seeping through
the blind at the window.   But which day?   Monday?

A door opened somewhere and he heard footsteps crossing the floor.   A face
appeared over him, a familiar face.   The man in the car.

"Where am I?" Nick mumbled through a furry mouth.   "What am I doing
here?"

The man leaned closer to the bed.   "You are here because I have stolen you."
The idea seemed to amuse him and he chuckled.

"Why?"   The room was beginning to swim before Nick's eyes.

"Don't try to talk.   We have no intention of harming you.   Just lie still and
relax."

"What's the matter with me?"

"A mild sedative.   Just something to keep you under control."

Nick tried to speak again, but the words would not come.   He closed his eyes
and slept . . .

When he awakened it was night again, or nearly so.   A shaded lamp glowed
dimly in one cormer of the room.   "Are you awake?" a girl's voice asked, in
response to his movement.

Nick lifted his head and saw a young brunette dressed in a dark turtleneck sweater
and jeans.   He ran has tongue over dry lips and finally found his voice.   "I guess
so.   Who are you?"

"You can call me Terry. I'm supposed to be watching you, but it's more fun if you're awake. I didn't give you the last injection of sedative because I want someone to talk to."

"Thanks a lot," Nick said, trying to work the cobwebs from his throat. "What day is it?"

"Only Monday. You haven't even been here twenty-four hours yet." She came over and sat by the bed. "Hungry?"

He realized suddenly that he was. "Starving. I guess you haven't fed me."

"I'll get you some juice and a doughnut."

"Where's the other one—the man?"

"Away somewhere," she answered vaguely. She left the room and reappeared soon carrying a glass of orange juice and a bag of doughnuts. "Afraid that's the best I can do."

"How about unlocking me?"

"No. I don't have the key. You can eat with your other hand."

The juice tasted good going down, and even the soggy doughnuts were welcome. "Why did you kidnap me?" he asked Terry. "What are you going to do with me?"

"Don't know." She retreated from the room, perhaps deciding she'd talked too much already.

Nick finished three doughnuts and then lay back on the bed. He'd been lured to that parking lot and kidnaped for some reason, and he couldn't believe the motive was anything as simple as ransom. The man on the telephone had identified himself as Max Solar, and asked if Nick had received his letter. Since kidnapers rarely gave their right names to victims, it was likely the man was not Max Solar.

"Terry," he shouted. "Terry, come here!"

She appeared in the doorway, hands on hips. "What is it?"

"Come talk. I feel like talking."

"What about?"

"Max Solar. The man who brought me here."

She giggled a bit, and her face glowed with youth. "He's not Max Solar. He was just kidding you. Do you really think someone as wealthy as Max Solar would go around kidnaping people?"

"Then what is his name?"

"I can't tell you. He wouldn't like it."

"How'd you get involved with him?"

"I can't talk any more about it."

Nick sighed. "I thought you wanted someone to talk to."

"Sure, but I wanted to talk about *you*."

He eyed her suspiciously. "What about me?"

"You're Nick Velvet. You're famous."

"Only in certain circles."

Their conversation was interrupted by the opening of a door. Terry scurried from the room and Nick lay back and closed his eyes. After a moment he heard Terry return with the man.

"What in hell is this bag of doughnuts doing on the bed?" a male voice demanded. "He's conscious, isn't he? And you've been feeding him!"

"He was hungry, Sam."

There was the splat of palm hitting cheek, and Terry let out a cry.

Nick opened his eyes. "Suppose you try that on me, Sam."

The man from the car, still looking bulky even without his tweed topcoat, turned toward the bed. "You're in no position to make like a knight in shining armor, Velvet."

Nick sat up as best he could with his handcuffed wrist. "Look, I've been slugged on the head, kidnaped, drugged, and handcuffed to this bed. Don't you think I deserve an explanation?"

"Shut him up," Sam ordered Terry, but she made no move to obey.

"You kidnaped me to keep me from seeing the real Max Solar, right?" Nick was guessing, but it had to be a reasonably good guess. The man named Sam turned on the girl once more.

"Did you tell him that?"

"No, Sam, honest! I didn't tell him a thing!"

The bulky man grunted. "All right, Velvet, it's true. I don't mind telling you, since you've guessed it already. Max Solar wrote you on Friday to arrange an appointment for this week. He wanted to hire you to steal something."

"And you kidnaped me to prevent it?"

The man named Sam nodded. He pulled up a straight-backed wooden chair and sat down by the bed. "Do you know who Max Solar is?"

"I've heard the name." Nick tried to sit up straighter, but the handcuff prevented him. "How about unlocking this thing?"

"Not a chance."

"All right," Nick sighed. "Tell me about Max Solar."

"He's a conglomerate. He owns a number of companies manufacturing everything from office machines to toothpaste. Last year while I was in his employ I invented a computer program that saved thousands of man-hours each year in bookkeeping and inventory control on his export and overseas operations. The courts have ruled that such computer programming cannot be patented, and I was at the mercy of Max Solar. He simply fired me and kept my program. For the past year I've dreamed of ways to get my revenge, and on Friday Terry supplied me with the perfect weapon."

Nick listened to the voice drone on, wondering where it was all leading. The man did not seem the type to resort to kidnaping, yet there was a hardness in his eyes that hinted at a steely determination.

"I'm a secretary at Solar Industries," Terry explained. "My office is right next to Max Solar's, and often I help his secretary when my boss is away."

Sam nodded. "Solar dictated a letter to Nick Velvet, asking for a meeting today. Terry brought me a copy, with a suggestion for revenging myself on Solar."

"You knew who I was?" Nick asked the girl.

"I had a boy friend once who told me about you—how you steal valueless things for people."

Sam nodded. "I figured up in the suburbs you probably wouldn't get Solar's letter till Monday—not the way mail deliveries are these days—but just to be safe I used his name when I phoned yesterday. See, I had to kidnap you and hold you prisoner till after the ship sails."

"Ship?"

"Solar was hiring you to steal something from a freighter that sails from New York harbor in two days."

"It must be something important."

"It is, but only to Max Solar. It would be worthless to anyone else."

Nick thought about it.

"That's not quite correct," he said.

"What do you mean?"

"You can revenge yourself on Solar by holding me prisoner, or you can hire me to steal this object and then sell it back to Solar."

"Why should I hire you? I have you already!"

"You have me physically, but you don't have my services."

"He makes sense," Terry said. "I hadn't thought about that angle. If Nick steals the thing, you can sell it to Solar for enough to cover Nick's fee plus a lot more. You'd be getting back the money Solar cheated you out of."

Sam pondered the implications. "How do we know you wouldn't go to the police as soon as you're free?"

"I have as little dealing with the police as possible," Nick said. "For obvious reasons."

Sam was still uncertain. "We've got you now. In forty-eight hours Max Solar will be in big trouble. Why let you go and take a chance on ruining our whole plan?"

"Because if you don't, you'll be in big trouble too. Kidnaping is a far more serious crime than blackmail. Unlock these handcuffs now and hire me. I won't press charges against you. I steal the thing, collect my fee, and you sell it back to Solar for a lot more. Everybody's happy."

Sam turned to Terry. When she nodded approval he said, "All right. Unlock him."

As soon as the handcuff came free of his wrist Nick said, "My fee in this case will be thirty thousand dollars. I always charge more for dangerous assignments."

"There's nothing dangerous about it."

"It's dangerous when I get hit on the head and drugged."

"That was Terry. She was hiding in the back seat of the car with a croquet mallet."

"You knocked me out with a croquet mallet?"

Terry nodded. "We were going to use a monkey wrench, but we thought it might hurt."

"Thanks a lot." Nick was rubbing the circulation back into his wrist. "Now what is it Max Solar was going to hire me to steal?"

"A ship's manifest," Terry told him. "But we're not sure which ship. We only know it sails in two days."

"What's so valuable about a ship's manifest?"

They exchanged glances. "The less you know the better," Sam said.

"Don't I even get to know your names?"

"You know too much already. Steal the manifest and meet us back here tomorrow night."

"How do I find the ship?"

"A South African named Herbert Jarvis is in town arranging for the shipment. He'd know which ship it is." Terry looked uneasy as she spoke. "I could go through the files at the office, but that might arouse suspicion. They might think it odd I took today off anyway."

"Shipment of what?" Nick asked.

"Typewriters," she said, and he knew she was lying.

"All right. But there must be several more copies of this ship's manifest around."

"The copy on the ship is the only one that matters," Sam said. "Get it, and we'll meet you here tomorrow night at seven."

"What about my car?"

"It's in the garage," Terry said. "We didn't want to leave it at the Mall."

Nick nodded. "I'll see you tomorrow with the manifest. Have my fee ready."

The house where he'd been held prisoner was in the northern part of the city, near Van Cortlandt Park. It took Nick nearly an hour to drive home from there, and another hour to comfort a distraught Gloria who'd been about to phone the police.

"You know my business takes me away suddenly at times," he said, glancing casually through the mail until he found Solar's letter.

"But you've always told me, Nicky! I didn't hear from you and all I could imagine was you were hit over the head and robbed!"

"Sorry I worried you." He kissed her gently. "Is it too late to get something to eat?"

In the morning he checked the sailing times of the next day's ships in *The New York Times*. There were only two possibilities—the *Fairfax* and the *Florina*—but neither one was bound for South Africa. With so little time to spare, he couldn't afford to pick the wrong one, and trying to find Herbert Jarvis at an unknown New York hotel might be a hopeless task.

There was only one sure way to find the right ship—to ask Max Solar. He knew that Sam and Terry wouldn't approve, but he had no better choice.

Solar Industries occupied most of a modern twelve-story building not far from the house where he'd been held prisoner. He took the elevator to the top floor and waited in a plush reception room while the girl announced his arrival to Max Solar. Presently a cool young woman appeared to escort him.

"I'm Mr. Solar's secretary," she said. "Please come this way."

In Max Solar's office two men were seated at a wide desk, silhouetted against the wide windows that looked south toward Manhattan. There was no doubt which one was Solar. He was tall and white-haired, and sat behind his desk in total command, like the pilot of an aircraft or a rancher on his horse.   He did not rise as Nick entered, but said simply, "So you're Velvet.   About time you got here."

"I was tied up earlier."

Solar waited until his secretary left, then said, "I understand you steal things for a fee of twenty thousand dollars."

"Certain things.   Nothing of value."

"I know that."

"What do you want stolen?"

"A ship's manifest, for the *S.S. Florina*.   She sails tomorrow from New York harbor, so that doesn't gave you much time."

"Time is no problem.   What's so valuable about the manifest?"

"A mistake was made on it by an inexperienced clerk.   All other copies were recovered and corrected in time, but the ship's copy got through somehow.   I imagine it's locked in the purser's safe right now.   I was told you could do the job.   I want this corrected manifest left in its place."

"No problem," Nick said, accepting the lengthy form.

"You're very sure of yourself," the second man said.   It was the first he'd spoken since Nick entered.   He was small and middle-aged, with just a trace of British accent.

Solar waved a hand at him.   "This is Herbert Jarvis from South Africa.   He's the consignee for the *Florina* cargo.   Two hundred and twelve cases of typewriters and adding machines."

"I see," Nick said.   "Pleased to meet you."

"You want some money in advance?   Say ten percent—two thousand?" Solar asked, opening his desk drawer.

"Fine.   And don't worry about the time.   I'll have the manifest before the ship sails."

"Here's my check," Jarvis said, passing it across the desk to Solar.   "Drawn on the National Bank of Capetown.   I assure you it's good.   This is payment in full for the cargo."

"That's the way I like to do business," Solar told him, slipping the check into a drawer.

As Nick started to leave, Herbert Jarvis rose from his chair.   "My business here is finished.   If you're driving into Manhattan, Mr. Velvet, could I ride with you and save calling a taxi?"

"Sure.   Come on."   Downstairs he asked, "Your first trip here?"

"Oh, no.   I've been here before.   Quite a city you have."

"We like it."   He turned the car onto the Major Deegan Expressway.

"You live in the city yourself?"

Nick shook his head.   "No, near Long Island Sound."

"Are you a boating enthusiast?"

"When I have time.   It relaxes me."

Jarvis lit a cigar.   "We all need to relax.   I'm a painter myself.   I've a lovely studio with a fine north light."

"In Capetown?"

"Yes.   But it's just a sideline, of course.   One can hardly make a living at it."   He exhaled some smoke.   "I act as a middleman in buying and selling overseas.   This is my first dealing with Max Solar, but he seems a decent sort."

"The *Florina* isn't bound for South Africa."

Jarvis shook his head.   "The cargo will be removed in the Azores.   It's safer that way."

"For the typewriters?"

"And for me."

After a time Nick said, "I'll have to drop you in midtown.   Okay?"

"Certainly.   I'm at the Wilson Hotel on Seventh Avenue."

"I need to purchase some supplies," Nick said.   He'd just decided how he was going to steal the ship's manifest.

The *Florina* was berthed at pier 40, a massive, bustling place that jutted into the Hudson River near West Houston Street.   Nick reached it in mid-afternoon and went quickly through the gates to the gangplank.   The ship was showing the rust of age typical of vessels that plied the waterways in the service of the highest bidder.

The purser was much like his ship, with soiled uniform and needing a shave. He studied the credentials Nick presented and said, "This is a bit irregular."

"We believe export licenses may be lacking for some of your cargo.   It's essential that I inspect your copy of the manifest."

The purser hesitated another moment, then said, "Very well."   He walked to the safe in one corner of his office and opened it.   In a moment he produced the lengthy manifest.

Nick saw at once the reason for Max Solar's concern.   On the ship's copy the line about typewriters and adding machines read: *212 cases 8 mm Mauser semi-automatic rifles.* He was willing to bet that Solar Industries was not a licensed arms dealer.

"It seems in order," Nick told the purser, "but I'll need a copy of it."   He opened the fat attaché case he carried and revealed a portable copying machine. "Can I plug this in?"

"Over here."

Nick inserted the manifest with a light-sensitive copying sheet into the rollers of the machine.   In a moment the document reappeared.   "There you are," he said, returning it to the purser.   "Sorry I had to trouble you."

"No trouble."   He glanced briefly at the manifest and returned it to the safe.

Nick closed the attaché case, shook the man's hand, and departed.   The theft was as simple as that.

Later that night, at seven o'clock, Nick rang the doorbell of the little house where he'd been held prisoner.   At first no one came to admit him, though he could see a light burning in the back bedroom.   Then at last Terry appeared, her face pale and distraught.

"I've got it," Nick said.   She stepped aside silently and allowed him to enter.

Sam came out of the back bedroom. "Well, Velvet! Right on time."

"Here's the manifest." Nick produced the document from the attaché case he still carried. "The only remaining original copy, showing that Solar Industries is exporting two hundred and twelve cases of semi-automatic rifles to Africa."

Sam took the document and glanced at it. For some reason the triumph didn't seem to excite him. "How did you get it?"

"A simple trick. This afternoon I purchased this portable copying machine from a friend who sometimes makes special gadgets for me. I inserted the original manifest between the rollers, but the substitute came out the other slot. It works much like those trick shop devices, where a blank piece of paper is inserted between rollers and a dollar bill comes out. The purser's copy of the manifest was rolled up and remained in the machine. The substitute copy that I'd inserted in the machine earlier came out the slot. He glanced at it briefly, but since only one line was different he never realized a switch had been made."

"Where did you get this substitute manifest?" Sam wanted to know.

"From Max Solar. I also got an advance for stealing the thing, which I'll return to him. I'm working for you, not Solar. And I imagine he'll pay plenty for that manifest. The clerk who typed it up must have assumed he had an export license for the guns. But without a license it would mean big trouble for Solar Industries if this manifest was inspected by port authorities."

Sam nodded glumly. "He's been selling arms illegally for years, mostly to countries in Africa and Latin America. But this was my first chance to prove it."

"I'll have my fee now," Nick said. "Thirty thousand."

"I haven't got it."

Nick simply stared at him. "What do you mean?"

"I mean I haven't got it. There is no fee. No money, no nothing." He shrugged and started to turn away.

Nick grabbed him by the collar. "If you won't pay for it, Max Solar will!"

"No, he won't," Terry said, speaking for the first time since Nick's arrival. "Look here."

Nick followed her into the back bedroom. On the rumpled bed where Nick had been held prisoner, the body of Max Solar lay sprawled and bloody. There was no doubt Solar was dead.

"How did it happen?" Nick asked. "What's he doing here?"

"I called him," Sam said. "We needed the thirty thousand to pay your fee. The only way we could get it was from Solar. So I told him we'd have the manifest here at seven o'clock. I left the front door unlocked and told him to bring $80,000. I figured $30,000 for you and the rest for us."

"What happened?"

"Terry arrived about twenty minutes ago and found him dead. It looks like he's been stabbed."

"You're trying to tell me you didn't kill him?"

"Of course not!" Sam said, a trace of indignation creeping into his voice. "Do I look like a murderer?"

"No, but then you don't look like a kidnaper either.   You had the best reason in the world for wanting him dead."

"His money would have been enough revenge for me."

"Was it on him?"

"No," Terry answered.   "We looked.   Either he didn't bring it or the killer got it first."

"What am I supposed to do with this manifest?" Nick asked bleakly.

"It's no good to me now.   I can't get revenge on a dead man."

"That's your problem.   You still owe me thirty thousand."

Sam held his hands wide in a gesture of helplessness.   "We don't have the money!   What should I do?   Give you the mortgage on this house that's falling apart?   Be thankful you got something out of Max Solar before he died."

Ignoring Nick, Terry asked, "What are we going to do with the body, Sam?"

"Do?   Call the police!   What else is there to do?"

"Won't they think we did it?"

"Maybe they'll be right," Nick said.   "Maybe you killed him, Terry, to have the money for yourself.   Or maybe Sam killed him and then sneaked out to let you find the body."

Both of them were quick to deny the accusations, and in truth Nick cared less about the circumstances of Max Solar's death than he did about the balance of his fee, and he saw no way of collecting it at the moment.

"All right," he said finally.   "I'll leave you two to figure out your next move.   You know where to reach me if you come up with the money.   Meanwhile, I'm keeping this manifest."

He drove south, toward Manhattan, and though the night was turning chilly he left his window open.   The fresh air felt good against his face and it helped him to sort out his thoughts.   There was only one other person who'd have the least interest in paying money for the manifest, and that was Herbert Jarvis.

He headed for the Wilson Hotel.

Jarvis was in his room packing when Nick knocked on the door.   "Well," he said, a bit startled.   "Velvet, isn't it?"

"That's right.   Can I come in?"

"I have to catch a plane.   I'm packing."

"So I see," Nick said.   He shut the door behind him.

"If you'll make it brief, I really am quite busy."

"I'll bet you are.   I'll make it brief enough.   I want thirty thousand dollars."

"Thirty . . . !   For what?"

"This copy of the ship's manifest for the *S.S. Florina*.   The only copy that shows it's carrying a cargo of rifles."

"The business with the manifest is between you and Solar.   He hired you."

"Various people hired me, but you're the only one I can collect from.   Max Solar is dead."

"Dead?"

"Stabbed to death in a house uptown. Within the past few hours."

Jarvis sat down on the bed. "That's a terrible thing."

Nick shrugged. "I assume he knew the sort of men he was dealing with."

"What's that mean?" Jarvis asked, growing nervous.

"Who do you think killed him?" Nick countered.

"That computer programmer, Sam, I suppose. That's his house uptown."

"How do you know it's Sam's house? How do you know about Sam?"

"Solar was going to meet him. He told me on the telephone."

It all fell into place for Nick. "What did he tell you?"

"That Sam wanted money for the manifest. That you were working for Sam."

"Why did he tell you about it?"

"I don't know."

"Let's take a guess. Could it have been because the check you gave him was no good? A man with Solar's world-wide contacts could have discovered quickly that there was no money in South Africa to cover your check. In fact, you're not even from South Africa, are you?"

"What do you mean?"

"You told me you're an artist, and since you volunteered the information I assume it's true. But you said you have a studio in Capetown with a fine north light. Artists like north light because it's truer, because the sun is never in the northern sky. But of course this is only true in the northern hemisphere. An artist in Capetown or Buenos Aires or Melbourne would want a studio with a good *south* light. Your studio, Jarvis, isn't in Capetown at all. It would have to be somewhere well north of the equator.

"And if you lied about being from South Africa, I figured the check drawn on a South African bank is probably phony too. You reasoned that once the arms shipment was safely out to sea there was no way Solar could blow the whistle without implicating himself. But when he learned your check was valueless, he phoned you and probably told you to meet him at Sam's house with the money or he'd have the cases of guns taken off the ship."

"You're saying I killed him?"

"Yes."

"You are one smart man, Velvet."

"Smart enough for a two-bit gunrunner."

Jarvis' right hand moved faster than Nick's eyes could follow. The knife was up his sleeve, and it missed Nick's throat by inches as it thudded into the wall. "Too bad," Nick said. "With a gun you get a second chance." And he dove for the man.

He remembered the address of Sam's house and got the phone number from a friend with the company. Sam answered on the first ring, sounding nervous, and Nick asked, "How's it going?"

"Velvet? Where are you? The police are here."

"Good," Nick said, knowing a detective would be listening in. "You did the right thing calling them. I don't know why I'm getting you off the hook, but tell them Solar's killer is in Room 334 at the Wilson Hotel on Seventh Avenue.''

"You found him?"

"Yeah," Nick said. "But he didn't have any money either."

It was one of the very few times Nick Velvet failed—that is, failed to collect his full fee.

One for Virgil Tibbs

At 11:31 A.M. on an unusually fine morning in Pasadena, California, the operator of a power shovel swung in full load of soil over the top of a heavy truck and pulled the release. Since the truck was almost full, a small shower of stones rattled off the sides, some loose dirt, and one human skull.

Fortunately Harry Hubert, male, thirty-one, was working close by. As he raised his arm to signal the truck driver to move on he looked down, then froze in his tracks. "Hold it!" he yelled.

He was not a superstitious man, but he did not want to handle the skull. He signaled the shovel operator to cease digging, pointed to what he had discovered, then waved his arms in the air to be sure that everyone understood that all work was to stop.

The shovel operator brought his machine to a halt and the truck driver shut off his engine.

Superintendent Angelo Morelli was sent for. Meanwhile, the truck driver got out of his cab and joined Hubert to find out what was wrong. He looked down at the object on the ground, bent over to examine it more closely, then spoke. "Alas, poor Yorick," he said.

He was an admirer of Sir Laurence Olivier.

Superintendent Morelli was a man accustomed to making decisions. It took him only seconds to assay the situation, then he sent for the police.

One of the all-white Pasadena patrol cars responded promptly. It arrived without lights or siren, and as the working officer driving it got out, Morelli wondered, What the hell. The officer was a woman and a comely one at that.

As soon as she was close enough, he read the nameplate over her right pocket. It said DIAZ.

Morelli checked her over. She was armed, of course; metal handcuffs were properly pouched on her belt, and there was even a small container of Mace visible.

The superintendent approached her. Although he was a rough-and-ready type, he also knew how to be diplomatic. "I certainly appreciate your quick response," he said. "However, I'm not sure this is suitable for a policewoman."

"I'm not a policewoman," she answered. "I'm a cop. Where's the fight?"

Morelli was amused. "No fight this time," he reassured her. "Do you get many of those?"

"I broke one up last night—knives in a bar. I have a suspect in custody."

"Then kindly step this way."

Officer Marilyn Diaz spent three minutes in a careful survey of the situation.
Then, despite her immaculate uniform, which was the same as the ones worn by
the male members of the department, she explored the fresh excavation and the
approximate spot where the skull had been unearthed.

She had one question for the shovel operator. "Is there any way you can tell,"
she asked, "how deeply that skull was buried when you dug it up?"

"No, ma'am, because I started my pass at the bottom of the cut and came up.
I would guess that it was somewhere near to the top."

"So would I," Diaz agreed. "Hold everything, will you?"

"Right."

Officer Marilyn Diaz, who is one of the particular prides of the Pasadena Police,
returned to her car and picked up the radio mike. Socially she was an attractive
and charming young woman; on the job she did not waste words. "I've got one
for Virgil," she reported. "At the Foothill Freeway construction site, near Raymond."

"Paramedics wanted?"

"No, human remains, but so far bones only."

"Anything else?"

"Yes," Diaz answered. "I've seen the skull. Unless I'm very wrong, the
victim was an eight-to-ten-year-old child."

On the wall of the small office he shared with his partner, Bob Nakamura, Virgil
Tibbs had a small sign posted. It read: *Write, for the night is coming.* He was
engaged in doing precisely that, presiding over a manual typewriter and punching
out the words of a report that, by police tradition, would be hopelessly pedantic
and at least twice the necessary length. He spent hours writing reports, as did
practically everyone else in the department. It was the curse of the profession.

His phone rang. He took the call, listened, then got up and put on his coat.
As the ranking homicide specialist of the Pasadena Police, the discovery of an
unattached skull was referred to him automatically. Ray Heatherton could have
handled it, but Ray was only too delighted to let Virgil Tibbs sit at the top of the
death-by-violence totem pole. Virgil had earned the spot many times over.

Virgil picked up an unmarked car, drove to the location, parked behind Marilyn
Diaz' unit, then walked over to where the people were gathered.

Superintendent Morelli saw him coming, noted that he was black, and remembered what he had read in the papers. "Is that Virgil Tibbs?" he asked Diaz.

"It is," she answered.

"He's good, I understand."

"The best."

Seconds later she made the introductions. Morelli shook hands, then got down
to business. "As soon as the skull showed up, we stopped everything immediately." He motioned to a hardhat who was waiting close by. "This is Harry
Hubert, he was the first to spot it."

Virgil listened to the man's account, then talked to the truck driver and the shovel operator. After that he addressed himself once more to Morelli. "I don't want to hold you up," he said. "I know that tying up men and equipment is costing you money and job delay. If you need the shovel somewhere else, I don't see any reason why you shouldn't move it. I'll need the truck until we can check the load in detail. Also, I want to go over the spot where the dirt is being dumped."

"I thought of that," Morelli said. "I stopped the unloading immediately. I don't believe anything has been moved since Harry saw that skull come off the truck."

"For that I'll buy you your lunch," Tibbs said.

"You're on."

"Fine. While we're eating, there are a few questions you might be able to answer for me."

Sergeant Jerry Ferguson headed the investigation team that arrived almost immediately thereafter. Since there was obviously pick-and-shovel work to be done, Superintendent Morelli assigned a half dozen men to work under Ferguson's direction. With Agent Barry Rothberg three of them left for the fill area where the dirt from the excavation was being dumped. At a convenient spot the filled truck that had taken the last load from the power shovel spread out what it had on board as another police unit arrived headed by Lieutenant Ron Peron.

Under careful examination the load that had been on the truck yielded up three additional bones and part of a spinal column. That grisly discovery was made shortly before Captain Bill Wilson arrived to see how the investigation was progressing.

By nightfall a set of foot bones that was almost intact had been discovered *in situ*. Its position suggested that the body, which had presumably been buried not long after death, had lain approximately four feet, three inches below the surface of the ground, with the head in an easterly direction. After extensive photographs had been taken, and measurements made, the few recovered bones were turned over to the Los Angeles County coroner. Even careful sifting gave no hope of recovering the complete skeleton, a point that disturbed Virgil Tibbs.

Satisfied that for the moment no more evidence would be found at the location, he authorized Superintendent Morelli to resume the construction work. He did ask that careful watch be kept while the remaining digging was done in the immediate vicinity—unauthorized burials were not always single projects. After the amount of searching that had already been done, he did not feel he could halt the important and expensive project any further without something definite in the form of additional evidence.

In the morning Tibbs went to work with grim determination. From the real-estate maps he located the exact piece of property that had marked the spot where the remains had been uncovered. It had been a single-family dwelling on a medium-sized lot in a definitely lower-class neighborhood. There had been no basement.

By the time he had these facts, the coroner's office called: the bone specialist was on the line. Virgil talked to the doctor for several minutes and was not

encouraged by the conversation.   From the skull it had been determined that the
deceased had been a child approximately eight years of age.   But no information
could be given either as to race or sex.   "You mean you can't say whether it was
a boy or a girl?" Tibbs asked.

"That's right.   The indications simply aren't present at that age."

"Can you make an informed guess?"

"Not based on what I have here."

The black detective was patient.   "What *can* you tell me?" he persisted.

"The individual is deceased.   Beyond that, only what you already have."

"Any dental data?"

"I should have mentioned that, forgive me.   So far as can be determined, and
this is pretty definite, the deceased never had any dental work done.   But this
doesn't necessarily indicate neglect; the subject could have been seen by a dentist
who found that no work was required."

"And the age of the remains?"

"Say from three years back.   There are several reasons why I can't be more
definite."

"I think I know what they are," Virgil said.   "Thanks, Doctor."

"You're most welcome."

Virgil turned to Bob Nakamura.   "All I have to worry about now is a missing
child, male or female, ethnic background unknown, who disappeared anytime from,
say, three years ago to you-say-when.   And the fact that all the bones were not
located after very careful search suggests that the corpse may have been cut up and
buried in various places."

Bob was sympathetic.   "Tough case, but not impossible.   You have the specific
house to work with—that should tell you a lot.   Better than that corpse in the
nudist park."

"Hell, yes, that took weeks."   And Virgil went back to work.

By noon he had the picture.   The house had last been occupied by an elderly
couple, Mr. and Mrs. Ajurian.   Mrs. Ajurian was recently dead; her husband was
in a nursing home in a senile condition.   The Ajurians had no known living relatives.
Before their occupancy the house had stood vacant for almost three years, tied up
in litigation because the owner had been killed in a car accident.

Prior to that the house had been rented on a month-to-month basis, frequently
to young people who had been required to pay in advance, and occasionally to
transient farm labor.   The house itself had been moved away when the area had
been cleared for the freeway.   It had been offered at auction, but no bids had been
received.

Two hours after lunch the house itself was located.   It stood, helpless and
unwanted, in a row of similar derelicts that had been parked in an available open
area.   As Virgil explored it minutely, he could not escape a feeling of profound
depression.   It was in a wretched state of outside repair and, if possible, was even
worse inside.

The single bathroom had been painted a particularly violent purple and despite
long disuse, it still carried a faintly unpleasant odor indicative of bad sanitation.

Where the telephone had been, the walls were covered with jottings in various hands; the smaller bedroom had children's crude drawings covering most of the wall space within their reach.   None of the drawings revealed any talent either in art or draftsmanship.

The floor in one closet was missing; the rectangular opening had the remains of a ledge that had once, obviously, held an unattached trap door.   There was, of course, nothing unusual in that—it was a conventional access hole—but something else about the house interested Tibbs.   When he had spent the better part of an hour examining the structure, he thanked the employee of the house mover who was serving as his guide.

"Did you find out anything?" the man asked, walking outside with Virgil.

"Yes, I think so."

"What?"

Virgil nodded down the long row of empty shells, the tombstones of what had once been homes.   "Did you notice anything different about this one?" he asked.

"Not particularly.   Most of them were in pretty bad shape when they came out here."

"It's at least two feet higher off the ground than any of the others," Tibbs said. "A little more than five feet between the surface of the ground and the bottom of the floor joists.   Room enough for a man to work in, if he had to."

Meanwhile, Bob Nakamura determined, by interviewing some of their one-time neighbors, that the Ajurians had been a quiet elderly couple who had never entertained and seldom went out.   They were judged to have been capable of only the simplest physical tasks.   No children had ever been seen on their premises.   The only criticism that the Nisei detective turned up was that they frequently cooked food so heavily spiced that the odor was objectionable.   A check of the records revealed that they had been on welfare.

During the time the house had stood vacant, it had been frequently used as a juvenile and young-adult rendezvous; several arrests had been made, but there had never been any indications of violence.

One former long-time resident of the street recalled a Mexican family that had lived in the house.   There had been eight or nine children; he did not remember the family name, but he did recall how the kids were incessantly running in and out and slamming the door each time.   He had been glad when they moved away. He also remembered a group of six young people, three long-haired males and three females, who had taken up residence, but who had been surprisingly quiet and peaceful.

By the time all this information had been gathered, another day had gone by.

Most of the next day went into a careful examination of all available missing-juvenile reports that fell within the proper time frame.   They added up to a heart-breaking number.   Dental charts ruled out most of them, but Tibbs was left with over fifty possibles and sixteen that offered the best prospects of a make.   When that tedious task had at last been completed, he sat back in his chair and began to think.

Bob Nakamura had seen him like that before, his eyes open but unfocused, his body relaxed.   After half an hour, Virgil stirred and Bob was prepared.   "It's a damn tough case," Bob said.

Tibbs nodded slowly.   "Yes," he agreed, "but if I can put one or two more things together, I may have it."

"Accidental death?" Bob asked.

Virgil shook his head.   "No—murder."

"The evidence of that is in the remains?"

"No."

"What else do you need?"

"I want to go back and re-examine that house.   But before I do that, I've got some other work to do."   He got up and stretched.   "I'll see you after a while," he said, and left.

The voter-registration lists gave him some information, much of it quite old. He went over the available data carefully, but found little to excite his interest. The Mexican family that had lived in the house had never registered anyone, a fact that suggested they might have been illegal immigrants—a major problem in Southern California.   On the other hand, it could have been indifference or an inability to understand English.

The welfare rolls were more productive.   From them Virgil learned that Emilio and Rosa De Fuentes, plus their nine children, had been publicly supported at that address for some time.

That was a breakthrough.   Knowing that welfare recipients often retained that status for years, he sent out a message through the network in California to learn if the same family was now being carried on the rolls elsewhere.   That accomplished, Virgil once more took refuge in his second-floor office in the old part of the Pasadena Police building, leaned back, and went into another session of concentrated thought.

When he finally came up for air, Bob Nakamura was back and ready to play straight man.   "Are you any nearer?" he asked.

"Yes."

"Fill me in."

Tibbs stirred.   "A lot of things are beginning to fit together.   My chief problem at the moment is the lack of hard data to back up some of my conclusions."

"Let's hear the conclusions."

"All right.   We begin with the Ajurians, the Armenian immigrants."

"You dug that far back?"

"No, but I know they were immigrants because of the way they cooked their food.   People direct from the old country tend to continue life as they knew it, particularly where diet is concerned.   Second- and third-generation offspring from that part of the world prefer less spicy food.   The Armenian part is easy because the name ends in *i-a-n*, something almost wholly Armenian."

"Go on."

"The evidence supports the fact that they were relatively feeble, and did not entertain, particularly children.   Also, I'm inclined to rule out the hippie sextet who lived in the house for a while.   I learned a lot from the drawings I found on the walls of one of the rooms."

"Explain."

Tibbs swung around to face his partner.   "Obviously they weren't made during the time the elderly Ajurians were occupying the house.   Yet they didn't remove them.   They were on the wall of what would have been the second bedroom.   The inference, therefore, is that they didn't remove the drawings because a fresh paint job was beyond their physical resources, or financial means.   I suspect they closed off that room and used it only for storage.

"The hippie sextet also left the drawings alone—perhaps they found them amusing.   It wasn't their house, they were simply living in it, and they probably favored self-expression.   They weren't made during that period since I have statements that no children were seen around the house while the hippies were there."

"The drawings could have been faked—done by an adult."

Tibbs shook his head.   "The only idea that holds water along that line would be an adult making them to entertain a child who used that room—but again, there were no children reported on the premises."

He stopped suddenly.   For a moment or two he stared off into space with his lips held tightly together, then a whole new expression took over his face.   "It's a long shot, but worth checking out."   He got up once more.

"Where are you going this time?"

"I need a social worker and a grocery store," Virgil answered.

The social worker proved to be unavailable.   After tracking her down, Tibbs learned that she had gone to Europe and was somewhere in Spain studying the guitar.   He made a note of her name and background, then began his canvas of the grocery stores.   That proved a much easier job; he hit pay dirt within an hour.

Sam Margolis had operated his small market and liquor store at the same location for many years.   He knew most of his customers well, and he recalled the De Fuentes family.   "Too damn many kids," he declared.   "She usually brought a lot of them with her and they couldn't keep their hands off anything.   They even swiped ice cubes and sucked on them."

"They were on welfare, I believe."

"Yeah, they were.   But the old man usually found enough money for a bottle. He wasn't a drunk, but he hit the cheap stuff a lot."

"Have you got any idea where they went?"

Margolis shrugged.   "Who knows?   And to be honest, who cares?   This is a cash business only—no checks except for welfare and payroll that I know.   Two will get you five they were wetbacks, or whatever they call them now.   And the woman—"   He shook his head.   "What he saw in her I'll never know.   She was built like a pile of mashed potatoes."

"You've helped me a lot," Tibbs said.   "More than you know.   One thing more if you can remember.   Were all the children that you saw normal, at least reasonably so?"

"All that I saw."

"And do you remember if they had a boy in his teen years, anywhere from about thirteen or fourteen up?"

Margolis was definite.   "Sure, Felipe.   He came to the store sometimes."

"What was he like?" Virgil asked.

"Another Mex kid," Margolis answered.

When Virgil Tibbs got back to his office, there was news for him: Mr. and Mrs. Emilio De Fuentes and their eleven children were on welfare in Modesto, California. In response Tibbs picked up his phone and called the police department there. When he had been put through to a detective sergeant, he made a request.   He described the family and supplied the welfare case number to make things as easy as possible.

"What I need," Virgil said, "is some information on when they reached Modesto and precisely when they went on welfare.   I'd like a copy of the original document accepting them as welfare clients.   Then, if it isn't too much trouble, I'd like the birth records of any children added to their family since they arrived up there. Especially an evidence of twins."

"Can do," the Modesto sergeant said.

After he finished the conversation Virgil left his office and went out for one more look at the abandoned house.   He stayed inside it for more than an hour, making an almost microscopic examination of the drawings that had first attracted his attention.   He satisfied himself that three children, apparently of different ages, had made them.

Child number one had been the oldest, but the drawings, eight of them, were also the simplest and the most repetitive.   Child number two had had a less steady hand, but more imagination.   Tibbs traced six of the drawings to his or her hand, and no two of them were similar.   Child number three appeared to have been the youngest since the drawings he or she had made were the lowest on the wall.   They were also the most varied and showed, on Tibbs' second examination, evidence of talent.

Despite the crudity of the draftsmanship, the third child had painstakingly tried to add background, drawing a horizontal line to suggest ground level in one instance and adding what was obviously the sun in another.   A third drawing showed experimentation; when a first attempt to draw a symmetrical figure had failed, the child artist had added lines until there were many arms and legs, and even the torso had a multiplicity of wavy outlines.

Virgil returned late to his office to find two messages.   One of them was a report that had come in from Modesto by teletype, the other was a penciled note from Diane Stone, the chief's secretary, that Chief McGowan would like to see him when he came in.

He put in a call to the chief's office, but McGowan had already left.   Virgil was glad of that because there were still some loose ends to tie up before he went upstairs.   Since the chief had sent for him personally, it did not require much deductive ability to know what was on the chief's mind.

A welfare report he had been waiting for was on his desk. From it he learned that the De Fuentes family had come from a small village in Mexico. That was a setback since it meant that his chances of getting accurate birthdates and related information were close to nil. Fortunately, there were other routes of inquiry.

Tibbs went home to his apartment and stretched out to rest. He wanted an expensive dinner, but it was his superstition to hold off splurging while he was still closing a case. There was still one very sticky fact to be established and while he was by that time reasonably confident, it still had to be rated as a long shot.

In the morning he visited the public school where some of the De Fuentes children had been enrolled. He did not trouble the office for official records, interviewing instead some teachers who had been on the faculty when the De Fuentes children had attended the school. The first three he spoke with could not help him much; one was resentful that he was there at all. "You haven't got any business prying into those people's lives," she told him. "You ought to be ashamed; you're a black man yourself and here you're trying to put down other people who have been discriminated against all their lives."

The gymnasium instructor was the one who came through. "I do remember the De Fuentes children very well," he told Virgil. "I was interested in them because one of the boys, Felipe, had remarkable athletic ability and exceptional reflexes. I think he could have made it all the way to the big time if he had really worked at it. But he showed no interest in baseball or basketball."

"Do you remember if he had any particularly close friends at school?" Tibbs asked.

"Yes, he did—several, as a matter of fact."

"May I have some names?"

"Yes, and you can get the addresses in the office if you need them. Willie Fremont, Cliff Di Santo, Trig Yamamoto, and—oh, yes, there was a girl too—Elena Morales."

By two in the afternoon Virgil Tibbs had determined that three of the families had moved away, but he had two forwarding addresses. He succeeded in locating the Yamamoto boy where he was working in the vegetable department of a supermarket. By a little after four he had found and also talked to the Morales girl who was a winsome little beauty and highly intelligent. She supplied him with the final data that he needed.

He went back to the office and called Mrs. Stone, to say that he was in if the chief still wanted to see him.

McGowan did. Virgil walked into the boss's office and sat down. When Diane handed him a cup of coffee, with cream and sugar exactly to his taste, he understood that he might be there for a little while.

"Virgil," the chief said, "I have a rather personal interest in the case you're working on—the child remains found during the freeway construction. Have you been able to make any progress?"

"I believe so, sir."

Captain Wilson arrived, and the chief filled him in.

"How much have you got, Virgil?" the captain asked.

"Since I'm not in court yet, and I don't have to provide absolute proof," Tibbs answered, "I can tell you that it's a case of premeditated murder. So far I can name the victim, give the time of death, and supply the motive. If all goes well, by tomorrow night I should have enough solid evidence for an indictment."

"Virgil," the chief said, "you never cease to amaze me. Instead of waiting for your report, suppose you bring us up to date now."

"All right, sir." Tibbs relaxed and enjoyed a little of his coffee.

"The preliminary work was quite simple," he began. "I located the plot, got the history of the dwelling that had been on it, and inspected the house itself. Fortunately it hadn't been destroyed, because there was quite a bit of evidence there, notably a series of children's drawings which were especially helpful."

"Children's drawings?" the chief queried.

"Yes, in fact they provided the essential clue when I finally had sense enough to see it. I completely missed it the first time."

"You must be slipping," the chief said.

"Undoubtedly, sir. Anyhow, without going into unnecessary details, I checked out the history of the house and satisfied myself that the most recent residents had all had one thing in common—no children were ever known to be on the premises during their tenure. There was a period of vacancy when children might have gone into the house to play, but I couldn't find any evidence to support that idea. It was also possible that someone could have taken a child there with criminal intent, but the available missing-persons reports tended to reduce the odds on that.

"So I focused my attention on a large Mexican family that had occupied the house about five years ago. There were nine children, ranging from a boy of fourteen to a one-year-old infant. I'm now satisfied that three of these children made the drawings I found on the walls of the second bedroom. Offhand I would fix their ages at about ten, nine, and eight, with the youngest the most talented of the three."

"That's interesting, I'm sure," Wilson said, "but where is it leading us?"

"Into proof of murder."

"You have my attention," the chief said.

"Consider first the fact that there were nineteen drawings and that they were done by three different children. There you have definite evidence of lack of family discipline. It was a rental property, but no regard was given to the rights of the owner—otherwise the children would have been restrained from drawing all over the walls of what was evidently their bedroom. And there was no indication of any effort whatever to remove the drawings when the family left. So we may conclude that the family in question was at the best irresponsible."

"I think I'm beginning to see something coming," Chief McGowan mumured.

"When this family lived in Pasadena, shortly before their departure, they had nine children. The family is now in Modesto and the latest head count is eleven."

"Which is not surprising," Captain Wilson commented.

"That's the key to the whole thing," Virgil said.

"Eleven children?"

"Exactly."

It was silent in the executive office for a few moments.   Then Chief McGowan leaned forward in his chair.   "I get it," he said.

Tibbs nodded.   "In a neighborhood like that, sir, with all the constant comings and goings and the frequent turnover in residents, hardly anyone, even the children's playmates, can keep track of every child in a family.   And I have now learned that since the family moved to Modesto, three more children have been delivered to them.   The birth records are on file and I have copies coming in the mail."

"Three more children.   Nine plus three are twelve.   But you said the latest count was only eleven," Captain Wilson noted.

"Yes, sir.   Now add to that these facts: we have a set of parents with a profusion of children.   I'm not putting down large families, but the De Fuentes family may have been blessed with more than they actually wanted.   They couldn't possibly support them—they were on welfare, and the mother was constantly pregnant.

"I was turning these thoughts over in my mind when an idea hit me.   What if one of those children had been particularly unwanted, because of being retarded or otherwise afflicted?   In most cases that wouldn't add up to murder, not by a wide margin, but here we are faced with the undisputable fact that a child of approximately eight years of age was buried under that house.

"If the child had died normally, since the family was already receiving assistance, some sort of funeral arrangements could have been made."

"Also," Captain Wilson added, "since they are Mexican, there is a good chance the family is Catholic.   The obvious absence of birth-control measures would support that.   If a child of theirs had died under acceptable circumstances, then they would want to have it buried in sanctified ground with the proper religious rites."

Tibbs nodded agreement.   "When I re-examined the house itself," he continued, "I checked carefully for any evidence that might reveal an abnormal child.   It was entirely possible, with all those children, such an unfortunate individual could be kept effectively hidden from the casual observation of the neighbors.   If the child's condition was bad enough, that would have been almost automatic.

"I found what I was looking for in the drawings I described.   One of them in particular.   It had been done by the youngest of the three child artists and this child, as I mentioned earlier, had some artistic ability.   He, or she, added touches of background and tried to make an actual picture.   One of these efforts showed a child with what at first appeared to be multiple arms and legs, and a torso of wavy outlines, drawn in apparently to get the right proportions.   Then I realized it wasn't that at all.   First, the other drawings done by the same child exhibited no such difficulty, in fact the proportions were quite good.   What the child was actually drawing was another child—"

"*Shaking!*" the chief interjected.   "A spastic!"

"That's it, sir.   Now I was confident that I knew why a large family might willfully dispose of one of its children.   Even death by accident wouldn't call for the extreme measure of burying a child under the house.   The answer was painfully apparent—a too large family with a problem child might make the terrible decision to simply get rid of it before moving on.   A family leaves one location with a large brood of children; it arrives at the next one, still with a large brood—who is going to notice that one is missing?"

"There are institutions," the chief said. "Surely they must have known that."

"Perhaps they did, but there is some indication that despite the fact the family had been on welfare for some time, it may have come to this country illegally. Also, unfortunately, there are many people to whom any kind of institution is terrifying. I believe they thought that what they planned would be simpler. Anyhow, the social worker's report on the family, which I dug out and read, lists a boy who would have been eight and a half when the family moved away. His name was Alberto. I checked with Modesto where the family is receiving assistance now. There is no Alberto. That is hard evidence. I suspect that if we confront the father with the facts we now have, he will admit to what he probably has rationalized as a mercy killing."

"I can't understand," Captain Wilson said, "how they expected to get away with it. What did they tell their other children?"

"Probably that Alberto had been taken away, or some other excuse. The older children might have been cautioned never to speak of their spastic brother in case it might harm their own images. They would understand that."

Tibbs stopped for a moment and locked his fingers tightly together as he frequently did when he was under mental stress. Then he looked up once more. "You see, sir, they *did* get away with it. The missing child died years ago—we know that— he was buried, and there he lay. No one ever raised a question so far as I have been able to learn, and I strongly doubt if anyone ever would. It was pure accident that the burial site was excavated for the new freeway, and even that could well have passed unnoticed if the skull had not rolled off the top of the load. If that truck had been half full or less when the bones were loaded, the chances are good they would never have been noticed."

Chief McGowan had one more question. "Did the social worker make any mention of an abnormal child in her report?"

Tibbs nodded. "Yes, sir, she did. But she called him an 'exceptional child,' which was the term just coming into use at that time. If the family saw the report, or was shown it, that phrase would probably not register with them, particularly since English is not their native language. I don't think, gentlemen, that we will have too much trouble in obtaining a confession."

And in that, too, he was right.

ERNEST SAVAGE

Doc Wharton's Legacy

I read the *Chronicle* story that evening at dinner; and when I got home and read the letter from Doc Wharton, I read the *Chronicle* story again.

The newspaper story said that Belcher and Crumb had been shot and killed by two Mountain County deputies named Arkins and Jellicoe. Belcher and Crumb were the two prison escapees and bank robbers every cop north of Bakersfield had been looking for lately. Arkins and Jellicoe, according to the story, had been patrolling one of the Mountain County roads near the Nevada border when they saw the body of a man on a dirt trail winding uphill from the road. He was dead. He'd bled to death from a gunshot wound in the belly. His name was Edward Wharton and he lived in a cabin farther up the trail and he hadn't been dead long.

Investigating, the two deputies came upon Belcher and Crumb near Wharton's cabin, and in the ensuing gunfight had shot them dead. In the two-column cut of Arkins and Jellicoe, they looked like the winner and runner-up in an idiot contest, but maybe they were thinking about the $8,000 reward that went with the two dead crooks.

I'd known Doc Wharton for fifteen years. I'd arrested him in the early '60s for practicing medicine without a license and failing to report a gunshot wound he'd treated. A couple years before that he'd lost his license for performing illegal abortions. The medical board agreed he was a good doctor—when he wasn't drunk—but that wasn't often enough to warrant his continued practice.

Personally, I liked the man. He seemed to have an affinity for the underworld, but I liked him anyway. He had style. I got a Christmas card from him every year, but the letter I got that night was the first. And the last. It was typed and full of errors and smears, which I won't attempt to reproduce. It follows in full:

Dear Sam:

A little while ago I killed two men who in turn killed me. I've got maybe 20 minutes to get this thing written and mailed.

I saw them come up from the road and when one of them split and circled to the rear of the cabin, I knew they were trouble. I got my gun, eased the front door open, and stood back in the shadows. The one out front was coming on at a crouch, a .45 automatic in his right hand. He was ready for war, Sam. When he was ten feet from the porch I hit him in the middle of the forehead and he went over like an acrobat.   He died instantly.

The other one came running around from the rear just as I stepped out on the porch.   We both fired at the same time.   His shot entered my upper abdomen between—I would guess—the transverse colon and stomach.   Tore up the pancreas and duodenum beyond a doubt, but didn't put me down.   My shot put him on his back.   It ruptured his sternum, probably ripped through the right auricle of his heart and lodged against a thoracic vertebra.

He was about two minutes dying.   I was able to get to him but there was nothing I could do.   He was a good-looking kid and had a pleasant soft smile on his face.   He told me to look in his jacket pocket before he died, and I did.   The enclosed is what I found.

Sam, I want you to see that Mitzi gets the reward.   I don't need to tell you how little I've been able to do for her, even from the first.   I haven't heard from her for a long time, but wherever she is I know she can use the money.   There is nothing else.

Now I'm going to try to put this thing in an envelope and get it down to the box before the juices run out.

> *Adutrumque paratus,*
> Edward Wharton, M.D. (erst.)

The enclosure was a Wanted poster, probably ripped from a post-office bulletin board.   Guys on the lam have an affinity for their own publicity.   It showed the usual pictures of Belcher and Crumb, recited their crimes, and offered $8,000 for them, dead or alive.   Lower middle class on the crook scale.

I got up from my desk, poured myself a brandy, and looked in my dictionary. *Adutrumque paratus* was Latin for "ready for either alternative."   I laughed.   As I said, Doc Wharton had style.   And a way of screwing things up to the bitter end.

Mitzi Wharton had been dancing topless when I first knew her, and I mean to advise, she was built for the work.   In the '60s she got herself picked up two or three times a year, but as far as I know she was never convicted of anything but damn foolishness.   She was about five-ten tall, but always carried herself straight with her chest out.   Most tall girls tend to slump, but not Mitzi.

Doc Wharton once told me she'd got into a fist fight with a boy her first day in kindergarten, and she'd had her dukes up ever since.   She had a face that shifted around between pugnacity and pulchritude.   She wasn't pretty in any ordinary way, but she was good-looking and had a lot of the Wharton style.

I hadn't seen her for months now and had no idea where she was living, but I didn't even bother to look her up in the book.   I called this desk sergeant I know and asked him to locate her for me and he said he would.

Then I wondered if I should put in a call for the Mountain County Sheriff and tell him he had a couple of cuties on his staff; but I figured he probably knew that already, and was maybe even party to his deputies' little deception.

Mitzi was in the slammer. When my friend, Mike Phelps, called back at 10:30 he said she'd been picked up around seven that evening for disturbing the peace and hitting a cop in the face with her handbag. "Which wouldn't have been so bad," Mike said, "except it had a sixteen-ounce jar of strawberry jam in it."

"Why'd she do that?"

"She said he called her a hooker."

"Is she?"

"Well, her means of support lacks a little something in the way of visibility, but she claims she isn't."

"How's the guy she hit?"

"He'll be eating soft food for a few days, they tell me, but outside of that he's okay."

I sighed. "Now what'll happen?"

"I don't know, Sam. She's at Central Station, not here, but it has the makings of a stand-off. Maybe if you call Lieutenant West over there you can get him to drop it. He's got a lot bigger fish to fry than her."

I thanked Phelps, then punched out the Central Station number and finally got West. He and I came up together in the Force and had good rapport. I'd quit after the strike, but he'd hung in there. He had two kids in college and couldn't afford to quit. Now he was having a bad night. The street rats were running and he had two knifings and a half-dozen other happenings on his hands. When I told him I'd pick up Mitzi at 8:00 A.M., he told me I could have her now if I wanted. But I didn't want.

The next morning, over breakfast, I let Mitzi read her father's letter and the Wanted poster. She had an interesting face to watch. It had matured some since I'd seen it last, but it had the old mobility I remembered, eyes, brows, and mouth moving with the sense of what she read. She smiled wryly at the end. She knew the Latin, which surprised me.

"Heaven or hell," she said. "He didn't care which, did he? He thought it was all here anyway. If he hadn't been my father, Sam, I would have killed him, I guess. A girl is supposed to have a thing for her father, isn't she? Maybe we did, in reverse."

It pleased me she hadn't mentioned the money first, but she got to it soon enough. "So now I'm an heiress, huh? Eight grand."

"There's a problem," I told her, and showed her the story in yesterday's *Chronicle*. Her face displayed hostility, her eyes fire as she read it. "The damn nerve of them!" she exploded. "Typical cops!"

"Don't generalize, Mitzi."

"You read it your way, Lieutenant, I'll read it mine."

"Drop the title, Mitzi. It's Sam Train now. I'm private."

"Couldn't live with it any longer, huh?"

"Never mind why. Do you want to go up there and get this thing straightened out, or not?"

"Why do I need you?" Her big green eyes flashed animosity at me as the symbol of everything she was accustomed to hold in contempt. It was an automatic reaction.   She'd belted a street cop in the face last night with sixteen ounces of strawberry jam and evidently taken a lick or two herself in return.   There was a mark under her right cheekbone that wasn't a makeup smear and wouldn't wash off with soap and water.   And it wasn't the only knock she'd taken from a cop in her thirty-two or thirty-three years.

"Think of me," I said, "as administrator of your old man's estate.   This letter gives me both the authority and the responsibility."

"At just how big a cut, *Mister* Train?"

"Just pay for the gas."

"I can get a car somewhere.   I don't need yours."

"But you need my letter, Mitzi."

"You guys've always got the last word, haven't you."   She added something in a deep throaty voice and slumped tiredly in her chair.   The desk cop at Central had told me she hadn't slept much last night in the tank, but then nobody does except the drunks.   In the moment's repose her face was lovely and I wondered, as I had wondered before, why some big rangy guy hadn't taken her in hand long ago.   I've even wondered once or twice why I hadn't myself.

She straightened abruptly in her chair, shucking off the fatigue, shoulders back, eyes engaging mine.   "Sam, is it real, the eight grand?"

"It's real, but we've got to go there and reclaim it."

"Fight 'em for it, huh?"

"If it comes to that, Mitzi."

"It'll come to that—it always does.   Damn it, what a world," she added, then raised her coffee cup and said, her eyes flashing again, "Well, *adutrumque paratus,* shamus."   She pronounced it suavely.

"We'll win," I said.   "Just leave the strawberry jam at home."

"Not a chance!   It's my shillelagh."

I took her to her apartment just off Van Ness and she said she was going to take her sweet time getting the stink of jail off her skin and I'd better come up.   If I were still on the Force I wouldn't have, but I was my own man now.

It was a dump on the outside, but had an almost nun-like neatness inside, as though in defiance of the other circumstances of her life—anyone's life in this town and time.   A cell of quiet in the midst of the storm.

A sleeping alcove behind drapes was off the main room and the drapes didn't quite meet the center after she'd drawn them.   I could see a slice of her bed and bits and pieces of her flitting around as she got undressed.   She didn't seem to care if I looked and nothing in me told me not to.   I'd seen everything there is to see in this town that shows everything there is to show, but that flitting, segmented display of a spectacular woman was as fresh and touching as a child's smile.   It moved me deeply in a strange new way.

I shook my head.   I'd made a quantum leap in a direction I not only didn't like, but that frightened me.   I'm a cop, an ex-cop, but I'm still a cop.   I deal in the brute, bloody rubble of civilization.   I'm not a lady's man.

"Hey, Sam," she hollered before she took her bath.   "Make some coffee if you want.   I got one of those Mr. Coffee things over there in the kitchen."

I did.   It was a relief.   To like her was one thing; to want her something else again.   Mr. Coffee talked me out of it.   But not for long.

We left town on the Bay Bridge and took 80 to Sacramento where we branched south.   She was wearing an expensive denim pants-suit that looked great on her. She'd got it as part of a modeling fee, she told me.

"That cop last night said you were a hooker," I said flatly, the thing coming alive again.

"And suffered pains for his error, Mr. Train."

"You're not a hooker?"

"We're all hookers, as the man said.   But if you mean what I think you mean, I'm not and never have been."

"Okay," I blurted, "that's okay."   It shouldn't have been important to me one way or the other, but it was and I couldn't suppress it.

I'd seen Mitzi maybe twenty times in the last ten-twelve years, sometimes on the street just in passing, or in a store, but mostly in the line of work.   She'd got picked up more times than a three dollar bill, usually for resisting arrest, or interfering with somebody else's arrest.   She wasn't a hippie or militant or revolutionary, but she had a sense of right and wrong that was up front and quick to express itself.

Once that I know of, the charge had been drunk and disorderly, but she wasn't a boozer in the usual sense of the word.   She wasn't anything that I could pin down.   Model?   Dancer?   Stripper?   Salesclerk?   "No visible means of support," the charge sheet had said last night; but that's what they put down when they arrest a mobster.

She had her head back and eyes closed, her long auburn hair draping over the seat of the car.   She spoke only when spoken to and I let her rest through most of the first 100 miles while I fought back this rising surge in me.   After the orderliness and discipline of nineteen years on the Force I was coming apart at the seams.

At 2000-feet elevation she seemed to respond to the sharply increased freshness of air and sat up straight, her eyes open.   The long flat Central Valley had been steeped in its usual haze, cutting visibility to a few miles and turning the mind in on itself.

We crossed State 49 a little west of Fiddletown in the old Mother Lode country and then picked up State 6 for the uphill run to Mountain City.   I'd never been this way before and neither had she.   She was studying the mountain scene with an alien's critical eye.

"What brought him up here?" she asked finally.   "He was a city man all his life.   He needed to live in a place where there's a bar on every corner."

"Maybe he grew out of that, Mitzi.   Maybe in the end he needed space and clarity and silence."

"That's a good definition of death, isn't it?"   She shuddered.   "Or maybe it's what life is supposed to be like, but we just forgot, all of us.   Maybe Pop was right.''

She was hugging herself, arms Xed across her chest.   She was beginning to mourn him and I felt pleased with her again.

A long time later she laughed briefly and said, "You know the thing about him that was so different?   He had manners, he was the last of the courteous men. Even when drunk.   I can remember him coming home in the middle of the night, bombed to the brows.   I would get up to make sure he didn't kill himself on the stairs and he would say, 'Forgive me for disturbing your rest, my dear.'   He must have said that to me a thousand times.   'Forgive me for disturbing your rest, my dear.' ''

"And did you?"

"No.   Not then.   I'm just beginning to now, but then I made him pay.   The young are the sternest judges, aren't they, Sam?   They're the ones who make the bombs.   They don't forgive you, they blow your head off.   Poor Pop, poor old Pop!   I really made him pay.   That's when I began taking my clothes off in public.''

"He resented that?"

"He thought it was bad manners.''   She looked gloomily out the window for a moment.   "And he was right.''

We got to Mountain City at 2:30.   Mountain City was about ten minutes long and four minutes wide, tucked between two craggy peaks that still had snow on their crowns.   One thousand, one hundred forty-four people, elevation 6,480 feet. Wine-sharp air.   Main Street was lined with red-brick structures that had been new in 1910.   One of them had a name that caught my eye as we drifted past—the Jellicoe Building; it was the name of one of the deputies in the *Chronicle* story, the tall one.

The Sheriff's headquarters was on the far edge of town.   It was a small, new, handsome structure made of native stone and set in a grove of dowager Douglas firs, the asphalted parking lot spreading between them like a flow of black lava. It was pretty and peaceful-looking.

Mitzi made no move to get out when I'd parked.   She was slumped against the door, crying softly now.   "I wonder where his body is," she said huskily.   "He told me once he wanted to be cremated and his ashes scattered out past the Golden Gate.   Maybe he thought it was symbolic of something.   I want to do that for him, Sam.''

"We'll find out where he is," I said.   "Come on in.''

"No, I'll wait," she mumbled.   "I just want to sit here for a while.   You got a tissue?''

"In the glove compartment," I said, and wanted urgently to draw her into my arms.   It was probably not the first time she'd cried in her thirty-three years, but it was the first time I'd seen her cry and it did something to me.   "Take your time," I said feebly.

Inside the building, the woman behind the counter was flanked by communication equipment, all of it silent for the moment.   She was reading the latest edition of the *Guinness Book of Records* and put it down, smiling.   A pile of yesterday's edition of the *Chronicle* was stacked on the counter between us.   I told her my name and that I wanted to see the Sheriff about the reward money, and I let her think I had it in my pants.

Within thirty seconds I was in the Sheriff's private office being invited to sit down.   I didn't.   I waited for the woman to close the door behind me and then handed the Sheriff Doc Wharton's letter and told him my story.   There was a stack of *Chronicles* on his desk too.   They would be an embarrassment to him soon.

Sheriff Mason had one of those faces that seem to be seven-eighths below the cheekbones, like Nixon's, with long curving jowls hammocked from the ears.   He read old Doc's letter slowly, then caught his face between his hands and pushed it around like a half-inflated volleyball.

"I knew it!" he muttered.   "I knew them two jackasses was conning me.   I knew damn well it couldn't be the way they said it was because the hole in that what's-his-name's head was a .45 hole if ever I seen one.   Grace!"   He hollered into his intercom, and I had a vision of Grace easing herself down off the ceiling.   "Get Arkins from acrost the street and tell him to get his butt in here right now and get Jellicoe on the radio and tell him to get his butt in here too—on the double!"

I sat down and watched Mason calm himself enough to read the letter again, his lips moving around like the open end of a hose.   "So Doc had a daughter," he said.

"Did you know Wharton?"

"Hell, everybody knew him.   He comes down—usta come down—durin' the ski season and help Doc Zerbo set bones.   Wouldn't take no fee for it 'cause he said he wasn't licensed, but Zerbo kept him in booze and food.   He's a real nice man.   Was.   Dammit, can't get usta him bein' gone.   What about the daughter?"

"You might say she's a chip off the old block."

"That'd make her a mighty nice girl, Mr. Train."

"She's got it in her," I said.   "What about the cabin, Sheriff?   Who owned it?"

"Hell, that place reverted to the State years ago.   Nobody owned it.   Doc just squatted there, and welcome—"

"Where's his body?"

"At Madison Funeral Parlor down the street.   We use it for a morgue.   I suppose she'll want him."

"She will."

Arkins came in after a brief knock on the door, and Mason made him sit down at the desk and read the letter while he and I watched his dark skinny face turn darker.   He read it twice, then turned it over and looked at the back, and then stared at the ceiling, sighing.

"We kinda wondered," he said finally, "what old Doc was doin' down by the mailbox, but the flag wasn't up so we—"

Mason smacked the desk.   "I s'pose if the flag *was* up you woulda took the letter outa the box, huh, Arkins?"

"Hell, no, Harry!   Fella don't fool with the mail, that's Federal.   We—"

"So what you done was local, is that it?   Just a little County offense, is that it?''

"Hell, Harry, we had no idea Doc Wharton had kin, did you?''

"What difference does that make?''

"Well, it makes *all* the damn difference, don't it?''

I was pleased with the way it was going.   I'd expected a fight, but not one I could just sit and watch like a tennis match.   The Sheriff was boiling but his hand, pawing at the pile of *Chronicles* as he talked, revealed the basic source of his concern. He could forgive Arkins and Jellicoe their little deception, I thought, but the problem now was what to do about it, how to deal with the publicity that had ensued.

"So now," Mason snarled, "I got a coupla heroes that oughta be slung in jail. I know why you did this, by God, Arkins, you been sneakin' over the border into Nevada again and losing at craps, ain't you?''

"Harry—''

"How much, dammit?''

"About twenty-seven hundred, but—''

"Good Godamighty!   How much into Jellicoe?''

"Nothin', Sheriff.   Johnny don't play no more.''

The Sheriff kneaded his jaws again and asked Grace through the intercom where Jellicoe was, for damn Pete's sake.

"He drove in the parking lot about five minutes ago," I heard her say, "but he hasn't come into the building yet.''

"Probably hit one of the trees out there," Mason muttered, "and is makin' out a phony accident report.   Mr. Train, I got to apologize for all this, sir.   I ain't *never* been so embarrassed by my men, and I tell you I've been embarrassed by 'em more times than one.''

"Nothin' wrong with Johnny," Arkins protested.   "Johnny's a good man, Harry, and you know it.   Nothin' much wrong with me neither that a forty-foot fence along the state line wouldn't cure.   I admit, I got this bug.''

Mason stared at his deputy in astonished incredulity.   "So there's nothin' wrong with Jellicoe, huh?   Mr. Train," he said, turning to me, "what would you call a deputy who carries skis in his patrol car from November to May and fishin' gear and a pick and shovel and a gold-pannin' pan all the rest of the year?''

I was growing wary.   "An outdoor man, to say the least.''

"Outdoor man!   Hell, he oughta be livin' in a tree.''

"He don't do none of them things on duty, though, Harry," Arkins said.   "His ma give him too much what-for after that last time.''

"I saw the name Jellicoe on a building in town," I said to the Sheriff.   "Is that him?''

"His family.   His grandpa built it.   His ma still owns it.''

"How old is he?''

"He's a thirty-five-year-old adolescent—goin' on thirty-four.''

"I don't care," Arkins said.   "Ain't nobody I'd rather have with me in a tight place than Johnny.''

"Well, there's that," Mason conceded.   "But otherwise, he don't hardly know the time of day, and if he don't get his butt in here—''

"I'll go get him," Arkins said, and picked up his hat from the desk and left the room in a hurry.

I smelled a scam.   The Sheriff's anguish was a bit too theatrical to suit the facts, a bit too diversionary.   And he and Arkins had fed each other lines like a veteran comedy team.   Arkins I'd judged to be about forty and a long-time deputy—on an easy first-name basis with the boss.

In one corner of the room by an outside door there was a fly-rod and creel and a pair of hip boots, so Mason himself was no stranger to the amenities of the region that he and his minions served.   It was then I noticed that Arkins had picked up Doc's letter along with his hat, but I didn't let Mason see the sudden awareness in my eyes.

"Sheriff," I said quietly, "I was a cop in San Francisco for nineteen years and one of the things I learned early was to make copies of any important papers in a case.   To save yourself further embarrassment, you'd better make sure Arkins brings that letter back with him when he comes."

Mason debated for a long moment, then decided to call the bluff.   "What letter, Mr. Train?"

"The letter he would have swiped from Doc Wharton's mailbox if he'd known it was there.   Don't dig the hole any deeper, Mason—it's just about the depth of a grave right now."

"No, sir, Mr. Train, you're bluffin'.   But don't get your hackles up.   I needed an edge on you and now I got it.   I don't want no bad publicity out of this thing— that's all.   I knew what the boys was up to and let 'em get away with it because I honestly didn't think Doc Wharton had a soul in the world to leave nothin' to and I'd enjoy seein' the boys get a dollar or two.   We get paid up here about as much as a ragpicker down below, and—"

"All right, Sheriff, what's your deal?"

"Let's split it."

"No way."

"Arkins needs $2700 for them skunks in Nevada.   The rest to the girl."

"No way.   Arkins should have known better."

"Everybody should know better than to gamble with them sharks over there, but nobody does.   What's your deal, Mr. Train?"

"All of it to the girl.   Your men can receive it publicly, then they turn it over to the girl, every cent."

Arkins tapped lightly on the door just then and came in, followed by a tall, good-looking blond man, Jellicoe.   Adolescent wasn't the word, I thought at first glance; naive maybe, a mountain man's face.

Mason spoke to Arkins.   "Did you show him the letter?"

"What letter?" Arkins said blandly.

"The letter, dammit!   How many letters we talkin' about this afternoon?"

"I showed him."   Arkins' eyes seemed to wince.

Mason said to Jellicoe, "Where in hell you been, Johnny?"

"There's this girl in the parking lot, Sheriff, crying."   He looked deeply concerned.   "I sat down with her in her car.   She's still crying."

"There's this girl in the parking lot, Sheriff, crying."   He looked deeply concerned. "I sat down with her in her car.   She's still crying."

"No damn wonder she's still crying.   Jellicoe, this here's Mr. Sam Train. He brought out the letter."

I stood up and traded a firm handshake with him.   He was an inch taller than I and I found myself stretching to my fullest height.   It had been a long time since I'd looked into eyes as clear and guileless as his, seen a smile as quick and warm. It made me uneasy.   "You musta been a good friend of Doc's," he said.

"I was, Jellicoe.   Were you?"

"Yes, sir!   I loved that man.   Everybody up here did."

"Was he dead when you found him?"   I asked it almost belligerently.   "Or just dying?   The story in the paper said he was dead but who knows about papers."

"He was dead, Mr. Train."   A frown was developing around his eyes.

"How do you know?"

"Well, I didn't know for absolutely sure, sir, until Doc Zerbo came out and said so.   But—"

"You radioed for Zerbo?"

"Yes, sir."

"While Arkins went up the hill to the cabin, is that it?"

He flashed a glance at Arkins.   "Yes, but—"

"And then you heard a lot of gunshots from the cabin area—and then what— ran up to see what happened?"

"Yes, sir, but—" He heaved an exasperated sigh and looked at Arkins again.

"And Arkins told you he'd just shot Crumb and Belcher and you and he would share this nice fat reward?"

"I didn't want any part of it, but Al—"   He broke off and stared at the wall behind me, almost reciting the rest of it.   "Al said that since he was going to tell everyone that I shot one of the two rats that killed Doc, because I would have if I hadn't stayed back to radio Zerbo, that we'd split the reward."

"So you didn't know until a few minutes ago," I said, "that Doc Wharton had killed them and not Arkins?"

"Yes, sir, that's right, but—"

"What difference does it make?" Arkins said.   He had stepped forward and was looking at Mason, not me.   "You knew all along that nothin' that tricky would ever cross Johnny's mind.   But like I said before"—now he was looking at me—"if I'd known Doc had kin, it'd never of crossed mine neither."

While Mason was staring bleakly at Arkins, Jellicoe was staring in wonder at me.   And when Mason started to say something to Arkins, Jellicoe cut him off. "Mr. Train," he blurted, "do you drive a Dart automobile?"   He had a glint in his eye, and something in his voice made us all look at him sharply.

"Yes, I do."

"Is that—is that Doc Wharton's daughter sitting in it crying?"

I sighed.   "Yes, it is."

"By golly!"   Jellicoe's tanned face flushed suddenly.   "I knew it was!   By golly, I just *knew* it was!"

He was turning back to the door as he spoke, on the run, and the Sheriff stood up and bellowed, "Jellicoe!" and I took three clumsy steps after his retreating back with the idea in mind of tackling him from the rear. I want her, she's mine! this voice in my head said clearly and I felt my neck grow thick with blood. I stopped after the third step, teetering on my feet, and the three of us stood there in various attitudes, looking at each other and the empty door.

"I had a hell of a time," Arkins said finally, "gettin' him to leave her. I never seen him like that before, Harry. I think he's in love."

"Good God!" Mason said. "So it's finally happened." He sat heavily in his chair again, shrewd eyes on mine, until mine dropped. "How old is she, Mr. Train?"

"In the low thirties." My voice was a growl.

"A nice age for a lady to be. And how old—if you don't mind my askin'—are you?"

"I mind your asking, Mason."

"You're not married, are you?"

"I mind your asking that too. We've still got this matter to settle, Sheriff." My breath was audible as I sat down again.

"Well, let's settle it, then. I'll take your deal and so'll Arkins. Al, give him back the letter—and don't ask me what letter."

Arkins slipped the letter from inside his shirt and handed it to me, and he too was giving me the jaundiced eye as my blood took its own sweet time cooling down. He didn't seem in the least concerned about his double deception. "I imagine," he said reflectively, "she's a handsome girl when her face ain't all screwed up with grief."

"Mind my askin'," Mason said, "what she is to you, Mr. Train?"

"I mind."

Mason clutched his face again, speaking between splayed fingers. "Maybe somebody oughta go out there and put a hobble on Johnny, Mr. Train. I mean, we frown on claim-jumpin' up here—any kind." He eyed me closely. "How much you expect to get from her eight thousand?—now that's a fair question, sir."

"I told her I'd bring her up for the price of the gas."

"Well, that could be a pretty penny, couldn't it? At least you're on a commercial basis with her—right?"

I should have said something flat and decisive right then, and cleared the air, but inside I was still waffling around like a wet-eared kid. She'd found a seam in my hide and slipped through to where I used to live, and I shouldn't have let her. Private eyes shouldn't allow themselves to make emotional ties with the civilian world. People aren't people to cops, even to ex-cops—they're suspects, or victims or perpetrators, present or future; they're cases. Cops have a terrible divorce rate and their kids are among the first to hit the skids. My mind ticked off the litany. And yet—

Mason bit the end off a cigar and lit it, taking his time giving me time. He was every bit as shrewd as he looked. "Arkins," he said finally, "maybe you'd better go get them two. We got to work out the details on this thing yet." When Arkins had gone, he said to me, "I've never been in on one of these reward deals, Mr. Train—how long's it usually take for the money to get here?"

"It varies, but not too long, Sheriff.   Three weeks maybe."

He was making conversation, and I thought vaguely I'd like to come up sometime and go fishing with him.   I bet he knows where every trout in the county is, and how to whistle it up.

Arkins appeared in the door.   "They're gone," he said.

"What!"

"I said they're gone, Harry.   Took off in Johnny's jeep."

"Well, I'll be damned!" Mason said, his eyes flicking to mine.   But there was no reaction in me now, no inner voice; the seam was sealed tight again, the blood cool.   They're not men and women, they're cases, open or closed.   The perpetrators, I said to myself, have fled.

They'd gone to Madison's Funeral Parlor, the Sheriff found out, and then to Jellicoe's house to meet his mother.   After that, his mother said over the phone, she didn't know where they'd gone, but she'd never seen Johnny so excited.   And she said she liked the girl right off, a real nice girl—Doc's daughter, would you believe?—and tall enough for once.   She made it sound as though she'd given her blessing to the trip, wherever it went, whatever it led to.

And I let Mason know that it had my blessing too, and I thought that Doc might join in the chorus himself, if he had a way of doing it.   And maybe, I thought to myself, he'd left Mitzi more than he knew, more than just a little money.

I asked Mason where Doc Wharton's cabin was and on my way home I stopped by.   It was about a hundred yards off the road, deep in the trees, and a slim finger of late sun touched the peak of the steep-sloped roof as I stood in the small clearing in front.   Here the trails of three men had crossed and ended in the inexorable geometry of life.

The silence was a palpable living thing there, full of suppressed sound.   You had the feeling it could burst into a mind-stunning roar at any moment and destroy you—as it had destroyed three men.

Doc's trail had ended here; and turning, to look outward, I thought that maybe Mitzi's had begun here.

I listened to the layered sound of silence for a while longer and then, in awe and some fear, took the next step along my own inexorable path.

"*Adutrumque paratus* to you too," I said cautiously.

And nothing happened.

KATHRYN GOTTLIEB

Dream House

I'd better begin at the beginning—but when, I ask myself, was that? The day, I suppose, when I agreed to buy the one-acre section of property at the south end of Phil Ritchie's farm. It was one of those days when for want of something better to do, for want of a home to go to, I hung around the station house for an hour after my tour of duty. I am that figure of fun, a small-town cop. Watch some television series and you'll know what I mean. They have small eyes and paunches, and sometimes they spit and beat up on the innocent. It makes my blood boil.

About that no-home-to-go-to business. I was married for over twenty years until my wife died last year, and what I can't understand is why the end of twenty years of an unhappy marriage can leave you feeling lost, at a loss, high and dry in a fog or a desert, take your choice, and without a future. It should be a time for rejoicing, right? Well, the older I get, and I'm forty-eight, the less I know about life. In fact, at my present rate of progress, I should be completely ignorant in another six months, give or take a few.

Well, as I say, on this particular day I ran into Phil Ritchie as I was heading back to my room in Mrs. Plauder's house, having sold my own house on the advice of my friends and enemies when Connie died. Let me give you one piece of advice: never listen to advice. They said the house was too big for me. Well, there are no apartments in this town for rent, and let me tell you that room of mine is big, but it's too small for me. Dismal, is what I was feeling. It's all very well to live in the present when you're a young kid; you can do it because there's that great big bank account of time and the unknown up ahead, but when you're my age and the present is all you've got, the absence of a desirable future invades the day you're living through and turns it black around the edges.

Phil Ritchie is the best type of man you find in a town like this, and I mean that as a compliment. He's a successful famer; he also owns the farm-equipment agency down in Skyton, and the only gas station on this stretch of Route 180. Everything brings in money, and with it all he is a calm, friendly, honorable guy who does a lot of good in town, and when he suggested that we stop for a beer and a bite to eat I was glad to go along and sit with him.

He got onto my mood right away and told me I was a damn fool for listening to people about selling my house in a hurry. Then he brightened up and said he had just the solution for me and although it entailed a bit of profit-taking for him, that wasn't the reason he was offering the idea, which turned out to be this: he owned a one-acre piece of land, wooded, lying at the extreme south end of his farm and between him and the county lands, which as far as he knew they weren't about to build anything on.   It would be an ideal place for me to build myself a house, he said, and start living like a human being again.

I asked him why I needed a house for one man.

"Get yourself a wife," he said.   He is also blunt.

I felt my face turn red.   "Like who?" I asked him.

"There are attractive women in town."

"Name one."

"Mary Ann Shifler."

We went up there just before twilight and looked at the piece of land.   It was beautiful, a little bit hilly, with a gentle slope running up from the road in a westerly direction, and covered with oak and dogwood except for a little glade right in the middle of it.   I knelt and scooped up a handful of earth and let it trickle through my fingers and it smelled of earth and spring and hope and I knew I would pay any price for that place.

"Name me a reasonable figure and I'll take it off your hands," I said.

He named a reasonable price, and we shook hands on it.

Ernie and Mary Ann Shifler ran the little grocery store half a block up from Headquarters next to the Texaco station.   It was the kind of place where they had a little bit of everything on the shelves, and if you couldn't find exactly what you wanted—well, you could find something else.   It wasn't a restaurant, or even a luncheonette, but you could get yourself a bit of breakfast there, and there'd be a little crowd in the place before half the town was out of bed.

On the coldest winter morning, you'd see their light go on upstairs over the store along about five o'clock in the morning, and then the light would go on downstairs and you knew they would—she would—be pouring the water into the big coffee urn and it was a friendly feeling it gave you, especially when you'd been on the desk or riding around all night.

When Ernie was still around, they used to serve the coffee from before six in the morning till about eight thirty, along with buttered rolls, or Ernie would cut you a piece of pie.   A friendly feeling, as I say, to watch the lights go on, but Ernie was not a friendly man.   He was big, broad-shouldered, nice-looking, I guess, but he never smiled.   The kind of man who talks too much or not at all, with a surly expression on his face to go with it.

And when he talked, the talk was unkind.   Maybe he resented being locked up behind that counter and waiting on people who were not his betters, and maybe he didn't make a good living in the store, but he was unpleasant in my judgment over and above what circumstances called for.

Some people said he beat his wife, and it is true she wouldn't show her face in the store for periods of time, but did he beat her?   Joe Patris swears he heard her screaming one night when he was driving by and he went and knocked on the door, and after a while Ernie opened up and Joe asked him if anything was wrong and Ernie said no. Joe said he'd like to talk to Mary Ann and Ernie said she's asleep and then he got a funny look on his face and said, all right, come on up, and they went up to the bedroom and she was sitting up pulling the bedcovers around her. She said, "What's wrong?" and Joe said, "I thought I heard you screaming," and she said, "You did. I was having a terrible nightmare." So what could Joe do but go away?

For a long while after Joe told me that, I pictured Mary Ann Shifler sitting up in her bed pulling those blankets around her. A beautiful woman. How could a man abuse a woman like that? And a nice person, too, just as sweet and cheerful and obliging as she was pretty. Sometimes I'd go in there to pick up cigarettes or odds and ends of groceries, and even while my wife was still alive I'd look at Mary Ann and think, God forgive me, if only I had a wife like that.

And then one night Ernie left her. Just walked out and never came back. You'd think she'd have been glad—everybody else in town who had dealings with him was glad—but it seemed to take her a while to get used to the idea. Probably couldn't believe her luck, I remember Joe saying. Well, I didn't understand it at the time, but now, as I say, I am a living witness to the fact that when a bad marriage ends, things don't necessarily get better right away.

But after a while Mary Ann perked up. She spruced up the store a lot, and she put in a line of ham and eggs along with the breakfast rolls, so I and a lot of the fellows got in the habit of dropping in there fairly regular.

I didn't need Phil Ritchie to tell me she was attractive. But until he mentioned her to me I had just never thought of her in a truly personal way, as maybe somebody who could care for me. The minute I thought of building the house on the acre up by the county farm, then everything changed, and I could see her in that house, my wife, cooking the ham and eggs for yours truly and forget the store. The funny part is, my reaction at first was to stay away from the store for a while. I didn't stop to figure it out, but I think maybe I didn't want to watch her waiting on a bunch of strange men. Not my wife.

And then one day I was walking past the store and there was nobody inside but Mary Ann, so I went in and walked up to her and said, "You and I are alone now. I don't mean there's nobody in the store. We're alone in life now. I want you to come have dinner with me." She said she'd like to do that.

I took her out to the Red Mill up near Slingerstown, not that I was trying to hide anything but I wanted to take her to a nice place where we wouldn't be surrounded by people we knew, so we could be alone together and get to know each other. After that we went up there most of the time, and sometimes out to Poole's place, which isn't as fancy as the Mill but was nice and clean and quiet and usually half deserted. I don't know how the Pooles made a living there, except that wasn't for me to worry about. But being a policeman, you get to thinking after a while that everything's your business; one of the hazards of the trade.

And being a policeman, I am also inclined to be blunt and come out with what's on my mind, so right off I asked her if she had divorced Ernie and she told me it was in the works.

And then, it couldn't have been two weeks later, but I couldn't have been more sure of what I wanted if I'd waited the rest of my life, I asked her to marry me, and she didn't look coy or stall me off.   She looked a little startled, and she said yes.

What a moment.

I never said a word to her about the new house I was going to build her, or about the dogwood and the oaks and all I was going to hand her on a platter, because I wanted to be sure it was me she wanted, and not something I could give her above and beyond the ordinary.   A feeling of modesty.   I wanted to be sure.

I guess you'd like to know what she looked like, although I cannot pretend it doesn't pain me to think of her in that personal way.   I am trying to be detached about things.   She was a nice height for a woman, just to my shoulder, with a lovely, shapely body, and long shiny hair about the color of a collie dog, one of the reddish brown ones, only sleek and glossy, and a lovely creamy complexion that set off her features so that even if they hadn't been beautiful they would have looked beautiful, and big clear light brown eyes of that shade you only see in natural redheads.

So I asked her, and she said yes, and then the tears rolled down her cheeks.

"Why are you crying?"

"I'm happy."

I put my hand over hers.   "I want you always to be happy."

The days started to get longer and I got in the habit of going up to my property in the early evenings when I wasn't with her and I'd just moon around.   The buds were swelling on the dogwoods and showing white in the cracks, while the oak trees were still looking like winter was never going to end.

On the first of April I hired a bulldozer from Phil and when I got up there I saw he had delivered it.   It had been run in to the edge of the glade, the way I asked, and neatly—count on Phil—with no trees disturbed; some brush lost, that was all, but of course we'd have to put in a driveway out to the road anyway, so that didn't matter.   The next day was Mary Ann's birthday, and I planned to spring the big surprise.

I picked her up at the usual time and asked her if she'd like to have dinner at the Red Mill or somewhere else, and she said wherever I'd like, and I said no, I'm asking you; so she said the Red Mill was fine, and then asked me where I was heading, since the Mill was in the opposite direction, and I told her I had something to show her.   Something *for* her, and her eyes lit up and she started to smile.   "I suppose you're looking for a little bracelet in a red box or something like that," I kidded her.

She shook her head.   "I don't know what I'm looking for.   I'm not looking for *anything*.   I'm happy just the way I am."

"You're going to be happier," I said.   "I've got you a house and lot."

"You what!"   She turned to me all agape, her eyes shining.   "What have you gone and done?"

"I bought us the prettiest piece of land for twenty miles around and you and I are going to build our house on it."

She wrapped her arms around me and landed me a kiss on my ear, don't ask me why.

"Hey!" I said. "Hey, I'm driving!"

She unwrapped her arms and faced front again, but I noticed she kept one hand on my shoulder that was nearer to her, as though she, well, didn't want to stop touching me. After a while she said, "Where is it?"

"You'll see."

"What's it like?"

"Beautiful. Oak trees. Dogwood. A hundred dogwoods getting ready to bloom. It's the one real piece of woods in five miles of town. Beautiful."

She didn't ask me again where it was. I guess she could see the way we were heading, and after a minute she dropped her hand from my shoulder and just sat there staring out the window on her side so I couldn't see her face.

After a while I pulled up to the side of the road under our trees and turned the motor off. "You've got a bulldozer in there," she said. Her voice had a funny tone to it; she was talking in the constrained kind of way that reminded me of when she was Ernie's wife.

I got out of the car, walked around, and opened her door. "What are you going to do?" she asked me.

"Come on," I said. I was impatient. "Let's walk over to where the 'dozer is. That's where we're going to build, right in the little open place. We won't have to touch a tree if you don't want to. It'll be just like a little private castle in the woods." I stretched my arm out, first one way and then the other, to the big open spaces of Phil's farm on the one side and the county lands on the other. "We'll be the lords of it all," I said.

She got out of the car then and stood beside me. Under the shade of the trees her face looked bleached out, and her eyes—I'll never forget her eyes—they looked huge, and hard to read. I took her hand. "Your hands are trembling."

"It's all too much," she said.

"It's beautiful, isn't it?"

She took a deep breath. "I'm grateful to you."

"Come on." I started up the path the bulldozer had crushed through the underbrush and we had got nearly to the clearing when she just sank down beside me. My first thought was that she had tripped over a root, but she hadn't gone down suddenly—she had seemed to drift down. She was kneeling and her head was hanging, and I bent down beside her and put my hand on her forehead. It felt all clammy and cold. She was muttering something and I had to get my head close and ask her what she was saying.

"Just I'm sorry. I'm sorry."

"It's all right."

"I've spoiled my birthday for you."

"It's all right."

"No."

"Are you sick?"

"You'd better take me home."

I was plenty worried about her, but she wouldn't let me come upstairs.   She insisted she was going straight to bed and then she'd be as right as rain in the morning.   She'd just been feeling queer all day, she said, but trying not to think about it, because of her birthday and all.

I said good night, but I was uneasy.   It even crossed my mind that she might be expecting, and what a feeling that was!   A father at my age!   Well, why not? She said she'd gotten her divorce papers, so we'd just hurry up and get married and ride out the gossip.   What did I care?   I rejoiced, but I was worried about her just the same.

And the worst of it was the next day it was impossible for me to call her, due to an outbreak of vandalism at the Regional High, the worst mess you ever saw, and the principal spitting with rage and one of the teachers hysterical, and I can't say I blame her.   I can understand crime, but there's something about that mindless kind of spite these kids go in for that gets you under the skin so that you feel almost capable of murder yourself and no better than they are.

It was nine o'clock before I got back to her place, and then I saw the lights were out, so I figured I ought not to disturb her.   But I was still worried.   If she was in bed that early, then didn't it mean she was still not okay?   Well, the morning would have to do.

In the morning the store was shut up tight and the lights were out.   I banged on the door for a while, then I figured I was drawing too much attention to myself and I went away.   The day was endless, and vile.   An old lady had been beaten to death and robbed, up on the Slingerstown Road.   The road to the Red Mill. It gave me a literal pain across my midsection to drive up that road that day, and I knew I wouldn't be driving up it again, except in the line of duty.

Her letter was waiting for me at the house when I came off duty.

"My heart is broken," she wrote, "and I only hope you will not be too unhappy. I have gone away.   I will not be back.   It was nothing you did.   No one was ever so wonderful to me.   But it wouldn't have worked out.   I can't say any more.

"Please see that the stuff in the refrigerator goes to the poor before it spoils, milk, eggs, and there is half a ham.   You could run it up to the Sisters of Charity in Slingerstown, they will know what to do with it.   I hope you don't mind my asking.

"I will ever love you."

It was that last line that got me, because it was poetry, and I believed it was true.   My throat got all tight and I couldn't have spoken if I had to, except that I did, I said her name, over and over.

I was awake until dawn, and then I took my car out and ran up to the cursed ground.   I climbed onto the bulldozer and began to move back and forth in the open space, as though I was digging a cellar.   I made twenty-seven passes—I didn't realize I had been counting—and then I saw it, and I let the load down back in the pit and climbed down and looked close.

A thigh bone was sticking out of the loam; not a horse's, not a dog's, not a part of any of the animals that run wild in the woods.

Ernie's.

I got back on the machine and scraped back all the earth into the pit that I had been piling at the edges, which seemed to take a very long time, and then I smoothed it out and spread out a load of brush and leaves over it.   All the time I felt very calm and full of hate and pity.   But more hate, for him that drove her to it.

Then I moved the bulldozer back out to the road and up the half mile to the side road into Phil's place, and came back to my car.

I guess the dogwoods bloomed, but I never went back to see them and I guess in God's good time the oaks leafed out.   What am I going to do with the place? I can't sell it because someone else will dig there and God knows what they will turn up.   My guess is a skull with a bullet hole.   And for myself, I never want to see the place again.   I told Phil I had changed my mind about building there.

"It's a shame," he said, shaking his head.   "That's a beautiful place."

But not a happy one.

JOYCE HARRINGTON

The Plastic Jungle

"If you stay in the Soft Goods you'll be all right."

My mother's voice comes to me and I go on combing my hair. My hair is quite long now. I haven't cut it for four years, except when my girl friend, Alexis, trims the ends. Alexis' family is Syrian and my mother doesn't like me to pal around with her. Oh, God! There she goes again.

"Don't go in the Housewares Department. Mimi, do you hear me? Don't even go near it. It's not safe. Answer me."

She's standing in the doorway. Momma, don't you want me to get you a nice new scrub brush so you can scrub out the rest of your life? No. Be nice to Momma, she's at a hard time in her life. My sister says. My sister who lives in Great Neck and doesn't have to listen listen listen, and come up with an answer. I put on some lipstick and try to say something.

"Momma, I'm only going to buy a bathing suit."

The lipstick is crooked and I wipe it off. Forget it. I stuff things into my shoulder bag. She comes into the room and sits down on the bed plop like that. She dumps herself down when she sits. Always. Like a sack of somebody else's dirty laundry she's carried around too long. The bed shakes.

"A bathing suit, anh. What, one piece or two?"

"I don't know, Momma. I'll see what they have. Maybe I won't get anything."

I'm ready to go, but I haven't been released yet. I have to wait until all the questions have been asked. Until all the wrong answers have been given. There aren't any right answers.

"A bikini? Don't bring home a bikini. You bring home a bikini, I'll send it right back."

She won't though.

"All right, Momma. No bikini."

"You're going with that Alexis? She's not a nice girl, Mimi. I saw her in the pizza place smoke a cigarette."

So what should she be smoking, a cigar? No. My mother is still fighting the Six Days' War. Alexis is an Arab guerrilla who kills Israeli babies. Would she like to see me in khaki shorts with a rifle on my back? Marching? Singing? Shooting Alexis? Would she?

"No, Momma.   I'm going by myself."

"Don't lie to me.   You never go downtown by yourself.   Why can't you go with a nice girl like Rose next door?"

"No, really, Momma.   This time I'm going alone."

Because Rose is a nice fat girl and it hurts both of us to go shopping together. Could you understand that, Momma?   That Rose couldn't wear a bikini, and she would have to say they all looked terrible.   And I would have to say something bitchy about her flab, and then we couldn't speak to each other for a week.

"You have enough money?"

Her hand is in her apron pocket pulling out the old black-leather change purse.

"Yes, I have enough.   I have to go now."

"Here.   Here, prices go up overnight.   Everything goes up, nothing comes down.   Just in case."

A weary crumpled five-dollar bill gets shoved into my shoulder bag.   At last I can go.   I head for the door.

"Thanks, Momma."

Her voice follows me to the front door.

"Be home for supper.   Be careful.   Don't go in the Toys, they're all plastic." Out.

I go along Westminster Road and turn toward the subway.   What do you do when your mother is crazy?   Is everybody's mother crazy or only mine?   She worries about plastic, she's afraid of it.   Never mind about drugs, about Vietnam, about crime in the streets.   My mother carries on a pogrom against plastic.

It's a menace, she says, and she won't have it in the house.   I have to keep all my records at Lex's house.   My sister says maybe she wouldn't be like this if my father was still alive and if my brother lived closer and if she wasn't having a hard time with the change of life.   If.   But the fact is that my father is dead and my brother lives in New Mexico and my mother is crazy.   Be nice, my sister says, go along with it.   It's harmless.

I reach the subway steps and go up.   The subway is out in the open here.   Not really elevated, but running on tracks above the ground.   Nice, to ride along seeing daylight and the backs of houses.   Alexis is waiting for me on the platform.

My brother the college professor in New Mexico sends his monthly letter with a check or his monthly check with a letter.   He helps out.   It's very hot in New Mexico, they moved from their apartment to a little house near the college, there's a nice back yard for Jemmy to play in, they are expecting another baby in October and he didn't write that sooner because he wanted to be sure everything was okay. His wife, Eleanor, had a miscarriage last year and Momma got so upset she had to go to bed for a week.

Momma reads me the letter after supper.   She cries.

"Why New Mexico," she moans, "so far away?   Might as well be China.   He couldn't get a job in New York?"

I'm eating my dessert while she's crying. She makes very good apple cake and my mouth is full of it. But I can't swallow.

"You could go visit them." I mumble around the cake and finally get it down. "You could go out there, take care of Eleanor, take care of Jemmy."

That does it. The tears disappear, dry as the Negev, dry as New Mexico, no more irrigation canals down the cheeks.

"Oh, yes, Madam. Who would take care of you? You are not yet as big as you think you are."

Right on, Momma. I'm not as big as I think. But who is? You, my little shriveled Momma with tear spots like watermelon pits on your blue wash-and-wear permanent-press coverall apron with a daisy on the pocket from Sears Roebuck?

"I could go and stay with Celia."

And spend the summer being built-in unpaid nosewiper for that batch of my mother's grandchildren. Listening to my beautiful sister, the heroic mother of three, complain about life as the doctor's wife. (He's never here when I need him, and when he is here he's too tired.) Who told her to marry the doctor?

"Momma."

That's right. Blow the nose. You look great. It's all red.

"Momma. I could go stay with Celia. You could go out to Sam and Eleanor."

More Kleenex. Stuff it in the pocket. What does she do with all that damp Kleenex? Iron it out and use it again? Put it away neatly in a drawer for my inheritance? I give and bequeath to my youngest daughter, Mimi the Nuisance, all the Kleenex I cried into during her lifetime.

"Celia has enough to worry about. You think she needs you besides?"

Thanks. That may be the nicest thing you've said to me all day.

I push back my chair and start to clear the table. The dishes are odds and ends of old sets, chipped and cracked, replacements picked out of dirty bushel baskets set out on the sidewalk in front of Benny's Bargain Bazaar. When my father died, the good dishes, two sets, were packed up and shipped out to Great Neck. To Celia because she has a family and keeps a kosher home. We don't bother any more. It's my personal opinion that Celia stayed kosher just long enough to get her hands on those dishes and, of course, when Momma comes to visit. I start to wash the crummy dishes.

"So where's the bathing suit? Let's see this year's free show at Jones Beach." She's still sitting at the table, sipping her third cup of tea. The tears are gone, the Kleenex is gone, and she's ready for the next round.

"It's in my room. I got a job, Momma." I'm splashing around with the brown soap and the greasy dishwater (Momma won't get detergent because it comes in plastic bottles) with my back to her waiting for the eruption. It doesn't come. Nothing.

"Did you hear me, Momma? I got a job." I look over my shoulder and she's sitting kind of crooked in her chair with her eyes closed and her mouth open and her face turning blue. I should have known.

Then I'm yelling, "Momma, stop it!" But she doesn't stop it. So I grab the bottle of ammonia from under the sink, and my hands are dripping dishwater all over the clean floor, and the bottle slips, of course, but I finally get it under her nose and she breathes again. She gasps, she wheezes, she groans, and a few more tears roll down the old tracks.

"Come on, Momma. Go to bed."

"How can I go to bed? You made such a mess on the floor. Now I'll have to mop it all over again."

"Never mind. I'll clean it up. You go to bed."

She lets me take her arm and start leading her out of the kitchen. She's all bent over like she's cuddling a pain next to her heart.

"I'm old and sick and all you want is to leave me. So get a job. What kind of a job could you get? You can't even wash dishes without flooding the kitchen." All this with more wheezes and groans, and she stumbles on the doorsill and nearly falls down. "It's just like the time with the plastic geraniums. Remember what the doctor said."

"Do you want a doctor now, Momma?"

"Who can afford a doctor? Who can afford to be sick? I'll go to bed and maybe I'll still be alive in the morning."

I get her into bed with two pillows and a heating pad. The television at the foot of the bed with the remote control next to her hand, this morning's *Daily News* and a copy of *TV Guide*. The television has plastic knobs, but somehow Momma missed that. As I head back to the kitchen to mop up the five water spots that make a deluge, her voice quavers after me.

"Mimi, be a good girl and bring a cup of tea and don't put too much sugar. And don't slop it in the saucer."

Okay.

While I'm waiting for the kettle to boil I'm thinking about Momma and the plastic geraniums. That was the start of it all. Almost a year ago. She had this box on the kitchen window full of plastic geraniums. She used to try to grow real ones but the window never got much sun, and she would forget to water them. So, okay, the plastic ones. They were bright red and always in bloom, and she liked them. No problems.

Then one day, she was hanging the laundry on the clothesline from that window, and she had a mild heart attack. That's what the doctor said. A mild heart attack. Take life easy, Mrs., and you'll be all right. You are not a young woman any more. You don't have to polish your house from morning to night. Did my dear Momma hear that? No.

When it was all over and she was back on her feet, all she could remember was that she was leaning over the geraniums and suddenly she couldn't breathe. The geraniums were out to get her. The plastic was stealing the air from her lungs. I came home from school one day and found her in the middle of one of the biggest house-cleanings I'd ever seen, even from Momma who is a champ in this field. And everything plastic was in the garbage can. Even my hair rollers and now I have to use frozen orange juice cans.

The kettle is screaming, so I make a cup of tea medium strong with a spoon and a half of sugar no milk and put a paper napkin on the saucer.   I take it in to her but she's asleep half sitting up with the lights on, the television on, the heating pad on.   I turn everything off and tiptoe back to the kitchen and drink the tea myself.   The job will be first on the agenda at breakfast.   If I like it maybe I won't go back to school in the fall.

The job is okay.   I mean, it's no big deal, but it's kind of fun and it's nice to have a little extra money.   Momma finally stopped moaning about it when she found out it was in the Infants' Wear Department where I would be relatively safe and I could get a nice discount on things for the grandbabies.   It's part time.   I work three days a week and still have enough time to go to the beach and get a decent suntan.   Alexis is working here, too, in the Bath Boutique, but I didn't tell Momma that.

Every morning Momma packs me a lunch in a brown paper bag which I am supposed to eat in the employees' lunchroom.   She's in one of her quiet periods now, knitting a sweater set with bootees for Sam and Eleanor's new baby.   Only complaining about the butcher (he's giving short weight), the heat (you don't feel it, Mimi, you spend all day in an air-conditioned store), and the plastic jungle (it sneaks up on you, Mimi, and soaks up all the air, so somebody should do something).

Every morning I take the brown paper lunch and shove it in my shoulder bag.   Thank God the shoulder bag is big enough and I don't have to carry the lunch in my hand like a little kid.   Sometimes I eat it, but sometimes Lex and I, we meet some guys we know from school, and then we goof around downtown at lunchtime and maybe have a hamburger or some pizza or something.

Momma should know, she'd really flip.   I wonder sometimes if I told her, which would be worse, throwing her lunch away or meeting guys.   With Momma you never know.

Every night we play twenty questions.   What did you do today, Mimi?   That's the way it starts.   Then I have to tell her every item I sold, who I sold it to, was she pregnant and how far along, what the grandmothers are buying, what new items the store has in for babies.   It's almost like she was jealous, like she wishes she could be me, working in that dumb store.   I mean the store is okay.   It's only that when I have to tell her all about it, it sounds so stupid.

And always the last question, the wrap-up like they say on the television news.   Did you eat your lunch, Mimi?   Someday the president of the store is going to call her up and say I'm sorry Mrs. but your daughter was eating your brown paper lunch today in the employees' lunchroom and she choked on it.

Tonight a surprise.   It's Thursday night and I've been working late.   Momma has a snack waiting for me on the kitchen table, and she's waiting for me with a funny smile on her face.

"Guess what, Mimila?"   She can't wait for me to sit down, wash my hands even.   It's like she's about to explode with something.   Maybe she won the lottery.   She thinks I don't know she buys tickets and hides them.

"What, Momma?"

"Tomorrow I'm coming downtown!   How do you like that?"   She sits back in her chair with her hands on her thighs and her elbows out like she's just been crowned Queen of England.

"That's great, Momma."   What are you gonna do?   It is great.   She hasn't been downtown since the plastic menace started.   Maybe she's getting herself straightened out.   Maybe she'll be all right now.

"One thing, Madam.   I'm going to check up on you.   See what kind of people you spend your days with.   You can't be too careful."

"Momma!   They're just people, salesgirls.   What's to be careful?"

"And, believe me, if there's any plastic in that Baby Department I'm getting you transferred out of there.   You'll thank me for it.   You'll see."

There's no stopping her now.   I'm wondering what happened today to set her off.   And I'm thinking what she'll do when she sees all the baby bottles and potty chairs and rattles and junk at the counter next to mine.

"Momma, I only sell beautiful baby blankets and beautiful cloth diapers and beautiful clothes for beautiful babies.   I don't touch any plastic.   You don't have to come."

"Oh, yes, Madam.   You don't want me to come."   Now she's standing over me triumphant, and my feet are hurting from standing all day, and my head is beginning to feel like my feet.

"You don't know what I saw today, do you?"   She's really in full swing now and all I can do is listen.   "Down by the bakery I was.   And out in front was a baby in a carriage drinking milk from a bottle.   The mother was in the bakery and the baby was outside.   So there I was looking in the window and thinking I might buy a loaf of seeded rye, and this baby starts crying and throws the bottle.   What happened, Mimi?   What happened?"

"Don't tell me.   Momma, where's the aspirin?   I got a headache."

"Don't try to change the subject.   The bottle didn't break.   The bottle did not break!   And why not?   *PLASTIC!*"

Momma is the picture of outrage, the protector of innocent babies from the plastic menace.   Her arms are flapping a mile a minute, and her little body is stiff with indignation.

"So what did you do, Momma?"

"What did I do?   What would you do?   I picked up that plastic bottle and I dropped it down the sewer.   That's what I did.   Some mothers don't care what happens to their babies.   The Mayor should make an emergency speech on television."

"Great, Momma.   Why don't you tell him?   In the meantime, is there any aspirin in the house?"

I'm holding my head in my two hands now because it feels like it's trying to break in half, and also so I can put my hands over my ears.

"There's some in my sewing box."   Momma never keeps medicine in the medicine chest.   God forbid anybody should be sick and not let her know about it.   "Don't take more than two."

She follows me into her bedroom while I look for the aspirin and back to the kitchen for a glass of water, and her voice never stops.

"So the second thing I'm going to do tomorrow is buy two dozen regular glass bottles and send to Eleanor.   They still make glass baby bottles, Mimi?   I can't depend on Eleanor to be careful.   She let Sam take a job so far away, how can I be sure she won't drown that baby in plastic?"

I swallow the aspirin and decide there's only one escape left.   "Momma, I'm going to take a hot bath."

"Don't fall asleep in the tub.   Remember, I'll see you in the Baby Department around eleven.   Maybe we'll have lunch in Schrafft's.   Sleep good, Mimila."

Later on I'm lying in bed watching shadows on the ceiling.   My head is calmed down and my feet are just tingling but not hurting.   Once in a while a car goes by and the lights race across the ceiling and down the wall.

I'm thinking about the times Momma and I used to go shopping and she knew that store inside out, where all the bargain counters were and what days there were special sales.   It used to be fun to go with her, even though she never let me pick out my own clothes.

I remember one time I got lost in the store and they took me to the office on the eighth floor and said they would make an announcement over the loudspeaker. But Momma was there in the office before we got there.   So we didn't get announced, and Momma only yelled at me a little, and then took me to the Toy Department and bought me a stuffed dog.

I'm lying here in bed thinking about those old things, and some tears are running down the sides of my head and getting in my ears, and I'm wishing for something to happen between now and tomorrow morning so Momma won't come downtown.

The next morning I'm dressed and out of the house before she gets up.   She'll be mad I didn't eat breakfast, but I stop at Lex's house and have coffee and Danish and tell her what Momma's up to.   Neither one of us can think of any way to head her off, so we go on to the store together.

All morning I'm so nervous I keep dropping things.   I give the wrong change for a twenty-dollar bill and the customer yells at me and I almost yell back at her. Finally it's time for my break and I meet Lex in the coffee shop, but I can't eat anything.   My hand is shaking so, of course, I spill my coffee all over the counter. The waitress comes to wipe it up and says "Clumsy" under her breath but just loud enough for me to hear, which she would never do if we were regular customers.

So I say, "Lex, I'm going back," and I go without leaving a tip and without even finishing my coffee break.

Angie, the regular full-time lady who works the baby counter with me, sees I'm not feeling so good, and she says, "It's not so busy right now, Mimi.   Why don't you put away some of that stock?"

So for the next half hour I have my mind occupied with sorting out little undershirts and nightgowns and training pants and stuff, and things are pretty quiet before the noontime rush, so I don't even notice when eleven o'clock comes and goes. And no Momma. I'm just sort of standing there in the middle of a pile of diapers, looking at the clock over the elevators which says a quarter after, and thinking, She's not coming. She's not coming.

Then the next to the last elevator opens and Alexis gets off and starts running toward me. Alexis is naturally very olive-skinned, but this is the first time I ever saw her look green.

I start to say "What's the matter?" But she grabs my arm and starts pulling me to the elevator and it's like she can't say anything, but she finally manages to get it out.

"Your mother!" she says and then clams up and won't look at me in the elevator. And I shout, "My mother what?" And I'm thinking all the things Momma could do to make Alexis look like that, and what was she doing on Alexis' floor anyway which has the Bath Boutique and Housewares and the Pet Shop.

And then the elevator is stopping and we're getting off, and over to the right there's a crowd of people. Alexis is pulling me that way and starts shoving through the crowd, and a fat lady says, "Who do you think you're pushing?" But Alexis just lets her have it in the corset and starts yelling to the store guards who are trying to hold everybody back. "Here she is, here's her daughter!" And then Alexis starts crying.

I still can't see anything, but one of the guards takes my hand and makes a path for me through the crowd. In the middle of the open space there's a little bundle on the floor covered with a plastic shower curtain. There are shoes sticking out at one end, and I can see that they are Momma's best comfortable shoes a little rundown at the heels. I don't want to see what's at the other end. Maybe it's some other old lady wearing Momma's shoes.

The guards are shouting, "Stand back, stand back! It's all over." But nobody moves, and I can hear a loud voice saying over and over, "I saw it happen. She got off the elevator and walked over here like she knew where she was going. Then all of a sudden she got this funny look on her face like she was lost. She looked like a little lost kid. And then she just fell down. I tried to get her sitting up, but she wasn't even breathing."

Then somebody is saying, "Are you the daughter?" My head is nodding yes, yes, yes, and I look and see it's the store manager and behind him is a short guy with a mustache and a black bag, and I guess he's the doctor. The store manager is holding my arm very tight like he's afraid maybe I'll scream or faint or something, and the doctor goes over and pulls back the shower curtain which is green with daisies all over it.

The doctor listens and looks and shakes his head, and then he looks up at me and says, "Is this your mother?" My head is still nodding yes, yes, yes, and Alexis is holding onto my other arm and bawling as if it was her mother. But I'm just standing there nodding and looking at Momma on the floor with a stack of yellow plastic dishpans on one side of her and a mountain of avocado-green plastic garbage cans on the other and at the end of the aisle a display of bright red plastic geraniums.

Some guys in white jackets come up with a stretcher on wheels, and the doctor is saying "Did she have a heart condition?   Is there somebody you can call?" And the store manager says, "You can call from my office."   So off we go to call Celia, with the store manager still hanging onto one arm and Alexis on the other, and she's saying, "You can come and stay with me."

But I'm thinking, now I'll have to go and live with Celia.   Unless I can go to stay with Sam and Eleanor.   And I'm thinking I won't have much trouble choosing between Albuquerque and Great Neck if I have any choice.   And then I'm thinking, I wonder how come I forgot to tell Momma they moved the Baby Department to the fourth floor and put the Housewares where the Baby Department used to be.

A As in Alibi

Detectives:
HOMICIDE SQUAD

Lieutenant Decker, the lean, gray-haired, gray-eyed Chief of Homicide, sat behind the beat-up desk in his tiny office and felt old. Empty inside. Past his prime. Licked, washed up. Twenty years ago he'd have shot fire and brimstone, and blasted this overweight slob into a confession.

But now—what? Here was Frank London, a half-baked, itinerant bum of a folk singer, sneering at him, sneering at the police. Logic hadn't worked, threats hadn't worked, the tricks of the trade hadn't worked. Nothing had even dented the guy, and Decker had nowhere to go. Not up, not down. Not sideways. Just stay put and molder away. Call the case a bust, put it in the Unsolved File, and know in his heart that he'd failed.

There was only one thing that Lieutenant Decker was sure of: Frank London had killed her. Decker knew it and London knew he knew it—which was why London had that smirk on his face. A big, round, oversized face with large agate eyes, cheeks like little red balloons, and that impossible, twisted handlebar of a blond mustache decorating his lip.

It was a grotesque mustache, braided like a quoit or a pretzel or a wicker carpet-beater. The Beatles had their hairdo, Groucho had his cigar—but this joker had his mustache; and he was making a monkey out of Decker and the Homicide Squad and the whole police department. And when they released London, somebody would be the fall guy and his name was Decker. William B. Decker, a cop for thirty-five years and head of Homicide for the last fifteen. The smart thing was to hand in his resignation, then go home and tell Martha, his wife. And move to Florida or California and never work, never worry, never be alive again.

Yeah? Not me, brother, not me!

Decker stared at the beefy hunk of beatnik in front of him and said, "Okay, let's go over it once more. You got to the cottage around five, her folks were already gone, and so you and Jodie rehearsed for a couple of hours. You left her a little before seven, walked up the path to the top of the cliff where your car was parked, and nobody saw you. A damn freak like you, and nobody ever noticed you!"

"The invisible man," London said tauntingly. His deep, resonant, troubadour voice separated every word and enunciated it with care. "I left, didn't I? Or do you think I'm still there?"

Decker knew that the car had been driven away around seven, although nobody could identify London as the driver.   "You got into your car," Decker said crisply, "drove home and took a shower.   Presumably to wash off the blood."

"There was no blood."

"What did you do with the towel?" Decker asked.   That was one of the few points he had.   London's landlady was certain that a towel was missing from London's bathroom, and Decker was convinced the folk singer had used it to wipe off the blood and then had disposed of it, along with the white polo shirt he'd been wearing.   "What did you do with the towel?" Decker asked again.

"I buttered it, put pepper and salt on it, and cut it into terrycloth canapés.   My usual dinner."

That was the way the interrogation had been going.   London kidding him, skating rings around him, and enjoying every minute of it.   Always the showman, always putting on an act.   And then London pulled a masterpiece of pure gall.   He took the unbelievably long braids of that fancy mustache of his, pulled one ropy end straight up, over his nose, and stretched the other end at a right angle, to his right. With Decker facing him, the mustache now looked like the two hands of a clock, pointing to nine o'clock.

Nine o'clock—the crucial time.

He did it solemnly, deadpan, and then he twisted his mustache back into its usual pretzel shape, sat there with that maddening smirk on his face, and clammed up. That was his answer: nuts to you, Lieutenant Decker.   And somehow, Decker felt he'd been given the clue to the puzzle—been given it by the man's brag and conceit; but Decker was just too dumb to figure it out.

Restraining an impulse to smack the guy, the Lieutenant thought back to the first, futile interview between them.   He'd been pretty sure, even then.   He'd asked questions, listened to answers, then sent London back to a cell for the night, while the Homicide Squad checked up on what London had said.

Orthodox procedure, and Decker thought he had the guy cold.   Duck soup, he'd told himself.   London's alibi depended on the time when the murder had been committed, and so he had simply set a clock on the scene of the crime to the hour of his alibi.   Which was a trick that had never fooled anybody, once a case was properly investigated.

Except this time.

Decker scowled.   "Then you went to the Red Grotto for your evening performance.   Jodie didn't come, and you went on stage alone."

"The show must go on," London said smugly.

Decker's adrenaline oozed out, and his face turned red.   "You sang *Frankie and Johnny*," he said tightly.   "Then you sang a new song, one you say you had just made up.   A few people remembered some of the words.   It started off—"

He picked up the sheet of paper on which he'd scrawled the beginning of the ballad, as some of the audience had recalled it.   He read it off starkly, prosaically. " 'My love has gone to a far country, My love has gone away from me, Sing die, goodbye, Oh, sigh, sigh, sigh.' "

"Nice song," London said judiciously.

"Where'd you learn it?"

"I made it up as I went along. It came naturally." London gave Decker a self-satisfied grin and added, "That's genius for you."

"You were singing her requiem. How did you know she was dead?"

"I didn't. I felt sad. Maybe it was telepathy. Maybe her spirit was in me, for those few minutes. The audience was so touched that for a few seconds nobody even applauded. Then their cheers rang to the rafters. It was a great moment."

The folk singer cocked his head to one side and grinned like an overfed gargoyle. "It was nine o'clock, exactly."

Decker glared, then spun around in his chair. The swivel squeaked. He reached for the doorknob, twisted it. He swung the door outward and gave it a kick. "Okay," he said in a dead voice. "You can go. You're free."

London jumped up with a shout and held out his hand. "Lieutenant, that's great! Thanks, Lieutenant, thanks."

Decker turned away.

"Look," London said, "don't take it like that. So you were wrong. Forget it. Enjoy yourself. I'm going to throw a party at the Red Grotto that this town's going to remember for years. I'm going to have all my friends there, including you. Lieutenant, be my guest—the guest of honor."

"Get the hell out of here," Decker said, barely spitting out the words.

London shrugged, grinned, and left.

Decker frowned as he slid his finger along the pieces of paper on his desk—the sheets with the words of the song and the timetable of the murder.

It was years since he'd blown his top and let a suspect see how infuriated he could become. Alone now, Decker asked himself where he'd gone wrong.

His investigation had been thorough, he'd examined the facts exhaustively. There were no loose ends, no doubts in his own mind. Jub Freeman, lab man and forensic scientist and a damn good one, had gone over every inch of the cottage, and the Homicide Squad had spent days questioning everybody who had been in the neighborhood. The picture was clear enough.

The Dorkins and the Finleys lived together—they had lived together for twenty years in the big stone house on Dixon Heights. Hannah Dorkin and Natalie Finley were sisters—their relationship was close. In his own mind, Bill Decker called it beautiful, and they were beautiful women in the fullness of maturity. Prominent in social work, married to eminent men, Hannah Dorkin and Natalie Finley were kind, gentle, rich in forgiveness. Decker wondered whether they'd forgiven London. And whether they'd ever forgive him, Lieutenant Decker.

Jodie Dorkin was the only young person in the household, and the Dorkins told the Lieutenant that, as a child, Jodie had sometimes got mixed up as to who were her father and mother, and who were her aunt and uncle. She solved the problem by loving them all equally.

Her father and uncle were distinguished men. Judge Dorkin was gruff, blunt, rigorous in his honesty and rocklike in his adherence to high principle. Decker knew him professionally and respected him for his clear mind and incorruptible character. Dorkin's clipped wit and his firm, impartial administration of justice had made enemies.   No upper court appointment for him.   Politics couldn't take away his distinction, but it had kept him from the advancement he so richly deserved.

Dr. Richard Finley was a small gentle man, a world-famous cardiologist and surgeon.   He was urbane, civilized, honored in his profession.   You looked at him and wondered how such an unobtrusive little man could have risen so far. But when he spoke, you began to understand why, and when you noticed the delicacy and strength of his hands, you knew there was talent in them.   He had the king's touch, which cured.

The four adults had gone down to their river cottage early that mild, summery Saturday afternoon.   The cottage was at the foot of the river bluff, just within the metropolitan limits.   A dozen other cottages were scattered along the bank of the river—pleasantly cool refuges in the heat, each of them with a dock and a boathouse built over the water.

Jodie was already at the cottage—she'd gone there the day before and stayed overnight.   At 18, she was interested in folk singing and had performed here and there as an amateur; but she hadn't been serious about it as a career until she met Frank London.   He had a good voice, he was an experienced performer, and on some level he and Jodie clicked.   Their voices complemented each other, but more than that, they gave each other style.   London's stature grew as some part of him softened and gained understanding, while Jodie acquired some of his confidence and bravura.   They were a team, and fast becoming the sensation of the small hootenannies.

Jodie had told her family that Frank was meeting her at the cottage, that they wanted to rehearse some new numbers.   The older people had never liked London, but they realized you don't have to like your colleagues in order to work with them. And Jodie had assured them there was nothing serious between her and Frank, and never would be.

"He likes me," she'd said.   "Maybe a little too much, but I know he's a heel. Except the times we're singing together, he rubs me the wrong way.   So you've nothing to worry about, any of you."

And they didn't.   They loaded the picnic basket in their boat, and went upriver. They didn't take watches, didn't know what time it was.   That was part of the fun, part of what made their outings so carefree.

"We go upriver," Dr. Finley said, "and land wherever we feel like, or else we just drift back.   We do it every weekend.   Sometimes we swim, sometimes we birdwatch, sometimes we just talk.   We eat when we're hungry.   Occasionally we stay out overnight.   We never know.   But we're free, we're completely eman- cipated from time."

Brother, Decker thought.   What a day to be emancipated!

They had returned after dark.   They had no idea what time it was.   Ten— twelve—two—they couldn't say.   They'd been immersed in a dream world and their senses were drugged, suspended, heavy with sound and sight and the richness of their own living.   Until they turned on the light in the living room of the cottage and saw Jodie.

She'd been stabbed with a kitchen knife.   There was blood.   There had been a fight.   She'd resisted.   Her clothes were torn.   In the course of the struggle her foot had apparently caught the cord of the electric clock, unplugged it, and sent it crashing down.   The cord was still hooked around her leg.

What the four grownups had subsequently gone through, they themselves could hardly relate.   Dr. Finley had examined Jodie.   Respiration had not entirely ceased. The doctor took over, and with the help of the others he improvised emergency techniques.   First-aid equipment and some of his basic instruments were in the cottage, so he tried to accomplish a medical miracle.

There was no phone, and even if there had been, no one would have bothered to summon the police.   Time was too important—a transfusion and manual massage of Jodie's heart were the only possible hopes, and they had to be done immediately, without moving her.

Natalie Finley had formerly been a nurse.   She assisted; she was familiar with the delicate and unusual operation that Dr. Finley had performed before, in hospitals. He made the incision and they stood by and did what he told them to.   They gave blood, under primitive conditions.

How long Finley worked on Jodie, none of them could tell.   An hour, three hours?   They hadn't the slightest idea.   But it was dawn when Finley finally gave up and told Judge Dorkin to trudge up the hill to the nearest phone and notify the police.

. When Decker got the call from headquarters, he tumbled out of bed and drove to the scene.   He saw the two women briefly, then got the basic facts from Judge Dorkin and Dr. Finley.   Frank London had presumably been there.   The clock had always kept accurate time.   Decker didn't touch it.   Jub Freeman would dust it for fingerprints and examine it and the cord for any possible physical evidence, no matter how minute.   The hands pointed to nine o'clock.

Decker had four homicide men at the scene before he and Mitch Taylor left to pick up London.   London was the obvious suspect and Decker woke him up, heard him mutter sleepily that he'd rehearsed with Jodie and left her around seven, maybe a little earlier, that she'd failed to show up at the Red Grotto, and so he'd gone on alone, and what the hell was this all about?

Decker told him and hauled him off to headquarters.   Decker's grilling was expert.   London was reticent about details and insolent in his general behavior, but Decker thought he had a pretty good case.   London had stabbed her, then set the hands of the clock to indicate nine, and figured he had a pretty good alibi.

He spent the day in jail while Decker gradually learned how a man can come to hate a clock.

His first theory—that London had set the clock after the stabbing—ran into immediate difficulty.   The time-set button was jammed and bent, and couldn't be moved.   Decker decided it was jammed because, when the clock fell, the button had hit the arm of a wicker chair.   Fragments of the wicker were wedged against the stem of the time-set, and there were clear marks on the chair to show where the clock had hit.

Microscopic examination made it seem highly unlikely that London had scraped off tiny bits of wicker and inserted them in such a way as to make the time-set inoperative. It was just one of those accidents. Therefore, London must have set the clock at nine *before* he committed the murder. That was Decker's first conclusion, in what he now thought of as his hours of innocence.

Medical evidence was consistent with placing the time of attack between seven and nine P.M. London had been there until almost seven, and everything in his background was against him. He'd been a juvenile delinquent in Chicago and had spent time in a reformatory. Later, he'd gone to New York and had become something of a Greenwich Village character. He sang and strummed in bars, drank too much, got into fights. He'd been arrested for assaulting a woman, but she'd refused to prosecute. There were rumors of other, similar incidents, although they hadn't got as far as a police blotter. He'd finally left New York, gone on tour, landed here, and met Jodie.

He was in love with her, according to everybody who knew the pair of them, but she would have no part of him. He'd made a few scenes at the Red Grotto, but she'd always managed to hold him off. To Decker, the picture of the murder was crystal-clear. Jodie and Frank London had been alone in that isolated river cottage. He'd tried to make love to her, she'd resisted, and he'd grabbed a kitchen knife and stabbed her in a violent rage.

So much for London. But granting him his nine o'clock alibi, it was reasonable to believe that a prowler had walked into the cottage after London had gone. The Homicide Squad combed the neighborhood for evidence of a stranger who might have assaulted and killed Jodie. No trace of an intruder had been found.

Which brought everything back to the clock.

It was an old battered clock, hexagonal in shape, and the numbers on the dial were indistinct. Nevertheless they were there, and the clock had stopped at nine. Decker bought two similar clocks and offered five bucks to any of his squad who could figure out how London could have jammed the time-set button in exactly the way it had been found. Nobody collected the five bucks.

It was a noisy clock, and the judge told him the family used to joke about it, referring to its death rattle. But it kept good time and they were sentimental about it, so they never replaced it.

"The electricity might have been cut off," the judge said.

"It wasn't," Decker said. "We checked that, for the last month. And we checked your fuse box. If it was keeping accurate time earlier in the afternoon, when you were still here, we have to assume it remained accurate."

The judge frowned. "I can't say that I really noticed."

But his wife had. "It was not only keeping time," Hannah Dorkin said quietly, "but the week before it had stopped making noises. I'm sensitive to sound, and I missed hearing the funny little rattle it always made. I mentioned it to Jodie, and she said she'd fix it, and she did."

"How?"

"She didn't tell me. We were making sandwiches and she was slicing some ham and she cut her finger. She went for a Band-Aid and we never finished the conversation."

Decker was still clinging to the idea that London had set the clock ahead to nine, and then murdered Jodie. Finally Dr. Finley scotched that theory.

"You couldn't set it," he said. "I tried to do something about the noise a few months ago, and I dropped it and bent that time-set button. Couldn't even turn it with a pair of pliers. But you couldn't hurt that clock. I checked it by my watch on Saturday, before we went out on the boat, and the clock was accurate."

The judge was philosophic in his point of view. "Lieutenant," he said, "we've both seen a lot of murders. The unbalanced man, the psychopathic killer without a motive—sometimes he commits a crime and isn't seen. Years later he's caught for something else and he confesses, and you just marvel at his luck, at the string of coincidences that made his escape possible."

"Not this time," Decker said. "London killed her."

"What does the D.A. say?" the judge asked.

"That he won't indict London until I can place him at the cottage at nine. And at nine—well—"

Decker turned away. At nine o'clock Frank London had been strumming a guitar at the Red Grotto and making public lament for Jodie Dorkin. He'd known she was dead, he'd practically advertised it. Therefore she'd been killed around seven—except that an unimpeachable clock said no.

Decker had traced Jodie's movements in detail; he had looked for a jealous suitor, for some clue that would provide a name, another person to question. Decker drew a total blank.

On Friday, the day before her death, Jodie had had an all-day swimming party at the boathouse. About a dozen teenagers had come in the morning and stayed until after dark, but most of them hadn't even been in the cottage. Around 6:30, however, two or three of them had gone there with Jodie to get food from the refrigerator; but they hadn't even noticed the clock.

Nothing unusual had happened. Nobody had got drunk. There were no fights, no incidents. Decker obtained a list of everybody who'd been at the party and checked out their whereabouts on Saturday. They could all account for themselves, and so it came back to London. Every time it came back to Frank London.

What, then, had gone wrong? Where had Decker slipped up?

Grunting, he yanked open the drawer of his desk. His favorite pencil, his personal diary. There on the bookcase, the small stuffed crocodile that brought him luck—or used to. He wondered whether to take it home with him, or to leave it here for his successor.

Fifteen years as head of the Homicide Squad, and what would he leave behind? What was personal to him in this tiny cubicle of an office that had held so much drama, had seen so many killers break down, confess, and walk out the door to their inevitable fate?

He sighed morosely. Tonight, London was setting up a celebration. He'd get drunk and shoot off his mouth about how he'd put one over on the police. Maybe Decker ought to go to that party, after all. Maybe London would give himself away.

Decker stepped outside and told the receptionist he was leaving for the day. In the corridor, he thought of going upstairs to the lab.   Jub Freeman was working on that robbery case.   The clock would be over in the corner, on the workbench near the window; but if Decker set eyes on the thing now, he was liable to smash it to pieces.

He went out to the parking lot, got in his car, and drove home.

Martha seemed to know.   She'd suffered these many years through all his moods, all his triumphs and despondencies, all the tough cases that woke him up in the middle of the night and sent him down to his desk in the small book-lined den, where he might scrawl out an idea, put together some outlandish logic, or connect two bits of apparently unrelated evidence that finally solved the unsolvable.

Tonight, she seemed to understand.   She was tender, quiet; she talked of small things in a low, comforting voice, while he sat on the couch and sipped at a double scotch.   After dinner he stalked out, got in his car, and went driving.

Anywhere.   Out to the river cottage.   Past the Red Grotto.   It didn't matter where.   He just wanted to be moving, to get away from himself and his problem.

He had a dozen bright ideas to explain how, although London had stabbed Jodie around seven, the clock had stopped at nine.   Maybe it had still been going after she'd been stabbed.   Maybe London had removed the glass over the dial of the clock after stabbing her, pushed the hands to nine, and then replaced the glass.

Decker swore.   He was kidding himself with wild theories that no jury would take seriously.   What he needed was a simple, down-to-earth explanation that would undermine the evidence of the clock and blast the cockiness out of London. He'd confess then.   No doubt about it.   Lieutenant Decker knew the type—he could handle guys like London.

Still driving aimlessly, Decker found himself rolling past headquarters.   There was a light on in the lab—Jub Freeman was apparently working late.   On impulse Decker swung through the arched entrance of the building and parked in his regular spot in the courtyard.   He got out of the car, strode through the lobby where a sergeant was seated at the long high desk, and went upstairs.

Jub, a stocky, cheerful, round-cheeked guy, dimpled up in a smile as he greeted Decker.   "Just checking up on a soil precipitation test that I started this afternoon," he said, putting down a test tube.   "Anything on your mind?"

"I got no mind," Decker said.   "When I give up on a jerk like London, I'm a nitwit.   No brains.   Low I.Q.   Been lucky up to now, but I got found out."

Jub corked the test tube carefully and placed it in a rack.   "He'll give himself away, some time.   He'll get drunk.   He'll brag about it to some dame.   Just wait, Lieutenant.   You'll get him."

"I can't wait.   You know what the papers are going to say tomorrow, don't you?   Then the Commissioner will have a little talk with me and—"   Decker shrugged despondently, noticed the Dorkin clock lying on a workbench near the window, and stalked over to it.

"Who the hell left it at nine o'clock?" he demanded bitterly.   "Somebody needling me?"   He plugged the cord in, then picked up the clock.

Jub said, "You've been working too hard.   Go away for a few days.   Rest up. Things will blow over."

Decker whirled, twisting his body. "Jub, don't try to—" He broke off, aware that the clock had started making its distinctive rattling.

As the six-sided clock now lay in Decker's hand, it was tilted sixty degrees, one side to the left—that is, counterclockwise. The numbers on the dial were faded and barely legible. If you told time simply by the position of the hands, they now indicated about ten minutes to seven.

The Lieutenant gasped. He shifted the clock back one side, clockwise. The dial now read nine o'clock. The barely visible numeral six was now at the base, and the rattling sound had stopped.

"So *that's* how Jodie 'fixed' it," Decker said in a low, somewhat awed voice. "She just turned it one side to the left. Look, Jub. Stand it up the way it's supposed to be, with six at the bottom, and it doesn't make any noise. But if you do this—"

He shifted it to the next left of the six flat sides, with the barely discernible numeral eight at the base. The noise started, and the dial now seemed to show ten minutes to seven. "And nobody noticed that she left the clock *standing on the wrong side*. After all, lots of clocks don't even have numerals and people tell time easily enough."

Jub nodded. "She must have done it on Friday, when she was there all day. Then on Saturday, after he stabbed her and looked down and saw the clock, London realized what a terrific break had been handed to him. Standing in the correct position, with six at the base, the clock showed the wrong time—not ten minutes to seven when he stabbed her, but nine o'clock—time enough for London to give himself an alibi!"

Decker, wonderment still on his face, patted the clock and broke into a broad grin. "Until now—but now we've got him," he said, "got him cold!"

URSULA CURTISS

The Pool Sharks

They came knocking at the door just as she was getting ready to leave for the hospital: two dark-eyed, dark-haired children she hadn't seen before in the month of living in the new house.

"Can we go swimming?" It was the boy, perhaps ten or eleven, holding his younger sister's hand with a firmness that suggested a frequent guardianship. Their fringed and upturned glances were hopeful but wary, in case of a rebuff, and Sarah smiled at them in spite of her own distraction.

"Well, not today, I'm afraid." She was careful not to explain that there wouldn't be anyone here for the next few hours, because the temperature was in the mid-nineties and with the confidence of childhood they wouldn't worry in the least about swimming unattended; it would strike them as much more fun. "Where do you live?"

The two round dark heads nodded obliquely across the field, which meant around the corner. What with the bulldozer and the cement mixer and then the various pickups with the company's name on the side, they had probably known to the minute when the swimming pool was completed and filled. (Tom had said, yesterday, "We'll probably have to establish some kind of rules, with the only private pool in the neighborhood, but let's face that when we come to it.")

Sarah suggested eleven o'clock the next morning, waited for a cautious few minutes after they were out of sight, then forgot them as soon as she was in the car.

It was only the second time she would be visiting her husband in the hospital. The first had been before dawn, when after what seemed like hours in the waiting room she had been allowed to go up to the fifth floor. She knew by that time that Tom's terrifying middle-of-the-night collapse had been caused by a bleeding ulcer, but she was still unprepared for his total pallor and the visible effort it cost him to open his eyes and smile faintly at her. It was clear that at this point her presence would do more harm than good, so she kissed him, drawing a black look from the nurse whose possession he now was, and said simply, "I'll be back."

In the corridor, following her out, the doctor was blunt. "It's a good thing you got him in here when you did, Mrs. Birchall. He's going to need another transfusion, and I want someone to have a look at his heart. Better wait until two or three o'clock this afternoon before you come in."

Meticulously, Sarah had split the difference; it was 2:30 when she left the elevator on the fifth floor of the hospital, followed the room-indicator arrow to 523, and felt an actual slam in her chest at the white-stubbled, scooped-out face that turned wearily on its pillow as she entered.   But—of course—this was a semi-private room and Tom's bed was the far one; she hadn't registered that fact in the small-hours panic.

She rounded the dividing curtain, and a lesser shock awaited her.   Tom wasn't sitting up as she had somehow expected but was lying flat and vulnerable, and although the dark suspended bottle was gone he was still very pale and his hand, when she took it and held it hard as she bent to kiss him, was cold.

She said, fast, "Tom, you look so much better.   I've brought"—she produced the small suitcase—"your robe and slippers and pajamas and things."   Her eyes were beginning to fill, and she turned briefly away as though a nurse had started into the room.   "And some stupid damn cherries and books.   How do you feel?"

"Better.   Really, better," said Tom, speaking in the light and careful way in which a man with a murderous headache might talk.   "This is an awful nuisance for you, driving all the way in."   He closed his eyes and opened them again.   "Did you have a swim?   Christen the pool?"   This time his smile was less effortful.   "Better hurry up."

Sarah was three and a half months' pregnant, although she had tried on her bathing suit the day before and no one would have guessed it.   "Not yet, I'm waiting for you.   As a matter of fact, though—"

She realized belatedly, with a kind of buried shock, that she could not present Tom with even the tiniest concern right now; she could not say that neighborhood children had already asked to swim in the pool which did not yet have its protective fence; could not inquire if they were insured against the kind of accident that might happen even if she were on the scene.

Depleted though he was, Tom was gazing at her and waiting for her to finish the sentence.

"—I imagine the water is fairly nippy, coming straight from the well," said Sarah, "and I wouldn't mind giving it a few days under the sun first.   When does the doctor think you can come home?"

Tom hadn't seen his own doctor yet, although three different ones had gone into a huddle over his electrocardiogram.   He thought he would have some kind of word around seven o'clock, when the doctor apparently made his rounds.   He said, "Don't drive all the way back in tonight, Sarah," and nodded at the telephone beside his bed.   "I can call you."

"So you can," said Sarah, and they both understood that she would be back there that evening.

Louis and Marisol—the girl's name was new and delightful to Sarah—arrived promptly at five minutes of eleven the next morning.   Sarah was ready for them, bathing-suited in case she had to jump in, giving them, briskly, a few elementary safety precautions.   They were not to run on the deck, or push each other into the pool. Although the water was nine feet at the deep end, they were to be careful diving and each to make sure that the other was visibly well out of the way.

She supposed as she spoke that she had the kind of unheard drone of their own mother, or teacher, but without Tom she felt a sharp concern in this particular situation.

They could swim; she made sure of that before she left the pool's edge for a basket chair under the trees where she could watch them while pretending to read. Louis had a sturdy windmilling stroke, Marisol, who had all the breath of a mosquito in her tiny two-piece suit, was less splashy and quietly determined.

Sarah gazed at them in a detached way; she had something new to think about.

Tom had had a wildly uneven heartbeat on admittance to the emergency room, and although the electrocardiogram had shown no sign of damage, the doctors were not quite satisfied and were attaching a monitor. Even in the event of the favorable outcome they cautiously expected, it would be at least a week before he could be discharged from the hospital. In the meantime he mustn't be worried in any way, but of course Mrs. Birchall would appreciate that.

. . . After an hour, with a little shrill dissension toward the end of it, Louis and Marisol climbed out of the pool, toweled themselves dry, bundled their belongings expertly onto their bicycles, and departed. Sarah only realized after she had said "Goodbye" that they hadn't been going to say anything at all. Swim, wrap-up, finish—as though it were a municipal pool. Oh, well, they were only children and maybe—cover-all excuse—they were shy.

They weren't shy. Sarah was making herself a glass of iced coffee late the next morning, as the most palatable way to drink the milk the doctor had ordered, when Louis and Marisol rounded the corner of the house. This time they were accompanied by two older boys, fourteen or fifteen, who stared appraisingly about them as they sauntered over the grass. One of them caught Sarah's eye through the kitchen window, appraised her as well, and kept on going.

She felt a quick, surprisingly sharp flash of anger. She had intended a pre-lunch swim—Tom had said last night, "Promise me you will. It's the least you can do for yourself with the heat and all your driving"—but that wasn't it. It was a feeling of being used, and used with a certain amount of mockery which said, "You're rich. You'd better fall over backwards about sharing your pool."

They weren't rich. They had only been able to buy this place because it was in need of so much basic repair, and more sensible people would have applied Tom's inheritance from an uncle to a lifetime roof for the house, a new heating system, and a remodeling of the smaller bathroom. Tom and Sarah had thought it all over and decided on a temporary roof job, sweaters and a little shivering for the first winter, guests who wouldn't mind the bath as it was—and a swimming pool.

She put down her glass of iced coffee, her heart beating quite hard and fast, and went outside. It was hot, she reminded herself, and after all what was there for these kids to do, miles outside the city in the tail-end of the summer when simply not being at school was no longer enough?

Louis and Marisol and one of the older boys were already in the water.   Sarah registered the fact that the other boy was not wearing swimming trunks but a pair of jeans which did not look particularly clean.   Sarah thought conscientiously: Maybe they can't afford—and the boy removed a wrist watch which had cost far more than a bathing suit, threw her a casual grin, and jumped feet first into the pool.

Sarah walked down the deck to where Marisol, who was infinitesimally more responsive than Louis, was sitting on a step.   Sarah said pleasantly, "Are these your brothers, Marisol?"

For some reason this was very funny.   Laughter erupted from the pool, accompanied by sidelong dark glances, flashing teeth, flung-back wet hair.   It crossed Sarah's mind that, hair or not, they looked a little like dangerous fish. *Stay friendly.* In five or six days Tom would be home, and he would know how to handle this.   She managed to keep the careful balance in her voice.   "Then introduce me, will you, please?   My husband's coming home for a swim at noon and he'll want to know who our visitors are."

The two pointed faces stared up from the blue water as if they knew no English at all, or they did but considered their names to be none of Sarah's business.   "He's Frank," volunteered Marisol, pointing, "and he's Jimmy."

Something decided Sarah not to press the matter further.   These new arrivals were also able to swim, so she went back into the house and stayed within earshot. It wasn't difficult; Louis and Marisol were far more boisterous in the company of their older friends, and the pool rang with shouts and huge splashes and simulated screams.   If they had been more likable boys Sarah would have gone out and said, "Would you try to be a little quieter, so I won't think someone's drowning?"   As it was, she bore the assault on her nerves until one of her frequent glances out the bedroom window showed her what was now going on.

They were all milling around the deep end of the pool while the older boys— Sarah had a reluctance to use their names even in her own mind, as if that implied a tenuous friendship or at least acceptance—cannonballed into the water, scrambling up the ladder again with an assembly-line effect.   With a vision of one of them landing on spindly little Marisol, she went rapidly outside and said firmly after two attempts to make herself heard, "Don't do that, please.   It could be quite dangerous."

There was a peculiar pause, indicating that she might or might not be obeyed. Louis and Marisol clung to the edge and gazed expectantly up at their friends, one of whom had been poised for another knees-tucked leap.   It was a matter of face. But that was saved by a shrug, a brief and indistinguishable mutter, an impish— smile?   No, a grimace—and then the boy's exaggerated daintiness as he sat down on the deck and lowered himself into the water.   Laughter all around.

And all wrong, thought Sarah dismally, retreating to the house again because to sit in the basket chair and watch them openly would be to pose a challenge which they might very well meet.   She had grown up with sisters; she didn't know how to treat boys.

Boys, or premature men?

She kept her occasional vigil, folding laundry on the bed—would they never go home?—and presently saw the jeaned one scramble out of the pool, consult his watch, gaze curiously at the house, and jump back in again.   She glanced at the bedside clock.   It was 12:20, and she had said her husband was coming home at noon to swim, and they were going to wait until he did.

Instantly, furiously, she got into her suit and a terry robe, caught up her bathing cap, and went outside.   She said with a steady smile, "Sorry, but it's time for my swim."

They all got out at once, and it was absurd to think that was mockery too, as though she had been an overseer appearing with a whip.   The pool thermometer had been wrenched from its nylon tie around the ladder's hand-rail and lay on the bottom near the drain.   It wasn't an earth-shaking matter, but the fact that they hadn't even bothered to dive for it was enough to make Sarah say casually, "By the way, no swimming tomorrow.   We're superchlorinating the pool."

We, evidence of strength.   And a mistake, as the first of a long line of excuses. ("We're expecting guests to swim all day.   My husband has a terrible case of impetigo.   We're keeping a school of piranhas for friends.")

They departed in silence, not pleased.   Sarah put on her cap, took off her robe, gazed at the water with its shifting pattern of gold, remembered the slippery, glistening jeans.   She did not swim.

Neither did she ask Tom's advice when she went to the hospital that night.   The monitor had shown nothing that couldn't be handled by medication, but although his color was better Tom was in a state of deep depression.   "Diet," he said. "Pills.   The baby will think I'm its grandfather."

Sarah suspected that wasn't quite all.   The other bed was flat and starchily immaculate: had that frail exhausted-looking old man really been judged fit to go home?   It was a case of cheering up rather than confiding any worries of her own, and when Tom finally roused himself to say, "Did you swim?" Sarah answered without hesitation, "Yes.   It was marvelous."

"How many lengths?"

It was a forty-foot pool.   "Ten," said Sarah, and Tom looked pleased and then said anxiously, "Don't overdo it, now.   What's the temperature?"

"Seventy-two," said Sarah, guessing, "and I won't overdo it, I promise."

The next day, after running the filter for four hours, she did swim, and the pool was all they had hoped for.   She recovered the thermometer from the bottom and re-tied it, and it must have been injured because it read only 68 degrees and the water was warmer than that.   Polished green leaves turned gently above her; she moved through an ice-blue taffeta rustle.   With a dim notion of undoing her lie to Tom she swam 20 lengths and then did some pleasurable dawdling.   It was a surprise to realize that she had better make the most of this, because tomorrow—

They came in force, Louis and Marisol, the two older boys, and two girls. Although the girls didn't look over 15, one of them was cradling an infant of two or three months.   Sarah's stomach muscles tightened involuntarily, because they had also brought beer and this was something she would have to put a stop to right away—Oh, God, if only Tom were home!

She went outside, her smile feeling varnished on, her heart thudding.   She was completely taken aback when the girl without the baby said courteously, "Mrs. Birchall, I'm Karen Sales, and I think you're awfully kind to let us swim.   Or are we interrupting?   Say the word and we'll take right off."

The practised air did not register at once, and Sarah heard herself answering that she could swim later.   Before she could mention the beer, the girl went on in a confidential tone, "Would you mind a little music, if we kept it down?   Tina"— she nodded at her encumbered friend—"has had sort of a rough time, and music soothes her."

Sarah swallowed.   "Oh, is that her own baby?"

"Well, hers and Jimmy's," said the girl.

Jimmy, whom Sarah had thought to be about fourteen and could be sixteen at the most—thin, dark, stringy-muscled.   She glanced about her, and there was a delicately nightmare quality in the sunlight; the baby, the beer being zipped open by people who, technically, were scarcely more than children.   And none of them invited.   She thought that no matter what Tom's condition was when she saw him this afternoon she would have to say, "What should I do?"

The instinctive answer wasn't necessarily the best.   Order them off—and have slashed tires and broken windows?   How could she even implement such an order? The boys were as tall as she was and undoubtedly stronger; the girls, busily making themselves comfortable, had an adamant air.   Even a casual day-by-day survey would have told them that she was alone here although she had been careful not to tell them so.

If she ordered them to go and they refused, or simply pretended not to hear, she would be infinitely worse off than now.

Wait it out, she told herself, this one last time.   Feeling, in her own backyard, as if she had invaded their territory and was being driven off, Sarah went back into the house.

Presently there was the sound of a car in the driveway.   More beer arrived, this time in bottles, borne by boys who appeared to be about eighteen.   Hard-rock music began to swell, not from a transistor but, when Sarah went transfixedly to the back door, a stereo hooked up to the outside light socket, from which they had removed the bulb.   The baby, presumably asleep, had been placed on a towel on the deck under the full burning force of the sun.

Sarah was fiercely glad, because it took this to strengthen her legs and give her no pause for further thought.   She ran outside, hearing a beer bottle shatter on the way, catching no particular eye but calling out imperatively, "Marisol, Louis—all of you!   I'm sorry, but we can't have this.   Leave, please, this minute."

A tremble caught her, late; she tried to conceal it by lifting her head militantly. A voice, she didn't know whose, shouted above the blaring music, "That's right, her old man's coming home for a swim."

Laughter, and then: "Who's she?"

"Chick that owns the house, man.   I vote we get out."

"Oh, right." Something thoughtful about it. "Don't want to bother the lady, it's her pool."

There was a scramble of tanned legs, and the afternoon had gone dangerously wrong: Louis and Marisol had pelted away without even taking their towels. Sarah couldn't identify the arm that pushed her—she hadn't even known that one of them was behind her. The water rushed up to meet her and then she was in the pool, clumsily, without a chance to dive, even her light clothing dragging at her. She kicked off her sandals at once, but shock and the naked fear she hadn't admitted to herself interfered with her breathing, and when she surfaced she was coughing and gasping.

And they were gazing down at her as if she were going to perform some interesting aquatic feat. Not children any more, but precocious young adults who had turned casually vicious at the end of a long hot summer because she, a newcomer at that, had something they did not. And now the power was reversed. Frank, or Jimmy, lifted the record player from the edge of the pool and poised it over his head. He said, "Gonna get a shock, Mrs. Birchall."

But that couldn't kill her—or could it? Sarah screamed, "Don't! I'm—" and found that even in this extremity she could not tell these savages that she was going to have a baby; it might act as a spur. From awe or a touch of fright, the girls had assumed expressions of—excitement?

Sarah swam toward the ladder, didn't dare grip the metal rails, swam away again. The record player seemed to blot out the sky. Then Karen who had spoken so politely had positioned herself at the pool steps. Spite hissed on the air like an invisible wind.

Sarah, who had swum twenty lengths without effort the day before, was already out of breath in this pinioned position—and nobody would come; nobody. They could play games with her as long as it entertained them, except that it wasn't a game any longer. Their control had left them the instant she hit the water.

In her terror her ears had begun to fill with a roaring—but it wasn't a distortion of her senses. Boy and record player were sent sprawling to the ground by the iron hand of huge, mustached Mr. Sandoval, who serviced the pool and carried fifty-pound bags of salt on one shoulder as though they were feathers.

The single roar—produced when he had been drawn to the pool by the sight of those intent and motionless backs—had been enough. Except for Sarah, Mr. Sandoval, and the abandoned record player, the back yard was empty.

Mr. Sandoval helped her out of the pool, keeping his look firmly at eye level because of her dripping, clinging dress. When he had asked her if she was all right, and she had nodded mutely because her mouth was trembling and she would cry if she tried to speak, he glanced down at the record player and said, "This yours? No?"—and gave it a demolishing kick.

He seemed to know intuitively that she had to be left alone for a few moments. He said cheerfully, "Better get on with my business here," and hefted the bag of salt he had dropped and vanished into the pump room with it.

Sarah stood motionless under the tree, gradually stopped shaking, then turned slowly to gaze at the pool. It was not contaminated *forever,* she thought fiercely;

that would have been the ultimate triumph.   They had gone, and she knew that with a witness, and such a witness as huge Mr. Sandoval, they would not come back.

She also knew that she would never tell Tom.

Mr. Sandoval backed his enormous frame out of the pump house, measured her, and judged her, by now, safe to address.   "Who were they?" he asked curiously.

The leaves turned gently overhead.   Had they swallowed those animal echoes forever?   "I don't really know," said Sarah.   "Just—kids."

JACK RITCHIE

Nobody Tells Me Anything

He was my first client.

"Mr. Turnbuckle," he said, "I'll pay you fifty dollars for each day's report. How does that strike you?"

It struck me as being a bit frugal, but possibly he was prepared to be generous with expenses. I voiced the thought. "Fifty dollars and expenses?"

"I don't forsee any expenses. Just fifty dollars for each day's report. Thirty reports."

I smiled tolerantly. "Fifty dollars a day for confidential investigation might have been a munificent sum twenty or thirty years ago, but by today's standards—"

He held up a hand. "It will not be necessary for you even to leave this office. Just sit down at your typewriter, insert the stationery of your agency, and type the reports, one after another until you are finished. Thirty reports to cover thirty days."

I glanced down at my notes, which consisted of just two words: Paula Smith. "You mean you *don't* want me to find this Paula Smith?"

"Exactly. I want you to do no searching at all. However, fill out your reports as though you had been exceedingly busy. Use your imagination. Trace her across the country—on paper—and finally lose her in, say, San Francisco or Seattle. Make it appear that you are sending your reports back here, where a secretary transcribes them, and forwards them to me."

I considered that. "Wouldn't it be cheaper if you had a few letterheads printed and then filled in the reports yourself?"

"I suppose so. But it would be quite a bother, and besides, I simply don't know the forms used, the methods of search, and the jargon or whatsoever used by private detective agencies, and I want these reports to appear as authentic as possible. I will also need thirty envelopes with your agency imprint."

I nodded to myself. He's going to mail the reports to himself—one at a time— and when they arrive, he intends to show them to one or more other people.

My client was a tall distinguished man in his fifties, graying at the temples, exceedingly well-dressed, and he had refused to tell me his name.

I consulted my sheet of paper again. "Is Paula Smith her real name?"

"Just fill out the reports."

"To whom shall I address the reports?"

"Leave that part blank.   I'll fill it in later myself."

I sighed.   "Just to recapitulate, we have a missing person, one Paula Smith. You do *not* want me to find her.   But she *is* missing, isn't she?   Have you gone to the police perhaps?"

He regarded me for a few seconds.   "Paula Smith is quite well and, I presume, happy.   You need to know no more than that.   How long will it take you to compile those reports?"

"Probably a week.   I'll have to do some research at the library—things like the names of streets, hotels, restaurants, and the like in various cities.   Where was Paula Smith last seen?"

"Why do you need to know that?"

"If she were last seen in the Sahara, I can hardly begin my report by taking up the trail at the North Pole."

He nodded reluctantly.   "Begin your report with the statement that you located the taxi which took her and her luggage from 'your residence' to the airport or the bus station.   You do not specifically need to know my address."

"What was the date and time she was last seen, and by whom?"

"You do not need to know by whom.   But she was last seen Sunday at approximately ten o'clock in the evening when she went up to her rooms.   Do you suppose I could have the first report by noon today?   I'd like to get on this as soon as possible before somebody else—"   He stopped and reached for his wallet. It was a fine piece of leather with the initials A.B. in one corner.   He handed me two twenties and a ten.

I took the bills.   "How did you happen to select my agency?"

"I walked through the yellow pages of the phone book and there you were." He went to the door.   "If you have any idea of following me, forget it.   I intend to take all due precautions."

When he was gone, I proceeded to think.

What did I have here?

I was being asked to fill out a series of false reports.   Why?   Obviously to fool someone—to make some person or persons think that this Paula Smith was indeed being searched for, though my client did not have the slightest desire in the world that she be found.

And what about the name Paula Smith itself?

Was the name fictitious?   Or did such a person really exist?

I reached for the telephone book and turned to the Smiths.   There were legions of them, of course.   Several Peter Smiths, but no Paulas or even P. Smiths.

And what about my caller, A.B.?

For one thing, he had said that he had walked through the yellow pages until he found my name and address.

But that was hardly possible since the name of my agency was not yet listed in the book.   I had just opened my office three weeks ago.   My name would appear in the next issue of the phone book which was not due for distribution for another two months.

Then why and how had he chosen me?

If not by means of the telephone book, had he simply wandered the corridors of downtown buildings until he saw the lettering on my door? Hardly likely. I am on the eighth floor of a twenty-six-story building and there are at least a hundred tall buildings in this city.

Or was it possible that he actually worked in this very building and that during the last three weeks while waiting for the elevator to take him up to his floor he had noticed my agency's name on the directory on the wall? And had it been filed in his memory bank until, when he needed the services of a private detective, it had suddenly leaped to his mind?

I rubbed my neck. Should I restrain my curiosity, mind my own business, and collect the $1500 as per order? Is that what an experienced private detective would do?

My phone rang. It was Ralph. He is a detective sergeant on the police force and I was his partner until three weeks ago.

"How are you doing, Henry?" he asked.

"I just got my first case."

"Congratulations. My wife and I were a little worried. I mean it's been almost a month since you opened your office."

I cleared my throat. "I just realized that most people consult the yellow pages of the phone book when they want to hire a private detective and I won't be in the book for another two months when the new edition comes out."

"You picked the wrong time of the year to open for business. Why not advertise in the newspapers?"

"I'm not sure that's professionally ethical."

"Henry, I wouldn't worry about ethical as far as the private detective scene is concerned. What's your first case about?"

"A missing person. Paula Smith."

"Smith? Well, I suppose the Smiths get lost now and then too. My wife's wondering if she should bring over some chicken soup or something?"

"No, Ralph. I'm doing just fine."

After he hung up, I went downstairs to the lobby and studied the directory next to the bank of elevators.

I found twelve companies and individuals listed under B. Albert Bancroft, Investments, seemed to be what I was looking for.

I went to the nearby public phone and turned the white pages of the book to the Bancrofts. I found only one Albert Bancroft listed.

I glanced at my watch. It was nearly ten in the morning. Where was Bancroft at this moment? Probably upstairs in his office poring over municipal bonds or something equally exciting.

I checked his address and phone number and then dialed.

The phone was picked up by a man who said, "Bancroft residence."

"Could I speak to Paula?"

There was a pause. "Paula?"

"Yes. Paula Smith."

Another pause. "I'm sorry, sir, but she is no longer in our employ."

Ah, so there really *was* a Paula Smith. And whom was I talking to? He had used the words "Bancroft residence," and had called me "sir." Was he the butler? After all, people who listed their trade as Investments and lived in Bancroft's neighborhood probably could afford to hire butlers. "Is this Jarvis?" I asked.

"No, sir. This is Wisniewski."

"Wisniewski?" I laughed lightly. "Jarvis. Wisniewski. I always seem to get those two names mixed. But you *are* the Bancroft butler, aren't you?"

"Yes, sir."

"Of course," I said. "Paula wrote to me about you."

"Miss Smith wrote to you about *me?*" He seemed cautious. "What did she say?"

"I don't remember the exact words, but they were nothing but good."

"Who is this speaking, sir?"

"John Smith. Paula's cousin, twice removed."

"I understood that she had no living relatives."

I chuckled. "I don't blame Paula for not mentioning me. But I'm on parole now. Did she leave a forwarding address?"

"No, sir."

"You mean she just disappeared into thin air?"

"Not exactly into thin air, sir. She just packed up during the night and left. I understand there was a note, sir, but it did not mention where she was going."

What had Paula's job been at the Bancroft's? Cook? I chuckled again and quoted H. H. Munro, better known as "Saki": "She was a good cook, as cooks go. And as good cooks go, she went?"

"Sir?" Wisniewski said.

I had evidently missed the mark. "The *last* place Paula worked, she was a cook," I said. "I just assumed—?"

"She was the housekeeper here, sir."

Housekeeper? What did housekeepers do? Oh, yes. They supervised the other servants, kept the household accounts, and generally feuded with the butler.

When I hung up, I pondered a few moments, then decided that further investigation at the scene was in order.

I left the phone booth for the multi-level garage where I park my car and drove to 217 Lake Crest Drive.

The entrance to 217 Lake Crest Drive was flanked by fifteen-foot stone pillars. The gates were open, but I had the feeling that a door-to-door salesman would hesitate before considering that an invitation to enter.

I turned into the driveway and followed it through the shade of elms and other greenery until I reached a large Tudor-style structure.

I parked, ascended the wide stairs, and used the knocker. While I waited, I watched an ancient gardener trimming a hedge.

To circumvent the possibility that Wisniewski might recognize my voice, I had intended to speak in a Scots burr, which I perfected while playing the part of

Macbeth in my senior year in high school, but a uniformed maid answered the door instead.   "Yes, sir?"

Where was Wisniewski?   Probably in the pantry polishing the silver or in the cellar turning wine bottles.

"Could I speak to Mr. Bancroft?"

"He is not at home, sir."

"Mrs. Bancroft?"

"I'm afraid not, sir.   She died three years ago."

That certainly eliminated her.   "Are there any other Bancrofts on the premises?"

"There is Miss Bancroft, sir.   Mr. Bancroft's daughter."

"She will do nicely."

"Who shall I say is calling, sir?"

"John P. Jones.   Attorney."

She left me there, but returned a minute later and led me to one of the drawing rooms.

Miss Bancroft appeared to be in her early twenties, wore shell-rimmed glasses, and had possibly been reading the open book on the cocktail table.

"I'm Marianne Bancroft," she said.   "What can I do for you?"

"I understand that you have in your employ one Miss Paula Smith?   Could I speak to her?"

"Paula?"   Marianne Bancroft shook her head.   "Paula is gone.   She left sometime before Monday morning when we were all asleep.   Bag and baggage. There was a note, but it didn't say where she was going."

"Did it say *why* she left?"

"She said she was just fed up here and had decided to move on.   Why do you want to find her?"

"Her uncle Theophilus Smith died and left her some money."

"Was it a lot?"

"Not really.   About a thousand.   I know very little about Paula Smith besides her name.   How old was she?"

"About forty.   But she looked younger when she tried."

"How long was she the housekeeper here?"

"Less than a year."

I noticed a framed photograph of three people on the corner shelf.   One of them was my client, Albert Bancroft, another Marianne, and the third probably Bancroft's son, a younger, thinner, and taller version of his father.

"Did anyone see Paula leave?" I asked.

"If they did, no one's said so."

I assumed a thoughtful pose.   "You don't suppose I could have a look at her room just on the off chance that there might be some indication of where she was going?   Perhaps some scrap of paper or some underlined portion of a bus schedule?"

She led me up to the third floor.   "You look familiar.   I could swear that I've seen you somewhere before."   She opened the door to Paula Smith's suite.   "Sitting room, bedroom, bathroom."

I opened the sliding doors to a large closet.   It was completely bare except for a few wire hangers, but the scent of perfume and powder still lingered.   "I always think of housekeepers as wearing uniforms.   With maybe a dress or two for going out?"

"Housekeepers don't wear uniforms anymore.   At least I can't think of any who do.   Paula probably had that closet full of clothes.   I know she was always sending things to the cleaners or getting them back.   Are you going to scour the ends of the earth until you find her?"

"Not for one thousand dollars.   We'll just put it in escrow and hope that someday she'll get in touch with somebody who'll tell her about us.   You don't happen to have a photograph of her?"

"No."

"What did she look like?"

Marianne shrugged.   "Quite tall and—well-developed.   Blonde."

"There isn't any shortage or anything of that nature in her household accounts?"

"Nobody's checked yet, but I doubt it.   I'm willing to bet that her books are in perfect order.   She was after bigger—"   She stopped.   "Are you sure you're not some kind of detective?"

I smiled.   "Well, there *is* quite a bit of detecting involved in tracing heirs." I moved to a door on the further wall of the bedroom and opened what appeared to be another closet or storage area.   A large steamer trunk stood upright but open. It appeared to be almost fully packed with dresses, skirts, and coats.

"Paula's?" I asked.

Marianne moved closer.   "It appears to be.   I recognize some of the clothes."

"Why would she leave this behind?"

"I don't know.   Maybe she intended to send someone back for it."

"But wouldn't she at least *close* the trunk and probably lock it before she left?"

"Perhaps she just decided that it was all too much to take along with her."

"It all looks like fairly good quality.   Would she abandon it?"

"Why not?" Marianne said a bit testily.   "She could always buy more.   She didn't leave here exactly empty—"   She stopped and smiled sweetly.   "Anything else?"

"Did Paula own an automobile?"

"No."

"Did she have any other luggage besides this trunk?"

"I seem to remember two suitcases when she came here."

"This note she left?   Do you mind if I see it?"

"It doesn't exist anymore.   I tossed it into the fireplace."

"Why?"

"Because I felt like it."

When I returned to my office, I phoned police headquarters and left a message for Ralph to call me when he next checked in.

Then I sat down at my typewriter and began composing my first report for Bancroft. At ten after eleven Ralph phoned.

"Ralph," I said, "I'd like you to find out if Paula Smith left a forwarding address at the post office and also if she had or has any savings or checking accounts in her own name. I'd do it myself, but you're on active duty and that opens doors and saves time.''

Ralph clicked his tongue. "Shame on you, Henry, using a public servant for private business. The post office will be easy, but the bank accounts won't—do you know how many banks there are in this town?''

"Try the branch banks in the Fiebrantz shopping center. It's only half a mile from the Bancroft place.''

"And what is the Bancroft place?''

"That's where Paula Smith worked until the night she disappeared.''

At noon, when Bancroft stepped into my office, I had two reports ready for him. "So far I trace her from your residence to a pizza parlor in Billings, Montana.''

He read and nodded. "These look fine.''

I offered him two envelopes. He put the second report into one of them, but not the first, from which I deduced that he intended to show the first report to someone immediately and did not want to wait out the time lag of mailing the report to himself.

He produced his wallet and handed me another $50 for the second report. "I'll drop in every day to pick up whatever reports you've finished.''

After he left, I paused to wonder again why he preferred to remain anonymous. Was he just embarrassed over the charade, or was he afraid that I might possibly attempt to blackmail him later. After all, he obviously had something to conceal and if I knew his identity I might find out what it was all about and attempt to profit from it.

Ralph phoned me in the afternoon. "The post office says that Paula Smith left no forwarding address. And according to the First National Branch at Fiebrantz, Paula Smith still has a checking account there. Balance $112.16. The bank's records show that she deposited her paycheck into the account each month and was usually overdrawn by the time the month was over.''

"Why would she leave $112.16 behind?''

"That isn't necessarily a final balance, Henry. There might be some checks outstanding. She could have closed the account for all practical purposes.''

"Ralph, when Paula left the Bancrofts' place she probably took along a couple of suitcases. She didn't own an automobile, so she must have taken a taxi.''

"I'll check on it. But maybe someone in the Bancroft house drove her to the airport or bus station or whatever.''

"If anybody did, he certainly hasn't volunteered the information.''

In the afternoon I dropped in at the main library for research that carried Paula from Billings to the Custer Battlefield National Monument and then on to the Cheyenne Frontier Days Rodeo.

That evening, at home in my apartment, I created and consumed my supper, and then sat down to TV, turning, as usual, to the educational channel. I was quietly engrossed in the history of barrel making when my door buzzer sounded.

I identified my caller immediately as Albert Bancroft's son. He looked even taller and thinner than his photograph.

He introduced himself. "My name is Jerome Bancroft. Are you the Turnbuckle of the Turnbuckle Detective Agency?"

I nodded.

He cleared his throat. "I understand that my father is employing your agency to search for Paula Smith? My father showed me your first report this evening and I memorized your letterhead." He stepped into the room. "I knew you wouldn't be in your office at this time of the night, of course, so I looked in the white pages of the telephone book. You are the only Turnbuckle listed."

I beamed proudly. "The Turnbuckle line is long but narrow. What can I do for you?"

He seemed uncomfortable. "Do you think your agency will find Paula?"

I shrugged. "One can only do one's best."

He took the chair I offered. "I don't know what father is paying you to search for Paula, but I'm willing to double it—if you do *not* find her."

I raised an eyebrow. Here was someone else who didn't want Paula Smith found and was willing to pay handsomely for it. "Why don't you want her found?"

"It's a personal reason. I really don't think it's necessary that you know."

I went to my TV set, which at the moment featured a cooper spoke-shaving some barrel staves, and turned it off. "I have the strangest suspicion about this case. Is Paula Smith still alive?"

He seemed surprised at the question. "Alive? Of course she's alive. I just don't want her to be found and persuaded to return."

"Do you know where she is now?"

"No."

"Why did she leave in the first place?"

Jerome Bancroft took half a minute to wrestle with a decision and then sighed. "I guess I might just as well give you the whole story. I *paid* Paula to leave. Twenty thousand dollars, to be exact. I felt that Paula had an undue influence on my father and that it was just a question of time before he asked her to marry him."

"You didn't think that Paula Smith was a suitable stepmother?"

"Frankly, no. As a matter of fact, she was considerably free with the amount of personal attention she paid to *me* too."

"You were attracted to her?"

"Actually she frightened me half to death."

"But still you were afraid that she might seduce you?"

"No. Frightened or not, I do have a mind of my own. I would have been able to resist her, regardless of temptation or perfume, both of which were considerable. But I was worried for Dad's sake. I don't know how strong he is in matters of this nature."

"Did the fact that Paula Smith, as your father's wife, would be in a position to claim a considerable share of your father's wealth disturb you?"

"Not particularly. Both Marianne, that's my sister, and I have quite enough money in our own right. Personally we both feel that Dad ought to remarry, but we can think of a number of more suitable candidates."

"So you offered Paula Smith twenty thousand dollars to leave the household?"

He frowned thoughtfully. "Now that I think it over, I'm not quite positive whether I offered or she *suggested* that I give her the money and she would leave. Anyway, I handed her twenty thousand in cash on Sunday afternoon. She promised that she would leave on Monday while Dad and I were at the office. She said she'd leave a note saying that she was just fed up with the job and had decided to get out. The note was so that Dad wouldn't think she'd been kidnaped or something and call the police."

"And she left the note?"

"Yes. On her bedroom dresser."

"But instead of leaving Monday she left sometime between ten P.M. Sunday, when she was last seen going up to her rooms, and seven A.M. Monday, when she was scheduled to report for duty, so to speak?"

"Yes. I don't know why though. Maybe she thought I'd think things over and demand the twenty thousand back. So she decided to skip while the skipping was good."

I debated whether to tell him that his father apparently had as little desire as he to have Paula Smith return, then I decided that this case needed a little more investigation first.

Jerome Bancroft brought out his checkbook. "How much would you like as a retainer?"

I pondered. What would your average private detective do? Take money for not doing a job for which he was already being paid for not doing? I'd have to think it over. "A retainer will not be necessary," I said. "I prefer to bill at the completion—or in this case, the noncompletion—of my job."

When he was gone, I turned on the TV set just in time to catch Winnebago Indians harvesting wild rice.

The next morning I completed several more reports tracing Paula Smith to Salt Lake City, where by finding a ticket stub in a room she had just vacated at the Excelsior Motel, I deduced that she had the night previous attended a concert of the Mormon Tabernacle Choir.

In the afternoon Ralph phoned.

"No taxi picked up a fare anywhere near the Bancroft residence either on Sunday or Monday," he said. "Maybe she phoned a relative or a friend to pick her up?"

"She told the butler she had no living relatives. As for friends outside of the household, I don't know. Nobody's mentioned any."

"If someone from the house drove her away, why is he so shy about mentioning it?"

"Maybe she wasn't alive when he drove her away."

Late in the afternoon a silhouette appeared at the opaque glass of my door and the knob turned.

Marianne Bancroft entered my office.

Her eyes widened. *"You? You* are the Turnbuckle Detective Agency?"

I thought for a flashing moment of telling her that I just happened to be visiting, but there I was coatless and before a typewriter.

So I admitted the fact. "Yes, I am Henry Turnbuckle. I'm sorry if I misrepresented myself yesterday, but it was necessary in my pursuit of information."

She regarded me with narrow-eyed suspicion, but nevertheless got to the point. "I understand that my father hired you to find Paula Smith."

I dodged the exact point delicately.   "I am in your father's employ, yes."

"All right.   I don't know what he's paying you to find her, but I'll double it if you *don't* find her."

I had heard those words before, of course, and I repeated my part of the dialogue. "Why don't you want her found?"

"I really don't think it is necessary you know."

I closed my eyes for a few reflective moments and then opened them.   "The pieces are beginning to fall into place.   You do not want me to find Paula Smith for the simple reason that you *paid* her to leave.   Possibly twenty thousand dollars?"

Naturally she was astounded.   "How did you know that?"

I tapped my forehead with a finger.   "Sheer deductive reasoning based solidly on coincidence.   And the reason you paid her to leave and do not want to have her found and returned is that you feel she was on the verge of entrapping either your father or your brother into matrimony."

She was, for the moment, speechless.

I smiled understandingly.   "My dear Miss Bancroft, neither your father *nor* your brother has the slightest desire ever to see Paula again.   As a matter of fact, your brother also offered me double what his father was paying me if I also did *not* find Paula."

She was confused.   "Why did father hire you in the first place, if he doesn't want Paula back?"

"I believe he was under the impression that your brother was infatuated with Paula.   She seems to have been clever at creating conflicting impressions.   It wouldn't surprise me at all if your father *also* was conned into paying her to leave. And it occurred to him that when Jerome discovered that Paula was gone, he might be heartbroken enough to decide to employ a private detective to find her.   And he might have, at that.   So to forestall that possibility, your father hired me not to look for her, but to prepare a number of reports to make it appear as though I was conducting an extensive search.   He would show them to Jerome to indicate that everything was already being done to find her."

Marianne sighed.   "I guess the three of us will just have to get together and compare notes."   She regarded me for a few moments and then frowned.   "Now I remember where I saw you before.   When the Culbersons had that break-in and jewel robbery at their place a couple of years ago, I dropped in because I wanted to hear all about it from Jenny Culberson.   The place was overrun with police and detectives."   She nodded reflectively.   "And you were there questioning one of the maids.   You and another man, both in plainclothes.   He was kind of chubby, with straw-colored hair."

"That was Ralph, my partner."

She stared at me accusingly.   "You're not a private detective, you're a public detective."

"Well, yes and no.   At the moment I'm on educational leave from the department. I'm doing my Master's on quasi-police organizations—like the Merchant Police, security guards, private detective agencies, and things like that. As part of my research, I'm putting in a spell as a private detective. My license cost me fifteen dollars, but I expect it's worth it."

She was still dubious. "You mean the police department put you on leave for something like that?"

I nodded. "Frankly, I *did* feel a little guilty about being absent from the force for one whole year and possibly letting them down in some way, but Captain Wilkerson was very understanding. He not only approved my application, but actually urged me to take the year off. As a matter of fact, he generously suggested that I make it two or three years."

She smiled faintly. "I know one thing for certain, Henry Turnbuckle, you'll never become a *rich* private detective."

I shrugged. "Well, I certainly have never expected to."

"I mean now that you've cleared the air, it isn't necessary anymore for either me or my brother to double the money Dad is paying you, is it? And as for Dad, I don't know what he's given you so far, but he really has no reason now to pay you any more, does he?"

Good heavens! She was right. In my moment of candor I had shot down my own financial balloon. I frowned. What would an experienced private detective do in a situation like this? Threaten to find Paula Smith on his own and bring her back unless the family paid? I rejected that after a few moments' consideration. No, that would be blackmail.

Marianne seemed about to pat me on the shoulder. "I'll tell you what, Henry, I'll take you home and the family will come through with some kind of settlement that won't leave you exactly empty-handed."

We used her car for the transportation to the Bancroft mansion and I'm afraid I was a bit moody during the ride. When we arrived, two other automobiles were parked in front of the house.

"Dad and Jerome are home," Marianne said. She led me to a drawing room where we found Bancroft Sr. and Jerome.

A large man, well over six feet tall, balding, and wearing a butler's uniform stood at the liquor cabinet making drinks. I deduced that this was Wisniewski.

Both of the Bancrofts blanched when they saw me.

"It's all right, Dad," Marianne said. "I'll explain everything." She did, and during the course of the explanation and clarification, I learned that Bancroft Sr. had also paid Paula Smith $20,000 to leave.

I had been thinking heavily while they talked and suddenly I saw the light at the end of the tunnel. "Ah, hah!" I said, gaining their attention.

I smiled tightly. "Paula Smith privately assured each one of you that she would leave secretly on Monday while all of you were gone from the house for one reason or another, presumably to 'prevent' some member of the family from pleading with her to remain. And yet she left suddenly the night before. Why?"

None of them had the answer.

I continued: "It is my belief that Paula Smith was murdered here sometime after ten P.M. on Sunday—when she was last seen alive—and before seven A.M. on Monday, when she normally assumed her duties for the day, and that her body was removed from the premises by her murderer.''

They blinked, of course, and Marianne said, ''Are you intimating that she changed her mind about going and that one of us killed her to get her out of the way?''

''No. I think she planned to go. She had milked all three of you for about as much as she could expect and she probably thought that you were on the verge of comparing notes and learning that none of you actually wanted her to remain. You might even decide to go to the police. After all, the entire scheme was a form of extortion. No, she had decided to leave, but before she could go voluntarily, she was murdered. You ask why? And by whom?''

None of them did, but I felt that the questions were implied.

''The Why is obvious,'' I said confidently. ''For the sixty thousand dollars in cash which she had accumulated.''

Albert Bancroft seemed shocked. ''I know that *I* certainly would not kill *anyone* for *any* amount of money.''

Jerome agreed. ''Neither would I. Besides, I couldn't strangle anybody. My wrists are too weak.''

I thought that over and regarded Jerome piercingly. ''What makes you think she was strangled?''

He shrugged. ''Nobody seems to have heard a shot and if a knife or a bludgeon were used, there would be blood sprayed about, I imagine, but nobody's mentioned any. So I opt for strangulation.''

He seemed to have a keen mind. I continued: ''The fact remains that Paula was murdered and that her murderer knew that she planned to leave on Monday and used that fact as a coverup for the murder. And after killing her he carried her body downstairs and put it into an automobile or a station wagon and then returned to her room, finished packing her suitcases, and then took them away with him.''

''Why didn't he take the trunk too?'' Marianne asked.

''Either he didn't know it was in that closet or, if he did, he probably felt that it was too great a risk attempting to carry a fully loaded trunk down three flights of stairs in the dead of night without making enough noise to waken someone. Or possibly he thought that each of you would just assume that Paula had decided at the last moment to abandon the trunk of clothes. After all, she had plenty of money to buy more.''

Marianne nodded. ''And you think that a man has to be the murderer because of the heaving and hauling involved with the body? After all, Paula was rather a full-bodied woman.''

''Exactly. And who in this household, besides your father and your brother, is capable of carrying a hefty body down three flights of stairs?''

''Who?'' Marianne asked.

I smiled. ''Shall we consider the gardener for a moment?''

''Hector?'' Marianne shook her head. ''He's sixty-five and I doubt if he weighs over one hundred and twenty pounds.''

I agreed. "You are quite right, Marianne. The murderer couldn't have been Hector."

Wisniewski had been doing make-work at the liquor cabinet so that he could remain in the room.

Now I turned to him and pointed triumphantly. "You, Wisniewski, *you* are the murderer of Paula Smith!"

He regarded me coldly. "Utterly ridiculous, sir. How could I possibly have known that Miss Smith had sixty thousand dollars in her possession?"

I chuckled meaningfully. "Miss Smith was a woman who, shall we say, came on strong. She lived in this house for almost a year, all the while apparently getting noplace at all with any member of the opposite sex, and frankly, in her case, I think that would have been both unendurable and unbelievable. She had to find some man who would prove more compliant and more willing—"

Wisniewski's crown reddened. "Preposterous, sir. She was definitely not my type."

Albert Bancroft was still aghast. "You mean that in this case it was the *butler* who did it?"

"Yes," I said firmly. "The butler." I scowled at Wisniewski. "And so there you were with a body on your hands. What did you do with it? Hide it on the grounds? No. A bit too risky. You might be seen or the body found at some future date. No, you had to take the body somewhere else to dispose of it. A lake? A river? But bodies have a nasty habit of floating to the surface eventually. Or did you bury Paula? Do you own some property around here? Perhaps a cabin on a lake? Certainly an ideal remote burial place."

There was silence.

The Bancrofts and Wisniewski had assumed a stance of deep thought.

After a while Marianne spoke. "Meadows is the murderer."

"Meadows?" I said. "Who is Meadows?"

"The chauffeur."

"Chauffeur?" I said. "What chauffeur?"

"He has quarters over the garage," Albert Bancroft said.

I frowned. "Nobody told me you had a chauffeur."

"Come to think of it," Jerome Bancroft said, "Paula and Meadows were a sort of package deal from that employment agency, weren't they, Marianne?"

I was getting a bit warm. "No one said a damn word about Meadows and Paula coming here at the same time from the same employment agency."

Wisniewski rubbed his chin. "Now that I reflect on it, there were a number of times when I saw the two of them together in what one might call close circumstances."

"Now look here," I said, my voice rising a bit. "How can anybody expect me to solve anything if I'm kept in the dark? No one even hinted that Paula and Meadows were the *least* interested in each other."

"Meadows is about twenty-five," Marianne said. "And Paula was at least forty and it was beginning to show. She must have told him about the sixty thousand dollars and they even planned on going away together. But he was getting tired of her and figured that this was the time to split, and with the money."

I glared out of the nearest window. "Suppositions, suppositions."

Wisniewski brightened. "I believe that Meadows once mentioned that his uncle had a hunting cabin on an acre of land up north. An ideal place to bury Paula. It's probably miles from neighbors."

I turned back to them. "Now there's another example. No one had the decency to tell me that Meadows had an uncle or that this mysterious uncle had a hunting cabin."

"The money," Marianne said. "If the police find the money on or near Meadows, that ought to incriminate him."

"Ha," I snorted. "But suppose they don't find the money on or near Meadows? Then what?"

"In that case they'll tell Meadows they're going to go over his uncle's land with a fine-tooth comb. That ought to crack him wide-open."

"Nonsense," I said. "Nobody cracks wide-open just because someone threatens to search the land around his uncle's hunting cabin."

Wisniewski phoned the police and told them what we knew and what we suspected.

When they arrived, they talked to Meadows and in the course of questioning mentioned that they were going to have a look at the land surrounding his uncle's hunting cabin.

Meadows cracked wide-open.

My phone rang.

It was Ralph. "Well, everything's wrapped up. Meadows led us to the spot where he buried Paula's body and her two suitcases. The money was hidden under the floorboards of his uncle's cabin."

My fingers paradiddled on my desk top. "I knew positively that the murderer had to be a man because to carry a deadweight body down three flights of stairs—"

"Actually he killed her in the garage," Ralph said. "He waited until she wrote the letter she was going to leave and then he lured her down there. Hit her over the head. We found bloodstains on the cement floor."

"Hm," I said thoughtfully. "Undoubtedly he used a tire iron."

"Henry," Ralph said. "You don't find tire irons around private garages anymore. The murder weapon was a geologist's hammer."

"What the devil was a geologist's hammer doing in a garage?"

"Meadows and Paula Smith were a team. They pulled the same stunt at other places. When the money ran out, they'd get another job and work the routine again. But Meadows got tired of Paula. She was a lot older than him. So Meadows decided that while it was a nice racket, he'd just as soon work with somebody younger. Like Fifi."

"Fifi?" I said. "Who's Fifi?"

"The Bancrofts' upstairs maid."

"Nobody told me that the Bancrofts had an upstairs maid named Fifi."

"She wasn't in on the murder, but Meadows told her about the racket and she was ready to take Paula's place. She's gaga about Meadows."

"Ralph," I said a trifle reproachingly, "nobody told me that Fifi was gaga about Meadows. If people persist in withholding information, it only makes things that much more difficult for me."

Soon after Ralph hung up, a familiar silhouette appeared against the glass of my door.

Marianne entered and smiled. "Hi. What time is it?"

I consulted my watch. "Two minutes to eleven."

My phone rang.

It was a woman's voice. "I suspect that my husband is having an affair and I'd like to have him followed."

I wondered idly how the caller had got my phone number. "Certainly, Madam. I'll put one of my best operatives on the job. Your name, please?"

"Darlington. Mrs. Darlington. Could I see you this afternoon?"

"Just one moment, please, I'll have to check my appointment book." I waited twenty seconds and then said, "Ah, yes. Would two o'clock be convenient? I have an opening then."

"Fine. I'll be there."

I put down the phone and smiled. "Well, Marianne, I've got another case. A Mrs. Darlington and possible infidelity."

Marianne nodded. "Winifred should have suspected long ago."

"Winifred?" I said. "Who's Winifred?"

"Winifred Darlington. I gave her your phone number and said to call at eleven. I'm just dying to find out who Edward's been going out with."

"Edward?" I said. "Who's—" I stopped. "Never mind. I can *guess* who Edward is and I have to guess because nobody ever tells me anything." I stalked to my filing cabinet and opened the bottom drawer. I pulled out the bottle and drank two stiff fingers of sherry.

CELIA FREMLIN

Etiquette for Dying

At what point, exactly, did the embarrassment—the sheer, cringing embarrassment of the thing—change over into fear? And then from fear into outright
terror, and the recognition of approaching tragedy?

Twisting the bedside lamp to a sharper angle, Agnes leaned closer, watching the
uneasy twitching of her husband's eyelids over his closed eyes. In the dim greenish
light the lines were sharply etched in the face sunk against the pillows, and he
looked suddenly, terrifyingly old. But of course illness—serious illness—can do
that to a person, even within a few hours.

How many hours? Glancing at Lady Olivia's bedside clock—for it was to their
hostess' bedroom that Bert had been carried, amid a muted turmoil of well-bred
dismay, after his collapse at the dinner table just as the salmon paupiettes were
being served—glancing at the clock, Agnes noted, with a sort of slow incredulity,
that it was still only a little after nine. Less than an hour had passed since Bert,
glass of whiskey still in his hand, had brought to a standstill in mid-sentence the
amusing anecdote he had been relating to his neighbor, the local M.P.'s wife, and
had quietly slewed sideways in his chair and come crashing to the floor, dragging
with him a great swath of shining linen tablecloth. With a dreadful clattering of
Georgian china and priceless glass, he had subsided into a crumpled heap on the
carpet, limbs twitching.

How *could* he! This (to her subsequent shame) had been Agnes' first and totally
spontaneous reaction to the catastrophe. How *could* he!—and in front of all these
important people too! Lady Olivia's antique dinner service, her precious glass!
Fury—a whole raging, bottled-up decade of it—boiled up in Agnes during those
microseconds of scandalized silence before the clamor began: the blinding, impotent
fury of a wife whose husband has disgraced her, has once again, and in the most
public and unforgivable way possible, humiliated her—humiliated himself—in front
of their friends.

No, not even friends. Friends, perhaps, could forgive these things, even within
a week or two laugh at them. "Do you remember that awful night when old
Bert . . . ?"—but Lady Olivia and her entourage were *not* friends, not in this sense.
They were too important to be friends, and too rich. All those smoothly successful
men, those straight-backed women aglitter with diamonds—they weren't *friends,*
but people whose favor must be sought, whose approval must be gained: tycoons,

diplomats, television personalities. The catastrophe *could* not have been more awful.

Because, of course, they would all have assumed that Bert was drunk. Agnes herself assumed it. All those whiskies before dinner, and then those soft-footed waiters padding round the table, filling his glass again, and yet again, even before the hors d'oeuvres were finished, knowing her husband's weakness, especially under stress.

Agnes had been watching every sip he took, counting every glass, ever since they'd arrived at the house. Even before they filed into the great dining room, her nerves were already at snapping point on his account; and when at last the crash came, the ghastly glittering slither of silver and precious glass, she had found herself praying, before she could stop herself, Please God, let him be dead! Please God, let him not be merely drunk! To *die* at an elegant dinner table—that is socially forgivable; but drunkenness, never.

He wasn't dead, of course; but nevertheless, everyone behaved beautifully, as of course they would in that kind of household. Without even a flicker of a glance toward her ruined dinner service or her smashed crystal goblets, Lady Olivia had calmed her guests, had had the victim carried solicitously and instantly upstairs to her own bedroom, and herself had telephoned the doctor.

"Suddenly taken ill," was the phrase she used, in tones of ringing concern, clearly audible through the great dining-room door; and neither by word nor by intonation had she given the faintest indication of being aware that the patient had simply passed out.

Such is breeding. Slinking shamefacedly upstairs behind her disgraced and unconscious husband, Agnes could not but be vaguely grateful for it. Though she could scarcely breathe for shame at the thought of what Lady Olivia must really be thinking, it was a relief that Lady Olivia could be counted on not to say it.

Brandy? Dinner sent up on a tray? Even a cup of tea? Agnes shook her head, still speechless with shame; and presently Lady Olivia, her duty by the two disgraced guests correctly, even graciously, performed, swept elegantly from the room.

What poise! What savoir faire! Crouched guiltily by her husband's bedside, Agnes could not help feeling a stab of unwilling admiration. By now the mess would have been unobtrusively cleared up, and the dinner party would be in full swing again, with Lady Olivia effortlessly setting her guests at ease, passing it all off as if this sort of thing happened every day.

Well, that's aristocracy for you, Agnes reflected wryly. Bred into the bones it was, over hundreds of years, this unflappable presence of mind, this imperturbable façade in the teeth of absolutely anything. Poor Bert, with all his passionate social climbing, he would never make it, never. It took a thousand years; and Bert, at forty-three, had been at the job for barely ten.

And anyway, just look at him! Couldn't even hold his liquor, let alone display these other, more regal, forms of self-command!

And it was now, looking down at her husband's still face in the green-shaded lamplight, that Agnes became conscious of her first qualm of fear.

Because this didn't look like drunkenness—not the kind of drunkenness she had grown used to over the years.   Where were the hiccups, where was the heavy, stertorous breathing, the throwing-up over someone else's carpet?   The awful insufferable humiliations rose up out of the past—and suddenly they seemed like mere pinpricks in the context of this new and unfamiliar dread.   She would have given anything now to see a return of the familiar, disgusting symptoms; how willingly would she have rushed at this very moment, in all the old familiar panic, for towel and basin to save Lady Olivia's heirloom bedspread!

But there was no need.   Not this time.   Already he had gone beyond this sort of thing.   In the greenish light she looked again at her husband's face, and it appeared waxen, and very still.   Even the twitching of the eyelids had ceased, and he lay as if dead, only the faint jerky rise and fall of the sheets showing that he was still breathing.   Breathing too rapidly, too unevenly, as if his lungs and heart were already faltering in their rhythm.

She wished desperately that the doctor would come.   Dare she make a fuss about it—ring the bell at the bedhead—bother someone?   Was it *done* to ring for your hostess' servants, even if someone was dying?

Turning the lamp away from Bert's face, she leaned over and tried once again to rouse him.

"Bert!" she said, quite loudly, "Bert, wake up!   It's all right, everything's going to be all right, Lady Olivia isn't angry, she—"

But it was no good.   She shook him, spoke loudly into his ear; but there was no drunken, inconsequential mumbling in response, no clumsy groping of half-conscious hands.   The hand she held in hers was limp and cool, it reminded her of lilies.   White lilies, and the proximity of death.

Death!   How could such a thing be possible?   Bert *dying*?   Greedy, self-indulgent, go-getting *Bert*?   Impossible!   Death just wasn't his thing!

When *would* the doctor arrive?   An hour now since he'd been summoned— surely he'd have realized that it was an emergency?   A man of forty-three collapsing suddenly—why it might be *anything*!

Heart attack?   Stroke?   Raking through her sparse medical knowledge, Agnes tried to recall those last minutes before the catastrophe.   Had Bert looked odd in any way?   Ill?   Had he been behaving strangely?   Certainly, in the drawing room before dinner, he had looked nervous and agitated.

From her observation point at the far end of the room, Agnes had watched him arguing heatedly with a slim supercilious young man—a television star, as she learned later—and losing the argument.   Not that she'd been able to hear from the distance what either of them was saying, but she could tell by the insolent set of Bert's shoulders, by the arrogant gesture with which he thrust his empty glass at a passing waiter, that he had been worsted.

But not ill, no.   Just at a disadvantage, and out of his depth in this company, and too proud, as always, to admit it to himself.

And at dinner?—the abortive beginnings of dinner, that is, which were all that either he or she was destined to enjoy.   From across the huge mahogany table she had watched him, with wifely anxiety, launching into conversation with Mrs. Beltravers, wife of the Conservative M.P., watched him boasting, as usual, describing how he'd used his influence to quash the Council's plans for a Remand Home just next to the Arts Centre—was he *sure*, Agnes remembered wondering, that this had been a Labour project and not a Conservative one?   Not that it mattered—you could see from Mrs. Beltravers' glazed expression that the affairs of her husband's constituency bored her into the ground.

And at least Bert was eating, Agnes remembered noting.   *That'll* settle all those whiskies, she had reflected with satisfaction, watching him polishing off a plate piled high with assorted hors d'oeuvres.   Duck pâté, jellied oysters, prawn darioles—wasn't it rather a faux pas, Agnes remembered wondering uneasily, to be eating the lot like this, as if he'd been starving for a week?

But now, sitting at his bedside in a growing turmoil of anxiety, Agnes had few thoughts to spare for the etiquette of the thing; ideas far more sinister were beginning to take possession of her.

Duck pâté!   You could get food poisoning from duck pâté.   And from shellfish too.   She'd heard of people collapsing like that, suddenly, from food poisoning, though of course it was more usual for the symptoms to appear after an hour or so.   On the other hand, if it was food poisoning, you'd expect the other guests to be affected too.   The chance that Bert alone—

Chance?   It was only now that Agnes became clearly conscious of the direction in which her uneasy thoughts were leading.   She felt herself gripped by a violent trembling; sweat broke out on her forehead and on the palms of her hands; her stomach seemed to be tying itself in knots within her.

Murder! Deliberately administered poison!   Poisoned pâté—or poisoned oysters?   Poisoned *anything*, in fact, from that lavish table, groaning with exotic and unfamiliar foods.   And Bert—poor gullible Bert, who for all his social pretensions knew no better than she did how these weird things *ought* to taste—poor Bert (and she could sympathize with this) would have swallowed *anything*, no matter how bitter or unpalatable, rather than show his unfamiliarity with such delicacies.

And if someone, knowing him well, aware of his hidden social ineptitude, and of his pride, and choosing to take advantage of this knowledge— But *who?* Who, of all this glittering throng, could be Bert's enemy?

Most of them—that was the answer.   A man like Bert, pushing his way ruthlessly to the top, thrusting aside everything and everyone that stands in his way—such a man is going to make enemies.   Somewhere along the way, had he pushed too hard?—trampled too blindly over feelings whose intensity he was unaware of?   Stirred up against himself a hornet's nest of revenge and hate?   Was this then, in the end, what Bert had earned for himself by all his struggles, all his social climbing, all his single-minded self-aggrandizement?   Murder, death by poisoning?

The sheer horror of the thing seemed to take Agnes' breath away; her head swam; her heart pounded in her ears.   The effrontery of it too!   The dreadful, cold-blooded simplicity of the method!   A little pharmaceutical knowledge, a little insight into Bert's vainglory and his precarious self-conceit, and the thing was in the bag.   A verdict of accidental food poisoning would be a near certainty.

Especially, of course, if *two* of the guests were known to have come down with it, one being lucky enough to have survived.   As Agnes, the blood pounding in her brain, slumped sideways in her chair and slipped unconscious to the floor, Bert slid swiftly from under the blankets and hurried to her side.

The carefully chosen green light already made her features look close to death, just as his had looked; but this time the illusion was fast becoming reality. For some minutes—maybe half an hour—he sat with his finger on her failing pulse, his ears intent on the harsh, uneven rattle of her breath. When both had finally ceased, he got to his feet and hurried quietly along the corridor to the head of the great curving staircase.

Peering, half hidden by shadows, over the oak bannisters, he was able to watch Lady Olivia ushering her guests from the dining room into the great hall; and when she managed, unnoticed by anyone, to flash a swift glance up in his direction, he gave her the thumbs-up sign.

It had all gone off like a dream.

HAROLD Q. MASUR

One Thing Leads to Another

It was an elegant building, tall and exclusive. The doorman, a resplendently caparisoned goliath, stood guard at the entrance like Leonidas defending the pass at Thermopylae. If you live in the Big Apple and can afford the protection, why not?

I paused alongside the revolving doors and stooped over to tighten a shoelace just as a taxi pulled up at the curb. Its occupant, apparently a paraplegic, struggled heroically to alight with the aid of aluminum crutches. As the doorman hastened across the sidewalk to assist, I ducked into the lobby, sprinted for the elevator, and jabbed the ninth-floor button.

Just before the door closed, I witnessed a miracle. The passenger suddenly straightened, tucked the crutches under his arm, saluted, and marched jauntily down the street. The doorman scratched his head in astonishment and then the elevator was lofting me skyward.

I found Lily Olson's door and rang the bell. It was opened by a spare, craggy-faced gent. "Mr. George Finney?" I asked.

"Who wants him?"

"This is for you, sir." I handed him a paper. "Summons and complaint. Finney versus Finney. Nonpayment of alimony and child support. Have a pleasant day."

There was a woman standing behind him, a striking blonde, thin-lipped now and furious. She ran to the house phone and as I walked back to the elevator I heard her chewing out the doorman, a venomous tirade in the lexicon of a mule-skinner.

On the way down I could not repress a smile of satisfaction. I had succeeded where two professional process servers had dismally failed to breach the building's security. Ordinarily, a lawyer does not serve his own papers. It's undignified. Nor do I generally handle cases of this kind. But Kate Finney had been recommended by an important client. She had a child from a previous marriage, legally adopted by Finney, and she desperately needed financial help.

She gave me the facts on the telephone. George Finney had walked out, left her and the child to shift for themselves, and had moved in with Lily Olson. She did not miss him, not on any emotional level. He drank excessively, worked sporadically, and could squeeze a dime until F.D.R.'s nose came out on the other side.

The elevator door opened on the lobby. The doorman was waiting. He towered over me, shoulders bunched, glowering and belligerent and spoiling for a fight. I handed him one of my cards.

"The name is Scott Jordan," I said. "Counselor and attorney-at-law. So if you decide to use your hands it won't cost me anything to sue the owners for aggravated assault. As a matter of fact, I'm perfectly willing to go a couple of rounds with you, but not at the moment. I'm due at my office for an appointment with the governor."

It gave him pause. The owner's wrath could be more catastrophic than Olson's abuse. While he was considering it, I slipped past him to the street and caught a cab back to the office.

Ten minutes later Danny Karr showed up. Danny, my new assistant, put some bills on my desk. He was grinning from ear to ear. "I returned the crutches, boss. Here's your change. How did you like my performance?"

"A bit gaudy," I said. "But the timing was fine and it worked."

"So how about a raise?"

"You had a raise last week."

"Inflation is killing me."

"You and everyone else. Learn to economize. Your time will come." And I was sure it would. Danny, only eight months out of law school, was young, eager, and bright. I moved some papers around on my desk. "On that environment case, where are those precedents I asked for?"

"We don't have the Minnesota Reports."

"Naturally. There are fifty states. Who has the shelf space? Use the Bar Association library."

"I'm not a member."

"I'm a member and you're my employee. Get over there tomorrow morning. Early, Counselor." He left and I phoned Kate Finney, asking her to stop by for trial preparation.

At four o'clock she arrived accompanied by Sara. The child had enormous eyes and an adult air of gravity. Kate, a slender, somewhat faded woman in her mid-thirties, introduced us. "This is Mr. Jordan, Sara. He's my lawyer."

"I don't like lawyers," Sara said.

"Why don't you like lawyers?" I asked.

"George says they're not honest. He says if you don't watch out, they'll steal you blind."

Her mother reprimanded her sharply. "Sara! Apologize at once."

"Okay," she said, not changing her opinion. "I apologize."

Keeping a straight face, I buzzed for Danny Karr. "Danny," I said, "this young lady is Sara Finney. Entertain her in your office while I talk to her mother."

Sara looked him over. "Are you a lawyer too?"

"Yes, ma'am."

She handed her small plastic purse to her mother. "Then you'd better hold this for me."

Danny rolled his eyes, beckoned, and she followed him out. Kate gestured helplessly. "I don't know what to do with that child."

"She'll grow out of it. Is George attached to her?"

"Hah! There is no room in George's emotional equipment for anyone but George. His ego is exceeded only by his selfishness and his penury. The man is incapable of sharing."

"You mentioned that he's a writer."

"Well, he's sold several short stories, but he drinks too much and he can't discipline himself to a full-time schedule."

"You said he has an independent income."

"Yes. From a trust fund administered by an old fossil of a lawyer he inherited from his parents."

"We'll levy an attachment against it."

She smiled. "I'd like to see his face."

"Tell me about Lily Olson."

"He met her through his literary agent, a man named Arnold Procter. She's a writer too, and fairly successful. She writes those romantic Gothic novels. After our last fight George went to live with her. Maybe she's more tolerant than I, or less sensitive." She paused and looked thoughtful. "I—er—have a confession to make." When I said nothing, she continued. "Last week a letter came for George from the editor of a magazine in Chicago. They used to correspond with each other and I guess he didn't know George had moved out. Anyway, I steamed it open. He said he liked the new story Procter had submitted and he would be sending a check to the agent at the end of the month."

"We'll get a court order restraining Procter from turning the money over to George until the determination of your case against him. There's really no way you can lose."

I spent some time preparing her for the court hearing and then I buzzed for Danny Karr. Sara was holding his hand and apparently had changed her mind about lawyers.

He accompanied Kate and Sara to the elevator and then came back, smiling.

I said, "Let's see how good you are, Danny." I told him to get the form book and to prepare a restraining order against Arnold Procter. "Complete the papers and serve them before you go home this evening."

Danny Karr spent the next morning at the Bar Association library. He checked into the office at noon and I saw at once that he was not himself. He seemed dreamy-eyed, dismantled. I had to snap my fingers to get his attention.

"Have you been smoking something, Counselor?" I asked.

He blinked and shook his head.

"You're in a trance, moonstruck. What gives?"

"I—I think I'm in love."

I did a double-take. "With little Sara Finney, for God's sake?"

"No, sir." He smiled foolishly. "With Amy."

"And who, pray, is Amy?"

He sighed. "Amy is a walking poem, a rainbow, a—"

"Whoa, boy! Settle down. Get your head together. Where did you meet this enchantress?"

"In Arnold Procter's office."

"Well, now, George Finney met a female in Procter's office and it changed his whole way of life. Is Amy a writer too?"

He shook his head. "She works for him. She's his secretary."

"Are you telling me you walked in there to serve some legal papers and beheld this vision and bingo, you were hooked, just like that?"

"Almost, Mr. Jordan. You see, Procter was out when I got there. Amy said he'd be back in fifteen minutes. So I waited. And we talked. I liked her. I asked her to have dinner with me last night and she said yes. So we went out and then I took her home and we sat up and talked until three o'clock this morning."

"You kissed her good night?"

"Uh-huh."

"And bells began to ring?"

He nodded, looking rhapsodic.

"I hope you didn't forget to serve that restraining order on her boss."

"I didn't forget. Business before pleasure."

"An excellent maxim, Danny. Never lose sight of it while you're employed in this office. Now go back to the library and finish your research."

My phone rang and Kate Finney was on the line. "Mr. Jordan," she said, sounding tense and subdued, "there's a policeman here. He says George is dead. He wants me to come to the morgue to identify the body."

"Let me talk to him." She put him on and I said, "I'm the lady's lawyer, officer. What happened?"

"Harbor Patrol fished a floater out of the East River early this morning. We got this address from his driver's license. They need the widow downtown for identification."

I spoke to Kate again. I told her to leave Sara with one of the neighbors and to cooperate. I promised to use my contacts at the Police Department for additional information.

My principal contact was Detective Lieutenant John Nola, Homicide, dark, lean, a resourceful and subtly intuitive cop. He sat behind his desk, a thin Dutch cigar smoking itself between his teeth, eyes unblinking, while I explained my connection with the deceased.

"Anything suspicious?" I asked finally.

"All we have now is that he was stoned. There was enough alcohol in his blood to float a rowboat."

"Then it could have been an accident."

"Or someone helped him over the edge. You know anything about his financial status?"

"He had an income from a trust fund."

"Who inherits?"

"The widow, probably."

He lifted an eyebrow. "And he'd strayed from the reservation, was living with another woman? He was tight and behind in his alimony?"

"No, Lieutenant. That's a bad hand. Mrs. Finney is not the type."

The eyebrow moved higher. "There are types of murderers, Counselor? Neatly pegged in categories? Make us a list, please. We can use it." He shook his head. "Tell me about the Olson woman."

I gave him what I had. He stood abruptly. "Let's check her out."

The taxpayers provided transport. At Lily Olson's building the same doorman recognized me and blocked our way. "No, you don't," he growled. "Not this time, buster. You're a cute one all right. You almost cost me my job. Now turn around and march, both of you."

But his truculence quickly evaporated at the sight of Nola's shield and was replaced by a lumpy smile of apology. He stepped aside. Nola pointed at the house phone. "Don't use that thing."

"Whatever you say, Lieutenant."

Lily Olson answered the doorbell. Nola identified himself. "And this one?" she demanded, indicating me with a thumb.

"His name is Jordan. He's a lawyer."

"A lawyer!" She snorted. "That explains the trickery. Do you know what he did, Lieutenant? He gained access to this building by subterfuge and served some legal papers on a guest of mine. Isn't there a law against that—criminal trespass or something?"

"I'll look it up," Nola said. "In the meantime I need some information. I understand you had a house guest, a Mr. George Finney."

"I still do."

"Any idea where he is at the moment?"

"No, I don't. He went for a walk the day before yesterday and hasn't returned."

"You're not concerned about his whereabouts?"

She shrugged. "George is a grown man. But he has a problem—drinking. He probably stopped off at a bar and got plastered. He knows how I feel about that, so he probably took a room somewhere to dry out. It wouldn't be the first time. Why are you asking these questions?"

"George Finney is dead."

She gasped. "Oh, no. How—how did it happen?"

"His body was found in the East River early this morning."

"Suicide?"

"We doubt it."

"Had he been drinking?"

"Heavily."

"Then it must have been an accident."

"From the amount of alcohol in Finney's blood we don't see how he could have reached the river under his own power."

"He liked to walk along the river. And he generally carried a flask in his pocket. Surely you don't suspect foul play."

"It's a possibility we have to explore.   Admittedly, he could have been the victim of a random mugging, or something more deliberate.   Did Finney have any enemies?"

"Everyone liked George."

"Including his wife?"

"There are always exceptions.   They fought a great deal."

"And he came to you for comfort?"

"Why not?   Life is short."

"It is indeed.   We'd like to look at his papers, his correspondence, anything he kept here."

"Do you have a warrant?"

"You invited us in."

"I'm inviting you out."

"It's too late, Miss Olson.   Finney is dead.   We don't need a warrant to examine his property."

"I think you do.   This is my apartment.   Ask your lawyer friend here."

He shook his head.   "One telephone call and I can have a warrant here within the hour."

She frowned and bit her lip.   She debated with herself and finally gestured ungraciously.   "Go ahead."

In the bedroom closet Finney's clothes yielded nothing.   There was a sunlit workroom at the end of the corridor.   It contained a filing cabinet, a shelf of reference books, and a large desk with an electric typewriter.   A bridge table in the corner held Finney's portable and an untidy pile of papers.   Nola gathered them into a bundle and we started to leave.

"How about his clothes?" Lily Olson called.

"Give them to the Salvation Army," I said and followed Nola out to the elevator and down to the street.

We parted.   He went back to the precinct and I returned to my office.   My secretary had left for the day.   Danny Karr was still at the Bar Association library. I was alone, correcting syntax on an appeals brief when I heard someone moving around in the outer office.   I got up and walked to the door for a look.

A young girl smiled at me.

"I'm supposed to meet Mr. Karr here at six," she said.   "I'm Amy Barth."

She was neither a rainbow nor a walking poem, but I could easily understand how the sturdy figure and the large eyes and the gamine grin could turn Danny Karr into a marshmallow.

I smiled back.   "How do you do, Amy.   I'm Danny's boss.   He should be back at any moment.   You can wait for him in my office, unless you'd prefer to sit out here and read the *Law Journal*."

"Oh, no," she said.   She perched herself on the red-leather chair, bouncing restlessly.   "Danny says you're probably the smartest lawyer in New York."

"Danny will be sadly disillusioned after he's been around for a while.   Is there something wrong with that chair?"

She giggled.   "Oh, no," she said, "the chair is fine.   It's just that I'm in very high spirits.   I work for a literary agency and such exciting things have been happening this week.''

''For example?''

''We're handling a new book by Lily Olson.   Do you know her work?   This one is different than anything she's ever written.   It's a political thriller called *The Machiavelli Project*.   It's about a millionaire vice-president who conspires to get rid of the president and take over the White House.''

''Sounds interesting,'' I said.

''It's a real cliffhanger.   Readers won't be able to put it down.   Mr. Procter got an enormous advance from the hardcover publisher and last Wednesday the paperback rights sold for one million dollars.   Three book clubs are taking it and all the major movie companies are bidding for the screen rights.   Some of Hollywood's biggest stars have called.''   She looked awe-struck and said in a hushed voice, ''I think I heard Gregory Peck's voice on the phone this morning.   I almost fainted.''

''Quite a blockbuster,'' I said.

''Mr. Procter never had one like this before.''

Danny arrived.   He saw Amy and his expression turned sappy.   They smiled at each other.   He approached and placed a sheaf of yellow legal cap on my desk. ''Here are my notes on the Minnesota Reports.''

''No, Danny,'' I said.   ''That's not the way to do it.   Who can translate your hieroglyphics?   Type them out.   Neatly.''

He looked stricken.   ''Now?''

''Tomorrow morning will do.''

''Yes, sir,'' he said gratefully and propelled Amy out of the office before I could change my mind.

I sat back and thought about Lily Olson's new novel.   Perhaps it was time for me to seek out a few writers as clients.   The paperback revolution and the money guarantees made the prospect extremely attractive.   I glanced at my watch and dialed Kate Finney's number.

''It was a dreadful ordeal,'' she told me.   ''I could hardly recognize George.''

''Is there anything I can do?''

''Would you take care of the funeral arrangements?''

''Of course.''

''And George's estate too?''

''If you wish.''

''Will the court hearing be postponed?''

''I'll call the clerk and explain the situation.''

After we broke the connection, I locked the office and headed across town to see Nola.   He seldom punched a clock when working on a case.   He had been studying Finney's papers.   I told him about Lily Olson's successful book.

He whistled.   ''At least two million in the till so far.   I guess I'm in the wrong business.''

''Finney's papers tell you anything?''

He shook his head.   ''Look for yourself.''

I pulled up a chair and started reading.   There was some correspondence from the lawyer handling Finney's trust fund, signed in a shaky hand; a note from a former army friend now living in Pocatello, Idaho; and a few letters from Kate complaining about support and threatening legal action.   Finney's notebooks interested me.   And so did a letter from Arnold Procter expressing mild interest in the outline for a prospective novel titled *The Long Night*.   The agent had reservations about Finney's ability to complete a full-length work.   He doubted that any publisher would commit himself to an advance.   As an alternative, he suggested finding a collaborator.

I was distracted by the ringing of Nola's phone.   He spoke briefly and I sensed his eyes watching me as I looked up.   He cradled the handset.

"The name Daniel Karr mean anything to you, Counselor?"

"Yes.   He's my assistant."

"He's in the Emergency Room at Manhattan General."

I sat erect.   "What happened?"

"Automobile accident.   Hit-and-run.   Compound fracture of the right leg, plus assorted contusions and abrasions.   He whispered your name several times before they put him under to set the bone."

I was on my feet and moving.   Nola came after me.   I said, "There was a girl with him."

"Amy Barth.   Same accident."

"Hurt badly?"

"She's dead."

Bile leaped into my throat.   I took the stairs two at a time.   In the street I started to flag a cab, but Nola shouldered me into a police car and snapped instructions at the driver.   The siren opened traffic like a carving knife.

We found Danny Karr propped up in bed, his face drawn and white, right leg supported in traction, head in bandages, plaster criss-crossing a cheek.   He said in a half-drugged voice, "They won't tell me about Amy, boss.   Can you find out how she is?"

"Later, Danny.   How did it happen?"

"Amy wanted to go home first and freshen up before dinner.   It's a brownstone on West 26th.   We came out and started to cross the street.   I heard some lunatic gun his engine and I started to turn, but it was too late.   He was right on top of us.   And then I felt the impact and I guess I passed out.   The next thing I knew I was in an ambulance.   They brought me here.   Did anything happen to Amy?"

I didn't have the heart to tell him.   Not yet, anyway.   I asked him if there was anything he needed, anything I could do, perhaps notify his parents.   They were retired and living in Florida and he didn't want to worry them.

Amy's people, however, would have to be notified.   I had no information for Nola except that she worked for Arnold Procter.   "Then that's the man we'll have to see," he said.   "Let's go."

The telephone directory supplied his home address in the exclusive Beekman Place area.   A townhouse, no less.   Procter was a man who did not believe in economizing.

Nola banged the knocker and a man opened the door.   My jaw fell.   Spare and craggy-faced, he stared back. Lazarus rising from the grave. The same man I'd seen in Lily Olson's apartment.

"Finney?" I said on a rising inflection.

"No, sir. The name is Procter—Arnold Procter."

"But you're the man I served with the summons."

"You made an unwarranted assumption, sir. I was visiting Miss Olson on business. You simply handed me that paper and left. What is it now? What do you want?"

"He's with me," Nola said, again presenting his credentials and identifying himself. "His name is Jordan."

"Scott Jordan? The lawyer?" Procter made a face. "I know the name. He dispatched one of his acolytes to my office yesterday with some kind of restraining order. A barrator, Lieutenant, this man is a compulsive barrator."

Nola glanced at me.

"Someone who practices barratry," I explained. "The excessive instigation and promotion of lawsuits."

He turned back to Procter. "You have an employee named Amy Barth?"

"I do."

"I have some sad news. She was struck by an automobile early this evening and killed."

"What?" He stared. "Oh, my God! That lovely child." He shook his head. "It doesn't seem possible. Come in, please." In the living room, his face grim, he shook a stern finger at Nola. "Those damned drunken drivers! Why do you grant them licenses to assassinate pedestrians? Amy Barth. What a dreadful waste!"

"Can you tell us how to reach her family?"

"I know only that she comes from the Midwest. Wichita, I believe. They gravitate here from the provinces, all the bright and eager youngsters, seeking adventure and opportunity." He gestured. "And Jordan? Why is Jordan interested? Because of the accident? Is he chasing ambulances?"

"Jordan's assistant was injured in the same accident."

"The young man should be warned, Lieutenant. He's courting eventual disbarment with his present affiliation."

And Mr. Arnold Procter, I thought, was courting a fat lip.

Nola said, "How long had the girl been working for you?"

"About a month."

"Did she ever discuss her personal affairs?"

"I do not encourage intimacies. We're under constant pressure at the agency. I imagine you could find the necessary information at the girl's apartment." He glanced at his watch. "I really don't have much time, Lieutenant. I'm due at an important meeting."

"Sorry. You'll have to resign yourself to being late."

Procter lifted his chin superciliously. "This city is suffering from a serious fiscal crisis. I understand we've been compelled to reduce the number of law-enforcement officers. Shouldn't you be out catching crooks?"

"That's exactly what he's doing right at this moment," I said.

His head swiveled. "What are you talking about?"

"I'm talking about embezzlement, Procter. I'm talking about murder. Where do you keep your car?"

"What car?"

"The car you parked near Amy's apartment early this evening, waiting for her to come out so you could aim it and step on the gas and put her away. My assistant was with her at the time, so he too was expendable. But it was Amy who caught the full impact."

"*Me?*" He flattened a palm against his chest. "Are you saying I killed Amy? I don't even own a car."

"Then you rented one. They'll check the rental agencies, Procter. Think about it. Did you return a car with a smashed headlight or a dented fender? Wiped clean of fingerprints?"

"Why in God's name would I want to hurt that girl?"

"Because she knew too much," I said. "She knew about all the money involved in Lily Olson's new book. Almost two million dollars or more. The first time your agency ever hit the jackpot. It might never happen again, either to you or to Lily Olson. Or to George Finney who conceived the idea and developed the plot and was entitled to half of the proceeds."

"Who says so?"

"Finney's notebooks. We have them in his own handwriting, elaborating on the same theme that appears in Olson's book, *The Machiavelli Project*. And a letter you wrote suggesting that he collaborate with some other writer. You put him in touch with Lily Olson. Those papers should have been destroyed, Procter, only the lieutenant showed up unexpectedly and seized them before you had a chance."

"I wrote him a letter, yes. But it referred to a different project."

"It referred to an outline called *The Long Night*. And Olson's book may even have been submitted under that title. Because at that time nobody anticipated this windfall. Shall we call the publishers and ask if they were involved in a change of title?"

It started a vein throbbing in his temple.

I said, "Finney's name had no currency in the publishing world. So he willingly agreed to let Olson appear as the sole author. As a matter of fact, he insisted on it. Because if his wife learned about any new source of income, she had a legal right to demand an increase in alimony. He wanted to avoid that. He hoped to squirrel the money away, so his selfishness played into your hands.

"But then lightning struck. You found yourself in possession of a blockbuster worth millions. Greed obliterated your ethics. You had an idea. You went to Lily Olson and sounded her out. You told her she had written the book, slaved over it for months, bled her talent. Why split with Finney? You made her a proposition. If Finney could be eliminated, with no risk to her, would she split his share with you. And she was receptive. So you worked it out. They celebrated their success and she got him drunk. Then you coaxed him into a car and he kept lapping it up while you drove to an appropriate spot along the river. You got him out, stoned and helpless, and gave him a push."

His mouth was open, breathing harshly, his face moist.

"It never ends," I said. "One thing leads to another. I sent my assistant to your office and he met Amy Barth and they became friends. That posed an instant threat. Because Amy knew about the collaboration. And she could kick over the pail by mentioning it. So she had to be silenced without delay and you took care of it. Who else knew where she lived? Who else had a motive? You, Procter, only you.

"You're finished, mister. They'll put it all together and when they start leaning on Lily Olson she'll come apart, trying to clear her own skirts. You haven't a prayer."

He sank into a chair and covered his face. Nola reached for the telephone and I heard him telling someone to pick up the Olson woman. I looked at Procter. All those snide comments about lawyers. And five will get you twenty, in about two minutes he'd be yelling his head off for one.

HENRY T. PARRY

Homage to John Keats

When Howard P. Ransom reached fifty-five, he retired from his job, sold his house, murdered his wife, and settled down in Rome, thereby fulfilling four long-cherished ambitions. He loathed his house, detested his job, hated his wife and loved the prospect of taking up life, late but renewed, in a foreign capital of endless attraction.

His job, he felt, was far beneath one of his talent but it paid so well that his love of money outweighed his distaste. His house was a constant burden, insatiable in its demands for repairs, rapacious in its tax requirements, an unstaunchable bleeding of the money and time that he would rather have spent on his boat. But it was his wife Hannah whom he regarded as the major obstacle to freedom and a new life.

As the years of their marriage passed, whatever of love and understanding there may have been had vanished, with Hannah exhibiting a half-hidden sufferance bordering on contempt, and he an impotent chafing and smoldering resentment. He found that the cute pussycat face of twenty-two became the snarling mask of a stalking tiger at fifty.

Hannah had adamantly refused to agree to a divorce, primarily because Howard wanted it. For Howard to have simply walked out was repellent to his nature, which required order and planning and abhorred loose ends and unfinished business. This plus the fatal flaw in the mind of every killer—the conviction that his action was justified—led him to the murder of his wife.

The act itself was simple, well planned, and swift. One of the few remaining things they did together was to take an occasional weekend cruise in the boat. Returning home just after dark one Sunday, they rounded the breakwater at the end of the Delaware-Chesapeake Canal and turned north against the ebbing tide where the river and bay met. Two miles upstream Howard put the engine on idle and came astern to where Hannah sat.

"I want you to put on this life jacket. The tide is ebbing quite strongly and there's all this debris floating about. If I have to make a quick turn and if you should be standing, you might go over the side."

"Oh, Howard, is that necessary? Such unusual precautions here on the river."

"This is practically the top end of Delaware Bay. And there's this heavy tanker traffic—"

"Oh, all right, all right. A lesson in geography. Always a lesson in some-thing."

"Just this one last lesson then."

She stood and he helped her into the life jacket, steadying her as she staggered slightly, and swiftly tied the ribbons. He could smell the perfume she used, a smell that he had come to loathe as much as once it had attracted him.

"Howard," her voice rose in bewilderment, "what have you done to this jacket? It weighs a ton."

"Yes," he agreed, "it's packed with lead"—and he pushed her over the stern.

The greasy water was barely disturbed as she went under. He switched on the spotlight and played it back and forth over the water. Crates, fruit baskets, odd pieces of lumber, all swam placidly by on the outward tide, but the surface betrayed no sign of what had happened.

For two hours he waited, to be sure that his plan had worked, and then headed for the nearest marina and a telephone to report his well-rehearsed story to the Coast Guard, with special care in placing the scene of the incident farther up the river than it had actually occurred.

It took Howard three months to make what he thought of as his getaway. Calls placed at lengthening intervals to the Coast Guard brought no news and elicited finally the opinion that there was no likelihood of the body being recovered.

The house was sold, removing forever the burden of wet basements, rising taxes, and ever more plentiful crops of crabgrass. Kindly neighbors offered sympathy and expressed understanding of his wish for a complete change of scene, expressions which Howard gravely accepted, inwardly relishing the contrast between his decently submissive outward manner and his inner satisfaction with the fruition of his plans.

Thoughtfully he arranged for a tombstone to be erected—a fact that was noted in the local paper—and had it incised with Hannah's name and the years of her birth and death, and, as indicative of his intentions, he had his own name added, followed by the year of his birth and a small uncarved rectangle in which at the proper time another year would be cut. With a touch of grim wholly uncharacteristic humor he thought that a suitable epitaph for Hannah might be "Lost at sea," but sensibly he restrained himself.

Late in the fall, after a dutiful and symbolic visit to the cemetery, Howard arrived in Rome. Through the columns of a newspaper aimed at the American tourist he rented a small furnished apartment in a converted palazzo on a street near the top of the Spanish Steps, a house reputed to have been owned by a cadet branch of the Medici.

After the spare trimness and openness of his suburban house he was struck by the stony, secretive exteriors of the Roman houses and the contrast with their ornate, pretentious interiors. His living room was furnished with heavy oaken furniture, elaborately carved; one chair with a faded damask cover on its tall back was supposed to have once been the property of the infamous Principe di Canisio who, it was said, had died in it, a messy affair of a jealous husband and a silken cord.

Dim acne-ed mirrors on the walls on each side of the door reflected windows with heavy velvet drapes looped back by tassled rope ties. It seemed that the same style of furniture that was suitable for the palazzo of a doge had been used in this small room, giving it a theatrical, shop-worn splendor. But Howard settled contentedly in these falsely elegant surroundings and gave himself over to the delights of leisurely explorations of the ancient city.

It was not until early summer that he saw Hannah. Or thought he saw Hannah.

He was returning from an afternoon of browsing among the many shops near the Piazza di Spagna and had begun to climb the magnificent stairway street of the Spanish Steps, the sweeping thoroughfare that leads majestically up to the Monte di Trinita. In the wall of the building to the right of the first landing was the shrine of millions of poetry-loving tourists, the window of the room where the poet Keats had died. He paused on the landing, looking up at the open window, and saw a woman looking down at him, a woman who resembled Hannah.

Shaken, he stared up at her, his mind rejecting the atavistic fear of the dead returned to life and telling himself to wait for a movement or gesture to dispel the likeness, for her aspect to shift from identity to mere similarity. The woman gazed down calmly, framed portraitlike in the window, an absent-minded half smile on her lips, and raised her hand; but whether or not the gesture was in greeting he could not determine. Then the woman slowly moved back from the frame of the window and was out of sight.

He stood and stared upward at the window not thirty feet away, his mind searching for the possibility of error in the execution of his plan, but at no point could he find a mistake. He was brought back to reality when he heard a passing American schoolteacher comment to her companion, "Look. Another poetry lover paying homage to John Keats." As they passed him he smelled the faint fragrance of the same perfume Hannah had used and he wondered if he had smelled it unknowingly as he looked at the woman in the window and if it had not added a subliminal reinforcement to a chance likeness.

He concluded that the resemblance was accidental, but from that time forward, before he fell asleep at night, he saw again the face and form of Hannah framed in the window.

A week later he saw her again.

It was during the intermission before the last act of "Aida," which was performed outdoors at the Baths of Caracalla. He strolled among the crowds under the lights along the wide paths that skirted the towering walls with their shadowed arches recessing into darkness. She was standing under an arch, well back from the walk and partially obscured by the shadow of a tree as well as by the shadows of the arch.

He stopped, the crowd moving slowly past him, and stared at the figure that stood dwarfed by the tall arch, hugging itself as if chilled and idly watching the passing crowd. Her eyes swept over him with no sign of recognition and then swung back to look at him uncertainly as if she were not sure she knew him, and then she turned away toward the interior darkness of the arch, on her lips the same half smile that he had seen from the Steps.

He pushed his way through the crowd toward her but the overhead lights flicked off and on several times to signal the end of the intermission.   By the time he made his way through the returning surge of the crowd she had vanished.   He made his way to the entrance where the patrons were returning to their seats and although he observed each one until the first aria was well under way he did not see her again.

Similarly after the performance he watched the main exit but saw no one who remotely resembled his dead wife.   But he found this occurrence less troubling than the previous one and although he thought about it constantly for days it did not cause the questioning and examination the first encounter had.   A resemblance, close enough to be sure, but it was not Hannah.   If it had been, he was certain she could not have resisted showing the new power which she would now have over him.

Three days later in the late afternoon he returned to his apartment, slipped his key into the handsome walnut door, swung the door inward, and froze.   Delusions of sight and errors in identification were always possible but there is no auto-suggestion in the sense of the smell.   The living room smelled faintly of Hannah's perfume.

Terror spurted in him but he forced himself to stride into the room.   Hannah sat in the Principe di Canisio's chair, her face as worn as the scarlet damask that covered the tall back of the chair, and in her hand was an ugly and unladylike .45 caliber automatic.   She pointed it upward, directly at his face, so that he looked into its cruel, uncompromising muzzle that seemed small for such a deadly object.

For several seconds they stared at each other wordlessly, the woman who should have been dead and the man who should have been free.   She waved the gun toward a slender gilt chair beside the door and he sat down facing her, the light from the window behind her chair making him feel, irrationally, that if only he could be in shadow he would be able to explain everything.

"How?" he managed to whisper.

"You thought of everything, Howard, everything but one small detail.   I surfaced under an upturned fruit basket and stayed there while you were making certain with the spotlight that you had murdered me.   My clothes made me buoyant for a time and the tide was carrying me downstream away from your light.   When I was in sufficient darkness I grabbed a floating timber and paddled to shore just below a refinery.   Murder and a polluted river, Howard!   Some form of repayment is indicated, don't you agree?

"I floundered through the marshes until I came to a highway and walked along it until I found a filling station.   It was closed but it was also a bus stop.   After an hour's wait, during which most of the water dripped out of my clothes—but oh, the smell—a bus marked Ocean City came in and I got on.   In the two-hour ride down the coast to Ocean City I planned what I would do.

"First of all, I couldn't let you, or anyone else, know I had survived.   You would surely try again.   I decided that this was no matter for the law and, besides, what could I prove?   I had $48 in my purse.   The next day I got a job as a summer waitress at a restaurant and worked there all summer under an assumed name.   I even got a new Social Security number.   I worked hard and they liked hard-working steady help who showed up seven days a week and didn't irritate the customers.   I also subscribed to our hometown paper so that I would have some way of finding out about you.   That tombstone now, that was touching.

"After the summer was over they offered me a job in their Florida place and I worked there until two weeks ago when I had enough money saved for this trip. The paper had reported your departure to live in Rome 'for an indefinite period,' it said, and how wrong that is now.   My one fear was that my money would run out before I located you.   I didn't realize how easy it is to find an American in Rome.   Just watch the tourist attractions long enough and you'll find them.

"I saw you first at the Colosseum one day and followed you to this address. I thought at the time what a fitting place the Colosseum would be to do what I had come to do if it weren't so public.   Too bad we didn't meet there by moonlight."

"May I get up and stand by the window?" he asked.   "I can't breathe."

"Do," she answered, "but don't get too close.   It's too late for accidents."

He walked to the window in the wall behind her chair and stood looking down into the street.   Shielded from her direct view by the tall back of her chair she was sitting in, he slowly slid one hand under the window drapery and unhooked the ropelike tie that looped the drape back.

"How did you get out of the life jacket?" he asked, not turning toward her chair.

"Oh, it almost worked.   But you made one mistake—one small detail.   When you tied the ribbons of the life jacket your reflexes took over.   You tied the same knot that you, and nearly everybody else, ties every day of their lives—a simple bow knot.   Under water I gave one pull at the ends of the ribbons and the knots came apart and I slipped out of the jacket.   It was simple compared to untying and taking off my sneakers under water as we used to do when I was a girl in camp.   If you had tied a good hard square knot, Howard, things would have been different for me.   And for you.

"If you're wondering about the gun, I borrowed it—stole it really—from the Florida restaurant.   They always kept one near the cash register."

He whirled from the window and leaped toward the back of her chair, the drapery tie outstretched between his hands.   Her first shot, fired in frightened reflex at his reflection, shattered the mirror on the wall opposite her chair.   Hanging over the chair back, he fumbled desperately to twist the rope tie around her neck.   She slid from the chair to the floor and fired backward and upward in the blind instinct of self-preservation.

Howard staggered backward from the impact of the shot, one hand jerking upward and holding the moth-eaten drapery tie as though in some baroque scalp dance, the other clutching the window drape which he pulled to the floor with him as he fell, his body becoming partly hidden in its pretentious folds.   She pulled herself to her feet and stood over the body, sickened at the reality of what her plans had brought to pass, and dreading the possibility of having to fire again.   But the thing that lay there was still and dead, the rope tie grasped in one hand.

She replaced the gun in her bag, inspected the room carefully to be sure she left no trail, and left the apartment without looking back.   She made her way through the streets to the top of the Spanish Steps, rejecting the waiting taxis in case the drivers would be questioned later.   Going down the long cascade of the Spanish Steps, she stopped at the landing one flight from the street below and looked up at the figures that drifted aimlessly past the open window of the room where Keats had died.

She wondered what historic shrine this house might be but knew that now she would never find out, any more than she would learn whether operas were performed in ruined bathhouses, as advertised.   She had already placed a foot on the next descending step when her body contracted with rigid terror.   Looking down at her from the open window of Keats's room was Howard, or a man who at this distance resembled Howard in startling detail.

He stood in full view immediately in front of the window, looking patient and expectant.   She stared up at him in a paralysis of fear; he gazed down at her with serene assurance.

Then the figure slowly disappeared backward into the room, smiling as if in anticipation and passing confidently, almost negligently, a faded rope tie through one hand and then the other.

VICTOR CANNING

A Stroke of Genius

Criminal:
LANCELOT PIKE

The Minerva Club, in a discreet turning off Brook Street, is one of the most exclusive clubs in London.   Members must have served at least two years in one of Her Majesty's Prisons and be able to pay £50 a year dues.   In the quiet of its Smoking Room, under the mild eye of Milky Waye, the club secretary, some of the most ambitious schemes for money-making, allied of course with evasion of the law, have been worked out.   But, although notoriety is a common quality among members, fame—real honest solid fame—has come to few of them.

Lancelot Pike is one of these few but, although he is still a member, he is not often seen in the august halls of the Minerva.   However, over the fireplace in the Smoking Room, hangs one of his greatest works—never seen by the general public— a full assembly, in oils, of the Management Committee of the club; it shows thirty figures of men whose photographs and fingerprints are cherished lovingly by Scotland Yard.

Lancelot's road to fame was a devious one and the first step was taken on the day that Horace Head, leaning against a lamppost in the Old Kent Road and reading the racing edition, saw Miss Nancy Reeves.   Without thinking, Horace began to follow her, some dim but undeniable impulse of the heart leading him.   And, naturally, Lancelot Pike, who was leaning against the other side of the lamppost, followed Horace, because he was Horace's manager and was not letting Horace out of his sight.

Horace Head at this time was at the peak of his brief career as a professional middleweight fighter.   He was younger then, of course, but still a wooden-headed, slow-thinking fellow with an engaging smile bracketed by cauliflower ears.   He was wearing a gray suit with a thick red line in it, a blue shirt, a yellow bow tie, and brown shoes that squeaked.

He squeaked away after Miss Nancy Reeves and there wasn't any real reason why he should not have done so.   She was a trim slim blonde with blue eyes and a pink and white complexion that made Horace think—and this will show how stirred up he was—of blue skies seen through a lacing of cherry blossoms.   It had been a good many years since Horace had seen real cherry blossoms too.

Lancelot Pike followed him.   Lancelot was a tall, slim, handsome, versatile number, with a ready tongue, a fast mind, and a determination to have an overstuffed bank account before he was thirty no matter what he had to do to get it. At the moment, Horace—at one fight a month—was his stake money.

If Miss Nancy Reeves knew that she was being followed, she showed no signs of it. She eventually went up the steps of the neighborhood Art School and disappeared through its doors.

Horace continued to follow. He was stopped inside by an attendant who said, "You a student?"

Horace said, "Do I have to be?"

"To come in here, yes," said the attendant.

"Who," said Horace, "is the poppet in the green coat with blonde hair?" He nodded to where Miss Nancy Reeves was almost out of sight up a wide flight of stairs.

"That," said the attendant, "is Miss Nancy Reeves."

"She a student?" asked Horace.

"No," said the attendant. "She's one of the art teachers. Life class."

"Then make me a student in the life class," said Horace, the romantic impulse in him growing.

At this moment Lancelot Pike intervened. "What the devil are you after, Horace? You couldn't paint a white stripe down the middle of the road. Besides, do you know what a life class is?"

"No," said Horace.

"Naked women. Maybe, men, too. You've got to paint them."

"To be near her," said Horace, "I'll paint anybody, the Queen of Sheba or the Prime Minister, black all over. I got to do it, Lance. I got this sort of pain right under my heart suddenly."

"You need bicarbonate of soda," said the attendant.

Horace looked at him, reached out, and lifted him clear of the ground by the collar of his jacket and said, "Make me a student."

Well, it had to be. There was no stopping Horace. Lancelot helped to fill out the form and, in a way, he was glad because he knew that the classes would keep Horace away from the pubs between training. Horace was the kind who developed an enormous thirst as soon as training was finished.

So Horace became a student in the life class. It was a bit of a shock to him at first. He came from a decent family of safe crackers, holdup men, and pickpockets. He didn't approve of naked women posing on a stand while a lot of people sat round painting them.

To do him credit, Horace seldom looked at the models. He sat behind his easel and looked most of the time at Nancy Reeves. Naturally he did very little painting— but he saw a lot of Nancy Reeves.

She was a nice girl. She soon realized that Horace was almost pure bone from the shoulders up; but she was a great believer in the releasing power of art, and she was convinced that Horace would never have joined the class if there had not been some deep-buried longing in him for expression.

Now Horace, of course, had not the faintest talent for drawing or painting; but, realizing that he could not sit in the class and do nothing, he would just smack an occasional daub of paint on his canvas in a way that loosely conformed to the naked shape of the model before him.   Nancy Reeves soon decided that Horace was— if he was going to be anything—an abstract painter.   She would come and stand behind him at times and her talk went straight over his head—but Horace enjoyed every moment of it.

After two weeks of this, Horace finally got to the point of asking her if she would go to a dance with him.   Surprisingly, she agreed, and she enjoyed it because, whatever else he was not, Horace was quick on his feet at that time and a good dancer.

Now, a week after the dance, Horace and Lancelot had fixed up a little private business which Lancelot had carefully planned for some time.   This was to grab the payroll bag of a local building firm when the messenger came out of the bank on a Friday morning.

Lancelot Pike had the whole thing worked out to the dot.   Horace would sit in the car outside the bank, and Lancelot would grab the moneybag as the man came to the bottom of the steps and they would be away before anyone could make a move to stop them.   It was a bit crude, but it had the merit of simple directness and nine times out of ten—if you read your papers—it works.

It worked this time—except for one thing.   The man came down the steps carrying the bag, Lancelot grabbed it and jumped into the car, and Horace started away; but at that moment the messenger shoved his hand through the rear window and fired at Lancelot Pike.

But the gun wasn't an ordinary one.   It was a dye gun full of a vivid purple stain.   The charge got Lancelot full on the right side of the face, ran down his neck, and ruined a good suit and a silk shirt.

Well, there it was.   They got back to the Head house, where Lancelot had a room, without any trouble from the police.   Lancelot nipped inside with the moneybag and Horace drove off to ditch the car.

When Horace returned he found Lancelot hanging over the wash basin trying to get the dye off.   But it wouldn't budge.   It was a good rich purple dye that meant to stay until time slowly erased it.

"You won't be able to go out for a while," said Horace.   "Months, maybe. The police will be looking for a purple-faced man."

"Lovely," said Lancelot savagely.   "So I'm a hermit.   Stuck here for weeks. You know what that's going to do to a gregarious person like me?"

Horace shook his head.   He didn't know what a gregarious person was.

"We got the money," he said.

"And can't spend it.   Can't put it to work to make more.   Cooped up like a prisoner in the Tower.   Me, Lancelot Pike, who lives for color, movement, people, the big pageant of life, and golden opportunities waiting to be seized."

"I could go to the chemist and ask him if he's got anything to take it off," suggested Horace.

"And have him go to the police once he's read the story in the evening newspaper!"

"I see what you mean," said Horace.

So Lancelot—very bad-tempered—was confined to his room.   For the first few days he kept Horace busy running to and from the public library getting books for him.   Lancelot was a talented, not far from cultured type—things came easily to him and idleness was like a poison in his blood that has to be worked out of his system.   But it was people and movement that he missed.   Every evening Horace had to recount to him all that he had done during the day and, particularly, how he was getting on with Miss Nancy Reeves at the Art School.

Curiously enough, Horace was getting on very well with her.   There was something simple, earthy, and engagingly wooden about Horace which had begun to appeal to Nancy Reeves.   It happens that way—like calling to unlike . . . think of the number of men, ugly as all get-out, with beautiful wives, or of dumb women trailing around with top intellects.

Anyway, Lancelot began to take a great interest in Horace's romance, and he knew that the time would come when Horace would ask the girl to marry him, and he was offering ten to four that she would not accept.

Horace wouldn't take the bet, but he was annoyed that Lancelot should think he had such a poor chance.

"What's wrong with me?" he asked.

"Nothing," said Lancelot, "except that you really aren't her type.   To her you're just a big ape she's trying to educate."

"You calling me a big ape?"

"Figuratively, not literally."

"What does that mean?"

"That you don't have to knock my head off for an imagined insult."

"I see."

"I wonder," said Lancelot.   "However, forget it.   You ask her and see what answer you'll get."

Meanwhile Lancelot helped Horace with his homework from the Art School.

Each week each student did a home study composition on any subject he liked to choose.   Lancelot got hold of canvas and paints and went to work for Horace. And then the painting bug hit him—and hit him hard.

He gave up reading books and papers, gave up listening to the radio and watching television, and just painted.   It became a mania with him in his enforced seclusion— and it turned out that he was good.   He had a kind of rugged, primitive quality, with just a lick of sophistication here and there which really made you stop and look.

Naturally, Nancy Reeves noticed the great improvement in Horace's work and her spirit expanded with delight at the thought that she was drawing from the mahogany depths of Horace's mind a flowering of his true personality and soul. There's nothing a woman likes more than to make a man over.   They're great ones for improving on the original model.

Well, one week when Lancelot's face had faded to a pale lilac, Horace came back from the Art School saying that the home study that week had to be "The Head of a Friend," and Lancelot said, "Leave it to me, Horace.   Self-portrait by Rubens.   Self-portrait by Van Gogh—"

"It's got to be a friend," said Horace. "I don't know no Rubens—"

"Quiet," said Lancelot, and he began to ferret for a canvas in the pile Horace had bought for him. As he set it up and fixed a mirror so that he could see himself in it, he went on, "How's tricks with the delicious Nancy?"

"Today," said Horace, "I asked her to marry me. A couple more good fights and with my share of the wages snatch, I can fix up the furniture and a flat."

"And what did she say?"

"She got to think it over. Something about it being a big decision, a reckonable step."

"Irrevocable step."

"That's it. That's what she said."

"Means she don't believe in divorce. If she says Yes, which she won't, you'll have her for life. When do you get your answer?"

"End of the week."

"Twenty to one she says No."

"You've lengthened the odds," said Horace, wounded.

"Why not? Deep knowledge of women. When they want time, there's doubt. Where there's doubt with a woman, there's no desire."

"Why should she have doubts? What's wrong with me?"

"You're always asking that," said Lancelot. "Someday somebody is going to be fool enough to tell you. Horace, face it—you're no Romeo like me. I've got the face for it."

"I love her," said Horace. "That's enough for any woman."

Lancelot rolled his eyes. "That anyone could be so simple! A man who has only love to offer is in the ring with a glass jaw. Now then, let's see." He studied himself in the mirror. "I think I'll paint it full face, kind of serious but with a little twinkle, man of the world, knowing, but full of heart."

Well, by the end of the week the self-portrait was finished and Horace took it along to the school. He set it up on the easel and pretended to be putting a few finishing touches to it. When Nancy Reeves saw it she was enraptured.

"It ain't," said Horace, who had learned enough by now to play along with art talk to some extent, "quite finished. It needs a something—a point of . . . well, of something."

"Yes, perhaps it does, Horace. But you'll get it."

She put a hand gently on his shoulder. They were in a secluded part of the room. "By the way, I've come to a decision about your proposal. It's better for me to tell you here in public because it will keep it on a calm, sane, level basis—a perfect understanding between two adult people who considered carefully, very carefully, before making an important decision. I feel that by producing in you this wonderful flowering of talent that I've completed my role, that I have no more to give. Marriage after this would be an anticlimax, since my attachment to you is really an intellectual and artistic one, rather than any warm, passionate, romantic craving. I know that you will understand perfectly, dear Horace."

"You mean, no go?" asked Horace.

Nancy nodded gently. "I'm sorry. But for a woman, love must be an immediate thing. There must be something about a man's face that is instantly compelling. Now take this painting of yours—there's a man's face that is full of the promise of romance, of tenderness and yet manly strength. I'd like to meet your friend."

For a moment Horace sat there, the great fire of his love just a handful of wet ashes. That Nancy Reeves could go for Lancelot just by seeing his portrait filled Horace with bitterness—a bitterness made even blacker by the fact that Horace had taken Lancelot's bet at twenty to one, and now stood to lose £100.

"You mean," said Horace, "that you could go for him?"

"He's certainly got a magic. You've caught his compulsive personality and—"

"You should really see him," said Horace jealously. "One-half of his face is as purple as a baboon's—well, like this—"

In a fit of pique, Horace picked up his brush, squirted some purple paint onto his palette, and slapped the purple thickly over the right side of Lancelot's face.

From behind him Nancy Reeves's voice said breathlessly, "But Horace—that's just the defiant abstract touch it needed! The unconventional, the startling, the emphatic denial of realism . . . Horace, it's staggering! Pure genius. Don't do a thing more to it—not another stroke!"

Horace stood up, looked at her, and said, "There's a lot more I could do to it. But if you like it so much—keep him. Call it 'A Painter's Goodbye.' " He walked out and he never went back to Art School again.

A week later, while Horace was sitting dejectedly in Lancelot's room watching him work at a painting, the local Detective-Inspector and a Constable walked in unexpectedly.

The Inspector nodded affably and said, "Hello, Horace. Evening, Lance. Forging old masters, eh?" He was in a good mood.

Horace gave him a cold stare, and Lancelot kept his hand up to his face to cover his pale lilac cheek.

The Inspector went on, "Funny—I never connected you two with that wages snatch. Bit out of your line. Thought it was strictly an uptown job."

He leaned forward and looked at the painting on which Lancelot was working. "Nice. Nice brushwork. Fine handling of color. Bit of a dabbler myself. Bitten by the bug, you know. Great relaxation. Go to all the exhibitions. They had one at the Art School yesterday. Picked up this little masterpiece by Horace Head."

The Constable stepped forward and brought from behind him Lancelot's self-portrait with Horace's purple-cheeked addition.

"Fine bit of work," said the Inspector. "Sort of neo-impressionistic with traces of nonobjective emotionalism, calculated to shock the indifferent into attention. It did just that to me—so you can take your hand away from your cheek, Lance, and both of you come along with me."

And along they went—for a three year stretch.

But it didn't stop Lancelot painting.   He did it in prison and he did it when he came out.   Gets 500 guineas a canvas now, and his name is known all over the country.

But he's not often in the Minerva Club.   His wife—who was a Miss Nancy Reeves—doesn't approve of the types there and rules the poor fellow with a rod of iron.

ELLERY QUEEN

The Odd Man

Detective:
ELLERY QUEEN

One of the unique encounters in the short and happy history of The Puzzle Club began, as so many interesting things do, in the most ordinary way.

That is to say, 7:30 of that Wednesday evening found Ellery in the foyer of Syres's Park Avenue penthouse aerie pressing the bell button, having the door opened for him by a butler who had obviously been inspired by Jeeves, and being conducted into the grand-scale wood-leather-and-brass-stud living room that had just as obviously been inspired by the king-sized ranchos of the Southwest where Syres had made his millions.

As usual Ellery found the membership assembled—with the exception, also as usual, of Arkavy, the biochemist whose Nobel achievement took him to so many international symposiums that Ellery had not yet laid eyes on him; indeed, he had come to think of the great scientist as yet another fiction his fellow members had dreamed up for mischievous reasons of their own.   There was Syres himself, their hulking and profoundly respected host—respected not for being a multimillionaire but for having founded the club; tall sardonic Darnell of the John L. Lewis eyebrows, the criminal lawyer who was known to the American Bar, not altogether affectionately, as "the rich man's Clarence Darrow"; the psychiatrist, Dr. Vreeland, trim and peach-cheeked, whose professional reputation was as long as his stature was short; and wickedly blue-eyed little Emmy Wandermere, who had recently won the Pulitzer Prize for poetry to—for once—unanimous approval.

It was one of the strictest rules of The Puzzle Club that no extraneous matters, not of politics or art or economics or world affairs, or even of juicy gossip, be allowed to intrude on the business at hand, which was simply (in a manner of speaking only, since that adverb was not to be found in the club's motto) to challenge each member to solve a puzzle invented by the others, and then to repair to Charlot's dinner table, Charlot being Syres's chef, with a reputation as exalted in his field as that of the puzzlers in theirs.   The puzzles were always in story form, told by the challengers seriatim, and they were as painstakingly planned for the battle of wits as if an empire depended on the outcome.

Tonight it was Ellery's turn again, and after the briefest of amenities he took his place in the arena, which at The Puzzle Club meant sitting down in a hugely comfortable leather chair near the super-fireplace, with a bottle, a glass, and a little buffet of Charlot's masterly canapés at hand and no further preliminaries whatever.

Darnell began (by prearrangement—the sequence of narrators was as carefully choreographed as a ballet).

"The puzzle this evening, Queen, is right down your alley—"

"Kindly omit the courtroom-type psychology, Counselor," Ellery drawled, for he was feeling in extra-fine fettle this evening, "and get on with it."

"—because it's a cops-and-robbers story," the lawyer went on, unperturbed, "except that in this case the cop is an undercover agent whose assignment it is to track down a dope supplier. The supplier is running a big wholesale illicit-drug operation; hundreds of pushers are getting their stuff from him, so it's important to nail him."

"The trouble is," Dr. Vreeland said, feeling the knot of his tie (I wonder, Ellery thought, what his analyst made of that—it was one of the psychiatrist's most irritating habits), "his identity is not known precisely."

"By which I take it that it's known imprecisely," Ellery said. "The unknown of a known group."

"Yes, a group of three."

"The classic number."

"It's convenient, Queen."

"That's the chief reason it's classic."

"The three suspects," oilman Syres broke in, unable to conceal a frown, for Ellery did not always comport himself with the decorum the founder thought their labors deserved, "all live in the same building. It's a three-story house . . ."

"Someday," Ellery said, peering into the future, "instead of a three-story house I shall make up a three-house story."

"Mr. Queen!" and Emmy Wandermere let a giggle escape. "Please be serious, or you won't be allowed to eat Charlot's chef-d'oeuvre, which I understand is positively wild tonight."

"I've lost track," Syres grumped. "Where were we?"

"I beg everyone's pardon," Ellery said. "We have an undercover police officer who's turned up three suspects, one of whom is the dope wholesaler, and all three live in a three-story house, I presume one to a floor. And these habitants are?"

"The man who occupies the ground floor," the little poet replied, "and whose name is John A. Chandler—known in the neighborhood as Jac, from his initials—runs a modest one-man business, a radio-and-TV-repair shop, from his apartment."

"The question is, of course," Lawyer Darnell said, "whether the repair shop is just a front for the dope-supply operation."

Ellery nodded. "And the occupant of the middle floor?"

"An insurance agent," Dr. Vreeland said. "Character named Cutcliffe Kerry—"

"Named what?"

"Cutcliffe Kerry is what we decided on," the psychiatrist said firmly, "and if you don't care for it that's your problem, Queen, because Cutcliffe Kerry he remains."

"Very well," Ellery said, "but I think I detect the aroma of fresh herring. Or am I being double-whammied? In any event, Cutcliffe Kerry sells insurance, or tries to, which means he gets to see a great many people. So the insurance thing could be a cover. And the top floor?"

"Is rented by a fellow named Fletcher, Benjamin Fletcher," Syres said. "Fletcher is a salesman, too, but of an entirely different sort. He sells vacuum cleaners."

"Door to door," Ellery said. "Possible cover too. All right, Jac Chandler, radio-TV repairman; Cutcliffe Kerry, insurance agent; Ben Fletcher, vacuum-cleaner salesman; and one of them is the bad guy. What happens, Mr. Syres?"

"The undercover man has been watching the building and—isn't the word tailing?—the three men, according to his reports to his superior at police headquarters."

"And just after he finds out who the drug supplier is," Darnell said mournfully, "but before he can come up with the hard evidence, he's murdered."

"As I suspected," Ellery said, shaking his head. "Earning the poor fellow a departmental citation and the traditional six feet of sod. He was murdered by the dope boy, of course."

"Of course."

"To shut him up."

"What else?"

"Which means he hadn't yet reported the name of the dope supplier."

"Well, not exactly, Mr. Queen." Emmy Wandermere leaned forward to accept the flame of Dr. Vreeland's gold lighter, then leaned back puffing like The Little Engine That Could on a steep grade. She was trying to curb her nicotine-and-tar intake, so she was currently smoking cigarettes made of processed lettuce. "The undercover man hadn't reported the drug supplier's name, true, but in the very last report before his murder he did mention a clue."

"What kind of clue?"

"He referred to the supplier—his subsequent killer—as, and this is an exact quote, Mr. Queen, 'the odd man of the three.' "

Ellery blinked.

"Your mission, Mr. Queen, if you accept it—and you'd better, or be kicked out of the club," said Darnell in his most doom-ridden courtroom tones, "is to detect the guilty man among Chandler, Kerry, and Fletcher—the one of them who's been selling the stuff in wholesale lots and who murdered our brave lad of the law."

"The odd man of the three, hm?"

Ellery sat arranging his thoughts. As at all such critical stages of the game, by protocol, the strictest silence was maintained.

Finally Ellery said, "Where and how did the murder of the undercover agent take place?"

Darnell waved his manicured hand, "Frankly, Queen, we debated whether to make up a complicated background for the crime. In the end we decided it wouldn't be fair, because the murder itself has nothing to do with the puzzle except that it took place. The details are irrelevant and immaterial."

"Except, of course, to the victim, but that's usually left out." Having discharged himself of this philosophical gripe, Ellery resumed his seat, as it were, on his train of thought.   "I suppose the premises were searched from roof to cellar, inside and out, by the police after the murder of their buddy?"

"You know it," Syres said.

"I suppose, too, that no narcotics, amphetamines, barbiturates, et cetera *ad nauseam*, no cutting equipment, no dope paraphernalia of any kind, were found anywhere in the building?"

"Not a trace," Dr. Vreeland said.   "The guilty man disposed of it all before the police got there."

"Did one of the men have a record?"

Miss Wandermere smiled.   "*Nyet*."

"Was one of them a married man and were the other two bachelors?"

"No."

"Was it the other way round?   One of them a bachelor and two married?"

"I admire the way you wriggle, Mr. Queen.   The answer is still no."

"The odd man of the three."   Ellery mused again.   "Well, I see we'll have to be lexical.   By the commonest definition, odd means strange, unusual, peculiar. Was there anything strange, unusual, or peculiar in, say, the appearance of Chandler or Kerry or Fletcher?"

Dr. Vreeland, with relish: "Not a thing."

"In a mannerism?   Behavior?   Speech?   Gait?   That sort of thing?"

Syres: "All ordinary as hell, Queen."

"In background?"

Darnell, through a grin: "Ditto."

'There was nothing bizarre or freakish about one of them?"

"Nothing, friend," Emmy Wandermere murmured.

Ellery grasped his nose more like an enemy.

"Was one of them touched in the head?" he asked suddenly.   "Odd in the mental sense?"

"There," the psychiatrist said, "you tread on muddy ground, Queen.   Any antisocial behavior, as in the case of habitual criminals, might of course be so characterized.   However, for purposes of our story the answer is no.   All three men were normal—whatever that means."

Ellery nodded fretfully.   "I could go on and on naming categories of peculiarity, but let me save us all from endangering Charlot's peace of mind.   *Did* the undercover man use the word odd to connote peculiar?"

The little poet looked around and received assents invisible to the Queen eye. "He did not."

"Then that's that.   Oh, one thing.   Was the report in which he fingered the supplier as being the odd man written or oral?"

"Now what kind of question is that?" the oil king demanded.   "What could that have to do with anything?"

"Possibly a great deal, Mr. Syres.   If it had been an oral report, there would be no way of knowing whether his word odd began with a capital O or a small o. Assume that he'd meant it to be capital O-d-d.   Then Odd man might have referred to a member of the I.O.O.F., the fraternal order—the Odd Fellows.   That might certainly distinguish your man from the other two.''

"It was a written report," Darnell said hastily, "and the o of odd was a small letter."

Everyone looked relieved.   It was evident that the makers of this particular puzzle had failed to consider the Independent Order of Odd Fellows in their scheming.

"There are other odd possibilities—if you'll forgive the pun—such as odd in the golf meaning, which is one stroke more than your opponent has played.   But I won't waste any more time on esoterica.   Your undercover man meant odd in the sense of not matching, didn't he?   Of being left over?''

"Explain that, please," Dr. Vreeland said.

"In the sense that two of the three suspects had something in common, something the third man didn't share with them—thus making the third man 'the odd man' and consequently the dope supplier and murderer.   Isn't that the kind of thing your undercover agent meant by odd man?''

The psychiatrist looked cautious.   "I think we may fairly say yes to that."

"Thank you very much," Ellery said.   "Which brings me to a fascinating question: How clever are you people being?   Run-of-the-game clever or clever-clever?''

"I don't think," Miss Wandermere said, "we quite follow.   What do you mean exactly, Mr. Queen?''

"Did you intend to give me a choice of solutions?   The reason I ask is that I see not one possible answer, but three.''

"Three!"   Syres shook his massive head.   "We had enough trouble deciding on one.''

"I for one," Counselor Darnell stated stiffishly, "should like to hear a for-instance.''

"All right, I'll give you one solution I doubt you had in mind, since it's so obvious.''

"You know, Queen, you have a sadistic streak in you?" barked Dr. Vreeland. "Obvious!   Which solution is obvious?''

"Why, Doctor.   Take the names of two of your suspects, John A.—Jac—Chandler and Benjamin Fletcher.   Oddly enough—there I go again!—those surnames have two points of similarity.   'Chandler' and 'Fletcher' both end in 'er' and both contain eight letters.   Cutcliffe Kerry's surname differs in both respects—no 'er' ending and only five letters—so Kerry becomes the odd surname of the trio.   In this solution, then, Kerry the insurance man is the supplier-killer.''

"I'll be damned," Syres exclaimed.   "How did we miss that?''

"Very simply," Miss Wandermere said.   "We didn't see it.''

"Never mind that," Darnell snapped.   "The fact is it happened.   Queen, you said you have three solutions.   What's another?''

"Give me a clue to the solution you people had in mind, since there are more than one.   Some key word that indicates the drift but doesn't give the game away. One word can do it.''

Syres, Darnell, and Dr. Vreeland jumped up and surrounded Emmy Wandermere. From the looped figures, the cocked heads, and the murderous whispers they might have been the losing team in an offensive huddle with six seconds left to play. Finally, the men resumed their seats, nudging one another.

Said little Miss Wandermere: "You asked for a clue, Mr. Queen. The clue is: clue."

Ellery threw his head back and roared. "Right! Very clever, considering who I am and that I'm the solver of the evening.

"You hurled my specialized knowledge in my teeth, calculating that I'd be so close to it I wouldn't see it. Sorry! Two of the surnames you invented," Ellery said with satisfaction, "are of famous detective-story writers. Chandler—in this case Raymond Chandler—was the widely acclaimed creator of Philip Marlowe. Joseph Smith Fletcher—J. S. Fletcher—produced more detective fiction than any other writer except Edgar Wallace, or so it's said; Fletcher's *The Middle Temple Murder* was publicly praised by no lesser mystery fan than the President of the United States, Woodrow Wilson. On the other hand, if there's ever been a famous detective-story writer named Cutcliffe Kerry, his fame has failed to reach me. So your Mr. Kerry again becomes the odd man of the trio and the answer to the problem. Wasn't that your solution, Miss Wandermere and gentlemen?"

They said yes in varying tones of chagrin.

Ordinarily, at this point in the evening's proceedings, the company would have risen from their chairs and made for Syres's magnificently gussied-up cookhouse of a dining room. But tonight no one stirred a toe, not even at the promise of the manna simmering on Charlot's hob. Instead, Dr. Vreeland uttered a small, inquiring cough.

"You, ah, mentioned a third solution, Queen. Although I must confess—"

"Before you pronounce your *mea culpa,* Doctor," Ellery said with a smile, "may I? I've given you people your solution. I've even thrown in another for good measure. Turnabout? I now challenge you. What's the third solution?" . . .

Ten minutes later Ellery showed them mercy—really, he said sorrowfully, more in the interest of preserving Charlot's chancy good will than out of natural goodness of heart.

"John A. Chandler, Cutcliffe Kerry, Benjamin Fletcher. Chandler, Kerry, and Fletcher. What do two of these have in common besides what's already been discussed? Why, they derive from trades or occupations."

"Chandler." The lawyer, Darnell, looked around at the others, startled. "You know, that's true!"

"Yes, a ship chandler deals in specified goods or equipment. If you go farther back in time you find that a chandler was someone who made or sold candles or, as in very early England, supervised the candle requirements of a household. So that's one trade."

"Is there another in the remaining two surnames?"

"Yes, the name Fletcher. A fletcher was—and technically still is—a maker of arrows, or a dealer in same; in the Middle Ages, by extension, although this was a rare meaning, the word was sometimes used to denote an archer.   In either event, another trade or occupation.

"But the only etymological origin I've ever heard ascribed to the name Kerry is County Kerry, from which the Kerry blue terrier derives.   And that's not a trade, it's a place.   So with the names Chandler and Fletcher going back to occupations, and Kerry to Irish geography, your Mr. Kerry becomes once again the unpaired meaning, the odd man—a third answer to your problem."

And Ellery rose and offered his arm gallantly to Miss Wandermere.

The poetess took it with a little shake.   And as they led the way to the feast she whispered, "You know what you are, Ellery Queen?   You're an intellectual *pack rat!*"

Hunting Accident

When I arrived in the office Tuesday morning Cord's wife was waiting for me. She didn't rise from the chair. I'd heard the news on the car radio and her grief didn't surprise me but it was mitigated by anger: she was in a rage.

"I'm sorry, Mrs. Cord. I just heard."

Her lips kept working and she blinked at me but she held her tongue; perhaps she was afraid of what might come out. Her natural appearance was drab but normally she managed attractive contrivances. This morning there was no makeup. She sat with her shoulders rolled forward and her arms folded as if she had a severe abdominal pain. Now she snarled—a visible exposing of teeth—and afterward she remembered herself, tried an apologetic smile, gathered herself with an obvious effort of will. Her wrath had rendered her quite inarticulate.

I tried to help. "I hope I haven't kept you waiting. I didn't expect—"

"I want you to help me, Bill. I want you to go up there."

Her voice had lost its customary music; it was like a smoker's morning voice—a deep hangover baritone. I stood at my desk unwilling to sit down. "Up where?"

"That place in Colorado. Whatever it's called."

"You'd like me to bring the body back? Of course."

"Bill, I want you to find out who was responsible." She spoke slowly with effort; the words fell from her with equal weight, like bricks. She said again, clenching a fist, "Responsible."

"The radio said it was an accident."

She watched me with her injured eyes. It rattled me. I said lamely, "My work's industrial security, Mrs. Cord. You seem to be asking me to investigate a homicide. It's a little out of my—"

"You don't like—you didn't like Charlie."

"Mrs. Cord, I—"

"Never mind. I didn't like him very much myself. But he was all I had."

"You need rest," I told her. I sat down behind the desk. "Have you seen a doctor?"

"He gave me a pill. I'll take it when I go home. Bill, you're the only one I trust to do this."

What a sad thing for her to say, I thought. I hardly knew her. She was the wife—the widow—of an acquaintance who'd been an executive in a neighboring department; I hadn't known Charlie Cord very well. She was right—I hadn't liked him, and therefore I'd avoided him when I could. Yet she'd come to me. Hadn't they any friends?

She looked down and saw her fist and unclenched it slowly, studying the fingers as if they were unfamiliar objects. She was waiting for me to speak; she almost cringed. I said, "I'm not sure I understand what you're asking me to do."

"Bill, nobody here cares about Charlie. Good riddance—that's what they'll be thinking. You know the gossip of course."

"Gossip?"

"Why Charlie married me. I've never been what you could call a glamour girl. But my father happens to be a director of the company with sixteen percent of the stock. When Charlie married me, he married sixteen percent of Schiefflin Aerospace and married himself into a forty-thousand-a-year job in the sales and marketing division. Charlie made his way well up in the world from the football team of a second-rate state university. That's what most everybody thinks of Charlie. That's *all* they ever think of him."

"Mrs. Cord, you're upset and that's understandable, but—"

She went on, not allowing me to interrupt further. "He wasn't likeable. He was a boor. He was a hearty backslapper, he was never sincere enough, he told outhouse jokes badly and too loudly. He affected garish jackets and ridiculous cars. He had a fetish for big-game hunting. But he did a good job for this company, Bill. People tend to ignore that—deliberately I'm sure, because no one likes to give credit to a person as obnoxious as Charlie. As Charlie was." Then her voice cracked. "He made my life miserable. Intolerable. But he was all I had. Can you understand that?"

"Sure." I tried to look reassuring.

"Bill, I want you to be the instrument of my revenge."

"Revenge? Wait a minute now, Mrs. Cord."

"He was mine and I was his."

"But apparently it was simply an accident."

"Accident? Maybe. He was shot twice." She paused as if to challenge me to contradict her. Then she said, "I've talked to my father. The company will voucher your expenses. There's a plane to Denver at half-past eleven." She stood up. "Find out how he was killed. And why. And who did it."

On the plane I reviewed what she'd told me about the death of Charlie Cord, what I'd already known, and what I'd learned from two brief phone calls to Colorado.

Six days ago Charlie had flown to Denver with his hunting gear, picked up a rental car at Stapleton Airport, and driven into the Rockies to a half-abandoned mining town called Quartz City. In Wild West days it had been a boom town; now it was a center for tourists and hunters.

Charlie had spent the night in a motel and in the morning by prearrangement he'd been picked up by a professional guide employed by Rocky Mountain Game Safaris, Ltd., a commercial hunting outfit. Charlie and the guide, a man named

Sam Mallory, had set out into the mountains in a four-wheel-drive truck with provisions and gear enough for ten days. Four days later Mallory returned to Quartz City in the truck with Charlie Cord's corpse in the back. Charlie had been dead, by then, about twenty-four hours.

According to the sheriff's office, Charlie had been shot twice through the chest by a .30-'06 rifle. Sam Mallory, the guide, professed to know nothing about the event. His deposition, prepared for the pending coroner's inquest, alleged that Mallory had been in the process of setting up camp on a new site to which they'd moved that morning; while Mallory was pitching the tents, he said, Charlie had taken his .303 rifle and climbed a nearby peak to reconnoiter and perhaps bag something for the supper pot.

About an hour after Charlie's departure from camp, Mallory heard two rifle shots on the mountain. He thought little of it at the time, assuming Charlie had shot some game animal. When Charlie didn't return within two hours, Mallory assumed Charlie had wounded the animal and gone after it, as any hunter must.

It wasn't until late afternoon—six or seven hours after he'd heard the shots— that Mallory became alarmed. After all, he deposed, Mr. Cord was an experienced hunter and had a compass and canteen with him; there was no reason for concern earlier.

Mallory went up the mountain but darkness fell before he found anything. Through the night he kept the campfire banked high to give Charlie a homing beacon, but Charlie didn't return and at dawn Mallory was back on the mountain tracking Charlie's boot prints; and at about 8:30 in the morning Mallory found him lying where he'd been shot. Mallory had backpacked the body down to the truck and driven straight to the sheriff.

The sheriff was a towering thin man with weathered blue outdoor eyes and a thatch of black hair. He went by the name of Bob Wilkerson. He poured me a cup of strong coffee to take the chill out of the autumn afternoon.

"Afraid I never met your friend while he was alive. They tell me he was— well, kind of loud." He smiled to take the edge off it.

The coffee was old but hot. "Have you found the rifle that shot him?"

"No. It was an 'ought-six, of course. We recovered both slugs from the body."

"Isn't that unusual?"

"Unusual? No. Why?"

I said, "A powerful rifle like that, wouldn't it tend to punch straight through a man and keep right on going? Or were they hollowpoints that explode on contact?"

He watched me gravely, then something like suspicion entered his face. "No, they weren't hollowpoints. Jacketed slugs—military style. They didn't expand hardly at all. But they were half spent by the time they hit him. That's why they didn't go on through."

"In other words he was shot from a considerable distance."

"Mr. Stoddard, you don't rightly believe a hunter could mistake a man for a buck deer at *close* range, do you?"

"Is that how it happened, then, Sheriff?"

"That's what it looked like to me. He was shot from a range of four hundred yards or better and it was an uphill trajectory. Fighting gravity and all, those slugs weren't going too fast when they hit him."

"Both bullets hit him in the chest?"

"Not more than three inches apart. One of them penetrated his heart."

"That's extraordinary shooting, wouldn't you say?"

"Or lucky shooting."

"Two shots within three inches of each other at four hundred yards, uphill?"

Wilkerson's shoulders stirred as if to dismiss it. "Let me lay it out for you, Mr. Stoddard. I just got back here an hour ago myself—spent the day up on that mountain with Sam Mallory. I expect you'll want to talk to him."

"If you don't mind."

"Surely. Anyhow, we went over the ground up there again. It's pret' near up to timberline, that area. Scrub trees, a lot of rocks, talus slopes, bare ground in patches here and there. You can pick up a track if you know what to look for but it ain't easy."

"And you found the killer's tracks?"

"Yes, sir." He refilled my cup and set the electric coffee pot back on the window sill. With his gangly frame and sharp Adam's apple he looked boyish, but he had to be at least forty. He went on, "The way Sam and I pieced it together, there was some fellow lower down over on the opposite slope, facing the mountain that your friend climbed over. This fellow, whoever he was—well, you've got to figure if he's up there with an 'ought-six rifle, then he's doing the same thing there that Mr. Cord's doing. Hunting. So this hunter looks across and sees Mr. Cord moving through the scrub oaks up there and he thinks it's got to be a deer or maybe an elk or an antelope or a bighorn sheep. Whatever he figures, he takes aim and he lets go two shots."

"What was Charlie wearing?"

"Buff-colored hunting coat. Bright red cap. We've got to assume the hunter didn't see the cap."

'Uh-huh," I said.

"After he fires the two shots, the fellow goes down one mountain and up the other to find out what he shot and whether it's dead."

"You managed to follow his tracks, then?"

"Yes, sir, we saw where he'd come across the canyon there. We saw where he came up to look at Mr. Cord's body. He sat himself down a while there. Probably shocked to realize he'd killed a man."

"And then the hunter just walked away?"

"Right back the way he came. We tracked him back to the point where he'd done the shooting from. Used a forked tree for a rifle rest. We found that."

"Where did the tracks go from there?"

"Into a shale slope. Nothing but loose rocks. Acres of them. No way to track the man through there." Wilkerson poured his own coffee, lifted it to blow on it, and watched me over the rim of the cup. "The way I size it up, Mr.

Stoddard, this hunter discovered he'd killed a human being by mistake and he sat there all gloomy-like, trying to think.   And after a while I expect he must have said to himself, 'Now this here poor man is dead and that's my own stupid fault for sure, but there ain't a thing I can do for him now.   If I was to take this body down and admit I was the one that shot him, why the sheriff just naturally he'd put me in jail and I'd go on trial for manslaughter or some damn thing and I could spend the next five years of my life in prison on account of this stupid accident.' ''

Wilkerson put his cup down.   "You see how it could have been."

"Yes."

"But this Mr. Cord was a valuable man to the big company you work for.   I guess they want more evidence than my guesswork.   So they've sent you up here to look around."

"I don't want to step on your toes," I said.   "I've got no official authority. But Charlie's widow and his father-in-law and the company I work for—yes, they'd like as many answers as we can find."

"I'm happy to help out however I can.   But I doubt we'll find much.   It ain't the first time we've had this kind of accident with hunters in these mountains and I expect it won't be the last."

"Does it happen often?"

"Sometimes five, six men get injured or killed up there in a single hunting season.   We get crowded with hunters up there, you know.   Some of them are city people that don't know half as much as they think they know.   Just last year we had three Milwaukee men in a party up in those canyons back of Goat Peak, all three of them were found dead at the end of the season.   Two of them had been shot with each other's rifles and the third one got shot by some 'ought-six. Wasn't much my office here could do about it except file the reports and notify the next of kin.   As long as the law allows men to go banging around mountains without so much as a hunting-license test to find out if they can recognize the difference between a human being and a cow, you're going to have accidents . . .''

When I left Wilkerson's office I drove the rent-a-car around to the buildings that housed Rocky Mountain Game Safaris, Ltd.   They were weathered barns and sheds; there was a corral with a few horses and a mule.   A terse old man in the tackroom told me Sam Mallory had left for the day.   The place smelled of leather and manure.   The old man gestured with a spade-bit bridle when he directed me to Mallory's house.

I felt as though I were going uselessly through the motions.   But I owed it, I supposed, to that sad angry lost woman who'd come to my office and I owed it to Schiefflin Aerospace.   The company had lived up to the moral stereotypes that are honored more often by empty lip service: Schiefflin had recovered me from a psychic gutter, reformed a tattered soul, brought me back to a life that seemed worth something after all.

It was a pleasant old frame house on a shady street behind a row of saloons and shops that had been restored for the tourist trade.   Sam Mallory surprised me: I must have expected to find a rustic old-timer.   He had a broad freckled young face and soft kindly gray eyes and blond hair tied back with an Apache-style headband. He was probably in his late twenties, no more.   He had a leggy young wife with a quick intelligent smile; she excused herself to go back through the house toward the wail of a baby.

Mallory knew who I was; obviously Sheriff Wilkerson had briefed him.   He offered me a drink and we sat in the front room surrounded by magazines and bookshelves and a few paintings.   The only outdoorsman touch was a tall rifle rack in one corner.   It held five rifles; they were locked in place with a chain.

He told me a number of things I already knew but I wanted his version.   He'd been with Wilkerson when they'd tracked the killer across the canyon.   "We didn't find his empties.   But then a lot of hunters pick up their brass.   Anyhow the sheriff tells me the slugs were fired by an old Springfield.   First World War type."

"When I was in the army," I said, "they still issued those to rifle competition teams.   It was a hell of an accurate weapon."

"I never saw one in the service myself.   We all had M-14's."

"You were in Vietnam?"

He nodded.

"What outfit?"

"Why?   Were you over there?"

"In the C.I.D., yes."   I smiled as if to apologize.

"Not a very popular outfit," Sam Mallory observed.   "I was just a grunt myself."   Then he grinned and put on a hillbilly twang: "Never had much truck with you hifalutin criminal-investigation types."   He sounded uncannily like Wilkerson when he did that.

"I didn't like the work much," I confessed.

"Then why are you still doing it?"

I said, "It's the only thing I know how to do well."

He gave me an up-from-under look as if to catch me off guard.   "You seem awfully low-key.   *Do* you do it well?"

"Usually."

"What have you found out so far?"

"Need to know, Sam?"

"No, I'm just curious.   What can you possibly have learned from me, for instance?"

I glanced toward his rifle rack.   "For one thing you haven't got a Springfield .30-'06 over there."

"You're acting as though it's a murder case.   As if I'm a suspect."

"Everybody is," I said.   "What did you think of Charlie Cord?"

"Obnoxious."   He didn't hesitate.

"That's the word most people use."

"Well, he liked to kill.   You know?"

"You're a hunters' guide.   You must see that all the time."

"Not really.   I'm a hunter myself but I'm no killer.   Not the way Cord was."

"I'm not sure what you mean by that."

"Sometimes I'll track a brown bear through those peaks two-three days and finally we'll stand face to face and I'll aim my rifle at him, and that's that. I hunt bears—to prove a point to myself, I guess—but I've never killed one."

"You mean you don't pull the trigger?"

"What would I do with a dead bear? I'm not a trophy collector and I don't like the taste of bear meat."

"But Charlie—?"

"He'd kill anything that moved. For fun."

"You must get a lot of clients like him."

"Not many. You'd be surprised. Most hunters have some dignity. And we're still carnivores, aren't we? Biologically there's nothing dishonorable about that. You can't condemn hunters if you eat meat yourself. But I'm talking about hunters. They eat what they kill. They make use of it. They don't just kill it for the fun of killing and leave it there to rot. You want another drink?"

"Not especially, thanks. Tell me, Sam, why'd you take up this line of work?"

"I like to think of myself as a pioneer mountain-man type. It's clean, you know. It keeps me outdoors."

"Clean," I said, "except when you have to go out with somebody like Charlie Cord."

"Yeah." He met my eyes and smiled. "Except then. Look, is this getting us anywhere?"

"Maybe. What was Charlie after? Specifically, what kind of game?"

"He said he wanted a bobcat and a mule deer buck."

"But?"

"He kept asking me about Rocky Mountain Goats."

"They're a protected species, aren't they?"

"What's left of them, yes."

"But he wanted one."

"One or a dozen. I think if he'd seen any goats he'd have killed them, yes."

"How was he with a rifle?"

"Good. Not spectacular, but good enough."

"Is it customary for the guide to stay in camp while the client goes out hunting?"

"Some hunters want you right with them all the time. But it wasn't unusual. He was just scouting around. He said he didn't want to waste his time sitting around watching me set up tents."

I unfolded my county map. "Show me where it happened."

He put his finger on it. "About there."

"Near Goat Peak." I folded it and put it in my pocket. "Anybody live up in that area?"

"It's National Forest. You can't own property up there."

"Sometimes you can lease it. Do you mind answering my questions?"

For the first time Mallory looked uncomfortable. It was subtle—I wouldn't have noticed it if I hadn't been waiting for it. A knotted muscle rippled briefly along his jaw; that was all. He said, "There's a sourdough who lives in a lean-to up there. Been searching for years—for the mother lode, I guess."

"What's his name?"

"I don't remember."

"Come on, Sam."

He pretended to be thinking, exercising his memory. Then he snapped his fingers. "Collins, that's it. Hugh Collins."

"I don't suppose he's got a phone."

Mallory laughed. "Up there?"

"I'd like to talk to him."

"What for?"

"He lives on Goat Peak. He may have seen someone."

"I doubt it. He lives on the far side of the peak."

"Can you take me up there? I'll pay for it."

"Waste of money."

"I want to talk to him," I said gently. "It'll go a little faster if you'd be willing to guide me."

"Suit yourself. We can leave in the morning."

"Make it ten o'clock. I've got something to do first."

You didn't put two jacketed .30-caliber bullets into a space smaller than a handspan at 400 yards without knowing what you were doing. That was what had stirred up my suspicions at first; it had been followed by improbabilities and too many coincidences.

The town didn't have a library or a newspaper. I had to get the information by phone from Denver. It took more than an hour and I was a few minutes late meeting Mallory. He had an old Dodge Power Wagon—four-wheel drive, winch, jerrycans, and canteens. A real wilderness rig. When I was a kid in the Southwest I'd known uranium prospectors who'd go out in Power Wagons and live out of them for months at a stretch and that was long before the fad for truck-mounted camper outfits.

We rolled out of town and Mallory put the truck up a steep dirt road through the pines. "Find out anything?" he asked.

I watched him while I spoke. "Seventeen hunters have died in this county in the past six years. Eleven of them in the vicinity of Goat Peak. Nine killed by .30-'06 bullets. Jacketed."

"Not surprising. That's what a lot of hunters carry. And Goat Peak's where most of the hunters go to set up their base camps." But he said it in a tight-lipped way.

I glanced at the carbine he had clipped to the inside of the door panel by his left knee. "What's that, a .30-.30?"

"Right. Saddle gun. For varmints."

"Tell me about Hugh Collins."

"Nice old guy. A gentleman. You'll see for yourself."

I said, "You didn't like it much in 'Nam, did you?"

"Did anybody?"

"Some did. We had to arrest some of them. The ones who learned to enjoy killing. Got so they'd kill anybody—our side or theirs or just neutral."

"Fragging?"

"Those. And others. Some of them just got bloodthirsty. Psychotic. They couldn't stop killing—didn't want to."

He said, "We had one of those in my outfit. One of the other guys fragged him—threw a grenade down his blankets while he was asleep. We never found out which guy did it but we figured he probably saved all our lives." He glanced at me. "It wasn't me."

"No. You never got into that bag, did you?"

Mallory said, "Too scared. And in the end I suppose I developed a respect for life. No, I never got to liking war."

"That wasn't war," I said.

"Shook you up, did it?"

"It was a long time before I got pulled back together. I had to have a lot of help."

He gave me a quick look and his eyes went back to the steep rutted road. "Shrinks? Psychiatrists?"

"Yes. And friends," I said. I opened up to him because it might inspire him to share confidences. "Mostly it was the interrogations that did it to me. The ones we arrested. The way they could talk about committing grisly murders— and laugh about it. I couldn't take it after a while. It was too grotesque. Terrifying. The bizarre became the commonplace. One day I just started screaming, so they sent me home."

"Rough," Mallory remarked.

I watched his profile. "Charlie Cord like to frag animals, didn't he, Sam?"

"You could put it that way," he replied, giving nothing away.

"He didn't have much respect for life."

"Not for animal life, at any rate." He turned the wheel with a powerful twist of his shoulders and we went bucking off the road up into a meadow that carried us across a rolling slope into a canyon. He put the Power Wagon into four-wheel drive and we whined up the dry gravel bed of the canyon floor. I was pitched heavily around and tried to brace myself in the seat.

It was past two o'clock when we reached Hugh Collins' lean-to. It was a spartan camp. A coffee pot and a few utensils were near the dead ashes of the campfire— he'd built his fireplace out of rocks. A cased rifle stood propped inside the lean-to. A bedroll, two canteens, a waterproof pouch with several books in it. No one was in sight, but we left the truck there and Mallory led the way through the forest. He was following tracks, although I couldn't discern them.

After a half-hour hike we heard the ring of a hammer against rock and presently we came upon the sourdough. He had a black beard peppered with gray; he wore coveralls and a plaid work shirt; he was short and built heavy through chest and shoulders. His eyes gleamed with an intelligence that seemed almost childishly innocent.

Mallory made introductions. "Mr. Stoddard's investigating the death of Mr. Cord."

"Who?"

"The hunter who got killed the other day over on the far side of the peak."

We hunkered in the shade. Hugh Collins had been whacking away at a rock face with his pointed hammer. I said, "Finding any color?"

"You always find color. Enough for day wages. I pan out a few hundred dollars a month. You wanted to ask about this hunter?"

"Someone shot him. Looking at the map, I thought the man might have come from this direction. I wondered if you might have seen anyone that day."

"What day was that exactly?"

"Sunday."

"Nobody came through this way Sunday."

"You didn't hear a couple of shots that day, then?"

Collins laughed. He showed good teeth. "I hear shots all the time. This time of year these hills are alive with idiot hunters."

An animal limped into sight and approached us hesitantly. It was a hardy-looking little creature; it had only three legs but it managed to hobble along with dignity and even grace.

Collins said, "All right now, Felicity," and snapped his fingers and the delicate little creature came to him and nuzzled his hand. Its left foreleg appeared to have been amputated at the shoulder. Collins said, "Felicity's a Rocky Mountain Goat. You don't see many."

"What happened to her leg?"

"That's how we got together, Felicity and I. Seven years ago—she was a yearling—some idiot hunter blew her leg off and I came across her half dead up there on the peak. Bandaged her up, looked after her. She's been with me ever since. Like the lion and Androcles." He scratched the goat's ears. After a moment she hopped away toward the woods. Collins looked up through the pines, evidently judging the angle of the sun. "You gentlemen hungry? Why don't we walk back to my camp?"

He served up a meal of beans and fritters and greens that he must have harvested from the mountain slopes. "Sorry there's no meat. I don't keep any on hand. Don't get many visitors."

"Are you a vegetarian?"

"Going on seven years now."

I said, "You don't talk like a back-country hermit, Mr. Collins."

"Well, I used to be on the faculty at the School of Mines down in Golden." He had an engaging smile. "I'm mainly anti-social. I prefer it up here. Of all the animals I've met, I find man the least appealing." The three-legged goat appeared and Collins fed it the last of his salad.

I'd seen the cased rifle when we'd arrived in camp; it was propped inside the lean-to. Now I walked to it and unzipped the leather case. I was sure before I opened it, but it needed confirmation. The old rifle shone with fresh oil—it was well cared for.

Collins and Mallory hadn't stirred from their places by the fireplace. Collins said in a mild voice, "That's a real old-timer, you know. Dates back to Black Jack Pershing's war."

"I know." I watched Sam Mallory get up and walk toward the Power Wagon. When he opened the door I said, "Leave the carbine there, Sam," and he looked at me—looked at the rifle I held—and closed the truck door with stoic resignation. I said to Collins, "Funny that a vegetarian keeps a rifle around."

"Varmints." He met my gaze guilelessly.

Mallory returned to the fire and sat. I said, "If I had this rifle tested by the crime lab in Denver, do you suppose they'd identify it as the weapon that killed Charlie Cord?"

I looked at Hugh Collins and then at the three-legged goat. She was curled up by the old man's side. I said, "What was he doing, Mr. Collins? Drawing a bead on Felicity here?"

"No. He was taking aim on a Bighorn Sheep. We've got a little flock of them up here. Seven or eight Bighorn Sheep. They're the last survivors of a multitude."

"How long do you expect to keep getting away with it?"

Sam Mallory said, "Sometimes you can't go by that."

I thought about the misery Charlie Cord had trailed around him. I remembered the face of the woman in my office and I looked at the half-asleep face of Felicity by Hugh Collins' side. I had an image of Charlie and I remembered the passionate happy killers who'd appalled me, sent me screaming toward lunacy; and I saw the calm faces of Collins and Mallory.

I said to Mallory, "You're a hunter who doesn't like to kill. You had to have a reason to work for killers. It was to lead them into this old man's trap, wasn't it? How long have you two known each other?"

"Sam's my nephew," Hugh Collins said. "We didn't see much of each other until he came back from Vietnam. That was his lesson—the way Felicity was mine."

I said to Mallory, "But you still eat meat."

"I'm his nephew and I'm his friend. I'm not his disciple."

Collins said, "Sam never shot any of them. That was me. I'd stalk them and watch them and decide whether they were hunters or criminals."

"Nine hunters in the past six years," I said.

"Eleven. Killers, Mr. Stoddard."

Mallory said, "I've guided hundreds of hunters through here."

Collins said, "You want to mind that trigger. She goes off easy."

I set the safety and put the rifle down against the lean-to and walked to the truck. I looked back at Mallory. "We'd better start back or it'll get dark before we're down off the mountain."

Mallory got to his feet, bewildered. I said, "I'll report that it was a hunting accident."

Collins scratched Felicity's chest and she pawed amiably at him with her one front hoof.   Mallory came past me and opened the truck door.   "You trust me next to this carbine?"

"Yes."

"Because you want us to trust you?"

"That's right," I said.   I went around and got in.   When I shut the door Mallory started the engine.   Collins appeared at the window.

He didn't offer to reach in and shake my hand.   But he smiled slightly.   "If you change your mind, don't go to Sheriff Wilkerson with what you know.   It would put him in a dilemma."

"I assumed he was in on it," I said.   "He had to be.   Otherwise he'd have compared the ballistics on those various .30-'06 bullets over the years and it would be public knowledge that they were all killed by the same rifle."

"All but two.   Last year that was.   I started shooting at one of them and the other two panicked and killed each other.   Damnedest thing I ever saw."

Mallory had the truck idling.   He said, "I still can't say I understand this."

I said, "Let's just say we're fellow veterans of the same war."

ANN MACKENZIE

I Can't Help Saying Goodbye

My name is Karen Anders I'm nine years old I'm little and dark and near-sighted I live with Max and Libby I have no friends

Max is my brother he's 20 years older than me he has close-together eyes and a worried look we Anders always were a homely lot he has asthma too

Libby used to be pretty but she's put on weight she looks like a wrestler in her new bikini I wish I had a bikini Lib won't buy me one I guess I'd stop being so scared of going in the water if I had a yellow bikini to wear on the beach

Once when I was seven my father and mother went shopping they never came home there was a holdup at the bank like on television Lib said this crazy guy just mowed them down

Before they went out I knew I had to say goodbye I said it slow and clear goodbye Mommy first then goodbye Daddy but no one took any notice of it much seeing they were going shopping anyway but afterwards Max remembered he said to Libby the way that kid said goodbye you'd think she knew

Libby said for gosh sakes how could she know be reasonable honey but I guess this means we're responsible for her now have you thought of that

She didn't sound exactly pleased about it

Well after I came to live with Max and Libby I knew I had to say goodbye to Lib's brother Dick he was playing cards with them in the living room and when Lib yelled Karen get to bed can't you I went to him and stood as straight as I could with my hands clasped loose in front like Miss Jones tells us to when we have choir in school

I said very slow and clear well goodbye Dick and Libby gave me a kind of funny look

Dick didn't look up from his cards he said goodnight kid

Next evening before any of us saw him again he was dead of a disease called peritonitis it explodes in your stomach and busts it full of holes

Lib said Max did you hear how she said goodbye to Dick and Max started wheezing and gasping and carrying on he said I told you there was something didn't I it's weird that's what it is it scares me sick who'll she say goodbye to next I'd like to know and Lib said there honey there baby try to calm yourself

I came out from behind the door where I was listening I said don't worry Max you'll be okay

His face was blotchy and his mouth was blue he said in a scratchy whisper how do you know

What a dumb question as though I'd tell him even if I did know

Libby bent down and pushed her face close to mine I could smell her breath cigarettes and bourbon and garlic salad

She said only it came out like a hiss don't you ever say goodbye to anyone again don't you ever say it

The trouble is I can't help saying goodbye

After that things went okay for a while and I thought maybe they'd forgotten all about it but Libby still wouldn't buy me a new bikini

Then one day in school I knew I had to say goodbye to Kimberley and Charlene and Brett and Susie

Well I clasped my hands in front of me and I said it to each of them slow and careful one by one

Miss Jones said goodness Karen why so solemn dear and I said well you see they're going to die

She said Karen you're a cruel wicked child you shouldn't say things like that it isn't funny see how you made poor little Susie cry and she said come Susie dear get in the car you'll soon be home and then you'll be all right

So Susie dried her tears and ran after Kimberley and Charlene and Brett and climbed in the car right next to Charlene's mom because Charlene's mom was doing the car pool that week

And that was the last we saw of any of them because the car skidded off the road to Mountain Heights and rolled all the way down to the valley before it caught fire

There was no school next day it was the funeral we sang songs and scattered flowers on the graves

Nobody wanted to stand next to me

When it was over Miss Jones came along to see Libby I said good evening and she said it back but her eyes slipped away from me and she breathed kind of fast then Libby sent me out to play

Well when Miss Jones had gone Libby called me back she said didn't I tell you never never never to say goodbye to anyone again

She grabbed hold of me and her eyes were kind of burning she twisted my arm it hurt I screamed don't please don't but she went on twisting and twisting so I said if you don't let go I'll say goodbye to Max

It was the only way I could think of to make her stop

She did stop but she kept hanging on to my arm she said oh god you mean you can make it happen you can make them die

Well of course I can't but I wasn't going to tell her that in case she hurt me again so I said yes I can

She let go of me I fell hard on my back she said are you okay did I hurt you Karen honey I said yes and you better not do it again and she said I was only kidding I didn't mean it

So then I knew that she was scared of me I said I want a bikini to wear on the beach a yellow one because yellow's my favorite color

She said well honey you know we have to be careful and I said do you want me to say goodbye to Max or not

She leaned against the wall and closed her eyes and stood quite still for a while and I said what are you doing and she said thinking

Then all of a sudden she opened her eyes and grinned she said hey I know we'll go to the beach tomorrow we'll take our lunch I said does that mean I get my new bikini and she said yes your bikini and anything else you want

So yesterday afternoon we bought the bikini and early this morning Lib went into the kitchen and fixed up the picnic fried chicken and orange salad and chocolate cake and the special doughnuts she makes for company she said Karen are you sure it's all the way you want it and I said sure everything looks just great and I won't be so scared of the waves now I have my bikini and Libby laughed she put the lunch basket into the car she has strong brown arms she said no I guess you won't

Then I went up to my room and put on my bikini it fitted just right I went to look in the glass I looked and looked then I clasped my hands in front I felt kind of funny I said slow and clear goodbye Karen goodbye Karen goodbye goodbye

EDWARD D. HOCH

Captain Leopold Plays a Hunch

Detective:
CAPTAIN LEOPOLD

The day was sunny, with an August warmth that hung in the air like an unseen cloud. It was the sort of day when children's voices carried far in the muggy atmosphere, when the slamming of a screen door or the barking of a dog could be heard throughout the quiet suburban neighborhood of Maple Street.

Out back, beyond the trees that marked the boundary of developed land, a group of boys barely into their teens stood watching while one of them fired a .22 rifle at a row of beer cans they had set up on a log. Presently the mother of the boy with the rifle appeared at the line of trees and shouted for him to stop. He did so, reluctantly, and the other youths drifted away. The boy with the rifle walked slowly back to his mother, his head hanging.

The afternoon settled into a routine of humid stillness, broken only by the rumble of an occasional delivery truck or the crying of a baby. It was nearly an hour later that the screaming started in a house on the next street, beyond the trees and across the open field.

Though the houses were some distance away, the screaming was heard quite clearly on Maple Street.

Lieutenant Fletcher took the call on Captain Leopold's phone, interrupting a department meeting on a recent wave of midtown muggings. Leopold, watching Fletcher's face from the corner of one eye, saw the blood drain from it.

"I'll be right home," Fletcher said and hung up. He turned to Leopold and explained. "I've got to get home, Captain. They think my kid might have killed somebody with his rifle."

"Go ahead," Leopold said. "Call me when you find out what happened."

He went on with the meeting, accepting suggestions from the other detectives and from policewoman Connie Trent, but his mind was on Fletcher. He hoped the news wasn't quite as bad as it had sounded on the phone. He and Fletcher had worked together for so many years that the troubles of one often became the worries of the other.

As soon as the meeting broke up he motioned Connie aside. "Try to find out what happened with Fletcher's son, will you? Let me know as soon as you hear anything."

"Right, Captain." Connie was tall and dark-haired, the brightest addition to

Leopold's squad since Fletcher had joined it eleven years earlier. She had beauty and brains, along with a superior arrest record that she had achieved while acting as an undercover narcotics agent. Leopold enjoyed talking to her, enjoyed looking at her deep green eyes and easy smile.

Within fifteen minutes Connie was back in his office. "It's not good, Captain. A man named Chester Vogel, a highschool teacher, was found shot to death in his living room. He was killed by a single .22 bullet that came through a back window of his house. The window faces a vacant lot where Fletcher's son was firing a .22 rifle at just about the time Vogel was killed."

"Damn!" Leopold frowned at his desk. "All right," he said finally. "I'd better get out there."

"Want me to come along?"

"No, Connie. I'm going as a friend, not as a detective." But he smiled and added, "Thanks for offering."

"I'll be here if you need me."

A police car was parked in front of Fletcher's white ranch home on Maple Street. Captain Leopold had been there a few times before—once for a summer cookout in the back yard when he'd felt oddly out of place as the only outsider in a close-knit family group. But he'd always liked Fletcher's wife Carol, a charming intelligent woman whose only fault was her heavy smoking.

Carol saw him coming up the walk now and opened the screen door to greet him. She was short and small-boned, looking far younger than her thirty-seven years. At that moment she might have been someone's kid sister rather than the mother of a fourteen-year-old boy. "Thank you for coming, Captain," she said simply.

"How are you, Carol? Is it young Mike?" He knew it was, because their other child was eight-year-old Lisa.

She nodded and pointed to the family room. Leopold went in, edging by the patrolman who stood in the doorway. Young Mike Fletcher was slumped in an armchair, staring at the floor. He did not look up as Leopold entered.

"Hello, Captain," Lieutenant Fletcher said quietly.

"What's the story?"

"I got Mike a .22 rifle last Christmas. I think I told you about it. He wasn't supposed to use it around here. This afternoon Carol caught him out in back with some other kids, shooting at beer cans. She made him come in, and then a while later she heard this screaming. Woman over on Oak Street came home to find her husband shot dead. Some of the neighbors remembered hearing the kids shooting, and the patrolman came over to find out about it."

Leopold looked questioningly at the officer in charge. "What do you think?"

"We'll run a check on the rifle, Captain, but there's not much doubt. Discharging a firearm out here is a violation. We'll have to book him for something or the guy's widow will be on our necks."

Leopold grunted. The man was a deputy sheriff, independent of the city police. He knew Leopold, of course, but there outside the city limits he wasn't impressed by detective captains. Leopold wished Fletcher had kept his family in the city, where he'd been obliged to live until the regulations for municipal employees were relaxed a few years back.

"It was an accident," Leopold pointed out. "And there were other boys involved."

"I did all the shooting," Mike said without looking up. "They were just watching. Don't bring them into it."

Leopold glanced at Lieutenant Fletcher's face and saw the torment in it. "Come on," he said to the boy. "Let's go for a walk out back. You can show me where it happened."

Mike nodded reluctantly and stood up. He was a good-looking boy with fashionably long hair and sideburns, dressed in jeans and a T-shirt. Leopold knew him only casually, but had always liked him. They went out through the kitchen, walking across the wide back yard like casual strollers on a summer afternoon. Leopold admired the close-cropped lawn and blooming rosebushes as only an apartment dweller could. He'd never owned a home of his own, even during his brief years of marriage. Now, passing uncomfortably through middle age, he often contemplated the simple joys of life that he had missed.

"Where were you standing when you shot at the cans, Mike?"

"Beyond those trees, Captain Leopold. Our yard ends at the trees, but we all go into the empty lots to shoot and stuff."

"Didn't you know discharging a firearm out here is against the law?"

"Yeah, I guess I knew it."

Leopold followed him between trees and found himself in a great open field overgrown with weeds and scrub brush. Had it not been for the line of houses some 300 yards away on the next street, he might have imagined himself suddenly transported to the countryside.

"Someday they'll build all this up," Mike said, "put a couple of streets through, build lots of houses. It won't be the same."

"Nothing stays the same, Mike." He stooped to pick up a punctured beer can. "Was this where the cans were?"

Mike nodded. "On the log."

Leopold turned and saw Fletcher walking out to join them. In that moment he was not a detective lieutenant or even a close friend. He was only a troubled father. "Find anything?" he asked.

"Beer cans. Bullet holes. What sort of rifle was it?"

"A pump-action .22. He wasn't supposed to fire it around here. I told him, his mother told him."

Leopold stared at the distant line of houses. "That's a long way for a .22 to carry and still have the impact to kill a man." Something was gnawing at him. It was only a hunch, but it was growing. He turned to the boy. "Did you fire toward that house, Mike?"

"No. I didn't even know which was Mr. Vogel's house till the policeman pointed it out."

"You can see the patrol car in the driveway," Fletcher said, pointing out a white ranch home in the middle of the row of houses.

"Did you fire in that direction, Mike?" Leopold asked again.

"No. At least, I don't think so."

"If you were standing here, you would have had to fire a good two feet to the left of your row of cans, and above them, to come anywhere near that house."

"I might have been wide on a few shots. I don't know."

"Let's just walk over there."

"I don't want to," Mike said.

"All of us do things we don't want to do. Come on."

Mike looked up at his father who nodded. But Fletcher stood back as the two started across the field. Perhaps he felt that his place was with his wife.

"Nice house," Leopold commented when they were almost there.

"Yeah. Oak Street is classier than Maple. I guess that's why they like that big empty lot separating us."

Leopold nodded to the pair of detectives in the living room of the sprawling home. His eyes went to the single hole where the bullet had passed through the window at the rear of the house. "A thousand-to-one chance," a detective said. "It was just bad luck, Captain."

"Seems so. Is Mrs. Vogel home?"

"I'm right here," a hoarse-voiced woman said from the kitchen. She was pale, a little overweight, and perhaps fifty years old. Once she might have been pretty, but today she was only sad-looking and alone.

"I'm Captain Leopold, Lieutenant Fletcher's superior in the city police. This is Mike Fletcher."

Mike stepped forward and tried to speak, but his voice broke when he saw the spots of blood on the white shag carpet at his feet. "No," he managed. "I didn't mean to—"

Mrs. Vogel stared at him with hard unyielding eyes. "You killed my husband," she said quietly. "I hope you rot in prison for it!" Then, turning to Leopold, she added, "Or will being a cop's son get him off?"

Before Leopold could reply, a much younger woman appeared from the kitchen and took Mrs. Vogel's arm. "Come on, Katherine. You've got to lie down. The doctor will be here soon with something to calm you."

"I am calm," Katherine Vogel replied, and indeed she seemed so. Bitter and accusing, but calm. She even glanced down at the watch on her left wrist as if to see what time it was. Nevertheless she allowed the younger woman to lead her off to the bedroom. One of the detectives looked at Leopold and shrugged.

When the young woman returned Leopold thanked her. She acknowledged the words with a nod and said, "I'm Linda Pearson from across the street. Just trying to help."

"She was the first one here after Mrs. Vogel found her husband," a detective explained.

Leopold nodded. "You heard her screams?"

"Yes. It was terrible. She'd been down the street talking to a neighbor and when she returned she found him dead."

"She seems to have calmed down quite a bit now."

"It's all inside.   I'm afraid she'll burst with it."   Linda Pearson was an attractive young woman, not more than thirty, who wore her long blonde hair in twin pigtails that made her seem even younger.

"You knew Mrs. Vogel and her husband well?"

She looked away.   "Just as neighbors.   I didn't see much of her."   She seemed reluctant to say more.

Leopold walked to the rear window and examined the bullet hole.   The shot had come from outside, all right, but somehow the whole thing still bothered him. His nagging hunch was back again.   "Was Mr. Vogel seated in that chair?"

"I think so," she answered.   "He'd fallen onto the rug by the time I got here."

Leopold bent to examine some indentations in the shag rug.   The chair seemed to have been moved several inches from its usual position.   "Come on, Mike," he said, straightening up.   "We'd better be getting back."

In the morning Leopold was restless and irritable.   He missed Fletcher, who'd taken the day off to be with Carol and the boy.   More than that, he wanted to help, but he didn't really know how.   When Connie Trent, filling in for Fletcher, brought his coffee, he looked at her and said, "Damn it, Connie, I want to help Mike!"

She sat down, crossing her legs with a whisper of nylon.   "What can you do?"

"That's the trouble.   I keep looking for something that isn't there, trying to find proof that he didn't do it.   I was awake half the night dreaming up nice neat theories.   Vogel having an affair with the girl across the street, his wife finding out, seeing Mike out shooting, and doing a little shooting herself."

"It's an idea," she admitted.

"But there's not a trace of evidence to back it up."

"What about the bullet?"

"Too mashed for a ballistics check.   But it was a .22 Long Rifle, the same type Mike was using."

"What will they do to him?"

"He's a juvenile, never in trouble before, and it surely was an accident.   He'll probably get off with a lecture from the judge unless Mrs. Vogel raises a stink about his being a detective's son.   He did break the law by just firing the rifle. But the thing that bothers me most is the effect on the boy, and on Fletcher and Carol.   The bad publicity, the civil suit for damages that Mrs. Vogel is bound to file."

"You can't do anything about that, Captain.   You can't invent a murder where none exists."

"I know that, Connie."

"Not even for Fletcher."

He sighed and turned toward the window.   "And yet, I have a hunch about Vogel's death—a feeling that the whole thing is just too pat.   The chair he was sitting in looked as if it had been moved.   Katherine Vogel glanced at her watch once while I was there.   Why would a woman whose husband has just been killed be so interested in what time it was?"   He paused a moment.   "More important, is there substance to any of this or am I merely concerned about Fletcher and his son?''

Connie had no answer, and she gave none.

Leopold parked his car at the corner of Oak Street and walked across to a yard where a man was mowing his lawn.   It was late afternoon, almost dinnertime, and in some yards families were preparing to eat outdoors.   The odor of charcoal cooking hung heavy in the air.

"You're Bob Aarons?'' Leopold asked the man with the power mower.

"That's right.''   He switched off the mower and frowned.

"I wonder if you could answer a few questions.   I'm Captain Leopold, investigating the death of Chester Vogel.''

"Terrible thing,'' the man said, his face relaxing a bit.   "I've been a friend of theirs for years.''   He was tall and middle-aged, with a ready smile when he cared to use it.

"I understand Mrs. Vogel was up here talking with you when it happened.''

"About that time, I guess, though the shooting might have stopped before she arrived.   We chatted a few minutes and then she went on home.   A few minutes later I heard her screams.   I reached the house just after Mrs. Pearson.''

Leopold nodded.   "Tell me, how did Vogel get along with his wife?   Any trouble there?''

"Not that I know of.''   The smile vanished.   "It was the kid on Maple Street that shot him, you know.   It wasn't Katherine Vogel.''

"I didn't say it was.''

"Just because the kid's father is a cop is no reason to let him off the hook.''

"Certainly not.''   Leopold could see he'd get nowhere here.   "Thanks for your time, Mr. Aarons.   I'll be going now.''

He turned to leave, but Aarons called him back.   "Look, you might talk to Linda Pearson about it.''

"What could she tell me?''

The man's face was blank.   "Ask her.''

"Come on, Mr. Aarons.''

The man stared down at the grass.   "In the house, right after I got there, Mrs. Pearson said Katherine had killed him.   That was before we knew what really happened, of course.''

"Of course.   Thanks, Mr. Aarons.   I'll talk to her.''

Linda Pearson came to the door at his first ring.   He identified himself and reminded her of their meeting the previous afternoon, but she still seemed reluctant to let him in.   "My husband's at the funeral parlor with Katherine Vogel.   I'm alone with the baby.''

"I'll only take a few minutes.''

"Oh, very well!''   She unlatched the screen door.   "A woman can't be too careful these days.''

Her house was a duplicate of the Vogel place across the street, though the décor carried out a more contemporary theme. "You were the first one over there after Katherine Vogel screamed, I believe."

"That's right. Mr. Aarons was right behind me."

"I was just talking to him. He said when you first saw the body you thought Mrs. Vogel had killed him."

"I—that was in the heat of the moment. It didn't mean anything."

"Sometimes the truth comes out in the heat of the moment."

"That wasn't the truth. The boy on the next street killed him."

"Why did you think it might have been Katherine Vogel?"

"I don't know." She glanced away, searching for the right words.

"Mrs. Pearson, forgive me, but were you having an affair with Chester Vogel?"

"Certainly not!" Her eyes blazed with fury. "You're sounding just like her!"

"Yes?" He smiled slightly. "More words in the heat of the moment?"

She started to turn away, then faced him again. "All right, I'll tell you. Katherine Vogel thought we were having an affair. She accused him of it and warned me to stay away from him. But I swear to you, there wasn't a word of truth in it! She's a suspicious old bitch who minds everybody else's business. He told me once that she threatened to kill him if she caught him fooling around."

The fury of her attack surprised Leopold. "Do you know if Vogel owned a gun of any kind?" he asked.

She nodded. "A target pistol. I saw it once. He kept it in the basement."

"A .22?"

"I don't know that much about guns."

Maybe, Leopold thought. Just maybe his hunch was beginning to pay off. "Thank you, Mrs. Pearson. You've been a big help."

Upstairs the baby started to cry.

Leopold stopped for a sandwich and then drove over to the funeral parlor in the early evening. It was an imposing colonial structure in keeping with middle-class suburban architecture. Leopold was surprised to find Fletcher lingering near the doorway as if awaiting some call.

"I thought I should come over," he explained. "I tried to get Mike to come, too, but he wouldn't."

"It's a terrible thing for him," Leopold said. His eyes were scanning the assembled mourners. "Is Linda Pearson's husband still around?"

"Dark blue suit. Straight ahead."

Harry Pearson was tall and virile, if somewhat older than his youthful wife. When Leopold motioned him aside to ask about Katherine Vogel, he drew in his breath and answered with some anger, "This is hardly the place for it, Captain."

Leopold glanced at the flower-draped coffin and agreed. "All right, let's go outside."

It was still daylight as they strolled across the blacktopped parking area behind the building. Harry Pearson swatted at a mosquito and asked, "Now, what was it you wanted?"

"What were Mrs. Vogel's relations with her husband?"

"Good, as far as I know."

"I've heard differently.   I've heard she was suspicious of him, jealous of other women, and that she even threatened to kill him."

He squinted at Leopold.   "Have you been talking to my wife?"

"Among others."

"Well, there's no truth in it.   Katherine Vogel is a fine woman.   A detective's son killed Chester, and there's nothing else you can make out of it."

Lieutenant Fletcher came out the back door at that moment, and Leopold knew he'd heard Pearson's last sentence.   Fletcher merely nodded and kept going to his car.   Leopold watched him in silence and then said, "All right, Mr. Pearson. Sorry to have taken your time."

He turned and followed Fletcher, catching him at the car.   "Want to stop for a beer?"

Fletcher turned to him, his eyes pained.   "Captain, I know what you're trying to do, believe me.   But it's no good.   We can't make a murder case out of this. Mike killed him, that's all there is to it."

"Mike says he didn't fire any shots in that direction.   I believe him, Fletcher."

"Then what happened?"

"She heard the shooting, got her husband's target pistol out of the basement, and shot him through the window herself."

"Without any neighbors seeing her?"

Leopold knew he was being unreasonable.   "All right," he agreed finally.   "Let me talk to ballistics again in the morning."

Fletcher managed a weak smile.   "Sure, Captain.   I appreciate everything you're trying to do.   So does Carol."

Leopold nodded.   They shook hands like two old friends who had just encountered each other briefly.   Then Fletcher got into his car and drove away.

In the morning Leopold went down to ballistics and talked to Sergeant Wolfer, a grumpy little man who was an expert at what he did.   "No chance for identification, Captain," he said immediately.   "The slug was too badly mashed."

"But it was a .22, the same as Mike Fletcher was firing?"

"That's right—a .22 Long Rifle."

"A rifle bullet?"

The little man sighed.   "Come on, Captain!   Do I need to lecture you on ballistics this morning?   Most .22 rifles and target pistols use the same ammunition. The majority of target pistols made today can fire .22 Long Rifle slugs."

Leopold persisted.   "What about penetration?   Mike's bullet would have traveled nearly three hundred yards."

"The bullet in Vogel's head penetrated only about an inch—just far enough to get mashed and drive some bone splinters into his brain.   I'm reading from the autopsy report now."

"Is that consistent with a shot from Mike's gun?"

"Within reasonable limits. Maybe there was a little extra powder in the cartridge."

"A .22 target pistol fired at close range would have penetrated deeper?"

"Maybe, maybe not."

"Damn it, Wolfer, I'm trying to conduct an investigation!"

"And I'm trying to help you. Many things can cause a bullet to lose penetrating power. The cartridges might have been old and damp, for one thing. Or the bullet could have been fired through something."

"Like a pillow, to deaden the sound of the shot?"

Wolfer nodded. "Like that."

"If somebody had a target pistol down in the basement for a long time, with old ammunition, and brought it up and fired it through a pillow, would it penetrate about the same distance as a bullet from a .22 rifle fired nearly three hundred yards away?"

Sergeant Wolfer thought about it. "Maybe, maybe not."

Leopold sighed and went back upstairs to his office. It was going to be that sort of day. Perhaps Fletcher was right. Perhaps he should forget the whole thing.

Young Mike Fletcher was waiting with his father in Leopold's office. "Captain, my dad wanted me to come see you," he said with hesitation.

"Sure, Mike. What is it?"

"He told me what you're trying to do for me and all that and I sure appreciate it, but—"

"But what?"

Mike hesitated, and Leopold repeated his question.

"Well, I told you I didn't remember shooting in that direction."

"Yes?"

"It wasn't true, Captain. I do remember. I remember the exact shot that did it. One of the kids accidentally hit my arm, and my aim went way off. I remember praying that it wouldn't hit anyone. It was high and to the left, right toward Vogel's house."

"I see," Leopold said.

Fletcher cleared his throat. "I thought you should know, Captain."

"Yes. Of course."

"Thanks again for what you tried to do for me," Mike said.

Leopold nodded. He waited until the boy left and then he said, "Get me some coffee, will you, Fletcher? I missed you yesterday. Connie had to do my running for me."

"Sure, Captain."

When they were settled over coffee Leopold asked, "When's Vogel's funeral?"

"Tomorrow morning."

Leopold sipped his coffee. It should have been over, but it wasn't. "Why did Mrs. Vogel glance at her wrist watch when I was there?"

"You're still on it, aren't you?   Even after talking to Mike?"

"I just want to know why the time interested her so much at that moment, with her husband dead."

"Maybe the time didn't interest her."

"Why else does someone look at their watch?"

Fletcher thought about that.   "To see if it's going?"

Leopold sat up straight.   "Of course!   Why didn't I think of that?   I forgot to take my watch off on the pistol range one day, and when I was firing left-handed the shock of the recoil stopped it."

"But why would a right-handed person fire a gun left-handed?"

"If she was holding something else in her right hand, Fletcher—something like a pillow to muffle the shot!"

"Captain—"

Leopold got to his feet.   "I'd better talk to Mrs. Vogel once more."

She answered the door dressed in black and looking as grim and defensive as he remembered her.   "Captain Leopold, isn't it?   I understand you've been questioning my neighbors."

"Only routine," he said.   "May I come in?"

"Routine when a detective's son shoots somebody?"

"May I come in?" he repeated.

"For a moment.   I have to be leaving for the funeral parlor."

He followed her into the living room, carefully avoiding the stains on the white rug.   He noticed that the window had been repaired, with the fresh pane of glass still bearing the window company's sticker.   He walked close enough to see the name: Empire Glass Company.

"They fixed it this morning, if that's what you're looking at."

"Fast work."   His eyes had gone to the wall opposite the window, to a spot that had been hidden behind the chair on his previous visit.   He could see a mark as if something had chipped the paint.

"Since when are city police concerned with a suburban crime, Captain Leopold?"

He ignored her question as he examined the wall.   "Mrs. Vogel, I'll admit this started out only as a hunch, but it's getting to be more than that now.   Mike Fletcher's bullet could have broken your window and hit the wall right here, leaving this mark before it fell, spent of all power, to the rug."

"That mark was caused a month ago when I tipped over a table while cleaning."

"I think you saw your opportunity, Mrs. Vogel, and you took it.   Perhaps your husband even kidded about how the bullet could have killed him if he'd been sitting in his favorite chair.   Somehow you kept him from phoning the police right away, maybe saying you'd call the boy's parents first.   Then you went down to the basement and got out his old .22 target pistol."

"Chester got rid of that long ago."

He ignored the interruption and went on.   "You shot him through the head with it, muffling the sound with a pillow held in your right hand.   Later, while I was here, you glanced at the wrist watch on your left hand to make sure the pistol's recoil hadn't stopped it.''

"Captain, if you repeat those charges I'll sue you for every cent you own!''

"That isn't much,'' Leopold said with a grim smile. "I'm only concerned about the boy, Mrs. Vogel. I don't want him going through life thinking he killed a man.''

"Get out of my house. I've listened to you long enough.''

Leopold felt a wave of helplessness wash over him. There was no way to prove it, no way even to prove to himself that his hunch was the truth. "What about the chair? You moved it to line up with the bullet hole in the wall, now you've moved it back.''

"Is it a crime to move one's furniture around?''

"Where's the broken window?''

"The glass company took it. There's no plot, Captain. It's all in your mind— every bit of it!''

And perhaps it was. That was the damnable part of it—perhaps she was right. "All right,'' he said finally. "I'll be going.''

She followed him to the door and slammed it behind him. He stood on the stoop for a moment, feeling old, and then started down the walk to his car. At least he could check on the glass. If he was going to do anything about Katherine Vogel, he'd need the windowpane to line up the bullet hole with the mark on the wall.

He drove over to the Empire Glass Company, a low cinderblock building in a nearby shopping plaza. The man at the counter remembered the Vogel job. "Sure, I replaced it just this morning.''

"She said you took the old window,'' Leopold told the man.

"Yeah, it's in the back. Heck, the bullet hole was just in one corner. We can cut it up for small panes.''

"I think I'll want that window,'' Leopold said. Then another thought struck him. "When did Mrs. Vogel call you to fix it? She didn't waste any time, did she?''

"No, the call came in day before yesterday, just after it happened, I guess. Only it was the guy that called, not her.''

Something churned in Leopold's stomach. "Guy? What guy?''

"The husband, Mr. Vogel. The one that died. I talked to him myself.''

"You're telling me it was Chester Vogel who called to report the broken window?''

"Sure.''

Leopold spoke very quietly. "But how could he have done that if he was killed by the same bullet that broke the window?''

The man shrugged. "I didn't read the details. I just knew he was dead.''

"I think you'd better come with me,'' Leopold said. "Right now.''

When Katherine Vogel opened the door Leopold said simply, "I just found out what your husband was doing while you were in the basement looking for his target pistol.''

Her eyes went from Leopold to the repairman. Leopold could see from her sagging face that it was all over.

HUGH PENTECOST

Jericho and the Studio Murders

Detective:
JOHN JERICHO

It was said of J. C. Cordell that he owned half of the world—oil, electronics, airlines, shipping, hotels, you name it. In an article about him Cordell was quoted as saying that he had the only three things in the world that could matter to any man. "I have my son, my health, and the wealth and power to live and do exactly as I please," he told his interviewer.

On a warm lovely summer day J. C. Cordell was deprived of one of those assets. His son lay dead in a small studio apartment in New York's Greenwich Village, with three bullet holes in his head. "The police suspect gangland revenge," an early radio report informed the world.

It revived an old waterfront story—old by at least two years. Special guards in the employ of J. C. Cordell had trapped some men trying to steal a cargo of expensive watch mechanisms from the hold of one of Cordell's ships. The guards had opened fire and one of the thieves was killed. The dead man turned out to be Mike Roberts, son of the reputed czar of the waterfront underworld, Reno Roberts. The word was out at the time that Reno Roberts would even that score with J. C. Cordell, but two years had gone by without reprisals, and Roberts' threats were forgotten.

Now J. C.'s only child, Paul Cordell, was dead, and the waterfront and the Village were alive with police trying to pin a Murder One rap on Reno Roberts and his men.

It was almost overlooked in the heat of that climate that a second man had died in the Village studio, also of gunshot wounds. He was the artist who lived there. Richard Sheridan was considered to have been an innocent and unfortunate by-stander. It turned out that J. C. Cordell indulged himself in the buying of paintings and sculpture. He had come across the work of Richard Sheridan in a Madison Avenue gallery, been impressed, and had commissioned Sheridan to paint a portrait of his son.

Paul Cordell had gone to Sheridan's studio in the Village for a series of sittings. Ever since the shooting of Reno Roberts' son on the waterfront and Roberts' threats, Paul Cordell had been accompanied everywhere by a bodyguard.

One had to assume that the tensions had relaxed after two years. The bodyguard, a private eye named Jake Martin, had grown fat and careless on his assignment. He had waited outside dozens of places where Paul was gambling or involved in one kind of party or another.   Jake Martin's life was almost entirely made up of waiting for Paul Cordell to satisfy his various appetites.

On that particular summer day Paul had told Martin that his sitting for Sheridan would last a couple of hours.   Certain that no one had followed them to Sheridan's studio, Martin had gone across the street to a bar to have himself a few beers.   It was a hot day.   While Martin was away from his post a killer had struck, wasting Paul Cordell and Richard Sheridan, the innocent bystander.

Telephone lines were busy with the story.   J. C. Cordell was in touch with the Mayor, the Waterfront Commission, the F.B.I.   Reno Roberts was going to have to pay for this.   The Mayor, in turn, was in touch with the Police Commissioner. Unless a cap was put on this case, fast, bloody waterfront violence was facing them.   A girl who had been with Paul Cordell only the night before called her friends.   My God, did you hear what happened to Paul Cordell?   And the news had spread like wildfire . . .

John Jericho was not in the habit of listening to the radio.   He didn't own a television set.   He had been working with a kind of burning concentration on a painting in his studio in Jefferson Mews at the exact moment when Paul Cordell and Richard Sheridan had been wiped out only a few houses down the block. When Jericho, six feet four inches of solid muscle, his red hair and red beard giving him the look of an old Viking warrior, got absorbed in a painting, the sky could have fallen in on Chicken Little and he wouldn't have been remotely aware of it.

Exhausted after the last brilliant strokes on his canvas, Jericho had thrown himself down on his bed and slept.   An unfamiliar creak in a floorboard would have awakened him instantly.   He heard the telephone ring, but it was a nuisance, so he ignored it.   But the caller was persistent, dialing the number every five minutes over a long stretch of time.   Finally, outraged, Jericho reached for the instrument on his bedside table and shouted an angry hello.

"Mr. Jericho?"   It was an unsteady female voice.   "This is Amanda Kent."

"Oh, for God's sake, Amanda."   Jericho glanced at his wrist watch.   "It's after one o'clock in the morning!"

"Did you hear what happened to Rick Sheridan?" the girl asked.

It was, perhaps, a notable question because all the people who had made all the phone calls during the evening had always asked: "What happened to Paul Cordell?"

Amanda Kent, Jericho had heard, had been desperately in love with Rick Sheridan.   To her Paul Cordell was a nobody, a zero.

To Jericho, Greenwich Village was a small town in which he lived, not a geographical segment of a huge metropolis.   He knew the shopkeepers, the bartenders and restaurant people, the artists and writers.   He knew the cops.   He knew the waterfront people who lived on the fringes of his "village."   The ships and the men who worked on the docks had been the subject matter of many of his paintings. He ignored the new drug culture.   He walked the streets at any time of day or night without any fear of muggers.   He was too formidable a figure to invite violence.

A little before two o'clock on the morning of Amanda Kent's phone call Jericho walked into the neighborhood police station and into the office of Lieutenant Pat Carmody.   Carmody, a ruddy Irishman with a bawdy wit when he wasn't troubled, was an old friend.   On this morning he was troubled.   He was frowning at a sheaf of reports, a patrolman at his elbow.   He waved at Jericho, gave the patrolman some orders, and leaned back in his chair.

"I expected you'd be showing up sooner or later, Johnny," he said.   "Young Sheridan was a friend of yours, I know."

"More than a friend," Jericho said.   "A protégé, you might say.   He mattered to me, Pat.   What exactly happened?"

"He was painting a portrait of Paul Cordell, J. C. Cordell's son," Carmody said.   "Damn good from what's there left to see.   You remember the rumble between J. C. Cordell and Reno Roberts?"

Jericho nodded.

"Ever since Roberts' son was shot by Cordell's watchmen, Paul Cordell has had a bodyguard—followed him everywhere, like Mary's little lamb.   He was a lamb this afternoon, all right, while Paul sat for his portrait.   Wandered off to pour a couple.   Hell, there hadn't been any trouble for two years.   Anyway, someone persuaded Sheridan to open his studio door and whoever it was blasted Paul Cordell and him.   No witnesses, nobody saw anyone.   No one admits hearing the shots.   Lot of neighbors at work that time of day.   Clean hit and run."

"And you think it was Roberts' man?"

"Who else?"   Carmody shrugged.   "Roberts bided his time, then ordered a kill.   Like always, when there's trouble on the waterfront, Reno was at his house on the Jersey coast with a dozen people to alibi him.   Not that he would pull the trigger himself.   He probably imported a hit-man from someplace out of the city, somebody who's long gone by now."

"No solid leads?"

"You mean something like fingerprints?"   Carmody made a wry face.   "Nothing.   No gun.   Meanwhile the town is starting to boil.   J. C. Cordell isn't going to wait for us to solve the case.   There's going to be a war, Cordell versus Roberts.   There's going to be a lot of blood spilled unless we can come up with the killer in the next few hours."

Jericho pounded on the door of Amanda Kent's apartment on Jane Street.   He could see a little streak of light under the door.   Amanda, he told himself, would not be sleeping this night.

She opened the door for him eventually and stood facing him, wearing some sort of flimsy negligee that revealed her magnificent body.   Amanda was a model, and stacked away in Jericho's studio were dozens of sketches of her body, drawn when she had posed for him professionally.

Amanda's physical perfection was marred now by the fact that she was sporting a magnificent black eye.

"Mr. Jericho!" she cried, her voice muffled, and hurled herself into his arms.

He eased her back into the apartment, her blonde head buried against his chest.

The small living room was something of a shambles—liquor glasses and bottles upturned on a small coffee table, ashtrays overflowing with cigarette butts, sketch-pad drawings scattered everywhere. Looking down over the girl's shoulder Jericho recognized Rick Sheridan's distinctive technique. Rick had evidently made dozens of drawings of Amanda's perfections.

Jericho settled Amanda on the couch and passed her the box of tissues on the coffee table.

"What happened to your eye?" he asked.

She gave him a twisted little-girl smile. "I bumped into a door," she said.

Her face crinkled into grief again. "Oh, God, Mr. Jericho, he was so young, so great, he was going so far!"

"I haven't come here to join you in a wake," Jericho said. He was remembering that after you had savored Amanda's physical perfection you were confronted with a very dull girl who delighted in cliché and hyperbole. "Why did you call me, Amanda?"

"Because I thought Rick's friends ought to know what happened to him," she said. "The radio and television are only talking about this gangster who was killed—as if Rick hadn't even been there. I thought his friends—"

"You've got it wrong," Jericho said. "It wasn't a gangster who was killed, it was a gangster they think did the killing."

"Only Rick matters to me," Amanda said. "Oh, God!" She looked up at him through one good eye and one badly swollen one. "There's no reason any-more for it to be a secret, Mr. Jericho. You see, Rick and I were having a—a—thing."

"Lucky Rick," Jericho said. "But spare me the details, Amanda. If you were that intimate with Rick you might be able to supply some information. Who would have wanted to kill Rick?"

Her good eye widened. "Nobody! It was this Cordell man they were after, wasn't it? Rick was shot because he could identify the killer. Isn't that the way it was?"

"Maybe," Jericho said. He appeared to be looking away into the distance somewhere. "But there's a chance it may have been some other way, doll. Did Rick have a row with anyone? Was there some girl who was jealous of the—the 'thing' you and Rick were having?"

"I was everything to Rick," Amanda said. "There hadn't been any other girl for a long, long time. Rick didn't have rows with people, either. He was the kindest, gentlest, sweetest—"

"He had the makings of a great painter," Jericho said. "*That's* the tragedy of it."

There was the sound of a key in the front-door lock. Jericho turned and saw a huge young man carrying a small glass jar in a hamlike hand.

"Oh, gee, you got company," the young man said. "How are you, Mr. Jericho?"

Jericho searched for the young man's name in his memory and came up with it. Val Kramer. He had grown up in the Village and was close to being retarded.

There had been moves to exploit his size and extraordinary strength. Someone had tried to make a fighter out of him, but he proved hopeless. Much smaller but faster and brighter men had cut him to ribbons.

He'd been tried as a wrestler, but he was no actor, the key to success in the wrestling game, and his only thought was to crush and possibly kill his opponents. He couldn't get matches. He was now, Jericho remembered, a kind of handyman and bouncer for a rather disreputable saloon on Seventh Avenue.

"I couldn't find a meat market open noplace, love," the giant said to Amanda. He grinned shyly at Jericho. "For her eye, you know." He advanced on the girl, holding out the glass jar. "Friend of mine runs a drug store on Hudson Street. I got him up and he gave me this."

"What is it?" Amanda asked.

Jericho saw what it was. There was a wormlike creature in the jar. Long ago leeches had been used to bleed people—the medical fashion of the time—and particularly to suck the black blood out of bruised eyes.

"You must put this little guy on your eye," Val explained to Amanda, "and he sucks out all the blues and purples." He was unscrewing the lid of the glass jar, fumbling with his clumsy fingers for the slimy slug.

Jericho felt a faint shudder of revulsion run over him. He remembered hacking his way through a Korean swamp with those dreadful bloodsuckers fastened to his chest, his arms, his legs.

Somehow the giant boy-man had Amanda helpless on the couch, pinioned by the weight of his body while he held her head still with his left hand and aimed the loathsome leech at her black eye with his right. Amanda screamed at him.

"No, Val! Please! No, *no*!"

"It's for your own good, Manda," the giant crooned at her.

"No!"

Then Val Kramer did an extraordinary thing. He lowered his head and fastened his mouth on Amanda's, smothering her scream. For a moment she resisted him, kicking and pounding at him with her fists. And then, suddenly, she was just as eagerly accepting him as she had been resisting, her arms locked around his neck. Gently Val managed to release himself and without any further outcry from Amanda placed the repulsive leech on her swollen eye.

"Have you fixed up in no time," Val said.

He stood up. Amanda lay still, her eyes closed, the leech swelling and growing larger as it sucked her blood.

Val Kramer gave Jericho a sheepish grin. "It's hard to convince anyone what's good for them," he said. "I gave Manda that black eye, so I'm responsible for fixing it up."

"She said she bumped into something," Jericho said.

"This," Kramer said, grinning down at his huge fist. "She was acting crazy about this artist fellow that got shot. She was going to run over there, get mixed up with the cops and all. I had to try to stop her, and somehow, in trying, I kind of backhanded her alongside the eye. I didn't mean to, of course."

"Of course," Jericho said. "But it was natural for her to want to go to Rick, wasn't it? She tells me they were pretty close."

Val Kramer looked up and the smile was gone from his face. "She belongs to me, Jericho," he said. "I can turn her on or off. You saw that just now, didn't you? She belongs to me."

Jericho took a deep breath and let it out in a long sigh. "Well, I'm sorry to have interfered with your blood-letting, Val," he said. He looked at Amanda, lying so still on the couch, her eyes closed, the leech swelling like an obscene infection. "I came because she called me."

"That was before I told her she could only get in trouble with Roberts' people if she stuck her nose in," Kramer said. "We appreciate your coming, though."

"My pleasure," Jericho said. "When Amanda comes to, tell her that."

Jericho walked west from Jane Street toward the waterfront. The scene in Amanda's apartment was something out of Grand Guignol, he thought. The girl, grief-stricken for a lost love, suddenly turned on by that giant child, submitting to his kiss, and to the disgusting creature held fixed on her eye. Jericho supposed that reactions to the physical were Amanda's whole life.

There was a house near the abandoned West Side Highway which Jericho had visited before. During a longshoremen's strike some years ago Jericho had done drawings and paintings of the violence, and he had met Reno Roberts and been invited to an incredible Italian dinner given by the crime boss. Reno Roberts had admired Jericho's size, his bawdy humor, and in particular his ability to draw extraordinary caricatures of the dinner guests. Jericho had earned a pass to the gangster's presence that night and he decided to use it now.

The security was unexpectedly tight. More than a block from the house Jericho was picked up by two of Roberts' men who recognized him.

"Better not try to see Reno this morning," they told him. "You heard what happened?"

"That's why I'm here," Jericho said. "I might be able to help him."

"He don't need no help," one of the men said.

"Everybody can always use help," Jericho said. "Ask Reno to let me see him for five minutes."

Reno Roberts was a short squat man, bald, with burning black eyes that were hot with anger when Jericho was ushered into his presence. A large diamond ring on a stubby finger glittered in the light from a desk lamp.

"Not a time for fun and games, Johnny boy," he said. "Pasquale says you want to help. What help? Can you turn off the cops?"

"Maybe," Jericho said.

"Can you turn off J. C. Cordell? Because he has his own army which won't wait for the police. A lot of us are going to die on both sides in the next forty-eight hours. I am supposed to have killed Paul Cordell."

"But you didn't," Jericho said.

"What makes you think I didn't?" Reno asked, his eyes narrowed. "J. C.'s people killed my boy Michael. We don't let such things pass in my world."

"But you did," Jericho said. "You let two years pass. You didn't strike when your anger was hot. Why? I'm guessing it was because your boy was involved in an unauthorized theft. The guards on Cordell's pier only did their duty. They didn't know whom they were shooting. You were filled with grief and sorrow, but there was no cause for revenge. Your boy pulled a stupid stunt and paid the price for it.''

"Not a bad guess," Reno said.

"So why strike back now, after two years?" Jericho asked. "And why do it so stupidly? That's not your style."

"Why stupidly?" Reno asked, his eyes bright.

"It would have been easy to finger Paul Cordell without having a witness present," Jericho said. "Why do it when it was also necessary to kill a completely innocent man? Why do it in broad daylight in a building where there might be other witnesses? Why choose a moment when Paul Cordell's bodyguard might walk in on you before the job was done? All those risks, Reno, when it could have been done with no risks. Not your style. Not professional.''

"Can you convince the cops and J. C. Cordell of that?" Reno asked.

"By producing the killer," Jericho said.

Reno leaned forward in his chair. "You know who it was?"

"A hunch, Reno. But I need your help."

"What kind of help?"

"I need you to persuade someone to talk to me without any holding back."

"Name him," Reno said. "And why are you doing this for me, Johnny boy? You don't owe me anything."

"Rick Sheridan was my friend. I owe him," Jericho said.

"I don't talk about my customers," Florio, proprietor of Florio's Bar & Grill, said to Jericho. He was a tall, thin, dark man who looked older than his fifty years. "You come into my place with some guy's wife and I don't talk about it. It's none of my business."

"But Reno has made it clear to you that you must talk," Jericho said.

"I would rather cut out my tongue than betray my friends," Florio said. "You are a friend of the cops."

"Didn't Reno tell you that I am also his friend?"

"The heat is on Reno. He would do anything to take it off."

"Maybe the people I want to talk about are not friends you would cut out your tongue to keep from betraying," Jericho said. "One of them works for you now and then. Val Kramer."

Florio's face relaxed.

"Poor dumb kid," he said. "Yeah, he fills in behind the bar when I'm short-handed."

"Yesterday?"

"From five in the afternoon till midnight. My regular bartender was home with the flu."

"My friend Rick Sheridan was murdered at about four in the afternoon. Did you know Rick?"

"Sure, I knew him. He came in here three, four times a week. A great guy. Very bad luck for him he was there when they hit Paul Cordell."

"If that's what happened," Jericho said. "Did you know Rick's girl, Amanda Kent?"

Florio laughed. "Rick's girl? He couldn't stand the sight of her. He used her as a model, I guess. She fell for him. She's a crazy kid, but he wanted no part of her. Only a couple of nights ago he told her off, right here in my place. He told her to get lost, to leave him alone."

"What do you know about Amanda Kent and Val Kramer? Is Val one of her lovers?"

"Oh, he was gone on her. Over his head gone. He followed her around like some faithful collie dog. But she had no time for him." Florio's face clouded. "Funny thing. She came in here with Val yesterday—at five o'clock—when he came on the job. She stayed here all night, till he went off at midnight. She left here with him then. When they came in at five we hadn't heard anything about the shooting. The news came over the radio a little before seven. Amanda went into a kind of hysterics, but she didn't leave. Some of the customers sat with her, tried to console her. You want to know who they were?"

Jericho shook his head slowly.

"I don't think so," he said. "She had hysterics, but she waited for Val Kramer to finish his tour, some five hours after she heard the news on the radio?"

"Yeah. I suppose—well, I don't know exactly what I suppose. Maybe she was afraid to go home. Maybe she thought Reno's boys might be after anyone who might have been around Sheridan's place at the time of the shooting."

"Are you saying Amanda was around Rick's studio at four o'clock?"

Florio shrugged. "I don't know for sure, Mr. Jericho. When the news came on the radio she had, like I told you, hysterics. She kept saying, over and over, 'I just saw him a little while ago!' "

"Did she get potted while she waited for Kramer?"

"Funny you should ask," Florio said, "because I remember being surprised that she didn't. She usually drank a lot. I figured she'd really go overboard when she heard about Rick Sheridan. But she didn't. She stayed cold-sober."

"And waited for Kramer?"

"Val would make her a perfect bodyguard," Florio said. "He's too stupid to be afraid of anybody or anything."

The gray light of dawn was sifting through the city's canyons when Jericho again knocked on the door of Amanda Kent's Jane Street apartment. It was Val Kramer who opened the door.

"Gee, Mr. Jericho, you got some news for us?" he asked.

"Perhaps," Jericho said. "May I come in?"

"Sure. Come in," the childlike giant said. "Have some coffee? I just made a fresh pot of coffee."

"I'd like that," Jericho said, moving into the apartment. "How's Amanda?"

"She's fine," Kramer said, his smile almost jubilant. "That blood-sucker really did his thing."

"Would you believe it?" Amanda asked from the bedroom doorway. She was still wearing the see-through negligee, but the swollen and discolored eye had vanished. "That little sucker really sucked. You found out something, Mr. Jericho?"

Jericho took the mug of hot coffee Kramer brought him. "I found out who killed Rick and Paul Cordell," he said quietly.

"Who?" they asked simultaneously.

"One of you," Jericho said, very quietly. He took a cautious sip of the scalding-hot coffee.

The childlike giant giggled. "You gotta be kidding," he said.

"I was never more serious in my life, Val," Jericho said.

The room was deathly still. Kramer looked at Amanda who had suddenly braced herself against the doorframe.

"I don't think you should say things like that, Mr. Jericho," the girl said, her voice shaken. "Because it's crazy!"

"Oh, it's crazy enough," Jericho said. "Rick had turned you down, Amanda, and he had to be killed for that. How crazy can you get? I came here to get you to turn over the gun to me, whichever one of you had it. I can't put it off, friends. There is about to be a war on the streets in which dozens of innocent people will die. So hand it over."

Val Kramer made a slow hesitant move toward the pocket of his canvas jacket. He produced a small pearl-handled gun that was almost hidden in his massive hand. He pointed it at Jericho, clumsily, like a man unaccustomed to handling such a weapon.

"It's too bad you couldn't mind your own business, Mr. Jericho," he said.

"Amanda called me, asked me for help," Jericho said, not moving a muscle.

"No such thing!" Amanda protested. "You were Rick's friend. I thought you should know what happened to him."

"Six hours after you'd heard the news? Why didn't you call me from Florio's bar? You were there for five hours after you heard the news."

"I—I was hysterical. I didn't have my head together," Amanda said. "After I got home I began to think of friends of Rick's who ought to be told."

"You wanted me to nail Val, didn't you, Amanda? Because you were afraid of him. When he found out you'd called me he hit you. You didn't bump into any door, did you, Amanda?"

"So I killed him," Val said, in a strange little boy's voice. "He couldn't get away with what he did to Manda. I went to his studio and I told him he had to pay for what he'd done to Manda, so I killed him. And I killed the guy who was there, because he could tell on me. I didn't know it was Paul Cordell and that it would make a lot of trouble. And now I'm going to kill you Mr. Jericho, because you can tell on me."

He lifted the gun a little so that it was aimed at Jericho's heart. Jericho threw the hot coffee full in the childlike giant's face. There was a roar of pain and Kramer dropped the gun as he lifted his hands to his scalded face. Then he lunged at Jericho.

It was a matter of strength against strength and skill. Jericho sidestepped the rush, and a savage chopping blow to Kramer's neck sent the giant crashing to the floor like a poled ox. He lay still, frighteningly still. Jericho bent down and picked up the little pearl-handled gun.

Then Amanda was clinging to him, weeping, "Oh, thank God, thank God!" she said. "I was so terrified of him!"

Jericho's fingers bit into her arms and held her away from him. "You scum," he said. It was more like a statement of fact than an angry expletive. "That poor guy would do anything on earth for you, including taking the rap for a murder you committed. Followed you around like a faithful collie dog, I was told. Followed you to Rick's studio yesterday afternoon. It was a habit with him—the faithful collie dog.

"He was too late to stop your killing a man who simply wasn't interested in what your body had to offer. 'Hell hath no fury—' He couldn't stop your killing, but he helped you get away. He took you to Florio's where he had to work. You stayed there for seven long hours. Why? Because you needed a bodyguard? Because you were grateful? No, because he had you cold and you knew you were going to have to do whatever he told you to do."

"No! No!" It was only a whisper.

"But you knew how to handle him, and you had to wait till it was possible. You knew that if you gave yourself to him he was yours forever, to handle as you pleased. You knew he would take the blame for you if the going got tough, no matter what. You waited for him all those hours in Florio's because until you could pretend that you cared for him he had you trapped. You took him home here and you offered him something he'd never really dreamed of having."

"I—I had no choice," Amanda said. "He killed Rick just like he said. I—"

"He hit you in the eye in some kind of struggle with you," Jericho said. "And because he really loves you, in his simple-minded and faithful way, he went out to find a piece of beef to put on your eye and when he saw there was no butcher shop open he found you that leech. While he was gone, you called me. You were already thinking of a way out. You would have fed me bits and pieces if I hadn't discovered them for myself. Unfortunately for you I found the right pieces and not the phony ones you'd have fed me."

"I swear to you—"

"It won't do, Amanda," Jericho said. "You're going out of here with me now, and just pray to God that your confession comes in time to stop blood from running in the gutters." He looked down at the unconscious giant. "And just pray that I can make that poor jerk believe that your body wasn't worth the price he was willing to pay. Get moving, Amanda."

EDGAR WALLACE

Warm and Dry

Detective:
SUPERINTENDENT MINTER

I went down to see Superintendent Minter just before the election began. He heard I was going to participate in the fray with a visible sneer on his homely face. "Politics!" he said. "Good Lord! At your time of life! Well, well, well! I've known a lot of fellows who took up that game, but nobody that ever made it pay, except Nippy the Nose, who used to travel the country and burgle the candidates' rooms when they were out addressing meetings.

"You know a lot about the hooks and the getabits of life, and you know that they're all specialists. If a man's a lob crawler—"

"What's a lob crawler? I've forgotten."

The Superintendent shook his head sadly. "You're forgetting everything," he said. "I suppose it's these politics. A lob crawler's a man who goes into a little shop on his hands and knees, passes round the counter, and pinches the till. There's not much of it nowadays, and anyway in these bad times there's nothing in the till to pinch.

"But once a lob crawler, always a lob crawler. If you go on the whizz—and I don't suppose you want me to tell you that whizzing is pocket-picking—you spend your life on the whizz. If you're a burglar, you're always a burglar. I've never yet met a burglar who was also a con man.

"That's the criminal's trouble—he's got no originality, and thank the Lord for it! If they didn't catch themselves, we'd never catch 'em. Nippy was an exception. He'd try anything once. If you went into the Record Office at Scotland Yard and turned up his M.O. card, which means—"

"I know what a *Modus Operandi* card is," I said.

The Superintendent nodded his head approvingly.

"That's right. Don't let these politics put business out of your mind. As I say, if you turned up his M.O. card you'd have a shock. He's been convicted of larceny, burglary, obtaining money by a trick, pocket-picking, luggage pinching—everything except blackmail. It's a funny thing that none of the regulars will ever admit they've committed blackmail, and there's not one of them that wouldn't if he had the chance.

"I used to know Nippy—in fact, I got two of his convictions. Nothing upsets a police officer more than these general practitioners, because we are always looking for specialists. We know there are about six classes of burglars. There's a class that never attempts to break into a live shop, by which I mean a shop where people are living in the rooms upstairs; and there's a class that never goes into a dead joint, which, you will remember, is a lock-up shop with nobody on the premises.

"And naturally, when we get a burglary with any peculiar features, we go through the M.O. cards and pick out a dozen men who are likely to have done the job, and after we've sorted 'em out and found which of 'em are in stir and which of 'em are out of the neighborhood, we'll pull in the remainder one by one and give them the once-over.

"So that when there was a real big bust in Brockley, and we went over the M.O. cards, we never dreamed of looking for Nippy, because he hadn't done that sort of thing before; and we wouldn't have found him, but we got the office from a fence in Islington that Nippy had tried to sell him a diamond brooch. When you get a squeak from a fence it's because he has offered too low a price for the stolen property, and the thief has taken it elsewhere.

"Nippy got a stretch, and the next time he came into our hands it was for something altogether different—trying to persuade a Manchester cotton man to buy a one-tenth share in a Mexican oil field. Nippy would have got away with the loot, but unfortunately he knew nothing about geography, and when he said that Mexico was in South Africa the cotton man got a little suspicious and looked up the map.

"Nippy was a nice fellow, always affable, generally well dressed, and a great favorite with the ladies. When I say 'ladies' I mean anybody that wore stockings and used lipstick.

"Nippy used to do a bit of nosing, too, but I didn't know he was making a regular business of it. Now, a nose is a very useful fellow. Without a nose the police wouldn't be able to find half the criminals that come through their hands. I suppose I'm being vulgar and ought to call them police informers, but 'nose' has always been good enough for me, because, naturally, I'm a man without any refinement.

"I happened to be walking down Piccadilly towards Hyde Park Corner one day when I saw Nippy. He tipped his hat and was moving on when I claimed him. 'Good morning, Sooper,' he said. 'I'm just on me way to the office. I'm going straight now. I'm an agent, you see, and everything's warm and dry. I've opened a little business in Wardour Street,' he said.

"Nippy had opened lots of businesses, mostly with a chisel and a three-piece jimmy, but I gathered that he had opened this one by paying the rent in advance. All criminals tell you they're going straight. Usually they're going straight from one prison to another. There are exceptions, but I've never heard of 'em.

"We had a few minutes' conversation. He told me where his office was, and I promised to look him up. He was so happy about me calling that I thought he was lying, but when I dropped in a few days afterwards I found that he had a room on the third floor.

"I expected to find that he was the managing director of the Mountains in the Moon Exploration Company, or else the secretary of a new invention for getting gold out of the sea. It was a bit surprising to find his real name, Norman Ignatius

Percival Philipson Young, on the glass panel. It was now that I found what he was agent for. He was standing in with the very fence who had given him away on his last conviction, and I suspected he was doing the same job.

"Anyway, he was full of information about various people, and he gave me a tip that afternoon to prove his—what's the phrase? yes, *bona fides*—that's French, isn't it? I made a pretty good capture—a man called Juggy Jones, who did a lot of automobile pinching, and was in with a big crowd up at Shadwell, who took the cars, repaired them, and shipped them off to India. There's many a grand family car running round Madras, loaded to the waterline with little Eurasians.

"Anyway, Juggy was a very sensible man, and if ever a thief could be described as intelligent, Juggy was that man. He didn't talk much.

"He was a big fellow, about six feet two, with a face as cheerful as the ace of spades. But if he didn't say much he did a lot of thinking.

"I took him out of a café, where he was having dinner with a lady friend, and we walked down to the station together and I charged him.

"He said nothing, but when he came up before the magistrate and heard the evidence and was committed for trial, he asked me to see him in his cell.

" 'I shouldn't be at all surprised, Sooper,' he said, 'if I know the name of the man who shopped me.'

" 'And I shouldn't be surprised either, Juggy,' I said, 'because you've known me for years.'

"But he shook his head and said nothing else. Somebody got at the witnesses for the Crown, and when they went into the box at the Old Bailey they gave the sort of evidence that wouldn't bring about a conviction, and it looked as if he was going to get an acquittal and something out of the poor box to compensate him for his wounded feelings, when the prosecuting counsel took a pretty strong line with one witness who, after he had changed his evidence three times, said just enough to convict Juggy on the count.

"He went down for a carpet. Am I being vulgar? Let me say he went down for six months, and a very lucky man he was. If we could have convicted him on the other indictments he'd have taken a dose of penal servitude.

"Naturally Nippy didn't appear in court, and I wondered what he was getting out of it.

"It was a long time afterwards that I found out there was a quarrel between the two rings as to who the stuff should be shipped to, and Nippy had been put in to make the killing. Nippy gave me one of two bits of information which were useful, but you could see that he was just acting for the fence. I made a few inquiries up Islington way, and I found out that whenever the police went to him to find out about stolen property, he referred them to the gentleman in Wardour Street who'd be able to tell them something.

"Now a thief who's earning a regular living has never got enough money, and I was pretty certain Nippy was doing something on the side, because he began to have his old prosperous look and started attending the races. As a matter of fact, though I didn't know it, he was working up a connection with a gang of luggage thieves. I found this out when he came on to my manor—into my division, I mean. I found him at a railway station acting in a suspicious manner, and I could have pinched him but, being naturally very kind-hearted with all criminals if I haven't enough evidence to get a conviction, I just warned him. Nippy was very hurt.

" 'Why, Sooper,' he said, 'I've got a good job. I'm warm and dry up in Wardour Street. Why should I lower myself to go back to my old sinful life? I haven't had a drink for three months, and I never pass the Old Bailey without taking off me hat to it.'

" 'There are two ways of being warm and dry, Nippy,' I said. 'One is to be honest, and the other is to get to Dartmoor, where I understand there is a fine system of central heating.'

"While this was going on, Juggy Jones came out of stir and reported to me. He'd got out with his usual remissions and I had a little chat with him.

" 'It's all right, Sooper,' he said. 'I'm going straight. I've had enough of the other game. How's Nippy—warm and dry?'

" 'Do you know him?' I asked.

"He thought a long time. 'I've heard about him,' he said.

"I should imagine he'd been doing a lot of thinking while he was in prison, and when I heard that he and Nippy had been seen together having a drink in the long bar, I thought it advisable to see Nippy and give him a few words of fatherly advice. But you couldn't tell anything to Nippy. He knew it all, and a lot more. He just smiled. 'Thank you, Sooper,' he said, 'but Juggy and I have always been good pals, and you couldn't wish to meet a nicer man.'

"According to his story, they had met by accident in the Haymarket. They'd had a drink together. I think Nippy was a bit jealous of Juggy, because he was one of the few crooks I have met who had saved money. He had enough money, anyway, when he was at the Old Bailey to engage a good mouthpiece, and he'd got a nice little flat in Maida Vale.

"One of my men shadowed Nippy and found he was in the habit of calling there, so if Nippy disappeared and his right ear was found on the Thames Embankment, I knew where the rest of the body would be. Not that crooks are that kind—they never commit murder.

"I only heard the rest of the story in scraps and pieces. But so far as I could make out, Nippy had been trying to get the man into the luggage crowd, which was silly because, as I have said before, a man who knocks off automobiles doesn't knock off anything else.

"Juggy said he would like to try the business, and he must have looked it over pretty thoroughly and taken an interest in it because one day he sent for Nippy to come to his flat and put him on an easy job that came off and brought him about £150.

"It's a simple trick. You have a car outside the station, and in it a little hand stamp and a case of type. You hang about the cloakroom till you see a man coming along carrying a bag in and taking his ticket. You've got a little bag of your own, containing a few well-worn bricks wrapped up in your favorite newspaper. You edge up behind him, and when he takes a ticket you check your bag and you receive a ticket. Now, suppose you receive Number 431. You know the ticket just before you was 430.

"You go outside to your little car. You have got a lot of blank tickets of all colors—they sometimes change the color—and you just make up the stamp to Number 430 and you stamp it. About three or four hours later along comes a gentlemanly-looking person, hands in the phony ticket Number 430 and claims the bag, and that's the end of it.

"One night, just as Nippy was going to bed, Juggy rang him up and asked him to come round to see him. When he got to the flat he told Nippy a grand story. It was about a man who traveled in jewelry and who was in the habit of taking one over the eight, and sometimes two. This fellow, according to Juggy, when he felt the inebriation, if you'll excuse the word, overtaking him, used to go to the nearest cloakroom and deposit all his samples in a bag which was kept in a case that you could open with a blunt knife or a celluloid card.

"According to Juggy, this fellow was coming to London from Birmingham, and the two arranged to shadow him. They picked him up at a railway station—a large fat man, who was slightly oiled. You may not have heard the expression before, but it means a man who has been lubricating—which is also a foreign expression, but you must go with the times.

"They tailed him till he went into a restaurant and met another man. He carried a bag, and he took out of this bag, and showed to the world, a large leather roll which he opened on the table. There were more diamonds in that roll than Nippy had ever heard of. When he saw it he began to breathe heavily through his nose.

"When they got outside the restaurant Nippy said to Juggy, 'Can't we get him in a quiet place and convert him to free trade? It's warm and dry.'

"But Juggy wouldn't have it. He said that this man, because he was in the habit of getting soused—which is another expression you may not have heard before, but it means the same thing—was always followed by a detective to watch him. Apparently, he wasn't an ordinary traveler—he was the head of the firm.

"So Nippy and Juggy followed him for a bit. He went into a bar and when he came out he couldn't have driven a car without having his license suspended for ten years. Sure enough he made for a railway station in the Euston Road, handed over the stock, and they watched it being locked in the safe.

" 'He'll do that every day this week,' said Juggy, 'but no time's like the present. You're a peterman, I'm not.'

"And then he told Nippy his plan. It was to put him in a packing case and deposit him in the cloakroom. 'It's Saturday night. They close the office at twelve, and all you've got to do is to get out during the night, open the safe, get the stuff, and I'll be down to collect you in the morning.'

"Nippy wasn't what I might describe as keen on the job, but he'd seen the diamonds and he couldn't keep his mind off them. Juggy took him down to a little garage off the Waterloo Bridge Road and showed him the packing case he'd had made.

" 'If you don't like to do it, I can get one of my lads who'll do the job for a pony and be glad of the chance. It's going to be easy to get, and we'll share fifty-fifty.'

"Nippy was still a bit uncertain. 'Suppose they put me upside-down?'

" 'Don't be silly,' said Juggy. 'I'll put a label on it: *This Side Up—Glass.*'

"Nippy had a look at the case. It was all lined, there was a nice seat, and although it was going to be a little uncomfortable there was a neat little pocket inside, with a flask of whiskey and a little tin of sandwiches.

" 'You won't be able to smoke, of course, but you won't be there more than seven hours. I'll notify the left-luggage people that I'm bringing the case in, and I'll slip the fellow a dollar and tell him not to put anything on top. All you've got to do is open the side of the case and step out. It'll be like falling off a log.'

"Nippy had a good look at the case. The side opened like a door. It didn't look hard at all. The only danger was that when they came in the morning to the cloakroom they'd find out that the safe had been opened.

" 'That's all right,' said Juggy. 'You needn't bust it. I've got a squeeze of the key.' He took it out of his pocket.

" 'That's all right,' said Nippy. 'It's an easy job. We'll be warm and dry on this.'

"About seven o'clock that night Nippy got inside the packing case and tried it out. The air holes all worked beautifully, so everything was as the heart could desire. He bolted the door on the inside, then heard somebody putting in screws on the outside.

" 'Hi!' said Nippy, 'what's the idea?'

" 'It's all right,' said Juggy. 'They're only fakes. They come out the moment you push the side out.'

"I don't know what happened to Nippy in the night, and I can't describe his feelings, because I'm not a novel writer. He heard cranes going and people shouting, felt himself lifted up in the air, heard somebody say, 'Lower away!' and he went down farther than he thought it was possible to go. And then Nippy began to realize that something had to be done.

"It was two hours before anybody heard his shouts, and at last the stevedores broke open the case and got him out. He was in the hold of a ship, and the packing case was labeled on the top: *Bombay. Stow away from boilers. Keep warm and dry.*

"It broke Nippy's nerve. He's in Parkhurst now, recuperating."

CELIA FREMLIN

A Case of Maximum Need

"**N**o, no telephone, thank you. It's too dangerous," said Miss Emmeline Fosdyke decisively; and the young welfare worker, only recently qualified, and working for the first time in this Sheltered Housing Unit for the Elderly, blinked up from the form she was filling in.

"*No telephone?* But, Miss Fosdyke, in your—I mean, with your—well, your arthritis, and not being able to get about and everything . . . You're on our House-Bound list, you know that, don't you? As a House-Bound Pensioner, you're entitled—well, I mean, it's a *necessity,* isn't it, a telephone? It's your link with the outside world!"

This last sentence, a verbatim quote from her just-completed Geriatric Course, made Valerie Coombe feel a little more confident. She went on, "You *must* have a telephone, Miss Fosdyke! It's your *right!* And if it's the cost you're worrying about, then do please set your mind at rest. Our Department—anyone over sixty-five and in need—"

"I'm not in need," asserted Miss Fosdyke woodenly. "Not of a telephone, anyway."

There had been nothing in the Geriatric Course to prepare Valerie for this. She glanced round the pin-new Sheltered Housing flatlet for inspiration, but she saw none. Its bland, purpose-built contours were as empty of ideas as was the incomplete form in front of her. "Telephone Allowance. In Cases of Maximum Need . . ."

It was a case of maximum need, all right. Valerie took another quick look at the papers in her file.

Fosdyke, Emmeline J. Retired dressmaker, unmarried. No relatives. One hundred percent disability: arthritis, diabetes, cardiovascular degeneration, motor-neurone dysfunction.

The case notes made it all so clear. Valerie glanced up from the precise, streamlined data and was once again confronted with a person—an actual, quirky, incomprehensible person, a creature whose eyes, sunk in helpless folds of withered skin, yet glittered with some impenetrable secret defiance.

Why couldn't old sick people just *be* old and sick, the poor girl wondered despairingly. Why did they have to be so many other things as well, things for which there was no space allotted on the form, and which just didn't fit in *anywhere?*

"But suppose you were *ill,* Miss Fosdyke?" Valerie hazarded, her eyes fixed on all that list of incapacitating disabilities. "Suppose—?"

"Well, *of course* I'm ill!" snapped back Miss Fosdyke. "I've been ill for years, and I'll get iller. Old people do. Why do I have to have a telephone as well?"

Valerie's brain raked desperately through the course notes of only a few months ago. Dangers to Watch Out For in Geriatric Practice. Isolation. Mental Confusion. Hypothermia. Lying dead for days until the milkman happens to notice the half-dozen unclaimed bottles . . .

An *easy* job, they'd told her back in the office—an easy job for Valerie's first solo assignment. Simply going from door to door in the Sheltered Housing block, and arranging for a free telephone for those who qualified, either by age or disability or both. She'd pictured to herself the gratitude in the watery old eyes as she broke the good news, imagined the mumbling but effusive expressions of gratitude.

Why couldn't Miss Fosdyke be like that? Eighty-seven and helpless—why the hell couldn't she?

"Miss Fosdyke, you *must* have a telephone!" Valerie repeated, a note of desperation creeping into her voice as she launched into these unknown waters beyond the cosy boundaries of the Geriatric Course. "Surely you can see that you must? I mean, in your situation—suppose you needed a doctor?"

"Nobody of my age needs a doctor," Miss Fosdyke retorted crisply. "Look at my case notes there, you can see for yourself the things I've got. Incurable, all of them. There's not a doctor in the world who can cure a single one of them, so why should I have to be bothered with a doctor who can't?"

Obstinate. Difficult. Blind to their own interests. Naturally, the course had dealt with these attributes of the aging process, but in such bland, nonjudgmental terms that when you finally came upon the real thing, it was only just recognizable.

But recognizable, nevertheless. Be friendly but firm, and don't become involved in argument. Smilingly, Valerie put Miss Fosdyke down for a free telephone, and left the flat, all optimism and bright words.

"Hope you'll soon be feeling better, Miss Fosdyke," she called cheerfully as she made her way out, and then on her long lithe young legs she almost ran down the corridor in order not to hear the old thing's riposte: "Better? Don't be silly, dear, I'll be feeling worse. I'll go on feeling worse until I'm dead. Everyone does at my age. Don't they teach you *anything* but lies at that training place of yours?"

"*What* a morning!" Valerie confided, half laughing and half sighing with relief, to her lunch companions in the staff canteen. "There was this poor old thing, you see, getting on for ninety, who was supposed to be applying for a free telephone, and do you know what she said . . . ?"

And while the others leaned forward, all agog for a funny story to brighten the day's work, Valerie set herself to making the anecdote as amusing as she knew how, recalling Miss Fosdyke's exact words, in all their incongruous absurdity: "No, no telephone, thank you. It's too dangerous."

Too dangerous! What *could* the old thing mean?   Ribald suggestions about breathy male voices late at night ricocheted round the table; anecdotes of personal experiences almost took the conversation away from Miss Fosdyke and her bizarre attitude, and it was only with difficulty that Valerie brought it back.

At *eighty-seven!*—she should be so lucky!—this was the general reaction of the others.   Of course, the girls admitted, one did read occasionally of old women being assaulted as well as robbed—look at that great-grandmother found stripped and murdered behind her own sweet-shop counter only a few months ago.   And then a few years back there had been that old girl in an Islington basement defending her honor with a carving knife.   Still, you couldn't say it was common.

"At *eighty-seven!*" they kept repeating, wonderingly, giggling a little at the absurdity of it.   Consciously and gloriously exposed to all the dangers of being young and beautiful, they could well afford to smile pityingly, to shrug, and to forget.

It was nearly three months after the telephone had been installed that Miss Fosdyke first heard the heavy masculine breathing.   It was late on a Sunday night—around midnight, as is usual with this type of anonymous caller—and it so happened that Miss Fosdyke was not in bed yet; she was dozing uneasily in her big chair, too tired after her hard day to face the slow and exhausting business of undressing and preparing for bed.

For it *had* been a hard day, as Sundays so often were for the inhabitants of the Sheltered Housing block.   Sunday was the day when relatives of all ages, bearing flowers and potted plants in proportion to their guilt, came billowing in through the swing doors to spend an afternoon of stunned boredom with their dear ones; or alternatively, to escort the said dear ones, on their crutches and in their wheel chairs, to spend a few hours in the tiny, miserable outside world.

Just *how* tiny and miserable it was, Emmeline Fosdyke knew very well, because once every six weeks her old friend Gladys would come with her husband (arthritic himself, these days) to take Emmeline to tea in their tall, dark, bickering home— hoisting her over their awkward front doorstep, sitting her down in front of a plate of stale scones and a cup of stewed tea, and expecting her to be envious.   Envious not of their happiness, for they had none, but simply of their marriage.   Surely any marriage, however horrible, merits the envy of a spinster of eighty-seven.

Especially when, as in this case, the marriage is based on the long-ago capture by one dear old friend of the other dear old friend's fiancé—a soldier boy of the First World War he'd been then, very dashing and handsome in his khaki battle dress, though you'd never have guessed it now.   Emmeline remembered as if it was yesterday that blue-and-gold October afternoon, the last afternoon of his leave, when she had lost him.

"He says you're frigid!" Gladys had whispered gleefully, brushing the golden leaves from her skirt, all lit up with having performed a forbidden act and destroyed a friend's happiness all in one crowded afternoon.   "He says . . ."

Details had followed—surprisingly intimate for that day and age, but unforget- table.   Only later, emboldened partly by old age and partly by a changing climate of opinion, had Emmeline found herself wondering how responsive Gladys herself had proved to be over the subsequent fifty-five years. Naturally Emmeline had never asked, nor would Gladys ever have answered. But maybe Gladys' tight bitter mouth and the gray defeated features of the once carefree soldier boy were answer enough.

The visit on this particular Sunday had been more than usually exhausting. To start with, there had been seedcake for tea instead of the usual scones, and the seeds had got in behind Emmeline's dentures, causing her excruciating embarrassment and discomfort; and on top of this, Gladys' budgerigar, who had been saying "Percy wants a grape!" at intervals of a minute and a half for the last eleven years, had died the previous Wednesday, and this left a gap in the conversation which was hard to fill.

And so, what with the seed cake and the car journey and the boredom and the actual physical effort of putting up with it all, Emmeline Fosdyke arrived back at the Sheltered Housing unit in a state of complete exhaustion. She couldn't be bothered even to make herself a cup of tea, or turn on the television; she didn't feel up to anything more than sitting in her armchair and waiting for bedtime.

She hadn't meant to fall asleep. She'd learned long ago that when you are old, sleep has to be budgeted just as carefully as money; if you use up too much of it during the day, there'll be none left for the night. So she'd intended just to sit there, awake but thinking of nothing in particular, until the hands of her watch pointed to a quarter to ten and it would be time to start preparing for bed.

But it is hard to think of nothing in particular after eighty-seven years. Out of all those jumbled decades heaped up behind, *something* will worm itself to the surface; and thus it was that as Emmeline's head sank farther and farther toward her chest, and her eyelids began to close, a formless, half-forgotten anxiety began nibbling and needling at the fringes of her brain—something from long, long ago, over and done with really, and yet still with the power to goad.

Must hurry, must hurry, must get out of here—this was the burden that nagged at her last wisps of consciousness. Urgency pounded behind her closed eyes—a sense of trains to catch, of doors to bolt, of decisions to make. And now there seemed to be voices approaching—shouts—cars drawing up—luggage only half packed.

Slumped in her deep chair, Emmeline Fosdyke's sleeping limbs twitched ever so slightly to the ancient crisis; the slow blood pumped into her flaccid muscles a tiny extra supply of oxygen to carry the muscles through the dream chase along streets long since bulldozed; her breath came infinitesimally quicker, her old lungs expanded to some miniscule degree at the need for running, running, running, through a long-dead winter dawn . . .

It was the telephone that woke her. Stunned by the suddenness of it, and by its stupefying clamor erupting into her dreams, Emmeline sat for a few moments in a state of total bewilderment. Who? Where? And then, gradually, it all came back to her.

It was all right. It was here. It was now. She, Emmeline Fosdyke, eighty-seven years old, sitting comfortably in her own chair in her own room on a peaceful

Sunday evening.   She was home.   She was safe—safe back from that awful outing to Gladys' house, and with a full six weeks before she need think about going there again.   There was nothing to worry about.   Nothing at all.   Nothing, certainly, to get her heart beating in this uncomfortable way, thundering in her eardrums, pulsing behind her eyes.

Except, of course, the telephone, which was still ringing.   Ringing, ringing as if it would never stop.   Who could possibly be telephoning her on a Sunday evening as late as—oh, dear, what *was* the time?   With eyes still blurred by sleep, Emmeline peered at her watch and saw, with a little sense of shock, that it was past midnight.

Midnight!   She must have been dozing here for hours!   That meant that even with a sleeping pill, she'd never—

And still the telephone kept on ringing; and now, her mind slowly coming into focus, it dawned on Miss Fosdyke that she would have to answer it.

"Hello?" she half whispered, her old voice husky and tremulous with sleep. Then from force of habit she said, "This is Emmeline Fosdyke, 497–6402. Who. . . ?"

There was no answer.   Only the slow measured sound of someone breathing— breathing loudly, and with deliberate intention; the sounds pounded against her ear like the slow reverberation of the sea.   In, out.   In, out.

For several seconds Miss Fosdyke simply sat there, speechless, the hand that clutched the instrument growing slowly damp with sweat, and her mind reeling with indecision.   During her long decades of solitary bed-sitter life, she'd had calls of this nature quite a number of times, and she knew very well there was no infallible method for dealing with them.   If you simply hung up without a word, then they were liable to ring again later in the night; if, on the other hand, you *did* speak, then they were as likely as not to launch forth immediately into a long rambling monologue of obscene suggestions.   It was a nerve-wracking situation for an old woman all on her own in an empty flat and late at night.

Miss Fosdyke decided to take the bull by the horns.

"Listen," she said, trying to speak quietly and control the quivering of her voice. "Listen, I don't know who you are or why you're calling me, but I think I ought to tell you that I'm—"

That I'm what?   Eighty-seven years old?   All on my own?   Crippled with arthritis?   About to call the police?

That would be a laugh!   Anyone who has been an elderly spinster for as long as Emmeline Fosdyke knows well enough what to expect from officialdom if she complains of molestation.   No, no policemen, thank you.   Not anymore.   Not ever again.

But no matter.   Her decisive little speech seemed to have done the trick this time.   With a tiny click the receiver at the other end was replaced softly, and Emmeline leaned back with a sigh of relief, even with a certain sense of pride in what she had accomplished.   Funny how these sort of calls always came when you were least prepared for them—late at night, like this one, or even in the small hours, rousing you from your deepest sleep.

Like that awful time five years ago—or was it six?—when she'd been living all alone in that dark dismal flat off the Holloway Road. Even now she still trembled when she thought about that night, and how it might have ended. And then there was that other time, only a few years earlier, when she'd just moved into that bed-sitter in Wandsworth. There, too, the telephone had only recently been installed, just as it had been here . . .

Well, I *told* her, didn't I? That prissy, know-it-all little chit of a welfare worker—no one can say that I didn't warn her! I *told* her that a telephone was dangerous, but of course she had to know better, she with her potty little three-year Training Course which she thinks qualifies her to be right about everything for evermore!

Training Course indeed!—as if life itself wasn't a training course much tougher and more exacting than anything the Welfare could think up, if it sat on its bloody committees yakketty-yakking for a thousand years!

Nearly one o'clock now. Emmeline still had not dared to undress, or to make any of her usual preparations for the night. Even though it was more than half an hour since she'd hung up on her mysterious caller, she still could not relax. Of course, it was more than possible that nothing further would happen, that the wretched fellow had given up, turned his attentions elsewhere. Still, you couldn't be sure. It was best to be prepared.

And so, her light switched off as an extra protection, and a blanket wrapped round her against the encroaching chill of the deepening night, Emmeline sat wide awake in the velvet darkness, waiting.

It was very quiet here in this great block of flats at this unaccustomed hour. Not a footstep, not a cough, not so much as the creaking of a door. Even the caretaker must be asleep by now, down in his boiler room in the depths of the building.

Emmeline had never been awake and listening at such an hour before. Her mind went back to earlier night calls when the sounds outside had grown sharper, louder. Did she hear them again?

Emmeline was trembling now, from head to foot. She'd never get out of it this time, never! Ten years ago—even five—she'd at least have been mobile, able to slip through a doorway, to get away from the house, and if necessary stay away for days, or even for weeks.

Not now, though. This time she would be helpless, a sitting duck. And as this thought went through her mind, she became aware, through the humming of her hearing aid, of a new sound, a sound quite distinct and unmistakable, the sharp click of the latch as her door handle was being quietly turned.

Softly, expertly, making no noise at all, Emmeline Fosdyke reached into the darkness for the long sharp carving knife that always lay in readiness.

It was a shame, really, having had to do this to them, after having been so nice to them on the phone, after having given them her name and everything, and encouraging them to think that her tense husky whisper was the voice of a young girl. It was a real shame; but then, what else could she have done?

In the deep darkness, the unknown male lips coarse and urgent against her own, she would have her brief moment of glory, a strange miraculous moment when it really seemed that the anonymous, ill-smelling mackintosh of some stranger was indeed a khaki battle dress of long ago, that the blind clutchings in the darkness were the tender caresses of her first love.   For those few wild incredible seconds, in the meaningless grip of some greasy, grunting stranger, she would be young again, and loved again, under the poignant blueness of a wartime summer sky.

During those mad brief moments she could allow hard masculine fingers to fumble with her cardigan in the darkness, and with the buttons of her blouse, scrabbling their way nearer and nearer . . . a shame it was, a crying shame, that at exactly that moment, just before the eager questing fingers had discovered the sagging, empty loops of skin and had recoiled in horror—that was the moment when she'd had to stab the poor nameless fellow, if possible in the heart.

Had to.   It was self-defense.   Even the law had agreed about that, on the rare occasions when the law had caught up with her.

She'd *had* to do it—*had* to stab them all, swiftly and surely, before they'd had a chance to discover how old she was.

"No, no telephone, thank you.   It's too dangerous"—for them.

CELIA FREMLIN

Dangerous Sport

"Darling, I'd just love to be able to stay. You know I would.
I'm just as disappointed as you are. But—"

But.

But, but, but. What would it be *this* time, Stella wondered bitterly. Whatever
it was, she'd have heard it before, that was certain. After five years of going
around with a married man, a girl knows his repertoire by heart.

But I have to help Wendy with the weekend shopping. *But* the man is coming
to fix the hot-water boiler. *But* I have to fetch Carol from the Brownies. *But*
Simon is away from school with a temperature. *But* I have to meet Aunt Esmé
at the airport.

This last had been the funniest "but" of all; and though in fact it had happened
quite near the beginning of her relationship with Gerald, it still made Stella laugh,
and grind her teeth, when she thought about it. For it had come so soon after that
golden September day when, lying in the long grass by the river outside Marlowe,
Gerald had been confiding in her, as married men will, about his loneliness. Even
as a child he'd been lonely, he told her.

"No brothers and sisters. Not even any uncles or aunts," he'd explained sadly.
"I used to long sometimes for one of those big, close, quarrelsome families, all
weddings and funerals and eating roast chicken and bread sauce at each other's
tables, and running down each other's in-laws. I yearned for a group larger than
just myself and my two parents—I wanted my own tribe, and that wonderful feeling
of *belonging*. Particularly at Christmas I used to feel . . ."

Stella couldn't remember, at this distance of time, what it was that Gerald used
to feel at Christmas—something about tangerines, and somebody else's grandfather
out in the snow sawing apple logs—or something; it was of no importance, and
that's why she'd forgotten it. What *was* important was the discrepancy she'd
instantly spotted between these maudlin reminiscences and the cock-and-bull story
about meeting "Aunt Esmé" at the airport.

She'd given him every chance. Why couldn't *Wendy* be the one to meet the
woman, she'd asked, watching him intently while she spoke. After all, she was
Wendy's aunt, not his—"Oh, no, darling, no, whatever gave you that idea? She's
my aunt. She was awfully good to me as a kid, and so I feel this is the least I
can do. It's an awful bore, but—you *do* understand, don't you, darling?"

Of course she'd understood.   That's what mistresses are for.

"Of *course*, darling!'' she'd said, not batting an eyelid; and afterward, how she'd laughed about it—when she'd finished crying!

She had to be so very careful, that was the thing: call Gerald's bluff even once, and the whole relationship could have been wrecked forever.   He had made it quite, quite clear to her, very early, that suspicion, jealousy, and possessiveness were the prerogatives of the wife, and of the wife alone.   It was in the nature of things (Gerald seemed to feel) that *Wendy* should cross-examine him about his business trips, ring up the office to check that he really was working late, go through his pockets for letters and for incriminating theater-ticket stubs; for *Stella* to do these things struck him as an outrage, an insult to the natural order of things.

"Look, darling,'' he'd said (and the cold savagery of his tone had seemed to Stella quite out of proportion to her very minor misdemeanor—a single tentative little phone call to his secretary asking, just simply asking, what time he was expected back from Wolverhampton), ''Look, darling, when a married man starts an affair, it's because he wants to get *away* from that sort of thing, not because he wants more of it!   He has enough trouble getting a few hours' freedom as it is, without having his mistress waiting for him like a cat at a mousehole every time he steps outside his front door!''

A speech both cruel and uncalled-for, and Stella had been dreadfully upset.   But being upset never got her anywhere with Gerald, it just made him avoid answering the telephone; and so after a while she'd stopped being upset, and had resolved to watch her step even more carefully in the future.   And so that was why, when the Aunt Esmé ''bit'' cropped up, she'd let it pass without a flicker of protest.   Dumber than the dumbest blonde she'd been, as she sleeked back her wings of black burnished hair and listened, her dark eyes wide and trusting, while he flounced deeper and deeper into a labyrinth of lies and evasions from which he would never (unless she, Stella, chose to assist him) be able to extricate himself.

For the lies hadn't ended with the meeting of ''Aunt Esmé,'' at the airport; they had gone on for weeks.   Because that hypothetical lady's visit had proved to be a long one, and packed with incident.   She had to be taken to the theater on just the night when Gerald usually went out with Stella; she caught the flu on the exact weekend when Gerald and Stella had planned a trip to the country; and when Stella herself caught the flu, she had to have it alone because it just so happened that Aunt Esmé had to be taken on a visit to an old school friend in Bournemouth at just that time.

And Stella had taken it all smiling.   Smiling, smiling endlessly down the telephone, making understanding noises, and never questioning, never protesting.   It had been over a year later (surely a *year* is long enough, surely no one could accuse her of checking up after a *year?*) before Stella had ventured, warily, and with lowered eyelashes, to ask after Aunt Esmé.   Had they seen her lately, or had a card from her, she'd asked innocently, one late December day when Gerald, preoccupied, filled and brimming over with family life, had driven over hastily with Stella's present.   Jewelry again, and expensive—Gerald was good at that sort of thing.

Stella thanked him prettily, even warmly; and then, still prettily, she tossed her bombshell into his face. "Have you heard from Aunt Esmé lately?" she asked, and enjoyed, as she only rarely enjoyed his lovemaking, the look of blank uncomplicated bewilderment that spread over his pink, self-absorbed features. Not even any wariness, so completely had he forgotten the whole thing.

"Aunt Esmé? Who's Aunt Esmé?" he asked curiously, quite unsuspicious.

Stella had intended it to stop there, to brush it off with a light "Oh, well, I must be mixing it up with some other family"; to leave him unscathed, untouched by guilt, and to savour her triumph in secret. But the temptation to go on, to spring the trap, was irresistible.

"Aunt *Esmé*, darling! You know—the one you had staying with you for all that time last winter"—and as she spoke Stella watched, with terror and with glee, the dawning of guilt and alarm in his plump lazy features. Fear, calculation, and panic darted like fishes back and forth across his countenance; and then he recovered himself.

Of course! How stupid! Dear old *Esmé,* she must mean! Not an aunt at all, but the old family governess from Wendy's mother's old home—the children had been taught to call her "aunt" because, you know . . .

And of course Stella *did* know, smiling and lying and letting him off the hook. She, too, had had an "aunt" like that in her childhood. An Aunt Polly (she quickly improvised) who had made gingerbread animals. Smiling, inventing, chattering, breathlessly easing the embarrassment, Stella was nevertheless already making her plans. In a year's time—or maybe two years—"How's your mother-in-law's old governess getting on?" she'd ask, all innocence, watching his face while he blundered into the trap. "*Governess?* But Wendy's mother never had—" And while his words stuttered into silence, she would be watching his face, never taking her eyes off it as it disintegrated into terror, bewilderment, and guilt.

Guilt, that was the important thing. Guilt so richly deserved and so long outstanding, like an unpaid debt. Such a sense of power it gave her to be able to call him to account like this, just now and again—a sense of power which compensated, in some measure, for the awful weakness of her actual position, the terrible uncertainty of her hold on him. To be able to make him squirm like this every so often was a sort of redressing of some desperate balance—a long-merited turning of the tables without which Stella sometimes felt she could not have gone on.

Oh, but it was fun too! A sort of game of catch-me-if-you-can, a fun game. Not quite as much fun, though, as it used to be, because of late Gerald had been growing more wary, less easily trapped. He was more evasive now, less buoyantly ready to come out with giveaway remarks like "*What* trip to Manchester, darling?" or "But they've never *had* measles." Now, before he spoke, you could see him checking through the lies he had told recently, his gray-green eyes remote and sly.

And as Gerald grew more wary, so did Stella grow more cunning. The questions by which she trapped him were never direct ones now, but infinitely subtle and devious. It was a dangerous sport, and, like all dangerous sports, it demanded skill and judgment, a sure eye and perfect timing. Push Gerald too far, and she

would have a terrible, terrifying row on her hands. "Possessive! Demanding!"—
and all the other age-old accusations hurtling round her head.

Push him not far enough, however, and the opposite set of mishaps would be
set in motion. He would start thinking he could get away with anything, leaving
her for days on end without so much as a phone call, and then turning up all smiles,
as if nothing had happened, and expecting her to cook him steak and collect his
shoes from the repairers. Taking her for granted, just as if she was a wife—and
what sensible woman is going to put up with all the disadvantages of being married
as well as all the disadvantages of not being?

It was a cliff-hanger business, though, getting the push exactly right. Only a
few months ago Gerald had actually threatened to leave her if she didn't stop spying
on him—though surely "spying" was an unduly harsh term to apply to Stella's
innocent little show of interest in the details of the business conference he'd pretended to attend the previous weekend?

"But darling, Lord Berners wasn't *at* the dinner!" she'd pointed out, with a
placating little laugh, just to save Gerald the trouble of inventing any more humorous
quotes from a nonexistent speech. "I read in *The Times* the next morning that"—
and at this, quite suddenly, he had gone berserk, and had turned on her like an
animal at bay. His rage, his dreadful, unwarranted accusations, were like nothing
she had ever heard before, and they threw her into such terror that she scarcely
knew what she was doing or saying.

In the end he had flung himself out of the flat, slamming the door on her tears
and screams, and vowing never to set foot in the place again. It had taken an
undated suicide note, no less, to bring him back again. It was just about as generous
a suicide note as any woman has ever penned to a recalcitrant lover, and Stella
still remembered it with a certain measure of satisfaction.

"You mustn't blame yourself, darling," she'd written. "It is my decision, and
mine alone. If I cannot face life without you, that is *my* problem, not yours. So
don't, my love, feel that you have to come rushing round when you get this letter.
The very last thing I want—or have ever wanted—is to inconvenience you in any
way, or make you feel guilty. By the time you get this, darling, I shall be
dead . . ."

The posts must have been slow that week, because it was nearly three days before
she at last heard his feet pounding up the stairs, and had started taking the pills,
stuffing them into her mouth in handfuls as he burst into the room.

It had been worth it, though. He'd been sweet to her for days afterward, visiting
her often in the hospital; and even after she got home, he'd continued to shower
her with presents, calling every day, and displaying in full measure all the remorse,
the tenderness, the self-recrimination that such a situation demands of a man.

Until, of course, he got bored with it. First bored, then resentful, and finally
beginning to throw the thing up to her in their arguments. "Blackmail," he called
it now whenever Stella tried to get him to do anything he didn't want to do; and
Stella began to realize, gradually, that she was right back at square one—having
to be careful, careful, knowing all the time that the only way she could hold him

now was by avoiding quarrels and by being infinitely tolerant and understanding—in short, by letting him get away with every bloody thing.

And this was why, this summer Saturday afternoon, Stella, her teeth set in a smile, was making herself listen without a murmur to what Gerald was saying. She had known, of course, the *kind* of thing it would be; married men always have such *righteous* reasons for letting you down.   Sick wives, kids on holiday, family visits—all perfectly uncheckable, and all revealing what a kind, compassionate, virtuous, dutiful creature the lying, treacherous creature really is.

So what was it *this* time?

Simon's Sports Day.   Gerald was potty about that son of his.

"You *do* understand, don't you, darling," he was pleading; and of course she understood very well, she understood that he preferred the prospect of watching a nine-year-old running across a field in gym shoes to the prospect of spending the whole long afternoon with his mistress, cool and mysterious in her darkened flat, the sunlight flickering across the bed through the slatted blinds.

"You see, darling, the thing is, he might *win!* Only nine and he might actually win the under-eleven two hundred and fifty yards!   He's a marvelous little runner, Mr. Foulkes tells me—a real athlete's body!"

A real athlete's body.   The light shining in Gerald's eyes was something Stella had never seen before.   For a few seconds she tried to imagine what it would be like to be the mother of that athlete's body, to have produced it jointly with Gerald, to have a right, now, to a share in that idiotic pride.   At the sight of those heavy, self-indulgent features thus irradiated, Stella felt a great darkness coming around her.   It came like a black monstrous wave, engulfing her, leaving her bereft of speech.

"I wouldn't miss it for a million pounds!" she heard him saying, from somewhere outside the swirling blackness.   "To hear his name called—Simon Graves—my own son!   And then the clapping, the cheers!   And him only nine!   The others are all over ten, darling, *all* of them!   He's the only nine-year-old who managed to . . ."

She preferred his lies, preferred them a thousand times.   How could she have guessed that the truth, when she finally heard it from those evasive, prevaricating lips, would hurt as much as this?

The school gates were propped wide-open and welcoming, and through them, in the blazing sunshine, trooped the mothers and the fathers, the sisters and the girl friends, the aunts and the uncles.   With their white sandals, their bright cotton dresses or pale freshly ironed slacks, women just like Stella, in their early thirties. Among so many, who was going to give her a second glance?   Unless of course, she gave herself away somehow—walking too fast maybe, or letting her eyes flit too anxiously from side to side?

The fathers were less numerous than their womenfolk, which made Stella's task that much easier; they stuck out among the bright dresses like the dark stumps of trees.   Stella's eyes darted from one to another of them ceaselessly, for he might be anywhere; and supposing—just supposing—he were to catch sight of her before she'd managed to locate him?

Not a big risk, really.   For she had the advantage that the hunter always has over the prey—she knew what she was looking for, and what she meant to do when she found it; whereas Gerald not only wasn't on the watch for her, he hadn't the slightest suspicion she could possibly be here at all.   On top of which she had, after a fashion, disguised herself with a pair of large round sunglasses, and a white silk bandanna wound tightly round her black shining hair.

Across the lawn, up under the avenue of limes, the slow procession wound, chattering, exclaiming, exchanging greetings; some were already fanning themselves against the heat.   Slowly, likewise, but with her heart hammering, Stella matched her pace with the rest; and it was not until she had settled herself on the grass at the far end of a long line of deck chairs facing the sports field that Stella began to breathe more easily.   Hemmed in by all these chairs, she could scarcely be seen from more than a yard or two away, and yet by craning her neck she could get a good view of the crowd still winding up from the school buildings.   Here and there a dark head, taller than the rest, would make her catch her breath; but always, it was a false alarm.

And now, here was the junior master walking up and down with his loudspeaker, announcing the order of events.   Already the crowd was falling into an expectant silence, the thousand voices dying away in wave after wave, fading away like the twitter of birds at twilight.   And still Gerald hadn't arrived.

Had he been lying to her after all?   Had his afternoon's truancy nothing to do with Simon's Sports Day, in spite of all those passionate declarations of paternal pride?   The swine!   The double-crossing, treacherous swine!   All that emotion wasted—not to mention having let herself in for a long hot afternoon of boredom, all for nothing!

I'll tell you, Gerald Graves!   I'll teach you to lie to me, make a fool of me! Thought you'd get away with it, didn't you?—*I'll* show you!

Already she could feel a line of sweat gathering under the bandanna, along her hairline; she'd never worn such a thing before, and by the Lord, she thought, I never will again!   *I'll* show him!

"Under sixteen hurdles . . ."

"Quarter mile, under fourteen . . ."

The sheer tedium of it was beginning to make Stella feel quite ill; her back ached, her eyes burned, and her brain felt half addled with heat and boredom.

Long jump.   High jump . . . on and on the thing droned; whistles blew, shouts exploded into the shimmering air and died away again; the clapping and the cheering rose, and fell, and rose again.   Cup for this, prize for that.   The sun beat down, the voices swelled and receded, and then, just when Stella was on the verge of sleep, she heard it.

"Simon Graves!   Winner of the under-eleven two hundred and fifty yards! Simon Graves!"

Stella was sitting bolt upright now, peering past the forest of chairs to get a glimpse of the sports field; but before she had time to locate the dark-haired little boy scuttling proudly toward the sidelines, she became aware of a little commotion going on in front of her and a few yards to the right.

"*Simon!* Our Simon! He's *done* it, Mummy! Daddy said he would! Oh, Simon—Si-i-i-mon!"

"Hush, darling, hush, Carol, you must sit down." A plumpish smiling woman was pulling at the sleeve of a wildly gesticulating little girl of about seven, urging her back into her seat. "Hush, Carol darling, not so loud. Simon'll be embarrassed. Oh, but won't Daddy be pleased!"

"Daddy will say," "Daddy will think"—and where the hell *was* Daddy, if one might inquire? "Wouldn't miss it for a million pounds," he'd said. Someone, somewhere, worth *more* than a million this bright afternoon?

Peering between the lines of chairs, Stella could see that the exultant mother and little sister were about to receive their hero. Pounding up the bank he came, wiry and brown and all lit up with triumph, hurling himself on his mother and sister amid a babel of congratulations.

Past the chairs, past the stirring smiling people, Stella watched, and kept very still. What *right* had the three of them to such joy, such total undiluted happiness? Didn't they know that the foundations of it were rotten, that their cosy little family life was based on a rotting, disintegrating substructure of lies and cheating? "Daddy" this and "Daddy" that—it made her feel quite sick to listen to the shrill little voices filled with such baseless adoration.

Quietly, unobtrusively, Stella got to her feet, and worked her way between the rows of chairs. She reached the little girl just when her mother and brother had turned away for a moment, receiving further congratulations. Quickly Stella dropped on her knees in front of the child, bringing their faces level.

"Do you know why your Daddy isn't here?" she said softly. "It's because he's spent the afternoon with me! In bed. Do you understand?"

The blank, almost stupid look on the child's face maddened her, and the blank look remained on the child's face. But Stella had the satisfaction, after she had squeezed back past row after row of chairs and had almost escaped from the enclosure, of hearing Carol, at last, burst into loud sobbing.

It was nearly ten o'clock when, at long last, she heard Gerald's step on the stairs; and even after all these hours she still could not have said if she had been expecting him to come, or to stay away.

He'd be angry, of course. But also, surely, relieved? Five years of secrecy was too much; it would be a relief to both of them to have it out in the open.

"Don't you agree, darling, that it is high time we had it out in the open?" she was asking, for the fourth or fifth time, of the silent slumped figure in the armchair. She'd been trying ever since his arrival to extract some sort of response from him. She'd tried everything, even congratulating him on his son's success.

"Pity you weren't there to see it," she'd been unable to resist adding; but even this had provoked from Gerald nothing more than the bald factual statement that he *had* seen it, thank you, from the Pavilion, where some of the fathers were helping to organize the boys.

Then more silence.   She tried again.

"I'm sorry, Gerald darling, if Carol—if the little girl—was upset.   I didn't mean to upset her, I just thought that the children should know about us.   I don't believe in lies and deceit with children.   I think they are entitled to the truth.   Oh, darling, please don't look at me like that!   It's been a shock, I know, but I'm sure that when you've had time to think about it, you'll see it's been for the best.   The best for *us*—and for Wendy too.   She can't have liked all this lying and deception all these years.   I'm sure she'd rather know where she stands, and be able to start making sensible plans for the future.

"I mean, Wendy looks quite a nice sort of person.   I don't think she'll make any trouble once she understands that we love each other.   Oh, darling, what *is* it?   Why don't you *say* something?   Look, let's have a drink, and relax, and think what we're going to do when the unpleasantness is all over.   This flat is a bit small for the two of us, but assuming that you'll be getting half of the value of your house, then between us we could—"

And now, at last, he *did* make a move.   He rose stiffly, as if he suffered from rheumatism, and went to pour them each a large glass of whiskey.   He handed her a glass in silence, and then, swallowing his at a gulp, he walked over to the table in the window where Stella's typewriter stood, open.   Laboriously, with one finger, he began to type.

Stella waited a minute, two minutes, then walked over to look.

> Gerald B. Graves
> 27 Firfield Gardens
> Sydenham Way

The long manila envelope stared up at her from the typewriter carriage; she watched, stupefied, while he finished the last few letters of the address.   Then—

"Whatever are you doing, darling?" she asked, with an uneasy little laugh.   "Are you writing a letter to *yourself?*"

And then she saw it, just by his right hand.   Her own suicide note of last autumn—*"By the time you get this, darling, I shall be dead . . ."*

"The handwriting will be unquestionably yours," he observed conversationally, "and the address will have been typed on your typewriter.   The postmark will also be right, as I shall post it myself, on my way out.   It should reach me at breakfast time the day after tomorrow, just in time to show to the police.   And now, my dear, just one more little job, and we shall be finished."

And as he stood up and turned toward her, the light from the lamp fell full onto his face, and she saw the look in his eyes.

"No!   No!" she gasped, took a step backward, and shrank, whimpering, against the wall.

"I intend it to look like suicide," he said, as if reassuring her; and as he moved across the carpet toward her, Stella's last coherent thought was: he will too!   He'll get away with it, he'll lie his way out of it, just as he's always lied his way out of everything!

How accomplished a liar he was, she knew better than anyone, for it was she who had trained him—trained him, like a circus animal, over five long years.

BRIAN GARFIELD

Charlie's Shell Game

By the end of the afternoon I had seen three of them check in at the reception desk and I knew one of them had come to kill me but I didn't know which one.

Small crowds had arrived in the course of the afternoon and I'd had plenty of time to study them while they stood in queues to check in at the reception desk. One lot of sixteen had come in together from an airport bus—middle-aged couples, three children, a few solitary businessmen; tourists, most of them, and sitting in the lobby with a magazine for a prop I wrote them off. My man would be young— late twenties, I knew that much.

I knew his name too but he wouldn't be traveling under it.

Actually the dossier was quite thick; we knew a good deal about him, including the probability that he would come to Caracas to kill me. We knew something of his habits and patterns; we'd seen the corpses that marked his backtrail; we knew his name, age, nationality; we had several physical descriptions—they varied but there was agreement on certain points: medium height, muscularly slim, youthful. We knew he spoke at least four languages. But he hadn't been photographed and we had no fingerprints; he was too clever for that.

Of the check-ins I'd spied at the Tamanaco desk, three were possibles—any one of them could be my intended assassin.

My job was to take him before he could take me.

Rice had summoned me back from Helsinki and I had arrived in Langley at midnight grumpy and rumpled after the long flight but the cipher had indicated red priority so I'd delivered myself directly to the office without pause to bathe or sleep, let alone eat. I was famished. Rice had taken a look at my stubble and plunged right in, "You're flying to Caracas in the morning. The eight-o'clock plane."

"You may have to carry me on board."

"Me and how many weightlifters?" He glanced at the clock above the official photograph of the President. "You've got eight hours. The briefings won't take that long. Anyhow you can sleep on the plane."

"Maybe. I never have," I said, "but then I've never been this exhausted. Have you got anything to eat around here?"

"No. This should perk you up, though—it's Gregorius."

"Is it now."

"I knew you'd wag your tail."

"All right, you have my attention." Then I had to fight the urge to look straight up over my head in alarm: Rice's smile always provokes the premonition that a Mosler safe is falling toward one's head.

"You've gained it back. Gone off the diet?" Now that he had me hooked in his claws he was happy to postpone the final pounce—like a cat with a chipmunk. I really hate him.

I said, "Crawfish."

"What?"

"It's what you eat in Finland. You take them fresh out of a lake, just scoop them up off the bottom in a wooden box with a chickenwire bottom. You throw them straight into the pot and watch them turn color. I can eat a hundred at a sitting. Now what's this about Caracas and Gregorius?"

"You're getting disgustingly fat, Charlie."

"I've always been fat. As for disgusting, I could diet it off, given the inclination. You, on the other hand, would need to undergo brain surgery. I'd prescribe a prefrontal lobotomy."

"Then you'd have no one left to spice your life."

"Spice? I thought it was hemlock."

"In this case more likely a few ounces of plastique. That seems to be Gregorius' preference. And you do make a splendid target, Charlie. I can picture two hundred and umpty pounds of blubber in flabby pieces along the ceiling. Gregorius would be most gratified."

He'd mentioned Gregorius now; it meant he was ready to get down to it and I slumped, relieved; I no longer enjoy volleying insults with him—they cut too close and it's been a long while since either of us believed they were jokes. Our mutual hatred is not frivolous. But we need each other. I'm the only one he can trust to do these jobs without a screw-up and he's the only one who'd give me the jobs. The slick militaristic kids who run the organization don't offer their plums to fat old men. In any section but Rice's I'd have been fired years ago—overage, overweight, overeager to stay in the game by the old rules rather than the new. I'm the last of the generation that puts ingenuity ahead of computer print-outs.

They meet once a month on the fifth floor to discuss key personnel reassignments and it's a rare month that goes by without an attempt being made by one of the computer kids to tie a can to my tail; I know for a fact Rice has saved me by threatening to resign: "If he goes, I go." The ultimatum has worked up to now but as we both get older and I get fatter the kids become more strident and I'm dubious how long Rice can continue the holding action. It's not loyalty to me, God knows; it's purely his own self-interest—he knows if he loses me he'll get the sack himself: he hasn't got anybody else in the section who knows how to produce. Nobody worthwhile will work for him. I wouldn't either but I've got no choice. I'm old, fat, stubborn, arrogant, and conceited. I'm also the best.

He said, "Venezuela is an OPEC country of course," and waited to see if I would attend his wisdom—as if the fact were some sort of esoterica. I waited, yawned, looked at my watch. Rice can drive you to idiocy belaboring the obvious. Finally he went on, "The oil-country finance ministers are meeting in Caracas this time. Starting Thursday."

"I haven't been on Mars, you know. They have newspapers even in Helsinki."

"Redundancies are preferable to ignorance, Charlie." It is his litany. I doubt he passes an hour, even in his sleep, when that sentence doesn't run through his mind: he's got it on tape up there.

"Will you come to the point?"

"They'll be discussing the next round of oil-price hikes," he said. "There's some disagreement among them. The Saudis and the Venezuelans want to keep the increase down below five percent. Some of the others want a big boost— perhaps twenty-five or thirty percent."

"I plead. Tell me about Gregorius."

"This is getting us there. Trust me."

"Let's see if I can't speed it up," I said. "Of course it's the Mahdis—"

"Of course."

"They want Israel for themselves, they don't want a Palestinian peace agreement, they want to warn the Arab countries that they won't be ignored. What is it, then? They've arranged to have Gregorius explode a roomful of Arab leaders in Caracas? Sure. After that the Arab countries won't be so quick to negotiate a Middle East settlement without Mahdi participation. Am I warm?"

"Scalding. Now I know you're awake."

"Barely."

The Mahdi gang began as an extremist splinter arm of the Black Septemberists. The gang is small but serious. It operates out of floating headquarters in the Libyan desert. There's a long and tedious record of hijackings, terror bombings, assassinations. Nothing unique about that. What makes the gang unusual is its habit of using mercenaries. The Mahdis—they named themselves after the mystic who wiped out Gordon at Khartoum—are Palestinian but they're Bedouins, not Arabs; they're few in number and they're advanced in age compared with the teenage terrorists of the PLO. The Mahdi staff cadre consists of men who were adults at the time of the 1947 expulsion from Palestine. Some of the sheiks are in their seventies by now.

Rather than recruit impassioned young fools the gang prefers to hire seasoned professional mercenaries; they get better results that way and they don't need to be concerned about generation-gap factionalism. They are financed by cold-blooded groups of various persuasions and motivations, many of them in Iraq.

They had used Gregorius at least twice in the past, to my knowledge; the Hamburg Bahnhof murders and the assassination of an Israeli agent in Cairo. The Hamburg bomb had demolished not only a crowd of Israeli trade officials but also the main staircase of the railroad station. The Cairo setup had been simpler, just one victim, blown up when he stepped onto the third stair of his entrance porch.

Gregorius was a killer for hire and he was well paid; apparently his fees were second only to those of Carlos the Jackal, who had coordinated the Munich athlete murders and the Entebbe hijack; but Gregorius always chose his employment on ideological grounds—he had worked for the PLO, the Baader-Meinhof Group, the Rhodesian rebels, the Cuban secret service, but he'd never taken a job for the West. Evidently he enjoyed fighting his own private war of liberation. Of course he was psychotic but there was no point dwelling on his lunacy because it might encourage one to underestimate him; he was brilliant.

Rice said, "We've got it on authority—fairly good authority—that the Mahdis have hired Gregorius for two targets in Caracas. Ministers. The Saudi and the Venezuelan. And of course whatever bonus prizes he may collect—bombs usually aren't too selective."

"How good is 'fairly good'?"

"Good enough to justify my pulling you off the Helsinki station and posting you to Venezuela."

"All right." If he didn't want to reveal the source he didn't have to; it wasn't really my affair. Need-to-know and all that.

Rice got down to nuts and bolts and that pleased me because he always hurries right through them: they bore him. He has a grand image of himself as the sort of master strategist who leaves tactical detail to junior staff. Unhappily our section's budget doesn't permit any chain of command and Rice has to do his own staff work and that's why we usually have to go into the field with a dearth of hard information; that's one reason why nobody else will work for him—Rice never does much homework.

"It could happen anywhere," he concluded. "The airport, a hotel lobby, a state banquet, any of the official ministerial meetings, a limousine. Anywhere."

"Have you alerted Venezuelan security?"

"I didn't have to. I've established your liaison out of courtesy."

In other words the tip had come from Venezuelan security. And they didn't feel confident of their own ability to contain Gregorius. Very astute of them; most small-nation security chiefs lack the humility to admit it when a job is too big for them.

Rice continued, in the manner of an afterthought, "Since we don't know where he plans to make the strike we've taken it upon ourselves to—"

"Is that a royal 'we'?"

"No. The fifth floor. As I was saying, it's been decided that our best chance at him is to lure him into the open before the ministers begin the conference. Of course he doesn't tempt easily."

Then he smiled. My flesh crawled.

"You're the bait, Charlie. He'll come out for you."

"In other words it's an open secret that I'll be in Caracas and you've spread the word where you know he'll hear it."

I brooded at him, hating him afresh. "Maybe you've neglected something."

"Oh?"

"Gregorius is like me in one respect. He's—"

"Young, fast, up-to-date, and sexy. Yes indeed, Charlie, you could be twins."

I cut across his chuckle. "He's a professional and so am I. Business comes first. He'd love to nail me. All right. But first he'll do the job he's being paid for."

"Not this time. We've leaked the news that you're being sent down there to terminate him regardless of cost. He thinks you're being set up to nail him *after* he exposes himself by blowing up a few oil ministers. He can't risk that—you got closer to nailing him than anybody else ever has. He knows if you're set on him again you won't turn loose until you've done the job. And he knows if he sets off a bomb while you're in earshot of it you'll reach him. He needs more lead-time than that if he means to get away."

And he smiled again. "He's got to put you out of the way before he goes after the ministers. Once the bombs go off he can't hang around afterward to take you on. He's got to do it first."

I said, "I've heard stronger reasoning. He's confident of his skills. Suppose he just ignores me and goes ahead with the job as if I weren't there?"

"He hates you too much. He couldn't walk away, could he? Not after Beirut. Why, I believe he hates you even more than I do."

Two years earlier we'd known Gregorius was in Beirut to blast the Lebanese-coalition prime minister. I'd devised one of the cleverer stunts of my long career. In those days Gregorius worked in tandem with his brother, who was six years older and nearly as bright as Gregorius. Our plan was good and Gregorius walked into it but I'd had to make use of Syrian back-up personnel on the alternate entrances to that verminous maze of alleys and one of the Syrians had been too nervous or too eager for glory. He'd started the shooting too early by about seven-tenths of a second and that was all the time Gregorius needed to get away.

Gregorius left his brother behind in ribbons in the alley; still alive today but a vegetable. Naturally Gregorius made efforts afterward to find out who was responsible for the ambush. Within a few weeks he knew my name. And of course Gregorius—that's his code name, not the one he was born with—was Corsican by birth and personal revenge is a religion with those people. I knew one day he'd have to come for me; I'd lost very little sleep over it—people have been trying to kill me for thirty-five years.

Just before Rice sent me to the airport he said, "We want him alive, Charlie."

"You're joking."

"Absolutely not. It's imperative. The information in his head can keep the software boys busy for eight months. Alive—it's an order from the fifth floor."

"You've already blindfolded me and sent me into the cage with him and now you want to handcuff me too?"

"Why, Charlie, that's the way you like it best, you old masochist."

He knows me too well.

I'd watched them check in at the hotel desk and I'd narrowed the possibilities to three. I'd seen which pigeonholes the room clerk had taken the keys from so I knew which rooms they were in. I didn't need to look at the register because it wouldn't help me to know what names or passports they were using.

It was like the Mexican Shell Game: three shells, one pea.   Under which shell is the pea?

He had to strike at me today because Rice's computer said so.   And it probably had to be the Tamanaco Hotel because I had studied everything in the Gregorius dossier and I knew he had a preference—so strong it was almost a compulsion—for the biggest and best old hotel in a city.   Big because it was easy to be anonymous there; best because Gregorius had been born dirt-poor in Corsica and was rich now; old because he had good taste but also because old walls tend to be soundproof.   In Caracas the Tamanaco was it.

It was making it easy for him, sitting in plain sight in the lobby.

Earlier in the day I'd toured the city with Cartlidge.   He looks like his name—all gaunt sinews and knobby joints.   We'd traced the route in from the airport through the long mountain tunnel and we'd had a look at the hotel where the Saudi minister was booked in; on my advice the Venezuelans made a last-minute switch and when the Saudi arrived tomorrow morning he'd be informed of the move to another hotel.   We had a look at the palace where the conference would take place and I inquired about the choice of halls: to forestall Gregorius, the Venezuelans had not announced any selection—there were four suitable conference rooms in the building—and indeed the final choice wouldn't actually be made until about ten minutes before the session began.   They were doing a good job.   I made a few minor suggestions and left them to it.

After lunch we'd set up a few things and then I'd staked myself in the Tamanaco lobby and four hours later I was still there.

Between five and six I saw each of the three again.

The first one spent the entire hour at the pool outside the glass doors at the rear of the lobby.   He was a good swimmer with the build and grace of a field-and-track contender; he had a round Mediterranean face, more Italian than French in appearance.   He had fair hair cut very short—crew cut—but the color and cut didn't mean anything; you could buy the former in bottles.   For the convenience of my own classification, I dubbed him The Blond.

The second one appeared shortly after five, crossing the lobby in a flared slim white tropical suit.   The heels of his beige shoes clicked on the tiles like dice.   He stopped at the side counter to make a phone call—he could have been telephoning or he could have been using it as an excuse to study my abundant profile—and then he went along to the bell captain's desk and I heard him ask the captain to summon him a taxi, as there weren't any at the curb in front.   His voice was deep: he spoke Spanish with a slight accent that could have been French.   He had a very full head of brown hair teased into an Afro and he had a strong actorish face like those of Italians who play Roman gigolos in Technicolor films.   He went right outside again, presumably to wait for his taxi.   I dubbed him The Afro.   If he'd actually looked at me I hadn't detected it—he had the air of a man who only looked at pretty girls or mirrors.

The third one was a bit more thickly muscled and his baldness was striking.   He had a squarish face and a high pink dome above it.   Brynner and Savalas shave their heads; why not Gregorius?   This one walked with an athlete's bounce—he came down about half-past five in khaki Bermudas and a casual Hawaiian tourist shirt; he went into the bar and when I glanced in on my way past to the gents' he was drinking something tall and chatting to a buxom dark-haired woman whose bored pout was beginning to give way to loose fourth-drink smiles.   From that angle and in that light the bald man looked very American but I didn't cross him off the list; I'd need more to go on.

I was characterizing each of them by hairstyle but it was useless for anything but shorthand identification.   Gregorius, when last seen by witnesses, had been wearing his hair long and black, shoulder-length hippie style.   None of these three had hair remotely like that but the sightings had been five weeks ago and he might have changed it ten times in the interval.

The Blond was on a poolside chaise toweling himself dry when I returned from the loo to the lobby.   I saw him shake his head back with that gesture used more often by women than by men to get the hair back out of their eyes.   He was watching a girl dive off the board; he was smiling.

I had both room keys in my pocket and didn't need to stop at the desk.   It was time for the first countermove.   I went up in the elevator and walked past the door of my own room and entered the connecting room with the key Cartlidge had obtained for me.   It was a bit elaborate but Gregorius had been known to hook a detonator to a doorknob and it would have been easy enough for him to stop a chambermaid in the hall: "My friend, the very fat American, I've forgotten the number of his room."

So I entered my room through the connecting door rather than from the hall. I didn't really expect to find anything amiss but I didn't want to risk giving Rice the satisfaction of hearing how they'd scraped sections of blubber off the ceiling.

Admittedly I am fat but nevertheless you could have knocked me over with a feather at that moment.   Because the bomb was wired to the doorknob.

I looked at it from across the room.   I didn't go any closer; I returned to the adjoining room, got the *Do Not Disturb* placard, went out into the hall, and hung the placard on the booby-trapped doorknob.   One of the many differences between a professional like Gregorius and a professional like Charlie Dark is that Charlie Dark tends to worry about the possibility that an innocent hotel maid might open the door.

Then I made the call from the phone in the adjoining room.   Within two minutes Cartlidge was there with his four-man bomb squad.   They'd been posted in the basement beside the hotel's wine cellar.

The crew went to work in flak vests and armored masks.   Next door I sat with Cartlidge and he looked gloomy.   "When it doesn't explode he'll know we defused it."   But then he always looks gloomy.

I said, "He didn't expect this one to get me.   It's a signal flag, that's all.   He wants me to sweat first."

"And are you?   Sweating?"

"At this altitude?   Heavens no."

"I guess it's true.   The shoptalk.   Charlie Dark has no nerves."

"No nerves," I agreed, "but plenty of nerve.   Cheer up, you may get his fingerprints off the device."

"Gregorius?   No chance."

Any of the three could have planted it.   We could ask the Venezuelans to interrogate every employee in the hotel to find out who might have expressed an interest in my room but it probably would be fruitless and in any case Gregorius would know as soon as the interrogations started and it would only drive him to ground.   No; at least now I knew he was in the hotel.

Scruple can be crippling.   If our positions had been reversed—if I'd been Gregorius with one of three men after me—I'd simply kill all three of them.   That's how Gregorius would solve the problem.

Sometimes honor is an awful burden.   I feel such an anachronism.

The bomb squad lads carried the device out in a heavy armored canister.   They wouldn't find clues, not the kind that would help.   We already knew the culprit's identity.

Cartlidge said, "What next?"

"Here," I said, and tapped the mound of my belly, "I know which one he is. But I don't know it here yet."   Finger to temple.   "It needs to rise to the surface."

"You *know?*"

"In the gut.   The gut knows.   I have a fact somewhere in there.   It's there; I just don't know what it is."

I ordered up two steak dinners from room service and when the tray-table arrived I had Cartlidge's men make sure there were no bombs under the domed metal covers.   Then Cartlidge sat and watched with a kind of awed disgust while I ate everything.   He rolled back his cuff and looked at his watch.   "We've only got about fourteen hours."

"I know."

"If you spend the rest of the night in this room he can't get at you.   I've got men in the hall and men outside watching the windows.   You'll be safe."

"I don't get paid to be safe."   I put away the cheesecake—both portions—and felt better.

Of course it might prove to be a bullet, a blade, a drop of poison, a garrote, a bludgeon—it could but it wouldn't.   It would be a bomb.   He'd challenged me and he'd play it through by his own perverse rules.

Cartlidge complained, "There's just too many places he could hide a satchel bomb.   That's the genius of plastique—it's so damn portable."

"And malleable.   You can shape it to anything."   I looked under the bed, then tried it.   Too soft: it sagged near collapse when I lay back.   "I'm going to sleep on it."

And so I did until shortly after midnight when someone knocked and I came awake with the reverberating memory of a muffled slam of sound.   Cartlidge came into the room carrying a portable radio transceiver—a walkie-talkie.   "Bomb went off in one of the elevators."

"Anybody hurt?"

"No.   It was empty.   Probably it was a grenade—the boys are examining the damage.   Here, I meant to give you this thing before.   I know you're not much for gizmos and gadgets but it helps us all keep in touch with one another.   Even cavemen had smoke signals, right?"

"All right."   I thought about the grenade in the elevator and then went back to bed.

In the morning I ordered up two breakfasts; while they were en route I abluted and clothed the physique that Rice detests so vilely.   One reason why I don't diet seriously is that I don't wish to cease offending him.   For a few minutes then I toyed with Cartlidge's walkie-talkie.   It even had my name on it, printed onto a plastic strip.

When Cartlidge arrived under the little dark cloud he always carries above him I was putting on my best tie and a jaunty face.

"What's got you so cheerful?"

"I lost Gregorius once.   Today I'm setting it right."

"You're sure?   I hope you're right."

I went down the hall.   Cartlidge hurried to catch up; he tugged my sleeve as I reached for the elevator button.   "Let's use the fire stairs, all right?"   Then he pressed the walkie-talkie into my hand; I'd forgotten it.   "He blew up one elevator last night."

"With nobody in it," I pointed out.   "Doesn't it strike you as strange?   Look, he only grenaded the elevator to stampede me into using the stairs.   I suggest you send your bomb-squad lads to check out the stairs.   Somewhere between here and the ground floor they'll doubtless find a plastique device wired to a pressure-plate under one of the treads, probably set to detonate under a weight of not less than two hundred and fifty pounds."

He gaped at me, then ran back down the hall to phone.   I waited for him to return and then we entered the elevator.   His eyes had gone opaque.   I pressed the lobby-floor button and we rode down; I could hear his breathing.   The doors slid open and we stepped out into the lobby and Cartlidge wiped the sweat off his face.   He gave me a wry inquiring look.   "I take it you found your fact."

"I think so."

"Want to share it?"

"Not just yet.   Not until I'm sure.   Let's get to the conference building."

We used the side exit.   The car was waiting, engine running, driver armed.

I could have told Cartlidge which one was Gregorius but there was a remote chance I was wrong and I don't like making a fool of myself.

Caracas is a curiously Scandinavian city—the downtown architecture is modern and sterile; even the hillside slums are colorful and appear clean.   The wealth of Twentieth Century oil has shaped the city and there isn't much about its superficial appearance, other than the Spanish-language neon signs, to suggest it's a Latin town.   Traffic is clotted with big expensive cars and the boulevards are self-consciously elegant.   Most of the establishments in the central shopping district are branches of American and European companies—banks, appliances, couturiers, Cadillac showrooms.   It doesn't look the sort of place where bombs could go off:

terrorism doesn't suit it. One pictures Gregorius and his kind in the shabby crumbling wretched rancid passageways of Cairo or Beirut. Caracas? No; too hygienic.

As we parked the car the walkie-talkies crackled with static. It was one of Cartlidge's lads—they'd found the armed device on the hotel's fire stairs. I'd been mistaken about one thing: it was a trip-wire, not a pressure plate. Again I'd forgotten how indiscriminate Gregorius could be, his indifference to the risk to innocents.

We had twenty minutes before the scheduled arrivals of the ministers. I said, "It'll be here somewhere. The bomb."

"Why?"

"It's the only place he can be sure they'll turn up on schedule. Are the three suspects still under surveillance? Check them out."

He hunched over the walkie-talkie while I turned the volume knob of mine down to get rid of the distracting noise and climbed out of the car and had my look around; I bounced the walkie-talkie in my palm absently while I considered the possibilities. The broad steps of the *palacio* where the conference of OPEC ministers would take place were roped off and guarded by dark-faced cops in Sam Brownes. On the wide landing that separated the two massive flights of steps was a circular fountain that sprayed gaily; normally people sat on the tile ring that contained it but today the security people had cleared the place.

There wasn't much of a crowd; it wasn't going to be the kind of spectacle that would draw any public interest. There was no television equipment; a few reporters clustered off to one side with microphones and tape recorders. Routine traffic, both vehicular and pedestrian. That was useful because it meant Gregorius wouldn't be able to get in close; there would be no crowd to screen him.

Still, it wasn't too helpful. All it meant was that he would use a remote-control device to trigger the bomb.

Cartlidge lowered the walkie-talkie from his face. "Did you hear?"

"No." I had difficulty hearing him now as well: the fountain made white noise, the constant gnashing of water, and I moved closer to him while he scowled at my own walkie-talkie. His eyes accused me forlornly. "Would it kill you to use it? All three accounted for. One in his room, one at the hotel pool, one in the dining room having his breakfast."

I looked up past the rooftops. I could see the upper floors of the Hotel Tamanaco—it sits on high ground on the outskirts—and beyond it the tiny swaying shape of a cable car ascending the lofty mountain. Cotton-ball clouds over the peaks. Caracas is cupped in the palm of the mountains; its setting is fabulous. I said to Cartlidge, "He has a thing about stairs, doesn't he."

"What?"

"The Hamburg Bahnhof—the bomb was on the platform stairway. The Cairo job, again stairs. This morning, the hotel fire stairs. That's the thing about stairways—they're funnels." I pointed at the flight of stone steps that led up to the portals of the *palacio*. "The ministers have to climb them to get inside."

"Stone stairs.   How could he hide a bomb there?   You can't get underneath them.   Everything's in plain sight.''

I brooded on it.   He was right.   But it had to be: suddenly I realized it had to be—because I was here and the Saudi's limousine was drawing up at the curb and it meant Gregorius could get both of us with one shot and then I saw the Venezuelan minister walk out of the building and start down the stairs to meet the limousine and it was even more perfect for Gregorius: all three with one explosion.   It *had* to be: right here, right now.

Where was the damned thing?   Where?

I had the feeling I needed to find the answer within about seven seconds because it was going to take the Venezuelan minister that long to come this far down the steps while the Saudi was getting out of the limousine; already the Venezuelan was nearly down to the fountain and the Saudi was ducking his berobed head and poking a foot out of the car toward the pavement.   The entourage of Arab dignitaries had hurried out of the second limousine and they were forming a double column on the steps for the Saudi to walk through; a police captain drew himself to attention, saluting; coming down the stairs the Venezuelan minister had a wide welcoming smile across his austere handsome face.

They'd picked the limousine at random from a motor pool of six.   So it couldn't be in the car.

It couldn't be on the steps because the *palacio* had been guarded inside and out for nearly a week and it had been searched half an hour ago by electronic devices, dogs, and human eyes.

It couldn't be in the fountain either.   That had been too obvious.   We'd exercised special care in searching the fountain; it had only been switched on ten minutes earlier.   In any case you can't plant a bomb under water because the water absorbs the force of the explosion and all you get is a big bubble and a waterspout.

In other words there was no way for Gregorius to have planted a bomb here. And yet I knew he had done so.   I knew where Gregorius was; I knew he had field glasses to his eyes and his finger on the remote-control button that would trigger the bomb by radio signal.   When the Saudi met the Venezuelan and they shook hands on the steps not a dozen feet from me, Gregorius would set it off.

Six seconds now.   The Venezuelan came past the fountain.

The walkie-talkie in my hand cracked with static but I didn't turn it up.   The mind raced at Grand Prix speed.   If he didn't plant the bomb beforehand—and I knew he hadn't—then there had to be a delivery system.

Five seconds.   Gregorius: cold, brutal, neat, ingenious.   Then I knew—*I* was the bomb.

Four seconds and my arm swung back.   It has been a long time since I threw a football and I had to pray the instinct was still in the arm and then I was watching the walkie-talkie soar over the Venezuelan's head and I could only stand and watch while it lofted and descended.   It struck the near lip of the fountain and for a moment it looked ready to fall back onto the stairs, but then it tipped over the rim and went into the water.

His reaction time would be slowed by distance and the awkwardness of handling binoculars and the unexpectedness of my move. Instinctively he reached for the trigger button, but by the time he pressed it the walkie-talkie had gone into the water. The explosion wasn't loud. Water blistered at the surface and a crack appeared in the surrounding rim; little spouts began to break through the shattered concrete; a great frothy mushroom of water bubbled up over the surface and cascaded down the steps.

Nobody was hurt.

We went into the hotel fast. I was talking to Cartlidge: "I assume the one who's still upstairs in his room is the blond one with the crew cut."

"How the hell did you know that?"

"He's Gregorius. He had to have a vantage point."

Gregorius was still there in the room because he'd had no reason to believe we'd tumbled to his identity. He was as conceited as I; he was sure he hadn't made any mistake to give himself away. He was wrong of course. He'd made only one but it was enough.

Cartlidge's bomb-squad lads were our flying wedge. They kicked the door in and we walked right in on him and he looked at all the guns and decided to sit still.

His window overlooked the *palacio* and the binoculars were on the sill. I said to Cartlidge, "Have a look for the transmitter. He hasn't had time to hide it too far away."

The Blond said, "What is this about?" All injured innocence.

I said, "It's finished, Gregorius."

He wasn't going to admit a thing but I did see the brief flash of rage in his eyes; it was all the confirmation I needed. I gave him my best Rice smile. "You'll be pleased to talk in time."

They searched him, handcuffed him, gave the room a toss, and didn't find anything; later that day the transmitter turned up in a cleaning-supplies cupboard down the hall.

To this day Cartlidge still isn't sure we got the right man because nobody ever told him what happened after we got Gregorius back to the States. Rice and I know the truth. The computer kids in Debriefing sweated Gregorius for weeks and finally he broke and they're still analyzing the wealth of information he has supplied. I'd lost interest by that time; my part of it was finished and I knew from the start that I'd got the right man. I don't make that kind of mistake; it didn't need confirmation from the shabby hypodermics of Debriefing. As I'd said to Rice, "The binoculars on the windowsill clinched it, of course. When the Venezuelan and the Saudi shook hands he planned to trigger it—it was the best way to hit all three of us.

"But I knew it had to be the Blond much earlier. I suppose I might have arrested him first before we went looking for the bomb but I wasn't absolutely certain."

"Don't lie," Rice said. "You wanted him to be watching you in his binoculars—you wanted him to know you were the one who defused him. One of these days your brain's going to slow down a notch or two.   Next time maybe it'll blow up before you throw it in the pond.   But all right, since you're waiting for me to ask—how did you pick the blond one?''

"We knew until recently he'd worn his hair hippie length.''

"So?''

"I saw him at the pool toweling himself dry.   I saw him shake his head back the way you do when you want to get the hair back out of your eyes.   He had a crew cut.   He wouldn't have done that unless he'd cut his hair so recently he still had the old habit.''

Rice said, "It took you twelve hours to figure that out?   You *are* getting old, Charlie.''

"And hungry.   Have you got anything to eat around here?''

"No.''

EDMUND CRISPIN

The Pencil

It was not until the third day that they came for Eliot. He had expected them sooner, and in his cold withdrawn fashion had resented and grown impatient at the delay—for although his tastes had never been luxurious, the squalid bedroom which he had rented in the Clerkenwell boardinghouse irked him. Now, listening impassively to the creak of their furtive steps on the staircase, he glanced at his gunmetal wristwatch and made certain necessary adjustments in the hidden thing that he carried on him. Then quite deliberately he turned his chair so that his back was toward the door.

His belated dive for his revolver, after they had crept up behind him, was convincing enough to draw a gasp from one of them before they pinioned his arms, thrusting a gun muzzle inexpertly at the back of his neck. Petty crooks, thought Eliot contemptuously as he feigned a struggle. And ''petty crooks'' again, as they searched him and hustled him down to the waiting car. Yet his scorn was not vainglorious. The hard knot into which his career of professional killing had twisted his emotions left no room even for that. Only once had Eliot killed on his own account—and that was when they had nearly caught him. He was not proposing to repeat the mistake.

It was a little after midnight and the narrow street was deserted. The big car moved off smoothly and quietly. Presently it stopped by an overgrown bomb site, blanched under the moon, and the blinds were drawn down. There they gagged Eliot, and blindfolded him, and tied his hands behind his back. When they found him submissive, their confidence perceptibly grew. Between them and Addison's lot, Eliot reflected as the car moved off again, there was little or nothing to choose: petty crooks all of them, petty warehouse thieves whose spheres of operation had happened to collide. That was why he was here.

He made no attempt to chart mentally the car's progress. He had not been asked to do that—and it was Eliot's great merit as a hired murderer that he was incurious, never going beyond the letter of his commission. Leaning back against the cushions, he reconsidered his instructions as the car purred on through London, through the night.

''Holden's people are getting to be a nuisance,'' Addison had said—Addison the young boss with his swank and his oiled hair and his Hollywood mannerisms. ''But if Holden dies they'll fall to pieces. That's your job—to kill Holden.''

Eliot had only nodded.   Explanations bored him.

"But the trouble is," Addison had continued, "that we can't find Holden.   We don't know where his hideout is.   That means we've got to fix things so that they lead us to it themselves.   My idea is to make you the bait."   He had grinned.   "Poisoned bait."

With that he had gone on to explain how Eliot was to be represented as a new and shaky recruit to the Addison mob; how it was to be made to seem that Eliot possessed information which Holden would do much to get.   Eliot had listened to what concerned him directly and ignored the rest.   It was thorough, certainly.   They ought to fall for it.

And to judge from his present situation, they had . . .

It seemed a long drive.   The only thing above all others that Holden's men wanted to avoid was the possibility of being followed, the possibility that he, Eliot, might pick up some clue to the hideout's whereabouts.   So whatever route they were taking, it certainly wasn't the most direct.

At last they arrived.   Eliot was pushed upstairs and through a door, was thrust roughly onto a bed.   A bed, he thought: good.   That meant Holden had only this one musty-smelling room.   All the more chance, therefore, that the job would come off.

He let them hit him a few times before he talked: his boyhood had inured him to physical pain, and he was being well paid.   Then he told them what they wanted to know—the story Addison had given him, the story with just enough truth in it to be convincing.   Eliot enjoyed the acting: he was good at it.   And they were at a disadvantage, of course, in that having left the blindfold on they were unable to watch his eyes.

In any case, Holden—who to judge from his voice was a nervous elderly Cockney—seemed satisfied.   And Holden was the only one of them who mattered . . . Before long, Eliot knew, the police would get Holden, and Addison too, and their small-time wrangling for the best cribs would be done with for good and all.   That, however, was of no consequence to Eliot.   All he had to do was to say his lesson nicely and leave his visiting card and collect his fee.

And here it was at last: the expected, the inevitable offer.   Yes, all right, Eliot said smoothly after a few moments of apparent hesitation; he didn't mind being their stool pigeon so long as they paid him enough.   And they were swallowing that, too, telling him what they wanted him to find out about Addison's plans, sticking a cigarette between his bruised lips and lighting it for him.   He almost laughed.   They weren't taking off the blindfold, though: they didn't trust him enough for that.   They were going to let him go, but in case he decided not to play ball with them, after all, they weren't risking his carrying away any important information . . .

Yes, they were going to let him go.   This is it, Eliot thought.   And delicately, as he lay sprawled on the bed, his fingers moved under the hem of his jacket, so that, hidden from his interrogators, something slim and smooth rolled out onto the bedclothes.

Fractionally he shifted his position, thrusting the object—to the limit that the rope round his wrists would allow—underneath the pillow.   It was a nice little thing, and Eliot was sorry to lose it: in appearance, nothing more than an ordinary mechanical pencil, but with a time fuse inside it and a powerful explosive charge. Addison had told him that it was one of the many innocent-looking objects supplied to French saboteurs during the Occupation, to be deposited on the desks of German military commanders or in other such strategic places.   And Eliot, who cared nothing for war but who was interested in any destructive weapon, had appreciated its potentialities.   As a means of murder it was chancy, of course: this one might kill Holden, or on the other hand it might kill a cleaning woman making up the bed.

But that was none of Eliot's business.   He was doing what he had been told to do, and whether it succeeded or not he was going to collect.

The return drive was like the first.   At the bomb site the gag and bonds and blindfold were taken off and presently Eliot was back at his lodginghouse door, in the gray light of early dawn, watching Holden's car drive rapidly away.

He mounted to his room, examined his damaged face without resentment in the mirror, and on impulse started to pack.   Then, tiring suddenly, he lay down on the bed and slept.

The pencil had been set to explode at eight . . .

It was a quarter to eight when Eliot woke, and the full light had come.   Finish packing first, he thought; then see Addison, report, and get paid off.   The early editions of the evening papers would tell him, before he caught the boat train, whether Holden was dead or not . . .

So he was shifting the pillows, to make more room on the bed for his shabby suitcase, just as the clock of St. John's struck the hour.

And that was when he saw the pencil.

For a second he stared at it in simple incomprehension.   Then understanding came.   Of course, thought Eliot dully, of course!   They weren't risking the secret of their precious hideout.   This is where they brought me to, after driving me round and round the streets.   This is where they questioned me—here in my own room!

Panic flooded him.   He ran.   From the bedside to the door was a distance of no more than three paces.

But the explosion had caught and killed him before his fingers even touched the doorknob.

VINCENT McCONNOR

Just Like Inspector Maigret

Detective:
GEORGE DRAYTON

The green park in the heart of London, to the passing eye, had not changed in half a century. But to George Drayton, born seventy-three years ago in a vast bedroom overlooking Knightswood Square, it had been altered in every possible way. Nothing was as it used to be.

He was the second person to enter the Square, fog or shine, every morning. Purdy, the gardener, was always the first, and Mrs. Heatherington the third. Actually she was fourth because her ancient Pekinese, Kwong Kwok, darted through the gate ahead of his mistress. That was how it had been for more than thirty years. Except that the gardener was never there on Sundays or bank holidays. On those days George Drayton was the first.

Every resident of the long rows of identical mansions surrounding Knightswood Square possessed a key which unlocked all the gates in the shoulder-high iron fence. A discreet sign near each gate warned that this was a private park.

George Drayton sniffed the morning air as he stepped out under the white-pillared portico and let the massive front door close itself behind him. He stood for a moment on the broad top step, eyes darting across the sunny Square in search of Purdy. A blue veil of smoke curled at the far northern corner. The gardener would be burning yesterday's accumulation of twigs and dead flowers. He daily raked every path and walk, picked up each fallen leaf and broken branch. Before dusk they were always neatly piled for burning the following morning.

The sun had climbed above the chimneys on the opposite side of the Square, dropping a curtain of haze across the elegant Regency façades so that all he could see was a blur of white columns against shadowed brick. It was going to be a pleasant August day. He would sit on his morning-bench under the protecting branches of the oak tree. There were several favorite benches he occupied, depending upon time of year and weather, but never the same bench, morning and afternoon.

George started down the shallow marble steps to the sidewalk and was careful not to drop his books or leather cushion. He carried three books into the park every morning. Today there was a new novel from his own publishing house and two detective novels.

"Morning, sir." Fitch, the caretaker, squinted up the basement steps where he was polishing the brass hand-rail. "Another fine day, sir."

"Splendid." He kept walking or Fitch would come charging up the steps for a chat that could delay him at least ten minutes. On those unfortunate mornings when it was impossible to escape, Mrs. Heatherington and Kwong Kwok always reached the Square ahead of him.

He hesitated at the curb and peered up and down for any moving vehicles. There was only the milkman pulling his small cart at the far end of the street. George walked more briskly as he crossed to the narrow pavement which edged Knightswood Square. Reaching the curb he slowed his steps again and headed for the nearest gate. He rested the cushion and books on the gate post as he felt in his pocket for the key. There was always a moment of panic when he was unable to find it among the jumble of loose objects. Blast! He would have to go all the way back to his flat. Fitch couldn't help him. None of the caretakers were permitted to have keys. Then his fingers touched cold metal and a sigh of relief escaped from his lips.

George unlocked the gate and stepped into the Square. He had made it ahead of the Pekinese.

Before closing the gate he removed his key from the lock and dropped it back into his pocket. Then, in a final burst of speed, he headed for the shaded morning-bench under the oak tree. He placed his leather cushion on the bench and sat on it, arranging the books beside him.

As he filled his first pipe for the day he let his eyes wander over the familiar mansions around the Square. George knew who lived behind every window. He also knew who slept late, who was ill, dying, or convalescent, and which wife had left which husband. His charwoman, Mrs. Higby, kept him informed. Twice a day she reported all the latest news of Knightswood Square. At the moment she complained that nothing much was happening. There had been little worth talking about since last year's murder. That sort of thing didn't happen often enough to please Mrs. Higby.

She came to him for several hours, every day but Sunday, and also did daily work in two other mansions on the Square. Late morning, while he sat in the park, Mrs. Higby would straighten the flat and cook his lunch. He always made his own tea but she would return, after finishing her other jobs, and prepare his supper before catching a bus home to Putney.

Each day as she served his lunch and supper she reported, with relish, the news of the day. He looked forward to Mrs. Higby's gossip because, otherwise, he would never know what was going on behind his neighbors' windows. It had been exasperating, last winter, when she was kept to her bed with the flu. He had hired a woman through an agency but she had known nothing about the other residents of the Square. It was as though his morning and evening papers had not been delivered for three weeks.

Purdy wheeled an empty barrow past, without a word, touching an earthy finger to his leather cap. He never paused for conversation until late in the afternoon.

George watched as the gardener settled down to work, digging at the roots of a rosebush. Then he turned to look across to the south side of the Square, but there was no sign of Mrs. Heatherington and her Pekinese.

He checked his watch.   9:36.   Six minutes late!   Very likely packing for her holiday.   She was taking an afternoon train from Victoria Station to Brighton where her daughter-in-law would be waiting to drive her across to Hove.   The old lady spent two weeks every August with her son and his family in their pleasant Georgian house overlooking the distant seashore.   Mrs. Higby had described the place to him, in detail, many times; she had heard all about it from her friend Mrs. Price, who came in twice a week to char for Mrs. Heatherington.

A blur of movement caught his eye at the opposite side of the park and he turned his head to see someone on a bicycle.   As his eyes adjusted to the distance he saw that it was Willie Hoskins who, once a month, washed every window facing the Square.   Each flat had its regular day for the window cleaner.

Willie braked his bicycle in front of Number 26, hoisted it across the pavement, and propped it against the railing of the basement areaway.

Then he lifted a bucket from the handlebar and carried it up the steps to the front door.   George could see the flash of color as the sun caught in Willie's red hair, noticed the yellow rubber gloves tucked under the wide leather belt that circled his waist, the faded blue shirt and trousers as the boy went into the house.   Boy?   He was a married man of twenty-three with a wife who, according to Mrs. Higby, regularly had him up before a local magistrate on charges of drunkenness, non-support, and knocking her about.

The tenants of the Square frequently threatened to dispense with Willie's services, but he would disarm them with his great smile, flashing white teeth and tossing his curly head.   It was suspected that Willie was not averse to tossing some of the ladies of Knightswood Square between washing windows.   "He's a complete rascal, he is!" Mrs. Higby would say.   "Always leave the front door wide when he does any windows where I be."

George turned to look, once again, for Mrs. Heatherington.   She was just coming down the front steps of the mansion where she had a second-floor-front flat.   The Pekinese was pulling on his leash, furious at being late, eager to get into the park. He yanked his mistress across the street and when she had unlocked the gate, sprang onto the grass jerking the leather leash out of her hand.   The small beast darted to a favorite bush as the old lady closed the gate and dropped the key into her handbag.   She crossed to the busy dog and bent stiffly to retrieve his leash.   Then, finally, she stood for a moment surveying the Square.

That was when George Drayton looked in another direction.   He had no idea whether Mrs. Heatherington could see him from that distance, but he didn't want her to think he was observing her.   So he always looked away.

He noticed Willie Hoskins washing a window on the third floor of Number 26— Colonel Whitcomb's flat.   A reflection of sunny sky gleamed from two panes he had already finished, but the others were dull with a month's accumulation of London soot.   As he watched the window cleaner work he could hear the scuffling sound of Mrs. Heatherington's footsteps approaching down the walk, and as she came nearer he sensed the soft padding of the Pekinese.   He turned to look and found that they were much closer than he had anticipated.

The Pekinese stalked past with majestic disdain but his mistress nodded and smiled.   George Drayton bowed as usual.   They never spoke.   In fact, he had never heard Mrs. Heatherington's voice except when she talked to the dog.

George watched them head for the north gate.   The old lady paused for a moment to speak to the gardener.   Usually she only nodded to Purdy.   Probably telling him that she was leaving on holiday.   The gardener touched his cap as she continued on her way out of the Square, toward the Old Brompton Road.   She would have final errands to do.   Small presents for her grandchildren.   Very likely a visit to her bank to withdraw money for the two-week holiday.

He wondered how old the dog might be.   A Pekinese, named Kwong Kwok, had accompanied Mrs. Heatherington back from China, more than thirty years ago, when she returned to London after the death of her husband.   Ever since there had been a Pekinese named Kwong Kwok, but it was impossible that the original dog could have survived so many years.   The dog was a constant topic of conversation among the charwomen.   To them and to George Drayton all Pekinese looked alike.

The first pram of the day, guided by a uniformed nanny, rolled into the Square as George picked up his small pile of books.   Soon there would be dark clots of nursemaids and prams.   Older children would avoid them and keep to the far side of the park where they could run and shout without glares and reprimands from the easily disturbed nannies.

He decided to put off reading the novel from Drayton House.   Since his retirement, eight years ago, they had sent him a copy of each new book but, too frequently, he only became upset when he read the pretentious trash his nephew was publishing. No point in getting into a temper on such a beautiful day.   He put the book aside and hesitated, deciding between the new Simenon and the new Christie.   This would be a perfect morning to read about Paris.   Simenon it would be . . .

As he turned to the first page he glanced across the Square to the dirt-encrusted windows of the third-floor flat where last year's murder had taken place.   They still remained curtained.   The Clarkson flat had never been rented.   And the murder remained unsolved.

For two hours he lost himself in a rain-drenched Paris.   Inspector Maigret sat in a small café, drinking calvados, listening to neighborhood gossip as he watched a house across the street where a man had been murdered.   Home for lunch with Madame Maigret in the apartment on the Boulevard Lenoir, then back through a cold drizzle to the café with its view of the bleak street.   Drinking toddy after toddy.   Smoking his pipe . . .

George put down the book and filled his own pipe.   Why couldn't he sit here and through pure deduction, like Inspector Maigret, solve last year's murder? Except that New Scotland Yard had put their best men on the Clarkson case and they had been unable to find any trace of the murderer.

As George lighted his pipe he noticed Mrs. Higby, parcels clutched in both arms, dart up the front steps of his building.   Another hour and she would have the flat in order and his lunch waiting.   Wouldn't she be surprised if he announced the name of the Clarkson murderer as he ate his noon chop!

He turned again to study the curtained windows of the murder flat.   The victim, young Mrs. Clarkson, had been separated from her husband, but not divorced. Harry Clarkson had an alibi for every minute of the afternoon when his wife was killed.   They had found her partially clothed body, sprawled across the bed, one silk stocking twisted around her throat and another stuffed into her mouth.   The newspapers said that she had not been attacked sexually.

Clarkson had testified, at the coroner's inquest, that he had not seen his wife in several months.   His solicitor sent her a monthly check and, regularly, tried to persuade her that a divorce would be wise; but she had refused to discuss such a possibility.   Her char told the police that Mrs. Clarkson entertained many male visitors.   She had never seen any of them but, every morning, she had to clean all the ashtrays.   Unfortunately, she had no idea how much money Mrs. Clarkson kept in the flat, so there was no way of knowing whether there had been robbery as well as murder.   The dead woman's purse, containing a few shillings, was found on her dressing table.

The police reported there had been no fingerprints.   All the locals were questioned—caretaker of the building, milkman, florist, laundryman, greengrocer, window cleaner, postman, delivery boy from the chemist shop.   Every name in Mrs. Clarkson's address book had been traced and interrogated.   Nobody knew anything.

A distant chime of bells brought George Drayton out of his dream of murder. Twelve o'clock.   He would finish the Simenon after lunch.   As he got to his feet he glanced, once again, at the Clarkson flat.   Maigret would have solved the mystery easily, sitting here in the Square, looking up at those curtained windows. But he, George Drayton, didn't have a suspicion of an idea—in spite of all the detective novels he had read and published.

He gathered up his books and leather cushion and headed for the gate.   As he walked down the path he noticed that the gardener was already wolfing a sandwich, perched between the handles of his barrow.   George looked for Willie Hoskins but the window cleaner had disappeared.   All the windows of Colonel Whitcomb's flat gleamed in the noon sunshine, reflecting bright rectangles of blue sky.

Instead of a chop there was cold salmon for lunch which he ate with appetite. He had all his meals at a small table in the study, surrounded by overflowing bookshelves and facing tall windows which overlooked the Square.

Mrs. Higby had her usual morning collection of gossip.   "That young American couple what sublet Number 29 are leavin' for Paris next week."

Yes, Maigret would have solved the Clarkson murder without difficulty.   Except that now the case was more than a year old and the clues would have long since vanished.

"The old gent in Number 12 is boozin' again.   Mr. Mortan, the super, had to help him out of his cab last night.   Carry him in to the lift an' up to his flat.   I've a lovely bit of Leicester for you."

He studied the curtained windows of the Clarkson apartment, across the Square, as he ate the cheese.   Curious that someone—the caretaker or the dead woman's solicitor—wouldn't have those unsightly windows washed.

"Mrs. Heatherington's off this afternoon on holiday.   Her an' that ol' dog.

This year she's told Mrs. Price, her char, not to come in while she's away.   Paid her two weeks' wages, she did.   Told her to have herself a bit of a rest.   Such a fine lady, Mrs. Heatherington.''

After lunch George placed his cushion on an afternoon bench near the northwest corner of the Square, his back to the sun.   He filled his pipe again and as he smoked he watched the renewed activity around him.

The gardener was pruning some kind of shrub near the rose arbor.   Most of the noisy older children had not reappeared.   Probably having an afternoon nap.   Several of the nannies had returned with their prams.   Or were these different nursemaids?   Some of them sat dozing in the warm sunlight.

He noticed that Willie Hoskins was now washing the windows of Mrs. Heatherington's flat.   Odd that the old lady would want them cleaned the afternoon she was going away.   Except that she had given her char a holiday, so there would be no one, these next two weeks, to let Willie Hoskins or anyone else into the flat.

George opened the Simenon and immediately returned to Paris.   He became so absorbed in Maigret's progress that he was no longer aware of the others in the Square.   Squealing children ran past him unheeded.   The distant chime of the bells on the quarter hours did not penetrate to his inner ear.   He was conscious only of the sounds and voices of Paris, just as Maigret heard them.

A sudden penetrating scream, shrill and sharp, pulled him back to London and Knightswood Square.

Some of the nursemaids still sat beside their prams.   The gardener was sweeping one of the walks.   No one in the Square seemed to have noticed the scream he had heard.   Or had he heard it?   And was the sound human or animal?   Perhaps one of the older children playing in the distance?   The sound was not repeated.

George raised his eyes to the windows of Mrs. Heatherington's flat.   Apparently the window cleaner had finished and gone on to his next job.   One of the windows had been left open and the curtains had not been drawn together.

He took out his watch and checked the time.   4:27.

Mrs. Heatherington would have telephoned for a cab and left for Victoria Station long before this.   Strange he hadn't noticed her departure.   He remembered the scene from other years.   Luggage brought down by the cabbie.   Last of all, the small wicker hamper containing the Pekinese.   He wondered if the old lady had forgotten to shut that window and close the curtains in the flurry of her departure.

He saw that he had finished all but a dozen or so pages of the Simenon.   The puzzle in the detective novel was nearly solved.

. . . Maigret was moving quickly now.   Each of the clues which had seemed so innocent before, had become ominous as the great French detective linked them together.

''Pardon me, sir.''

George looked up from his book to see the gardener with a large bouquet of yellow roses in his hand.

''Told Mrs. Heatherington I'd have these for her.   Fresh cut.   So they'd last till she got to Hove.''

"They're very beautiful."

"Said she'd get them before she took off.   But I never seen her go."

"Didn't notice her leave, myself.   I was reading."

"Guess I'll take them home to the Missus.   S'prise the old girl."   Purdy held
the bouquet in front of him, carefully, as he started back up the walk.

George reopened the Simenon.   As he read on, something seemed to shadow
the final pages of the book.   The printed words faded together and his thoughts
wandered.

Why had Mrs. Heatherington forgotten the bouquet of roses?

And why hadn't she shut that window before she left on her holiday?   And
closed those curtains?

. . . Maigret had crossed the street and was climbing the stairs to the floor where
the murder had taken place.

There had been no fingerprints in the Clarkson apartment because the murderer
had, obviously, worn gloves.

It was a dog that had screamed.   George was certain of it now.

Could it have been Mrs. Heatherington's dog?   Why would the Pekinese make
such a sound?   It seldom even barked.   Of course there were other dogs in the
mansions around Knightswood Square.

. . . Maigret was now standing in the dark hall, outside the murder apartment,
listening at the door.

Too bad Mrs. Clarkson had not owned a dog.   Might have saved her life.

George glanced across to the curtained windows of the Clarkson flat again.

Those dirty windows.   Disgraceful.

Dirty windows!

George whirled to look again at Mrs. Heatherington's windows.   Something
wrong there!

The open window had been completely washed.   All its panes sparkled in the
afternoon sunlight.   And the window next to it reflected blue sky in every rectangle
of gleaming glass.   But the other two windows were still dull with grime.

Half the windows of Mrs. Heatherington's flat had not been cleaned—
Why?

Had Willie Hoskins seen something inside Mrs. Heatherington's living room?
Something that had stopped him in the middle of his job?

And why the devil hadn't the old lady shut that window and closed those curtains
before she left to catch her train?

Why had she gone off without that bouquet of roses the gardener had cut for
her?

Yellow roses.

Something else yellow—

The window cleaner's gloves!   That was it!   Willie Hoskins always wore yellow
rubber gloves.

No fingerprints.

Why had the Pekinese screamed?

What possible reason—

"Murder!" The terrible word exploded from his throat. "Murder!" He was on his feet, pointing up at Mrs. Heatherington's open window.

Everyone in Knightswood Square had turned to stare. Purdy was running toward him across the grass.

"Up there! Mrs. Heatherington! Hurry, man! Get the police!"

The gardener, without pausing to ask questions, raced toward the nearest gate, at the southern end of the Square.

George Drayton collapsed onto his leather cushion, exhausted and out of breath. All he would ever be able to remember of the next hours would be a blur of strangers.

Arrival of the first policeman.

Cars screeching to a stop.

Dark-suited men hurrying to Mrs. Heatherington's flat.

The ambulance.

A clutter of curious people gathering on the sidewalk.

White-uniformed figures carrying something down the steps.

His bench surrounded. The dark-suited men. Polite questions. How did he know what had happened? What had he seen? Had he heard something? The dog? Questions ran together until they gave him a headache.

He finally managed to get home to the quiet of his flat where he stretched out gratefully on the sofa in his study . . .

Mrs. Higby wakened him. "You're a hero! Saved the old lady's life, you did! They say another hour an' she'd have been a goner. Just like her dog. Poor little beast. His head bashed in—"

"Mrs. Heatherington? Is she—"

"In hospital. They had to operate. But she's goin' to be fine. I just talked to Mrs. Price, her char, and the police told her. They say the old lady's money was stolen. What she took out of the bank for her holiday. Afraid your supper's goin' to be late this evenin'."

The telephone rang.

Mrs. Higby hurried to snatch it from the desk. "Mr. Drayton's residence . . . What is it, love? What's happened now? . . . Fancy that!" She turned to pass on her information. "It's me chum, Mrs. Price. They've caught Willie Hoskins! Drunk in a Chelsea pub. The old lady's money still in his pocket." Her eyes widened as she spoke into the phone again. "He didn't! Well, I never."

She turned back toward the sofa. "He's confessed to killin' Mrs. Clarkson last year. I always said he was a rascal."

George Drayton smiled. He had solved the Clarkson case. And he had done it without moving from his bench in Knightswood Square.

. . . Just like Inspector Maigret.

DOUGLAS SHEA

Advice, Unlimited

Mr. Gihon Gore
$c/_o$ Chutney & Chives, Inc., Publishers
New York, N.Y.
Dear Mr. Gore:
   Although your mystery stories have not been exactly unheard of by me, last week was the first occasion I had to pick one up and read it.   I am speaking of *Brent's First Case*.   Generally speaking I found the book adequate but there were two errors in Chapter 21.   You speak of the killer African bees navigating to the bedroom of elderly pig-iron heiress Harriet Heald (a) by polarized light from the sky and (b) by being attracted to the interior of the bedroom by the phlox-scented room-freshener spray used by Miss Heald.   I'll take the easy one first.
   Bees are *never* attracted to phlox, Mr. Gore.   Their tongues are too short to reach the nectar deeply buried within the flowers.   The bees know this and you might say that they wouldn't even stick out their tongues (ha, ha) at phlox scent.   Try cyclamen scent.   Your bees will go bananas over that one.
   Now about that polarized light bit.   It is true that bees do navigate by polarized light from the sky but never (I repeat, *never*) on cloudy days.   You have to have blue sky in order to detect polarized light at certain angles to the sun.   Cloud particles destroy the effect by scattering the light.
   What to do?
   The cloudy day seems necessary in order to give Miss Heald her attack of sinus migraine, an attack which brings old Dr. Physick tottering to her bedside so that they can be killed by bee venom together.   On the other hand, if the sun isn't shining, forget the polarized light.
   Thinking the matter through, I believe that skilled replotting of Chapters 21, 22, 23, and 24 might turn the trick.   You might want to consider this in your next edition of *Brent's First Case*.

> Very truly yours,
> George Ohm
> Associate Professor of Science
> Dimwiddie University
> Glen Cove, L.I., N.Y.

From: Quentin Quarles, Editor
Chutney & Chives, Inc., Publishers
New York, N.Y.

As Mr. Gore now receives several thousand items of mail a year, it is not possible for him to answer you personally.   Hence this form letter designed to answer 95% of the questions he is asked.

His home address is Waldorf Towers, New York, N.Y.; his London office $^c/_o$ Cratchit and Marley, Solicitors, 54 Dewlap Road, London N22, 4PP.

Biographical details will be found in *Who's Who, Contemporary Authors, Contemporary Novelists, Dictionary of International Biography, Celebrity Register, Britannica 3*.   See also profile in *Time* of September 12, 1972.

Mr. Gore has now written 37 books.   See above references, or the list in any recent edition.

Permission to quote should be directed to Chutney & Chives, Inc.

Mr. Gore *never* supplies photos or autographs.   Also he cannot autograph and mail back books.

Lecture requests are no longer accepted.   Nor can questions be answered about how to plot good mystery stories.   The only advice he can give to beginners is this: Read, read, read.   Read at least one book a day.   Also write, write, write. And remember one thing about getting fresh ideas; there is no substitute for living. As Ernest Hemingway said, "Writing is not a full-time occupation."

Mr. Quentin Quarles, Editor
Chutney & Chives, Inc., Publishers
New York, N.Y.
Dear Quentin, Quentin, Quentin:

I return your form letter herewith, having studied it carefully.   I took your advice, Quentin: you told me to read, read, read, and to write, write, write.

Please refer to page 209 of *The Case of the Undertaker's Hat*.   See where Gore sends the hemophiliac crashing through a thin sheet of invisible glass blocking the garden path?   Another no-no, Quentin.   Fact is, there's no such thing as "invisible" glass.   Gore means nonreflective glass, sometimes called invisible glass by tyros.   Such glasses have the light that they would reflect at normal incidence almost completely suppressed by interference.

But the condition for said destructive interference can be fulfilled for only one wave length.   This is usually chosen to be near the middle of the visible spectrum. The reflection of red and violet light is then somewhat larger and these two colors combine to form purple.

Take a look at a coated lens in a camera.   See the purplish hue?   A sheet of glass that color across anybody's path would stand out like your ears, ears, ears, old friend.   No matter what wave length you try to suppress, others will be reflected. And that's the name of the game.   That seems to knock out Chapters 11 and 12, also pages 209 through 218, also Chapters 23, 24, and 25.   I don't know how you fix up *that* mess.   Sorry about that.

George Ohm

Mr. Quentin Quarles, Editor
Chutney & Chives, Inc., Publishers
New York, N.Y.
Dear Quentin:
   Where are you: I miss those little inspirational words of yours.
   Incidentally, I found some more boo-boos—in *The Slim Man*.   Say please and
I'll tell you what they are.   Pretty please, Quentin?

George Ohm

Memo: From the suite of Gihon Gore
To: George Ohm
   Get lost.

Gihon Gore

GG: Louise L'Erotique
cc: Quentin Quarles

Memo: From George Ohm
To: Gihon Gore
   I have your little note.   Gore, you need help and I'm here to give it to you.
Let's begin with *The Slim Man*.
   In one scene you have The Slim Man, astronomer Herschel Skyanier, look
through the eyepiece of the Hale Telescope on Palomar Mountain while the tube
of the instrument is lowered for routine inspection.   If I read you correctly, and I
believe I do, Skyanier thereby witnesses a murder being committed five miles down
the mountain slope.   Gore, there's so much wrong with that that I hardly know
where to begin—but I'll try.
   In the first place, you can't even deflect the tube of a modern astronomical
telescope to the horizon, let alone point it down a mountain slope.   Take a look
at a picture of any observatory anywhere in the world, Gore.   Notice the position
of the slit in the dome.   In the case of the Hale Telescope of which you write, the
floor on which the mountain of the instrument rests is 75 feet below the level of
the slit.   What I'm saying is that with one of these big babies you can only look
up at the sky—never down.
   And another thing: the field of view of any large telescope is so small that even
if you could look at a murderer five miles away about all you'd see would be a
nose or an eyebrow.   Finally, Gore, the image would be *inverted*.   You see, they
don't bother with erecting eyepieces on astronomical telescopes.   It's an absolutely
unnecessary refinement.   Ask yourself the question: what's up, what's down in
the case of the heavenly bodies? and you'll have the answer why.
   You slipped up badly in *The Slim Man*, Gore.   Tonight I'm going to rifle
through *The Affair at Byles* to see if I can be of use to you there.   Don't lose
heart.
   Yours for Science,

George Ohm

Mr. Gihon Gore
Waldorf Towers
New York, N.Y.
Dear Mr. Gore:

You have scarcely had time to digest the information I sent you re *The Slim Man*, but I wanted you to know that I have finished *The Affair at Byles* and I think we are in *real* trouble this time.

As you tell it, Thedabara Gam, spoiled, filthy-rich heiress to the Gam millions, is giving a lawn party at Byles, her family estate, for a small gathering of 200 persons come to honor her engagement to Herman Opdyke, polo-playing scion of her father's business associate. Meanwhile, unbeknown to all, Shamus McGillicuddy, Miss Gam's jilted ex-suitor, just back from the Amazon, has secreted himself in the third cook's tent, murder burning in his black heart.

At an opportune moment McGillicuddy sticks the tip of an Orinoco blowgun through the tent fly and lets Opdyke have it full in the chest with a curare-dipped dart. In the resulting confusion he thereupon escapes through the back of the tent, disguised as an attendant bearing a tray of petits fours, ladyfingers, and strawberry preserves.

Oh, this is dreadful! How shall I begin?

Item Number One. Curare is a highly unreliable poison, its toxicity varying greatly with its source and method of preparation. See *The Merck Index* or any of the several pharmacopoeias. More than that, curare isn't nearly strong enough or quick-acting enough. I myself would prefer to use sodium cyanide. Sodium cyanide is freely soluble in water. It can also be readily obtained since it is widely used in extracting gold and silver ores, in electroplating baths, in fumigating citrus and other fruit trees, and in disinfecting ships, railroad cars, warehouses, etc. Only four to eight grams of this chemical would prove lethal to a horse.

Dissolve a thimbleful of the crystals in a tablespoonful of water when your murderer is ready to go and you've got it made. Have him carry the solution to the scene of the crime in a small plastic-capped vial. The victim who receives a shot of this will die in seconds.

Item Number Two. The blowgun. Do you have any idea how long an Orinoco Indian blowgun is? Well, it would reach from the ground almost to a man's armpit. Try sawing it off to a more practical length and you destroy its accuracy. How did McGillicuddy carry that monstrosity to Byles?—tucked down his pants' leg and up his shirt? Really, Gore, you'd have a veritable stiff before you ever got to the murder. May I suggest replacing the blowgun with a tranquilizing gun and a tranquilizing dart? It seems so obvious to me.

Yours for Science,

George Ohm

Look, Ohm:

I've had you pegged for some time. You're a medical school dropout with a useless smattering of sixth-grade science. You have such a gnawing sense of inferiority that it gives you a compulsion to pester famous people with your paranoid prattle.   If Einstein were living, I'll swear you would be deluging him with a one-sided tirade about his mistakes in the theory of relativity.   Now don't bother me any further with your puerile disquisitions, Ohm.

Be sure you hang onto my letters, though.   The autographs may bring you a buck or two when you come to a decrepit old age.

Gihon Gore

GG: Louise L'Erotique

Dear Mr. Gore:

"Puerile disquisitions," eh?   Hoity-toity now!

As for saving your letters, be informed that I use them for a very special purpose. I do find that 20-pound bond paper a little abrasive, though.   How much would you want to switch to a 9-pound weight?

Well, Gore, I've prayed with you and I've wrestled in spirit with you and I finally see that I've wasted my time.   *En garde* now, Gore!

I see you don't know about my fall and winter Saturday night lectures on popular science.   Yes, pompous one, I circulate up and down a good part of the Atlantic seaboard, stopping off at many of the smaller colleges where I have an invitation to speak.   I kick off this season's series this coming Saturday night right here in Peter Piper Hall at good old Dimwiddie.

Guess what this season's topic is, Gore?   "Scientific Boo-boos in the Works of a Famous Mysterymonger."   Do you like the title?   Well, guess who I'm going to talk about?

Do you know how popular you are on college campuses, Gore?—almost as popular as Tolkien with his Hobbit stories.   Think of the rage and disgust of all those students when the word starts to pass that their idol has typewriter keys of clay.

I'll bury you, buster!

Yours for Science.

George Ohm

INTERIM REPORT

From: Seymour Kravitz, Detective

To Inspector Attila Hund, Homicide

(on cassette tape)

I arrived at Peter Piper Hall, Dimwiddie University, at 8:52 P.M. approximately 25 minutes after the commission of the crime.   The body of the victim, George Ohm, white, 34, had not been touched, being still in place on the platform where it had fallen.   Death was due to a hypodermic dart which still protruded from the upper left quadrant of the victim's chest.   The Medical Examiner reports that the dart, of the type used to tranquilize animal subjects, had been filled with a concentrated aqueous solution of either potassium or sodium cyanide.   (Details later on receipt of report of analysis from Departmental chemist.)

A quick-witted student, Gary Cooper Rabinowitz, white, 21, had taken temporary charge pending my arrival and no one had left the theater.

"A Chinese detective with a Jewish name!" exclaimed Gary when I introduced myself. "Welcome, *landsman!*"

"Yes. And you should be a good Jewish boy and help me further so that we may find the murderer and give him such a hurt that he will pray for the death of ten thousand tickling nightingales' tongues."

My words seemed to strike a responsive chord in Gary who I later learned is an exchange student from Sweden.

There were 47 persons in the theater—36 students and 11 senior citizens who excitedly explained to me that they were receiving Social Security benefits and didn't want any further trouble with the government. All 47 persons were eventually released.

The theater is a small one, seating approximately 300 persons. The front platform on which Ohm was standing is elevated about three feet above floor level. Entry to the theater is gained by means of two sets of double doors, right and left, leading in from a spacious corridor. Between the two entrances is a single door leading to a projection booth. As seen from within the theater, the projection booth is a mat-black boxlike structure closed on three sides except for the usual small projection ports which in this case are about eight feet above theater floor level.

An important witness was Willie Crumble, black, 21, who was sitting in the center of the theater two rows from the back and just under the line of sight from the projection ports. Willie was anxiously awaiting the arrival of his girl friend and kept turning and glancing toward first one entrance, then the other. Willie is prepared to swear that no one entered or left the theater after Professor Ohm— Associate Professor of Science at the institution—began to speak.

Only about a half dozen sentences of Ohm's lecture were delivered when the tragedy occurred. No one knows the import of the lecture except that it had to do with technical or scientific mistakes in the writing of mystery fiction. No notes were found, either on the platform or in Ohm's bachelor apartment.

According to a majority of witnesses, Ohm had just uttered the partial sentence, "And so tonight I want to tell you about—" when there was a very faint *throop* sound whose point of origin in the theater could not be determined. Ohm fell backward, flung his arms wide, and emitted a single unintelligible guttural groan that sounded like *Gorrr-r-r!*

And that was it. He died immediately after.

Ohm seems to have been a man of catholic tastes. On the night stand beside his bed were three paperbacks by Mickey Spillane; in the library-study the complete set of Beilstein's *Organischen Chemie*. Over the desk hung framed pictures of Olga Korbut and Thomas A. Edison. He evidently had no enemies, according to the consensus of all students interviewed.

You know my methods, Inspector. I was able to deduce that the lethal dart had come from one of the two projection ports and such indeed proved to be the case. The booth door in the corridor was secured, but I was easily able to open it with a picklock. Inside I found a dart gun on the floor just under the right port. Against it was propped a 3-by-5-inch unlined white index card bearing the legend

in block letters: STOLEN FROM THE NASSAU COUNTY SPCA.   PLEASE RINSE THOR-
OUGHLY AND RETURN.

According to our handwriting expert the card was lettered by a right-handed
person using his left hand.   No fingerprints were found anywhere except for some
smudged repetitions on the cylindrical sides of the projection lenses, obviously
accumulated there by the projectionist.   There was a faint fragrance of Brut cologne
pervading the air.

There was a curious circular smudge on the end of the dart gun barrel and I was
almost immediately able to deduce what it was.   The gun was used with an
appurtenance which had been tossed or had rolled into one corner.   It is probably
the first time in history that a tranquilizer gun was used with a silencer.

Inspector, there is really nothing by which to get hold of this case.   The Saturday
night cultural events at the University are largely informal affairs, no admission
being charged, and it is this very informality that allowed the murderer to come
and go as he chose.

The homicide itself has the simple line that marks the hand of a master.   Hsi
Tz'u Chuan says that what is easy is easy to know; what is simple is easy to follow.
One part of me wants to believe this—to keep delving and triumph—but another
part remembers what the Talmud says: Much talk, much foolishness.

Inspector Hund, I reluctantly have to report to you that at last we seem to have
stumbled on The Perfect Crime.

BARRY PEROWNE

Raffles and the Dangerous Game

All of a sudden, in the fog that blanketed London one midwinter evening, the tall figure of a policeman loomed up at a street corner and, waving a red lantern, brought a hansom jingling to a standstill.

"Sorry, gentlemen," he told the passengers, who happened to be A. J. Raffles and myself, Bunny Manders, "this street is closed."

I had spent the past couple of hours watching Raffles win his match in a tennis tournament in progress at Lord's Cricket Ground, where the building which houses the court for the gentlemanly game of "real" tennis, or *jeu-de-paume*, is for a spectator about the chilliest place in town.

So, being anxious to thaw myself out with a rum toddy or two at my flat, where Raffles would drop me off on the way to his own bachelor chambers in The Albany, I protested to the bobby.

"But look here," I said to him, "this is Mount Street. I live in this street."

"Well, sir," he replied, "there's been a gas explosion in a house along there on the left."

"You describe, more or less," I said, startled, "the area where *I* live! Raffles, if you'll excuse me—"

Leaving him to pay off the cabbie, I sprang out of the hansom and, breaking into a run along Mount Street, saw above the roof of some house ahead a dull red glow pulsing in the fog. The glow faded out as I arrived upon the scene, but the gabled roof from which clouds of smoke and steam were now billowing up was that of the very house in which I had my domicile.

I stopped dead, incredulous. The windows of the flat on the top floor, the fourth, and of my own flat on the third floor, were shattered, and a brass-helmeted, thigh-booted fireman was in the act of clambering from a ladder into my living-room.

"Mr. Manders!" a voice called to me.

I looked round. Firemen's lanterns and the lamps of three Fire Brigade vehicles, one of them of the new horseless type, pallidly mitigated the fog, and I saw that the man who had called to me was Hobday, the hall porter of the house. He was talking to three of the residents.

"Who would have thought it?" said Hobday, as I went over to him. "A gas explosion in *Mount* Street, sir!   In the top flat, it was—Major Torrington's, just above yours, Mr. Manders.   The Major was out at the time—still is.''

"Luckily for him," said Charles Chastayne, who occupied the other flat on my floor.   A typical man-about-town, who played cards in the best clubs and probably, I suspected, derived his income from it, he was in evening dress, his cape and silk hat blotched with some sort of white stuff.   "I'd only just come in, Manders," he told me, "when the big bang shook the whole house."

"Anyone hurt?" asked Raffles, who had joined us.

"No, sir," said Hobday.   "I had my hands full getting Lady Davencourt an' her marmosets out of her first-floor flat, into a cab an' off to her sister's.   But, my word, I was worried about Miss Van Heysst here, who's unfamiliar with the premises as yet.   It was lucky a few lights stayed on for a minute or two, or she mightn't 'ave found her way out, plunged in the dark, an' come over panicky, bein' foreign.''

"I do not at all panic in the least, Mr. Hobday—*though foreign*," said Miss Marika Van Heysst, whose accent was as charming as her person and who had moved recently into the flat below mine.   "Only, see now how it is with us!   We have run out safely, yes, but the firemen say we cannot go back in.   We say, for how long?   They only shake their heads.   So we are become refugees in the fog, and your London fog is so *cooold!*''

She drew more closely about her a cloak like Red Riding Hood's, but Miss Van Heysst's cloak, its hood framing her enchanting young face and flaxen hair, was as blue as her forlorn, appealing eyes.

"You make a sensible point, Miss Van Heysst," agreed the man who occupied the other flat on her floor.   A handsome naval officer with a staff job at the Admiralty, he was in uniform, his cap and greatcoat marred here and there with white smears.   "Since we're not allowed back in the house," he said, "there's no point in our standing here in the cold.   Miss Van Heysst, may I suggest that I seek a cab for you and escort you to a hotel I know of?''

"Oh, Commander Rigby, that would be kind, for if I am lost in the fog alone and meet with your Jack the Ripper, then yes, I panic very much—being foreign," said Miss Van Heysst, with a flash of her lovely eyes at Hobday as she accepted Clifford Rigby's proffered arm and went off with him into the fog.

"You can trust the Navy with a pretty young woman," said Chastayne, the cardplayer.   "Or can you?"   He shrugged cynically.   "No business of mine. I must go and find somewhere to pig it temporarily myself.   Good night, Manders.''

Only then, as Chastayne left us, did it dawn on me that the white smears on his evening-cape and on Rigby's greatcoat must have been caused by ceiling plaster falling when the explosion shook the house—and a sudden thought threw my mind into a cerebral commotion.

"Raffles," I blurted, "I'll just pop up to my flat—see the damage.''

He gripped my arm, restraining me.   "Nonsense, Bunny, you won't be allowed in.   You can have my spare room in The Albany.   I take it your goods and chattels are insured, so you've nothing to worry about.''

But I knew otherwise—knew it so damnably well that I did not sleep a wink in his spare room and, while still the lamps were dim yellow blurs in the murk of what passed for dawn, I inserted my key into the front-door lock of the now silent house in Mount Street.

In the dark hall I stood listening.   All was still.   I struck a match.   The light quivered on the walls of the water-drenched, chaotic hall.   On a coffer stood a candelabrum with three unused candles in it.   Their wicks spluttered wetly but finally lit and, my heart thumping, I stole up the stairs.

The sodden carpet was blotched with plaster-white bootprints all the way up to the second floor, where my candles showed the landing littered with chunks, still wet, of lath-and-plaster.   The ceiling must have come down at the moment of the explosion, and down with the ceiling must have come a package of mine—a package so private that, under a sawn section of floorboard in a corner of my living-room immediately above this landing, I had kept the package hidden on the laths between the floor-beams.   I peered up, holding my candles higher, and their light showed me the exposed floor-beams and, dangling down from a hole between them, a corner of my water-soaked carpet.

My package must have fallen, with the lath-and-plaster, onto this second-floor landing.   I searched vainly through the debris lying here, then crept on up to my living-room, which was a shambles, and checked the hole from above.   But there was no possible doubt about it.   My package was gone.

I slunk out of the house.   I had rather have blown out my brains than tell Raffles what I had now to tell him, but I forced myself to walk back to The Albany, where I found him at breakfast.

The lights were on, a coal fire burned cheerfully in the grate, and Raffles, immaculate in tweeds, a pearl in his cravat, his keen face tanned, his dark hair crisp, looked up from *The Times* propped against the coffee-pot.

"Chafing-dishes on the sideboard, Bunny.   Ring for more toast."

"I don't want any," I said.   I sat down.   "Raffles, I've had a shock.   Due to that damned explosion last night, some private papers of mine have—gone astray. They were wrapped in a yellow silk muffler patterned with red *fleurs-de-lys,* the package tied with cord, the knot sealed with red wax."

"A colourful package, Bunny, and valuable-looking.   Some fireman at work in your flat has probably spotted the package and taken charge of it for you.   What *are* these papers—or are they so private you'd rather not tell me?"

"I'd rather not tell you," I said, "but I must.   Raffles, you know that ever since we were at school together I've had a sort of—well, a compulsion to write? If one has that sort of compulsion, one naturally writes about things that have made a strong impression on one's mind.   Somehow, writing them down is the only way one can get them *off* one's mind—especially if they're things it would be suicide to talk about to other people.   So these private writings of mine are accounts, no names or details changed or omitted, of some—recent experiences of ours."

"Ours?"

"Raffles," I muttered, "that package contains full accounts of six of our—criminal adventures."

Silence. Only the rustle of the fire in the grate, the quiet ticking of the clock above it. Then I heard Raffles cross to the fireplace. I thought it was to get the poker, and my scalp tingled in anticipation of a terminal impact upon it. But he was only lighting a cigarette with a spill. I sensed him standing there on the hearthrug, his grey eyes looking down at me, studying me with a clinical detachment. At last he spoke, his tone even.

"I now know, Bunny," he observed, "why it's said, of people with the strange compulsion to write, that they've been *bitten by the tarantula.*' "

He asked me then for further details, and I explained that the package, which did not have my name on the outside, must have been found on the second-floor landing.

"Raffles," I said, "your cricket's made your name very well known. If whoever's found that package opens it to see whom it belongs to, and sees your name in a criminal context on every page of those manuscripts, the finder may hand them to the police!"

"Who, if they once start inquiries," Raffles said, "could be a bit awkward."

"We must get out of the country—immediately!"

"And, not knowing whether the police have or have not got that package, have to spend the rest of our lives in Callao?"

"Why Callao, Raffles?"

"Because, as the famous rhyme says, Bunny: 'Under no condition is extradition allowed from Callao'! No, we've got to try to trace your package. It may be unopened. We'd better not make overt inquiries in person. I'll get Ivor Kern, our invaluable 'fence,' to put some of his snoops on to this. Take a room at your club, Bunny. A red light glows for us in the fog. If the light should glow redder still, I'll get word to you. Meantime, keep a suitcase packed handy for instant travel."

All the things in my flat had been ruined by water from firehoses. I had to buy a suitcase and new togs. And towards the end of a week of torturing suspense, I returned to my club after a fitting at my tailor's and was told that Raffles was waiting for me in the Hastings Room.

I hared up the handsome marble staircase and found Raffles, alone except for a whisky-and-soda, sitting in a saddlebag chair under a dismal great painting, *The Trial of Warren Hastings*.

"Well, Bunny," Raffles greeted me, "we've had a communication."

"From the police?"

"No," said Raffles. "From the Tarantula."

He handed me a large envelope, which had been opened, and with shaking hands I drew out the contents—about forty pages of my own handwriting, held together with a paper clip.

"One of your six manuscripts," Raffles said. "Came in my mail this morning. No message with it. None needed. The sender holds five more of your writings. This one, obviously, is to serve notice on us."

"Notice?"

"Of the Bite To Come," Raffles said.

It came three agonizing days later.   It was another of my manuscripts.   Raffles showed it to me in the Hastings Room.   Attached to the manuscript was a type-written message:

"To.   A. J. Raffles, Esq.:—

"There now remain in the hands of the present writer four further manuscripts from the pen of your confederate, the ineffable Manders.

"To hand these manuscripts to Scotland Yard, and so end the career of an individual who, little suspected of being a criminal, frequents high social and sporting circles, would be less to the purpose of the present writer than to exchange the manuscripts in return for services rendered.

"Here, Mr. Raffles, is the particular service required of you:

"Sir Roderick Naismith, a pillar of the British Treasury, frequently has with him, when he leaves his office in the evening. a small dispatch-case.   Invariably is this so on Friday evenings, when no doubt his dispatch-case contains matter for study in his Hampstead home over the week-end.

"In winter, however, Sir Roderick does not go directly home, but proceeds in a cab to Lord's Cricket Ground, where, at 6:30 on Friday evenings, he exercises himself at the aristocratic game of 'real' tennis.

"To you, Mr. Raffles, a familiar of that exclusive haunt of the nobility and squirearchy, the building which houses the 'real' tennis court at Lord's, an oppor-tunity to acquire Sir Roderick's dispatch-case should readily present itself.

"On Friday evening, therefore, you will obtain that dispatch-case.   You will then return to your chambers in The Albany, where, it has been ascertained, the window of your chambers at the rear of the building overlooks Vigo Street.   You will place in that window of yours, as a signal that the service has been duly rendered, a reading-lamp with a green shade.   You will then receive, by second post the following day, instructions regarding arrangements for the exchange of Sir Roderick's dispatch-case in return for your confederate's manuscripts.

"Failure on your part to carry out the specified service will result in the delivery of your partner's manuscripts to Scotland Yard."

"Oh, dear God!" I said.

"Sir Roderick Naismith's match at Lord's on Friday evening," Raffles said, "is one in the intermediate stages of the tennis tournament.   He'll be playing against a distinguished soldier, a Field-Marshal—Kitchener of Khartoum."   Raffles' eyes glittered.   "Bunny, the Tarantula—so to call that unknown person—has made a significant slip in this missive, a slip that may well indicate a curious element in this whole situation.   The ball's now in my court—and I intend to play it."

"How?"

"By doing, more or less, as the Tarantula demands," Raffles said.   "But, Bunny, I think you'd do well to keep out of this from here on."

"I got you into the situation," I said, "and I damned well intend to see it through with you—come what may."

He raised his glass to me.

So the following evening, Friday, found us arriving together, in one of those taximeter-cabs currently challenging the supremacy of London's hansoms and "growlers," at Lord's, the headquarters of world cricket.

The stands and terraces, gaily stippled in summer with the confetti hues of men's blazers and ladies' parasols, loomed now deserted, spectral in the persistent fog. Only from the tennis-court building, in its secluded corner of the famous demesne, did gleams of gaslight faintly mitigate the dank, muffling vapour.

Capped and ulstered, we entered the building.   Just inside the entrance stood a glass case.   In this was housed the token trophy of the tournament—token only, as it was one of the priceless treasures at Lord's and never left the ground.   Warped, time-blackened, wormeaten, the long-handled, curved, stringless old racquet in the glass case was a reminder of that long ago day when a monarch of France had presented to a monarch of England, as they met in conclave among the pennoned pavilions and glittering shields and lances of the armoured chivalry of both nations, on a French meadow, a gift of tennis balls.

Now, from the unseen court to our left, sounded hollow thuds and bangs, and from the changing-room, to our right, emerged a wiry man carrying a huge basket loaded to the brim with tennis balls of a type little changed since that far-off day of the two monarchs.

" 'Evening, Mole," said Raffles.

"Good evening, Mr. Raffles," said Mole, the resident professional.   "Come to see the match?   Lord Kitchener and Sir Roderick Naismith are in the court now, warming up.   I'm just going in to mark for them."

He went off with his heavy basket, and Raffles strolled over to the door of the changing-room, glanced in casually, then returned to me.

"Just three men in there, Bunny," he murmured.   "Let's hope they decide presently to watch the match.   Meantime, we'll watch it ourselves."

Gripping my arm, he opened a door to the left, closed it behind us, and in the almost total darkness of the restricted space for spectators steered me to the rearmost of a half-dozen spartan benches.   Through the interstices of a protective net I saw the reflector-shaded, wire-caged gaslights which from aloft shed down their brilliance solely on to the court proper, a stylized version of a barnyard of some ancient abbey in the Avignon of Pope Joan, or Cahors of the turreted bridge, or grey-walled Carcassonne of the many candlesnuffer towers.

But whereas medieval monks, banging balls at each other across a net slung between the monastery cow byre and the barn wall, had played this tennis stripped to their hairshirts, the two gentlemen now in the court here—one of the only eight such courts in England, including Henry VIII's at Hampton Court—were in white flannels and sweaters.

"In these troubled times, Bunny," Raffles murmured, "when a European monarch's keeping half of the world nervous by his rapid expansion of his High Seas Fleet, it's good to see Kitchener looking fit."

I nodded, my gaze on the powerful figure, granite jaw, heavy moustache, and challenging steel-blue eyes of the great soldier, with whom the distinguished senior civil servant, gaunt, grey-haired, shrewd-faced Sir Roderick Naismith of the Treasury, markedly contrasted.

From the marker's niche to the left of the court, where a section of penthouse roof simulated the eaves of a cow byre, Mole appeared, carrying his basket of tennis balls, which he emptied into a trough that already contained hundreds.   And the match now began, but here in the dark I was trying to discern how many shadowy figures were spaced about on the benches in front of Raffles and myself. There were, as far as I could make out, only about half-a-dozen spectators—members here, of course—but presently I became aware of three more men quietly entering. Closing the door behind them, they groped their way to the front bench.

Raffles breathed in my ear, "The three from the changing-room. Sit tight!"

Silent as a ghost, he was gone from my side. I forced myself to keep my eyes on the game. Sir Roderick was serving, sending the ball, struck underhand, sliding along the penthouse roof. The ball, falling at the far end, was emphatically struck back across the centre net by Lord Kitchener. Sir Roderick's return went high, the ball banging hollowly against a piece of wood—shaped like a Gothic arch and simulating a monastery pigeon-cote—on the wall behind Kitchener.

"Fifteen thirty," chanted Mole, the marker, as the players changed ends. "Thirty fifteen—chase four."

The game continued, the players changing ends as service was won or lost. Twanging of racquets, thudding of balls, thumping of plimsolled feet echoed hollowly in the court.

"Better than three," rang the voice of Mole. "Deuce!"

Vicariously, I was with Raffles, breaking now into Sir Roderick's locker in the changing-room. Or surprised red-handed at the job? I did not know. Crypt-cold as it was here in the dark, my gloved hands were clammy with sweat. Because I could not keep a pen out of them, Raffles now risked total ruin—and the grim lines of Omar Khayyam rang in my ears: *The Moving Finger writes, and, having writ—*"

" 'Vantage," chanted Mole. "Game! Game and set to Lord Kitchener!"

The players met in mid-court to mop their faces with towels proffered to them by Mole from his marker's niche between the netted apertures which represented the window-openings of a monastery cow byre. Sir Roderick's pale face looked as cool as ever, but the hero of Khartoum was considerably ruddier as he dried his brow and his heavy great moustache.

"Have at you again, Naismith," I heard him growl.

"Good-oh, Field-Marshal," said Sir Roderick.

Half-way through the second set, I became aware, with a start, of a shadow at my side. Raffles was back.

Neither of us said a word until the match was over, with victory to Kitchener, and we made our way out from the tennis-court building into the fog shrouding the cricket ground, when I ventured to ask Raffles how he had got on.

"I'll tell you when I've thought it over," he said. "Let's see if we can find a cab of some sort. I'm hoping there may be a message for me at The Albany."

When we reached his chambers and with a match he popped the gas-globe alight, we saw an envelope lying on the doormat. He tore the envelope open, read the message enclosed, thrust it into his ulster pocket.

"From Ivor Kern," he said. "Come on, we've a call to make."

"On Ivor?"

"No, Bunny. On the Tarantula!"

He turned out the gas, hurried me out of the building by the front entrance to Albany Courtyard and Piccadilly, where we were fortunate enough to get a cab, a four-wheeler.   Telling the cabbie to drop us at the corner of Church Walk, Kensington, Raffles thrust me into the dark, cold interior of the cab and, as the horse jingled us off westward, gave me a cigarette.

"Now, Bunny," he said.   "Consider your lost package.   On the night of the explosion in the Mount Street house, just three people passed along the second-floor landing in making their hasty exits from the house.   Any one of those three could have spotted and snatched up your valuable-looking package—and, oddly enough, when we had our brief conversation with them in the street each of them was wearing a garment which could have concealed the package.   Charles Chastayne was in evening-dress—with cape.   Miss Van Heysst had thrown on a hooded cloak—as blue as her eyes.   Commander Rigby was in uniform, with a deep-pocketed Navy greatcoat."

A match flared.   We dipped our cigarettes to the flame Raffles held in his cupped hands.

"I had Ivor Kern," he went on, "set his snoops to find out where those three persons had taken up their respective temporary abodes—and keep an eye on them. Then came the Tarantula's missive—with its significant slip, the reference to 'the British Treasury.'   Any English person would say, simply, 'the Treasury.'   So here was a hint that the writer of the Tarantula missive was a foreigner—and one of our three suspects is a foreigner."

"Miss Van Heysst!"

"Yes, but she couldn't have written that letter, Bunny.   Her English is charming, but if she'd written that letter there'd have been more slips, more foreign locutions. No, if it were she who snatched up your package, she must have shown it to someone—the person, a foreigner fluent in English and well informed on English ways and values, who wrote the Tarantula letter.   So who—and what—*is* this person with the very sharp bite?"

Our cab was jingling past the muffled gaslamps and flickering fog-flare braziers of Hyde Park Corner.

"And just what," Raffles said, "is the youthful, seductive Miss Van Heysst? A new resident, she moves into a flat adjoining that of Commander Clifford Rigby. A gas explosion puts them on the street.   At whom, Bunny, was Miss Van Heysst's forlorn plea of fearing to meet Jack the Ripper in the fog subtly directed, and who takes it up with the gallantry to be expected of the Navy and promptly tucks Little Blue Riding Hood under his wing?   Commander Rigby.   And what, in these times when the clang of shipbuilders' hammers is resounding threateningly to us across the North Sea, is Rigby?   He's a naval officer—*with a staff job at the Admiralty.*"

"Oh, dear God!" I said.

"What an adroit little opportunist," said Raffles, "is Miss Van Heysst!   But, Bunny, though it seemed to me that a curious element was beginning to creep into this matter of your lost manuscripts, it struck me as odd that the Tarantula was anxious to view the documents in a dispatch-case of a senior civil servant at the *Treasury*.   If the Tarantula is what I was beginning to suspect, it would have been more understandable if the documents he wanted stolen belonged to, say, Field-Marshal Lord Kitchener.   Why those of a senior civil servant at the *Treasury?* I decided to have a look at Sir Roderick's documents, in the changing-room at Lord's this evening, and find out.''

"And you did?''

"I did," said Raffles.   "Naturally, I left the documents intact and Sir Roderick's dispatch-case and locker relocked.   What the Tarantula, as a foreigner, doesn't realise is that a member at Lord's does *not,* however dire his need, rob another member.   It's simply not done.   But a brief skim through Sir Roderick's documents made all plain to me.   He's an impostor!''

"Sir Roderick Naismith's an impostor?   Raffles, that's incredible!''

"But true, Bunny.   He's a senior civil servant, but not at the Treasury.   That ostensible occupation of Sir Roderick's is a mask for his real one.   He's the head of our Secret Security Service.''

"I never knew we had such a thing!''

"How could you?'' said Raffles.   "It's secret.''   He peered out into the fog. "We'll be arriving any minute now," he said, and he went on, "I've no doubt now that the Tarantula is a spymaster.   He's evidently learned Sir Roderick's real occupation.   And what the Tarantula is anxious to find out is whether any of the agents whose activities in this country he directs and controls are under suspicion. And, significantly enough, Bunny, in Sir Roderick's dispatch-case there's a pen-cilled list of five names, each with some personal particulars noted against them. The list is headed: 'For expulsion from England subject to Firm Evidence of Es-pionage Activity.' Among the names is that of Miss Van Heysst of Mount Street. But *not* the name of the Tarantula.''

"You know his name, then?''

"It's in the note I had just now from Ivor Kern," Raffles said.   "One of his snoops, who'd traced Miss Van Heysst to a respectable hotel, Garland's, near the Haymarket Theatre, was keeping an eye on her.   It seems that this afternoon she went, by a circuitous route, to Richmond Park, a place usually deserted on a foggy afternoon.   She met a man at the Priory Lane gate, had a brief talk with him.   As I'd instructed, any person she met with was to be followed.   So Ivor's snoop followed the man.   He lives on the first floor of Number Eight, Church Walk, Kensington.   So we're now about to visit him in his spidery lair," Raffles said, "and return his Tarantula bite!''

We were, as always, unarmed, and I was taut with apprehension as Raffles paid off our cab at the corner of Church Walk and we walked along that silent side-street.   Here and there, dim light from curtained windows faintly blurred the fog.

"Here we are, Bunny," Raffles said, "that house with the number 8 barely visible on the front-door fanlight.   He's probably in that first-floor where faint edges of light show around the window-curtains.   No doubt he's waiting impatiently for word from whatever minion he has skulking in Vigo Street, at the back of The Albany, that a green-shaded reading-lamp has appeared at the window of my chambers.   H'm!   Now, how're we to trap this hairy Tarantula?''   Raffles thought for a moment. "Tell you what, Bunny. We'll get him worried. Got plenty of small change in your pocket?"

"A fair amount, Raffles."

"Good. Now, I'm going to try that front door. It'll probably be locked, but may not be bolted—in which case the little implement I used on Sir Roderick's locker at Lord's should serve our purpose. If I can get into the house, you keep well back in the fog and toss coins up at that first-floor window. The man's almost certainly armed, so my prudent course will be to steal in on him from behind when his back's turned as he peers out of the window."

Instantly grasping Raffles' strategy, I whipped off my gloves, took a handful of small change from my pocket as he moved silently up the two steps to the door under the dim fanlight. As I watched his shadowy figure at work on the door, a vertical line of light suddenly appeared there—and vanished instantly as Raffles, entering, soundlessly closed the door.

Drawing back into the fog, I tossed up a coin at the first-floor window. I heard a tinkle against the glass, a second tinkle as the coin dropped down into the railed basement area. No movement of the curtains ensued, so I tossed up another coin— another—and another. Suddenly, the faint lines of light that edged the window-curtains vanished. Drawing back further into the fog, I sensed, my heart thumping, that the curtains had been parted a little and that some evil, spider-like creature, crouching there at the window of the now dark room, was glaring out balefully into the fog.

Listening intently, I heard no sound from within the room, but I saw the light go on again. For a second Raffles showed himself to me between the curtains, then he closed them. I waited, swallowing with a parched throat. It seemed a long wait before the front door of the house silently opened and closed, and Raffles rejoined me.

We picked up a cab in Kensington High Street, and Raffles gave the cabbie an address in Hampstead.

"I'm afraid, Bunny," he said, "I had to violate a rule of ours and use a modicum of violence. I banged the Tarantula's head hard against his floor, to stun him while I relit the gaslight he'd turned out. Still, he was beginning to come round as I left. He'll find he's lost your four manuscripts. They were on his desk. Here they are, still loosely wrapped in your yellow silk muffler.

"There was a locked drawer in his desk. The lock presented no problem. So we're richer by about one thousand pounds—spies' wages, I imagine. I also abstracted from the drawer a batch of the Tarantula's papers—which provide, I fancy, all the 'firm evidence' Sir Roderick Naismith needs to justify some expulsions from this country. I noticed Sir Roderick's Hampstead address on letters in his document-case at Lord's, so we'll drop these papers he needs through his letter-box, then drive to Piccadilly Circus and see if we can buy a few flowers."

I was at a loss to divine why he should want flowers at this hour. However, late as it was when we got back from our Hampstead errand and paid off our cab in Piccadilly Circus, we found this hub of London an oasis of activity in the blanketing fog.   The theatres and music-halls were disgorging their second-house audiences, the gin palaces their inebriates, into the blurred glow from gaslights and the naked flicker of naphtha fog-flares.

Police whistles shrilled above the clip-clop of hoofbeats, harness-jingle of hansoms, fourwheelers, and rumbling omnibuses, and mingled with the honking of occasional taximeter-cabs and the raucous cries of the Piccadilly flower women sitting beside their big baskets at their usual receipt of custom on the steps of the Eros statue.

"Oy, misters, you gents there!"   A cheeky-looking wench, much shawled and petticoated, with a feather boa, a huge hat bedecked with ostrich plumes, and high-heeled button boots, brandished a great bunch of chrysanthemums at Raffles and myself.   "Out lyte, you are!   Bin on the spree, you two 'ave!   You'd best tyke a few flowers 'ome—beautiful chrysanths, fresh as a dysy—to sweeten yer little bit o' trouble-an'-strife!"

"On behalf of my friend here," said Raffles, "I'll give you a sovereign for that fine bunch of chrysanthemums, and if you'd care for an extra half-bar, you can deliver them for him at your leisure.   The place is not far.   It's just off the Haymarket there—a hotel called Garland's.   Hand the flowers in at the desk and say they're for Miss Van Heysst, as a *bon voyage* gift from A Gentleman of Mount Street.   Are you on?"

"Mister, for an extra 'arf-bar, the w'y tryde's bin to-night in this bleedin' fog," said the wench, "I'd walk as far as Seven Dials for yer wiv me whole bloody basket!"

So Raffles gave her the extra half-sovereign and, raising our caps to the wench, we walked across the misty Circus towards the nearby Albany.

"There are games, Bunny, *and* games," Raffles remarked thoughtfully.   " 'Real' tennis is an old one, but espionage is an older one still—and much more dangerous. As far as women are concerned, only a brave woman would play it.   It's to be hoped that Miss Van Heysst doesn't continue her activities in the pay of the Wilhelmstrasse, or—in the troubled state of Europe to-day—she may come to a bad end.   That would be a pity, because she's not only an exceptionally attractive and very young woman, but also a brave one."

"Yes," I said.

"So I think, Bunny," Raffles said, "although she was a fellow resident of yours in Mount Street for only a short while, it would be nice for her to have a small tribute of flowers from you, to take with her when Sir Roderick Naismith has her escorted aboard the Harwich to Hook-of-Holland boat to-morrow.   I wish we'd seen more of her.   She's a most interesting person.   According to some particulars against her name in Sir Roderick's list, her real surname is Zeller—and she's believed to use aliases other than Van Heysst."

"Other aliases?" I said.

He nodded.

"One of them, noted against our Little Blue Riding Hood in Sir Roderick's list, is rather striking," Raffles said.   "Mata Hari."

JEAN L. BACKUS

Last Rendezvous

I resented the old woman's approach, not having driven 150 miles along a rugged coast highway to be an unwilling dinner partner at Little River Inn. Particularly so early in my short stay.   But I'd been told thirty or forty years ago that a lady was always kind to old people since she herself would be old one day, and perhaps unhappy and lonely as well.   Now my time had come, and I had no need to be reminded of my age and circumstances.   But as usual I hated to be in the position of rejecting anyone.

"No," I said, as she stood waiting by my table, "nobody's with me.   I'm alone."   Which was the solitary truth—family dead, friends dead or moved away, everyone I'd ever loved gone.

"It's not good for a woman to eat by herself," she said, sitting in the opposite chair.   "And that makes two of us.   What are you drinking?"

"Gin and tonic, no fruit."   Even then I should have told her I was in a poor mood for company, because her voice and gestures jangled my nerve ends.   I looked at her more closely.   Short gray hair, carelessly brushed, a blue pants suit, wrinkled and slightly soiled; she looked neglected.   My own hair was white, but so far I had not neglected my appearance.

"Why, that's what I drink too," she said, beaming.   "I'll have one tonight, I think.   Where are you from?"

"The Bay Region."

"I used to live there," she said.   "I live here now.   This is as close to a home as I'll ever get, unless they put me in the booby hatch someday.   What are you going to eat?"

"Petrale sole."   I'd stayed at the inn and dined in this room at this table before. Tonight the sole, tomorrow night the salmon.   The next morning I'd be gone, leaving behind all that was precious and good in my life.   Only memories now, but once a man had sat opposite me at this table, he down from the north, I up from the south.

For fourteen years we'd met every other month for a weekend together, walking on the beach at the mouth of the river, driving around the headland to watch the surf on the rocks at sunset, and retiring to the same cottage after a superb and leisurely dinner.

"And apricot cobbler."   I spoke aloud, out of my thoughts.

"We have rhubarb cobbler tonight," the hostess said at my side.   And to the woman across from me, "Miss Barnes, did you ask the lady if she minded your sitting with her?"

"Yes, I did."   Miss Barnes flushed unbecomingly.   "She didn't tell me I couldn't."

I said, "Perhaps you'll excuse me after all.   I intend to eat very slowly tonight, and I have something serious to think about."   Immediately I wished I'd kept still. Miss Barnes looked about to weep.   But it was too late.   The hostess, after a prolonged argument, led her away to another table, somewhere behind me.

The waitress brought me a bowl of clam chowder, and normally I'd have savored every spoonful.   As it was, I could hardly swallow.   By the time the salad arrived, however, my thoughts were back on Jim and how he'd always ordered oil and vinegar while I took the roquefort dressing.

Food had been one of the things we had in common, although he was married, a drygoods merchant in Eureka, while I was single, a librarian from Concord.   I had hobbies and friends, I kept up with the news and theaters and concerts, I read a lot; I was fairly well content.   When I met him, he had no interest beyond his work and his children, whom he adored and for whom he maintained the semblance of a marriage.   Periodically he had to get away from his wife, and one time we turned up separately here at the inn.   Our rooms happened to be next to each other, and on our way to dinner we collided as we locked our doors.

But we sat at separate tables to eat.   I certainly hadn't thought of a possible friendship, much less an affair, on that first meeting.   Yet, as we acknowledged later, both of us felt the impact of looking at a stranger and thinking how nice it would be if we could have been together.

Call it luck as I did, or fate as Jim did, we kept colliding all the next day—in the village, up Fern Canyon, and finally on the headland at sunset.   "This is silly," Jim said as he left his car to come sit in mine.   "Tomorrow let's spend the day together."

It took another accidental weekend before I accepted what Jim said had been obvious and inevitable to him from the beginning.   Probably it was his immediate honesty about his family situation that persuaded me to let my unexpectedly insistent fantasies become a reality, because I was never in any doubt as to the source of his interest in me, and if I were honest, the source of my interest in him.   We represented adventure without danger, excitement without consequences, love without responsibility . . .

Behind me, Miss Barnes asked for a doggie bag because her little dog was starving, she said, and anyway, she couldn't eat all her sole.   Suddenly I couldn't finish mine either.

The hostess came to refill my water glass.   "Sorry about that," she said quietly. "Poor Miss Barnes has a habit of accosting the other guests, and tonight you were elected.   It must be very annoying; I do apologize."

"It's all right," I told her.   "Only I feel sorry for her because she seems so lonely, and—well, isn't she a bit out of touch?"

"Out of touch," the hostess said.   "She's senile, poor thing.   I'm afraid we're going to have to do something about her.'' I winced and covered it with a cough. Then she added, ''Oh, you aren't eating. Isn't the fish all right?''

''It's perfect, thank you.''

She nodded and moved away, while I took another bite of sole, remembering how Jim had always called it ambrosia and said we were the gods. Laying my fork down again, I got out a cigarette and my lighter.

''Could I have that little bit of fish you're not going to eat?'' Miss Barnes asked, right at my elbow. ''It's for my dog.''

''What about bones? I never give my dog fish for fear of his choking on a bone.''

''My dog eats anything I give her,'' Miss Barnes said, holding her doggie bag open. Then she leaned closer, her voice barely audible. ''That's a lie. I want the fish for my lunch tomorrow. You see, retirement isn't all it's supposed to be these days.''

Silently I transferred the remnant of my sole to the doggie bag and was relieved when the waitress came to lead Miss Barnes back to her own table.

Thought of my own retirement, not so far off now, was so unnerving that I left the dessert, finished my coffee, and went out through the bar onto the long front porch of the old inn, with the rose vines climbing up to the wooden scrollwork of the gabled windows and eaves. In front was the parking area where my car stood among others, and beyond the highway running below the property were the rocks with the sea pounding the shore under the dark old windblown cypresses.

I considered what I wanted to do and decided to get my Sheltie and feed him before we walked down the hill to the beach.

Miss Barnes was right behind me. ''Is your doggie with you?''

''Locked in the car.''

''Oh, dear, they say it's dangerous leaving children and animals in locked cars.''

''I left the window partly open,'' I said. ''Anyway, I'm going to feed him now and then go to bed.''

Her smiled faded. ''Oh, dear. I thought maybe you and I could go for a walk.''

''Not tonight.'' And hastily I added, ''Thanks.''

''I'm sorry.'' Her eyes filled with weak tears. ''I'm being tiresome, aren't I? It's a part of growing old not to know when you're being tiresome. That and being retired. What about you? Are you retired?''

''Not yet.'' But I would be. Any day now.

She shook her head. ''You won't find it easy when you do. People die or drop away from you, and finally you're alone, with nothing but your regrets to sustain you.'' She looked far out to sea where a fishing vessel was beating the waves back to port. ''I was young once, you know, and there was a man who found me attractive. But nothing came of it.''

''Why not? Did you quarrel?''

''Oh, it was my fault.'' She faced me, lips quivering. ''You see, I didn't trust him. He said he would leave his wife for me, but I thought he was just trying to—oh, you know. Then he died, and I discovered he'd gone ahead and started a divorce.   If he'd lived, I think he would have come after me again.   By the time I found out what I truly wanted, it was too late."

"I'm sorry," I said, and helpless to comfort her, I escaped to my car, put Star on his leash, and took him to my room for his meal.   He gobbled it as usual, finding no strange smell from the phenobarb I'd put in the food I'd brought from home.

When I was sure Miss Barnes had disappeared, I took Star down the path through the red alders and young firs, past the Oregon grape and elderberry bushes, and across the highway to the beach at the mouth of the river.   Here the water was calm, and I let Star run in and out of the waves, his barking already muted and uncertain.   He got all wet and shook himself feebly when I whistled him back and restored the leash.

He was my second Sheltie, Jim having given me both dogs to remind me of him during our separations, he said.   When the first Star sickened and died, I was inconsolable and felt it was a bad omen.   But Jim simply went out and bought the second puppy for me.   Now the second Star was twelve years old and I couldn't bear to see the way he was aging, because it was like a reflection of my own state.

We walked around to the point where I stood hypnotized by the surf pounding up and over the glistening black rocks and falling back, leaving ruffles of white foam . . .

"The seahorses are riding high tonight," Jim said in my ear.

I felt his arm around me, and leaned back wanting only to preserve and extend the love and security he gave me.   Wanting it harder and oftener as the years rolled by, worrying that he was tired of me, resenting the sterile two months between our weekends, frequently mistrusting his ultimate intentions.   In this I was unreasonable, for I'd known from the beginning ours would be love without responsibility, but the force of resentment swept me along anyway.

And sensing this in me, he tried to make it all right again by saying, "Oh, God, I'd give my life to go south with you tomorrow."

"Do it then."

"I can't.   You know I can't, not unless—"

"Not unless she divorces you, which she won't, or the children become mature enough not to be damaged."   I threw back the words he always used whenever I spoke of the future.   Not that I often did, because I respected his love for his children, his desire to protect them, or their image of him.   But that didn't prevent the slow rot of distrust from growing in my mind . . .

I sighed and turned to go, thinking of Miss Barnes.   "I thought he was just trying to—oh, you know."

My poor old Star came dragging after me, already asleep on his feet from what I'd put in his food.   Finally I had to pick him up and carry him like a baby in my arms.   He died an hour after I got back to my room, and I sat weeping all night because I lacked the courage to finish what I'd started.

When daylight came, I wrapped the body in a blanket and carried it out to the car where I placed it on the passenger seat.   Then I sat beside him until it was time for the dining room to open.

I couldn't eat, but the coffee helped, and so did being seated at the table near the fireplace where Jim and I had always sat. Until the last morning when I'd come here alone while he still slept in the cottage we'd shared for the past two nights.

Presently I went out to the car again, and with Star's body beside me, drove off to visit our favorite headland and sit watching the water burst on the rocks for the rest of the day. I'd have given anything to bury Star there under a carpet of Indian paintbrush, lupines, and poppies, but it was public property.

I returned to the inn after sundown and had barely seated myself and ordered a drink in the dining room when Miss Barnes came to my table.

"Good evening," she said, face aglow. "How's your sweet little dog today? Not locked in the car again, I hope."

"My dog? Star?" I swallowed. "Oh, he died last night."

"Why, you poor thing! What happened?"

"Please. If you don't mind, I can't talk about it."

"Of course not. I'll sit down and keep you company—"

"Please don't, Miss Barnes. Please leave me alone."

The hostess heard me and led the old woman away.

I ordered the salmon and toyed with it. After refusing berry cobbler, I went straight to my room and sat down to wonder what I should do about Star's body, which was still in the car. I couldn't think where to take it, or whom to ask for help. All I could think about was poor old Miss Barnes, and how in a way I resembled her: not accosting strangers in the dining room, not yet; but inside, where it counted, and where I'd worked for eight long years to contain it. Now, if I could, I had to recall the last night Jim and I ever had together. Not as I would like to remember it, but as it really happened . . .

He had said that his wife was going to tell his children if he didn't give me up.

"Oh, Jim, no! She wouldn't."

"Well, she said she would. And it will devastate the kids. The youngest isn't quite fifteen, and I can't stand even the thought of their disillusion and hurt."

"What did you tell her then?"

"I said I'd think about it."

He didn't look at me as he spoke, and believing he'd already made his choice, I lost control. I said unspeakable things, made unreasonable accusations and threats. I was beside myself, and all the resentment and distrust in my festering mind came out until at last we faced each other, pale and shaking, utterly washed up, and we both knew it.

Jim was the first to break the silence. "Before I left home, I thought of another way, if you're willing. I'd rather die with you than live without you."

Shaken to my fibers, I finally agreed.

So we made our pact and went to bed for the last time, close and warm together as if nothing had changed. Only in the morning he didn't wake up—and I did.

After weeping for a time, I'd gone for breakfast which I didn't eat and driven straight home, a journey I don't remember. Nobody ever came after me, though I presume his wife must have had difficulty convincing the authorities who she was because nobody would have recognized her as the woman who'd been registered as Jim's wife so often at the cottage.

Later when I went to Eureka and read his obituary in the local paper, I discovered she'd had enough influence to hush up the circumstances.   Death from a heart attack, the notice read.   But it should have said murder, because at the last minute and without saying so to Jim, I had panicked and failed to keep the suicide pact we'd made . . .

I stirred at last, calm and not unhappy as I got the bottle and swallowed the rest of the phenobarb tablets Jim had handed me eight years ago on the night, when in my madness, I believed he intended that only I should die . . .

EDITORIAL POSTSCRIPT

The story you have just read was nominated by MWA (Mystery Writers of America) as one of the five best new mystery short stories published in American magazines and books during 1977.

JOHN BALL

Virgil Tibbs and the Cocktail Napkin

The 134 freeway is reasonably well lit as it passes through Glendale so that Mrs. Robert Shozinsky had no difficulty as she drove carefully only a little over the legal limit of 55 miles per hour. Because she was alone in her car, she had the doors locked. As soon as she passed the city limits the roadway became much darker, particularly when it began the long climb up toward the Arroyo Seco bridge that led into Pasadena.

The freeway had been carved out of the side of a substantial hill, one that would have been called a mountain in many other places; consequently it was both isolated and very dark at two o'clock in the morning. Since the only illumination Mrs. Shozinsky had was provided by her own headlights, she did not see the body until she was almost on it.

Her fingers locked with sudden panic as she swerved her car; her knuckles went white against the steering wheel. For the first few seconds she was unable to realize exactly where she was, then she saw that she had reached the top of the long grade, and the first lights of Pasadena were visible ahead. Although the freeway was almost deserted at that hour on Monday night, she used her turn signal as she pulled off to the right. She was a knowledgeable woman and she remembered there were emergency telephones approximately every quarter mile along the right of way.

She saw one about 200 feet ahead. She let her car come to a stop beside it, and seconds later she was in communication with the operator at the Zone Five headquarters of the California Highway Patrol.

"There's a man lying on the freeway," she reported, "on his face, all sprawled out. I—I almost ran over him. Please come quickly!"

"Right now," the operator assured her. He made note of the phone number she was calling from and popped the slip on the conveyor belt.

The dispatcher put the call on the air promptly and also notified the Fire Department paramedics. Four minutes later Mrs. Shozinsky had company—a one-man CHP unit arrived at almost the same moment the red paramedic unit rolled up, silently but with lights flashing. No one used sirens on the freeway system; they had proved to be too dangerous.

The body was spreadeagled on the concrete pavement in the Number Four lane, lying almost directly opposite the sign that marked the city limits of Pasadena.

The paramedics went to work immediately while the highway patrolman set out emergency flares.   It did not take them long.   The taller of the two men gave the verdict.   "Dead," he said simply.   Then he asked, "Whose jurisdiction is it?"

The patrolman couldn't answer that immediately.   Instead he went on the air with the suggestion that both Pasadena and LAPD be notified.   Meanwhile, the paramedics covered the body and informed the coroner's office.   By the time they had finished and were ready to pull away, a white Matador patrol car from Pasadena was just rolling up.   The two officers were getting out of their vehicle when a Los Angeles black and white appeared.

The highway patrol officer thanked his informer for her cooperation and sent her on her way after he had taken her name and address.

The four newly arrived officers surveyed the situation and mutually determined what they had.   One man from each team radioed in, at almost the same time.   "Homicide," the Pasadena officer reported to his dispatcher.   "Possible 187.   Request full backup."

The dispatcher alerted the watch commander, Lieutenant Robenson, who wanted to know the exact location.   "Is that in our jurisdiction?" he asked.

"I think so, but Bob Watson also asked for a full backup."

Code 187 meant murder, so Robenson did not hesitate.   He called out a homicide team that would respond with its specially equipped vehicle, then he dialed an unlisted number on his personnel index.   Virgil Tibbs answered the third ring.

"Good morning, Virg," Robenson said.   "Rise and shine.   Apologize to the young lady, I assume there is one, and come on in.   We have a nice dead body for you."

"I don't want a dead body," Tibbs replied, "I want to get some sleep."

He hung up after that, because any further conversation would be pointless, and dressed quickly.   He ran his hand across the skin of his face, but despite the stubble, he decided not to take time to shave.

The black detective found a small mob scene when he arrived at the point on the freeway, close to Malcolm Street, where the body had been found.   The Pasadena Police had put a full homicide team into action and the LAPD had sent an even larger contingent.   Obviously, the question of jurisdiction had not been clarified.   Both teams were busy taking photographs and making the usual measurements while two men from the coroner's office waited patiently to remove the body.

Virgil went quietly to the place where the body lay, removed the cover, and began a swift careful examination.   He had barely started when a tall, powerfully built man in plainclothes appeared at his side.   "May I see your ID, please," he asked.

A uniformed Pasadena sergeant answered for Virgil.   "He's with us—our top homicide man."

The Los Angeles man remembered what he had heard about Pasadena's specialist.   "Virgil Tibbs?" he asked.

Tibbs rose and shook hands.   "Tim Yost," the tall man introduced himself.   "That whitehead over there is Vince Scott, my partner."

"Nice to know you," Tibbs said.

"I don't know why they called you out, Virgil.   The body is in Los Angeles and it's our headache."

"Assuming the sign is accurately placed," Tibbs countered, "from the hips down it's in Pasadena."

"Look, Virgil, the guy was shot in the head—one neat hole right in the forehead. On this side of the freeway he had to be coming from Los Angeles.   Somebody made the hit in a car, then dumped him out.   It's ours all the way."

"Suppose," Virgil suggested, "that the car stopped and he got out.   Not a-likely place, but I'm assuming he wasn't given any choice.   Then he was shot. The hole in the forehead fits and that would keep any blood out of the car."

"Remote, but possible," Yost conceded.

"The man fell where he was found.   I didn't get very far with my examination, but if he had been thrown from a moving vehicle, there would be abrasion marks, particularly on his exposed skin.   There don't seem to be any.   That points to his having been put out, and then shot."

"So?" Yost asked.

"Notice the position of the feet.   He was standing in Pasadena when he was shot—from the hips down he's clearly on the left side of the sign.   He fell forward, partly into Los Angeles, after he was fatally wounded.   It's our case."

It was an impasse which for the moment no one was in a position to resolve. "Have you IDed the victim?" Tibbs asked.

"Yes, there were some things in his pockets—nothing very significant.   Look, the powers that be will settle whether you'll be handling this one or Vince and me, so for the moment why don't we avoid duplication of effort?"

"I'll agree to that," Virgil said.   "But I'd still like to know exactly what was in his pockets."

"Just the usual things—a wallet, pocket comb, ballpoint pen, some change, a key case, a handkerchief, and a cocktail napkin."

Tibbs made a swift decision.   "You take the body and all the personal effects. Let me have the napkin.   I'll work on that."

Yost looked at his partner for a moment of silence, then the two men seemed to agree by telepathy.   "It's a deal," Yost declared.

The napkin had the name of a bar printed across one corner.   Apart from that it was very ordinary, exactly like tens of thousands of others produced in quantity by the same supplier.   It was relatively fresh and clean; the only marking was a faint ring on the middle of the printed side where a cocktail or some other drink had once stood.   The ring was a light reddish color, and apart from that, the napkin was entirely unmarked.

Knowing the ways of bars, Virgil Tibbs spent the morning in his office preparing for a court appearance coming up later in the week.   Then, after his usual lunch of a sandwich and a large glass of milk, he took a plain car off the police lot and headed into Los Angeles.   Halfway down the Pasadena Freeway he picked up the microphone clipped to the dash and advised the LAPD that he was coming into their jurisdiction. He gave no reason and he was not asked for one.

Locating the bar had been a simple matter of checking the phone book; it was on the west side of the city in a respectable neighborhood.

At a little after two Kitty and Sam's Bar was open for the early-afternoon trade. As Tibbs walked inside he saw that the place was almost deserted, a situation that suited him perfectly. He sat down on a bar stool and noted that the napkin the bartender placed before him was an exact duplicate of the one he had in his pocket.

"I'm a police officer," Tibbs said quietly. "I came by for a little information."

"I'd like to see some ID," the bartender said.

Virgil opened the thin leather folder he carried and displayed his badge. The barman nodded.

Virgil produced the cocktail napkin he had and laid it carefully on the bar. "I believe that a man was in here last night who took this away with him," he said.

"That's possible, it's one of ours. What time last night?"

"I don't know, perhaps around midnight. It was probably last night because the napkin isn't crumpled or pocket-worn. If he'd had it for two or three days, it wouldn't look this fresh."

The bartender nodded again. "I'll buy that. Can you describe him?"

"Possibly, but something else first. You noticed the ring on the napkin?"

"Sure, of course. Nothing unusual about that."

"What I'd like," Tibbs continued, "is to have you show me the glass that fits that ring. It would be a tall one without a stem, because a stemmed glass wouldn't leave that kind of ring."

"It might. A stemmed glass could have been standing on the bare bar and then set on the napkin. That would do it." The bartender was beginning to enjoy himself.

Virgil shook his head. "The man wasn't sitting at the bar. He was at one of the tables. As a wild guess, I'd say somewhere in the back."

"Because he didn't want to be seen?"

"Possibly, but the napkin gave me the idea."

"How?"

"First, it's almost impossible to keep a bar constantly clean and dry—some moisture is almost inevitable when the bar is in heavy use. Did you have a good crowd?"

"Yes, we did."

"Then the bar was probably moist if not wet, but the back of the napkin hasn't been dampened; you can see that."

The bartender turned the napkin over and studied its reverse side. As Tibbs had said, it showed no trace of ever having been wet. "So you figure that your man wasn't at the bar, but was at a table that had been wiped dry."

"Exactly. And if you had a good crowd, and he came in late as I think he might have, he would have most likely taken a rear table—one that hadn't been used and therefore was still dry."

"That's kinda far-fetched, isn't it?" the barman asked.

"Maybe, but the table part is worth a bet, I think. Now, will you see about matching a tall glass onto the ring on the napkin?"

The man behind the bar found the right one on his second try. It matched the stain perfectly.

Virgil set the glass to one side on the bar. "Now that we know the kind of glass, it narrows the number of possible drinks. You notice the color of the ring— it has a reddish tinge."

The bartender thought for a few seconds, then he snapped his fingers. "I just remembered," he said. "It might be it. Every bar gets some strange orders now and then, but last night somebody ordered a Harvey Wallbanger without the vodka— just the orange juice and the Galliano."

"Which could leave a ring of about that color?"

"I'd say so, yes. That is, if the drink ran over a little, and that happens all the time."

"Now we're getting somewhere," Tibbs said. "Tell me about the customer with the odd taste in drinks."

The man behind the bar shook his head. "I didn't even see him. One of the girls served him. I think it was Elsie."

That was a setback, but only a minor one. Elsie was due in within the half hour and patience being one of Tibbs's virtues, he was willing to wait. A few customers drifted in, but they settled themselves in booths and closed out the rest of the world. The bartender came back to Virgil once more. "Have one on the house while you're waiting?" he asked.

"On duty," Tibbs answered.

The barman filled a tall glass with ice and ran some Coke inside. He added a few drops of something and dropped in a cherry. "A little specialty of my own," he said. "No voltage at all, but nice."

There was no way that could be refused. Virgil tried it and found the drink unexpectedly pleasant. He sipped it and then downed half of it in a burst of thirst-quenching satisfaction. Ten minutes later the bartender made him another.

Elsie arrived a few minutes late—a tall leggy girl with a costume cut low enough to stir the customers' interest, but not low enough to gratify it to any measurable degree. She was a cocktail waitress with just the right manner to keep her clear of unwanted involvements and still earn her the maximum in tips.

After introductions, she settled down in a booth with Tibbs for a few minutes of conversation. Fortunately she was intelligent and had a good memory. "I know the man you want," she said after she had been briefed. "He came in last night about eleven or so, I don't remember the exact time. He was alone. When he ordered that unusual drink, I was certain he was waiting to meet someone. Nobody would come in here to pay a dollar and a half for four ounces of orange juice and a little Galliano—the solitary drinkers go for the heavy stuff, straight doubles and things like that."

"Where did he sit?"

Elsie gestured toward the back. "One of those tables, I can't say definitely which one. He sat where he could see everyone who came in and out."

"How did he treat you?"

"Very nicely. He was polite, gentlemanly, easy to deal with."

"Under the influence at all?"

The girl shook her head. "Not at all—stone-cold sober, and believe me, I know."

"And did someone join him?"

"Yes, a man did after a while, I can't say just when because it was quite busy at that time."

"Do you remember anything about the man?"

"Somewhat, I'd never seen him in here before. Not a very big man. Dark complexion, olive skin, but that's a guess with the lights we have in here." She hesitated.

"But not a black man," Tibbs finished for her.

She nodded. "That's right. One more thing I can tell you about him—he had a very odd nose. It was big and had two or three ridges or bumps on it. It was almost funny."

Virgil got up. "That ought to do it. Did you notice if they went out together?"

"Yes, they did. Funny nose had a drink, a quick one, and then they left."

Virgil gave a brief description of the man who had been found dead on the freeway and mentioned how he had been dressed. The girl nodded promptly. "That's him," she said. "The nice guy who was waiting, the one who drank the Wallbangers without the vodka."

Halfway home on the Pasadena Freeway, Tibbs received a radio call. On responding, he was asked to switch to tac. two. As soon as he had done so, he was told that Tim Yost of the LAPD wanted to meet him. Yost and his partner, Vince Scott, were at the West Valley station, which was a good distance away. Tibbs said he would be there in about forty-five minutes. Back came a reply that Yost and Scott would come to see him.

As soon as he returned to his own headquarters Virgil headed directly for the intelligence unit and sat down with Jim Larsh who worked that section. He produced his description of the man with the odd nose, supplied the m.o. of the homicide, and through Larsh let the computers go to work. Well before his colleagues from Los Angeles arrived, he had most of the information he wanted. He lacked a photograph, but that could be obtained as soon as it was needed. Meanwhile, the fingerprint classification was quite adequate.

Just off the executive offices on the fourth floor, the PPD had a small conference room. When Yost and Scott got there Tibbs took them up, then carefully shut the door. "Very nice of you guys to come by," he said.

Yost, as the senior member of the team, took over. "Virgil, we want to thank you for responding to that homicide on the freeway. We've got a ruling that it's our case, so you don't have to worry about it anymore. It's a little heavy and we're laying on a maximum effort. We think we can crack it in forty-eight hours."

"Fine," Tibbs said. "Has the word been passed to our department that we're out of it?"

"I think so," Scott answered.

"Then I'm relieved." Virgil took his time. "Do you mind telling me one thing?" he asked.

"Sure, go ahead."

"When did the victim graduate from the academy?"

Yost and Scott exchanged quick glances that showed visible concern, then Yost became firmer. "What do you know?" he asked.

Virgil relaxed. "Some facts, some conjectures. Mixing them up, I'd say the victim was an LAPD officer, recently out of the academy, never on the street, and pulling his first undercover assignment. He had been put in against the big boys and that was a mistake, because he wasn't ready for that yet. Somewhere along the line they made him, just about the time something fairly big was about to go down. They didn't play around; they set him up for a meet, got him in a car, then terminated him. Putting him right on the line between two jurisdictions was deliberate. Would you care for a description of the man who suckered him in?"

"Damn it!" Yost muttered.

"Who've you been talking to?" Scott asked tightly.

Yost leaned forward. "Right now I want to know how you got all that—and in so little time. This operation was supposed to be totally leakproof—we've been on it for weeks. If I've got to see your chief, I want to know who opened the door, even to another department."

"Would you guys care for some coffee or a cold drink?" Tibbs asked. "Nothing fancy, but we have some machines that put out the usual stuff."

"You said that you have a description," Scott said. "We'd be very interested in that."

The black detective allowed himself to smile. "Courtesy of the Pasadena Police Department, I can give you a fairly hot suspect. Description: five feet seven and a half, olive complexion, dark hair, slight scar on the back of his right hand, and a large nose broken at least twice and badly reset, if at all."

Scott responded with sudden interest. "Right—we know him."

"So do we," Tibbs continued. "Rafael Monza, sometimes known as Nosey. A specialist in the use of small-caliber arms and also good with a knife. Two convictions for 211, two for assault with a deadly weapon. Out on parole as a reformed and now valuable member of society."

Yost was deadly serious. "Virgil, if you can establish a positive link between Monza and our boy—any evidence at all that they had ever even met—you've done us a helluva service."

Virgil put the cocktail napkin onto the table. "There's your lead," he said. "It's all you gave me, but fortunately all I needed. I've got two witnesses for you and both, I'm sure, will cooperate, since they've already talked to me. Respectable people, no record—I checked them out. They'll make a good impression on the grand jury."

Yost and Scott were silent for a moment. There was communication between them, but none of it had to be spoken. Then Scott looked up. "Anything else?" he asked.

"Just one thing. After you left the place where the body was discovered, I went back for another look. You know how the freeways are landscaped—it's a very nice job most of the time. That shallow hillside was covered by an eight-inch-high growth that left a few traces."

"Just what are you telling us?" Yost inquired.

"Your man was shot in Pasadena, just over the line. Then the body was dragged back a few feet and put under the sign deliberately to create a police problem. But if you don't choose to tell anyone that, I don't think I will either."

MICHAEL GILBERT

The Happy Brotherhood

The Grants lived in Kennington. Mr. Grant worked in an architect's office in the City and had inherited the small terrace house on Dodman Street. It was convenient, since he could reach the Bank Station in ten minutes on the Underground. But it was not a neighborhood which he found really congenial. There was Mr. Knowlson, who worked in insurance and lived two doors up. But most of the inhabitants of Dodman Street were uncouth men, with jobs at railway depots—men who went to work at five o'clock in the morning and spent their evenings in public houses.

Mr. Grant had often spoken to his wife of moving out to the suburbs, where people went to their offices at a rational hour and spent the evenings in their gardens and joined tennis clubs and formed discussion groups. The factor which tipped the balance against moving was Timothy. Timothy was their only child and was now fourteen, but with his pink and white face and shy smile he could have been taken for eleven or twelve. After a difficult start he was happily settled at the Matthew Holder School near the Oval, and sang first treble in the choir at St. Mark's.

"It would be a pity to make a change now," said Mrs. Grant. "Timothy's easily upset. I've put his dinner in the oven, so I hope he won't be too late back from choir practise. If his dinner gets dried up he can't digest it properly."

At that moment Timothy was walking slowly down the road outside St. Mark's. He was walking slowly because, if the truth were told, he had no great desire to get home. When he did get there, his mother would make him take off his shoes and put on a dry pair of socks and would sit him down to eat a large and wholesome meal, which he did not really want, and he would have to tell his father exactly what he had done in school that day and—

A hand smacked him between the shoulder blades and he spun around. Two boys were standing behind him, both a little older and a lot bigger than Timothy. The taller one said, "It's a stickup, Rosebud. Turn out your pockets."

Timothy gaped at him.

"Come on, come on," said the other one. "Do you want to be ruffed up?"

"Are you mugging me?"

"You've cottoned quick, boyo. Shell out."

"I'm terribly sorry," said Timothy. "But I've actually only got about ten pence on me. It's Thursday, you see. I get my pocket money on Friday."

He was feeling in his trouser pocket as he spoke and now fetched out a fivepenny piece and a penny and held them out.

The taller boy stared at the money, but made no move to touch it. He said, "How much pocket money do you get every week?"

"A pound."

"So if we'd stuck you up tomorrow, we'd have got a quid?"

"That's right," said Timothy. "I'm terribly sorry. If you're short tonight I could show you how to make a bit perhaps."

The two boys looked at each other, then burst out laughing.

"Cool," said the tall one. "That's cool."

"What's the gimmick?" said the second one.

"It's the amusement arcade in the High Street. There's a big slot machine, tucked away in the corner, and no one uses it much."

"Why no one uses that machine is because no one ever makes any money out of it."

"That's right," said Timothy. "It's a set-safe machine. I read about it in a magazine. It's a machine that's organized so that the winning combinations never come up. A man comes and clears the machines on Friday. By this time it must be stuffed with money."

"So what are you suggesting we do? Break it open with a hammer?"

"What I thought was, it's plugged into a wall socket. If you pulled out the plug and broke the electric circuit *while it's going,* the safety mechanism wouldn't work. It would stop at some place it wasn't meant to stop, so you'd have a good chance."

The two boys looked at each other, then at Timothy.

Timothy said, "It would need three people. One to distract the attention of the attendant. You could do that by asking him for change for a pound. The second to work the machine and the third to get down behind and jerk out the plug. I could do that. I'm the smallest."

The tall boy said, "If it's as easy as that why haven't you done it before?"

"Because I haven't got—" said Timothy and stopped. He realized that what he had nearly said was, "Because I haven't got two friends."

"We'd better go somewhere and count it," said Len. Their jacket pockets were bursting with twopenny bits.

"That bouncer," said Geoff. He could hardly get the words out for laughing. "Poor old sod. He just *knew* something was wrong, didn't he?"

"He was on the spot," agreed Len. "He couldn't very well say, that machine's not meant to pay off. He'd have been lynched. Come on."

Since the "come on" seemed to include Timothy he followed them. They led the way down a complex of side streets and alleys, each smaller and dingier than the last, until they came out almost onto the foreshore of the Thames. Since the dock had been shut two years before, it had become an area of desolation, of gaunt buildings with shuttered windows and boarded doorways.

Len stopped at one of these and stooped. Timothy saw that he had shifted a board, leaving plenty of room for a boy to wriggle under. When they were inside and the board had been replaced, Geoff clicked on a flashlight. Ahead were stone stairs, deep in fallen plaster and less pleasant litter.

"Our home away from home," said Len, "is on the first floor. Mind where you're walking. Here we are. Wait while I light the lamp."

It was a small room. The windows were blanked by iron shutters. The walls, as Timothy saw when the pressure lamp had been lit, were covered with posters. There was a table made of planks laid on trestles, and there were three old wicker chairs. Timothy thought he had never seen anything so snug and cozy in the whole of his life.

Len said, "You can use the third chair if you like."

It was a formal invitation into brotherhood.

"It used to be Ronnie's chair," said Geoff with a grin. "He won't be using it for a bit. Not for twelve months or so. He got nicked for shoplifting. They sent him up the river."

"Your folks going to start wondering where you are?"

"No, that's all right," said Timothy. "I can say I went on to the club after choir practise. It's a church club. The vicar runs it."

"Old Amberline? That fat poof."

Timothy considered the Reverend Patrick Amberline carefully and said, "No. He's all right."

Mr. Grant said, "Timmy seems very busy these days. It's the third night running he's been late."

"He was telling me about it at breakfast this morning," said Mrs. Grant. "It's not only the Choir and the Youth Club. It's this Voluntary Service Group he's joined. They're a sort of modern version of the Boy Scouts. They arrange to help people who need help. When he leaves school he might even get a job abroad. In one of those depressed countries."

"Well, I suppose it's all right," said Mr. Grant. "I used to be a Boy Scout myself once. I got a badge for cooking too."

They were busy weeks. For Timothy, weeks of simple delight. Never having had any real friends before, he found the friendship of Len and Geoff intoxicating. It was friendship offered without reserve, as it is at that age.

He knew now that Len was Leonard Rhodes and Geoff was Geoffrey Cowell and that Len's father was a market porter and Geoff's worked on the railway. He had enough imagination to visualize a life in which a boy was not expected to come home until eleven o'clock at night, a life in which you had to fight for everything you wanted, a life which could be full of surprising adventures.

The first thing he learned about was borrowing cars. This was an exercise carried out with two bits of wire.   A strong piece, with a loop at the end, which could be slipped through a gap forced at the top of the window and used to jerk up the retaining catch which locked the door.   Timothy, who had small hands and was neat and precise in his movements, became particularly skillful at this.

The second piece of wire was used by Len, who had once spent some time working in a garage, to start the engine.   After that, if no irate owner had appeared, the car could be driven off and would serve as transport for the evening.   Timothy was taught to drive.   He picked it up very quickly.

"Let her rip," said Geoff.   "It's not like you were driving your own car and got to be careful you don't scratch the paint.   With this one a few bumps don't matter."

This was on the occasion when they had borrowed Mr. Knowlson's new Ford Capri.   Timothy had suggested it.   "He's stuck to the television from eight o'clock onwards," he said.   "He wouldn't come out if a bomb went off."

The evening runs were not solely pleasure trips.   There was a business side to them as well.   Len and Geoff had a lot of contacts, friends of Geoff's father, who seemed to have a knack for picking up unwanted packages.   A carton containing two dozen new transistor pocket radios might have proved tricky to dispose of. But offered separately to buyers in public houses and cafés and dance halls, they seemed to go like hot cakes.   Len and Geoff were adept at this.

The first time they took Timothy into a public house the girl behind the bar looked at him and said, "How old's your kid brother?"

"You wouldn't think it," said Geoff, "but he's twenty-eight.   He's a midget. He does a turn in the halls.   Don't say anything to him about it.   He's sensitive."

The girl said, "You're a ruddy liar," but served them with half pints of beer. Mr. Grant was a teetotaler and Timothy had never seen beer before at close quarters. He took a sip of it.   It tasted indescribable.   Like medicine, only worse.   Geoff said, "You don't have to pretend to like it.   After a bit you'll sort of get used to it."

Some nights they were engaged in darker work.   They would drive the car to a rendezvous, which was usually a garage in the docks area.   Men would be there, shadowy figures who hardly showed their faces.   Crates which seemed to weigh heavily would be loaded onto the back seat of the car.   The boys then drove out into the Kent countryside.   The men never came with them.

When the boys arrived at their destination, sometimes another garage, sometimes a small workshop or factory, the cargo was unloaded with equal speed and silence, then a wad of notes was pushed into Len's hands.

The only real difference of opinion the boys ever had was over the money.   Len and Geoff wanted to share everything equally.   Timothy agreed to keep some of it, but refused any idea of equal sharing.   First, because he wouldn't have known what to do with so much cash.   More important, because he knew what it was being saved up for.   One of the pictures on the wall of their den was a blown-up photograph of a motorcycle—Norton Interstate 850 Road Racer.

"Do a ton easy," said Len.   "Hundred and thirty on the track.   Old Edelman

at that garage we go to down the docks says he can get me one at wholesale.   How
much are we up to?''

As he said this he was lifting up a board in the corner.   Under the board was
a biscuit tin, the edges sealed with insulating tape.   In the tin was the pirates'
hoard of banknotes and coins.

''Another tenner and we're there,'' said Geoff.

Timothy still went to choir practise.   If he had missed it his absence would have
been noticed, and inquiries would have followed.   The Reverend Amberline usually
put in an appearance, mainly to preserve law and order, and on this occasion he
happened to notice Timothy.   They were practising the hymn from the Yattenden
hymnal, *O quam juvat fratres.*   ''Happy are they, they that love God.''

The rector thought that Timothy, normally a reserved and rather silent boy, really
did look happy.   He was bubbling over, bursting with happiness.   ''Remember
now thy Creator,'' said the Reverend Amberline sadly to himself.   ''In the days
of thy youth.''   How splendid to be young and happy.

That evening Detective Chief Inspector Patrick Petrella paid a visit to Mrs. Grant's
house in Dodman Street.   He said, ''We've had a number of reports of cars being
taken away without their owner's consent.''

''That's right,'' said Mr. Grant.   ''And I'm glad you're going to do something
about it at last.   My neighbor, Mr. Knowlson, lost his a few weeks ago.   He got
it back, but it was in a shocking state.''

''Yesterday evening,'' said Petrella, ''the boys who seem to have been responsible
for a number of these cases were observed.   If the person who observed them had
been a bit quicker, they'd have been apprehended.   But she did give us a positive
identification of one lad she recognized.   It was your son, Timothy.''

''I don't believe it,'' said Mr. Grant, as soon as he had got his breath back.
''Timothy would never do anything like that.   He's a thoroughly nice boy.''

''Can you tell me where he was yesterday evening?''

''Certainly I can.   He was with the Voluntary Service Group.''

''The people at Craythorne Hall?''

''That's right.''

''May I use your telephone?''

''Yes.   And then I hope you'll apologize.''

Three minutes later Petrella said, ''Not only was he not at Craythorne Hall on
Wednesday evening, but he's never been there.   They know nothing about him.
They say they only take on boys of seventeen and over.''

Mr. Grant stared at him, white-faced.

''Where is he now?''

''At choir practise.''

''Choir practise would have been over by half-past eight.''

''He goes on afterwards to the Youth Club.''

Petrella knew the missioner at the Youth Club and used the telephone again.

By this time Mrs. Grant had joined them.   Petrella faced a badly shaken couple.
He said, "I'd like to have a word with Timothy when he does get back.   It doesn't
matter how late it is.   I've got something on at the Station which is going to keep
me there anyway."

He gave them his number at Patton Street.

The matter which Petrella referred to was a report of goods stolen from the
railway yard, being run to a certain garage in the docks area.   It was out of this
garage, at the moment that Petrella left Dodman Street, that the brand-new shining
monster was being wheeled.

"She's licensed and we've filled her up for you," said Mr. Edelman, who was
the jovial proprietor of the garage.   "The petrol is on the house."   He could
afford to be generous.   The courier service the boys had run had enriched him at
minimal risk to himself.

"Well, thanks," said Geoff.   He was almost speechless with pride and excitement.

"If you want to try her out, the best way is over Blackheath and out onto the
M.2.   You can let her rip there."

Geoff and Len were both wearing new white helmets, white silk scarves wrapped
round the lower parts of their faces, black leather coats, and leather gauntlets.   The
gloves, helmets, and scarves had been lifted the day before from an outfitter's in
Southwark High Street.   The coats had been bought for them by Timothy out of
his share of the money.   Len was the driver.   Geoff was to ride pillion.

"Your turn tomorrow," said Geoff.

"Fine," said Timothy.   "I'll wait for you at our place."

"Keep the home fires burning," said Len.   "This is just a trial run.   We'll be
back in an hour."

"And watch it," said Mr. Edelman.   "There's a lot of horsepower inside that
little beauty.   So don't go doing anything stupid."

His words were drowned in the roar of the Road Racer starting up.   Timothy
stood listening until he could hear it no longer.

Petrella got the news at eleven o'clock that night.

"We've identified the boys," said the voice on the telephone.   "They both
lived in your area.   Cowell and Rhodes.   I can give you the addresses."

"Both dead?"

"They could hardly be deader.   They went off the road and smashed into the
back of a parked lorry.   An A.A. patrol saw it happen.   Said they must have
been doing over ninety.   Stupid young fools."

The speaker sounded angry.   But he had seen the bodies and had sons of his
own.

The Cowells' house was nearer, so Petrella called there first.   He found Mr.
and Mrs. Cowell in the kitchen, with the television blaring.   They turned it off
when they understood what Petrella was telling them.

"I warned him," said Mr. Cowell.   "You heard me tell him."

"You said what nasty dangerous things they were," agreed his wife. "We didn't even know he had one."

"It was a brand-new machine," said Petrella. "Any idea where he might have got it from?"

"Tell you the truth," said Mr. Cowell, "we haven't been seeing a lot of Geoff lately. Boys at that age run wild, you know."

"We've brought up six," said Mrs. Cowell, crying softly.

Mr. Cowell said, "He and Len were good boys really. It was that Ronnie Silverlight led them astray. Until they ganged up with him we never had no trouble. No trouble at all."

It was one o'clock in the morning by the time Petrella got back to Patton Street. The desk sergeant said that there had been a number of calls. A Mr. Grant had rung more than once. And a boy who said he was Len Rhodes's brother was asking for news.

"How long ago was that?"

"About ten minutes ago."

"That's funny," said Petrella. "I've just come from the Rhodes'. And I don't think Len had a brother. What did you tell him?"

"I just gave him the news."

"What did he say?"

"Nothing. He just rang off. I think he was in a phone booth."

At this moment the telephone on the desk rang again. It was Mr. Grant. His voice was ragged with worry. "It's Timothy," he said. "He's not come home. You haven't—"

"No," said Petrella, "we haven't got him here. Is there any other place he might have gone? Has he got any friends?"

"We don't know anyone round here. He wouldn't just have walked out without saying anything. His mother's beside herself. She wanted to come round and see you."

"I don't think that would do any good," said Petrella. "We'll do what we can." He thought about it, then said to the desk sergeant, "Can you turn up the records and find out what happened to a boy named Ronald Silverlight? He was sent down for petty larceny about two months ago. One of the Borstal Institutes. See if you can find me the Warden's telephone number."

In spite of being hauled from his bed the Warden, once he understood what Petrella wanted, was sympathetic and cooperative. He said, "It's a long shot, but I'll wake Ronnie up and ring you back if I get anything."

Ten minutes later he came through again. He said, "This might be what you want. I gather they were using some derelict old building down in the docks area. It wouldn't be easy to describe the location. The best plan will be to send the boy up in a car. It'll take an hour or more."

"I'll wait," said Petrella.

It was nearly four o'clock in the morning before the car arrived, with a police driver, and Ronnie Silverlight and a guard in the back.   Petrella got in with them and they drove toward the river.

"You have to walk the last bit," said Ronnie.

Petrella thought about it.   There seemed to be too many of them.   He said, "I'll be responsible for the boy.   You two wait here."

When they got to the building Ronnie said, "We used to shift the bottom board, see, and get in underneath.   It'll be a tight squeeze for you."

"I'll manage," said Petrella.

He did it by lying on his back and using his elbows.   When he was inside he clicked on the flashlight he had brought with him.

"Up there," said Ronnie.   He was speaking in a whisper and didn't seem anxious to go first, so Petrella led the way up.

When he opened the door, the first thing that caught his eye was a glow from a fire of driftwood in the hearth which had burned down to red embers.   Then, as his flashlight swung upward, the white beam showed him Timothy.   He had climbed onto the table, tied one end of a rope to the beam, fixed the other in a noose round his neck, and kicked away the plank.

Petrella put the plank back and jumped up beside him, but as soon as he touched the boy he knew that they were much too late.   He had been dead for hours.

He must have done it, thought Petrella, soon after he had telephoned the station and heard the news about Len and Geoff.   And he made the fire to give him some light to see what he was doing.

"It's Timmy Grant, isn't it," said Ronnie.

"Yes," said Petrella.   "It's Timmy."   He was thinking of all the things he would now have to do, starting with breaking the news to his parents.

"He was a good kid," said Ronnie.   "Geoff wrote me about him."

Petrella's light picked up a flash of white.   It was a piece of paper that had fallen off the table.   On it was written, in Timothy's schoolboy script, two lines. Petrella recognized them as coming from a hymn, but he did not know, until Father Amberline told him long afterward, that they were from the hymn the choir had been singing that evening.

> *And death itself shall not unbind*
> *Their happy brotherhood.*

Petrella folded the scrap of paper and slipped it quickly into his pocket.   It was against all his instincts as a policeman to suppress evidence, but he felt that it would be too brutal to show it to Mr. and Mrs. Grant.

THOMAS WALSH

The Sacrificial Goat

They met one bright August afternoon in one of the elegant red and gold Hotel Versailles elevators, and since it was a bit crowded at the moment they had to stand close together, though without touching. Yet even on that first occasion, in the way that such people instinctively recognize each other's morality and inclinations, there was something communicated between them. They touched eyes for only a brief instant, yet even so the man knew the woman from then on, and the woman the man.

They were very careful, however. Mistakes were always possible. So it was mid-October before the man rented a small furnished apartment on East 78th Street under the name of Robinson, after which the woman came over there to spend a few hours in the afternoon with him about twice a week. They were both experienced in such matters, the man very experienced, and after he had made sure there was an automatic elevator in the building and no doorman, everything could be managed with the most admirable discretion.

Nobody knew about them. Nobody suspected about them. But something unforeseen happened. Little by little the thing got more serious, or perhaps only more passionate, and by January it had become very serious. That was when they began to think with increasing hatred of the one person who stood in their way. Without that one person they would have more money than they could use. Without him they could have everything they wanted and enjoy a long happy life together.

At first, however, they only considered the thing silently, in their thoughts. But one afternoon the man remarked as if jokingly how fortunate it would be if only some sort of accident occurred, and the woman responded in the same manner. But an accident, the man pointed out, might be very dangerous for them. Details could go wrong; mistakes could be made; everyone concerned, husband or wife, son or daughter, would be thoroughly checked out, even down to the hotel staff— unless, of course, someone else could be found who obviously had the means, the motive, and the opportunity to eliminate that one person.

After that, no longer jokingly, they began to discuss who the someone might be. First, there must be no question as to his identity. And second, the police must be made to realize at once who had done the thing and the reason for it. If that part could be set up, only one very simple question remained. Who would the tool of murder be? Whom would they pick as the sacrificial goat?

Finally the solution presented itself and they both immediately understood it was the perfect solution. Soon a pleasantly conspiratorial excitement carried them ahead faster and faster, and by the last week in January, with every possible difficulty taken care of, they arranged the whole thing from beginning to end.

The Versailles was an old but still extremely elegant New York hotel. It had been designed by a famous architect many years ago, and though by now its quiet but luxurious high-society tone had perhaps faded a little, it still was considered by all the right people as far superior to the newer and more commercial establishments. It had a famous Garden Room, several expensive restaurants much too costly for the common herd, and half a dozen exclusive shops—jewelry, interior decorating, gentlemen's furnishings, and three French couturiers all just off the main lobby.

It was no longer, however, as in its first haughty years, restricted as to all minorities, and although its employees were screened much more carefully than the patrons upstairs, a few blacks and Puerto Ricans were beginning to be accepted. It had twenty-odd floors, and on the north side a magnificent view over Central Park. Every floor had a desk clerk and a page boy, and the page boy on the 17th floor was named Ramon Rodriquez.

One day he was on duty from seven in the morning until twelve noon, and again from six until nine in the evening. On the following day, conversely, he worked from twelve noon until six. He was a slim undersized boy with black hair and cheerfully glistening black eyes, only fifteen years old—but the Versailles, needing a page boy, had not bothered to make sure that he was old enough to work full time according to the laws of New York State. Interviewed only by the bell captain, he was paid no more than the minimum wage—one reason perhaps that the Versailles needed a page boy—and out of that, the bell captain said, the Versailles would deduct $5 a month to keep his uniform cleaned and pressed. But in addition, it was also explained to Ramon, there would be a great many tips from all the rich society people who patronized the Versailles and those tips would be entirely Ramon's.

So Ramon expected great things for himself on his first job, although he soon discovered that the tips were more a promise than an actuality. Most of the better suites on the 17th floor were reserved for permanent guests, and all had maids who answered the door. It happened, consequently, that when Ramon delivered a package to one of the suites, or ran an errand for the occupant, the only thanks he got, if that, was a nod from the maid.

There were no more than a few generous exceptions. A rich mining man named Mr. Lahrheim in 1734 gave Ramon a dollar for anything he did, and a Mrs. McLeod in 1748 gave him a crisp five-dollar bill every Saturday morning, although she required less service from him than anyone on the whole floor. But most of the other permanent guests, in sharp distinction, must have thought that what Ramon did for them was well covered by the exorbitant rent they paid the Versailles, and that there was no need of further largess.

And Ramon did a great many things for them which most never even thought about.   On early mornings, for instance, he delivered newspapers to their doors, which they could read while having breakfast comfortably in bed; and on Sunday mornings, when the papers were five or six times the daily size, he had to go downstairs on the service elevator three or four times, pile the papers onto a cart, then wheel the cart from Suite 1701 at the northwest corner of the Versailles to Suite 1794 at the southwest corner.   He ran all their errands, brought all their packages, since no outside delivery boy was ever admitted into the Versailles corridors, and twenty or thirty times a day, when a guest was out, he took a telephone message from Miss Riley, the floor clerk, and then hung it on the proper doorknob for the guest's return.

In between times he had to sit on a small straight-backed chair by Miss Riley's desk, and when a guest appeared, was required to jump up, ring for the elevator, and then stand as rigidly at attention as a West Point cadet until the guest had been wafted down.   On Christmas morning, when he also had to work, he did that for old Mrs. Terwilliger in 1707.

"Oh, yes," old Mrs. Terwilliger beamed, toddling into the floor clerk's office with a nurse supporting her on one side and a uniformed chauffeur on the other— on her way, probably, at that time of the morning, to one of the more exclusive Park Avenue churches.

"Christmas Day.   We mustn't forget the boy, must we?   Now let me see."

And Ramon had great expectations at that moment.   For month after month he had done chore after chore for Mrs. Terwilliger, but never yet had he been given so much as a five-cent piece for any of them.   His expectations proved much too optimistic, however.   Mrs. Terwilliger rummaged through her purse, then rummaged again.

"Oh, dear," she exclaimed.   "It appears that I—would you have change for a dollar, Miss Riley?"

And Miss Riley, who liked Ramon very much, made a great show of examining her desk drawer.

"No," she said.   "I'm very sorry, Mrs. Terwilliger.   But no, I haven't."

"Oh, dear," Mrs. Terwilliger repeated, hesitating with anxious distress for a moment, then reluctantly extending the dollar bill.   "Then I suppose—well, Christmas Day, after all.   Here you are, boy."

Then the elevator went down and Miss Riley violently slammed in her desk drawer.

"Mean, miserable old bitch," she said.   "Change for a dollar!   It's a wonder she didn't want change for a dime, Ramon."

But still Ramon liked his job very much.   The long and quiet Versailles halls, finished with subdued elegance in gold and green, were a great change for him from Spanish Harlem, and on his early morning shifts there were always wheeled breakfast trays outside many of the guest suites.   Then Arturo the waiter would allow him to help himself to a leftover sausage or some buttered toast, and whatever remained in the silver coffee pots.   In that way Ramon could have a fine breakfast for himself, leaving a little more at home for his four smaller brothers and sisters, although he had to be careful that none of the guests came along and caught him.

They would probably have been very indignant at such low-class vulgarity in the Versailles and in all likelihood have reported it at the main desk on their way out.

Ramon even liked his gray and blue Versailles uniform. He always kept it immaculately neat—and of course his shoes polished, his hair brushed, and his fingernails cleaned, as the bell captain had impressed on him. But then Ramon had a certain ambition. He hoped, by hard and painstaking attention to duty, to become in time a bellhop down in the main lobby where he had heard that the tips amounted to more than $100 a week. And the sum would make a vast difference at home where Ramon was the only breadwinner. Therefore he was always quickly and cheerfully responsive to a guest's need, tip or no tip, and off like a flash to get them toothpaste or cigars from the drug store downstairs, or *Fortune* magazine or a Paris newspaper from the hotel newsstand.

There was an electric signboard on the wall over Miss Riley's desk, and on that, when a guest pressed the bell in his room, the corresponding number would appear— 1714, 1729, 1765. Then Ramon, after pushing up the release disk so that the number dropped back into place, would be up and away on the instant. And every night at home, when he had to crowd into a rickety daybed with his two little brothers, he would first pray fervently for the bellhop's job, so that in his first months at the Versailles there was never any kind of mark against him.

Only a bare year out of San Juan, Ramon was a very good boy, and a very innocent boy, with almost no experience in the world. The man and the woman had chosen him out of sure instinct. Ramon had no money, no influential friends, and no way to get himself even half-competent legal help. And early in February it developed that if Arturo and Miss Riley liked him, there were other members of the Versailles staff who did not like him at all.

That proved itself one night when two security men appeared in the hall and beckoned him out silently from Miss Riley's desk. Each of them took him by an arm, gripping him painfully, and the blond, very good-looking one even twisted his arm painfully. They marched him down to the service stairway and there, with the hall door closed behind them, the blond security man immediately slapped him across the mouth.

"Know what we got here?" he remarked to the other one. "A real smart little operator, Walter. Okay. I guess what we have to do now is to show him pretty damned quick just how smart he is to try and pull something like this."

"Guess we will," Walter said, and smashed Ramon's head into the wall. "Now tell me something, you little punk. You deliver a package to 1727 about six thirty tonight?"

Ramon was frightened and in much pain. He backed against the wall, shaking his head. It was not to deny that he had delivered the package to Mr. Curtis in Suite 1727. It was to show that in his pain and confusion he did not quite understand what they were asking him.

"No?" Walter said, smacking him again. "You mean you didn't? You mean the maid never left you all alone in the living room when she went inside to get the receipt signed, and that you weren't standing right beside old man Curtis' coin case when she came out with it? You better own up, punk, or me and Harry are going to knock the hell out of you. Where did you hide that coin you stole? What did you do with it? Take a look in his pockets, Harry.''

But in Ramon's pockets there were only the few tips he had made, a subway token, and his locker key. That Harry handed to Walter.

"Probably stashed it away down there," he said. "Check it out, Walter. I'd bet on the thing.''

Then, all alone, Harry twisted Ramon's arm even more viciously and kept on slapping his face. He also said things, but Ramon—fifteen years old, after all— was in no condition to understand what they were. He did not want to cry, but he had to. He crouched lower against the wall, shielding his face.

Walter came back.

"Nope," he said. "Nothing at all. Only his overcoat ain't there. Nothing but a crummy old sweater.''

"Ees all I have to wear," Ramon whispered to them. "Ees all I have.''

"That right?" Harry said. Crisply curling, reddish-gold hair; coldly sharp blue eyes with thick lashes; hard, hatingly contemptuous grin. "Then maybe they'll give you one up the river, because that's where you're going straight from here, cutie. You got just one chance before we take you around to the precinct house. What did you do with that coin you took? Where did you hide it?''

"No coin," Ramon whispered. "No, no. I bring the package, yes. I wait for the maid to come back. But—''

They led him out into the hall and down to Suite 1727, where Mr. Curtis and Mr. and Mrs. Purnell, his daughter and son-in-law from 1739, were talking together in front of the door.

"Well, here's your answer," Harry said, brutally slapping Ramon's head forward. "He's the one stole it, Mr. Curtis, sir. We checked it all out for you, Walter and me, and the maid said he's the only one she left into your suite tonight. So it's got to be him. It's the only answer. No one else could have taken it.''

Mr. Curtis glanced in helplessly at a glass-topped case, just like a museum case, that stood against one wall of the foyer. Each coin in there was nestled in a circle of red velvet that fitted exactly around it. One circle was empty. Mr. Curtis was a coin collector.

"Well, I know it was there," he said. "And now it isn't. And I paid over $15,000 for it in London last year. I'm sure you're right, men. But why you employ boys of this type—''

Mrs. Curtis came out of Suite 1727. She was a slim platinum-blonde, much younger than her husband, and had the aloof, haughtily disinterested expression of the fashion model she had been before Mr. Curtis married her. There was a coin in her right hand.

"Is this what you're so concerned about?" she asked calmly. "Really, Charles. I said that you only mislaid it somewhere. I found it under some letters on your desk inside. And you yourself put it down there last night after showing it to Ted Bannister and his wife. I saw you do it.''

Mr. Curtis' mouth gaped.

"But I put it back in the case," he cried. "I did, Adele. I remember coming out into the living room after the Bannisters left and—"

"Oh, Daddy," Mrs. Purnell said, making an impatient gesture. "You remember so many things lately that you don't do at all. You forgot your dinner appointment with us only last Saturday. And you forgot about that Charity Ball at the Waldorf. I don't know what's getting into you."

"But I only made a mistake in the dates," he insisted feebly. "That's all, Barbara. I just—"

There was a pause. Mrs. Curtis and Mrs. Purnell murmured together. Mr. Purnell shook his head sadly. Harry and Walter glanced slyly at each other, grinning. But nobody looked at Ramon or appeared to notice the tears on his face. It was just as if Ramon were not present.

"Well, I guess it's all right," Mr. Curtis said finally to Harry and Walter. "I'm so sorry, so sorry, men. But I could have sworn—"

After that, rubbing the back of his gray head wearily, he went into 1727, with the other members of his family following him. The door closed, and after it had, Harry uttered a curt, jeering laugh.

" 'I'm so sorry,' " he mimicked. " 'So sorry, men.' But not a damn dime for us, Walter, not even after I told him all the trouble we went to. Only the best people here, hah? But all I hope is that they come up here some night and clean out the whole damn suite on him."

And Ramon was left all alone in the hall, with not one word of regret or apology having been spoken to him. It was at least five minutes before he could go back to the office again and face Miss Riley. His head hurt. His eyes felt hot and dry. But worst of all he felt deeply ashamed. It was as if no one had realized that Ramon was a human being. It was as if he had been, not only to Harry and Walter, just nothing at all.

About a week after that, a few minutes before nine in the evening and just as Ramon was preparing to go off duty, they found Curtis' body sprawled in front of the coin case in Suite 1727. It was Harry, making one of his regular house rounds, who saw the door to 1727 half open and discovered Mr. Curtis with blood all over his white evening shirt, and the one coin again missing from its place in the glass-topped museum case.

After that many things happened. Policemen came up by way of the service elevator, first two in uniform, then several more in ordinary civilian clothes. There was a great deal of feverish but subdued excitement in the 17th floor corridor, and even Mr. Lenormand the manager appeared, wringing his hands and whispering in agitated low tones to Walter and Harry by the side of Miss Riley's desk. But soon Mr. Lenormand, very distinguished-looking in a tail coat and white tie, nodded as if distractedly at Harry, and Ramon was again marched down to Suite 1727 where he had to close his eyes and swallow three times at the way Mr. Curtis looked.

By that time there were a great many other men in the suite. Some measured things; some took pictures; and some spoke to the maid, then to Mrs. Curtis, who looked very pale and shaky, though without tears. But Mrs. Purnell sobbed quietly in one corner, while Mr. Purnell stared out of the window at Central Park.

It was all very frightening to Ramon, the way all the policemen kept whispering to Harry and then looking around at him, and it was only a little better when a tall slim man with hard eyes and a saturnine face had Ramon sit down on the couch with him—the only time Ramon had ever been permitted to sit in Suite 1727.

But the man had a calm quiet voice, almost a friendly voice, and could speak Spanish to Ramon. At first he asked very simple questions—how old Ramon was, whether he went to church, and how long he had been working at the Versailles. But Ramon hardly knew what he answered, having to close his eyes when they lifted Mr. Curtis' body onto a stretcher, covered it with a gray blanket, and carried it off in the direction of the service elevator so that none of the other guests would see it. Then only the slim man was left, and Harry and Mr. Lenormand, until another man came in from the hall holding something that was wrapped carefully in a white cloth.

Then all the men turned around to look at Ramon again, and the tall slim one, who had been called Lieutenant Da Costa by the others, walked across the room holding the white cloth in his hand.

He put his other hand under Ramon's chin and made him look straight into his eyes. Then he opened the cloth very suddenly, without even the least warning, and Ramon saw all the blood that had been wiped off on it, and under the blood a razor-sharp knife with a wood handle. It was done so suddenly that Ramon started to shake all over, and then he closed his eyes from the knife. But Da Costa forced his head back and turned over the knife.

"R.R.," he said, pointing a forefinger at two initials on the handle. "You see that, Ramon? And you just told me what your name is—Ramon Rodriquez. How about those initials, then? Is this your knife? Did you ever see it before?"

"I do not know it," Ramon whispered. "I swear, senor. I never see it before."

Harry came over to them.

"What the hell are you wasting time for?" he demanded angrily. "Just slap it out of him, Lieutenant. What else do you want? Mr. Curtis mislaid that same coin last week and this little jerk heard how much it was worth—about $15,000. We heard Mr. Curtis say that himself, all of us. So this little punk snuck in here to grab it tonight and Mr. Curtis caught him. And all of these people are the same kind, aren't they? Ain't one of them that doesn't have a knife handy, just in case."

"One of these people myself," Da Costa murmured, still looking down at Ramon. "But I never owned or used a knife in my life. And you know what, Hannegan? A lot of us don't."

"Well, of course," Hannegan said, coloring a bit. "Didn't mean anything like that, Lieutenant. Only trying to say—"

"Yes, I know," Da Costa put in. "How about the coin, O'Brien? Anybody find it yet?"

"Not yet," O'Brien said. "But it's around somewhere, Lieutenant. Got to

be. Miss Riley says the kid ain't been off the floor since about 8:15. The last
call he answered was at eight o'clock when somebody wanted him in 1735. Right
down the hall.''

"How long did the call take him?''

"Not long at all, Miss Riley says. He was always quick as a shot, according
to her. She's sure he was back again in about two minutes. All he had to do
for 1735 was take some letters and drop them down the mail chute in Miss Riley's
office.''

"So all in two minutes,'' Da Costa murmured, "he goes down to 1735, passes
1727 here on the way back, finds the door open or at least unlocked, comes in and
opens the coin case, takes the right coin out, stabs Curtis when he's caught doing
it, then walks back to the floor office cool as a cucumber, after dropping the knife
behind that hall radiator where you found it, and sits down again just like nothing
has happened. Not excited at all; not in any kind of crazy panic—and only fifteen
years old, he tells me. All he says to Miss Riley is about the money he's saving
up for his little sister's birthday next week. How about that, Hannegan? He sure
knew how to handle himself, didn't he? *All* in two minutes?''

"Well, like I said,'' Hannegan said, shrugging insolently. "Them people.
Maybe Miss Riley got a degree in child psychology, Lieutenant. You ought to
ask her.''

"Maybe I ought to start asking a lot of people,'' Da Costa said. "Starting with
you. Were you up on this floor any time tonight before you discovered the body
in here?''

"Yeah, flew up,'' Harry Hannegan said, and laughed jeeringly. "Why, none
of the elevator operators saw me. Go ahead. Ask them.''

"Stairs,'' Da Costa murmured. "Service stairs. And deserted, I should imagine, about nine-tenths of the time.''

"I was up here a bit earlier,'' Mr. Lenormand said, wiping his face harriedly
with the flowing linen handkerchief that he took out of his breast pocket. "Mr.
Curtis wanted to discuss the menu for a dinner he was giving for a few friends
tomorrow night in the Garden Room. Then when I came out, I passed Mr. Purnell
in the hall. I believe he can verify that, if you think it's necessary.''

"We will,'' Da Costa said. "Although it looks like the boy, all right. He
made a very serious mistake talking to me, even if he doesn't realize that he did.
All we need to prove on him now is that he stole the coin and we have him dead
to rights.''

"Lost his nerve,'' Harry suggested, "and got rid of it. Probably threw it down
one of the toilets.''

"Or better yet,'' Da Costa thought, "dropped it down the mail chute with those
letters from 1735. What's your first mail pickup in the morning, Hannegan?''

"I think eight o'clock,'' Hannegan said. "That right, Mr. Lenormand?''

"I believe so,'' Mr. Lenormand said, still wiping his face. "But a thing like
this to happen at the Versailles! My God!''

"Then have somebody here when the mailman comes around,'' Da Costa ordered.
"If we find the coin down there, we got Ramon. Once we face him with that,

we'll give him half an hour downtown with Frank Sandstrum and we'll have the whole story.''

But still the man and the woman were very careful, even after it became known the next morning that the coin had been found right where Da Costa had suggested it would be. They arranged a meeting only two weeks later at the East 78th Street apartment. The man got there first and the woman had just taken off her coat when the hall door opened. Da Costa and O'Brien walked in.

"Nice little place," Da Costa said, glancing around casually. "Not so high-toned as the Versailles, of course—but fair enough for what you needed. How long you been meeting here?''

The woman sat down as suddenly as if her legs had given way under her, but the man had better control of himself.

"Now just a minute," he blustered. "You have nothing against us. What we're doing here is our own personal business.''

Da Costa cuffed him across the mouth with hard knuckles.

"From a kid named Ramon," he said. "Keep your mouth shut. I don't have to ask what you did because I know it already. You got damned cozy at the Versailles first, meeting each other nearly every day there, and then you got even more cozy in this place. You—'' he glanced contemptuously at the woman "—had to set up the first scene. I mean how the old man forgot the coin, or apparently forgot it, leaving it on his desk when he hadn't left it there at all. You also made out that he had begun forgetting a lot of things, giving him the wrong dates for appointments and so on till he began to believe it himself. In addition, you made sure that he said right in Ramon's hearing how much the coin was worth, and if he hadn't said it you'd have slipped it in yourself. Following me so far?''

Neither one answered. The man sat silently. The woman, shaking her head time after time, had become pale as death.

"Then we might as well proceed," Da Costa went on. "I had to prepare the ground too, because I know kids like Ramon, and I knew by the way he acted that he didn't even understand what was happening to him. So I told you"—glancing down contemptuously at the man—"how important the coin was and how Ramon made a very serious mistake when he was talking to me. Well, the coin was important, important as all hell, because whoever took it out of the case obviously killed the old man. Where to find it, though? It could have been hidden in any place at all in the Versailles, if Ramon hadn't taken it.

"So I made another suggestion while we were all in the same room. I suggested that maybe Ramon dropped it down the mail chute, and asked what time the first pickup was the next morning. Only before that I had O'Brien get in touch with the post office and they sent a man up here to open the chute right away, take the letters out, and close it up again, empty.

"And what do you know? The letters from 1735 were in there already, just like Ramon said—but the coin wasn't. Next morning, though, with a lot of other letters, there it was. Which meant that whoever dropped it into the chute, it wasn't Ramon. It couldn't have been. He was in our hands already. See what I mean?''

There was still dead silence. The man had put his head in his hands. The woman had begun to weep brokenly.

"Guess you do," Da Costa said, his lips curled. "You figured that coin would be the last thing to damn the kid, only it turned out to be the one thing that nailed you. So if it couldn't be Ramon, it had to be somebody else. Who? That was the poser.

"Well, it was quite a little trouble for us, but from then on everybody involved was given a good careful tail wherever he went.

"So what do you think happens? Our hero here leaves the Versailles at two o'clock this afternoon, and his dear lady fifteen minutes later. Then where do you suppose they both come? Right here. And then where do you suppose we come? Right here too. All we have to do then is talk to the superintendent downstairs, get his passkey—and here we are. We know how long ago you rented the place; we know how long you've been coming here; and so all we have to do is to leave it to a jury as to what the reason might be.

"Slap the cuffs on them, O'Brien. I want them to feel it just the way a little Puerto Rican kid did when I had to do it to him, even if it was only for show that time. Now come on. Up on your feet, both of you. You get one phone call apiece to any lawyer you want, but I'll lay fifty to one that no lawyer can help you. Anybody talking?"

There did not appear to be. Mrs. Curtis, her face stony-hard under the tears, stood up like a sleepwalker. Across from her, his head still in his hands but his eyes open and staring down with savage hopelessness at the brilliantly polished tips of his black shoes, sat the Versailles manager, Mr. Lenormand.

PATRICIA HIGHSMITH

When in Rome

Isabella had soaped her face, her neck, and was beginning to relax in the spray of deliciously warm water on her body when suddenly—there he was again! An ugly grinning face peered at her not a meter from her own face, with one big fist gripping an iron bar, so he could raise himself to her level.

"Swine!" Isabella said between her teeth, ducking at the same time.

"Slut!" came his retort. "Ha, ha!"

This must have been the third intrusion by the same creep! Isabella, still stooped, got out of the shower and reached for the plastic bottle of yellow shampoo, shot some into a bowl which held a cake of soap (she removed the soap), let some hot shower water run into the bowl and agitated the water until the suds rose, thick and sweet-smelling. She set the bowl within easy reach on the rim of the tub, and climbed back under the shower, breathing harder with her fury.

Just let him try it again! Defiantly erect, she soaped her facecloth, washed her thighs. The square recessed window was just to the left of her head, and there was a square emptiness, stone-lined, between the blue-and-white tiled bathroom walls and the great iron bars, each as thick as her wrist, on the street side.

"Signora?" came the mocking voice again.

Isabella reached for the bowl. Now he had both hands on the bars, and his face was between them, unshaven, his black eyes intense, his loose mouth smiling. Isabella flung the suds, holding the bowl with fingers spread wide on its underside.

"Oof!" The head disappeared.

A direct hit! The suds had caught him between the eyes, and she thought she heard some of the suds hit the pavement. Isabella smiled and finished her shower.

She was not looking forward to the evening—dinner at home with the First Secretary of the Danish Embassy with his girl friend; but she had had worse evenings in the past, and there were worse to come in Vienna in the last week of this month, May, when her husband Filippo had to attend some kind of human-rights-and-pollution conference that was going to last five days. Isabella didn't care for the Viennese—she considered the women bores with nothing on their minds but clothes, who was wearing what, and how much did it cost.

"I think I prefer the green silk tonight," Isabella said to her maid Elisabetta, when she went into her bedroom, big bathtowel around her, and saw the new black dress laid out on her bed. "I changed my mind," Isabella added, because she remembered that she had chosen the black that afternoon.   Hadn't she?   Isabella felt a little vague.

"And which shoes, signora?"

Isabella told her.

A quarter to eight now.   The guests—two men, Filippo had said, besides the Danish secretary who was called Osterberg or Ottenberg, were not due until eight, which meant eight thirty or later.   Isabella wanted to go out on the street, to drink an espresso standing up at the bar, like any other ordinary Roman citizen, and she also wanted to see if the Peeping Tom was still hanging around.   In fact, there were two of them, the second a weedy type of about thirty who wore a limp raincoat and dark glasses.   He was a "feeler," the kind who pushed his hand against a woman's bottom.   He had done it to Isabella once or twice while she was waiting for the porter to open the door.   Isabella had to wait for the porter unless she chose to carry around a key as long as a man's foot for the big outside doors.   The feeler looked a bit cleaner than her bathroom snoop, but he also seemed creepier and he never smiled.

"Going out for a caffé," Isabella said to Elisabetta.

"You prefer to go out?" Elisabetta said, meaning that she could make a caffé, if the signora wanted.   Elisabetta was forty-odd, her hair in a neat bun.   Her husband had died a year ago, and she was still in a state of semi-mourning.

Isabella flung a cape over her shoulders, barely nodded, and left.   She crossed the cobbled court whose stones slanted gently toward a center drain, and was met at the door by one of the three porters who kept a round-the-clock guard on the palazzo which was occupied by six affluent tenants.   This porter was Franco.   He lifted the heavy crossbar and opened the big doors enough for her to pass through.

Isabella was out on the street.   Freedom!   She stood tall and breathed.   An adolescent boy cycled past, whistling.   An old woman in black waddled by slowly, burdened with a shopping bag that showed onions and spaghetti on top, carelessly wrapped in newspaper.   Someone's radio blared jazz through an open window.   The air promised a hot summer.

Isabella looked around, but didn't see either of her nuisances, and was aware of feeling slightly disappointed.   However, there was the bar-caffé across the street and a bit to the right.   Isabella entered, conscious that her fine clothes and well-groomed hair set her apart from the usual patrons here.   She put on a warm smile for the young barman who knew her by now.

"Signora!   Buon' giorno!   A fine day, no?   What is your wish?"

"Un espress', per piacere."

Isabella realized that she was known in the neighborhood as the wife of a government official who was reasonably important for his age which was still under forty, aware that she was considered rather rich, and pretty too.   The latter, people could see.   And what else, Isabella wondered as she sipped her espresso.   She and Filippo had a fourteen-year-old daughter in school in Switzerland now.   Susanna.

Isabella wrote to her faithfully once a week, as Susanna did to her.   How was Susanna going to shape up?   Would she even *like* her daughter by the time she was eighteen or twenty-two?   Was Susanna going to lose her passion for horses and horseback riding (Isabella hoped so) and go for something more intellectual such as geology and anthropology, which she had shown an interest in last year? Or was she going to go the usual way—get married at twenty before she'd finished university, trade on her good looks and marry "the right kind of man" before she had found out what life was all about?   What *was* life all about?

Isabella looked around her, as if to find out.   Isabella had had two years of university in Milan, had come from a rather intellectual family, and didn't consider herself just another dumb wife.   Filippo was good-looking and had a promising career ahead of him.   But then Filippo's *father* was important in a government ministry, and had money.   The only trouble was that the wife of a man in diplomatic service had to be a clothes-horse, had to keep her mouth shut when she would like to open it, had to be polite and gracious to people whom she detested or was bored by.   There were times when Isabella wanted to kick it all, to go slumming, simply to laugh.

She tossed off the last of her coffee, left a five-hundred-lire piece, and turned around, not yet leaving the security of the bar's counter.   She surveyed the scene. Two tables were occupied by couples who might be lovers.   A blind beggar with a white cane was on his way in.

And here came her dark-eyed Peeping Tom!   Isabella was aware that her eyes lit up as if she beheld her lover walking in.

He grinned.   He sauntered, swaggered slightly as he headed for the bar to a place at a little distance from her.   He looked her up and down, like a man sizing up a pick-up before deciding yes or no.

Isabella lifted her head and walked out of the bar-caffé.

He followed.   "You are beautiful, signora," he said.   "I should know, don't you think so?"

"You can keep your filthy ideas to yourself!" Isabella replied as she crossed the street.

"My beautiful lady-love—the wife of my dreams!"

Isabella noticed that his eyes looked pink.   Good!   She pressed the bell for the porter.   An approaching figure on her left caught her eye.   The bottom-pincher, the gooser, the real oddball!   Raincoat again, no glasses today, a faint smile. Isabella turned to face him, with her back to the big doors.

"Oh, how I would like to . . ." the feeler murmured as he passed her, so close she imagined she could feel the warmth of his breath against her cheek, and at the same time he slapped her hip with his left hand.   He had a pockmark or two, and big cheekbones that stuck out gauntly.   Disgusting type!   And a disgusting phrase he had used!

From across the street, Peeping Tom was watching, Isabella saw; he was chuckling silently, rocking back on his heels.

Franco opened the doors.   What if she told Filippo about those two?   But of course she had, Isabella remembered, a month or so ago, yes.   "How would *you* like it if a psychopath stared at you nearly every time you took a shower?" Isabella had said to Filippo, and he had broken out in one of his rare laughs.   "If it were a *woman* maybe, yes, I might like it!'' he said, then he had said that she shouldn't take it so seriously, that he would speak to the porters, or something like that.

Isabella had the feeling that she didn't really wake up until after the dinner party, when the coffee was served in the living room.   The taste of the coffee reminded her of the bar that afternoon, of the dark-haired Peeping Tom with the pink eyes walking into the bar and having the nerve to speak to her *again*!

"We shall be in Vienna too, at the end of the month," said the girl friend of the Danish First Secretary.

Isabella rather liked her.   Her name was Gudrun.   She looked healthy, honest, unsnobbish.   But Isabella had nothing to say except, "Good.   We shall be looking forward," one of the phrases that came out of her automatically after fifteen years of being the wife-of-a-government-employee.   There were moments, hours, when she felt bored to the point of going insane.   Like now.   She felt on the brink of doing something shocking, such as standing up and screaming, or announcing that she wanted to go out for a walk (yes, and have another espresso in the same crummy bar), of shouting that she was bored with them *all*, even Filippo, slumped with legs crossed in an armchair now, wearing his neat, new dinner suit with a ruffled shirt, deep in conversation with the three other men.   Filippo was long and lean like a fashion model, his black hair beginning to gray at the temples in a distinguished way.   Women liked his looks, Isabella knew.   His good looks, however, didn't make him a ball of fire as a lover.   Did the women know that, Isabella wondered.

Before going to bed that night, Isabella had to check the shopping list with Luigi the cook for tomorrow's dinner party, because Luigi would be up early to buy fresh fish.   Hadn't the signora suggested fish?   And Luigi recommended young lamb instead of tournedos for the main course, if he dared say so.

Filippo paid her a compliment as he was undressing.   "Osterberg thought you were charming."

They both slept in the same big bed, but it was so wide that Filippo could switch his reading light on and read his papers and briefings till all hours, as he often did, without disturbing Isabella.

A couple of evenings later Isabella was showering just before seven P.M. when the same dark-haired creep sprang up at her bathroom window, leering a "Hello, beautiful!   Getting ready for me?"

Isabella was not in a mood for repartée.   She got out of the shower.

"Ah, signora, such beauty should not be hidden!   Don't try—"

"I've told the *police* about you!" Isabella yelled back at him, and switched off the bathroom light.

Isabella spoke to Filippo that evening as soon as he came in.   "Something's got to be done—opaque glass put in the window—"

"You said that would make the bathroom too humid."

"I don't care!   It's revolting!   I've told the porters—Giorgio, anyway.   He doesn't do a damned thing, that's plain!   Filippo?"

"Yes, my dear.   Come on, can't we talk about this later?   I've got to change my shirt, at least, because we're due—already."   He looked at his watch.

Isabella was dressed.   "I want your tear-gas gun.   You remember you showed it to me.   Where is it?"

Filippo sighed.   "Top drawer, left side of my desk."

Isabella went to the desk in Filippo's study.   The gun looked like a fountain pen, only a bit thicker.   Isabella smiled as she placed her thumb on the firing end of it and imagined her counterattack.

"Be careful how you use that tear-gas," Filippo said as they were leaving the house.   "I don't want you to get into trouble with the police just because of a—"

"*Me* in trouble with the police!   Whose side are you on?"   Isabella laughed, and felt much better now that she was armed.

The next afternoon around five, Isabella went out, paid a visit to the pharmacy where she bought tissues and a bottle of a new eau de Cologne which the chemist suggested, and whose packaging amused her.   Then she strolled toward the bar-caffé, keeping an eye out for her snoops as she went.   She was bareheaded, had a bit of rouge on her lips, and she wore a new summer frock.   She looked pretty and was aware of it.   And across the street, walking past her very door now, went the raincoated creep in dark glasses again—and he didn't notice her.   Isabella felt slightly disappointed.   She went into the bar and ordered an espresso, lit a rare cigarette.

The barman chatted.   "Wasn't it a nice day?   And the signora is looking especially well today."

Isabella barely heard him, but she replied politely.   When she opened her handbag to pay for her espresso, she touched the tear-gas gun, picked it up, dropped it, before reaching for her purse.

"Grazie, signora!"   She had tipped generously as usual.

Just as she turned to the door, the bathroom peeper—her special persecutor—entered, and had the audacity to smile broadly and nod, as if they were dear friends. Isabella lifted her head higher as if with disdain, and at the same time gave him an appraising glance, which just might have been mistaken for an invitation, Isabella knew.   She had meant it that way.   The creep hadn't quite the boldness to say anything to her inside the caffé, but he did follow her out the door.   Isabella avoided looking directly at him.   Even his shoes were unshined.   What could he do for a living, she wondered.

Isabella pretended, at her door, to be groping for her key.   She picked up the tear-gas gun, pushed off its safety, and held it with her thumb against its top.

Then he said, with such mirth in his voice that he could hardly get the words out, "Bellissima signora, when are you going to let me—"

Isabella lifted the big fountain pen and pushed its firing button, maneuvering it so that its spray caught both his eyes at short range.

"Ow!—Ooh-h!"   He coughed, then groaned, down on one knee now, with a hand across his eyes.

Even Isabella could smell the stuff, and blinked, her eyes watering.   A man on the pavement had noticed the Peeping Tom struggling to get up, but was not running to help him, merely walking toward him.   And now a porter opened the big wooden doors, and Isabella ducked into her own courtyard.   "Thank you, Giorgio."

The next morning she and Filippo set out for Vienna.   This excursion was one Isabella dreaded.   Vienna would be dead after eleven thirty at night—not even an interesting coffee house would be open.   Awful!   But the fact that she had fired a shot in self-defense—in attack—buoyed Isabella's morale.

And to crown her satisfaction she had the pleasure of seeing Peeping Tom in dark glasses as she and Filippo were getting into the chauffeured government car to be driven to the airport.   He had stopped on the pavement some ten meters away to gaze at the luggage being put into the limousine by the liveried driver.

Isabella hoped his eyes were killing him.   She had noted there was a box of four cartridges for the tear-gas gun in the same drawer.   She intended to keep her gadget well charged.   Surely the fellow wasn't going to come back for more!   She might try it also on the feeler in the dirty raincoat.   Yes, there was one who didn't mind approaching damned close!

"Why're you dawdling, Isabella?   Forget something?" Filippo asked, holding the car door for her.

Isabella hadn't realized that she had been standing on the pavement, relishing the fact that the creep could see her about to get into the protective armor of the shiny car, about to go hundreds of kilometers away from him.   "I'm ready," she said, and got in.   She was not going to say to Filippo, "There's my Peeping Tom."   She liked the idea of her secret war with him.   Maybe his eyes were permanently damaged.   She hoped so.

This minor coup made Vienna seem better.   Isabella missed Elisabetta—some women whose husbands were in government service traveled with their maids, but Filippo was against this, just now.   "Wait a couple of years till I get a promotion," Filippo had said.   Years.   Isabella didn't care for the word year or years.   Could she stand it?   At the stuffy dinner parties where the Austrians spoke bad French or worse Italian, Isabella carried her tear-gas gun in her handbag, even in her small evening bag at the big gala at the Staatsoper.   *The Flying Dutchman*.   Isabella sat with legs crossed, feet crossed also with tension, and dreamed of resuming her attack when she got back to Rome.

Then on the last evening Filippo had an "all-night meeting" with four men of the human-rights committee, or whatever they called it.   Isabella expected him back at the hotel about three in the morning at the latest, but he did not get back till seven thirty, looking exhausted and even a bit drunk.   His arrival had awakened her, though he had tried to come in quietly with his own key.

"Nothing at all," he said unnecessarily and a little vaguely.   "Got to take a shower—then a little sleep.   No appointment till—eleven this morning and it won't matter if I'm late."   He ran the shower.

Then Isabella remembered the girl he had been talking to that evening, as he smoked a fine cigar—at least, Isabella had heard Filippo call it "a fine cigar"—a smiling, blonde Austrian girl, smiling in the special way women had when they wanted to say, "Anything you do is all right with me.   I'm yours, you understand?   At least for tonight."

Isabella sighed, turned over in bed, tried to sleep again, but she felt tense with rage, and knew she would not sleep before it was time for breakfast, time to get up.   Damn it!   She knew Filippo had been at the girl's apartment or in her hotel room, knew that if she took the trouble to sniff his shirt, even the shoulders of his dinner jacket, she would smell the girl's perfume—and the idea of doing that revolted her.   Well, she herself had had two, no three lovers during her married life with Filippo, but they had been so brief, those affairs!   And so discreet!   Not one servant had known.

Isabella also suspected Filippo of having a girl friend in Rome, Sibilla, a rather gypsy-like brunette, and if Filippo was "discreet," it was because he was only lukewarm about her.   This blonde tonight was more Filippo's type, Isabella knew. She heard Filippo hit the twin bed that was pushed close to her bed.   He would sleep like a log, then get up in three hours looking amazingly fresh.

When Isabella and Filippo got back to Rome, Signor Sore-Eyes was on hand the very first evening, when Isabella stood under the shower about seven thirty in the evening.   Now that was fidelity for you!   Isabella ducked, giggling.   Her giggle was audible.

And Sore-Eyes' response came instantly: "Ah, the lady of my heart is pleased! She laughs!"   He had dropped to his feet, out of sight, but his voice came clearly through the stone recess.   "Come, let me see more.   *More!*"   Hands grasped the bars; the grinning face appeared, black eyes shining and looking not at all damaged.

"Get lost!" she shouted, and stepped out of the shower and began to dry herself, standing near the wall, out of his view.

But the other nut, the feeler, seemed to have left the neighborhood.   At least Isabella did not see him during three or four days after her return from Vienna. Nearly every day she had an espresso at the bar-caffé across the street, and sometimes twice a day she took taxis to the Via Veneto area where a few of her friends lived, or to the Via Condotti for shopping.   Shiny-Eyes remained faithful, however, not always in view when she came out of her big doors, but more often than not.

Isabella fancied—she liked to fancy—that he was in love with her, even though his silly remarks were intended either to make her laugh or, she had to admit it, to insult and shock her.   It was this line of thinking, however, which caused Isabella to see the Peeping Tom as a rival, and which gave her an idea.   What Filippo needed was a good jolt!

"Would you like to come for after-dinner coffee tonight?" Isabella murmured to Shiny-Eyes one day, interrupting his own stream of vulgarity, as she stood not yet pushing the bell of her house.

The man's mouth fell open, revealing more of his stained teeth.

"Ghiardini," she said, giving her last name.   "Ten thirty."   She had pushed the bell by now and the doors were opening.   "Wear some better clothes," she whispered.

That evening Isabella dressed with a little more interest in her appearance.   She and Filippo had to go out first to a "buffet cocktail" at the Hotel Eliseo.   Isabella was not even interested in what country was host to the affair.   Then she and Filippo departed at ten fifteen in their own government car, to be followed by two other groups of Americans, Italians, and a couple of Germans.   Isabella and Filippo were earlier than the rest, and of course Luigi and Elisabetta already had the long bar-table well equipped with bottles, glasses, and ice, and platters of little sausages stuck with toothpicks.   Why hadn't she told Shiny-Eyes eleven o'clock?

But Shiny-Eyes did the right thing, and arrived just after eleven.   Isabella's heart gave a dip as he entered through the living-room door, which had been opened by Luigi.   The room was already crowded with guests, most of them standing up with drinks, chattering away, quite occupied, and giving Shiny-Eyes not a glance. Luigi was seeing to his drink.   At least he was wearing a dark suit, a limp but white shirt, and a tie.

Isabella chatted with a large American and his wife.   Isabella hated speaking English, but she could hold her own in it.   Filippo, Isabella saw, had left his quartet of diplomats and was now concentrating on two pretty women; he was standing before them while they sat on the sofa, as if mesmerizing them by his tall elegant presence, his stream of bilge.   The women were German, secretaries or girl friends.   Isabella almost sneered.

Shiny-Eyes was nursing his Scotch against the wall by the bar-table, and Isabella drifted over on the pretense of replenishing her champagne.   She glanced at him, and he came closer.   To Isabella he seemed the only vital person in the room. She had no intention of speaking to him, even of looking directly at him, and concentrated on pouring champagne from a small bottle.

"Good evening, signora," he said in English.

"Good evening.   And what is your name?" she asked in Italian.

"Ugo."

Isabella turned gracefully on her heel and walked away.   For the next minutes she was a dutiful hostess, circulating, chatting, making sure that everyone had what he or she wanted.   People were relaxing, laughing more loudly.   Even as she spoke to someone, Isabella looked in Ugo's direction and saw him in the act of pocketing a small Etruscan statue.   She drifted back across the room toward him. "You put that back!" she said between her teeth, and left him.

Ugo put it back, flustered, but not seriously.

Filippo had caught the end of this, Isabella speaking to Ugo.   Filippo rose to find a new drink, got it, and approached Isabella.   "Who's the dark type over there?   Do you know him?"

Isabella shrugged.   "Someone's bodyguard, perhaps?"

The evening ended quietly, Ugo slipping out unnoticed even by Isabella.   When Isabella turned back to the living room expecting to see Filippo, she found the room empty.   "Filippo?" she called, thinking he might be in the bedroom.

Filippo had evidently gone out with some of the guests, and Isabella was sure he was going to see one of the blondes tonight.   Isabella helped herself to a last champagne, something she rarely did.   She was not satisfied with the evening after all.

When she awakened the next morning, at the knock of Elisabetta with the break-fast tray, Filippo was not beside her in bed.   Elisabetta, of course, made no comment. While Isabella was still drinking caffè latte, Filippo arrived.   All-night talk with the Americans, he explained, and now he had to change his clothes.

"Is the blonde in the blue dress American? I thought she and the other blonde were Germans," Isabella said.

Now the row was on. So what, was Filippo's attitude.

"What kind of life is it for *me*?" Isabella screamed. "Am I nothing but an *object*? Just some female figure in the house—always here, to say *buona sera*—and smile!"

"Where would I be without you? Every man in government service needs a wife," replied Filippo, using up the last of his patience. "And you're a very good hostess, Isabella, really!"

Isabella roared like a lioness. "Hostess! I detest the word! And your girl friends—*in this house*—"

"Never!" Filippo replied proudly.

"Two of them! How many have you now?"

"Am I the only man in Rome with a mistress or two?" He had recovered his cool and intended to stand up for his rights. After all, he was supporting Isabella and in fine style, and their daughter Susanna too. "If you don't like it—" But Filippo stopped.

More than ever, that day, Isabella wanted to see Ugo. She went out around noon, and stopped for an americano at the little bar-caffé. This time she sat at a table. Ugo came in when she had nearly finished her drink. Faithful, he was. Or psychic. Maybe both. Without looking at him, she knew that he had seen her.

She left some money on the table and walked out. Ugo followed. She walked in an opposite direction from the palazzo across the street, knowing that he knew she expected him to follow her.

When they were safely around another corner, Isabella turned. "You did quite well last night, except for the attempted—"

"Ah, sorry, signora!" he interrupted, grinning.

"What are you by profession—if I dare to ask?"

"Journalist, sometimes. Photographer. You know, a free-lance."

"Would you like to make some money?"

He wriggled, and grinned wider. "To spend on you, signora, yes."

"Never mind the rubbish." He really was an untidy specimen, back in his old shoes again, dirty sweater under his jacket, and when had he last had a bath? Isabella looked around to see if anyone might be observing them. "Would you be interested in kidnaping a rich man?"

Ugo hesitated only two seconds. "Why not?" His black eyebrows had gone up. "Tell me. Who?"

"My husband. You will need a friend with a gun and a car."

Ugo indulged in another grin, but his attitude was attentive.

Isabella had thought out her plans that morning. She told Ugo that she and Filippo wanted to buy a house outside of Rome, and she had the names of a few real-estate agents. She could make an appointment with one for Friday morning, for instance, at nine o'clock. Isabella said she would make herself "indisposed" that morning, so Filippo would have to go alone. But Ugo must be at the palazzo with a car a little before nine.

"I must make the hour the same, otherwise Filippo will suspect me," Isabella explained. "These agents are always a little late. You should be ten minutes early. I'll see that Filippo is ready."

Isabella continued, walking slowly, since she felt it made them less conspicuous than if they stood still. If Ugo and his friend could camp out somewhere overnight with Filippo, until she had time to get a message from them and get the money from the government? If Ugo could communicate by telephone or entrust someone to deliver a written message?

Either way was easy, Ugo said. He might have to hit Filippo on the head, Isabella said, but Ugo was not to hurt him seriously. Ugo understood.

A few moments later, when they parted, everything was worked out for the kidnaping on Friday morning. Tomorrow was Thursday, and if Ugo had spoken to his friend and all was well, he was to give Isabella a nod, merely, tomorrow afternoon about five when she would go out for an espresso.

Isabella was so exhilarated she went that afternoon to see her friend Margherita who lived off the Via Veneto. Margherita asked her if she had found a new lover. Isabella laughed.

"No, but I think Filippo has," Isabella replied.

Filippo also noticed, by Thursday afternoon, that she was in a merry mood. Filippo was home Thursday evening after their dinner out at a restaurant where they had been two at a table of twenty. Isabella took off her shoes and waltzed in the living room. Filippo was aware of his early date with the real-estate agents, and cursed it. It was already after midnight.

The next morning Elisabetta awakened them with the breakfast tray at eight thirty, and Isabella complained of a headache.

"No use in my going if you're not going," Filippo said.

"You can at least tell if the house is possible—or houses," she replied sleepily. "Don't let them down or they won't make a date with us again."

Filippo got dressed.

Isabella heard the faint ring of the street-door bell. Filippo went out. By this time he was in the living room or the kitchen in quest of more coffee. It was two minutes to nine. Isabella at once got up, flung on a blouse, slacks and sandals, ready to meet the real-estate agents who she supposed would be twenty minutes late, at least.

They were. Elisabetta announced them. Two gentlemen. The porter had let them into the court. All seemed to be going well, which was to say Filippo was not in view.

"But I thought my husband had already left with you!" She explained that her husband had left the house half an hour ago. "I'm afraid I must ask you to excuse me. I have a migraine today."

The agency men expressed disappointment, but left in good humor finally, because the Ghiardinis were potentially good clients, and Isabella promised to telephone them in the near future.

Isabella went out for a pre-lunch cinzano, and felt reassured by the absence of Ugo. She was about to answer a letter from Susanna which had come that morning when the telephone rang.   It was Filippo's colleague, Vicente, and where was Filippo?   Filippo was supposed to have arrived at noon at Vicente's office for a talk before they went out to lunch with a man who Vicente said was "important."

"This morning was a little strange," Isabella said casually, with a smile in her voice, "because Filippo went off with some estate agents at nine, I thought, then—"

"Then?"

"Well, I don't know.   I haven't heard from him since," Isabella replied, thinking she had said quite enough.   "I don't know anything about his appointments today."

Isabella went out to mail her letter to Susanna around four.   Susanna had fallen from her horse taking a low jump, in which the horse had fallen too.   A miracle Susanna hadn't broken a bone!   Susanna needed not only new riding breeches but a book of photographs of German cathedrals which the class was going to visit this summer, so Isabella had sent her a check on their Swiss bank.   As soon as Isabella had got back home and closed her door, the telephone rang.

"Signora Ghiardini—" It sounded like Ugo speaking through a handkerchief. "We have your husband.   Do not try to find out where he is.   One hundred million lire we want.   Do you understand?"

"*Where* is he?" Isabella demanded, putting on an act as if Elisabetta or someone else were listening; but no one was, unless Luigi had picked up the living-room extension phone.   It was Elisabetta's afternoon off.

"Get the money by tomorrow noon.   Do not inform the police.   This evening at seven a messenger will tell you where to deliver the money."   Ugo hung up.

That sounded all right!   Just what Isabella had expected.   Now she had to get busy, especially with Caccia-Lunghi, Filippo's boss, higher than Vicente in the Bureau of Public Welfare and Environment.   But first she went into her bathroom, where she was sure Ugo would not be peering in, washed her face and made herself up again to give herself confidence.   She would soon be putting a lot of money into Ugo's pocket and the pocket of his friend—whoever was helping him.

Isabella now envisaged Ugo her slave for a long time to come.   She would have the power of betraying him if he got out of hand, and if Ugo chose to betray *her*, she would simply deny it, and between the two of them she had no doubt which one the police would choose to believe: her.

"Vicente!" Isabella said in a hectic voice into the telephone (she had decided after all to ring Vicente first).   "Filippo has been kidnaped!   That's why he didn't turn up this morning!   I've just had a message from the kidnapers.   They're asking for a hundred million lire by tomorrow noon!"

She and Filippo, of course, had not that much money in the bank, she went on, and wasn't it the responsibility of the government, since Filippo was a government employee, an official?"

Vicente sighed audibly.   "The government has had enough of such things. You'd better try Filippo's father, Isabella."

"But he's so stubborn!—The kidnaper said something about throwing Filippo in a *river*!"

"They all say that.   Try the father, my dear."

So Isabella did. It was neariy six P.M. before she could reach him, because he had been "in conference." Isabella first asked, "Has Filippo spoken to you today?" He had not. Then she explained that Filippo had been kidnaped, and that his captors wanted 100,000,000 lire by tomorrow noon.

"What? Kidnaped—and they want it from me? Why *me*?" the old man spluttered. "The government—Filippo's in the government!"

"I've asked Vicente Carda." Isabella told him about her rejection in a tearful voice, prolonging her story so that Filippo's predicament would have time to sink in.

"Va bene, va bene." Pietro Ghiardini sounded defeated. "I can contribute seventy-five million, not more. What a business! You'd think Italy . . ." He went on, though he sounded on the brink of a heart attack.

Isabella expressed gratitude, but she was disappointed. She would have to come up with the rest out of their bank account—unless of course she could make a deal with Ugo. Old Pietro promised that the money would be delivered by ten thirty the following morning.

If she and Filippo were due to go anywhere tonight, Isabella didn't give a damn, and she told Luigi to turn away people who might arrive at the door with the excuse that there was a crisis tonight—and they could interpret that as they wished, Isabella thought. Luigi was understanding, and most concerned, as was Elisabetta.

Ugo was prompt with another telephone call at seven, and though Isabella was alone in her bedroom, she played her part as though someone were listening, though no one could have been unless Luigi had picked up the living-room telephone. Isabella's voice betrayed anxiety, anger, and fear of what might happen to her husband. Ugo spoke briefly. She was to meet him in a tiny square which Isabella had never heard of—she scribbled the name down—at noon tomorrow, with 100,000,000 lire in old bills in 20,000 and 50,000 denominations in a shopping bag or basket, and then Filippo would be released at once on the edge of Rome. Ugo did not say where.

"Come *alone*. Filippo is well," Ugo said. "Goodbye, signora."

Vicente telephoned just afterward. Isabella told Vicente what she had to do, said that Filippo's father had come up with 75,000,000 and could the government provide the rest? Vicente said no, and wished Isabella and Filippo the best of luck.

And that was that. So early the next morning Isabella went to their bank and withdrew 25,000,000 lire from their savings, which left so little that she had to sign a check on their Swiss bank for a transfer when she got home. At half-past ten a chauffeur in uniform and puttees, with a bulge under his tunic that must have been a gun, arrived with a briefcase under each arm. Isabella took him into the bedroom for a transfer of money from the briefcases into the shopping bag—a black plastic bag belonging to Elisabetta. Isabella didn't feel like counting through all the soiled banknotes.

"You're sure it's exact?" she asked.

The calm and polite chauffeur said it was. He loaded the shopping bag for her, then took his leave with the briefcases.

Isabella ordered a taxi for eleven fifteen, because she had no idea how long it might take her to get to the little square, especially if they ran into a traffic jam somewhere. Elisabetta was worried, and asked for the tenth time, "Can't I come with you—just sit in the taxi, signora?"

"They will think you are a man in disguise with a gun," Isabella replied, though she intended to get out of the taxi a couple of streets away from the square, and dismiss the taxi.

The taxi arrived. Isabella said she should be back before one o'clock. She had looked up the square on her map of Rome, and had the map with her in case the taxi driver was vague.

"What a place!" said the driver. "I don't know it at all. Evidently you don't either."

"The mother of an old servant of mine lives here. I'm taking her some clothing," Isabella said by way of explaining the bulging but not very heavy shopping bag.

The driver let her out. Isabella had said she was uncertain of the house number, but could find out by asking neighbors. Now she was on her own, with a fortune in her right hand.

There was the little square, and there was Ugo, five minutes early, like herself, reading a newspaper on a bench. Isabella entered the little square slowly. It had a few ill-tended trees, a ground of square stones laid like a pavement. One old woman sat knitting on the only sunlit bench. It was a working-class neighborhood, or one mainly of old people, it seemed. Ugo got up and walked toward her.

"Giorno, signora," he said casually, with a polite nod, as if greeting an old acquaintance, and by his own walking led her toward the street pavement. "You're all right?"

"Yes. And—"

"He's quite all right. —Thank you for this." He glanced at her shopping bag. "Soon as we see everything's in order, we'll let Filippo—loose." His smile was reassuring.

"Where are we—"

"Just here," Ugo interrupted, pushing her to the left, toward the street, and a parked car's door suddenly swung open beside her. The push had not been a hard one, only rude and sudden enough to fluster Isabella for a moment. The man in the driver's seat had turned half around and had a pistol pointed at her, held low on the back of the front seat.

"Just be quiet, Signora Isabella, and there will be no trouble at all—nobody hurt at all," the man with the gun said.

Ugo got in beside her in back and slammed the door shut. The car started off.

It had not even occurred to Isabella to scream, she realized. She had a glimpse of a man with a briefcase under his arm, walking only two meters away on the pavement, his eyes straight ahead. They were soon out in the country. There were a few houses, but mostly it was fields and trees. The man driving the car wore a hat.

"Isn't it necessary that I *join* Filippo, Ugo?" she asked.

Ugo laughed, then asked the man driving to pull in at a roadside bar-restaurant.

Here Ugo got out, saying he would be just a minute.   He had looked into the shopping bag long enough to see that it contained money and was not partly stuffed with newspaper.   The man driving turned around in his seat.

"The signora will please be quiet," he said.   "Everything is all right."   He had the horrible accent of a Milan tough, attempting to be soothing to an unpredictable woman who might go off in a scream louder than a police siren.   In his nervousness he was chewing gum.

"Where are you taking me?"

Ugo was coming back.

Isabella soon found out.   They pulled in at a farmhouse whose occupants had evidently recently left—there were clothes on the line, dishes in the sink—but the only people now in the house seemed to be Isabella, Ugo, and his driver chum whom Ugo called Eddy.   Isabella looked at an ashtray, recognizing Filippo's Turkish cigarette stubs, noticed also the pack empty and uncrumpled on the floor.

"Filippo has been released, signora," Ugo said.   "He has money for a taxi and soon you should be able to phone him at home.   Sit down.   Would you like a coffee?"

"Take me back to Rome!" Isabella shouted.   But she knew.   They had kidnaped *her*.   "If you think there is any *more* money coming, you are quite mistaken, Ugo—*and you!*" she added to the smiling driver, an old slob now helping himself to whiskey.

"There is always more money," Ugo said calmly . . .

"Swine!" Isabella said.   "I should have known from the time you first stared into my bathroom!   That's your real occupation, you creep!"   A fear of assault crossed her mind, but only swiftly.   Her rage was stronger just now.   "After I tried to—to give you a break, turn a little money your way!   *Look* at all that money!"

Eddy was now sitting on the floor counting it, like a child with an absorbing new toy or game, except that a big cigar stuck out of his mouth.

"Sit down, signora.   All will be well when we telephone your husband."

Isabella sat down on a sagging sofa.   There was mud on the heels of her shoes from the filthy courtyard she had just walked across.   Ugo brought some warmed-over coffee.   Isabella learned that still another chum of Ugo's had driven Filippo in another car and dropped him somewhere to make his own way home.

"He is quite all right, signora," Ugo assured her, bringing a plate of awful-looking sliced lamb and hunks of cheese.   The other man was on his feet, and brought a basket of bread and a bottle of inferior wine.   The men were hungry.   Isabella took nothing, refusing even whiskey and wine.   When the men had finished eating, Ugo sent Eddy off in the car to telephone Filippo from somewhere.   The farmhouse had no telephone.   How Isabella wished she had brought her tear-gas gun!   But she had thought she would be among friends today.

Ugo sipped coffee, smoked a cigarette, and tried to assuage Isabella's anger.   "By tonight, by tomorrow morning you will be back home, signora.   No harm done!   A room to yourself here!   Even though the bed may not be as comfortable as the one you're used to."

Isabella refused to answer him, and bit her lip, thinking that she had got herself into an awful mess, had cost herself and Filippo 25,000,000 lire, and might cost them another 50,000,000 (or whatever she was worth) because Filippo's father might decide not to come up with the money to ransom her.

Eddy came back with an air of disappointment and reported in his disgusting slang that Signor Ghiardini had told him to go stuff himself.

"What?" Ugo jumped up from his chair. "We'll try again. We'll threaten—didn't you threaten—"

Eddy nodded. "He said . . ." Again the revolting phrase.

"We'll see how it goes tonight—around seven or so," said Ugo.

"How much are you asking?" Isabella was unable to repress the question any longer. Her voice had gone shrill.

"Fifty million, signora," replied Ugo.

"We simply haven't got it—not after *this!*" Isabella gestured toward the shopping bag, now in a corner of the room.

"Ha, ha," Ugo laughed softly. "The Ghiardinis haven't got another fifty million? Or the government? Or Papa Ghiardini?"

The other man announced that he was going to take a nap in the other room. Ugo turned on the radio to some pop music. Isabella remained seated on the uncomfortable sofa. She had declined to remove her coat. Ugo paced about, thinking, talking a little to himself, half drunk with the realization of all the money in the corner of the room. The gun lay on the center table near the radio. She looked at it with an idea of grabbing it and turning it on Ugo, but she knew she could not keep both men at bay if Eddy woke up.

When Eddy did wake up and returned to the room, Ugo announced that he was going to try to telephone Filippo, while Eddy kept watch on Isabella. "No funny business," said Ugo like an army officer, before going out.

It was just after six.

Eddy tried to engage her in conversation about revolutionary tactics, about Ugo's having been a journalist once, a photographer also (Isabella could imagine what kind of photographer). Isabella was angry and bored, and hated herself for replying even slightly to Eddy's moronic ramblings. He was talking about making a down payment on a house with the money he had gained from Filippo's abduction. Ugo would also start leading a more decent life, which was what he deserved, said Eddy.

"He deserves to be behind bars for the protection of the *public!*" Isabella shot back.

The car had returned. Ugo entered with his slack mouth even slacker, a look of puzzlement on his brow. "Gotta let her go, he may have traced the call," Ugo said to Eddy, and snapped his fingers for action.

Eddy at once went for the shopping bag and carried it out to the car.

"Your husband says you can go to hell," said Ugo. "He will not pay one lire."

It suddenly sank into Isabella. She stood up, feeling scared, feeling naked somehow, even though she still wore her coat over her dress. "He is joking.

He'll—'' But somehow she knew Filippo wouldn't. "Where're you taking me now?"

Ugo laughed. He laughed heartily, rocking back as he always did, laughing at Isabella and also at himself. "So I have lost fifty million! A pity, eh? Big pity. But the joke is on *you!* Hah! Ha, ha, ha! Come on, Signora Isabella, what've you got in your purse? Let's see." He took her purse rudely from her hands.

Isabella knew she had about twenty thousand in her billfold. This Ugo laid with a large gesture on the center table, then turned off the radio.

"Let's go," he said, indicating the door, smiling. Eddy had started the car. Ugo's happy mood seemed to be contagious. Eddy began laughing too at Ugo's comments. *The lady was worth nothing!* That was the idea. *La donna niente,* they sang.

"You won't get away with this for long, you piece of filth!" Isabella said to Ugo.

More laughter.

"Here! Fine!" yelled Ugo who was with Isabella in the back seat again, and Eddy pulled the car over to the edge of the road.

Where were they? Isabella had thought they were heading for Rome, but wasn't sure. Yes. She saw some high-rise apartment buildings. A truck went by, close, as she got out with Ugo, half pulled by him.

"Shoes, signora! Ha, ha!" He pushed her against the car and bent to take off her pumps. She kicked him, but he only laughed. She swung her handbag, catching him on the head with it, and nearly fell herself as he snatched off her second shoe. Ugo jumped, with the shoes in his hand, back into the car which roared off.

To be shoeless in silk stockings was a nasty shock. Isabella began walking—toward Rome. She could see lights coming on here and there in the twilight dimness. She'd hitch a ride to the next roadside bar and telephone for a taxi, she thought, pay the taxi when she got home. A large truck passed her by as if blind to her frantic waving. So did a car with a single man in it. Isabella was ready to hitch a lift with anyone!

She walked on, realizing that her stockings were now torn and open at the bottom, and when she stopped to pick something out of one foot, she saw blood. It was more than fifteen minutes later when Isabella made her painful way to a restaurant on the opposite of the road where she begged the use of the telephone.

Isabella did not at all like the smile of the young waiter who looked her up and down and was plainly surmising what must have happened to her: a boy friend had chucked her out of his car. Isabella telephoned a taxi company's number which the waiter provided. There would be at least ten minutes to wait, she was told, so she stood by the coat rack at the front of the place, feeling miserable and ashamed with her dirty feet and torn stockings. Passing waiters glanced at her. She had to explain to the proprietor—a stuffy type—that she was waiting for a taxi.

The taxi arrived, Isabella gave her address, and the driver looked dubious, so

Isabella had to explain that her husband would pay the fee at the other end.   She was almost in tears.

Isabella fell against the porter's bell, as if it were home itself.   Giorgio opened the doors.   Filippo came across the court, scowling.

"The taxi—" Isabella said.

Filippo was reaching into a pocket.   "As if I had anything left!"

Isabella took the last excruciating steps across the courtyard to the door out of which Elisabetta was now running to help her.

Elisabetta made tea for her.   Isabella sat in the tub, soaking her feet, washing off the filth of Ugo and his ugly chum.   She applied surgical spirits to the soles of her feet, then put on clean white woolen booties and a dressing gown.   She cast one furious glance at the bathroom window, sure Ugo would never come back.

As soon as she came out of her bathroom, Filippo said, "I suppose you re-member—tonight we have the Greek consul coming to dinner with his wife.   And two other men.   Six in all.   I was going to receive them alone—make some excuse."   His tone was icy.

Isabella did remember, but had somehow thought all that would be canceled. Nothing was canceled.   She could see it now: life would go on as usual, not a single date would be canceled.   They were poorer.   That was all.   Isabella rested in her bed, with some newspapers and magazines, then got up and began to dress. Filippo came in, not even knocking first.

"Wear the peach-colored dress tonight—not that one," he said.   "The Greeks need cheering up."

Isabella began removing the dark blue dress she had put on.

"I know you arranged all this," Filippo continued.   "They were ready to kill me, those hoodlums—or at least they acted like it.   My father is furious!   What stupid arrangements!   I can also make some arrangements.   Wait and see!"

Isabella said nothing.   And *her* future arrangements?   Well, she might make some too.   She gave Filippo a look.   Then she gritted her teeth as she squeezed her swollen feet into "the right shoes" for the evening.   When she got up, she had to walk with a limp.

NEDRA TYRE

Locks Won't Keep You Out

L eave me alone.

Terror of you paralyzes me, nails me to the threshold. My hands hesitate to open a door. I'm afraid you're on the other side.

I can't sleep. After short troubled naps I wake with the sensation you've been hovering over me. These last few days I've convinced myself it's safe to walk only when the sun is shining so I'll be warned of your presence by your shadow.

I don't go to museums anymore. They have too many dark and secluded nooks where you could find me.

My concert tickets go unused; in the darkened auditorium when the music reaches a crescendo you could easily crush out my life while my shouts of protest are drowned by the percussion instruments.

My mail goes unanswered and I refuse invitations. I've lied out of attending committee meetings, pretending that minor illnesses keep me from dinners and parties.

I've never been a coward—what had to be faced I faced. Yet I can't face your malice.

Perhaps you're enraged because I have ignored you. No, ignored is too strong a word. Disdained would be a more accurate way of putting it. I suppose I do have some of Aunt Carrie's arrogance. She wasn't a snob. She just had a way of walking straight past some people without seeing them—she didn't seem to know they were there. I honestly didn't know you were there. I couldn't believe it when you began to threaten me. When I realized your intentions were deadly, that it was my life you were after, I refused to believe it. I called myself an imaginative fool.

Why I despise you most of all—rather, why I despise my fear of you most of all—is that my fear makes me oblivious of everything else. I don't even notice the weather. I have loved weather, no matter what form it takes. Its ridiculous caprices that can begin a morning at twenty degrees and a few hours later have the thermometer soaring to summer heat—those caprices have delighted me. Hot. Cold. No extreme mattered. I responded to it all with joy.

Now I don't pay any attention to the weather, and since I don't notice its vagaries the weather has turned into my enemy. I find myself shivering, not having put on warm enough clothing. I plunge into rain without an umbrella or sink ankle-deep in puddles without my boots.

One day my fear of you made me panic and I telephoned the police for protection. My damsel-in-distress, ladylike trills had an immediate effect.   Within minutes a policeman arrived at my door.

But I had no crime to report, only your vague threats.   I began to apologize for having summoned the policeman on a fool's errand.   Immediately he reassured me.   I had reason to be afraid, he insisted, as he looked around at the paintings and the silver.   He hoped I had good locks.   And surely I wasn't ever foolish enough to let anyone enter whom I didn't know.

If only I could tempt you with the things I've accumulated, appease you with a minor Gauguin or a George III silver beaker.

The policeman went around appraising the security, suggesting a stronger lock here and there.

Locks won't keep you out.   You're not interested in valuables.   What you're after is my life.   I'm positive of that.   Yet never before have I felt the inevitability of anything; life has always offered many paths and one could easily retreat from a path already begun.   Trips to be taken always held as many choices as there were air routes and if one residence didn't prove satisfactory there were dozens of houses and apartments—a planetful of locations—to select from.   A jewel could be recut and reset and a joyless love affair ended.   To be pleased was only a matter of making another and wiser choice.

But there is no choice now.

The paths have all converged and they lead straight to you.   They lead to my death from you.

If only these last days were free of dread and the short time remaining to me were not ruined by constant apprehension.   I should have thought that when one knows she is looking on something for the last time it would be with a heightened response.   Flowers are blooming—roses and lilies-of-the-valley are bursting with beauty and fragrance.   The shelves are heavy with books I've promised myself the pleasure of reading again.

But the flowers might as well be rank and the books printed in Sanskrit for all the delight they will ever give me.

It isn't as if I haven't made preparations for death.   My last will and testament has been sensibly drawn.   My daughter is well provided for; *objets d'art* are to go to museums; and there are legacies and keepsakes for my friends.

I detest myself for this cowardly preoccupation with my annihilation.   Newspapers and TV and the radio should have hardened us all to death—hundreds dashed to death in tornadoes shown on the TV shortly before dinner, thousands demolished in a tidal wave in the paper read with the morning coffee, unnumbered victims crushed in earthquakes announced on the radio as one sips a cocktail before lunch.

Death and danger are everywhere and much closer home than the announced tragedy delivered with the morning paper along with the advertisements of month-end clearance sales or reported on TV between the detergent commercials.   There can be a car out of control only a block away or a fire can devour a house on the next street.

But all those tragedies are dealt by destiny impersonally and without malice.

There's nothing impersonal in your malice toward me.

Please—I beg you—leave me alone. I was a dutiful child. I obeyed my parents. I was polite to my elders. I was a loving wife and a conscientious mother. I've been committed to good causes.

Only listen to that—you have me whining—I've been degraded by you. I'm trying to cash in my chits of good behavior. I'm sniveling for mercy, sucking up to you for leniency.

The telephone is ringing. I'm not going to answer it. I know it's you. I know what you'll say.

The ringing goes on and on and on. Finally it stops. After a while there's a harsh knock on the door. Then two hands are pounding. The bell works perfectly. Yet the person outside is too excited to use the bell. It can't be you. You're much too sneaking to knock and ask for admission.

I open the door and my daughter is standing outside. I am always amazed by her beauty and her lack of knowledge of it or at least of her refusal to take advantage of it. How lovely to have a child like her.

"Mama," she says, "what on earth's the matter?" Not even a frown of worry can disturb her beauty. "I telephoned and there was no answer and suddenly I realized that it's been a week since you've called. I know how busy you are but you've never gone this long before without phoning me. Darling, come home with me now. It would be such a pleasure to have you. Please?"

I love my daughter and her husband and her children, but I can't infect their house with my fear. I can't spoil their happiness. I can't have you following me there. I beg off with a promise to come as soon as I can manage.

When she has kissed me and left I begin to work compulsively.

I polish silver. I tidy the broom closet. I arrange pots and pans in neat rows and realign the already regimented rows of canned food on the pantry shelves.

Mollie won't like this. She hates for me to tidy the kitchen or to polish the silver. Again and again she has said she ought to be out working for a woman who needs her more than I do. She says it makes her feel I no longer trust her to do the job I pay her to do.

But I must occupy myself. I must somehow black out my terror of you.

The shelves are in meticulous order and the silver glistens. The kitchen is spotless.

There's nothing else to do.

Yet I must occupy myself.

I can play solitaire.

There's something infinitely soothing in knowing that the cards may all be played one upon the other, black and red in descending order. At least there's a possibility that they may all find their prescribed places.

I don't often win. Still it's possible. And when I do win there's such a feeling of exuberance. Once I even won twice in succession. I wonder how often that has happened. I'm sure the probability of winning twice in succession in solitaire is most unlikely.

I take the cards from the second drawer of the red lacquered desk and then sit down at the fruitwood card table.   I like the feel of the cards.   As I riffle them they flutter like a bird beating its wings in my hands.

I play the first card.

It's the ace of spades.

Death.

I won't believe it.   I refuse to believe it.

Somehow my fear of you has infected the cards.

Yet I know the cards can't respond to my fear.   There is no such thing as inanimate objects responding to human moods and emotions.   My terror cannot have summoned up the card that signifies death.

Perhaps my fear did infect the cards.

If the mind can influence cards, then I will influence them.   I pick the cards up from their various small stacks and shuffle them again.   I must concentrate on a good luck card.   The nine of hearts or the ten of diamonds—or, best of all, the ace of diamonds.

I shuffle and riffle the cards.   Again, against my palms there is that feeling of the heartbeat of a bird or some small caged animal.   I distribute the cards and prissily take time to make the seven stacks symmetrical.

I turn the first card face upward.

The ace of spades.

I push the ace of spades from me, then grasp it and try to tear it.   It remains intact and blood oozes from the thin cut the card has made on my right forefinger.

I need reassurance—not reassurance from a wise professional or a dear friend but from a very particular source.

The walls of my large apartment seem to contract.   I must escape before they crush me.

I go outside and hail a taxi, and as I enter it I repress my fear.   I insist to myself that I'm on a lark, a small diversion, something foolish, but forgivable; any bored housewife could understand my action.

When I've ridden several miles I dismiss the taxi and tip the driver lavishly as if he's done me a special favor or service.   I have not been let out at my real destination and must walk four blocks to my goal.

Outside there is a sign of a large hand marked like a road map, but its routes are the life line, the heart line, the line of destiny, and beneath it in small letters there is a legend: *Madame Sybil—the Past, Present, and Future.*

I have teased my friends who have come here and have smiled over their insistence that they don't believe a word of what Madame Sybil says; but going to her is fun, like getting a new hairdo or finding an unexpected bargain in an antique shop. But I had no such feeling now.   I was here from absolute necessity.

I pushed the bell.

There was a long wait and the door was jerked open.

Madame looked like someone caught unaware.   She had the petulance of someone aroused needlessly from sleep.   Grease was smeared around her mouth beyond the splotched and spotted lipstick.   Her tongue explored her teeth, as if for bits of food, and I realized I must have surprised her at a meal.   She had the ruffled, somewhat annoyed air of someone summoned to an emergency; there was nothing about her of a sybil who could foretell the future or divine the past or give me sage counsel on how to act.   But with a commanding motion that contradicted her disheveled appearance, she waved me down the hall to a doorway, then swept past me.

In a room cluttered with furniture she squinted against the sun eking through the slats of some dirty and disjointed Venetian blinds, and with theatrical flicks of her wrist she adjusted the blinds so that we were in darkness.

Then from somewhere behind me a thin light wavered and a candle projected unsteady shadows on the walls.   There was another flickering of a match and almost immediately I began to smell incense of such stifling intensity that I coughed. Madame slid into a chair across from me at the heavily draped table and said, "Ten dollars."   Her voice was as bland and impersonal as that of a checkout clerk at a supermarket counter demanding the amount to be paid for a cart of groceries.

I fumbled in my pocketbook.   I shuffled through credit cards and dry-cleaning tickets and at last found some money.   A lizard's tongue could not have been as quick as her hand darting for the money and there was a detour into her large bosom to bank the fee before her hands came to rest in her lap.

I waited for her to speak, to ask me why I was here, what I wanted to know. But there was only silence.   After a while I was about to question her when she said angrily, "I can't tell you anything."

"I don't understand," I said.   "You tell other people things.   You've talked to a number of my friends and acquaintances.   Last week you told Eloise Smithson she was going to get a legacy."

"I can't tell you anything," she said again, as if I hadn't heard her the first time.   "Take your money and leave."   Her right hand dived inside her bodice and then my bill sailed across the table and lighted like a crippled moth on the sleeve of my coat.   "Take the money and go."   Her voice was shrill.

I did not move.   Then she screamed at me.   She was like a very poor actress overplaying a scene.   Her mouth curled in anger.   "Leave this house at once," she ordered.

I left with as much dignity as I could muster.   Even as she shrieked at me to leave I got up slowly and smoothed my skirt and tucked the money back into my bag and snapped the fastener and walked down the dim hall with composure, but once I was on the street I began to run.

I thrust people aside.   I scrambled onto a bus, then got off.   I took another bus in the direction from which I had just come.   I was like a spy in a third-rate film who is trying to shake pursuers.   I ran down an alley.   I lost myself in the crowds of a department store.

I was trying to evade you.

Then I took a taxi home, to be swallowed up by the lobby of the apartment house where I live.   Far beyond me, as unapproachable as an astronaut in orbit, was the receptionist behind the shield of a heavy glass partition.   Nearer was the bank of elevators.   I knew that none of my dodges or detours had worked and that you were in one of the elevators waiting for me.

I dared not risk taking an elevator.   I left the elevators and skirted the gigantic plants in their huge cachepots that lined the passage to the stairway.   I pulled at the door beneath the discreet sign marked STAIRS and scurried up the steps.   I was tempted to stop at each landing to rest but fear of you made me race to my floor and terror forced me to brush so close against the wall of the corridor that paint scaled off onto my sleeve.

I had to stop for breath and I looked through one of a long row of tall windows hung with full thick draperies.   I knew you were hiding somewhere in that endless line of heavily swathed windows.   I looked down on the lawn with its neatly clipped boxwood hedges and rosebushes bulging with blooms, and then I ran down the gantlet of windows expecting you to grab me.

At my door I pawed through my bag for the key.   My trembling hand made it clatter outside the lock.   I finally inserted the key and entered my apartment.

With the double-locked door at my back I whimpered with relief, but fear had drained me.   I stood as still as an autistic child, as if any movement from me might arouse your wrath.

At last I fell across the bed in exhaustion and went to sleep, and then, after a while I awoke.   My bed was a grave.   I couldn't move.   Wind blew through the windows.   The curtains fluttered, swirled—one reached out and stroked my cheek. I had left the windows beside my bed open and the fire escape was just outside. It was an invitation to you to enter, an overt sign of welcome.   I was like a virgin who invites rape.   I was like a miser who entices thieves.

I glanced at the clock.   Another night is over.   There is some small comfort in the precise and orderly ticking of the clock, but only dread in the prospect of another day that will wither and become rancid by my fear of you.

Suppose I were to surrender.   I'm weary of suspense.   I'm tired of being wary.

But I won't surrender.   Keep away from me.   Mollie will be here soon.   She'll protect me from you.   I think that's her key in the lock now.   Don't touch me. Keep away—

"I think she was afraid of you, Doctor."

"No, Mollie, she wasn't afraid of me.   We've known each other since childhood. There was only one thing in the world for her to be afraid of—death."

CELIA FREMLIN

Waiting for the Police

The topsoil had been easy. He remembered how lightly the spade had tossed the loose earth this way and that in the moonlight. For those first minutes it had all been as effortless as in a dream—the strange euphoria of the previous evening was still flowing strongly in his veins, giving his thin young arms the strength, almost, of a grown man.

But two feet down he came to the clay—the sullen, sodden, implacable London clay; and it was only then that the dreamlike omnipotence began to drain out of him. Now the sweat of terror began to glisten on his forehead and his skinny adolescent arms began to quiver with exhaustion.

The length was all right. The uprooted dahlias and the shaggy, seeding willow-herb lay blanched in the moonlight along half the length of the devastated autumn flowerbed. But only two feet deep! It would have to be deeper than that, much deeper. Four feet? Six? Years of wide but desultory reading of lurid paper-backed stories had not provided him with this sort of solid, factual information; but any fool could see that a depth of two feet would not be enough.

He was crying now, in a sort of weak fury at the obstinate, devilish clay. He would have stamped and stormed at it, throwing a tantrum like a toddler, if it had not been for all those silent, curtained windows overlooking, like lightly closed eyes, the whole row of little back gardens. Any moment now one of those sleeping eyes might open, with a streak of yellow light between the curtains, and a sly sleepy voice would call out, "What's going on there?" or maybe, more raucously, "Shut that bleedin' row!"

This soft squelch of spade on clay—*was* it a bleedin' row? Of course it was— it seemed to him that it must be heard for miles! And then there would be more voices, more cracks of light, eyes everywhere, queries called across the cloying darkness. Would it be best, when all this began happening, to make a clean breast of it? To tell them straightaway, in a ringing shout, before they came flitting out of the doors and alleyways, over the fences, like ghosts attracted by the smell of blood, to find out what was going on?

"I have killed my love," he would yell to them across the gardens, across the closed, listening night swept silent by the moon. "I have killed my love, my only love. She was with Cyril—Cyril from the Gas Board offices, with his posh voice and natty suit. She was standing by the front door, I could see her face in the moonlight, and when she saw me coming she laughed. She pointed, and she whispered to Cyril, and then he laughed, too.

"That was their last laugh, though, the last laugh they'll ever have. He ran away like I've never seen a man run, nor even a rat; and her, she's lying there in the passage where I dragged her. I hope—yes, the thing I hope most of all—is that she was still alive just long enough to see him run like that, see him run away like a rat, and never lifted a finger to protect her! That's what I hope—she was alive just long enough to see—to see it, and to know it, before she died."

The clay, the damnable accursed clay! Tears of fury and terror streaked the boy's thin moon-blanched face; his breath came in feeble sobs, like the sobs of the wet clay under the onslaughts of his jabbing spade.

But he did not give up. He couldn't give up, for soon it would be dawn, and then bright morning, and the cover of darkness would be gone. So he struggled on, and gradually, inch by inch, as if dragging at the very intestines of the earth, he got the clay to move; and presently, into his trance of exhaustion, there came, dully, the knowledge that the hole was deep enough at last. As deep as it would ever be. Deep enough anyway, for his love, his sweet treacherous love.

Oh, but the dangers still ahead! With morning, the neighbors would come. "Getting busy in the garden, eh? Them dahlias—you didn't oughter 'a' pulled up them dahlias, not while they're still flowering. What a shame! Just look at them, all them colors!"

"To plant a new lilac, you say? But you didn't need to've cleared the whole bloomin' bed, a whole six foot of it, just to plant a lilac bush! Besides, what does a young lad like you want with a lilac? It's only a rented room you got in there, innit? You'll be gone off, lad, somewheres else, that's for sure, long before that lilac can bloom!"

But as the days went by, the questioning died down. Gradually the horticultural experts of the little street lost interest in the boy's folly, and turned their attention back to their own gardens; and at last the boy himself began to sleep again at night, instead of lying tense as whipcord through the black hours, waiting for the police to come for him.

And so the autumn passed, and a long sodden December, and while it was still winter, before even the crocuses had begun to show their first leaves, tiny green things had already begun to sprout in the flat untidy soil above his own true love. Weeds, presumably, but he never found out for certain; nor did he ever know whether the lilac bloomed, for, just as the neighbors had predicted, before this could possibly have happened, he was gone.

"Now, come along, Mr. Parsons! Drink up! Just look at Mrs. Carruthers, she's on her second cup already, you're getting left all behind. Come on, Mr. Parsons, wakey, wakey! What's the good of bringing you out into the garden for your tea when you just—oh, dear! Shall I hold the saucer for you? There, is that better? Can you manage now?"

The young woman's voice went on and on, bright and bracing, but he had been at the Old People's Home a long time now, and he no longer listened. Nor was he bothered any longer by the sweet tepid tea which his throat was obediently gulping from the expertly tipped cup.

He was aware only of the lilac in full bloom, above and all around him, and the sweet May breeze stirring the mauve blossoms, heavy with bees.   Now that he was more than ninety years old, he was finding it hard to distinguish the sweet summer days, one from another, over the long years.

He was a little confused, too, about the lilacs—so many of them there had been, in gardens here and gardens there, blooming and fading, through ninety springtimes. By now they were all the same lilac, and beneath it lay his love, his first and only love, with her bright hair and her green enchanting eyes.

Over the long years he had waited for the police; but they had never caught him, never even suspected anything.   He recalled how, over the years, the guilt and terror had gradually faded, to be buried at last, forever, under the turmoil of the rushing adult years.   Marriage—children—work; success and failure; and more work; they had come and gone, and now at last he was close to her again, close to his first love, as lovely still as on the day he had killed her.

Killed her.   How thankful he was now that he had done it!   That he had killed her then, on that moonlit autumn night, in the full flower of her loveliness, more than seventy years ago!   A murderer in shining armor, he had saved her from this Old People's Home as surely as St. George had saved his princess from the dragon.

They would never get her now!   Not for her the shameful, slobbering gulps of tea from a cup that her trembling hands could no longer manage; not for her the wheel chair, or the bright, professional voices impatiently jollying her through the dim dead days.

Not for her the crutches, the pointless tottering round and round the smooth, terrible lawns.   Not for her the ill-fitting teeth, the mislaid spectacles, the endless, feeble bickering of the old, as thin as the mewing of seagulls left stranded by a tide that has gone out too far ever to turn again.

"Thank God I murdered you, my darling," he murmured into the lilac-scented air; and the nurse, noticing that old Mr. Parsons was mumbling to himself again, and slobbering over his cup, decided it was time to wheel him indoors.

PATRICIA McGERR

Nothing But the Truth

That Sunday was, in its beginning, no different from any other Sunday. I got up about 7:30 and put the coffee on to boil while I shaved and dressed. Then I had my usual breakfast—corn flakes and milk, toast with grape jelly, and coffee. I was finishing the second cup when the bell rang to let me know that a car was driving into the service station.

I hurried down the stairs, through the office, and out to the pumps. It was a '69 Pontiac with out-of-state tags and it took 12.8 gallons of high test. I entered the sale in my log, noting the time as 8:15, then went back to my living quarters to make the bed and wash the dishes.

It was kind of chilly for the end of April, so I pulled a sweater on over my work shirt. With the chores done, I settled down in the office to tot up the week's receipts and write an order for the supplies I needed for the month ahead.

Business is always slow on Sunday mornings. My station is at the junction of State Highway 40 and the road to Morristown. That's a town in name only—a two-block business district surrounded by farms—and the people don't do much Sunday gadding. It's a good day for paperwork and I finished with only two interruptions, both from the highway. A '66 Mercury took 12 gallons of regular and a '63 Volks wanted directions to a turnoff he'd missed a mile and a half back.

I was putting the order into its envelope when I heard the first car on the Morristown road. By the sound it was traveling faster than is safe or legal on the two-lane gravel surface that is still as winding as the cowpath that provided its original design. There's a stand of timber behind my station, so I can't see vehicles till they're almost here. This one hardly slowed for the turn into the station and pulled up beside the pumps with tires screeching. It was Chad Bascom in his '72 Chevy.

"Fill 'er up, Gimpy," he said.

I walked to the back of the car with the heat starting someplace near the bottom of my stomach and rising in waves to the top of my head. My fingers were unsteady when I unscrewed the top of his gas tank and I was afraid, when I set the nozzle down, he'd hear the clatter and get satisfction from knowing he'd pushed me once more to blind and trembling rage.

You'd think that after twenty years I'd be immune to Bascom's insults, that a single word, so often repeated, would have lost its power to send my blood pressure

403

soaring.   I stood still while three gallons flowed through the hose and while I built
a fantasy of lighting a match and bringing gas and flame together to turn his car
into a fiery coffin.   Then, as the throbbing in my temples eased, I picked up the
spray bottle and paper towels and cleaned his back window.   When that was done
I did the same to the front, keeping my lips tightpressed to hold back an answer
to anything he might say.   But today, for a change, he didn't keep on riding me,
just sat in stony silence till I was forced to speak.

"Check under the hood?" I asked.

"The way you move," he snapped, "that would take all day.   Put the lid on
and let me out of here."

The pump cut off at 13.2.   I squeezed out a few more drops to make it an even
$5 and capped his tank.   He thrust a $5 bill at me and had the car moving almost
before I could step out of the way.   I went into the office, put the money in the
register, looked at the clock on my desk, and entered it in the log: "10:10—13.2
regular—$5."

Then I stood at the window and watched Chad Bascom's car head north on the
highway.   There's a straight stretch of almost a mile with good visibility, but even
after he was out of sight I still stood there with my eyes on the white-lined asphalt.
Going to the city, I thought, on his way to a good time—with Ruth, predictably,
left behind.

I wasn't really seeing the highway.   My thoughts, as always after an encounter
with Chad, turned inward.   Gimpy he'd called me and gimpy he'd made me.
Time had honed my anger to a bitter edge and my hatred now had a depth and
hardness that would have been beyond my capabilities at the time it happened.

I was a year out of Ag College then and had put my savings into the old Mullen
place.   The mortgage payments were manageable, the spring weather benign, and
a good crop would have permitted me to buy a tractor and modernize the kitchen.
After the harvest Ruth Hadley and I were going to be married.   We weren't
engaged—folks in our community don't formalize things that way; but ever since
high school it was taken for granted that as soon as I was able to make my own
way and had a place to take her, it would be Ruthie and me for life.   Nobody had
to tell me how lucky I was.

Ruth wasn't the prettiest girl in our class.   Thelma Frankes, with her blonde
curls and china-blue eyes, had that distinction.   But in any group it was Ruth your
eyes kept coming back to.   Her dark brown hair had a sheen that caught the play
of light and shadow.   Her eyes were brown too and held a glint of humor that
even her most serious mood couldn't quite vanquish.   What held attention, though,
was her sheer aliveness, the sense she passed to all around of a deep and bubbling
joy.

I never knew what she saw in me.   I was that nice Sprague boy.   Good old
Nate Sprague.   Steady, honest, hard-working, dependable.   All the adjectives
were dull.   But Ruth looked at me as if we shared a wonderful secret.   And I
could never look at her without a sense of inner singing.   Not in those days.

That June was the fifth reunion of our high-school graduating class.   We met
in the gym and danced to records and reminisced.   There were platters loaded with

sandwiches and a bowl of punch made from grape juice blended with ginger ale. Chad Bascom's class was holding its tenth reunion in the cafeteria. Late in the evening he crossed the hall to the gym. I was dancing with Ruth when I noticed him first. He was standing near the door looking over the crowd with something in his expression that was like a cattleman at an auction. I wondered whom he was looking for and then forgot him until a few moments later I felt a sharp rap on my shoulder.

"Cutting in, partner," he said.

That's an alien custom in our county. When we bring a girl to a party we dance with her all evening. Or maybe, if two or three couples come together, we trade off a few dances within the group. But Chad was an older man with big-city ways. I looked at Ruth and she gave her little what's-it-matter shrug, so I let him dance with her.

At the time it didn't seem important. I leaned against the wall and watched them. Together they made a very pretty picture. Like him or not, no one could deny Chad's handsomeness. He was big, well over six feet, with rock-hard muscles. And he was a far better dancer than I. Ruth's natural rhythm matched his and they seemed to float across the floor as a single body.

"Better watch out, Nate." A classmate stopped beside me, only half kidding. "That Bascom's a grade-A wolf."

I knew Chad's reputation, but it didn't worry me. I was too sure of Ruthie. When the dance ended he kept his arm around her and guided her to the refreshment table. I followed and saw him fill two paper cups from a pint bottle he took from his back pocket.

"This'll put back our bounce," he said.

"No, thank you," she refused politely. "I'd rather have punch."

"Punch with no punch in it." He pushed his own brew toward her. "Come on, baby, live a little."

I went to the bowl, ladled punch into a cup, and carried it to Ruth. Chad gave me an ugly look.

"Don't crowd me, youngster," he said. "I'm taking care of the lady."

I tried to ignore him and offered her the cup. He knocked it out of my hand and purple drops spattered her white linen dress. She looked frightened. Chad, I realized, had already drunk most of his pint.

"Let's go home, Nate," she said.

"Yes, sure." I moved to her side, but Chad put the flat of his hand on my chest and pushed me away.

"Stay out of this, small fry," he warned. "I said I'd take care of the lady." He took Ruth's arm, tightening his hold as she tried to pull away. "I'll see you home, baby, by the longest way round."

I sprang at him with a fist that was aimed at his chin but landed on his shoulder. His surprise and my momentum nearly knocked him off balance, but my advantage was brief. He was four inches taller and forty pounds heavier. Almost before I knew it I was on the floor with a feeling that the room was rocking like a boat. He nudged my side with the steel-tipped toe of his boot.

"Get up, boy," he ordered.   "I got some more things to show you."

I tried to raise my head and focus my eyes.   Chad drew back his foot and kicked me with stunning force.   The last thing I saw was his mouth stretched in an exultant grin.

I was in the hospital for five months.   The hip bone was shattered and at first it looked as if I'd spend the rest of my life on crutches.   Twice Ruth drove ninety miles to visit me.   The first time I asked her not to come again.   The second time I had the doctor tell her that seeing her was bad for my morale.   That was true.   I'd been shamed in front of her and I couldn't stand being reminded of that or of all that I'd so nearly had and lost.

Later they moved me to a hospital in another state where there was a surgeon especially skilled in bone grafts.   The operation was successful and I came home almost as good as new, except that my left leg was two inches shorter than my right.

While I was healing, my neighbors pitched in to save my crop.   And the county sheriff had a long talk with Chad.   He offered him a choice—pay my medical bills or face trial on assault charges.   As a result I left the hospital in fair financial condition.   But a farmer needs to work on two good legs.   So I sold my land and made a down payment on this gas station.   With the second story fixed up as a small apartment it makes a good enough living for a man alone.

Since Ruth and I weren't formally engaged, there was nothing to break off.   I kept away from her and when her mother called or her friends came round I told them it was over and Ruth should forget me.   A woman like Ruth deserves a whole man and I just couldn't take her pity.   Chad moved quickly to fill the vacuum and those same friends described the smoothness of his operation.

When sober and trying, Chad could display great charm.   He came to her first with profuse apologies for his behavior while under the influence.   He let her know that he was taking care of my medical expenses, but he carefully neglected to mention Sheriff Crane's alternative.   He took her to movies and dances and was always a perfect gentleman.   He won her mother with flattery and her younger brother with presents.   He told her he loved her and needed her and wanted nothing in life so much as to make her happy.

Six months after I began living above my service station, Ruth became Mrs. Chad Bascom.

I tried not to hate him.   A man shouldn't be held responsible for what he does when he's drunk.   I had been a fool to stand up to him.   He hadn't taken Ruth from me, I'd given her up.   Those were the things I told myself to hold down the bile that surged up at the thought of him.   After a while I was able, most of the time, to put him out of my mind.

He seldom patronized my station and I seldom left the premises.   It was painful going out among my old friends with things so changed and I had everything I needed right at home.   The weekly bookmobile supplied plenty of reading material, and daily banter with my customers was sufficient social life.   So I was a long time learning how things really were between Ruth and Chad.

I heard a few things.   People who came by the station dropped hints that he was giving her a bad time.   They told stories about his jealousy, how he raged if she smiled too brightly at another man.   Some even said he beat her, that they'd seen bruises on her face and arms.   But I know how easily gossip starts in a small town and how quickly it can grow.   I didn't encourage them to talk and dismissed their tales as puffed-up versions of normal crises in married life.   Perhaps, I told myself, they were exaggerating on purpose, thinking it would cheer me to believe the marriage had turned sour.   Then Ruth's mother began to call me and I discovered the reports weren't exaggerated at all.

Mrs. Hadley and I had been close in the early days.   My own mother died when I was thirteen and in high school and when I was eating more dinners at the Hadley house than at home, I had started to call her Ma.   She seemed to like it and joked sometimes about my being the first young man to choose a mother-in-law ahead of a wife.

For the first few years after the marriage I didn't hear from her.   Then Ruth's brother went off to college and Mrs. Hadley's arthritis got so bad she couldn't go out much.   I guess that gave us a special bond—both alone, both crippled.   Anyway, she began to phone and tell me her worries.   Mostly they had to do with Chad's treatment of Ruth.

"Ruthie doesn't tell me half of it," she said.   "She tries to pretend everything's all right.   But I've seen her eyes red and puffy with crying.   Sometimes there are black and blue marks she can't hide.   And I've heard him yell at her as if she were his servant.   Remember, Nathan, how bright and pretty she always was? You wouldn't know her now."

Others too spoke of these changes.   Ruth had lost her looks and her vitality, and she seemed to care little about her appearance.   Chad no longer had cause for jealousy, but that didn't improve his temper.   Instead he berated her for being such a poor stick that no other man would look at her.   It was as if he'd set out deliberately to break her spirit and then, having succeeded, made the deterioration that he caused another mark against her.   He used it too as excuse for infidelity.

He drove often to the city, sometimes stayed two or three days.   The rumor was he had a woman there.   On his return he'd be more cruel than ever to Ruth, as if that was a way of working off his guilt.

I didn't want to hear these things, but I couldn't endure not knowing either. One of the worst times was after her miscarriage.   She was in the hospital for nearly a week and Mrs. Hadley was barely coherent when she told me about it.

"He hit her in the stomach," she sobbed.   "A woman four months pregnant! Now she can't have children, the doctor says.   But maybe that's a blessing.   It's bad enough what he's done to my girl, but to see an innocent little one at his mercy—who could bear it?   You should have married her, Nathan."   It was the nearest she ever came to reproach me.   "When you turned away from her he was there.   And none of us saw the brute inside him."

Ruth's friends tried to persuade her to leave him.   Some thought he should be sent to jail and Sheriff Crane went to the hospital to ask if she was willing to bring charges.   But she gave everyone the same answer.   Chad was her husband.   She'd promised to honor and obey him for better or for worse and she was bound, whatever he did, by that promise. If there's a thin line between a saint and a fool, Ruth Bascom walked very close to that line.

A peculiar thing happened after that. Chad began coming more and more often to my service station. Some perverse streak seemed to make him want to draw me into the orbit of their discontent. The purchase of a few gallons of gas bought him the right to rail at his wife's misery and my helplessness.

"You ought to give me a discount," he said once. "That gimp leg of yours cost me a packet. Maybe you think your girl was my payoff. Boy, was I ever fooled! You should come out some time and see the sourpuss bag of bones she's turned into. Could it be you knew something I didn't?"

I learned to say nothing, not even to look at him, just to fill his tank, take his money, and pretend not to hear his taunts. But they got under my skin, every one of them, and grated long after he was gone. Sometimes he thought up small meannesses, like buying just one gallon of gas and asking me to check the battery and all the tires. He watched with a sneering smile as I hobbled and bent my way around the car. "Shake that short leg," he jeered. "I've places to go even if you don't." I gritted my teeth and told myself that if he got the spite out of his system here, maybe he'd take less home to Ruth.

So I felt relieved, that Sunday morning, because he was in and out of the station in such a hurry and with so little to say. I serviced three more cars before going upstairs to make myself a liverwurst sandwich and reheat the coffee. I had just returned to the office when the phone rang. It was Mrs. Hadley.

"Oh, Nathan!" Her voice was strange, low and breathy as if each word was pulled from a deep pit. "Nathan, is that you?"

"Yes, Ma. Is something wrong?"

"You haven't heard yet? Oh, Nathan!"

"What is it? Has something happened to Ruth?"

"My poor girl!" It was a drawn-out wail. "Nathan, he's killed her."

"My God!" Blood rushed to my head and I grasped the edge of the desk to keep from falling. "How—what—"

My disturbance neutralized hers. She told me the story in a flat tone as if it had grown stale with repetition.

"I didn't go to church this morning, my arthritis was that bad. Instead I listened to Pastor Meyer on television. His text was 'Blessed are they who suffer persecution for justice's sake,' and it was beautiful. He could have been talking about Ruthie, I thought, and as soon as he finished I called to tell her what he said. But we only talked for two or three minutes when she said, 'I've got to go now, Ma. Thanks for calling,' in that scared voice she uses when he comes into the room and catches her at something he doesn't like. 'I've got to go now, Ma. Thanks for calling.' Those are the last words I'll ever hear her say."

"What did he do to her?" My fingers ached from the tight grip I had on the phone.

"Maybe she told him about Pastor Meyer's sermon." She went on as if she hadn't heard my question. "Maybe she repeated the part about people who suffer in doing their duty and earn a high place in heaven. That might have set off one

of his rages.   He doesn't like her talking to me anyway.   I shouldn't have called.
It's my fault what happened.''

"What did he do to her?''

"Joachim and Kitty found her.''   Kitty is Ruth's cousin, but they were as close
as sisters.   ''They drove round that way, thinking if he wasn't home she might
like to go to church with them.   When they didn't see his car, they went up to
the back door.   They saw her through the window.   She was dead, Nathan.   She
was already dead.   He'd hit her—like he was always hitting her—but this time he
broke her neck.''

"He was here, Ma.''   I said the first thing that came into my head, trying to
shut out the picture her words made.   ''He stopped here for gas, then drove off
toward the city.''

"They'll catch him, Nathan.   They'll bring him back and make him pay for
what he's done.''

"Yes, Ma,'' I said, ''he'll pay.''

For a long time after she hung up I sat and stared at the phone as if it might
have more to tell me.   Dead, I thought.   Ruth is dead.   All our dreams, all we
planned to do together, and this is how it ends.   But our dreams and plans were
twenty years out of date and what had ended for her was pain and humiliation and
despair.   I couldn't, in honesty, mourn her death.   On an obscure impulse, seeking
a share in her last moments, I went to my bookshelf, pulled out my Bible, and
opened it to the Sermon on the Mount.

"Blessed are the poor in spirit . . .   Blessed are the meek . . .   Blessed are
they who suffer persecution for justice' sake, for theirs is the kingdom of heaven.''
Ruth was poor in spirit.   Ruth was meek.   Ruth was persecuted.   She lived by
those words and she died by them.   Had she, at the last, found comfort in her
mother's quotation from the TV preacher's sermon?

I put the Bible down and my thoughts turned from Ruth to Chad.   Now I
understood his haste, why he didn't play his usual games with me.   He had just
killed her and was making his escape.   His tank was low and he couldn't risk
running out of gas on the road.   If I had looked at him I might have read what he
had done in his face.   How long was it, I wondered, between the murder and the
time I saw him?

The county paper was on my table.   It comes out on Thursdays and carries the
television schedule for the week.   I spread it out and ran my eyes up the Sunday
column till they reached Pastor Meyer's name.   He was on, it told me, from 9:30
to 10:00 A.M.   So Mrs. Hadley had called Ruth at ten o'clock.   And Chad had
driven into my station a few minutes later.

It took several seconds for the two facts to meet in my mind and register.   It
wasn't possible.   It couldn't have happened that way, it absolutely couldn't.   The
Bascom place is twenty-five miles from here over a very rough and winding road.
The best driver, the fastest driver, can't make it in less than forty minutes.   Chad
must have left home before the TV program even began.

So Mrs. Hadley had to be mistaken.   She'd listened to some other preacher.
I looked again at the newspaper schedule.   There's only one channel that reaches

our area.   Its first Sunday program, from 8:00 to 9:00 A.M., was made up of children's cartoons.   From 9:00 to 9:30 the Department of Agriculture had a special report.   Pastor Meyer's sermon was the only one Ruth's mother could have heard. And my own log proved that Chad left my station with a filled tank at 10:10.

He must have gone back, I reasoned.   That's the only answer.   He couldn't have been home when Mrs. Hadley phoned Ruth.   After he left here he must have remembered something he'd forgotten and circled back.   He found Ruth doing something he disapproved—like getting ready to go to church—and struck her down.

It was the only answer, but it wasn't a good one.   I remember how long I'd stood at the window after Chad was out of sight, speeding toward the city.   The only road from the highway to his house is the one that goes by my station.   And I'm conditioned to be aware of every passing car.   How could he have turned round, come back, and gone down that road without my knowing?   Especially on Sunday morning when traffic is so light.   It could only have happened when I was servicing another car, perhaps with my head under the hood.

That theory lasted a short while, till the Kroehler brothers brought in their Ford pickup.   It took only 4.4 gallons, so I knew they'd come to find out if I'd heard the news and how I was taking it.   I said yes, I'd heard, and didn't tell them any more.   But that didn't stop them from sharing the news they'd gathered elsewhere.

Jointly the Kroehlers play the role of town crier.   They'd talked to Joachim and learned, among other things, that it was 10:40 when he and Kitty got to the Bascom house.   He was sure of the time because the church service began at 11:00 and they were worried about being late.   So there was no way that Chad could have made it home ahead of Joachim and Kitty.

For a moment I toyed with the notion that he'd left her dying but not dead, that she'd lived a half hour or so, long enough to receive her mother's call.   One of the Kroehlers answered that question without my asking it.

"She died instantly, the doc said," he reported.   "Didn't suffer at all, Nate, if that's any consolation to you."

"And Chad will get his just deserts," his brother added.   "The sheriff ought to be back with him pretty soon."

"They've caught him?" I asked.

"Sure.   He has a woman in the city.   The sheriff's known about her for a long time—he doesn't miss many tricks, old Crane doesn't—and he figured that's who he'd run to.   The sheriff phoned the city police, they went round and picked him up, and Crane and his deputy drove in to get him.   Reckon Chad thought he had more time to plan a getaway.   Ordinarily it might have been a day or so before anybody found Ruth's body.   Joachim and Kitty stopping by was his bad luck."

I didn't contradict him and a few minutes later they drove away.   I went into the office, entered their 4.4 gallons in the log, and gazed at the earlier entry. "10:10—13.2 regular—$5."   Chad hadn't killed Ruth and the proof was right in front of me.   I realized then that what had borne me up, what had made Ruth's death a tolerable fact, was the belief that it carried the seeds of Chad's destruction.

He had at last done something for which he would be punished—punished to the full extent of the law.

Now that prop was pulled from under me. Someone else had murdered Ruth. A stranger, perhaps a tramp. I didn't care who had done it. All that mattered was that Chad was not guilty and would go free. He was probably lording it over the sheriff right now, showing him up in front of the city police as a hick who went chasing after the wrong man while the right one got away.

I was surprised, therefore, about an hour later to get a call from Sheriff Crane.

"Mrs. Hadley says she called you about Ruth," he began. "A bad business, Nate."

"Yes."

"You told her Chad got gas at your place?"

"That's right."

"Good. I'll be right over to talk to you. Your evidence should fill in the last gap in our case against him."

"You've arrested Chad?"

"Just locked him in the jail." There was grim satisfaction in his tone. "His next stop will be the state prison."

"You still think he did it?"

"Not a doubt in the world."

"But he—he hasn't confessed, has he?"

"Chad? Not a chance! He denied everything and then clammed up. You don't catch him doing anything to make my job easier. See you in a few minutes, Nate."

So Chad was in jail charged with murder. At least he'd have a bad hour or so. Until the sheriff heard my story and went back to set him free. Was I the only one who'd seen him, the only one who could swear he was miles away from home at the time of the murder? God in heaven, I prayed, don't play that kind of trick on me. Don't make me the instrument of Chad's freedom.

Yet there it was in my logbook, in black and white, in my own handwriting—the incontestable proof of his innocence.

But he's not innocent! The protest was thunder in my brain. He's black with guilt. What if he didn't strike the final, fatal blow? What he did to Ruth, day in, day out, was worse than murder. He deserves a murderer's penalty. Everybody in town will agree to that. I'd be nobody's hero if I saved him. So why do it? Why should I give Chad an ironclad alibi?

The more I thought about it, the more right it seemed. Chad had been arrested for Ruth's murder. Without my evidence he would be tried and convicted—not a shadow of doubt about it. All I had to do was fudge the time a little, say it was later when he came to my station. Or perhaps it would be best to be vague. Might have been 10:30, I'd say, or maybe 11:00. It's quiet here on Sunday morning, so I don't pay much attention to what time it is. That way I wouldn't need to perjure myself, probably wouldn't even be called as a witness. Chad would be convicted without my saying a word.

I closed the log and pushed it under the order forms in the bottom drawer of my desk.   No one even knew I kept a log.   There was no reason for anyone else to see it.   Twenty years, I told myself.   Twenty years since he crippled me and stole my girl.   But I mustn't think of that.   Not about my own injury.   I was seeking retribution for Ruth.   That mustn't be tainted with thoughts of personal revenge.

Vengeance is mine, says the Lord, I will repay.   The long-forgotten text came unwanted to my mind.   But the Lord, I answered, uses human agents.   And there's justice, the purest kind of justice, in convicting Chad for Ruth's murder. The person who killed her only stopped her breathing, her suffering.   The life that person took today ended many years ago and Chad was the destroyer.   He deserves to pay for that and I have no obligation to testify in his defense.

There had been, I realized suddenly, something odd in my conversation with the sheriff.   It was Mrs. Hadley who told him about Chad's stopping here for gas. Chad hadn't mentioned it.   Why not, I wondered.   Ruth was alive when he left home and he knows that I can help establish the time.   Why hadn't he said so?

The answer to that was easy.   He knows how much I hate him.   He's sure I'll never lift a finger to help him.   He didn't send the sheriff to me because he was afraid I'd seize the chance to lie and make it worse for him.   I'd only be doing what Chad expects, acting as he would if he were in my place.

With that thought I knew exactly what I had to do.   One Chad Bascom in this world is enough.   I could not—no matter how righteous the words in which I cloaked my motive—remake myself in his image.   When the sheriff drove up to the door I was waiting with the logbook in my hand.

He sat in my office and went over it again and again, as if I might, in repeating it, change my story.   The logbook lay open on the desk between us.

"You're sure that's the record of Chad's buy?"   Crane's index finger moved on to the line below.   "Not this one?   The later time would fit."

"I'm positive he's the one at ten past ten," I said wearily.   "I remember his snapping that $5 bill at me.   And the 10:55 entry shows a quart of oil.   Chad got nothing but gas."

"That pulls it apart.   I checked the television station to confirm the time and text of Pastor Meyer's sermon.   He talked about blessing the persecuted and went off the air at 9:58.   Ruth was alive and talking to her mother at ten o'clock.   So your story gives Chad an airtight alibi."

His tone was angry, blaming me for the flaw in his case.   "When it comes to credibility he couldn't have a better witness.   His woman would protect him, he might have gotten a pal to lie for him.   He could even bribe a stranger.   But you, Nate—when you testify on Chad's side it has to be the truth."

"Yes," I said, "it's the truth."

"Funny thing," Crane went on.   "Chad's been taken off the hook by the testimony of the three people who'd most like to make him pay for what he did to Ruth—her mother, her cousin Kitty, and you."

And me, I added mentally.   A sanctimonious fool who couldn't keep his mouth shut.

"Nothing left but to go back to the jail and turn him loose."   His lips twisted in a humorless smile.   "With apologies yet."

The bell rang and I left him sitting there while I went out to fill another tank. When I came back he was pacing the length of the office with an air of great impatience.   I wondered why he hadn't left.

"Go on."   He waved me to the desk.   "Write up your sale."

I did so and he moved round beside me.   "Is that"—he pointed to the desk clock—"your only timepiece?"

"I've a watch upstairs.   I don't wear it when I'm working.   That clock keeps good time."

"Okay, let me see what you just wrote."

Puzzled, I pushed the log toward him and let him read the last line: "5:20—11.3 gallons high test—$4.55."

"Then it's all right."   He let out his breath in a long sigh.   "We've got Chad tied up in a neat package."

"I don't understand."

"This is the last Sunday in April, Nate.   Daylight Saving Time began this morning, but you didn't turn your clock forward."   He thrust his left arm in front of my face, pushed back the sleeve.   His watch said 6:20.   "Chad was here not at 10:10, but at 11:10—one hour later than you thought."

LLOYD BIGGLE, JR.

Have You a Fortune in Your Attic?

Detective:
GRANDFATHER RASTIN

It was a sight Borgville had never seen before and most likely would never see again, and I almost missed it.

It had been raining hard all morning, and for want of anything else to do I was down in the cellar getting in some target practice with my air rifle. I had a couple of windows open, and when I heard something that sounded like a herd of cows stampeding along the sidewalk, naturally I went to look.

It was Doc Beyers' wife, and she was *running!*

Mrs. Beyers prides herself on being the most sedate woman in Borgville—though as Grandfather says, she really hasn't much choice. There's so much of her to move around that it's only a question of doing it sedately or staying put. She even holds her laughs down to chuckles because of what she'd have to move if she cut loose with anything more violent than that. If I'd known she was going to be running in front of our house, I'd have set up some chairs and charged admission.

I watched her until she started up our walk, and then I headed for the stairs. I got to the front hall just as she came stumbling across the porch. My Grandfather Rastin had seen her coming, and he was waiting at the front door. He helped her out of her raincoat, and she gasped, ''Elizabeth . . .'' and collapsed onto the sofa.

''Take it easy,'' Grandfather said.

''Elizabeth . . .''

''Elizabeth will keep for a couple of minutes. She's standing out on her porch now, looking over this way, so she can't be in very bad shape. Wait till you get your breath back.''

For the next ten minutes Mrs. Beyers panted on the sofa, and was hushed up by Grandfather every time she opened her mouth. I came close to dying of curiosity, but Grandfather sat down and rocked as if it was an ordinary social call. He always says the first lesson a man has to learn from life is patience, and in eighty years he'd learned it pretty well.

Finally Mrs. Beyers got a grip on her breathing, and Grandfather let her talk.

''Elizabeth found a violin in her attic!'' she said.

Grandfather nodded. ''You don't say. That'd be . . .''

''It's a Strad—Strad—''

''Stradivarius? You don't say. That'd be . . .''

"It's worth a fortune."

"You don't say. That'd be Old Eric's fiddle. I heard him play it many times, when I was a boy. I often wondered what happened to it."

"It's a godsend, what with Elizabeth needing money for Ellie's wedding. She wants you to come and see it."

"I've seen it," Grandfather said. "Many times. Old Eric was quite a fiddler in his day."

"He lived to be a hundred and two," Mrs. Beyers said.

"A hundred and three. And he loved to tell about the time . . ."

"Will you come and see it?"

"I suppose."

We got our raincoats and went back to Elizabeth Peterson's house with Mrs. Beyers, all three of us walking very sedately.

Elizabeth Peterson has been a widow for more years than I am old, and in a friendly sort of way half the women in Borgville hate her. She's the example everyone holds up to them. She has no regular income at all, and has to work at anything offered to her at Borgville wages, which aren't much; but somehow she manages wonderfully well.

Lately, though, she'd been worried. Her daughter Ellie, the prettiest girl in Borgville, was graduating from high school and getting married. Her fiancé was Mark Hanson, whose father is our Village President, and President of the Borgville Bank, and the richest man in town. Naturally, Mrs. Peterson wanted her daughter to have the prettiest wedding and the biggest and best reception in the history of Borgville, if not the whole state of Michigan; but she didn't have any money.

So I wasn't surprised to find her hardly touching the floor as she paced up and down her porch waiting for us. Even I had a vague notion that a genuine Stradivarius might be worth a lot of money.

"Do you think it really is?" she asked Grandfather, all out of breath, as if she, rather than Mrs. Beyers, had been doing the running.

"Of all the things I'm not an expert in," Grandfather said, "it's violins. But I'll take a look. How'd you happen to find it?"

"It was more a matter of remembering it than finding it. It's been up there in the corner of the attic for years, and I guess I just forgot it was there. The funny thing is, I knew all the time it was valuable. It's a tradition in the Peterson family. My husband told me once that when he was a little boy playing in the attic, his mother would tell him not to go near Grandpa Eric's fiddle, because it was a valuable instrument. It never occurred to me that the value could be measured in money."

"It's the usual way of doing it," Grandfather said.

"Anyway, yesterday at the church social Miss Borg gave a talk about people finding fortunes in their attics—in old stamps and books and things; so afterwards I asked her just as a joke—about old violins, and she came by today, and—come in and see it."

Miss Borg was still there, standing by the big round dining-room table. She's a little old lady with white hair, and she looks nothing like the terror she is teaching history at Borgville High School.   The violin was on the table, and she was gazing at it as if it were the Holy Grail in Tennyson's *Idylls of the King,* which is one of the numerous epics the students at Borgville High have stuffed into them.

The violin looked like something that might possibly raise nine cents at a rummage sale.   The case was a battered old thing of wood.   The hinges were missing, and it had been held together with a couple pieces of rope.   The one string left on it had snapped, and the whole contraption was falling apart.   There were loose pieces in the bottom of the case, and on the violin there was a big crack along one side, which meant that whatever else it might do, it would never hold water.   There was loose hair all over the place, except on the bow where it belonged.

Miss Borg said when she was a little girl she heard the Peterson family legend about Old Eric's valuable violin, but she doubted that anyone, including Old Eric, ever realized just how valuable it was.   She shined a flashlight down into the violin, and said, "Look!"

Grandfather looked, and then I looked.   Pasted inside the violin was a piece of paper, brown with age, and on the paper were some letters.   The ink had faded, and some of it was illegible, but with Miss Borg's help I was able to make out: . . . *adivarius Cremon* . . .

"That's the label," Miss Borg whispered.   "See—it says so right here."   She had a thick book called *Biographical Dictionary of Musicians*, and under "Stradivari, Antonio," it said, "His label reads: 'Antonius Stradivarius Cremonensis. Fecit Anno. . . .' "

Grandfather scratched away at his head.   "I guess it might say that.   The only way to tell whether or not it's genuine is to take it to an expert.   I suppose if it's a valuable instrument it could be fixed up."

"A violin maker could take it all apart and put it together again," Miss Borg said.   "It would be as good as new.   Better.   An old instrument is always better than a new one."

"Maybe," Grandfather said.   "My advice would be not to get excited about it until you hear what an expert has to say."

Mrs. Peterson wasn't listening.   "What do you think it's worth?"

"I've heard that Stradivarius violins bring as much as fifty thousand dollars," Miss Borg said.   "Or more.   Of course some are worth more than others.   Even if it isn't one of the best ones it should bring quite a lot.   Five or ten thousand dollars, at least."

"Five or ten thousand!" Mrs. Peterson said.

"Since it's Saturday, you won't be able to do anything with it before the first of the week," Grandfather said.   "First thing Monday morning."

"Five or ten thousand!" Mrs. Peterson said again.   Most likely she'd just moved the wedding reception from the church basement to the big room above the Star Restaurant.

"Maybe there's someone in Jackson who'd know about it," Grandfather said. "On Monday. . . ."

Mrs. Peterson still wasn't listening.   She looked again at the violin—looked at it as if she was seeing it for the first time—and then she sat down and started to cry. Grandfather dragged me out of there, and on the front porch we met Hazel Morgan, Dorothy Ashley, and Ruth Wood, all coming to see the violin. Half a dozen others were on their way, from various directions. It was then I noticed that Mrs. Beyers hadn't come in with us. She was out spreading the Good Word . . .

Grandfather hadn't anything to say on the way home, or even after we got there.

As soon as it stopped raining he went over to Main Street to borrow the Detroit paper from Mr. Snubbs, who runs the Snubbs Hardware Store; and the rest of the day, whenever I mentioned the violin, he hushed me up.

"Whether or not a violin was made by Stradivarius is just not the kind of question I can settle," he said. "I refuse to waste any energy even thinking about it."

"Miss Borg shouldn't have spouted off about all those dollars before they find out for sure," I said.

"Miss Borg should be shot."

On Saturday night all the stores in Borgville stay open late so the farmers can spend the money they were too busy to spend all week, and almost everyone comes to town. That night the talk up and down Main Street was about Elizabeth Peterson's violin. Suddenly everyone in town remembered hearing a grandfather, or an uncle, or some elderly person down the street tell about what a remarkable fiddler Old Eric Peterson was, and what a valuable violin he had.

The queer thing was that my Grandfather Rastin, who usually remembers such things better than anyone else, was acting skeptical about the whole business.

He and some other old-timers were sitting on the benches in front of Jake Palmer's Barber Shop, and when Grandfather suggested that it might be better to get an expert's opinion before sticking a price tag on the violin, Nat Barlow got pretty hot about it.

"Everyone knows it's valuable," he said. "My father heard Old Eric say so himself. Anyway, Old Eric played dances all over this part of the state, even some in Detroit, and everyone said he was the best fiddler they'd ever heard. Why wouldn't he have a valuable violin?"

"Is Sam Cowell in town tonight?" Grandfather asked.

"Haven't seen him," Nat said.

"How much would you say his car is worth?"

Everyone laughed.

"That pile of junk?" Nat said.

"There isn't a better driver in Borg County than Sam Cowell," Grandfather said. "Seeing as he's such a good driver, why wouldn't he have a valuable car?"

That shut Nat up for the next hour or so.

"I've been trying to remember a few things about Old Eric," Grandfather said. "He loved to talk about the time he played for Ole Bull, and Ole Bull. . . ."

"Who—or what—is Ole Bull?" someone asked.

"He was a famous Norwegian violinist. One of the greatest," Grandfather said. "He was touring the country giving concerts, and Old Eric went way off to Cincinnati, or Chicago, or somewhere to hear him. He took his fiddle along, on the chance of picking up some money along the way, and after the concert he got to meet Ole Bull. He introduced himself as another Norwegian fiddler, and Ole Bull asked him to play. Old Eric . . .''

The crowd wasn't much interested in Ole Bull.

"They tell me a Wiston reporter was over to see Elizabeth this evening," Bob Ashley said. "There'll be a piece about the violin in the Wiston newspaper."

"Got your oats in yet, Bob?" Grandfather asked.

"I don't suppose a Stradivarius violin turns up every day," Bob said.

That was when Grandfather headed for home, looking mighty disgusted. I caught up with him and asked for his version of the Peterson family legend.

"I never heard of any legend," he said. "Old Eric may have told his family something about that violin, and whatever he told them was so, because Old Eric was no fool. If it was a Stradivarius violin he'd have known it, and so would everyone else in Borgville, which makes it seem odd that I never heard anything about it. On the other hand, I do remember *something* about Old Eric's fiddle, but I haven't been able to recollect what it is."

After Sunday dinner the next day, we sat on our front porch and watched the procession to Elizabeth Peterson's house. Those who hadn't seen the violin yet wanted to see it, and a lot of those who'd seen it wanted to see it again, and traffic on our street was heavy.

Then Mark Hanson came by. He was home from the University for the week-end, and on his way to an afternoon date with Ellie. Mrs. Beyers met him in front of our house, and made some crack about him marrying an heiress, and he shrugged and came up on the porch to talk to Grandfather.

"Family tradition to the contrary," he said, "I don't think that violin is worth a button. And it can't possibly be a Stradivarius. It has a very odd shape—too short and too wide. Did you notice?"

"One violin looks just about like another one to me," Grandfather said.

"I talked to Mr. Gardner—he's the orchestra director at Wiston High School. He says thousands of violins have a Stradivarius label, but all it means is that the violin maker *copied* a Stradivarius violin, or tried to. This one isn't even a good copy."

"What does Ellie think about all this?" Grandfather asked.

"Oh, she agrees with me, but we're both worried about her mother. The truth will be a terrible blow to her, and there doesn't seem to be a thing we can do about it. Mr. Gardner is coming over this evening to see the violin. Most likely one look is all he'll need."

"If it's the wrong shape, as you say, then anyone who knows violins would see that right away. When is he coming?"

"He wasn't sure—sometime after eight."

"I'll be over," Grandfather said. "I'd like to hear what he has to say."

"Glad to have you," Mark said. "But please don't tell anyone else he's coming. What he has to say may not be good news, and I don't want a big audience there."

Mark went after Ellie, and the two of them walked back up the street hand in hand, Ellie looking pretty in a new spring dress and Mark admiring her as a fiancé should.   By that time I'd gotten tired watching the procession, so I went off to play baseball; but I made a point of being on hand when Grandfather went over to Peterson's that evening.

News has a way of getting around in Borgville, and there was a good crowd there—enough to fill the parlor, anyway.   Mrs. Peterson bustled about, happy and excited, trying to feed everyone.   The Peterson family legend got another kicking around, and every now and then someone would go into the dining room for another look at the violin.

It was nearly nine o'clock when Mr. Gardner came up the street, driving slowly and looking for house numbers, which very few houses in Borgville have.   He had to be introduced to everyone, and he went through the motions of this in a very abrupt way, as if he wanted to get on with the business at hand.   I noticed when I shook hands with him that his hands were white and soft, and sometimes he would bow to a lady and show the bald spot at the top of his head.

"It's in here," Mark said finally, and led him into the dining room.   Miss Borg and Mrs. Peterson and Ellie went along.   The rest of us crowded up to the big arch that separates the dining room from the parlor, and watched.

Miss Borg tried to give Mr. Gardner the flashlight, so he could see the label, but he waved it away.   "I don't care what's written inside," he said.   He picked up the violin, and it came out of the case trailing loose parts.   He looked at it, turned it over for a glance at the bottom, and put it back.

There wasn't a sound in the house.   In the parlor everyone had stopped breathing.

I will say this for him—he didn't prolong the suspense.

Mrs. Peterson's face went suddenly white.   "You mean—it isn't worth anything?"

"Worth anything?"   Mr. Gardner snorted.   Grandfather snorts sometimes, when he's real disgusted, but this was a different kind of snort.   A nasty kind.   "It's worth something, I suppose.   If you had it fixed up, which would cost—oh, maybe fifty dollars, if you include a new case—then you might be able to sell it for twenty-five.   My recommendation is that you burn it—there are enough bad violins around.   One less would make the world a better place—a better place for violin teachers, anyway."

He left without waiting to be thanked—though Mrs. Peterson was in no condition to thank him anyway.   Everyone else left right after him, except Miss Borg, who was indignant, and Grandfather, who seemed very thoughtful.

"The idea!" Miss Borg said.   "Why, he didn't even look at the label!"

"If you don't mind . . ." Mrs. Peterson said.   Then she started to cry, and it wasn't at all like the crying she'd done when she thought the violin was worth a lot of money.

"Don't burn it just yet," Grandfather said to Ellie.   "I want another look at it myself."

Ellie nodded, and Mark showed us to the front door.

"Well," I said to Grandfather as we crossed the street, "I guess the wedding reception is back in the church basement."

He didn't seem to hear me. "I finally remembered something," he said.

"Something about the violin?"

"It was such a long time ago. I was only a boy, you know, when Old Eric died, But it seems . . ."

He went straight up to the rocking chair in his bedroom, where he usually takes his problems, and he was still rocking when I went to bed. I couldn't see how rocking would turn Mrs. Peterson's piece of junk into a valuable violin, but I didn't ask him about it. There are times when it is better not to bother Grandfather with questions, and one of them is when he's in his rocking chair.

In the morning it seemed as if all his rocking was wasted, because Sheriff Pilkins dropped in while we were still at breakfast, to ask Grandfather if he'd heard anything about a burglary the night before.

"Not yet, I haven't," Grandfather said. "Where was it?"

"Elizabeth Peterson's house," the Sheriff said. "Someone stole a violin."

Grandfather and I yelped together. "Violin!"

"Yep. She had this violin on her dining-room table, and when she came down this morning it was gone. Naturally she can't remember the last time she bothered to lock her doors. Funny thing, though—the burglar wasn't really stealing it. He was buying it. He left her an envelope full of money."

"How much money?" Grandfather asked.

"A thousand dollars."

Grandfather whistled, and I dropped the toast into my cereal. "Last night Mr. Gardner said that violin might be worth twenty-five dollars if she spent fifty dollars fixing it up," I said.

"So I heard," the Sheriff said. "There are some funny angles to this case. How many people knew she had what might be a valuable violin?"

"Half of Borg County," Grandfather said.

"Right. And how many of them knew this Mr. Gardner said the violin was practically worthless?"

"Those that were there last night, and whoever they managed to tell before they went to bed. Maybe about a fourth of Borg County."

"That leaves a lot of people who didn't know."

"You won't have any trouble narrowing down your list of suspects," Grandfather said. "There aren't very many people around here who'd have a ready thousand dollars for a speculative flutter on a violin."

"Tell me something I don't know."

"How is Elizabeth taking it?"

"Not very well. She's pretty blamed mad about the whole thing. She's sure now that the violin is worth a fortune, and someone is trying to do her out of it."

"It's just possible that taking a thousand dollars for that violin is more of a crime than stealing it."

"That's what I think myself. But Elizabeth is certain the thief wouldn't have left the thousand if he hadn't known it was worth a lot more. She wants her violin back, and hang the money. Which is why I'm here. You didn't chance to notice any suspicious-looking characters hanging around last night, did you?"

"Borgville doesn't have any suspicious-looking characters," Grandfather said.

"They're all suspicious-looking to me. Look—I know you can come up with information I can't touch. Let me know if you find out anything."

Grandfather nodded. "I'll go have a talk with Elizabeth, and look around."

So Grandfather went to Peterson's, and I went to school. Miss Borg intercepted me in the hallway, and asked me if I'd heard the news. She seemed excited about it—in fact, until I could get to a dictionary I thought she was excited to the point of being sick, because she said she felt vindicated.

I didn't go home for lunch, so I don't know how Grandfather spent the day. Sheriff Pilkins passed the time working, which is something he has no natural aptitude for, and when he came to see Grandfather that evening he was looking glum.

"I have a list of suspects," he announced.

"Good," Grandfather said. "Then you're further along than I am."

Normally it would cheer the Sheriff up to find he's ahead of Grandfather in anything, but this time it seemed to make him mad. "Lucy Borg," he said, "was pretty irked at what Gardner said about the violin. She could have taken it with the idea of getting another expert opinion on it."

"Somehow I can't see Lucy burgling a house. And where would she get a thousand dollars?"

"Then there's this Gardner—he could have lied about the violin, and then stolen it so he could sell it himself. Elizabeth favors this theory."

"Why?"

"Who knows why a woman thinks anything? Gardner supports a big family on a schoolteacher's salary, and he wouldn't have been able to lay his hands on a thousand dollars on a Sunday night. Then there's Pete Wilks, who lives on Maple Street right behind Peterson's. He took an unusual interest in that violin."

"He had an old violin of his own," Grandfather said. "He was interested in finding out if his might be valuable. There is also the question of where he would get a thousand dollars. The money complicates things."

"It sure does. My favorite would be Mark Hanson. It's common knowledge that the Hansons tried to give Elizabeth money for the wedding, and she wouldn't take it. Mark could have used this as a back-handed way of making her take the money, and the Hansons are one family that could come up with a thousand dollars in a hurry. The only trouble is, they didn't do it. Mark was with Ellie until nearly midnight, and then his folks drove him back to Ann Arbor and stayed there overnight."

"So where does that leave you?" Grandfather asked.

"Nowhere!"

"I have an idea or two. Let's go see Elizabeth."

Mrs. Peterson met us at the door, and she didn't waste any time showing what was on her mind. "Did you get it back?" she asked the Sheriff.

Sheriff Pilkins sputtered all over the place. I guess law officers don't like blunt demands for quick results. They'd rather talk about all the progress they're making, which they can do without getting any results at all.

"Did you think over what we talked about this morning?" Grandfather asked.

"I certainly did," Mrs. Peterson said.   "I want the violin."

"Give me the money, then, and I'll try and get it back for you."

The Sheriff stared at Grandfather.   "Where are you going to get it?"

"The law isn't involved in this," Grandfather said.   "Party unknown bought Elizabeth's violin for a thousand dollars.   The transaction isn't satisfactory to her, so she's going to take the violin back and return the money—if I can arrange it, that is."

"Baloney!" the Sheriff shouted.

"I don't see that there's much you can do about it."

The Sheriff didn't seem to, either, and he stood there glaring at Grandfather. I'm not one who cares much for art, but I never get tired of watching the way his face changes color when he and Grandfather meet head-on.

Finally he stomped down off the porch, muttering something about accessories, and withholding information, and interfering with legal processes.   Mrs. Peterson came back with an envelope and handed it to Grandfather.

"You understand," Grandfather said, "that if Gardner turns out to be right about the violin you've made a bad deal for yourself."

"We went through all that this morning," she said.   "I want the violin."

"I'll get it for you if I can."

Grandfather stuffed the envelope into his shirt pocket, and the two of us went home.

I'd like to tell you all about Grandfather's system for tracking down a thief, but I can't.   I expected him to make a mysterious telephone call as soon as it got dark, and then head for a meeting in some alleyway.   Instead, he sat down and read all evening, and he was still reading when I went to bed.

In the morning, when I went down to breakfast, the violin was lying on *our* dining-room table.

"Where'd you get it?" I asked.

"You're most as bad as Pilkins.   What difference does it make?   Elizabeth will be satisfied, the person who took it is satisfied, and beyond that what happened is nobody's business."

After breakfast he took the violin over to Elizabeth Peterson, who was very happy to have it back—that is, she was happy until later that day, when Mr. Hanson drove her to Jackson to see a violin repair man there.   This man told her even more emphatically than Mr. Gardner that the violin was nothing but junk, and he didn't think it would be worth twenty-five dollars even if it was fixed up.

The violin went back to the Peterson attic, and Mrs. Peterson started all over again to try to figure out how to pay for a big wedding and reception without any money, and Sheriff Pilkins stopped by three times a day the rest of the week in the hope of prying the name of the violin thief out of Grandfather.

Other than that, nothing happened.   That is, I thought nothing happened, but on Friday, Jimmy Edwards, whose mother works in the telephone office at Wiston, asked me how come Grandfather was getting all those long distance telephone calls.

"What long distance telephone calls?" I asked.

"How would I know if you don't?" Jimmy said.   "All I know is, Mom said your Grandfather has been getting calls from all over—New York, Los Angeles, Chicago . . .''

"I don't know," I said, "but I'm sure going to find out."

But I didn't. All Grandfather did when I asked him was grunt and shrug. All Friday evening he grunted and he shrugged, and all Saturday morning, until about ten o'clock. Then a big limousine such as had never before been seen in Borgville drove up in front of our house. A chauffeur in a fancy uniform popped out and opened the rear door, and a tall, gray-headed man got out and walked up to our house.

Grandfather met him on the porch.

"You're Mr. Rastin?" the man asked.

Grandfather nodded, and shook hands with him.

"Where is it?" the man asked.

"Across the street," Grandfather said.

They headed for the Peterson house, with me tagging along, and Grandfather introduced the man to Mrs. Peterson—his name was Edmund Van Something-or-other—and sent Ellie chasing up to the attic after the violin.

We sat down in the parlor and waited.

"Has it been in your family for a very long time?" Mr. Van asked.

"It belonged to my husband's great-great-grandfather," Mrs. Peterson said.

"You don't say. Treasures are often preserved in this way. My first Stradivarius violin . . ."

Ellie bounced in, all out of breath, and carefully placed the violin on a coffee table beside Mr. Van. She untied the knots and took off the top of the case, and then she scooted back out of the way, as if she expected Mr. Van would be throwing the violin at someone as soon as he saw it.

He did look at the violin. He looked at it once, with an expression of disgust such as I never hope to see again. Then he picked up the loose lid of the case, and held it on his lap looking at the violin bow that was hooked onto it.

"François Tourte!" he said.

"The label is under that little doohicky that screws in and out," Grandfather said.

"Under the frog. Yes. It really has a label?"

He unscrewed something or other, fished a magnifying glass out of his pocket, and said, speaking very softly, "This bow was made by François Tourte in 1822, aged seventy-five years. Splendid! Tourte never branded his bows, and rarely labeled them."

"Is it genuine?" Grandfather asked.

"Unquestionably genuine."

"I had no way of knowing. A label, of course, can be stuck onto anything."

"Unfortunately true. Even a violin such as that one—" he made a face, "—could have a Stradivarius label. But craftsmanship cannot, as you say, be stuck on. One look at the shape of the head—Tourte. It still has the original frog—Tourte. The thickness of the shaft, the narrow ferrule—all unmistakably Tourte. And it's in remarkably fine condition. The grip is a little worn. The slide, too, but not badly. The man who owned this bow knew its value. I stand by my offer. I'll pay four thousand dollars for it.''

He looked at Mrs. Peterson, and for a long moment she couldn't find her voice. "You want to buy the violin?" she stammered.

Mr. Van winced. "Not the violin. The bow. This bow, Ma'am, was made by François Tourte, who was to the violin bow what Stradivarius was to the violin. And more. There were great violin makers before Stradivarius, but Tourte created the modern bow—its design, its materials, to some extent its mechanics. Without the Tourte bow, string instrument technique as we know it would be impossible, and the work of the great instrument makers would to a considerable extent be wasted. Will you sell the bow for four thousand dollars, Ma'am?''

"It's a very good offer," Grandfather said.

Mrs. Peterson still didn't seem to understand. "You mean—the violin . . ."

Mr. Van clapped his hand to his forehead. "The violin I do not want, but I'll buy it if I must. What is it worth? Five dollars? Ten? I'll give you four thousand and ten dollars for the violin and the bow.''

"Oh," Mrs. Peterson said. "You just want the bow. I'll sell that, and keep the violin as a—a memento.''

"Splendid!" Mr. Van whipped out a check book and began to scribble. He presented the check, shook hands with everyone present, and walked back to his car carrying the lid of the case with the bow still hooked onto it. He carried it the way I've seen couples carry their first baby when they bring it home from the hospital.

Mrs. Peterson sat down and gazed at the check for a long time. "I don't know how to thank you," she said. Then she started to cry, and Ellie looked as if she wanted to cry, too, and it was as good a time as any for Grandfather and me to get out of there, which we did.

"Sheriff Pilkins will have a fit," I said, when we got back to our porch.

"It'll do him good," Grandfather said.

"He'll say anyone who stole something worth four thousand dollars belongs behind bars, and he'll threaten to put you there if you don't tell him who it was.''

"Let him threaten," Grandfather said. "That was one crime that will stay unsolved permanently.''

"How'd you know the thing was valuable?''

"Something I remembered Old Eric saying. He played for Ole Bull, and he had a bow that was better than anything Ole Bull had. Ole Bull tried to buy it from him. I figured if the bow was good enough back in the eighteen sixties, or whenever it was, for a great violinist to want it, it might still be worth something. But none of these local experts thought to look at the bow. The violin was unbelievably bad, and it distracted their attention. So when I got the chance I looked at the bow, and I found that label. I told Professor Mueller, at Wiston College, and he said a Tourte bow might be worth a fair amount of money, and the person who'd pay the most for it would be a collector of old instruments.''

"Why not a violinist?" I asked.

"A bow can be made today that plays just as well as that one. Maybe a little better, for all I know. It's the same as with postage stamps. An old stamp may be worth hundreds of dollars, but you can buy one at the post office for four cents that will do just as good a job of getting a letter through the mails. Professor Mueller got the word around to some collectors, and this man made the best offer, so I told him to come and see the bow.''

"Then Old Eric knew the bow was valuable, rather than the violin, but after he died the family legend got things twisted.''

"I suppose."

"That still doesn't explain who stole the violin.''

"Like I said, that's one crime that won't ever be solved," Grandfather said.

"I'm not so sure," I said. "I think I can figure it out myself. Someone thought the violin just *might* be worth something in spite of what Mr. Gardner said. So he went to Mr. Hanson, and said, 'Look, we should get this violin to a genuine expert, but of course there's a good chance that it really isn't worth anything, so why not do it this way. You put up a thousand dollars, and I'll steal the violin and leave the money. If it turns out to be worth more, we can give Mrs. Peterson the difference. If it turns out to be worthless, she'll still have the thousand dollars for the wedding. She wouldn't accept the money as a gift, and now that Mr. Gardner has said the violin is junk she wouldn't sell it to us for a thousand dollars, because she'd figure that would be the same as a gift. But if we steal it, and leave the money, she'll think the thief didn't know it was junk and she's made a good deal for herself.' The only trouble was, Mrs. Peterson thought otherwise, and called in the Sheriff and messed everything up.''

"Not bad," Grandfather said. "It only goes to show that you can't figure out in advance how a woman will react to anything.''

"And of course there was only one person who had any reason to think the violin—or the bow—might be valuable even after Mr. Gardner said it was nothing but junk.''

Grandfather grinned. "Right again. I stole it myself.''

LAWRENCE G. BLOCHMAN

The Killer with No Fingerprints

Detective:
DR. DANIEL WEBSTER COFFEE

The place was almost a shambles when Max Ritter, Lieutenant of Detectives, arrived. All the living-room furniture was slashed or overturned. Chair legs and lamps littered the apartment. So many light bulbs had been broken that the police had to work by flashlights until more bulbs could be sent up. The bed was a rat's nest of bloody tatters, and a trail of gore led from the bedroom through the living room into the bathroom.

The dead man was lying in the bathroom in a pretzel-like posture that would have made a Ringling Brothers contortionist green with envy. He had one foot in the toilet bowl, one arm in the wash basin, and his head in the bathtub. The wood-handled long-bladed kitchen knife which had carved hieroglyphics into his torso had been left lying on the bathroom floor. So had a cheap plastic raincoat which the murderer had obviously worn to protect his clothing, as well as the crumpled bloody towels with which he had wiped his hands and probably his shoes.

The house phone was off the hook and lay on the floor—a fact which led to the early discovery of the crime. The desk clerk of the Westside Residential Hotel had plugged a jack under a signal light that had suddenly flared for Apartment 26. He had said "Office" several times, but got no response. He thought he heard curious sounds in the background and repeated "Office" three more times. When he heard what he thought was the sound of a door closing, he had run up the stairs—the self-service elevator was somewhere in the stratosphere—and had banged on the door of Apartment 26. When there was no response, he ran back down the stairs and called the police. He made no attempt to enter the apartment with his passkey until the squadcar cops arrived. Why should he, a law-abiding and unarmed citizen, usurp the unquestioned duty of the uniformed forces of the law?

While the print men, photographers, and other technicians were picking their way gingerly through the mess in Apartment 26, Lieutenant Ritter was collecting pertinent data. But the swarthy, lugubrious beanpole of a detective found the desk clerk, the manager, and the neighbors singularly uninformative. It seemed incredible to Ritter that such a desperate life-and-death struggle could have gone on without arousing some auditory interest; yet this appeared to be the case. The man and wife across the hall were addicted to loud television—the wife was rather deaf—and the people in the apartment next door were out for the evening. The girl at the end of the hall had taken a sleeping pill and even slept through five minutes of door pounding by the police.

Neither the desk clerk nor the house manager was of much help at first. The desk clerk, a young man with curly brown hair, long eyelashes, and suspiciously red lips, was terribly, terribly bored and terribly, terribly vague about who had entered and left the lobby during the evening. The manager said that the dead man had registered three weeks previously as Gerald Sampson of New York, although he agreed with the desk clerk that the deceased had a pronounced Southern accent.

Lieutenant Max Ritter was convinced that the dead man's name was not Sampson and that he had not come from New York. In the wastebasket of Apartment 26 the Lieutenant had found an envelope addressed to Mr. Paul Wallace, General Delivery, Northbank, and postmarked Baton Rouge, Louisiana. There was no return address on the envelope and no letter inside the envelope or in the wastebasket.

In a dresser drawer, under a pile of expensive shirts, Ritter found a Social Security card in the name of Paul Wallace and a passbook showing a balance of $1706 in a Cleveland bank to the credit of P. L. Wallace. In an envelope stuffed into the inside pocket of a Brooks Brothers sports jacket hanging in a closet, the detective found an envelope containing a dozen newspaper clippings about a young singer named Patty Erryl.

Even in the smudged halftone pictures, Patty was a comely lass, apparently not far out of her teens, brimful of that intangible effervescence which is the exclusive property of youth. In most of the poses her eyes glowed with the roseate vision of an unclouded future. Her blonde head was poised with the awareness of her own fresh loveliness. Patty Erryl was quite obviously a personality. Moreover, Lieutenant Ritter concluded as he read through the clippings, Patty had talent.

Patty had been singing in Northbank night clubs for the past year. Just a month before the sudden demise of Mr. Paul Wallace, she had won the regional tryout of the Metropolitan Opera auditions. In a few weeks she would go to New York to compete in the nationally broadcast finals.

Ritter took the clippings downstairs and reopened his questioning of the bored desk clerk.

"Ever see this dame?" He dealt the clippings face up on the reception desk.

"Ah? Well, yes, as a matter of fact I have." The clerk fluttered his eyelashes. "I saw the pictures in the papers, too, even before I saw the girl, but I somehow didn't connect the one with the other. Yes, I've seen her."

"Did she ever come here to see this bird Wallace?"

"Wallace? You mean Mr. Sampson?"

"I mean the man in Twenty-six."

"Ah. Well, yes, as a matter of fact she did."

"Often?"

"That depends upon what you call often. She's been here three or four times, I'd say."

"Do you announce her or does she go right up?"

"Well, the first time she stopped at the desk. Lately she's been going right up."

"What do you mean, lately? Tonight, maybe?"

"I didn't see her tonight."

"If she comes here regular, maybe she could go through the service entrance and take the elevator in the basement without you seeing her?"

"That's possible, yes."

"Does she always come alone?"

"Not always. Last time she came she brought lover boy along."

"Who's lover boy?"

"How should I know?" Again the clerk fluttered his eyelashes. "He's a rather uncouth young man whom for some reason Miss Erryl seems to find not unattractive. She apparently takes great pleasure in gazing into his eyes. And vice versa."

"But you don't know his name?"

"I do not. We don't require birth certificates, passports, or marriage licenses for the purpose of visiting our tenants."

"You're too, too liberal. You let in murderers. Did lover boy ever come here without lover girl?"

"He did indeed. He was here last night raising quite a row with the gentleman in Twenty-six. When he came down he was red-faced and mad as a hornet. Right afterward the gentleman in Twenty-six called the desk and gave orders that if lover boy ever came back, I was not to let him up, and that if he insisted I was to call the police. Lover boy had been threatening him, he said. But I think he came back again tonight."

"You think?"

"Well, I had just finished taking a phone message for one of our tenants who was out, and I turned my back to put the message in her box when this man went by and got into the elevator. I only had a glimpse of him as the elevator door was closing, but I'm sure it was lover boy. I shouted at him but it was too late. I tried to phone Twenty-six to warn Mr. Sampson—"

"Wallace."

"Wallace. But there was no answer, so I assumed he was out. Then a few minutes later the phone in Twenty-six was knocked off the hook."

"Did you see lover boy come down again?"

"Now that you mention it, no, I didn't—unless he came down while I was up banging on the door of Twenty-six."

"Or took the car down to the basement and went out the service entrance, maybe?"

"You're so right, Lieutenant. Or he could have been picked up by a helicopter on the roof." The clerk giggled.

"Very funny." Ritter advanced his lower lip. "Any other non-tenants come in tonight since you came on duty?"

"Traffic has been quite light this evening. There was the blonde who always comes to see the man in Sixty-three on Wednesdays. There was a boy from the florist's with roses for the sick lady on Nine, and there was an elderly white-haired gent I assumed to be delivering for the liquor store on the corner.''

"Why?"

"Well, he had a package under his arm and it was about time for Miss Benedict's daily fifth of gin, so—''

"What time do you call 'about time'?''

"About an hour ago.''

"This was before Wallace's light went up on your switchboard?''

"About twenty minutes before. Now that I think of it, I didn't see him come down either. Of course, with all the excitement—''

"That makes two for your helicopter,'' the detective said. "Let me know if you think of any more.''

Ritter went upstairs again for another look at the dead man and to wait for the coroner who had been summoned from his weekly pinochle game but had not yet arrived. At least this was one case the coroner could not very well attribute to heart failure—"Coroner's Thrombosis,'' as Dr. Coffee called it—since the cause of death was plainly written in blood.

The dead man had been on the threshold of middle age. His temples were graying and there was gray in his close-cropped beard. The beard, instead of giving him an air of distinction, left him with a hard ruthless face.

His features were regular, except perhaps for his earlobes which were thick, pendulous, and slightly discolored as though they had been forcibly twisted.

Whoever killed Mr. Wallace-Sampson must have really hated him to have done such a savage knife job on him. Why, then, would the victim have admitted a man who was such an obvious and determined enemy? Could the murderer have obtained a key from some third party?

Ritter's reverie was interrupted by the approach of Sergeant Foley, the scowling fingerprint expert.

"Lieutenant,'' he said, "we got something special here. I think we're stuck with a sixty-four-million-dollar question and with no sponsor to slip us the answer.''

"You mean you can't make the stiff?''

"Oh, the stiff's a cinch. We haven't made him yet, but we got a perfect set of prints and he's old enough so he must be on file somewhere in the world. But the murderer—no soap!''

"Sergeant, you surprise and grieve me,'' Ritter said. "With my own little eyes I see five perfect bloody finger marks on the bathroom door.''

"Finger marks yes,'' said Sergeant Foley, "but prints no.''

"Meaning what?''

"Meaning no prints. No ridges, no pore patterns, no whorls, no radial loops, no ulnar loops—no nothing.''

Ritter frowned. "Gloves?''

"We usually get *some* sort of pattern with gloves, even surgical gloves sometimes, although they're hard to identify. But here, nothing—and I mean *nothing*.''

"The knife?''

"Same thing. It wasn't wiped. Bloody finger marks, yes—prints, no. The knife, by the way, comes from the kitchenette here."

Max Ritter scratched his mastoid process. He pursed his lips as though rehearsing for a Police Good Neighbor League baby-kissing bee. Then he asked, "Your boys finished with that phone, Sergeant?"

"Yup. Go ahead and call."

A moment later Ritter was talking to his private medical examiner, Dr. Daniel Webster Coffee, chief pathologist and director of laboratories at Northbank's Pasteur Hospital.

"Hi, Doc. Get you out of bed? . . . Look, I got something kind of funny, if you can call homicide funny . . . No, the coroner's a little late, but this one he can't write off as natural causes. A knife job, but good. Like a surgeon, practically . . . No, I don't think there's anything you can do tonight, Doc. I already emptied the medicine chest for you, like always. But if I can talk the coroner into shipping the deceased to your hospital morgue for a P.M. . . . You will? Thanks, Doc. I think you're going to like this one. The killer's got no fingerprints . . . No, I don't mean he left none; he's *got* none. Call you in the morning, Doc."

When Dr. Coffee returned to the pathology laboratory after the autopsy next morning, he handed two white enameled pails to his winsome, dark-eyed technician and said, "The usual sections and the usual stains, Doris. Only don't section the heart until I photograph the damage."

Doris Hudson lifted the lids from both pails and peered in without any change of expression on her cover-girl features.

"Lieutenant Ritter is waiting in your office, Doctor, talking to Calcutta's gift to Northbank," she said. "If you agree that Dr. Mookerji is not paid to entertain the Police Department, I could use him out here to help me cut tissue."

Doris's voice apparently had good carrying qualities, for the rotund Hindu resident in pathology immediately appeared in the doorway and waddled into the laboratory.

"Salaam, Doctor Sahib," said Dr. Mookerji. "Leftenant Ritter is once more involving us in felonious homicide, no?"

Dr. Coffee nodded.

"Hi, Doc," said Ritter. "What did you find?"

"The gross doesn't show much except that the deceased died of shock and hemorrhage due to multiple stab wounds in the cardiac region and lower abdomen. As you know, Max, I won't have the microscopic findings for a day or so."

"Did you shave off the guy's whiskers?"

"That's not routine autopsy procedure, Max. But it's pretty clear that he grew a beard to hide scars. There's old scar tissues on one cheek, on the chin, and on the upper lip."

"He also grows the bush to hide behind." Max Ritter grinned. "Doc, the guy's a con man and a small-time blackmailer. I wire the Henry classification to the F.B.I. last night and I get the answer first thing this morning. His name's

Paul Wallace, with half a dozen aliases. He's got a record: four arrests, two convictions. Two cases dismissed in New York when the plaintiffs, both dames, withdrew their complaints. Last four years are blank, the F.B.I. says, at least as far as Washington knows.''

"What about the murderer with no fingerprints?'' the pathologist asked.

"That's what I want to talk to you about, Doc. Since this Wallace is a crook, maybe the guy that knifed him is another crook he double-crossed. Maybe the butcher boy had a little plastic surgery on his fingers.''

"I don't know, Max.'' Dr. Coffee shook his head, then with one hand brushed an unruly wisp of straw-colored hair back from his forehead. "I've never seen a first-class job of surgical fingerprint elimination. Did you ever see the prints they took off Dillinger's corpse? His plastic job was a complete botch. No trouble at all to make the identification.''

"Then how do you—?''

"Give me another forty-eight hours, Max. Meanwhile, what progress have you made running down blind leads?''

Ritter told the pathologist about Patty Erryl and her visits to the dead man's apartment with and without "lover boy''; also about the bored and vague desk clerk's recital, and about his own conclusions.

"This white-haired old geezer with the package under his arm is definitely not delivering gin to Miss Benedict in Seven-oh-two for any liquor store within half a mile,'' said Ritter. "I checked 'em all. Could be that his package was the plastic raincoat I found in the bathroom.

"Anyhow, I just come from talking to this Patty Erryl, the opera hopeful.'' Ritter brought forth his envelope of clippings and spread them on Dr. Coffee's desk. "Look, Doc. A real dish. Not more than twenty. Born in Texas, she says—some little town near San Antonio. Grew up in the Philippines where her father was a U.S. Air Force pilot. He was killed in Korea. Her mother is dead too, she says. I ain't so sure. Maybe Mama just eased out of the picture, leaving little Patty with a maiden aunt in Northbank—Aunt Minnie Erryl. Anyhow, little Patty studies voice here in Northbank with Sandra Farriston until Sandra is bounced off to join Caruso, Melba, and Schumann-Heink. Remember Sandra? Then Patty goes to New Orleans to study with an old friend of Sandra's for a few years, she says. Then she comes back to Northbank to live with Auntie Min and sing in night clubs, under Auntie Min's strictly jaundiced eye. Then all of a sudden she wins this Metropolitan Opera audition tryout—''

"What about lover boy?''

"I was just coming to that, Doc. Seems he's a reporter on the Northbank *Tribune*. Covers the Federal Building in the daytime and the night-club beat after dark. Name's Bob Rhodes. He's the one who pushes her into the opera auditions. Quite a feather in his cap, to read his night-club columns. He thinks he discovers another Lily Pons.''

"What has he been seeing Wallace about?''

"I don't know yet.'' Ritter pushed his dark soft hat to the back of his head.

"Seems last night's his day off and I can't locate him.   I'm on the point of putting out a six-state alarm for him, but little Patty talks me out of it.   She guarantees to produce him for me at eleven o'clock this morning.   Want to come along?"

"Maybe I'd better.   How does the girl explain her visits to Wallace?"

"She don't know he's a crook, she says.   Friend of her dad's, she says.   Ran into him in New Orleans when she was studying music down there, then lost sight of him for a few years.   When he sees her picture in the papers after she wins that opera whoopdedoo, he looks her up here in Northbank.   She goes to see him a few times to talk about her family and maybe drink a glass of sherry or two.   That's all.   She has no idea who killed him or why."

"What about that stuff you collected from the medicine cabinet in Wallace's bathroom?"

"I got it here."   Ritter pulled a plastic bag from his bulging pocket.   "It ain't much.   Aspirin, toothpaste, bicarb, hair tonic, and this bottle of pills from some drug store in Cleveland."

Dr. Coffee uncorked the last item, sniffed, shook a few of the brightly colored tablets into the palm of his hand, sniffed again, and poured them back.   He picked up the phone.

"Get me the Galenic Pharmacy in Cleveland," he told the operator.   A moment later he said, "This is Dr. Daniel Coffee at the Pasteur Hospital in Northbank.   About a month ago you filled a prescription for a man named Wallace.   The number is 335571.   Could you read it to me?   Yes, I'll wait . . .   I see.   Diasone.   Thank you very much.   No, I don't need a refill, thank you."

Dr. Coffee's face was an expressionless mask as he hung up.   He pondered a moment, then picked up the phone again.   He dialed an inside number.

"Joe?   Coffee here.   Has the undertaker picked up that body we were working on this morning? . . .   Good.   Don't release it for another half hour.   Dr. Mookerji will tell you when."

The pathologist took off his white jacket, hung it up carefully, and reached for his coat.   He took the detective's arm and marched him out of the office.   As he crossed the laboratory, he stopped to tug playfully on the tail of the Hindu resident's pink turban.

"Dr. Mookerji," he said, "I wish you'd go down to the basement and wind up that autopsy I started this morning.   I need more tissue.   I want a specimen from both the inguinal and femoral lymph nodes, and from each earlobe.   When you're through, you may release the body.   Doris, when you make sections from this new tissue, I want you to use Fite's fuchsin stain for acid-fast bacilli.   Any biopsies scheduled, Doris?"

"Not today, Doctor."

"Then I won't be back until after lunch.   Let's go, Max."

The office bistro of the Northbank *Tribune* staff was on the ground floor of the building next door.   There reporters and desk men could refuel conveniently and could always be found in an editorial emergency.   It was whimsically named "The Slot" because the horseshoe bar was shaped like a copy desk with the bartender dealing fermented and distilled items to the boys on the rim—like an editor meting out the grist of the day's news for soft-pencil surgery.

There was a pleasant beery smell about the place, and the walls were hung with such masculine adornment as yellowing photos of prizefighters and jockeys, moth-eaten stags' heads, mounted dead fish, a few Civil War muzzle-loaders, and framed *Tribune* front pages reporting such historic events as the sinking of the Titanic, the surrender of Nazi Germany, the dropping of the first atomic bomb, and the winning of the World Series by the Northbank Blue Sox.

The masculine decor was no deterrent, however, to invasion by emancipated womanhood.   A series of stiffly uncomfortable booths had been erected at the rear of the barroom, and from one of them, as Dr. Coffee and Max Ritter entered, emerged a dark-eyed, flaxen-haired cutie who, from the swing of her hips as she advanced toward the two men, might have been a collegiate drum-majorette—except for the set of her jaw, the intelligent determination in her eyes, and the challenge in her stride.

"Hi, Patty," said Lieutenant Ritter.   "Where's the fugitive?"

"Fugitive!"   The girl flung out the word.   "I warn you, I'm not going to let you frame Bob Rhodes.   Who is this character you've brought along—a big-shot from the State Police, or just the F.B.I.?"

"Patty," said Ritter, his Adam's apple poised for a seismographic curve, "Dr. Coffee is maybe the only friend you and your lover boy have in the world—if you're both innocent.   Doc, meet Patty Erryl, the girl who's going to make the Met forget Galli-Curci, or whoever they want to forget this year.   Where's Bob?"

"He's been delayed."

"Look, Patty baby, if you insist on obstructing justice, I'll have lover boy picked up wherever he is and we'll take him downtown for questioning without your lovely interfering presence."

"Don't you dare.   If you—"

"Just a minute, Max," Dr. Coffee cut in.   "Remember I've never met Miss Erryl before.   I may have a few questions—"

The pathologist was interrupted by a crash near the entrance.   A man, sprawled momentarily on all fours, immediately rose to his knees, trying to recapture the bottles that were spinning off in all directions.

Patty Erryl sped to his rescue.   She caught him under the armpits, straining to get him to his feet.   "Bob, please get up.   They're trying to railroad you, and I'm not going to let them."

"Come, my little chickadee, there's no danger."   Rhodes had recaptured three of the elusive bottles.   "There are no witnesses.   There is no evidence.   I did not kill Fuzzy Face."

"Bob, you've been drinking."

"No, my little cedar wax-wing.   Only beer.   My own.   If only Mr. Slot would stock my Danish brand.   You know I never drink until the sun is over the yard-arm.   Which reminds me.   We have passed the vernal equinox.   The sun must be over—"

"Bob!"

"Rhodes," said Max Ritter, "the desk clerk saw you at the Westside last night."

"That near-sighted pansy!" Rhodes exclaimed. "Don't you ever try to prove anything by his testimony. And don't tell me that anything I say may be used against me, because even if this place is bugged I'll deny everything. You've drugged me. You've beaten me with gocart tires. You've kicked my shins black and blue. I'll swear that you've—"

"Stop it, Bob."

"May I ask a question, Mr. Rhodes? I'm Doctor—"

"Sure, you're the learned successor to Dr. Thorndyke, Dr. Watson, Dr. Sherlock, Dr. Holmes, Dr. . . . Indeed, I've heard about you, Dr. Sanka. Go ahead and ask."

"What were you doing at the Westside Apartment Hotel last night?"

"I was on assignment."

"From whom?"

"I'm not at liberty to say. The highest courts of this state have ruled that a newsman is not required to reveal his sources. Privileged communication."

"This ain't a matter of privileged communication," Ritter said. "This is a matter of murder in the first degree. Look here, Rhodes—"

"Just a minute, Max. Mr. Rhodes, were you inside Apartment Twenty-six last night?"

"No."

"Did you see a man named Paul Wallace last night?"

"No."

"But you know that Paul Wallace was killed in Apartment Twenty-six last night, don't you?"

"Sure. I read the papers even on my day off."

"Did you see anyone go into Apartment Twenty-six last night?"

"No."

"Did you see anyone come out?"

Rhodes hesitated for just the fraction of a second before he said, "No."

"What were you doing on the second floor of the Westside?"

"I was playing a hunch. I'm a great little hunch player."

"You make mincemeat of Wallace's lights and gizzard on a hunch?" Lieutenant Ritter asked.

"Down, Cossack!" said Rhodes. "Down. Roll over. Sit up. Beg . . ."

"Bob, you're not making any sense," the girl broke in. "Lieutenant, I'll tell you why he was at the Westside. He had an awful fight with Paul Wallace the night before last. You see, Bob and I are very much in love, and Bob is terribly jealous. He thought Paul Wallace had designs on my virtue, so Bob told him if he as much as invited me to his apartment again, he would kill him."

"And last night he made good his threat?"

"Of course not. Last night I told Bob he was being silly and he would have to go around and apologize to Paul Wallace. Only he couldn't apologize because nobody answered when he knocked on the door. I guess Mr. Wallace was already dead."

From the expression on Bob Rhodes's face, Dr. Coffee judged that at least part of the girl's story was new and startling to him.

"Patty," said Ritter, "if this guy Wallace was so buddy-buddy with your family, how come your Auntie Min never heard of him?"

"Because I never spoke of him in front of Auntie Min.   Auntie is a real spinster. She thinks all men are creatures of the devil.   If she ever thought that I went to see Mr. Wallace alone, she'd simply die, even if he is old enough to be my father."

"Is he your father?"

"No, of course not.   Lieutenant, why don't you let Bob go home and sober up? You'll never get a straight story out of him in this condition."

Ritter ignored the suggestion.   "Getting back to your Auntie Min," he said, "how come she wasn't worried to death about you being alone with that voice coach of yours 'way down south in New Orleans?"

Patty laughed.   "He's even older than Mr. Wallace."

"What was his name, Miss Erryl?" Dr. Coffee asked.

The girl hesitated.   "You wouldn't recognize it," she said after a moment. "He wasn't very well-known outside of the South.   In the French Quarter they used to call him Papa Albert."

"No last name?"

"That was his last name—Albert."

"Address?"

"Well, he used to live on Bourbon Street, but the last I heard he was going to move away."

"To Baton Rouge?"

"I—I don't know where he is now."

"Didn't he write to you from Baton Rouge?"

"No."

"Or to Mr. Wallace?"

"I'm sure I don't know."

"Do you know of anyone who might have written to Mr. Wallace from Baton Rouge?"

"I . . . I . . ."   Patty Erryl suddenly covered her face with her hands and burst into tears.

"Lay off the gal, will you, Cossack?"   Rhodes stood up, swinging a full beer bottle like an Indian club.   "If you have to work off your sadistic energy somewhere, call me any day after dark and I'll give you some addresses which I suspect you already know.   You can bring your own whips, if you want, and—"

"Sit down, Mr. Rhodes."   Dr. Coffee gently removed the bottle from the reporter's hand.   "Miss Erryl, I happened to listen to the broadcast of your operatic audition.   I thought you did a first-rate job.   I particularly admired the way you sang *Vissi d' Arte*. Do you have any real ambition to sing La Tosca some day?"

The girl's weeping stopped abruptly.   She stared at the pathologist for a moment. Then she said, "Why do you ask that?"

"You seemed to have a feeling for the part of Floria Tosca," Dr. Coffee said. "I'm sure you must be familiar with the libretto.   You are, aren't you?"

Patty Erryl's lips parted.   She closed them again without saying a word.

"Come on, Max," Dr. Coffee said.   "Miss Erryl is right.   I think you'd better tackle Mr. Rhodes when he's more himself."

"But Doc, he admits—"

"Let's go, Max.   Goodbye, Miss Tosca.   Goodbye, Mr. Rhodes."

As the police car headed for Raoul's Auberge Française (one flight up) where since it was Thursday, Dr. Coffee knew they would be regaled with *Quenelles de Brochet* (dumplings of fresh-water pike in shells), Max Ritter said, "Doc, I shouldn't have listened to you.   I should have taken that wisecracking reporter downtown."

"You won't lose him, Max.   I saw some of your most adhesive shadows loitering purposefully outside The Slot."

"You never miss a trick, do you, Doc?" Ritter chuckled.   "Doc, you don't really believe that a guy gets that squiffed so early in the day just because he can't apologize to a dead swindler, do you?"

"Hardly, Max.   But a man might get himself thoroughly soused if he realized he was seen heading for the apartment of a man with whom he had quarreled the night before and who had since been murdered.   My guess is that he spent the rest of the night ducking from bar to bar, trying to forget either that he killed a man or that he had certainly maneuvered himself into the unenviable position of appearing to have killed a man."

As they waited for a light to change, Ritter asked, "What was that crack of yours about Tosca?"

Dr. Coffee laughed.   "Pure whimsy.   Probably unimportant.   I wanted to watch the girl's reaction."

"You sure got one.   What's the angle?"

"Max, why don't you drop in at the Municipal Auditorium when the Metropolitan Opera troupe stops by for a week after the New York season?"

"Doc, you know damned well I never got past the Gershwin grade.   Who's the Tosca?"

"Floria Tosca is the tragic heroine of a play by a Frenchman named Sardou which has become a popular opera by Puccini.   Tosca is a singer who kills the villain Scarpia to save her lover, an early Nineteenth Century revolutionary named Mario, and incidentally, to save her honor.   As it turns out, her honor is about all that is saved because everybody double-crosses everybody else and there are practically no survivors.   But it's a very melodious opera, Max, and I think you might like it.   Listen."   Dr. Coffee hummed *E Lucevan le Stelle*.   "Da da da deee, da da dum, da dum dummmm . . ."

"You think we got a Patty La Tosca on our hands, Doc?"

"It's too early to tell, Max.   Right now, though, I'd say it might be a sort of Wrong-Way Tosca.   Instead of Floria Tosca killing Scarpia to save Mario, Mario may have killed Scarpia to save Tosca.   Only I'm not sure who Mario might be. I'll know more tomorrow or the next day.   I'll call you, Max."

Dr. Coffee was reading the slides from the Wallace autopsy.   The Fite stains provided colorful sections.   The acid-fast bacteria appeared in a deep ultramarine.

The connective-tissue cells were red, and all other elements were stained yellow. He raised his eyes from the binocular microscope and summoned his Hindu resident.

"Dr. Mookerji, I want you to look at this section from the femoral lymph node. You must have seen many like it in India."

Dr. Mookerji adjusted the focus, moved the slide around under the nose of the instrument, grunted, and held out a chubby brown hand.

"You have further sections, no doubt?"

"Try this. From the right earlobe."

Dr. Mookerji grunted again, then twisted the knobs of the microscope in silence.

"Hansen's bacillus?" ventured Dr. Coffee.

"Quite," said the Hindu. "However, am of opinion that said bacilli present somewhat fragmented appearance. Observe that outline is somewhat hollowish and organisms enjoy rather puny condition if not frankly deceased. Patient was no doubt arrested case?"

"The patient is dead," said Dr. Coffee, "but I'll go along with you that it wasn't Hansen's bacillus that killed him. It rarely does. In this case it was a knife." He stared into space as he toyed with the slides in the rack before him. After a moment he asked, "Doris, when is that New Orleans convention of clinical pathologists that wanted me to read a paper, and I replied I didn't think I could get away?"

Doris consulted her notebook. "It's tomorrow, Doctor."

"Good. Doris, be an angel and see if you can get me a seat on a plane for New Orleans tonight. Then try to get me Dr. Quentin Quirk, medical officer in charge of the U.S. Public Service Hospital at Carville, Louisiana. Make it person to person. Then get me Mrs. Coffee on the other line."

In five minutes Dr. Coffee had reservations on the night flight to New Orleans, had instructed his wife to pack a small bag with enough clothes for three days away from home, and was talking to Dr. Quirk in Louisiana.

"This is Dan Coffee, Quent. I'm coming down to your shindig tomorrow after all . . . Sure, I'll read a paper if you want. I don't care whether it's in the proceedings or not. Will you let me ride back to your hospital with you after the show? Fine. I've always wanted to see the place. See you tomorrow then, Quent. 'Bye."

The pathologist had barely replaced the instrument when Max Ritter walked into his office and tossed a pair of very thin rubber gloves to his desk.

"Developments, Doc," the detective said. "I just come from Patty Erryl's Auntie Min's place. She happens to have five pairs of surgeon's gloves in the house. Seconds, she says. Big sale of defective gloves at the five and ten. Forty-nine cents a pair because they're imperfect but still waterproof. She buys six pairs for herself and Patty to wear when they do the dishes. But there's only five pairs there when I find 'em. She can't remember what happened to the missing pair. She says she thinks Patty threw 'em out because they split."

"So you think old Auntie Min wore the defective surgical gloves to kill Wallace?"

"I don't say that. But this lush Rhodes is at her house practically every night to sell his bill of goods to Patty. If he should have grabbed that sixth pair of surgeon's gloves one night, it might explain why there ain't any fingerprints."

"Max, have you arrested Rhodes?"

"Not exactly. But the chief is getting impatient. I'm holding Rhodes as a material witness."

"Good lord! Well, at least I won't have to face Patty when she starts raising hell to get lover boy out of custody. I'm going to Louisiana tonight, Max. If it's at all possible, don't prefer charges until after I get back. I have a hunch I may pick up a few threads down there. Do you have that letter with the Baton Rouge postmark?"

"Sure."

"And a photo of Patty Erryl?"

"A cinch."

"Wish me luck, Max. I'll call you the minute I get back—maybe before, if I run into something hot and steaming."

Dr. Coffee savored the applause with which the convention of pathologists greeted his paper on *Determination of the Time of Death by the Study of Bone Marrow*. He also savored two days of gastronomic research: *Pompano en papillote* at Antoine's and *Crab Gumbo chez Galatoire*, among other delights. Then he drove northwest along the Mississippi with his old classmate at medical school, Dr. Quentin Quirk.

Except for an occasional mast which poked up above the levees, Old Man River was carefully concealed from the Old River Road. The drive through the flat delta country was enlivened by the pink-and-gold bravura of the rain trees, the smell of nearby water hanging on the steamy air, and the nostalgic exchange of medical school reminiscences—who among their classmates had died, who had gone to seed, who had traded integrity for social status, who had gone on to be ornaments to the growing structure of the healing sciences.

Dr. Coffee carefully avoided mentioning the real purpose of his visit even after the moss-hung oaks and the antebellum columns and wrought-iron balconies of the entrance and Administration Building loomed ahead.

It was Dr. Coffee's first visit to Carville. In spite of himself, he was surprised to find that the only leprosarium in the continental United States should be such a beautiful place. He knew of course that modern therapy had removed most of the crippling effects of the disease, which was not at all the leprosy of the Bible anyhow, and that even the superstitious dread was fading as it became generally known that the malady was only faintly communicable.

Yet as Dr. Quirk gave him a personally conducted tour of the plantation—the vast quadrangle of pink-stucco dormitories, the sweet-smelling avenue of magnolias leading up to the airy infirmary, the expensive modern laboratories, the Sisters of Charity in their sweeping white cornettes, the gay parasols in front of the Recreation Hall, the brilliantly colored birds, the private cottages for patients under the tall pecan trees beyond the golf course—Dr. Coffee wondered how it was possible for the old stigma to persist in the second half of the Twentieth Century. When he settled down to a cocktail in Dr. Quirk's bungalow, however, he remembered what he had come for.

"Quent," said Dr. Coffee, "I've seen Hansen's bacillus only twice since we've left medical school, while you've been living with it for years.   Didn't we read something in Dermatology 101 about leprosy affecting fingerprints?   Some Brazilian leprologist made the discovery, as I remember."

"That's right—Ribeiro, probably, although several other Brazilians have also been working in that field—Liera and Tanner de Abreu among them."

"Am I dreaming, or is it true that the disease can change fingerprint patterns?"

"Definitely true," said Dr. Quirk.   "Even in its early stages, the disease may alter papillary design.   The papillae flatten out, blurring the ridges and causing areas of smoothness."

"Do the fingerprint patterns ever disappear completely?"

"Oh, yes.   In advanced cases the epidermis grows tissue-thin, the interpapillary pegs often disappear, and the skin at the fingertips becomes quite smooth."

Dr. Coffee drained the last of his Sazarac, put down his glass, and gave a rather smug nod.

"Then I've come to the right place," he said.   "Quent, you may have a murderer among your patients—or among your ex-patients."

"Murderer?   Here?"   Dr. Quirk got up and pensively tinkled a handful of ice cubes into a bar glass.   "Well, it is possible.   Over the years we have had three or four murders at Carville.   When did your putative Carvillian commit murder?"

"Last Wednesday night," said Dr. Coffee, "in Northbank.   The murderer left bloody finger marks but no distinguishable prints.   I suspect the victim might also have been a one-time patient of yours.   There was Diasone in his medicine chest, and at autopsy I found fragmented Hansen's bacilli in the lymph nodes and in one earlobe.   Did you know a character named Paul Wallace?"

"Wallace?   Good lord!"   Dr. Quirk shook Peychaud bitters into the bar glass with a savage fist.   "That no-good four-flushing ape!   Yes, Wallace has been in and out of here several times.   Whenever he gets into trouble with the law, he tries to scare the authorities into sending him back here.   'You can't keep me in your jail,' he says.   'I'm a leper.   You have to send me to Carville.'   But I wouldn't take him back anymore.   He's an arrested case.   Last time he tried to dodge a conviction, I sent him back to serve time.   I knew he'd end up in some bloody mess.   Who killed him?"

"Somebody who must have loathed his guts enough to cut them to pieces.   It was a real hate job—by a man with no fingerprints."

Dr. Quirk shook his head.   "I can't imagine—"

"Quent, did you ever see this girl before?"   Dr. Coffee opened his brief case and produced a photo of Patty Erryl.

Dr. Quirk squinted at the picture, held it out at arm's length, turned it at several angles, squinted again, brought it closer, then slowly shook his head.

"No," he said.   "I don't think—"   Suddenly he slapped his hand across the upper part of the photo.   "Sorry," he said.   "Change signals.   Her hair fooled me.   I never saw her as a blonde before.   That's Patty Erryl."

"An ex-patient?"

Dr. Quirk nodded.   "She came to Carville as a kid.   Her father was an Air

Force officer in the Far East. She was raised out there—Philippines, I think; one of the endemic areas, anyhow. When her father was killed in Korea, her mother brought her back to the States. The girl developed clinical symptoms. Her mother brought her to Carville and then faded out of the picture.''

"Did she die, too?"

"I'm not sure. Maybe she remarried. Anyhow, she never once came to Carville to visit Patty. Patty responded very well to sulfones and when she was discharged as bacteriologically and clinically negative, an aunt from somewhere in the Middle West came to get her."

"That would be Auntie Min of Northbank," said Dr. Coffee. "How long ago was Patty discharged?"

"Two or three years ago. Do you want the exact date?"

"I want to know particularly whether Paul Wallace was a patient here while Patty was still in Carville."

"I'm not sure. I'll check with Sister Frances in Records." Dr. Quirk poured fresh Sazaracs.

"No hurry. I suppose you know that Patty is quite a singer."

"Do I! When she sang in the Recreation Hall, radio and television people used to come down from Baton Rouge to tape her concerts."

"How far away is Baton Rouge?"

"Oh, twenty, twenty-five miles."

"Did Patty's voice develop spontaneously, or did she have a coach?"

"Well, I guess you could say she had a coach of sorts."

"Papa Albert?"

Dr. Quirk's teeth clicked against the rim of his cocktail glass. His eyebrows rose. "You come well briefed, Dan."

"Where does Papa Albert live? Baton Rouge?"

Dr. Quirk laughed briefly. "For twenty-five years," he said, "Carville has been home to Albert Boulanger. He was a promising young pianist when the thing hit him. This was before we discovered the sulfones, so he was pretty badly crippled before we could help him. Hands are shot. He can play a few chords, though, and he's still a musician to his fingertips."

"Fingertips with papillae and interpapillary pegs obliterated?"

Dr. Quirk looked at the pathologist strangely. He muddled the ice in the bar glass, and squeezed out another half Sazarac for each of them. He took a long sip of his drink before he resumed in a slow, solemn voice.

"Patty Erryl was a forlorn little girl when she came here," he said, "and Albert Boulanger sort of adopted her. He taught her to sing little French songs. When she began to bloom, he fought off the wolves. He would invite her to his cottage out back to listen to opera recordings evening after evening.

"She was an early case. She could have been discharged in three years, except that she wanted to finish her schooling here. I think, too, that she appreciated what Papa Albert was doing to bring out the music in her. He was like a father to her. And since she scarcely knew her own father, she was terribly fond of the old man."

Dr. Coffee drained his glass again. "I suppose your records will show that Albert Boulanger was here at Carville last Wednesday night."

"I'm afraid not." Dr. Quirk frowned. "He had a forty-eight-hour pass to go to New Orleans last Wednesday. He wanted to see his lawyer about a new will. The old man hasn't long to live."

"I thought people didn't die of Hansen's disease," Dr. Coffee said.

"Boulanger has terminal cancer. He found out just two weeks ago that he's going to die in a month or two."

"Could I speak to him?"

"Why not?" Dr. Quirk picked up the phone and dialed the gate. "Willy, has Mr. Boulanger come back from New Orleans? . . . Yesterday? Thanks." He replaced the instrument. "I'll go with you," he said. "Papa Albert has one of those cottages beyond the golf course. We won't move him to the infirmary until he gets really bad."

Albert Boulanger must have been a handsome man in his youth. Tall, white-haired, only slightly stooped, he bore few external signs of his malady. Only the experienced eye would note the thinning eyebrows and the slight thickening of the skin along the rictus folds and at the wings of the nostrils.

As Dr. Coffee shook hands, he saw that Papa Albert had obviously suffered some bone absorption; his fingers were shortened and the skin was smooth and shiny.

"I stopped by to bring you greetings from Patty Erryl in Northbank," Dr. Coffee said, "and to compliment you on the fine job you did on Patty's musical education."

Papa Albert darted a quick, startled glance at Dr. Quirk. He apparently found reassurance in the MOC's smile. He coughed. "I take no credit," he said. "The girl has a natural talent and she's worked hard to make the best of it."

"I hope she wins the opera finals," the pathologist said. "Did you get to see her when you were in Northbank on Wednesday?"

Papa Albert looked Dr. Coffee squarely in the eyes as he replied without hesitation, "I've never been in Northbank in my life. I was in New Orleans on Wednesday."

"I see. Did you know that Paul Wallace was killed in Northbank last Wednesday night?"

"Paul Wallace is not of the slightest interest to me. He was a blackguard, a swindler, a thoroughly despicable man."

"Do you have a bank account in Baton Rouge, Mr. Boulanger?"

"No."

"But you did have—until you sent about $1700 to Paul Wallace."

"Why would I send money to a rotter like Wallace?"

"Because you love Patty Erryl as if she were your own daughter. Because you'd do anything to stop someone from wrecking her career just as it's about to start."

"I don't understand you." Papa Albert wiped the perspiration from his forehead with the back of his hand. He coughed again.

"Mr. Boulanger, you and I and Dr. Quirk know that there are dozens of maladies more dreadful and a thousand times more infectious than Hansen's disease.   But we also know that the superstitious horror of the disease is kept alive by ignorance and a mistaken interpretation of Biblical leprosy which equates the disease with sin.   Despite the progress of recent years there is still a stigma attached to the diagnosis.

"Suppose, Mr. Boulanger, a blackmailer came to you or wrote to you making threats that suggested a newspaper headline such as 'Girl Leper Barred from Met After Winning Audition.'   Wouldn't you dig into your savings to prevent such a headline?   And if the blackmailer persisted, if his greed increased, I can even envision—"

"Dr. Coffee, if you want me to say that I'm happy that Wallace is dead, I'll do so gladly and as loudly as I can.   But now . . ."   Papa Albert had begun to tremble.   Perspiration was streaming down his pale cheeks.   "Now, if you will excuse me . . .   Dr. Quirk has perhaps told you of my condition—that I'm supposed to get lots of rest.   May I bid you good evening, Doctor?"

He tottered a little as he walked away.

The drainage ditches were aglitter with the eerie light of fireflies as the two doctors left Papa Albert's cottage.

"What do you want me to do, Dan?" Dr. Quirk asked.

"Nothing," Dr. Coffee replied, "unless you hear from me."

Max Ritter was at the Northbank airport to meet Dr. Coffee.

"News, Doc," he said, as the pathologist stepped off the ramp.   "Rhodes has confessed."

Dr. Coffee stopped short.   "Who did what?"

"Rhodes, the lush, the lover boy, the star reporter and the talent scout.   He signed a statement that he killed Wallace."

Dr. Coffee managed a humorless laugh.   "Tell me more," he said as they passed through the gate and headed for the parking lot.

"While you're away I took a gander at the phone company's long-distance records. I find two calls in one week from Patty Erryl's number to the same place in Louisiana.   Who makes the calls?   Not me, says Auntie Min.   Must be a mistake, says Patty.   Not two mistakes, says Ritter.   Then Rhodes comes clean.   *He* makes the calls.

"Patty is terrified of this Wallace character, but she runs to see him every time he raises his little finger.   Why?   Well, Rhodes phones a newspaper pal in Louisiana to smell around a little, and he finds out Wallace is blackmailing Patty. Seems when she was studying music down there she got mixed up with a crummy bunch and got caught in a narcotics raid.   She's let off with a suspended sentence but the conviction is a matter of record.   Wallace finds out about it and starts putting the screws on her, so Rhodes kills him.   So I lock him up."

"That poor, love-sick, courageous, gallant liar!" said Dr. Coffee as he climbed into Ritter's car.   "Let's go right down to the jail and let him out."

"But Doc, Rhodes confessed!"

"Max, Rhodes is making a noble sacrifice, hoping, I'm sure, that he can beat the rap when he comes up for trial.   He's given you a confession he will surely repudiate later if it doesn't endanger Patty.   He's confessed so that you will not run down those long-distance phone calls and discover they were from Patty to the Public Health Service Hospital in Carville, Louisiana."

"The phone company didn't say anything about Carville.   The number was a Mission number out of Baton Rouge exchange through Saint Gabriel."

"Exactly.   All Carville numbers go through Baton Rouge and Saint Gabriel, and the exchange is Mission."

And Dr. Coffee told Ritter about Carville, Hansen's disease, and Papa Albert Boulanger.

"I'm positive, Max, that Papa Albert is the white-haired man with the package under his arm—the man the clerk at the Westside saw get into the elevator shortly before Wallace was killed on Wednesday," he said.   "I'm also sure that he was paying blackmail to protect Patty.

"When Papa Albert found out two weeks ago that he didn't have long to live, he decided that before he died he would get Wallace out of Patty's life forever. Northbank is only two hours from New Orleans by jet.   He could have come up by an early evening plane, killed Wallace, and been back at his New Orleans hotel by midnight.   He'll have an alibi, all right.   Who wouldn't perjure himself for a man with only a month or two to live."

"But Doc, if he's going to die anyhow, why doesn't he just give himself up, say he did it for Patty, and die a hero?"

"Because that would undo everything he's been willing to commit murder for. That would connect Patty with Carville.   And let's face it, Max, the stigma of Carville is still pretty strong poison in too many places."

"Not for Rhodes it ain't.   Or don't you think he knows?"

"He knows.   But he's an intelligent young man and he's in love with Patty."

"I still don't see what Rhodes was doing at the Westside the night of the murder if he didn't kill Wallace."

"He'll deny this, of course, but I see only one explanation.   Papa Albert didn't have Wallace's address—Wallace has been getting his mail at General Delivery. My guess is that Boulanger called Patty, probably from the airport, to get the address.   And Patty, realizing after she had hung up what the old man was intending to do, sent Bob Rhodes out to the Westside to try to stop him.   Rhodes got there too late."

"Do you think we can break Boulanger's alibi, Doc?"

"I'm sure you could build a circumstantial case.   You could dig up an airline stewardess or two who could identify him as flying to and from New Orleans the night of the murder—he's a striking-looking old gent.   You could subpoena bank records in Louisiana to show that he withdrew amounts from his savings account approximating Wallace's deposits in Cleveland.   Maybe the desk clerk at the Westside could identify him.   But you'll have to work fast, Max.   Otherwise you'll have to bring your man into court on a stretcher."

"You really think he's going to die, Doc?"

"Sooner than he thinks, I'd say. The metastases are pretty general. The lungs are involved—he has a characteristic cough. The lymph nodes in his neck are as big as pigeons' eggs. With luck he may last long enough to hear Patty sing in the finals—La Tosca, I hope. Unless, of course, you start extradition proceedings."

The detective swung his car into the "Official Vehicles Only" parking space behind the county jail.

"I dunno, Doc," he said as he switched off the ignition. "Maybe we ought to let God handle this one."

RICHARD LAYMON

Paying Joe Back

Folks say everything changes, but that's not so. I've lived in Windville all my life, and Joe's Bar & Grill looks just the same to me as always.

It has the same heavy steel grill, the same counter, the same swivel stools. Those long tables sticking out of the walls aren't much different than they were thirty years back, when Joe opened up—just older and more beaten up. The booth cushions got new upholstery seven years back, but Joe had them fixed up in the same red vinyl stuff as before, so you can't hardly tell the difference.

Only one thing has changed about Joe's place. That's the people. Some of the old-timers keep dropping by, regular as clockwork. But time has changed them considerably. Lester Keyhoe, for instance, fell to pieces after his wife kicked over. And old Gimpy Sedge lost his conductor job, so he just watches the train pull in and leave without him, then comes by here to tie one on with Lester.

Joe's gone, too. Not *gone*, just retired. I've kept the place going for the past three years, since I turned twenty-one. When Joe isn't shooting deer in the mountains, he comes in for coffee and a cinnamon bun every morning. He likes to keep an eye on things.

I sure wish he'd been after deer the morning Elsie Thompson blew in.

The place was empty except for me and Lester Keyhoe, who was sitting down the bar where he always does, getting a start on the day's drinking.

I was toweling down the counter when the car pulled up. I could see it plain through the window. It was an old Ford that looked like somebody'd driven it a dozen times back and forth through Hell. It sputtered and whinnied for a minute after the ignition key was turned off.

I stopped toweling and just stared. The old gal who jumped out of the Ford was a real sight—short and round, dressed in khakis, with gray hair cut like Buster Brown, and wearing big wire-rimmed glasses. She chewed on some gum like she wanted to kill it. A floppy wicker handbag hung from her arm. I said, "Get a load of this," to Lester, but he didn't even look up.

The screen door opened and she stumped towards the counter in her dusty boots. She hopped onto the stool in front of me. Her jaw went up and down a few times. One time when it was open, the word "coffee" came out.

"Yes, ma'am," I said, and turned away to get it.

"Does this establishment belong to Joseph James Lowry from Chicago?" she asked.

"Sure does," I said, looking at her.

Behind the glasses her round eyes opened and shut in time with her chewing mouth. She gave me a huge grin. "That's mighty good news, young man. I've been driving through every one-horse town west of Chicago looking for this place, looking for Joe Lowry and his damned tavern. There's a place called Joe's in every single one of them. But I knew I'd find Joe Lowry's place sooner or later. Know why? Because I've got will power, that's why. When do you expect him in?"

"Well . . . what did you want to see him about?"

"He *is* coming in?"

I nodded.

"Good. I expected as much. I'm only surprised not to find him behind the counter."

"You know him, huh?"

"Oh, yes. My, yes." Her eyes turned sad for a second. "We used to know each other very well, back in Chicago."

"How about if I give him a ring, tell him you're here?"

"That won't be necessary." Snapping her gum and grinning, she opened the handbag on her lap and pulled out a revolver. Not a peashooter, either—one of those long-barreled .38's. "I'll surprise him," she said. Her stubby little thumb pulled back the hammer and she aimed the thing at me. "We'll surprise him together."

I didn't feel much like talking, but I managed to nod my head.

"What time will Joe be in?" she asked.

"Pretty soon." I took a deep breath and asked, "You aren't planning to shoot him, are you?"

She pretended like she didn't hear me, and asked, "How soon?"

"Well . . ." Far away, the 10:05 from Parkerville let loose its whistle. "Well, pretty soon, I guess."

"I'll wait for him. Who's that slob over there?"

"That's Lester."

"Lester!" she called.

He turned his head and looked at her. She waved the gun at him, grinning and chewing, but his face didn't change. It looked the same as always, long and droopy like a bloodhound's, but more gloomy.

"Lester," she said, "you just stay right on that stool. If you get up for any reason, I'll shoot you dead."

His head nodded, then turned frontwards again and tipped down at his half-empty glass.

"What's your name?" she asked me.

"Wes."

"Wes, keep Lester's glass full. And don't do anything to make me shoot you. If some more customers come in, just serve them like everything is normal. This

revolver has six loads, and I can take down a man with each.   I don't want to.
I only want Joe Lowry.   But if you drive me to it, I'll make this place wall-to-
wall corpses.   Understand?''

"Sure, I understand."   I filled Lester's glass, then came back to the woman.
"Can I ask you something?''

"Fire away.''

"Why do you want to kill Joe?''

She stopped chewing and squinted at me.   "He ruined my life.   That's enough
reason to kill a man, I think.   Don't you?''

"Nothing's a good enough reason to kill Joe.''

"Think so?''

"What'd he do to you?''

"He ran off with Martha Dipsworth.''

"Martha?   That's his wife—was.''

"Dead?''

I nodded yes.

"Good.''   Her jaw chomped, and she beamed.   "That makes me glad.   Joe
made a mistake, not marrying me—I'm still alive and kicking.   We'd be happily
married to this day if he'd had the sense to stick with me.   But he never did have
much sense.   Do you know what his great ambition was?   To go out west and
open up a tavern.   Martha thought that was a *glorious* idea.   I said, 'Well, *you*
marry him, then.   Go out west and waste your lives in the boondocks.   If Joe's
such a romantic fool as to throw his life away like that, I don't want him.   There're
plenty of fish in the sea.   That's what I said.   More than thirty years ago.''

"If you said that—'' I stopped.   You don't catch me arguing with an armed
woman.

"What?''

"Nothing.''

She shifted her chewing gum over to one corner of her mouth and drank some
coffee.   "What were you going to say?''

"Just . . . well, if you said they could get married, it doesn't seem very fair of
you to blame them.''

She put down the cup and glanced over at Lester.   He still sat there, but he was
staring at the gun.   "When I said that about the sea being full of fish, I figured
it'd only be a matter of time before I'd land a good one.   Well, it didn't work out
that way.''

She chewed a few times, gazing up at me with a funny distance in her eyes as
if she was looking back at all the years.   "I kept on waiting.   I was just sure the
right man was around the next corner—around the next year.   It finally dawned
on me, Wes, that there wasn't ever going to be another man.   Joe was it, and I'd
lost him.   That's when I decided to gun him down.''

"That's—''

"What?''

"Crazy.''

"It's justice.''

"Maybe the two of you could get together. He's unattached since Martha died. Maybe—"

"Nope. Too late for that. Too late for babies, too late for—"

All at once Lester flung himself away from the bar and made a foolish run for the door. The old gal swiveled on her stool, tracked him for a split second, then squeezed off a shot. The bullet took off Lester's earlobe. With a yelp he swung around and ran back to his stool, cupping a hand over what was left of his ear.

"You'd better pray nobody heard that shot," she said to both of us.

I figured nobody would. We were at the tail end of town, so the closest building was a gas station half a block away. The cars passing by on the highway kicked up plenty of noise. And around here, with all the hunting that goes on, nobody pays much attention to a single gunshot unless it's right under his nose.

But I was nervous, anyway. For five minutes we all waited without saying a word. The only sound was her gum snapping.

She finally grinned and squinted as if she'd just won a raffle. "We're in luck."

"Joe's not," I said. "Neither's Lester."

Lester said nothing. He was pinching his notched ear with one hand and draining his glass with the other.

"They shouldn't have run," the woman said. "That was their mistake—they ran. You aren't going to run, are you?"

"No, ma'am."

"Because if you do I'll shoot you for sure. I'll shoot anyone today. Anyone. This is my day, Wes—the day Elsie Thompson pays Joe back."

"I won't run, ma'am. But I won't let you shoot Joe. I'll stop you one way or another." I went over to fill Lester's glass.

"You can't stop me. No one can stop me. Nothing can. Do you know why? Because I've got will power, that's why."

Grinning mysteriously, she chomped three times on her gum and said, "Today I'm going to die. That gives me all the power in the world. Understand? As soon as I gun down Joe, I'll drive out of this burg. I'll get that old Ford up to seventy, eighty, then I'll pick out the biggest tree—"

I made a sick laugh, and came back to her.

"Think I'm fooling?" she said.

"No, ma'am. It's just kind of funny, you talking like that about crashing into a tree. Not funny ha-ha, funny weird. You know what I mean?"

"No."

"That's 'cause you don't know about Joe. He crashed into a tree—an aspen, just off Route 5. That was about three years back. Martha was with him. She got killed, of course. Joe was in real bad shape, and Doc Mills didn't give him much chance. But he pulled through. His face got so broken up he doesn't look quite right, and he lost the use of an eye. His left eye, not his aiming eye. He wears a patch over it, you know. And sometimes when he gets feeling high, he flaps it up and gives us all a peek underneath."

"You can stop that."

"He lost a leg, too."

"I don't want to hear about it."

"Yes, ma'am. I'm sorry. It's just that . . . well, everyone that crashes into a tree doesn't die."

"I will."

"You can't be sure. Maybe you'll just end up like Joe, hobbling around half blind on a fake leg, with your face so scarred up that your best friends won't recognize you."

"Shut up, Wes."

She stuck the pistol into my face, so I slowed down and said quietly, "I just mean, if you want to make sure you die, there's a concrete bridge abutment about a mile up the road."

"Warm up my coffee and keep your mouth shut."

I turned around to pick up the pot. That's when I heard the footsteps outside. Boots against the wood planks out front, coming closer. I faced Elsie. She grinned at me. Her jaw worked faster on the gum. Her eyes squinted behind her glasses as the unsteady clumping got louder.

Through the window I saw his mussy gray hair, his scarred face with the patch on his left eye. He saw me looking, smiled, and waved.

I glanced at Lester, who was holding a paper napkin to his ear and the glass to his mouth.

Elsie pushed the pistol close to my chest. "Don't move," she whispered.

The screen door swung open.

Elsie spun her stool.

"Duck, Joe!" I cried out.

He didn't duck. He just stood there looking perplexed as Elsie leaped off the stool, crouched, and fired. The first two bullets smacked him square in the chest. The next hit his throat. Then one tore into his shoulder, turning him around so the last shot took him in the small of the back.

All this happened in a couple of seconds as I dived at Elsie. I was in mid-air when she wheeled on me and smashed me in the face with the barrel. I went down.

While I was trying to get up, she jumped over the body and ran out. I reached the door in time to see her car whip backwards. It hit the road with screeching brakes, then laid rubber and was gone from sight.

I went back inside.

Lester was still sitting at the bar. His stool was turned around, and he was staring at the body. I sat down at one of the booths, lit a cigarette, and kept Lester company staring.

We spent a long time like that. After a while I heard the sheriff's siren. Then an ambulance's. The cars screamed by and faded up the road in the direction of the bridge abutment.

"My God!" The big man looked at me, then at Lester, and knelt down over the body. He turned it over. "Gimpy," he muttered. "Poor old Gimpy." He patted the dead conductor on the back, and stood up. His eyes questioned me.

I shook my head. "Some crazy woman," I muttered. "She came in here dead set to kill you, Dad."

MICHAEL GILBERT

The Merry Band

Detective:
SERGEANT PATRICK PETRELLA

The late-afternoon sun, shining through the barred skylight, striped the bodies of the four boys sprawled on the floor. Nearby the Sunday traffic went panting down the Wandsworth High Street, but in this quiet, upper back room the loudest noise was the buzzing of a bluebottle. The warm, imprisoned air smelled of copperas and leather and gun oil.

The oldest and tallest of the boys was sitting up, with his back propped against the wall. In one hand he held a piece of cloth, something that might once have been a handkerchief, and he was using it to polish and repolish a powerful-looking air pistol.

"They're beauties, ent they, Rob?" said the fat boy. He and the red-haired boy both had guns like their leader's. The smallest boy had nothing. He couldn't take his eyes off the shining beauties.

"Made in Belgium," said Rob. "See that gadget?" He put the tip of his finger on the telltale at the end of the compression chamber. "You don't just open it and shut it, like a cheap air gun. You pump this one up slowly. That gadget shows you when the pressure's right. It's accurate up to fifty yards."

"*It* may be accurate," said the fat boy. "What about us? I've never had a gun before."

"We'll have to practise. Practise till we can hit a penny across the room."

"Why don't we start right now, Rob?" said the red-haired boy. "These things don't make any noise. Not to notice. We could chalk up a target on the wall—"

"Yes?" said Rob. "And when the geezer who owns this shop comes up here tomorrow morning, or next week, or whenever he does happen to come up here, and he finds his wall full of air-gun pellets, he's going to start thinking, isn't he? He's going to check over his spare stock and find three guns missing. Right?"

"That's right," said the fat boy. "Rob's got it figured out. We put everything else back like we found it, it may be months before he knows what's been took. He mayn't even know anyone's broke in."

The leader turned to the smallest of his followers. "That's why you can't have one, Winkle," he said. "There's plenty of guns in the front of the shop, but we touch one of them, he'll miss it."

"That's all right, Rob," said Winkle. But he couldn't keep the longing out of his voice.   To own a big bright gun!   A gun that went *phtt* softly, like an angry snake, and your enemy fifty yards away crumpled to the ground, not knowing what had hit him!

"What about Les?" said the red-haired boy.

"What about him?"

"He'll want a gun when he sees ours."

"He'll have to go on wanting.   If he's not keen enough to come with us on a job like this."

" 'Tisn't that he's not keen," said the fat boy.   "It's his old man.   He's pretty strict.   He locks his bedroom door now.   Where can we practise, Rob?"

"I've got an idea about that," said the tall boy.   "You know the old Sports Pavilion?   The Home Guard used it in the war, but it's been shut up since."

The boys nodded.

"I found a way in at the back, from the railway.   I'll show you.   There's a sort of cellar with lockers in it.   That'll do us fine.   We'll have our first meeting there tomorrow.   Right?"

"Right," they all said.   The red-haired boy added, "How did you know about this place, Rob?"

"My family used to live round here," said the tall boy.   "Before my Ma died, when we moved up to Highside.   As a matter of fact, I was at school about a quarter mile from here."

The fat boy said, "I bet I get a strapping from my old man when I get home. He don't like me being away all day."

"You're all right," said Winkle.   "You're fat.   It don't hurt so much when you're fat."   He looked down with disgust at his own slender limbs.

It was nine o'clock at night nearly a month after that talk and in quite another part of London that Fishy Codlin was closing what he called his Antique Shop. This was a dark and rambling suite of rooms, full of dirt, woodworm, and the household junk of a quarter of a century.   Codlin was in the front room, locking away the day's take when the two boys came in.

"You're too late," he growled.   "I'm shut."

He noticed that the smaller of the boys stayed by the door, while the older came toward him with a curiously purposeful tread.   He had a prevision of trouble and his hand reached out for the light switch.

"Leave it alone," said the boy.   He was a half-seen figure in the dusk.   All the light seemed to concentrate on the bright steel weapon in his hand.   "Slip the bolt, Will," he added, but without taking his eyes off Codlin.   "Now you stand away from the counter."

Codlin stood away.   He thought for a moment of refusing, for there was nearly £25 in the box, the fruits of a full week's trading.   But he was a coward as well as a bully and the gun looked real.   He watched the notes disappearing in the boy's pocket.   When one of the notes slipped to the floor the boy bent down and picked it up, but without ever removing his steady gaze from the old man.

When he had finished, the boy backed away to the door.   "Stay put," he said. "And keep quiet for five minutes or you'll get hurt."

Then he was gone.   Codlin breathed out an obscenity and jumped for the telephone.   As he picked it up, "I warned you," said a gentle voice from the door.   There was a noise like a small tire bursting and the telephone twisted round and clattered to the floor.

Codlin stood, staring stupidly at his hand.   Splinters of vulcanite had grooved it, and the blood was beginning to drip.   He cursed, foully and automatically.   Footsteps were pattering away along the road outside.   He let them get to the corner before he moved.   He was taking no further chances.   Then he lumbered across to the door, threw it open, and started bellowing.

Three streets away Detective Sergeant Petrella, homeward bound, heard two things at once.   Distant shouts of outrage and, much closer at hand, light feet pattering on the pavement.   He drew into the shadow at the side of the road and waited.

The two boys came round the corner, running easily, and laughing.   When Petrella stepped out, the laughter ceased.   Then the boys spun around and started to run the other way.

Petrella ran after them.   He saw at once that he could not catch both, so he concentrated on the younger and slower boy.   After a hundred yards he judged himself to be in distance and jumped forward in a tackle.   It was high by the standards of Twickenham, but it was effective, and they went down, the boy underneath.   As they fell, something dropped from the boy's pocket and slid, ringing and spinning, across the pavement.

"Of course you've got to charge him," said Haxtell later that night.   "It's true Codlin can't really identify him, but the boy had a gun on him and he was running away from the scene of the crime.   Who is he, by the way?"

"His name's Christopher Connolly.   His father's a shunter at the goods depot. I've left them together for a bit, to see if the old man can talk some sense into him."

"Good idea," said Haxtell.   "Can we get anything on the gun?"

"It's an air pistol.   Therefore no registration number.   And foreign.   Newish. And a pretty high-powered job.   If it's been stolen we might have it on the lists."

"Check it," said Haxtell.   "What about his pockets?"

"Nothing except this."   Petrella pushed across a scrap of paper.   It had penciled on it: WILL BE AT USUAL PLACE 8 TONIGHT.

"What do you make of it?" said Haxtell.

"It depends," said Petrella cautiously, "if you think the dot after the first word is a full stop or just an accident."

Haxtell tried it both ways.   "You mean it could be a plain statement: 'I will be at the usual place at eight o'clock tonight.'   Or it could be an order, to someone called Will."

"Yes.   And Codlin did say that he thought he heard the bigger boy address the smaller one as Will."

"Is Connolly's name William?"

"No, sir.   It's Christopher George.   Known to his friends as Chris."

"What does he say about the paper?"

"Says I planted it on him.   And the gun, of course."

"I often wonder," said Haxtell, "where the police keep all the guns they're supposed to plant on criminals.   What about the other boy?"

"He says that there was no other boy.   He says he was alone, and had been alone, all the evening."

"I see."   Haxtell stared thoughtfully out of the window.   He had a sharp nose for trouble.

"One bright spot," he said at last.   "Codlin always marked his notes.   Ever since he caught an assistant trying to dip into his till.   He puts a letter C in indelible pencil on the back."

"That might be a help if we can catch the other boy," agreed Petrella.   He added, "Haven't I heard that name Codlin before?   Something about a dog."

"He tied his dog up," said Haxtell.   "A nice old spaniel.   And beat him with a golf club.   Fined forty shillings.   It was before your time."

"I must have read about it somewhere," said Petrella.

"And if you think," blared Haxtell, "that's any reason for not catching these— these young bandits—then I dare you to say it."

"Why, certainly not," said Petrella hastily.

"This is the third holdup in a fortnight.   The third that's been reported to us. All with guns—or what looked like guns.   Now we've caught one of them.   We've *got* to get the names of the other boys out of him.   For their sake as much as anything.   Before someone really gets hurt."

"I expect the boy'll talk," said Petrella.

Haxtell nodded.   Given time, boys usually talked.

But Christopher Connolly was an exception.   For he said nothing, and continued to say nothing.

The next thing that happened, happened to old Mrs. Lightly, who lived alone in a tiny cottage above the waterworks.   Her husband had been caretaker and she had retained the cottage by grace of the management as long as she paid the rent of ten shillings a week.   Lately she had been getting irregular in her payments and she was now under notice to move.

The evening after the capture of Connolly, just after dark, she heard a noise down in her front hall.   She was a spirited old lady and she came right out, carrying a candle to see what it was all about.

On the patched linoleum lay a fat envelope.   Mrs. Lightly picked it up gingerly and carried it back to the sitting room.   She got very few letters, and, in any case, the last mail had come and gone many hours earlier.

On the envelope, in penciled capital letters, were the words:

EIGHT WEEKS RENT FROM SOME FRIENDS.

Mrs. Lightly set the candle down on the table and with fingers that trembled tore open the flap.   A little wad of notes slid out.   She counted them.   Two pound notes and four ten-shilling notes.   There was no shadow of doubt about it.   It was four pounds.   And that was eight weeks' rent.

Or, looked at in another way, suppose it was seven weeks' rent.   That would have the advantage of leaving ten shillings over for a little celebration.   The whole thing was clearly a miracle; and miracles are things which the devout are commanded to commemorate.

Mrs. Lightly placed the notes in the big black bag, folded the envelope carefully away behind a china dog on the mantelshelf, and got her best black hat out of the closet.

On the same evening, shortly after Mrs. Lightly left her cottage, four boys were sitting in the basement changing room of the old Sports Pavilion.   A storm lantern, standing on a locker, shed a circle of clear white light around it, leaving the serious faces of the boys in shadow.   The windows were carefully blacked out on the inside with cardboard and brown paper.

"I don't like it, Rob," the black-haired boy was saying.   He was evidently repeating an old argument.

"What's wrong with it?" said the tall boy.   He had a curiously gentle voice.

"Old Cator's what's wrong with it.   He's a holy terror."

"He's a crook," said the fat boy.

The small boy said nothing.   His eyes turned from one to the other as they spoke, but when no one was speaking they rested on the tall boy, full of trust and love.

"Isn't it crooks we're out to fix?" said the tall boy.   "Isn't that right, Busty?"

"That's right," said the fat boy.

The black-haired boy said, "Hell, yes.   But not just any crooks.   Cator's got a night watchman.   And he's a tough, too.   As likely as not, they both carry guns."

The tall boy said, "Are you afraid?"

"Of course I'm not afraid."

"Then what are we arguing about?   There's four of us.   And we've got two guns.   There's two of them.   When we pull the job, maybe only one'll be there. This is something we've *got* to do.   We need the money."

"Another thing," said the black-haired boy.   "Suppose we don't give quite so much away this time."

"You mean, keep some for ourselves?"

"That's right."

"What for?"

"I could think of ways to use it," said the black-haired boy, with a laugh.   He looked round, but neither of the others had laughed with him.   "All right," he said.   "All right.   I know the rules.   Let's get this planned out."

"This is how it is, then," said the tall boy.   "I reckon we'll have to wait about a week—"   He demonstrated, on sheets of paper, with a pencil, and the four heads came close together, casting long shadows in the lamplight.

Next morning Petrella reported to Superintendent Haxtell the minor events of the night.   There was a complaint from the Railway that some boys had broken a hole in the fence below the Sports Pavilion.

"Apart from that," said Petrella, "a beautiful calm seems to have fallen on Highside.   Oh—apart from Mrs. Lightly."

"Mrs. Lightly?"

"Old Lightly's widow.   The one who lives in the cottage next to the waterworks."

"Was that the one there was a bit in the papers about how she couldn't pay her rent?"

"That's right," said Petrella.   "Only she got hold of some money and that's what the drinking was about.   It was a celebration.   She seems to have drunk her way steadily along the High Street.   Mostly gin, but a certain amount of stout to help it down.   She finished by busting a shop window with an empty bottle."

"Where'd she got the money from?"

"That's the odd thing.   She was flat broke.   Faced with eviction, and no one very sympathetic, because they knew that as soon as she got any money she'd drink it up.   Then an angel dropped in, with four quid in an envelope."

"An angel?"

"That's what she says.   A disembodied spirit.   It popped an envelope through the letter box with four ten-shilling notes and two pound notes in it."

"How much of it was left when you picked her up?"

"About two pounds ten," said Petrella.

"I don't see anything odd in all that," said Haxtell.   "Some crackpot reads in the papers that the old girl's short of money and how her landlord's persecuting her, and he makes her an anonymous donation, which she promptly spends on getting plastered."

"Yes, sir," said Petrella.   He added gently, "I've seen the notes she *didn't* spend.   They're all marked on the back with a C in indelible pencil."

"They're *what*?"

"That's right, sir."

"It's mad."

"It's a bit odd, certainly," said Petrella.   Something, a note almost of smugness in his voice, made the Superintendent look up.   "Have you got some line on this?"

"I think I might be able to trace those notes back to the boy who's been running this show."

"Then we don't waste any time talking about it," said Haxtell.   "We need results and we need 'em quickly."   He added, with apparent inconsequence, "I'm seeing Barstow this afternoon."

Petrella's hopes, such as they were, derived from the envelope, which he had duly recovered from behind the china dog on Mrs. Lightly's mantelshelf.   The name and address had been cut out, but two valuable pieces of information had been left behind.   The first was the name *Strangeway's* printed in the top left-hand corner.   The second was the postmark, the date on which was still legible.

Petrella knew Strangeway's.   It was a shop that sold cameras and photographic equipment, and he guessed that its daily output of letters would not be large.   There was a chance, of course, that the envelope had been picked up casually. But equally, there was a chance that it had not.

Happily, the manager of Strangeway's was a methodical man. He consulted his daybook and produced for Petrella a list of names and addresses. "I think," he said, "that those would be all the firm's letters that went out that day. They would be bills or receipts. I may have written one or two private letters, but I'd have no record of them."

"But they wouldn't be in your firm's envelope."

"They might be. If they went to suppliers."

"I'll try these first," said Petrella.

There were a couple of dozen names on the list. Most of the addresses were in Highside or Helenwood.

It was no use inventing an elaborate story. He was too well known locally to pretend to be an insurance salesman. He decided on a simple lie.

To the gray-haired old lady who opened the door to him at the first address he said, "We're checking the election register. The lists are getting out of date. Have you any children in the house who might come of age in the next five years?"

"There's Jimmy," said the woman.

"Who's Jimmy?"

She explained about Jimmy. He was a real terror. Aged about nineteen. Just as Petrella was getting interested in Jimmy she added that he'd been in Canada for a year.

Petrella took down copious details about Jimmy. It all took time, but if you were going to deal in lies, it was well to act them out.

That was the beginning of a long day's work. Early in the evening he came to Number 11 Parham Crescent. The house was no different from a million others of the brick boxes that encrust the surface of London's northern heights.

The door was opened by a gentleman in shirtsleeves, who agreed that his name was Brazier and admitted having a sixteen-and-a-half-year-old son named Robert.

"Robert Brazier?"

"Robert Humphreys. He's my sister's son. She's been dead two years. He lives here—*when* he's home."

Petrella picked up the lead with the skill of long experience. Was Robert often away from home?

Mr. Brazier obliged with a discourse on modern youth. Boys nowadays, Petrella gathered, were very unlike what boys used to be when he—Mr. Brazier—had been young. They lacked reverence for their elders, thought they knew all the answers, and preferred to go their own ways. "Sometimes I don't see him all day. Sometimes two days running. He could be out all night for all I know. It's not right—Mr.—um—"

Petrella agreed that it wasn't right. Mr. Brazier suffered from bad breath, which made listening to him an ordeal. However, he elicited some details. One of them was the name of the South London school that Robert had left eighteen months before.

Petrella did some telephoning, and the following morning he caught a bus and trundled down to Southwark to have a word with Mr. Wetherall, the headmaster of the South Borough Secondary School for Boys.   Mr. Wetherall was a small spare man with a beaky nose and he had been wrestling for a quarter of a century with the tough precocious youths who live south of the river.   The history of his struggles was grooved into his leathery face.   He cheerfully took time off to consider Petrella's problems; all the more so when he discovered what was wanted.

"Robert Humphreys," he said.   "I had a bet with my wife that I'd hear that name again before long."

"Now you've won it, sir."

"Yes," said Mr. Wetherall.   He gazed reflectively round his tiny overcrowded study, then said, "This is a big school, you know.   And I've been here, with one short break, for more than ten years.   Maybe two thousand boys.   And out of all that two thousand I could count on the fingers of one hand—without using the thumb—the ones whom I call natural leaders.   And of those few I'm not sure I wouldn't put Robert Humphreys first."

Mr. Wetherall added, "I'll tell you a story about him.   While he was here, we were planning to convert a building into a gymnasium.   I'd got all the governors on my side except the Chairman, Colonel Bond.   He was opposed to spending the money, and until I'd won him over I couldn't move.

"One day the Colonel disappeared.   He's a bachelor who spends most of his time at his Club.   No one was unduly worried.   He missed a couple of governors' meetings, which was unusual.

"Then I got a letter.   From the Colonel.   It simply said that he had been thinking things over and had decided that we ought to go ahead with our gym.   He himself wouldn't be able to attend meetings for some time, as his health had given way."

Petrella goggled at him.   "Are you telling me—?" he said.

"That's right," said Mr. Wetherall calmly.   "The boys had kidnaped him. Robert organized the whole thing.   They picked him up in a truck, and kept him in a loft, over an old stable.   Guarded him, fed him, looked after him.   And when they'd induced him to write that letter they let him out."

"How did they disguise themselves?"

"They made no attempt to disguise themselves.   They calculated, and rightly, that if the Colonel made a fuss people would never stop laughing at him.   The Colonel had worked the sum out too, and got the same answer.   He never said a word about it.   In fact, it was Humphreys who told me.   It was then that I made my confident prediction.   Downing Street or the Old Bailey."

"I'm afraid it may be the Old Bailey," said Petrella unhappily.

"It was an even chance," said Mr. Wetherall.   "He was devoted to his mother. If she hadn't died, I believe there's hardly any limit to what he might have done. He's with an uncle now.   Not a very attractive man."

"I've met him," said Petrella.   As he was going he said, "Did you get your gym?"

"I'll show it to you as we go," said Mr. Wetherall.   "One of the finest in South London."

It took another whole day for Petrella to finish his inquiries, but now that the clue was in his hand it was not difficult to find the heart of the maze. It had been a day of blazing heat; by nine o'clock that night when he faced Superintendent Haxtell, hardly a breath was moving.

"There are four of them," he said. "Five with Chris Connolly, the one we caught. First, there's a boy called Robert Humphreys. His first lieutenant's Brian Baker, known as Busty."

"A fat boy," said Haxtell. "Rather a good footballer. His father's a pro."

"Correct. The third one is Les Miller."

"Sergeant Miller's boy?"

"I'm afraid so, sir."

The two men looked at each other. Sergeant Miller was Petrella's opposite number at Pond End Police Station.

"Go on," said Haxtell grimly.

"The fourth, and much the youngest, is one of the Harrington boys. The one they call Winkle. His real name's Eric, or Ricky. There seems to be no doubt that the air guns they've been using were stolen from a shop in Southwark, which is, incidentally, where Humphreys went to school."

"And Humphreys is the leader?"

"I don't think there's any doubt about that at all, sir. In fact, the whole thing is a rather elaborate game made up by him."

"A game," said Haxtell, pulling out a handkerchief and wiping the sweat from his forehead.

"Of Robin Hood. That's why they used those names. Fat Brian was Friar Tuck, red-headed Chris was Will Scarlet, Les was the Miller's son. And Ricky was Allen-a-Dale. Robert, of course, was Robin. I believe that historically—"

"I'm not interested in history. And you can dress it up what way you like. It doesn't alter the fact that they're gangsters."

"There were two points about them," said Petrella. "I'm not suggesting it's any sort of mitigation. But they really did adhere to the ideas of their originals. They didn't rob old women or girls—and they're usually the number-one target for juvenile delinquents."

Haxtell grunted.

"They chose people they thought needed robbing." Petrella caught the look in his superior's eye and hurried on. "And they didn't spend the money on themselves. They gave it away. All of it, as far as I can make out. To people they thought needed it. More like the real Robin Hood than the synthetic version. Hollywood's muddled it up for us.

"You hear the kids saying, 'Feared by the bad. Loved by the good.' But that wasn't really the way of it. Robin Hood didn't rob people because they were bad. He assumed they were bad because they were rich. He was an early Communist."

Petrella stopped, aware that he had outrun discretion.

"Go on," said Haxtell grimly.

"Of course, he's got idealized now," Petrella concluded defiantly. "But I should think the authorities thought *he* was a pretty fair nuisance—when he was actually operating—wouldn't you?"

"And you suggest, perhaps, that we allow them to continue their altruistic work of redistributing the wealth of North London?"

"Oh, no, sir.   We've got to stop them."

"Why, if they're doing so much good?"

"Before they get hurt.   As you said yourself."

Haxtell was spared the necessity of answering by a clatter of feet in the corridor and a resounding knock at the door.   It was Detective Sergeant Miller, and he had his son with him.

"Good evening, Miller," said Haxtell.   "I was half expecting you."

"I've brought my boy along," said Sergeant Miller.   He was white with fury. "He's got something he's going to tell you."

The boy had been crying, but was calm enough now.   "It's Humphreys and the others," he said.   "They're going to do Cator's Garage tonight.   I wouldn't agree to it.   So they turned me out of the band.   So I told Dad."

Just so, thought Petrella, had all great dynasties fallen.   He was aware of a prickling sensation, a crawling of the skin, not entirely accounted for by the onrush of events.   He looked out of the window and saw that a storm had crept up on them. Even as he watched, the first thread of lightning flicked out and in, like an adder's tongue, among the banked black clouds.

Les Miller was demonstrating something on the table.

"They've found a way in round the back.   They get across the canal on the old broken bridge, climb the bank, and get in a window of an outhouse, which leads into the garage.   There's a watchman, but they reckon they can rush him from behind and get his keys off him.   Cator keeps a lot of his money in the garage."

Petrella said, "I expect that's right, sir.   We've had our eyes on that gentleman for some time.   If he's in the hot-car racket he'd have no use for checks or a bank account."

"We'd better warn Cator," said Haxtell, "and get a squad car round there quick. What time's the operation due to start?"

Before the boy could answer, the telephone sounded.   Haxtell picked off the receiver, listened a moment, and said, "Don't do anything.   We'll be right around," and to the others, "It has started.   That was the watchman.   He's knocked one boy out cold."

As Petrella ran for the car the skies opened and he was wet to the skin before he reached the car.

Outside Cator's Garage, a rambling conglomeration of buildings backing on the canal, they skidded to a halt, nearly ramming a big green limousine coming from the opposite direction.   Herbert Cator jumped out, pounded up the cinder path ahead of them, and thumped on the door.

The man who opened the door looked like a boxer gone badly to seed.   The right side of his face was covered with blood, from a badly torn ear and a scalp wound.   He was holding a long steel poker in one hand.   "Glad you've got here," said the man.   "Three of the little scum.   I got one of 'em."

He jerked his head toward the corner where fat Friar Tuck lay on his face, on the oil-dank floor.

"Where are the others?" said Haxtell.

"In there." He pointed to the heavy door that led through to the main workshop. "Don't you worry. They won't get out of there in a hurry. The windows are all barred."

Haxtell walked across, slipped the bolt, and threw the door open.

It was a big room, two stories tall. The floor space was jammed with cars in every stage of dismemberment. The top was a clutter of hoisting and lifting tackle, dim above the big overhead lights.

"Come out of there, both of you."

"The big one's got a gun," said the watchman. "He nearly shot my ear off."

"Keep away then," said Haxtell. He turned back again and said in a booming voice, "Come on, Humphreys. And you, Harrington. The place is surrounded."

As if in defiant answer came a sudden deafening crash of thunder. And then all the lights went out.

"Damnation," said Haxtell. Over his shoulder to Petrella and Miller he said, "Bring all the torches we've got in the car. And the spotlight, if the flex is long enough—"

Cator said, "Hold it a moment. Something's alight." A golden-white sheet of flame shot up from the back of the room. Cator said thickly, "They've set fire to the garage, the devils."

In the sudden light Petrella saw the boys. They were crouching together on an overhead latticework gantry. Cator saw them, too. His hand went down and came up. There was the roar of a gun, once, twice, before anyone could get at him. Then Petrella was moving.

The light showed him the iron ladder that led upward. He flung himself at it and went up. Then along the narrow balcony. When he reached the place where he had seen them, the boys had gone. He stood for a moment. Already the heat was becoming painful. Then, ahead of him, he saw the door to the roof. It was swinging open.

As he reached it the whole of the interior of the room went up behind him in a hot white belch of flame.

Out on the roof he found the boys. Ricky Harrington was on his knees, beside Humphreys. The flames, pouring through the opening, lit the scene with cruel light.

Petrella knelt down beside him. One look was enough.

"He's dead, ent he?" said Ricky, in a curiously composed voice.

"Yes," said Petrella. "And unless the fire engine comes damned quick, he's going to have company in the next world."

The boy said, "I don't want no one to rescue me." He ran to the side of the building, vaulted the low coping, and disappeared. Petrella hurled himself after him.

He was just in time to see the miracle. Uncaring what happened to him, Ricky had landed with a soft splash in the waters of the North Side Canal.

"If he can do it, I can," said Petrella. "Roast or drown." He jumped. The world turned slowly in one complete fiery circle, and then his mouth was full of water.

He rose to the surface, spitting.   There was no sign of the boy.   Petrella tried to think.   They had jumped from the same spot.   There was no current.   He must be there.   Must be within a few yards.

He took a deep breath, turned over, and duck-dived.   His fingers scrabbled across filth, broken crockery, and the sharper edges of cans.   When he could bear it no longer he came up.

At the third attempt his fingers touched clothing.   He slithered for a foothold in the mud and pulled.   The small body came with him, unresisting.

A minute later he had it on the flat towpath.   He was on the far side of the river, but even so he had to stagger twenty or thirty yards and turn the corner of the wall to escape the searing blast of the heat.

Then he dumped his burden and started to work, savagely, intently fighting for the life under his hands.

It was five minutes before Ricky stirred.   Then he rolled onto his side and was sick.

"What's happened?" he said.

"You're all right," said Petrella.   "We'll look after you."

"Not me, him."   Then he seemed to remember, and sat still.

In the sudden silence Petrella heard a distant and plaintive bugle note.   He knew that it was only the hooter, from the goods depot, but for a moment it had sounded like a horn being blown in a lonely glade; blown for the followers who would not come.

L. E. BEHNEY

Tales from Home

I: The Man Who Kept His Promise

Long evening shadows of live oak and chaparral stretched across the rutted wheel tracks as Kendricks rode his tired mare down the hill into town.

He was a tall square-shouldered man, rimed with dust and sweat, and he held himself stiffly erect in the saddle as the mare picked her way down the main street through a confusion of riders, buggies, and wagons.

Except for the crowd of farmers, cowboys, and mill men that filled the street, Oak Flat might have been any one of the dozens of small towns that Kendricks had ridden into in the past few weeks—a cluster of frame houses, a string of high-fronted stores, a mingled smell of dust, manure, and smoke.

Kendricks reined the mare over to the town's livery stable and swung stiffly from the saddle. He peered into the dark interior of the frame building, then rapped sharply on the open door. A balding man wearing a leather apron came limping out.

"We got no more room—full up," he said, grinning.

"Is there another stable in town?" Kendricks asked.

"No, ya just bet there ain't," the man said, "but fer a buck ya can turn yer hoss out in the corral back of the stable."

"For five could you find her a stall, a measure of oats, and give her a rubdown?"

"Fer five—silver—I could do a lot of things," the man said, suddenly respectful. He took the mare's reins as Kendricks fished the coins out of his pocket. "When'll ya be wantin' her? Tomorrow, I guess, after the show's over, huh?"

The tall man untied his saddlebags and slung them over his shoulder.

"Is there a hotel in town?"

"Yes, sir, ya bet there is, right down the street. The Antlers—but I'll bet they're full up too. It ain't every day business is this good. Ya just bet it ain't."

Kendricks walked down the board sidewalk, his boot heels thumping hollowly. Teams and wagons lined the hitch rails in a yellowish haze of dust. Some of the farmers had brought their families with them. They had unhitched their horses and fed them hay. The women were busy spreading quilts in the wagon beds and handing out food to their noisy youngsters.

Kendricks stepped into the first saloon he came to. He put his saddlebags on the bar, pulled off his dusty hat, wiped his sweaty face on his shirt sleeve, and ordered a beer. No need to ask the usual questions this time. Aching with weariness, he let his body sag against the stained and polished wood.

The beer was warm and flat, but it quenched his thirst.   He drank slowly, listening to the boisterous flood of talk and laughter that swept around him.   The bartender wore a broad happy grin—it was a great day for business.   Abruptly Kendricks paid for his drink and left.

The hotel lobby was crowded.   Kendricks pushed his way to the desk and asked for a room.

"You gotta be kidding," the clerk said, cleaning his fingernails with a penknife. "There ain't been a room here since this morning."

"Any other hotel in town?"

"Nope," the clerk shrugged.   He glanced slyly at Kendricks.   " 'Course, if ya don't mind payin' a little extra, I mought just manage to squeeze ya in with a feller in Room Twelve."

"I don't mind."

"In that case it'll be four dollars—in advance, that is."

Kendricks paid him and laid his saddlebags on the desk.

"I'm going out for a while.   Put these up for me."

"Well, I dunno as I want—"

"Do it, and I'd not like to see anything happen to them."

"All right.   Yes, sir."

Kendricks went back to the busy street.   In the middle of the square formed by the town's only crossroads a wooden structure towered stark and raw.   Men were still working on it, clinging like flies to the two uprights, lifting a heavy cross beam into place.

Kendricks walked across the square and looked up at it.   One of the onlookers nudged him with a bony elbow.

"Stranger here, ain't ya?   Never seen no better lookin' gallows, now did ya? By golly, we don't have many hangin's, but when we do we fix things up good and proper."

The thud of workmen's hammers echoed back from the store fronts.

"Where's the Sheriff's office?" Kendricks asked.

"Right down there," the man pointed with a gap-toothed grin.   "Ol' Matt Starrett, he don't go much for fancy hangin's, but Geary had a lot of friends in these parts, and there ain't a hell of a lot Ol' Matt ken do about it."

The Sheriff was sitting alone in his office behind a battered oak desk.   As Kendricks entered he swung around, grimly alert, a small man with the toughness of worn leather and sharp, cold gray eyes.

"I'm Bill Kendricks," the tall man said slowly.   "I've come a long ways."

The Sheriff stood up.   He wore a heavy revolver in a low-slung holster and he moved as though the weapon were a natural part of him.

"Kendricks," he said.   "Any relation of the boy's?"

"Brother."

A flicker of light touched the Sheriff's cold eyes.   "Sorry about the mess out there," he said.   "Some fools'll make a circus out of anything—even a hanging."

"Yes," Kendricks said.

"The boy got any other kinfolks?"

"Folks are both dead."

"I suppose you wanta see him?"

"Yes."

Kendricks stood stolidly while the Sheriff ran his hands over his tall body.

"You'd be more of a fool than you look if you tried to break him out."

"Yes," Kendricks said again.

"Come along," the Sheriff said.   He took a large ring of keys from his desk drawer and led the way out the back of his office into a debris-littered alley.

The jail stood by itself—a small squat building of stone with a metal roof and a heavy ironbound door.   The Sheriff, watching Kendricks steadily, fumbled with the keys, then opened the door.   It swung back on protesting hinges and a hot, fetid smell curled out of the darkness inside.

"You stand right there in the door where I can see you," the Sheriff said, and stepped aside.

Kendricks stood in the doorway and peered into the dark.   The only light and air came from a small barred window up near the ceiling, and in spite of the thick stone walls the heat was stifling.   The room was divided by a grille of iron bars into a narrow hallway and two cells.   Each cell contained a bunk, a rusty pail, and a heavy chain riveted to an iron ring set into the stone floor.

One cell was empty.   In the one next to the door the chain was padlocked around the bare ankle of a man lying on his face on the narrow bunk, his blond head buried in his arms.   In the sticky heat he was shivering, and his sweat-soaked clothing clung to his thin body.

"Tod," Kendricks said.

The man on the bunk jerked.   He leaped to his feet and flung himself against the bars.   The chain on his leg clattered across the rough floor.   His young face was gray and waxy beneath the soft, pale stubble of his beard.   As his startled eyes fixed on Kendricks they glittered with a sudden wild hope.

"Bill!" he cried shrilly.   "I knew you'd come!   You couldn't let me die like this!   I sent you word—weeks ago.   What took you so damn long?   Tomorrow they're gonna hang me.   Tomorrow—"   His thin gray fingers clutched the bars.

"I happened to hear," the older man said.   "I haven't been home since you run off.   I been looking for you."

The boy tried to smile.   Tears trickled down his cheeks and his mouth twisted grotesquely.   "Sure I left," he said.   "I wanted to see something—to do something—'fore I got so old and settled down.   You can understand that, can't you, Bill?"

"I can't understand you killing a man."

"I never killed nobody!"

"A couple of witnesses and the judge and jury thought you did.   They said you bushwhacked a man named Abe Geary—shot him down after he licked you in a fair fight."

"It weren't a fair fight!   The damned bully!"   The boy's reddened eyes narrowed.   "I tell you I didn't kill him.   But anyway, what difference does it make?"   His thin, high-pitched voice dropped to a whisper.   "You gotta get me out of here.   You got no time to do it legal.   The Sheriff's got the keys.   Half the time there ain't even a guard.   I don't give a damn how you do it, Bill—but you gotta get me outta here!''

"I think you did kill Geary."

"What if I did?   He had it comin'.   You swore to Ma you'd look after me. When she was dyin' you swore to her on the Bible that you'd take care of me. You never broke a promise in your life, Bill.''

"I don't aim to break my word now, Tod," the older man said heavily.   "I looked after you for years—getting you out of scrapes, trying to see to it you did what was right and honorable.''

"You get me out of this," the boy panted.   "You get me out of here and I'll do like you say.   You won't never have no more trouble with me again—I swear you won't.''

"You can't give a man back his life.''   Kendricks turned away slowly, his square shoulders sagging.

"Wait!" the boy shouted.   "Bill, you can't leave me here!   Bill!''   He pressed his face against the bars and stretched out his hands with desperate appeal. The older man looked at him, seeing the bony wrists, the thin white arms, the frightened childish face, the mop of straw-colored hair.

"You done talkin' to him?" the Sheriff called out.

"Yes," Kendricks said.   As he walked down the alley he heard the Sheriff slam the heavy door shut and lock it and he heard his brother's hysterical screaming.

Kendricks walked back to the hotel, got his saddlebags, and went upstairs to Room 12.

It was empty and he pulled off his boots and lay down on the bed.   After a time the town grew quiet and a small plump man in a checked suit stumbled happily into the room, undressed, and tumbled into bed beside Kendricks where he fell instantly asleep, snoring loudly and smelling of cheap whiskey.

Kendricks, awake in the dark, thought of his brother.   Not the Tod who was a sniveling wretched man in the jail cell, but the boy he once was, bright-eyed and laughing.   The daydream was so real that the older man groaned and buried his face in the hard pillow.

Toward morning he slept fitfully and awoke as the sky grew light in the east. He slid off the bed quietly so that he would not disturb his snoring companion and went to the window.   Already the people camped in the streets were stirring.   The smoke of a small campfire rose across the bright sky, and a horse stamped and whickered.

Kendricks pulled on his boots, splashed water into the basin, and washed his face.   He took his razor from his saddlebags and shaved carefully, using the hotel's cracked and smelly bar of soap.   He emptied the basin into the slop pail, rinsed the basin, wiped it dry, and hung the towel neatly in place.   He put on a clean shirt and combed his thick hair.

On the street, beneath the hotel window, people were beginning to pass, their shoes drumming on the boards, their voices low-pitched and full of nervous excitement.

Kendricks took a .45 Colt revolver from his saddlebags.   He checked the action, loaded it, and put it inside the waistband of his pants under his shirt.   He went down the stairs and joined the crowd as it moved like a fast-flowing river toward the square.

The gallows towered overhead, the splintery green lumber glistening with pitch drops in the early morning sunlight.   As Kendricks stepped into the open square, the crowd that had been pushing and shoving and fighting for the best view grew suddenly silent and intent.

The door of the Sheriff's office opened and a small procession emerged.   A pale young preacher came first, his hands clasped in prayer.   After him came the Sheriff and a grim-faced deputy supporting between them the prisoner in a white shirt and dark trousers, his hands bound behind him.   Two other men, solemn and dressed in black suits, followed.

Kendricks walked slowly forward.   The street was silent except for the soft sluff-sluff of shoes in the powdery dust.   The stumbling prisoner, his mouth hanging slack, his face beaded with sweat, stared with unbelieving horror up at the waiting noose.

The tall man reached the procession.

"Out of the way, Kendricks," the Sheriff said sharply.   "There's nothing you can do now."

The boy's terrified eyes fixed on his brother's face.   "Bill!" he screamed. "Help me!   Don't let them!"

He flung himself toward Kendricks, dragging the Sheriff and the deputy with him.

"Help me!"

With one smooth quick motion the tall man drew the Colt from his shirt front, cocked it, and fired point-blank into the boy's chest.

The prisoner's thin body jerked back and a bright fountain of blood gushed from the wound.   The boy's childish face lost its sudden look of incredulous bewilderment and took on the blank and impersonal stare of death.

Kendricks dropped the revolver in the blood-spattered dust.   "I promised Ma I'd look after him," he said.   "I promised her he'd never hang like his Pa did."

II: Why Don't You Like Me?

Lying on her back under the old truck and tightening the last of the oil pan bolts, Luddy didn't here the Jeep drive into the yard until it pulled up close to the machine shed and stopped.

She wiggled out from under the truck as Sheriff Fred Kyle swung his big booted feet to the ground.

"Hello, Luddy," he said politely enough.   He ought to be polite—after all she had a vote the same as anyone else in the county; but she could see in the way his gray eyes passed over her coolly, indifferently, what he thought—like all the others—that if a woman worked with her hands and didn't stay dressed up pretty with her hair curled and her face painted—

"Hello, Fred," she said, making her voice deep and still.   She picked up a rag and wiped her grease-blackened hands.

"Thought I'd better come by and tell you," he said.   "Man broke out of jail last night.   We were holding him for murdering a couple of women with a knife. He's dangerous.   I'm not trying to scare you, Luddy, but it would be a good idea if you stayed in town nights till we get him."

She laughed harshly.   "No man 'ud bother me, Sheriff," she said.   "Besides I got a twelve-gauge shotgun in there and I know how to use it."   Probably better'n you do, Sheriff—little Freddie Kyle she'd gone to school with and licked at everything, even baseball and arithmetic.   Now he was the Sheriff acting smart and wearing a tin badge, and telling her to go stay in town.

The late afternoon sun shone on his short blond hair, on his tanned skin, on the bulge of muscles under his neatly pressed khaki shirt.   At least the soft-skinned, cow-eyed Eva Petrie he'd married kept his shirts ironed.

"You've been running this place nearly ten years, haven't you, Luddy?   Ten years since your Pa died?"   He looked around at the straight, tight fences, the painted barns, the fat cattle grazing in the lush pasture, the newly mown hayfields. "You're doing a fine job.   A man couldn't do better."

"Thanks," she said wryly, "and I'm nearly thirty and I've never been kissed!" She knew she had said the sudden, almost irrational thought aloud when he looked at her sharply.   That's what came of being alone so much, of never having anyone to talk to; thoughts became words, and words thoughts, without reason or purpose.

She felt her whole body grow stiff and hot with embarrassment.   She looked away from the sharp-eyed Sheriff and saw one of his deputies sitting in the Jeep, a beefy, round-faced man grinning contemptuously at her.

"Get out of here," she said thickly, "and take that gawking ape with you."

Fred Kyle was frowning at her.   "We came here to warn you, Miss Vadick," he said with cold formality.   "This man we're looking for seems harmless.   He's only twenty and he looks as sweet and innocent as a young angel, but he's a psychotic killer and he'd as soon shove a knife into you as eat breakfast.   I'd be within my duty to order you into town until we catch him—you living alone this way, miles from anyone."

"You don't order me anywhere, Fred Kyle, I won't go.   I've got my stock to look after and my work to do.   Now get out, both of you!"

Kyle shrugged.   "All right," he said.   "If you see anyone suspicious you let me know."

"I'll do better'n that.   I'll catch him for you and deliver your killer all tied up neat with pink ribbons."

"If you see him, you call us, Miss Vadick.   He's tall and thin, has black hair and eyes, and as far as we know he's still wearing the county's blue shirt and jeans. And let me warn you again that he's dangerous."

Kyle got into the Jeep and drove rapidly out of the yard.

Luddy stood with her hands on her hips watching them until they were out of sight up the winding road across the hillside.   She let her rigidly held body slump. "Fred Kyle always was a fool," she said angrily.

She pulled her watch out of her pocket and looked at it.   Five o'clock—time to start the chores.   She rinsed her rough, greasy hands in stove oil and washed with soap at the hand pump in the yard.   She fed the chickens and gathered the eggs.   She got the two milk pails in the house and went to the barn.   She drove the cows in from pasture and milked, she fed the calves and turned the cows out, and gave hay and water to the big white bull in his strong log pen.

She carried a pail of milk to the spring house and strained the foamy liquid into graniteware pans.   She went to the field and fueled the engine that ran the pump and changed the water into three checks in the hayfield for the night.   It was dark when she came into the house.

She lighted a lamp, set it on the table, opened a can of beans, fried a slab of bacon, and heated the coffee left in the pot from breakfast.   She ate her supper, piled the dishes in the dish pan, poured a dipper of water over them, and wiped out the crusted frying pan with a piece of newspaper.

She picked up the lamp and paused to look around the kitchen.   It was cluttered and dirty; cobwebs festooned the walls and the once white curtains were stiff with dust.   She thought of Fred Kyle and his scrubbed pink neck and freshly ironed shirt.   Eva—she'd been the most helpless little thing, squealing at bugs and looking up at Fred through her eyelashes—

"She got him, didn't she?" Luddy said.   She stumped down the hall to her bedroom, blew out the light, undressed in the dark and crawled into her bed.

Sleep with its welcome oblivion wouldn't come.   Outside in the dark the pump engine throbbed and crickets and frogs chorused.   Her mind churned, her tortured thoughts like sparks from a fire that brightened and dimmed and twisted in bitter remembrance. She saw herself as a child always alone, always left out of the others' games and parties, shy, painfully self-conscious of her homely face and plain ill-fitting clothing.

Memory was like a rasping of sharp fingers across a raw wound.   She twisted in anguish remembering her cringing, her fawning, her begging—who wants the candy out of my lunch?—do you want my doll, I don't want her anymore—I'll do your homework for you—can't I go too?—oh, Fred, why don't you like me?— why don't you like me?

She flung herself out of bed, lighted the lamp, and stared at herself in the mirror above the dresser.   Her face peered back at her from the fly-specked dark, a gargoyle face, wrinkled, weathered, with hooded glaring eyes—

With a sudden moan she picked up her heavy shoe and beat it against the glass. The mirror shattered into a cascade of silvery fragments.   Sobbing convulsively, she put out the light, threw herself back on the bed, and at last slept . . .

In the morning the torment of the night seemed like a dream.   She dressed— careful not to look at the shattered mirror—and did her morning chores.   She changed the water, ate breakfast, and worked on the old truck.   By noon she had it running.   In the afternoon she cleaned out ditches, finished the irrigating, and built another calf corral.

That evening as she brought in the cows she thought she saw a movement in the willows along the creek that divided her farm from her nearest neighbor.

"A big dog," she said, "or one of Milt's calves. He better not say I stole it. I'll take a club to him."

She watched the willows furtively as she went about her chores. At sundown she saw with a quick surge of excitement the figure of a man standing just inside the brushy cover. He was tall and thin; his hair was dark and he was staring intently up toward the farm buildings.

"He's hungry," she said. "He'll come."

When she had finished the chores she went into the house and got her shotgun down from the bedroom shelf, wiped it with an oily rag, and loaded it with buckshot.

She didn't eat. Holding the cocked weapon she sat on the front porch and waited. The quartering moon made a faint light. After a while she saw a movement near the barn and a tall, thin figure came stealthily toward the house.

"Hold it!" she called. "I've got you covered!"

The man turned and leaped away. She fired both barrels at his wispy shadow, but he vanished without an outcry. She reloaded the shotgun and got a flashlight. There were tracks in the soft dust, but no drops of blood.

Luddy didn't think of calling the Sheriff. She sat all night on the porch with the shotgun across her knees, but by the light of dawn he had not appeared again. She kept the weapon handy as she went about her work, but she saw no trace of the fugitive.

At noon, when she went into the house, he was sitting at her kitchen table with his hands quietly folded, looking up at her. She knew him instantly. He had *Kings County Jail* stenciled in black across the front of his worn blue shirt.

She felt a moment's wild panic. Then she pointed the shotgun at him and he smiled.

"You don't need that, Luddy," he said. "I won't hurt you. I'm your friend."

His lips barely moved when he talked. It was as if his mind talked to her mind—but she could hear his voice as deep and clear as a great bronze bell. The voice soothed her and she was no longer afraid. Her knees felt as weak and wobbly as a newborn calf's. She leaned the shotgun against the wall and sat down across the table from him.

He sat quietly, still smiling at her. His crisp dark hair curled on his high forehead; his eyes were large and as liquid and deep as the dark still pools beneath the willows along the creek; his skin was the silken gold of fall leaves; his features were perfectly molded and the perfection of his smiling mouth made her shiver. Even his hands, with their tracery of blue veins, were beautiful—with long tapering fingers and just a dusting of black hairs on the backs.

"You must be hungry," she said breathlessly. "Let me get you something to eat."

"Thank you, Luddy," he said. "You are very kind."

It wasn't strange that he knew her name. Everything about him was as familiar and real as her own being. She heard herself babbling as she stoked the stove and got out her pots and pans.

"The Sheriff was here—did you know that?   He said you were dangerous, that I should call him if I saw you."   She laughed, glancing at him, then pulled her lips down over her uneven teeth, knowing that she was especially hideous when she laughed; but his face did not turn from her.   He watched her, smiling gently, his eyes warm and bright.

She put on fresh coffee to boil, sliced bacon, diced potatoes with onions for frying, brought cold fresh milk and a bowl of cream from the spring house, picked a colander of strawberries from the neglected garden.   Each time she went out of the house she hurried back, her heart pounding, cold with the fear that he would be gone; but he remained at the table and watched her with his black liquid eyes.

When the food was ready they ate.   Luddy kept right on talking.   It was wonderful to have someone to talk to.   She knew he must hate her, that she must sound like a fool, but still the words bubbled out of her mouth like an inexhaustible spring.

"It wasn't always like this," she said, gesturing at the dirt-encrusted room. "When Papa was alive and I kept house for him I had everything so neat and clean you wouldn't believe it.   I had everything so tidy."

He nodded.   "Of course you did, Luddy."

"It's different now," she said.   "I don't have time.   Something has to go."

"You're very wise, Luddy."

When they had finished eating she fell silent as she stacked the dishes.   He'd been hungry; he'd come to eat, and in a few moments he'd be gone.

She said, "They're looking for you everywhere.   They want to kill you."

He nodded and his eyes looked sad.

"You could stay here," she said.   "You'd be safe.   I'd look after you and hide you."

He shook his head.   "I must go."

"No!" she cried, "I won't let you!   You don't know how much they hate you— how much they want to kill you!"

"Dear Luddy," he said sadly, "how good you are.   But I must go."

He stood up.   He moved with a sinuous grace and ease that seemed effortless. He seemed to flow across the floor toward the door.

She snatched up the shotgun.   "Don't leave me!" she cried.

He stopped and looked at her with the faintest smile on his curved lips.

She held the shotgun steady.   Where could she put him?   It had to be a safe place, a strong place, one that he couldn't get out of and where they'd never find him.   The grain bin in the barn.   It was built of two layers of tongue-and-groove siding, sheathed with tin and bolted to a concrete foundation.   It had a heavy door and two small heavily screened windows for ventilation.

He made no objection as she ordered him across the yard to the big barn.   He went quietly into the small, square, dark little room and he sat on the floor watching her with his faint little smile as she brought him bedding and a jar of water.   She put a heavy padlock through the hasp of the door.

"It's for your own good," she called, "so's you'll be safe.   They won't find you here."

She hung the key on a nail in the barn wall and leaned the shotgun in the corner beside the grain bin.   She felt strange, almost dizzy and light-headed.   The afternoon sunlight that poured in through the barn's wide door seemed unbearably bright.

She went to the house and spent the rest of the afternoon cleaning it.   By evening the floors shone, the windows were clean, the curtains washed.   After the chores were done that evening, she fixed a tray of food and carried it out to the barn.   She unlocked the grain bin in a sudden panic that he would be gone, but he was there sitting quietly in a corner on his bedding.

The next day she went into town and recklessly bought meats and vegetables and canned goods and even a carton of ice cream wrapped in newspapers to keep it cold.   She went to a store and bought him a fancy shirt and a pair of slacks and a belt with a gold buckle.

When she got back to the farm she carried the clothes and the ice cream out to the barn and they ate the ice cream and while she turned her back he changed into the new clothes and flung his old ones into a corner.

The next few days were the happiest of Luddy's life.   She seemed to live for the times when she could sit on an old apple box in the grain bin talking to the stranger.   She poured out her heart to him, telling him everything that had ever happened to her, and he listened sympathetically.   He never scolded or seemed shocked or repulsed.   He sat as still as a carved wax figurine, his head tilted a little forward, his bright dark eyes fixed on her face.

Her thoughts centered on her prisoner.   What could she fix for him that he would like?   What could she think to tell him that he would find amusing?   What small comfort would he enjoy?   But he asked for nothing.   He seemed content.

A week after Luddy had locked the fugitive in the grain bin, Sheriff Fred Kyle drove into the farm yard.   Luddy was carrying the milk pails out to the barn to start her evening chores.   She stopped as Kyle swung down from his Jeep.   He was alone this time.   He looked fat and coarse, not handsome at all, in the reddish evening sunlight.

Luddy watched him coldly.   "Well," she called, "what do you want?"

He grinned and seemed pleased about something.   "I just came in to tell you, Miss Vadick.   We caught that killer, so you can relax."

"You caught him?" she asked stupidly.

"Sure—that fellow I was telling you about—the one that killed those women."

"Oh," Luddy said.

"Caught him between here and town just this afternoon.   Thought you'd want to know.   You don't have to worry anymore."

Luddy screamed.   Her limp fingers dropped the milk pails.   She ran across the yard toward the barn.   Kyle stared after her with a puzzled frown.   Then he shrugged and followed her.

She ran to the grain bin, snatched the key from the nail, and fumbled with the padlock.   Her fingers were so clumsy that it took her a long time to get the lock open and throw back the door.

He was there.   He sat on the bed and smiled at her.   His eyes were luminous in the gloom, like the eyes of a cat.   The gold buckle on his belt glimmered in the faint light.

Then she understood.   Fred Kyle had tricked her with his lies and she, like the poor stupid fool she was, had led him straight to the fugitive.

She turned blindly toward the door and, whimpering like a mortally wounded animal, seized the shotgun that leaned against the wall.   As the Sheriff stood silhouetted against the light, peering into the dark barn from the wide doorway, she shot him.   His heavy body jerked back as though he had been struck by a huge fist.   He fell and twitched a little, then lay with his astonished face staring sightlessly up into the bright evening sky.

Luddy dropped the shotgun and ran back to the grain bin.

In the shadowy dark she called, "Come!   Come quick!   We gotta—"

He was gone.   The bin was empty.

She dropped to her knees and lighted the lamp with shaking fingers.   There was nothing in the tiny square room—nothing but a pile of neatly folded blankets, a gray plaid shirt still in its cellophane envelope, a pair of slacks with pristine creases, and a gold-buckled belt in an unbroken plastic holder.   On the floor around the bedding were plates and bowls of food in varying stages of decay.

Luddy cried out wildly.   She crawled across the floor to the corner where he had discarded his clothing.   Only two ragged burlap sacks lay crumpled in the dust.

DAVIS GRUBB

Cry Havoc

In 1923 the family Pollixfen migrated from Eire to settle in the small Ohio river town of Glory, West Virginia.   Sean Pollixfen was a big florid boast of a man of common heritage.   His wife, Deirdre, was a lady of gentle breeding; raised in a Georgian townhouse in Dublin's Sackville Street, she deplored Sean's harsh upbringing of their only child—ten-year-old Benjamin Michael.

The Pollixfen house was a rambling one-story structure with a great blue front door and slate flagstones set level with its threshold.   Their nearest neighbor was a man named Hugger who dwelt a good three blocks up Liberty Avenue.

When the Thing began, it was an autumn night at supper.   Benjy abruptly laid down his knife and fork and tilted his ear, harking.   "But for what?" Sean asked him.

"I was listening for the auguries of the War that's coming, sor."

"Wisht, now, boyo!" cried Sean.   " 'Tis 1932.   The Great War ended fourteen years ago this November.   And surely there's not another one in sight."

Sean paused, reminiscing, smiling.

"Still, somehow I'd favor another War," he said.   "I'm proud to be wearing the sleeve of this good linen jacket pinned up to me left shoulder.   I lost that hook at First Ypres.   Yet, despite that, it was a Glory."

Benjy made no reply, though a moment later he left the table, went to the bathroom, and threw up his supper.

Next morning at eight two men pulled up in a truck out front.   Moments later they had laboriously borne a huge pine crate to the flagstone threshold and rang the bell.   Sean, on his way to his Position at the Firm, answered their ring.

"Is this here the residence of Master Benjamin Michael Pollixfen?"

"It is that," Sean replied, rapping the crate with his malacca cane.   " 'Tis another gift for me boy Benjy from his Uncle Liam in Kilronan.   He's always sending the lad a grand present, no matter what the occasion!"

That night when they had finished supper, Sean went to Benjy's room.   He stared at the great crate's contents, all ranked round the room so thick that one could scarce walk among them.   There were 5000 miniature lead soldiers—Boche, French, and English.   There was every manner of ammunition and instrument of warfare, from caissons and howitzers to hangars and tarmac for the landing fields of the miniature aircraft of all varieties and types—from Gotha bombers for the Boche to D.H.4's for the British and Bréguets for the French.

"Now Liam is showing good sense," Sean said. "Rocking horses were fine for you a year ago. But you're ten now, Benjy. 'Tis time you learned the lessons of Life's most glorious Game!"

Benjy stared at the little soldiers, cast and tinted down to the very wrinkle of a puttee, the drape of a trenchcoat. Moreover, no two soldiers wore the same facial expressions. Benjy could read in these faces Fear, Zest, Valor, Humdrum, Cravenness, Patriotism, and Sedition. And somehow each of them seemed waiting. But for what? For whom? Sean missed seeing these subtleties. . Yet Benjy saw. And Benjy knew. Aye, he knew all too well.

"They are green, dads," Benjy said. "Green as the turf of Saint Stephens Green park. The British officers are just days out of Sandhurst, the gun crews hardly a fortnight from the machine-gun school at Wisquies. They don't know the noise of a whizgang from a four-ten or a five-nine. Yet once they've been through a bloody baptism such as Hannescamps or the Somme they'll know. Aye, they'll know then."

"And what would *you* be knowing of Hannescamps or the Somme?" Sean chuckled.

Benjy made no reply.

And so the three strange weeks of it began. Benjy spent every waking hour working feverishly in the great black lot of nonarable ground beyond Deirdre's flower-and-kitchen garden. While about him all the world seemed filled with the sound of locusts sawing down the great green tree of summer.

Benjy carved out the laceries of trenches with his Swiss Army knife. He found strips of lath and split them to lay down as duckboards. He sandbagged the trenches well in front. Beyond this he staked, on ten-penny nails, the thin barbed wire which had come on spools in the great crate. Some distance to the rear of both sides he set up his little field hospitals, and his hangars and the tarmac fields for the little fighter, reconnaissance, and bombing planes.

At the kitchen door Sean would watch the boy and listen as Benjy chanted songs that Sean and his man had sung at Locrehof Farm or Trone Woods once they'd billeted down for a night in some daub-and-wattle stable. He could fairly smell the sweet ammoniac scent of the manure of kine, lambs, and goats, and the fragrance as well as the Gold Flake and State Express cigarettes they smoked, saving only enough to barter for a bottle or two of Pichon Longueville '89 or perhaps a liter of Paul Ruinart.

Strange to relate, it had not yet begun to trouble Sean that the boy knew of these things, that he sang songs Sean had never taught him and sometimes in French which *no one* had ever taught him. As for Benjy he soon began to show the strain. Deirdre's scale in the bathroom showed that in ten days he had lost twelve pounds. He seldom finished supper. For there was that half-hour's extra twilight to work in. Sean gloated. Dierdre grieved.

"Why in Saint Brigid's blessed name don't you put an end to it?" she would plead.

"No, woman, I shan't."

"And why not then?"

"Because me boyo shall grow up to be what I wanted for myself—a soldier poet more glorious than Rupert Brooke or the taffy Wilfred Owen."

"And them dead of their cursed war—dead before they could come to full flower of Saint Brigid's sacred gift."

"So much the better," Sean replied icily one night. "We must all die one day or another. And no man knows the hour. Death it has no clocks. Moreover, we are Pollixfens. Kin on me father's side to Eire's glory of poets—William Butler Yeats."

"But Yeats died in no war," Deirdre protested.

"Better he had," Sean said. " 'Twould have increased his esteem a thousandfold."

Deirdre went off to bed weeping.

Next night in Benjy's room Sean spoke his dreams out plain.

" 'Tis stark truth, old man," he said. "Real War is a rough go. But there is that Glory of Glories in it."

Benjy said nothing.

"Don't you understand me, boyo? Glory!"

"I see no Glory," said the child. "I see poor fools butchering each other for reasons kept secret from them. Oh, they give reasons. King and Country. They leave out, of course, Industry. No, dads, there are no fields of Honor. There are only insane abattoirs."

Sean colored at this, got up and strode from the boy's room. Yet a minute later, unable to contain himself, he was back.

"Now, boyo!" he cried out. "Either you shed from yourself these craven, blasphemous, and treasonable speculations or I shall leave you to grow up and learn War the hard way. As did I."

"And what might that mean, sor?"

"It means that I shall go to Al Hugger's ga-rage and fetch home three ten-gallon tins of petrol and douse the length and breadth of your little No Man's Land of toys and then set a lucifer to it."

"That would be a most fearsome mistake, sor. For on the morning when the little armies came they were mine. Now I am Theirs. And so, poor dads, are you."

"That does it then! 'Tis petrol and a lucifer for all five thousand of the little perishers!"

Benjy smiled. Sadly.

"But 'tis no longer a skimpy five thousand now, man dear. 'Tis closer to a million. Perhaps more. Even files-on-parade could not count their hosts."

"Wisht, now! How could that be? Did Liam send you another great crate?"

"No, sor. There's been Conscription on both sides. And enlistments by the million. A fair fever of outrage infects every man and boy of the Kings Realm from Land's End to Aberdeen since Lord Kitchener went down in one of his Majesty's dreadnaughts off the Dolomites. Then there's Foch and Clemenceau and Joffre. They've whipped up the zest of Frenchmen to a pitch not known since the days of Robespierre and Danton in the Terror. In Germany the Boche seethe at every word from Hindenburg or Ludendorf or Kaiser Willie.''

Benjy chuckled, despite himself.

"Willie—the English King's cousin! Willie and Georgie! Lord, 'tis more of a family squabble than a War!''

He sobered then.

"No, sor,'' Benjy said. "Cry havoc now and let loose the dogs of War!''

Sean stared, baffled.

"Tell me, boyo. If you loathe War so, why do you go at your little War game with such zest?''

"Why, because there's twins inside me, I suppose,'' Benjy replied, and press him as he might, Sean could elicit no more from the boy.

Sean's face sobered. He went off with a troubled mind to Dierdre in their goosedown bed. Lying there on his back he could hear Benjy singing an old war ditty—*The Charlie Chaplin Walk.* Sean's batman, a Nottinghamshire collier, had used to sing that before the Somme. Sean was drowsy but could not sleep. Yet soon he roused up wide-waking from the drowsiness. Was it thunder he heard out yonder in the night? And that flickering light across the sill of the back window. Was it heat lightning?

He stole from Deirdre's sound-sleeping side and stared out the rear window. A river fog lay waist deep upon the land. Among the tinted autumn trees the cold sweet light of fireflies came and went as though they were stars that could not make up their minds. Yet the flashes and flames that flickered beneath the cloak of mists on the black lot were not sweet, not cold.

Sean could hear the small smart chatter of machine guns. There were the blasts of howitzers and whizbangs and mortars. Above the shallow sea of leprous white mists the Aviatiks and Sopwith Strutters swooped and dove and Immelmanned in dogfights.

Far to the rear Sean could see Benjy in his peejays, standing and watching. The child's wild face was grievous and weeping. He had flung out his spindly arms as if transcendentally to appease the madness to which he bore such suffering witness.

Sean crept shivering back into the bed. He lay awake, again thinking of Liam's great gift that had come to life, proliferated, and had now taken possession both of himself and Benjy.

And it went on thus. For another two weeks. Then one morning all was changed. Pale, half staggering from lack of sleep and haggard-eyed from poring over the war map thumbtacked to his play table beneath the gooseneck lamp's harsh circle of illumination, Benjy—almost faint—came down to breakfast all smiles.

"What does that Chessy cat grin on your face mean, boyo?'' Sean asked.

"C'est la guerre, mon vieux, c'est la guerre!'' cried Benjy. "But last night the news came through—''

"C'est la guerre and so on,'' Deirdre intervened.   "And what might that alien phrase mean to these poor untutored ears?''

" 'Tis French,'' Sean said.   "That's War, old man, that's War.''

"But now—tomorrow night at midnight—it will be over!'' Benjy cried brightly.

"Tomorrow night and midnight be damned!'' Sean exclaimed.   *"Tonight* at midnight it shall end!   I am unable to endure another night of it, and so I have determined to end it all myself!   Benjy, I swear now by the holy martyred names of the Insurrection of Easter '16—Pearse, Casement, John Connolly, and the O'Ra-hilly—that I shall not let this thing possess the two of us for even one night more! I shall end it with me petrol and me lucifer at midnight tonight!''

"Lord save us, dads, you mustn't talk so!'' cried Benjy.   "Word has been flashed to all forces up and down the lines that the cease-fire is set for tomorrow's midnight.   Already the gunfire is only token.   Already the men crawl fearlessly over sandbags and under the barbed wire and march boldly into the midst of No Man's Land to embrace each other.   They barter toffees and jars of Bovrils and tins of chocs for marzipan and *fastnacht krapfen* and strudels and *himbeer kuchen!* They show each other sweat-and-muck-smeared snapshots of mothers, sweethearts, and children back home.   Men who a day ago were at each others' throats!''

Deirdre watched and listened, helpless, baffled, appalled.

"No matter to all the sweet sticky treacle of your talk!'' Sean cried.   "I'll not let this madness take possession of our home!   So 'tis petrol and a lucifer to the whole game tonight at the strike of twelve!   And a fiery fitting end to it all!''

"Bloody ballocks to that!'' shouted Benjy, outraged.

"Go to your room, boy,'' Sean said, struggling to control himself.   "We have man's words to say.   Not words for the hearing of your mum.''

A moment later Sean was strutting the length and breadth of Benjy's bedroom like a bloated popinjay.   His swagger stick was in his hand; it seemed to give him back some of his old lost Valor, some long mislaid or time-rotted Authority.   As he walked he slapped it in vainglorious bellicosity against his thigh.

Benjy watched him solemnly, sadly.   "They'll not let you do this thing,'' he said.   He paused.   "Nor shall I.''

Sean whirled, glaring.

"Ah, so it has come to that then!'' he barked out in the voice of a glory-gutted martinet.   " 'Tis they shan't and I shan't and you shan't, eh?   Well, we shall see about that!   I am King of this house.   And I am King of all its environs!''

"No,'' Benjy said, his face above the war map tacked to his table.   "You are no King.   You are a King's Fool.   Though lacking in a King's Fool's traditional and customary wisdom and vision.''

Sean broke then.   In a stride he crossed the room and slashed the boy across the face with the swagger stick.

A thin ribbon of blood coursed down from the corner of Benjy's mouth.   A droplet of it splattered like a tiny crimson starfish or a mark on the map to com-memorate some dreadful battle encounter.

"King, I say!   King!''   Sean was shouting, pacing the room again.   There was a livid stripe across the child's cheek where the leather had fallen.   But there was even more change in Benjy's face.   And even something newer, something darker in the mind behind that face.   The boy smiled.

"Come then," Benjy said softly.   "Let us sit a while and tell sad stories of the Death of Kings."

The next day neither child nor father spoke nor looked each other in the eye. When occasionally they would be forced to pass in a corridor, it was in the stiff-legged, ominous manner of pitbulls circling in a small seat-encircled arena.   Dierdre, sensing something dreadful between them, was helplessly distraught.   For what did she know of any of it, dear gentle Deirdre?

Benjy did not appear for supper.   Sean ate ravenously.   When he was done he drove his car into town and came back moments later with the three ten-gallon tins of petrol.   He ranked them neatly alongside the black lot's border.

At nine Sean and Dierdre went to bed.   For three hours Sean lay staring at the bar of harvest moonlight which fell across the carpet from the window sill to the threshold of the bedroom door.   Now and again half-hearted gunfire could be heard from the black lot.   Soon Sean began speaking within himself a wordless colloquy. Fear had begun to steal from him.   Misgivings.   He could not forget the Thing he had seen in the boy's face after the blow of the stiff, hardened leather.   He could never forget the strange new timbre of the boy's voice when he spoke softly shortly after.

As the great clock in the hallway struck the chime of eleven thirty, Sean decided to forego the whole headstrong project.   Let the cease-fire come in its ordained time.   What could another twenty-four hours matter?   There was scarcely any War waging in the black lot anyway.   Cheered by his essentially craven decision he started, in his night shirt, down the hallway toward Benjy's room to inform him of his change of mind.

Within ten feet of the boy's bolted door Sean came to a standstill.   He listened. It was unmistakable.   The tiny quacking chatter of a voice speaking from a field telephone.   And Benjy's murmurous voice giving orders back.   Only one phrase caught Sean's ear.   And that phrase set beads of sweat glistering on his face in the pallid gaslight of the long broad hallway.   The words were in French.   But Sean knew French.

"On a besoin des assassins."

Sean felt a chill seize him, shaming the manhood of him.   "We now have need of the assassins."

Shamed to the core of his soul, Sean fled back to the bedroom.   With his one arm he turned the key in the back door.   With that same arm he fetched a ladder-back chair from against the wall and propped the top rung under the knob.   Then he hastened to the bureau drawer where he kept the memorabilia of his old long-forgotten War and fetched out his BEF Webley.

The pistol was still well greased.   It was loaded, the cartridge pins a little dark with verdigris but operable.   Then Sean went and lay atop the quilt, shivering and clutching the silly, ineffectual pistol in his hand.

That was when he first heard them.   Myriad feet; tiny footsteps and not those of small animals with clawed and padded paws. Boots. Tiny boots. The myriad scrape of microscopically small hobnails. Boots. By the thousands. By the thousands of thousands. And then abruptly above their measured, disciplined tread there burst forth suddenly the skirl of Royal Scots' Highlanders' bagpipes, the rattle of tiny drums, the piercing tweedle of little fifes, the brash impudence of German brass bands.

Deirdre still slept. Even the nights of the War in the black lot had never wakened her. It was to Sean's credit that he did not rouse her now. For, as never before in his life—not even in the inferno of First Ypres or the Somme—had he so craved the company of another mortal. A word. A touch. A look.

Abruptly, just beyond the door, there was a command followed by total silence. Sean chuckled. They were not out there. It had been a fantasy of his overwrought mind. A nightmare—a *couchmare* as the French call it. But his tranquillity was shortlived. He heard a tiny voice in German crying orders to crank a howitzer to its proper angle of trajectory. Another shouted command. Sean sensed, with an old soldier's instinct, the yank of the lanyard. He heard the detonation, felt the hot Krupp steel barrel's recoil, saw flame flare as the shell blasted a ragged hole in the door where the lock had been.

The impact flung the door wide and sent the chair spinning across the moonlit carpet. And now, in undisciplined and furious anarchy, they swarmed across the door sill like a blanket of gray putrescent mud. Gone from them were the gay regimental colors, the spit-and-polish decorum of the morning of the great crate's arrival. Now they were muck-draped and gangrenous, unwashed and stinking of old deaths, old untended wounds. Some knuckled their way on legless stumps. Others hobbled savagely on makeshift crutches.

Sean sat up and emptied every bullet from the Webley into their midst. He might as well have sought to slaughter the sea with handfuls of flung seashells. All of them wore tiny gas masks. A shouted command and small steel cylinders on miniature wheeled platforms were trundled across the door sill and ranked before the bed. Another shout and gun crews of four men each wheeled in, to face the bed, behind the gas cylinders, ten Lewis and ten Maxim machine guns.

At a cry from the leader these now began a raking enfilade of Sean's body. He had but time to cross himself and begin a Hail Mary when the cocks of the little gas cylinders were screwed open and the first green cloud of gas reached his nostrils. Enveloped in a cloud of gas, the big man uttered one last choking scream and slid onto the carpet and into their very midst.

In a twinkling they swarmed over him like a vast shroud of living manure. They stabbed him with the needle points of their tiny bayonets, again and again. At last one of these sought out and found the big man's jugular vein. A shouted command again. The lift and fall of a bloody saber.

"All divisions—ri' tur'!"

And to a man they obeyed.

"All divisions—'orm rank!"

Again they obeyed.

"All divisions—quick 'arch!"

And with pipers skirling, drums drubbing, fifes shrilling, and brass bands blaring they went the way they had come.   The siege was a *fait accompli*.

Awakened by all the gunfire and clamor at last, and at the very moment of the door's collapse, Deirdre sat up, watching throughout.   First in smiling disbelief, then in fruitless attempt to persuade herself that she was dreaming it all, then in acceptance, and, at last, in horror.   Now as the first wisps of the chlorine stung her nostrils she went raving and irreversibly insane, sprang from her side of the bed, and hurtled through the side window, taking screen and all, to tumble onto the turf three feet below.

In the hushed autumn street of the night Deirdre, beneath the moon and the galaxies and the cold promiscuous fireflies, fled back into the hallucination of Youth returned.   She raced up and down under the tinted trees.   She twirled an imaginary pink lace parasol as if doing a turn on a small stage.   She chanted the Harry Lauder and Vesta Tilley ballads from the music halls of her Dublin girlhood.

Wakened by all this daft medley of unfamiliar songs, Al Hugger, the nearest neighbor, took down his old AEF Springfield rifle and came to the house to discover what calamity had befallen it.

When, at last, he stood in the bedroom doorway, he looked first at the monstrous ruin which had been Sean, humped in his blood on the carpet by the bed.   Then Hugger saw the blasé and unruffled figure of Benjy, clad only in his peejays and sitting straight as the blackthorn stick of a Connaught County squire in the ladder-back chair now back against the wall.   Almost all the gas had been cleared from the room by the clean river wind which coursed steadily between the two open windows.

"No one," Hugger said presently—more to himself than to the child—"shall likely ever know what happened in this room tonight.   Better they don't.   Yes, I hope they don't.   Never.   For there is something about it all—something—"

Benjy yawned.   Prodigiously.   He smiled hospitably at Al Hugger.   He looked at the thing—like a great beached whale—on the carpet by the bedside.   He yawned again.

"C'est la guerre, mon vieux, c'est la guerre," he said.

HAROLD Q. MASUR

Murder Never Solves Anything

Albert Osborn was an ambitious young man, volatile, brash, self-confident. But all these characteristics quickly dissolved under the pressure of calamitous events. I found him sitting disconsolately in his cell at the 19th Precinct, subdued and chastened.

"Thank God," he said fervently, clasping his hands in supplication. "Thank God you're here, Mr. Jordan."

"I heard the news, Albert. Did you kill her?"

He swallowed and shook his head.

I had first met Albert two years ago when he'd bought a junior partnership in a Wall Street brokerage firm, using money borrowed from a doting aunt, Mrs. Agnes Mahler, a fluttery, powder-haired lady, the childless widow of a wealthy scrap-metal dealer. Albert had retained me to handle the legal details. And until this morning, apparently, he'd had no further need for a lawyer.

Now Aunt Agnes was dead. Someone had banged an ancient Grecian urn against the base of her skull. And within twenty-four hours New York's finest had put the arm on Albert Osborn, the victim's only living relative and sole legatee under her last will and testament.

"How come they nominated you, Albert?" I asked.

"We had a terrible fight, Aunt Agnes and I," he said miserably. "One of her neighbors heard us and told the police."

"A fight about what?"

"I needed some money and Aunt Agnes lent it to me, but her check bounced."

"How much money?"

"Eighty thousand dollars."

I lifted an eyebrow. "I thought that all the partners in your firm, Zachary and Company, were making a bundle. What happened?"

He sighed. "Do you know about the two-thousand percent rule?"

"Vaguely. Refresh my recollection."

"Brokers operate on borrowed money, mostly lent by banks. The Stock Exchange prohibits us from raising more than twenty times our net capital. Zachary and Company exceeded the limit."

"Using what as collateral?"

"Unregistered stock."

"That's against the law, Albert."

"I know. I know. And when the bank caught on, they called in the loan immediately and notified the Exchange. The Board of Governors gave us an ultimatum: raise enough cash within a week to take us out of violation or suffer a suspension. So Mr. Zachary laid an assessment on every partner for his proportionate share. My contribution was the smallest, eighty thousand dollars. I was strapped, Mr. Jordan. Like everyone else I'd taken a bath when the market got clobbered."

"So you appealed to Aunt Agnes."

"I had no choice. If I couldn't raise the money, I'd lose my interest in the firm."

"And your aunt agreed?"

"Willingly. She'd just returned from a long Caribbean cruise and was in a good mood. She drew a check to my order, I deposited it and gave one of my own to Mr. Zachary."

"They bounced?"

"Like rubber balls. Both marked INSUFFICIENT FUNDS. Here. He took Mrs. Mahler's check from his pocket and proffered it. "Mr. Zachary," he continued, "was very chilly. He gave me forty-eight hours to make good or clear out my desk." Albert's chin went out of control. "My future, everything, all down the drain."

"Take it easy," I said. "What happened next?"

"I was wild. I went storming over to my aunt's apartment. I ranted and berated her and called her all sorts of names. I have a terrible temper, Mr. Jordan. I'm not proud of myself."

"Did she offer an explanation?"

"She kept shaking her head. She said the bank must have made a mistake. But banks don't make mistakes like that, Mr. Jordan." He blinked. "I admit I made a lot of noise—but I didn't kill her."

"Did she have any enemies?"

"I don't think so."

"Close friends?"

"The lady next door. Mrs. Stewart—Claire Stewart. They visit back and forth all the time. It was Mrs. Stewart who told the cops about our fight. Listen, this is an awful place. Can't you get me out of here on bail?"

"Not likely, if you're indicted for homicide. But I'll see what I can do."

He sat, deflated and forlorn, watching dismally as the turnkey let me out. Over at Homicide the cops were disgorging information with all the prodigality of a slot machine. So I appealed to Detective Lieutenant John Nola and got little more than consideration.

"Counselor," he told me, "this time you've got a loser. The accused needed money. He was slated to inherit the victim's estate. He was angry at her and he threatened her. There was no sign of a forced entry. Nothing missing. His fingerprints were on the murder weapon. All of which gives us that unholy trinity— means, motive, and opportunity. The Grand Jury will vote a true bill and we're going to process your client into the slammer for life plus forty. You'll never prove him innocent."

"I don't have to, Lieutenant. That's a legal presumption in his favor. You fellows have to prove him guilty."

He simply smiled and shifted one of those thin Schimmelpenninck cigars to the other side of his mouth. I walked out, flagged a cab, and drove to the site of the crime—an old dowager of a building on Park Avenue operated now by an economy-minded landlord. Self-service elevator and no doorman. Claire Stewart's apartment was listed on the directory. I identified myself and she buzzed me in.

I had been expecting one of the victim's contemporaries, someone's ancestor, shrunken, wrinkled, arthritic. Instead I was greeted by a tall abundant redhead in her early forties, vital and vivid, totally feminine, and given to bravura flourishes. I sat in her sumptuous living room and listened.

"I really don't know whether Albert killed his aunt or not," she said. "I merely told the police what I heard. This building is one of the old ones, you know, solid, with very thick walls, and we don't usually hear our neighbors. But oh, my, Albert was in a state. Turned up to several hundred decibels. And the language! I haven't heard words like that since I divorced my first husband."

"For example?"

"I will not repeat such obscenities."

"If it goes to trial the prosecutor may insist."

"In open court? Why, that's disgusting!"

"Did Albert threaten his aunt?"

"Not in so many words. He told her she was a deceitful, stingy old woman who had outlived her usefulness. I just hope he remembers those words when he's in a wheel chair in some nursing home. Did you know they found his fingerprints on the murder weapon? A Sixteenth Century urn that Agnes' dear departed husband had smuggled out of one of those Greek islands. It was Mr. Mahler's most prized possession and after he was cremated, Agnes kept his ashes in it. Isn't that touching? And then because it was used in such a terrible way all the ashes spilled out and were trampled into the carpet by the police. I think that's sacrilegious. Agnes simply venerated those ashes."

"Would Mrs. Mahler open the door for anyone who rang?"

"Are you kidding? This city is a jungle. People are being mugged and killed all over the place. Agnes was super-cautious. She would never have admitted a stranger. But she would certainly have opened the door for Albert, especially if she thought he had returned to apologize."

"Did you speak to her after he left?"

"She came here straightaway and confided in me. She was terribly upset. She simply could not understand why the bank had refused to honor the check. And she used my phone to call the bank and tell them they had made a very costly error and that she was going to hold the bank responsible. She said she would be down there first thing in the morning for a full explanation. But of course she never did go. Poor dear."

"Who found the body?"

"A cleaning lady who came every morning. When nobody answered her ring she called the super and he used his passkey."

"I take it he notified the police, Mrs. Stewart."

"Yes. And please, don't be so formal. Call me Claire. Your first name is Scott, isn't it? Do you like duck?"

"I beg your pardon?"

"Duck is my favorite dish. I prepare it even better than Maxim's in Paris. I'd like to invite you to dinner some evening this week."

"I'll have to check my appointment book and call you back."

"My number is unlisted." She scribbled it on a card and came over and tucked it into my breast pocket, smiling warmly. "Murray Hill 4-0040. Call soon."

I promised and departed hastily.

Agnes Mahler's bank was the Gotham Trust. I knew it well. The Madison Avenue branch has a most impressive facade. I headed for the desk of Mr. Harry Wharton, third vice-president, a neat compact man with a salesman's smile and a tax collector's eyes. The smile faded as I explained the situation.

"Mrs. Mahler," he said, "was a valued depositor of this institution. A little vague and confused at times, but otherwise no problem. She traveled frequently and had a custodial account. We held her securities, clipped her coupons, collected her dividends, and I advised her on investments and made quarterly reports. Her death shocked us. Of course we stopped all activity in her account until the estate goes through probate. You say one of her checks bounced? Impossible. She was a wealthy woman. Let me check it with Martin Schorr, our assistant cashier."

He dialed three digits on the intercom. "Schorr? Front and center. On the double. And bring the file on Mrs. Agnes Mahler."

A moment later Schorr came trotting through the door, a slight clerical specimen with thick glasses. He was clutching a bulky folder.

"Just tell me," Wharton demanded curtly, "why we refused to honor a check on Mrs. Mahler's account?"

"Insufficient funds, sir."

"Nonsense! Mrs. Mahler keeps much more than eighty thousand dollars in her savings account. We automatically transfer funds to cover her checks."

"There have been heavy withdrawals over the past few weeks."

"By whom?" I asked.

"The depositor, sir." Schorr opened the folder and showed me a bunch of withdrawal slips.

I examined them. But I knew that Agnes Mahler had been out of the country during that time. She could not possibly have conducted these transactions. I had the check she'd given Albert in my pocket. I took it out and compared its signature with those on the withdrawal slips. They were not even remotely similar.

"Someone goofed," I told Wharton. "The signatures on these withdrawal slips are forgeries."

"What? What are you talking about?"

I showed him. He riffled the file for Agnes Mahler's original signature card, then visibly relaxed. "You're mistaken, Counselor. Here is the card Mrs. Mahler signed when she opened the account.   The handwriting is identical with the with-drawal slips.''

"Then the card is also a forgery, Harry.   I have the check Mrs. Mahler gave Albert Osborn.   It was written in his presence, so the signature has to be genuine. Observe the capital 'M' in Mahler.   A simple letter.   Now look at the fancy loops and flourishes on the card and on the withdrawal slips.   No similarity at all.''

Wharton frowned.   "Perhaps Osborn is lying.   Perhaps he wrote the check himself.''

"Then he would have done a much better imitation.   He would have made at least a minimal attempt to copy her signature.   But we have other ways to learn which signature is genuine.   We can compare it with the handwriting on her will, which was attested by two witnesses.   Easier still, go back four or five months and compare it with earlier withdrawal slips.''

He nodded and rummaged in the file.   His face turned grim.   He had to clear his throat twice, then he made a gesture of total resignation.   "I'm afraid you're right, Counselor.   The handwriting *is* different.   Somebody must have pulled the original signature card and substituted a forged one.''

"Clever,'' I said.   "Any withdrawals under the new signature would check with your records and be honored.   Had to be one of your own people, Harry, fleecing the account.   Probably with an outside confederate, a woman who pretended to be Mrs. Mahler.   Better tag your employee before he guts the whole damn bank.''

Wharton made a face.   "Counselor, almost every employee in this institution has access to the signature files.   Tellers and cashiers are constantly comparing against those cards.''

"I take it you're insured.''

"Of course we're insured.   But with every fraud and embezzlement our pre-miums soar.''   He turned to the assistant cashier.   "We'll need a complete audit of Mrs. Mahler's account, from the ground up.   Start it rolling at once.''   After Schorr had left, he appealed to me.   "Where do we start?   We bond all our people. We check their backgrounds.   And still this sort of thing goes on.   How can you keep people from stealing?''

"Easy,'' I said.   "Triple all employees' salaries and remove the temptation or the need.''

That suggestion did not sit well.   He gave me an aggrieved look.   "Do me a favor, Jordan.   Take your ideas and—''

"Don't say it, Harry.   Bankers are supposed to be dignified.   You know you'll have to replace all that money in Mrs. Mahler's account.   It may ultimately belong to my client.''

"Only if you prove him innocent.''

He was right.   The law is clear.   A legatee cannot profit by his own misdeeds. He may not accelerate his bequest by liquidating the testatrix.

But the picture was no longer entirely bleak.   Back at my office I thought about it.   I knew now that someone else may have had a motive to silence Mrs. Mahler. And I needed to know more about that someone else.   The only source of infor-mation I could think of was Claire Stewart.   I am not especially fond of duck, either roasted, stewed, or fricasseed. But a lawyer often makes sacrifices for the sake of his client. So I reached into my breast pocket for the card bearing her telephone number.

I stared at it, my eyes wide, my pulse quickening—stared at the "M" in Murray Hill with its fancy loops and flourishes. Calligraphy identical with the "M" in Mahler on the substituted signature card in the bank's file. Identical with the handwriting on the recent withdrawal slips.

I did not phone her. Instead I rang Macbeth—Fitz Macbeth, that is—the private eye who practically has a monopoly on investigative work for lawyers. He has a large staff and a number of free-lance operatives on call, all ex-cops who had opted for early retirement.

He listened to me and said, "You want around-the-clock surveillance of Mrs. Claire Stewart. Starting when?"

"This minute."

"For how long?"

"Until further notice."

"And your description is adequate?"

"The lady is *sui generis*. Nobody around quite like her."

"It's going to cost, Counselor."

"Fitz, have I ever skunked you on a bill?"

He laughed and broke the connection.

I finished the afternoon working on other matters, then took some papers home with me. I ate a solitary TV dinner and was correcting syntax on a pending appeal when the call came—from one of Macbeth's men reporting that Claire Stewart had left her apartment at 9:42 P.M. to rendezvous with a man at a nearby cocktail lounge. Was I interested? I was. He gave me the address and I hurried out and flagged a cab.

I recognized the operative loafing against a light pole. "Still in there," he told me.

I headed for the bar, chin tucked in, hat pulled down. I ordered intently. They seemed to be arguing. Martin Schorr looked nervous and Claire Stewart was grim. She had her bravura flourishes under control, trying not to attract attention.

This was neither the time nor the place for a confrontation. I ducked out quickly, face averted. "Okay," I told the operative. "Stick with her until the next shift arrives. Can Fitz reach you if necessary?"

He showed me a small box. "Fitz gives me a beep, I call him back from the nearest booth."

Several times in the past both the D.A. and the police have accused me of withholding evidence material to the solution of a felony. The felony here was top drawer. Homicide. So I decided to play this one according to the book. I found Lieutenant Nola at home, watching a televised ballet on NET, one of those thin Dutch cigars smoking itself between his teeth.

He shut off the set and listened while I dumped it in his lap—the bank swindle, the cast involved, the whole works. I said, "You spoke to Mrs. Stewart. You had a chance to size her up."

He rolled his eyes.

"Exactly," I agreed. "And a man like Schorr, a wallflower type, unprepossessing, deprived, he'd be an easy mark for Mrs. Stewart with all those obvious charms. She'd have no difficulty enlisting his cooperation. What I think happened, one of them panicked when Agnes Mahler blew the whistle and phoned the bank. They took advantage of the fight between Albert and his aunt to divert suspicion to Albert. Mrs. Stewart volunteered that information pretty quick."

He studied the card with her telephone number. "You're certain this handwriting matches those forged signatures?"

"Without question."

"No shenanigans, Counselor?"

"My hand on the Bible, Lieutenant."

"You're saying that Schorr supplied a blank signature card and she filled it out and he substituted it for the original?"

"Yes."

"And where would the Stewart woman get blank checks or a passbook for withdrawals?"

"She and the victim were always visiting back and forth. She could easily have lifted them while Mrs. Mahler was in the kitchen or the bathroom."

"Wouldn't Mrs. Mahler have noticed their absence?"

"Ordinarily, yes. But Mrs. Stewart probably waited until just before Agnes took off on a long cruise."

He pursed his lips. "Damned careless of the Stewart dame to let you have a copy of her handwriting."

"I never said she had a full deck, Lieutenant. She was probably trying to cultivate me, hoping to wheedle information or exert influence if I got too close."

Nola stood up. "Schorr sounds like the weak partner in this conspiracy. Let's sweat him first. If he cracks we should have no trouble with the lady." He pointed to a telephone book. "Check the man's address."

He managed to commandeer a prowl car. It took us to a five-story walkup on Second Avenue. I anticipated little trouble with Martin Schorr. He possessed neither the Byzantine shrewdness nor the toughness of his accomplice. We found his door partly open—in that neighborhood a fearless act, or a careless one, or perhaps he was expecting someone.

But Schorr didn't even know his door was open. A bullet hole in the left temple had stopped him from worrying about such matters. Or anything else.

Nola bent and touched the corpse. "Still warm," he said harshly. "Dammit, we couldn't have missed the perpetrator by more than minutes." He used the dead man's phone and called it in, then looked at me. "Off the top of my head. The obvious conclusion. A dead accomplice cannot share the loot or implicate his partner. I think we should brace the lady while her adrenalin is still pumping."

"Let me make a call first," I said. "It may save us time." I got through to Macbeth. "Fitz, contact your man and get me a quick rundown on Mrs. Stewart's activities during the past hour. Ring me at this number. It's urgent."

Nola's technical support, with sirens, and Macbeth's response arrived simultaneously. I picked up the handset. Fitz said, "Here it is, Counselor. The lady and her escort left the cocktail lounge about fifteen minutes after you did. They separated immediately. She walked home and he flagged a cab in the opposite direction. She hasn't left her apartment since."

"No other exit?"

"Only the service door, in clear view."

I relayed the information to Nola. "It shoots down your theory, Lieutenant. Schorr was still alive when she left him."

"Then the lady will keep for a while. Where can I get some background on Schorr?" Nola asked.

"From Mr. Harry Wharton, Schorr's boss at the Gotham Trust."

On our way Nola made only one comment, directed at his driver. "Shut off that damn siren."

Wharton's apartment was far more impressive than Schorr's. He was, after all, in a higher bracket. I introduced Nola and gave Wharton the news about his cashier.

He gaped at us, incredulous. "Schorr an embezzler? Dead? I can't believe it."

"Did the man have any relatives?" Nola asked.

"I don't think so." Wharton shook his head. "Do you know the name of his accomplice?"

"Yes."

"Did she kill him?"

"We have evidence to the contrary."

"How did you manage to identify her?"

"The accomplice blundered and disclosed her identity to Jordan."

"Is the accomplice in custody?"

"Not yet," I interjected. "We had a theory, Harry, and then Schorr's death put a different face on it. We had to scrub our inference that it was Schorr who devised the swindle and set it up. I don't think he had anything at all to do with it. May I use your phone?"

I did not wait for permission. I dialed the Murray Hill number and when I had her voice on the line I said in a tense mimicking whisper, "Claire? Harry. No time to explain. Clear out. Fast."

Sudden alarm strained her voice. "What is it, Harry? What happened?"

I hung up.

The color had run out of Wharton's face. It was now stiff with restraint, tissue-gray, his eyes fixed on mine. I said, "That's all the confirmation I need, Harry. It struck me less than a minute ago. You wanted to know if we had identified Schorr's accomplice and then you asked if *she* killed him. We never told you it was a woman."

He swallowed hugely. "My God, Jordan, that was a natural assumption. It was a woman who withdrew the money."

"Yes. But your calling the accomplice 'she' and 'her' opened my eyes. Then I suddenly remembered your response at the bank—as if you knew nothing about

Agnes Mahler's call after her check bounced.   Not likely, Harry.   Who would she ask for?   *Only you,* Harry.   You handled her account.   You gave her advice. You visited her apartment to discuss investments.   And that's where you met Claire Stewart.   She's hard to resist.   She made a play for you and you tumbled.   She's a lady with expensive tastes and the liaison must have required a lot of money. Whose idea was it to plunder the Mahler account?   Yours or hers?''

He made a desperate reach for words.   "You're mistaken, Jordan, terribly mistaken!''

"I don't think so, Harry.   Mrs. Mahler threatened to blow the whistle.   It would start an investigation that could sink you.   You needed time to cover yourself. And the old lady was expendable.   So you paid her a visit.   She would certainly open the door for her banker.   You saw the urn and you used it.   But murder never solves anything, Harry.   It only creates new problems.   And one of those problems was Martin Schorr.

"He was nosing around.   He probably knew you had something going with Claire Stewart—she may have picked you up at the bank several times.   I think he knew her name because she too was a depositor at the bank.   She must have opened an account as an excuse to see you during the day.

"As soon as Schorr checked her signature he was in the picture.   It gave him what he needed, a chance to cut himself in for a piece of the action.   And he figured the lady would be easier to handle.   A very risky undertaking, after what happened to Mrs. Mahler.   So of course Schorr had to be eliminated, and quick. So you moved immediately, right after Claire phoned and told you what he wanted.''

Wharton appealed to the lieutenant.   "Not true.   Not a word of it.''   But his voice lacked conviction.

I said coldly, "You shot him, Harry.   Did you get rid of the gun?   A professional would have dropped it off the Staten Island ferry or one of the bridges.   But you're not a professional.   So it's probably hidden right here in this apartment.   The lieutenant's men know how to search and when they find it, your goose is cooked. They'll collar Mrs. Stewart and she'll sing her lungs out, pinning it on you, trying to clear her skirts.''

Nola got to the phone and snapped out an All Points Bulletin on the lady.   It sent Harry Wharton into a tailspin of despair.   He sank into a chair and lowered his face into his hands.

"All right, Lieutenant,'' I said.   "This one is all yours.   Now do me a favor, please.   Call the D.A. and start the ball rolling so I can spring my client.   I have to earn my fee.''

"You've already earned it.   But how can Osborn afford your usual whopping fee if he's broke?''

"You forget,'' I said.   "Albert is still Mrs. Mahler's sole legatee.   There's a sizeable estate involved, especially after the bank replaces all that embezzled loot.''

Nola grinned.   "Well, Counselor, he owes you more than a fee.   If you ask me, he owes you his skin.''

RUTH RENDELL

A Drop Too Much

You won't believe this, but last Monday I tried to kill my wife. Yes, my wife, Hedda. And what a loss that would have been to English letters! Am I sure I want to tell you about it? Well, you're not likely to tell her, are you? You don't know her. Besides, she wouldn't believe you. She thinks I'm the self-appointed president of her fan club.

The fact is, I'm heartily glad the attempt failed. I don't think I've got the stamina to stand up to a murder inquiry. I'd get flurried and confess the whole thing. (Yes, thanks, I will have another drink. My back's killing me—I think I've slipped a disk.)

Hedda and I have been married for fifteen years, and I can't complain she hasn't kept me in the lap of luxury. Of course I've paid my own price for that. To a sensitive man like myself it is a little humiliating to be known as "Hedda Hardy's husband." And I don't really care for her books. It's one thing for a man to write stuff about soldiers of fortune and revolutions in South American republics and jet-set baccarat games and seductions on millionaires' yachts, but you expect something a little more—well, delicate and sensitive from a woman. Awareness, you know, the psychological approach. I've often thought of what Jane Austen said about the way she wrote, on a little piece of ivory six inches wide. With Hedda it's more a matter of bashing away at a great rock face with a chisel.

Still, she's made a fortune out of it. And I will say for her, she's generous. Not a settlement or a trust fund though, more's the pity. And the property's all in her name. There's our place in Kensington—Hedda bought that just before house prices went sky-high—and the cottage in Minorca, and now we've got this farmhouse in Sussex. You didn't know about that? Well, that's crucial to the whole thing. That's where I made my abortive murder attempt.

Hedda decided to buy it about six months ago. Funnily enough, it was the same week she hired Lindsay as her secretary. Of course she's had secretaries before, must have had half a dozen, and they've all worshipped the ground she trod on. To put it fancifully, they helped fill my cup of humiliation. (And while on the subject of cups, old man, you may refill my glass. Thank you.)

I'll tell you what I mean. They were all bitten by this Women's Lib bug, so you can imagine they were falling about with glee to find a couple like us. And though I manage to be rather vague about my financial position with most of our friends, you can't keep things like that dark from the girl who types the letters to your accountant, can you?   The fact is, Hedda's annual income tax alone amounts to—let me see—yes, almost six times my whole annual income.

Those secretaries were mistresses of the snide comment.   What did you say? All right, I don't mind admitting it; a couple of them were my mistresses too.   I had to prove myself a man in some respects, didn't I?   But Lindsay—Lindsay's different.   For one thing, she'd actually heard of *me*.

When Hedda introduced us, Lindsay didn't come out with that It-must-be-wonderful-to-be-married-to-such-a-famous-writer bit.   She said, "You write that super column for *Lady of Leisure,* don't you?   I always read it.   I'm crazy about gardening."

My heart warmed to her at once, old man.   And when Hedda had finished making poor sweet Lindsay type about twenty replies to her awful fan letters, we went out into the garden together.   She's really very knowledgeable.   Imagine, she was living with her parents in some ghastly suburban hole and doing their whole garden single-handed.   Mind you, though, it's living in the suburbs that's kept her so sweet and unspoiled.

Not that it was just that—I mean the gardening bit—that started our rapport. Lindsay is just about the most beautiful girl I ever saw.   I adore those tall delicate blondes who look as if a puff of wind would blow them away.   Hedda, of course, is handsome after a fashion.   I daresay anyone would get a battered look churning out stuff about rapes and massacres year after year between breakfast and lunch.

The long and the short of it is that by the end of one week I was head over heels in love with Lindsay.   And she feels the same about me.   What did you say? You should be so lucky?   I reckon I deserved every bit of luck I could get in those ruddy weeks while Hedda was buying the farmhouse.

Honestly, Hedda treats me the way some men treat their wives.   Pours out all her troubles, and if I don't grovel at her feet telling her how wonderful she is, she says I don't know what it is to have responsibilites and that, anyway, I can't be expected to understand business.   And all this because the house agent didn't phone her at the precise time he'd promised to and the seller got a bit uptight about the price.   I don't blame him, the way Hedda drives a hard bargain.

(Another Scotch?   Oh, well, if you twist my arm.)   Hedda got possession of the place in March and she had an army of decorators in, and this firm to do the carpets and that one to do the furnishings.   Needless to say, I wasn't consulted except about the furniture for what she calls my "den."   Really, she ought to remember it isn't lap dogs who live in dens.

It's an extraordinary thing how mean rich people can be.   And quixotic.   The thousands she spent on that wallpaper and those Wilton rugs, but when it came to the garden she decided I could see to all that on my own, if you please.   Hedda really has no idea.   Just because I happen to know the difference between a calceolaria and a cotoneaster and am able—expertly, if for once I may blow my own trumpet—to instruct stockbrokers' wives in rose pruning, she thinks I enjoy nothing better than digging up half an acre of more or less solid chalk.   However, when I said I'd need to hire a cultivator and get the Lord-knows-how-much top soil and turfs, she was quite amenable—*for her*—and said she'd pay.

"I don't suppose it'll come to more than a hundred or so, will it?" she said. "With the stock market the way it is, I don't want to sell any more shares."   Just as if she was some poor little housewife having to draw it out of Post Office savings. And I knew for a fact—Lindsay had told me—she was getting £50,000 for her latest film rights.

She'd had the old stables at the end of the garden converted into a double garage. You can't park on the road itself—there's too much through traffic; but there's a drive that leads down to the garage between the garden and a field.   Not another house for miles, by the way.   But the garden was a real wilderness and at that time you had to plow through brambles and giant weeds to get from the garage to the house.   Taking care, I may add, not to fall down the well on the way.   Oh, yes, there's a well.   Or there was.

"I suppose that'll have to be filled in," I said.

"Naturally," said Hedda.   "Or are you under the impression I'm the sort of lady who'd want to drop a coin down it and make a wish?"

I was going to retort that she'd never dropped a coin in her life without knowing she'd get a damn sight more than a wish for it, but she'd just bought me a new car so I held my tongue.

I decided the best thing would be to fill the well up with hardcore, concrete the top, and make a gravel path over it from the garage entrance to the back kitchen door.   It wasn't going to be a complicated job—just arduous—as the brickwork around the well lay about two inches below the level of the rest of the garden. The well itself was very deep, about forty feet, as I knew from measuring with a plumb line.

However, I postponed filling in the well for the time being.   Hedda had gone off to the States on a lecture tour, leaving mountains of work for poor little Lindsay— a typescript to prepare about a million words long, and the Lord knows how many dreary letters to write to publishers and literary agents and all those people for whom the world is expected to stop when Hedda Hardy is out of the country.

Still, since Hedda had now established her base in Sussex and had all her par- aphernalia there, Lindsay was down there too and we had quite a little honeymoon. I can't begin to tell you what a marvel that girl is.   What a wife she'll make!— for some other lucky guy.   I can only say that my wish was her command.   And I didn't even have to express my wish.   A hint or even a glance was enough, and there was the drink I'd just begun to get wistful about, or a lovely hot bath running or a delicious snack on a tray placed right there in my lap.

It made a change for me, old man, the society of a really womanly old-fashioned woman.   D'you know, one afternoon while I happened to be taking a little nap, she went all the way into Kingmarkham—that's our neighboring town—to collect my car that had been serviced.   I didn't have to ask, just said something about being a bit weary.   And when I woke up, there was my car tucked away in the garage, and Lindsay in a ravishing new dress tiptoeing about getting our tea so as not to disturb me.

But I mustn't get sidetracked like this. Inevitably we began to talk of the future. Women, I've noticed, always do. A man is content to take the goods the gods provide and hope the consequences won't be too difficult. It's really quite offputting the way women, when one has been to bed with them once or twice, always say, "What are we going to do about it?"

Mind you, in Lindsay's case I felt differently. There's no doubt, marriage or not, she's the girl for me. I'm not used to a sweet naiveté in the female sex—I thought it had died with the suffrage—and to hear the assumptions Lindsay made about my rights and my earning power et cetera really did something for my ego. To hear her talk—until I set her right—you'd have thought I was the breadwinner and Hedda the minion. Well, you know what I mean. Unfortunate way of putting it.

We were bedding out plants one afternoon when Lindsay started discussing divorce.

"You'd divide your property, wouldn't you?" she said. "I mean, split it down the middle. Or if you didn't think that quite fair to her, she could keep this place and that sweet cottage in wherever-it-is, and we could have the Kensington house."

"Fair to her?" I said. "My dear girl, I adore you, but you don't know you're born, do you? All these hereditaments or whatever the lawyers call them are *hers*. Hers, lovey, in *her* name."

"Oh, I know that, darling," she said. By the way, she really has the most gorgeous speaking voice. I can't wait for you to meet her. "I know that. But when you read about divorce cases in the papers, the parties always have to divide the property. The judge makes a—a what's-it."

"An order," I said. "But in those cases the money was earned by the husband. Haven't you ever heard of the Married Women's Property Act?"

"Sort of," she said. "What is it?"

"I'll tell you what it means," I said. "It means that what's mine is hers and what's hers is her own. Or, to enlarge, if she fails to pay her income tax *I'm* liable, but if I fail to pay mine the government can't get a bean out of *her*. And don't make me laugh, sweetheart," I said, warming to my theme, "but any idea you may have about a division of property—well, that's a farce. There's nothing in English law to make her maintain me. If we got divorced I'd be left with the clothes on my back and the pittance I get from *Lady of Leisure*."

"Then what are we going to do about it?" she said.

What a question! But, to do her justice, she didn't make any silly suggestions as to our living together in a furnished room. And she was even sweeter to me than before.

Of course she loves me, so she doesn't feel it a hardship to run around laying out my clean clothes and emptying my ashtrays and fetching the car round to the front door for me when it's raining. But I know she thought I'd have a shot at Hedda, ask her to let me go and make a settlement on me. I could picture Hedda's face! Having a deeply rooted idea that she's the most dynamic and sexy thing since Helen of Troy, my wife has never suspected any of my philanderings and she hasn't an inkling of what's in the wind between me and Lindsay.

The funny thing is, I had an idea that if I did tell her she'd just roar with laughter and then say something cutting about church mice and beggars who can't be choosers. Hedda's got a very nasty tongue. It's been sharpened up by writing all that snappy dialogue, I suppose.

Anyway, when Hedda got back she wasn't interested in me or Lindsay or all those petunias and antirrhinums we'd planted. The first thing she wanted to know was why I hadn't filled in the well.

"All in good time," I said. "It's a matter of priorities. The well can get filled in anytime, but the only month to plant annuals is May."

"I want the well filled in now," said my wife. "I'm sick of looking at that disgusting heap of hardcore out there. If I'd wanted to look at rocks I'd have bought a house in the Alps."

What I'd said about priorities wasn't strictly true. (Thanks, I will have that topped up, if you don't mind.) I didn't want to fill in the well because I'd already started wondering if there was any possible way I could push Hedda down it. It had become a murder weapon, and to fill it up with hardcore now would be like dropping one's only gun into the Thames off Westminster Bridge.

Hedda hadn't made a will, but so what? As her widower, I'd get the lot. All through those hot weeks of summer while I stalled about the well, I kept thinking of Lindsay in a bikini on Hedda's private beach in Minorca—only it would be my private beach—Lindsay entertaining guests in the drawing room in Kensington, Lindsay looking sweet among the herbaceous borders at the farm, *my* farm. And never a harsh word from her or a snide remark. I'd never again be made to feel that somehow I'd got an invisible apron on. Or be expected to—well, accede to distasteful demands when I had a headache or was feeling tired.

But how do you push an able-bodied woman of thirty-eight, five feet ten, a hundred and fifty-two pounds, down a well? Hedda's an inch taller than I am and very strong. Bound to be, I suppose, with all the T-bone steaks she eats. Besides, she never goes into the garden except to walk across it from the garage to the back kitchen door when she's put her Lincoln Continental away. I thought vaguely of getting her drunk and walking her out there in the dark. But Hedda doesn't drink much and she can hold her liquor like a man.

So the upshot of all this thinking was—nothing. And at the beginning of this month Lindsay went off for her three-weeks' holiday to her sister in Brighton. I'd no hope to give her. Not that she had a suspicion of what was going on in my mind. I wouldn't have involved a sweet little innocent like her in what was, frankly, a sordid business.

As we kissed goodbye, she said, "Now, remember, darling, you're to be extra specially loving to Hedda and get her to settle a lump sum on you. Then afterwards, when it's all signed, sealed, and settled, you can ask for a divorce."

I couldn't help smiling, though I felt nearer to tears. When you come across ingenuousness like that, it revives your faith in human nature. And when you come to think of it, old man, what an angel!   There she was, prepared to endure agonies of jealousy thinking of me making love to Hedda, and all for my sake. I felt pretty low after she'd gone, stuck at the farm with Hedda moaning about not knowing how to get through all her work without a secretary.

However, a couple of days at bashing away on the typewriter with two fingers decided her.   She couldn't get a temporary typist down in Sussex, so she'd go back to Kensington and get a girl from the nearest agency.   I wasn't allowed to go with her.

She stuck her head out of the Lincoln's window as she was going off up the drive and pointed to the heap of hardcore.

"Faith doesn't move mountains," she yelled.   "The age of miracles is past. So let's see some damned action!"

Charming.   I went into the house and got myself a stiff drink.   (Thanks, I don't mind if I do.)   It was fair enough being alone at the farm, though painful in a way after having been alone there with Lindsay.   A couple of postcards came from Lindsay—addressed to us both for safety's sake—and then, by a bit of luck, she phoned.   Of course, I told her I was going to be alone for the next three weeks, and after that she phoned every night.

Remember how marvelous the weather was last week and the week before?   Not too hot, but ideal for a spot of heavy engineering in the open air.   I was just resigning myself to the fact that I couldn't put off filling in the well a day longer when I got this brilliant idea.

Oddly enough, it was television that inspired me.   Hedda doesn't care for watching television, though we've got two big color sets which she says, if you please, she bought for my benefit.   I hardly think it becomes her to turn up her nose at the medium, considering what a packet she's made out of getting serials on it.

Be that as it may, I don't much enjoy watching it with her supercilious eye on me, but I'm not averse to a little discriminating viewing while she's away.   It must have been the Friday night I saw this old Hollywood film about some sort of romantic goings-on in the jungle.   Dorothy Lamour, I think it was, and Johnny Weissmuller—it was that old.   But the point was, there was a bit of wild animal trapping in it, and the way the intrepid hunter caught this puma thing was by digging a trough right on the path the hapless beast frequented and covering it up rather cunningly with branches and leaves.

It struck me all of a heap, I don't mind telling you.   The occasion called for opening a bottle of Hedda's Southern Comfort.   In the morning, a wee bit the worse for wear, I spied out the land.   First of all I needed a good big sheet of horticultural polythene, but we'd already got plenty of that for the cloches in which I was going to have a stab at growing melons.   Next the turfs.   I drove over to Kingsmarkham and ordered turfs and the best quality gravel.   The lot was delivered on Monday.

By that time I'd got all the surrounding ground leveled and raked over, smooth as a beach after the tide's gone out.   The worst part was getting rid of the hardcore. Hedda was damned right about faith not moving mountains.   It took me days.   I had to pick up every chunk by hand, load it onto my wheelbarrow, and cart it about a hundred yards to the only place where it could be reasonably well concealed, in a sort of ditch between the greenhouse and the boundary wall. Must have been Thursday afternoon before I got it done to my satisfaction. I remember reading somewhere that the human hand is a precision instrument that some people use as a bludgeon. I wish I could use my hands as bludgeons. By the time I was done, they looked as if they'd been through mincing machines.

I waited till nightfall—not that it mattered, as there wasn't an observer for miles, apart from a few owls and so on—and then I spread the polythene over the mouth of the well, weighting it down not too firmly at the edges with battens. The lot was then covered with a thin layer of earth so that all you could see was smoothly raked soil, bounded by the house terrace, the really lovely borders of annuals that Lindsay and I had planted, and the garage at the far end.

I was pretty thankful I'd got those turfs and that gravel well in advance, I can tell you, because the next day when I went to start my new car, I couldn't get a squeak out of it. Moxon's, who service it for me, had to come over from Kingsmarkham and pick it up. Some vital part had conked out, I don't know what—I leave all that mechanical stuff to Hedda. But the thing was, I was stranded without a car which rather interfered with my little plan to surprise Lindsay by popping down to Brighton for her last week.

She, of course, was dreadfully disappointed that she wasn't going to get her surprise. "Why don't I come back and join you, darling?" she said when she phoned that Saturday night.

And get wind of what was going on down the garden path?

"I'd much rather be with you by the sea," I said. "No, I'll give Moxon's a ring Monday morning. If the car's ready I'll just have to stagger into Kingsmarkham on the eleven-fifteen bus and collect it. It's only an hour's run to Brighton. I could be with you by lunchtime."

"Heaven," said Lindsay, and so it would have been if Hedda hadn't sprung a little surprise of her own on me. Luckily—with my heavenly week ahead in view—I'd laid all those turfs and made a neat gravel path from the garage to the back kitchen door when, on Sunday night, Hedda phoned. She'd got all her work done, thanks to the efficiency of the temporary girl, and she was coming down in the morning for a well-earned rest. By twelve noon she'd be with me.

But I didn't feel dispirited and there didn't seem any point in phoning Lindsay. After all, we were soon going to be together forever and ever. Before I went to bed I made a final survey of the garden. The path looked perfect. No one would have dreamed it hid a forty-foot death trap going down into the bowels of the earth.

That was last Sunday night, the night the weather broke, if you remember. It was pelting down with rain in the morning, but I had to go out to establish my alibi. I caught the 10:15 bus into Kingsmarkham to be on the safe side. When Hedda says twelve noon, she means twelve noon and not a quarter past. But, by George, I was nervous, old man. I was shaking and my heart was drumming away. As soon as the Olive and Dove opened I went in and had a couple of what the doctor would have ordered if he'd been around to do an electrocardiograph. And I chatted with the barmaid to make sure she'd know me again.

At twelve sharp I beetled down to Moxon's. Couldn't have given a damn whether the car was ready or not, but if Moxon's people were talking to me face to face at noon, the police would know I couldn't have been at the farm pushing my wife down a well at noon, wouldn't they? The funny thing was, this mechanic chappie said my car had been taken back to the farm already. The boss had driven it over himself, he thought, though he couldn't be sure, having only just got in.

Well, that gave me a bit of a turn and I had a very nasty vision of poor old Moxon walking up to the house to find me and—however, I needn't have worried. I was just getting on the bus that took me back when I saw Moxon himself zoom by in his Land Rover with the towrope.

It was still pouring when I reached home. I nipped craftily round the back way and in by the garage. Hedda's Lincoln and my little Daf were there all right, the two of them snuggled up for all the world like a couple of cuddly creatures in the mating season.

Out of the garage I went on to my super new path. And it was as I'd planned—a big sagging hole edged with sopping wet turf where the well mouth was. I crept up to it as if something or someone might pop out and bite me. But nothing and no one did, and when I looked down I couldn't see a thing but a bottomless pit, old boy.

Never mind the rain, I thought. I'll get into my working togs, clear the well mouth of polythene, and call the police. Here is my wife's car, officer, but where is my wife? I suspect a tragic accident. Ah, yes, I have been out all morning in Kingsmarkham, as I can prove to you without the slightest difficulty.

I was fantasizing away like this, with the rain trickling down between my raincoat collar and my sweater, when there came—my Lord, I'll never forget it!—the most ear-splitting bellow from the house. In point of fact, from the kitchen window.

"Where the flaming hell have you been?" Only she didn't say "flaming," you know. "Are you out of your damned mind? I come here to find the place piled high with your filthy cigarette butts and not a duster over it for a fortnight. Where have you been?"

Hedda.

I nearly had a coronary. No, I'm kidding. I had the first symptoms. Pain up my left side and in my arm. I thought I'd had it. I suppose the fact that Hedda and I do have a perfect diet, the very best of proteins and vitamins, stood me in good stead when it came to the nitty-gritty.

Well, I sort of staggered up the path and into the kitchen. There she was, hands on hips, looking like one of those what's-its—Furies or Valkyries or something. (Sorry, I've had a drop too much of your excellent Scotch.)

I could have done with a short snort at that moment. I didn't even get a cup of coffee.

"One hell of a landscape gardener you are," Hedda yelled at me. "A couple of drops of rain and your famous path caved in. Lucky for you it happened before I got here. I might have broken a leg."

A leg, ha ha! Of course I realized what had happened.   The water had collected in a pool till the polythene had sagged and the battens finally had given way.   I would have to run into a wet spell, wouldn't I, after the heat wave we'd been having?

"You didn't put enough of that hardcore down," said my wife in her psychopathic bird-of-prey voice.   "Damn it, you live in the lap of luxury, never do a hand's turn but for that piddling-around-the-peonies column of yours, and you can't even fill in a damned well.   You can get right out there this minute and start on it."

So that's what I did, old man.   All that hardcore had to be hauled back by the barrow-load and tipped down the well.   I worked on it all afternoon in the rain and all yesterday, and this morning I made another path.   It's messed up my back properly, I can tell you.   I felt the disk pop out while I was dropping the last hundredweight in.

Still, Hedda had bought me that German stereo system I've been dreaming of for years, so I mustn't grumble.   She's not a bad sort really, and I can't complain that my every wish isn't catered to, provided I toe the line.   (No, I'd better not have any more.   I'm beginning to get double vision, thanks all the same.)

Lindsay?   I expect her back on Monday and I suppose we'll just have to go as before.   The funny thing is, she hasn't phoned since last Saturday, though she doesn't know Hedda's back.   I called her sister's place this morning and the sister went into a long involved story about Lindsay going off, full of something about a surprise for someone—but Hedda came in and I had to ring off.

I can use your phone, old man?   That's most awfully nice of you.   I don't want the poor little sweet thinking I've dropped her out of my life forever.

FLORENCE V. MAYBERRY

The Grass Widow

I used to watch Jim Gibbs walk past our house on his way to visit Mrs. Tichenor. Back then I didn't call him Jim. I was only fourteen and he was around thirty—thirty-one to be exact—and I was trained to say Uncle or Aunt to old people if they were close friends and Mr. or Mrs. or Miss if they weren't. So Jim was Mr. Gibbs to me.

He went by every day to visit Mrs. Tichenor. Shameful, folks in town said, all except his relatives and maybe they did too on the quiet. Mrs. Tichenor was a grass widow, which is what they called a divorced woman in those days. Or so she said, but she might not be divorced at all, according to the gossip I heard—did anyone ever see her divorce papers? Dying too. Her lungs were bad and Doc Williams told his wife, who told everyone, that Mrs. Tichenor was likely on her deathbed.

With all that facing Jim Gibbs, it was a shame that a well-off man like Jim, who belonged to one of the best families in West Texas, would take up with her. Besides, he scarcely knew her. He met her at a church sociable before she got so housebound, and fell head over heels in love with her then and there.

Actually—and that was odd in a town of less than 2,000 people—I had never seen Mrs. Tichenor. She had been in town not quite a year, had come from Pennsylvania to Texas to get well.

She didn't go to the same church as our family, and I was in school most of the time. By the time I heard enough about her to be curious she was already too sick to leave her house, and before that she stayed home and did what fancy sewing anyone would give her to eke out the little she had brought with her.

I heard Papa tell Mama that, seeing he owned the bank, he always knew how much money everybody had. But with Jim Gibbs visiting her every day, carrying an armload of groceries—well, she didn't need much.

I heard, too, that she had a little girl. The child was young, so her minister's wife said, and stayed with relatives back in Pennsylvania. Back then, in a little Texas town like ours, folks didn't pay too much mind to germs, but the minister's wife said Mrs. Tichenor did. She knew she had consumption and wouldn't let the child be with her.

This was just before World War I and ideas about morals were different then. Divorced women weren't looked on kindly, sick or well. Folks figured they had feisty ways else they would have clung to their husbands till death did them part. My mother did with my father.

Jim always walked fast, or rode fast on Big Ben, on his way to Mrs. Tichenor's, and slow when he left. Once I was sitting under the lilac bush as he walked towards town in the twilight and I saw tears on his cheeks. It was the first time I had ever seen a man cry, and it was especially shocking for a man like Jim to do it. He was tall and strong, good-looking in a redheaded kind of way, a cowman who could ride range with the best of his hired hands, mend fence, brand, and with a hard business head on his shoulders besides, so my father said. My father should have known because he had a hard business head too—he owned half of the town and ran the other half.

When I watched Jim walk by crying, I thought: Mr. Gibbs is in love with that bad woman and she's been mean to him—they say sick people complain a lot. Seeing him that way gave me shivers, because at fourteen I was getting ready for love. It was a terrible feeling, but beautiful at the same time. I began to wish someone would love me like that.

My mother felt sorry for Mrs. Tichenor—said she was too sick to do for herself and Jesus taught, let him without sin cast the first stone, and besides Jim Gibbs never visited her at night, only in the daytime when a neighbor might drop in on them any minute. For instance my mother did, carrying with her a slab of pie or a plate of chicken and dumplings or a fresh loaf of bread—different things, so the poor soul would have something decent to eat. But Mama would never let me go with her.

One afternoon my father came home early from the bank and found my mother gone. When she came back with her empty dish, he bullied her until she told him where she had been. He railed around and ordered her never to set foot again in that whore's house. "What's a whore, Mama, what's it mean?" I asked after my father had stormed back downtown.

"Katy, what were you listening for?" Mama asked sharply, her eyes pink.

"I was out in the porch swing. How could I help hearing with Papa yelling?"

"Don't be sassy, young lady, talking about your Papa that way!" Mama always stuck up for Papa no matter what he did or said, and he was a terror.

"What's a whore?" I asked Gladys, my best chum at school.

"Oo-o-ooh, Katy Prendergast, you're talking nasty, and said a bad word!" she screamed. She did it in the school yard and next thing I was in the principal's office and he was asking what I said, and I wouldn't tell him because he was a man. Neither would Gladys for the same reason, but she told me she was never going to speak to me again and would tell her mother who would tell my mother. But next day she threw her arms around my neck and cried and said she hoped to die, she'd never tell on me. Only she still wouldn't say what whore meant.

Jim Gibbs usually visited Mrs. Tichenor along about four in the afternoon, most times bringing groceries. Once I saw him carrying a sack that had *Sotheby's Yard Goods and Dresses* printed on it. Clothes for Mrs. Tichenor, must be. Was that what whore meant? A man buying clothes for a woman who wasn't his wife?

A few times Jim came with Dr. Williams, riding Big Ben alongside the doctor's buggy. One of those times, after the doctor came out of Mrs. Tichenor's house—she lived just up the road from us—I watched the pair of them standing at the gate a long time. Then Jim went back into the house, his head bent and his shoulders slumped as though he carried a heavy load.

Mama was always in our house or in the garden when I came home from school. I was the youngest child by twelve years, my brother and sister already married and living in Amarillo and Dallas. My father had laid down the law, as he did about everything. He told Mama to always be home when I was out of school—and so must I, no lollygagging around with schoolmates, girls couldn't be trusted alone, no telling what they'd be up to.

So it was a shock one day when I came home and Mama wasn't there. She came back soon, though, running down the path from the direction of Mrs. Tichenor's house, pink in the face and out of breath with hurry.

"You've been up at Mrs. Tichenor's again, haven't you, Mama?"

"Hush!" she said, scared like, looking around as though my father might be home. "Mind your manners, Miss, don't you be questioning your Mama."

"You have been! And after Papa said you couldn't."

"So I have!" she said, as flip as I might have said it to anyone but Papa. "So I have. The poor thing, she can barely down a bowl of soup. Jim Gibbs does his best, but he don't know how to take care of a sick woman, shouldn't be doing it anyway. Now if you know what's good for you, you'll not tell your father a thing about it. It was only my Christian duty."

I had no intention of telling my father. But I saw my chance—to set eyes on Mrs. Tichenor. Perhaps if I could see her I would know what a whore is. "I won't tell, Mama, if—"

Mama looked startled. "*If* what, Miss Sassbox?"

"If you'll let me go with you tomorrow when you take something for her to eat. Mama, I bet you've been taking her things all along, probably every day. Please let me go with you, Mama. If Papa comes home before we do we can just say we've been—oh, anywhere, visiting, shopping. Mama, if she's dying like they say, it can't hurt just to see her."

Mama looked uncertain. "They say consumption is catching."

"Only if you eat out of their dishes without scalding them first, or they cough in your face. I read about it. Please!"

"I'll see."

"Tomorrow?"

"We'll see. Maybe you'll sass your teacher like you do me and be kept after school. Then it'll be too late for visiting."

I figured then she would let me go with her. I was never kept after school. I was a good scholar. Besides, my father was chairman of the school board.

I was so excited at school next day that I shivered off and on even though the late spring day was warm. "Are you sick, Katy?" the teacher asked. "If you don't feel well, perhaps you had better go on home now." If it had been afternoon when she asked that, I would have taken her up. But it was morning and there was still noon dinner to be eaten with Papa. "I feel fine. Just a little draft maybe." Which was silly, it was warm as all getout.

Mama had chicken and dumplings for noon dinner, green onions and radishes out of our garden, peas in cream sauce, lemon pie with high brown-tipped meringue. The dinner put Papa in a good mood, he didn't growl at us once. "Good gal," he said to Mama, and she blushed. Maybe from being pleased, maybe from a guilty conscience, maybe from both.

That afternoon at school I put on a little for the teacher—I shivered every time she looked my way. "Katy, you are shivering! You certain you feel all right?"

"Well—maybe I *should* go home."

I walked slow across the school yard in case the teacher was watching, then ran the rest of the way home. Leaving early was better—no schoolmates to see Mama and me go into Mrs. Tichenor's house. "I got let out early, was all through with my class work," I fibbed to Mama. "Let's go now before there's a chance of Papa coming home."

"I declare," Mama said uncertainly. "Truth is, I'd been meaning to go up early to keep you from coming along. But now you're here, I suppose—" She turned back into the kitchen and picked up a little basket with a white fringed napkin across it. "Poor thing, she don't eat enough to keep a bird alive, but chicken and dumplings may tempt her."

It was queer the way I felt as Mama and I walked to Mrs. Tichenor's house. As though I were taking a long journey into some foreign country. Scared and excited. Jim's horse, Big Ben, was tied to the hitching post in front of her house, tossing his head against flies that lit on his neck. Big Ben's coat was red as fire, like Jim Gibbs' hair, and he was a real beauty. Fire in Big Ben too—finest horse in all that cow country, folks said. So Mama and I knew Jim had come early too to visit Mrs. Tichenor.

"Mind your manners," Mama whispered as she knocked on the screen door. "And stop staring."

It was Jim who came to the door. "Howdy, Mrs. Prendergast, Miss Katy, come right in."

"I brought a little something for Mrs. Tichenor," Mama said, holding out the basket but walking right inside at the same time. "How's she feeling today?"

"Well—" Jim hesitated like he didn't want to go on with that, and looked over his shoulder towards the back of the house. "Not too—"

And there she was. Just suddenly. Standing in the archway that led into the back parlor. The wide opening framed her almost like she was on a stage, with the sun from the sitting-room's west window floodlighting her face. My tongue turned dry, and I realized my mouth was hanging open. I shut it and swallowed. Mrs. Tichenor was as beautiful as an angel.

All my life long, either before or after, I never saw another woman as beautiful as Mrs. Tichenor. No wonder Jim fell in love with her at first sight. And stayed in love.

She was wearing a loose white robe, its sleeves wide and full like wings, which helped the angel look.   Her hair hung down her back in soft black waves, and her eyes were just as black.   Creamy pale skin, except for a pink flush on her cheeks.   Slender and almost as tall as Jim.   She was so beautiful she made me hurt.

"You're so kind to me, Mrs. Prendergast, I do thank you."   Her voice was beautiful too, soft and breathy with a city sound to it.   "And is this young lady your daughter whom I've never met before?"

"Yes, my youngest.   Katy—Katy, meet Mrs. Tichenor."

"Pleased to meet you, Ma'am," I whispered.

"Won't you sit down and visit a while?"   When Mrs. Tichenor smiled, her eyes glowed like there were soft-shaded lamps behind them.

"Thank you, but we have to get right back home," Mama said nervously.   "Got some garden stuff to fix for supper.   Shall I just put this chicken and dumplings in the kitchen?   Brought gravy to go with it—tastes pretty good heated up."

"I'll take them, Ma'am," Jim said, smiling.   You could tell he liked Mama.

"Oh, well, I could—"   She handed the basket to Jim.   "No hurry about getting the basket and dishes back.   I can pick them up tomorrow."

"I'll carry them back," Jim said.

Mama looked flustered, like a pin was stuck in her and she didn't want to let on.   "Oh, no, please don't bother.   I'll take them now, save you the trip.   I'll just put the chicken and gravy in something here—"

"Yes, that would be better," Mrs. Tichenor said, still smiling, but the lamps had turned out behind her eyes.   Anybody but a fool could tell that Mama didn't want somebody at our house to know she had come here.   "You shouldn't trouble so much for me, but I'm truly grateful.   I haven't felt like eating but now I do—everything you cook is so delicious.   What a pretty daughter you have—you must be very proud of her."

"Pretty is as pretty does," Mama said prissily.   Then flushed.   Because there was never anyone so pretty as Mrs. Tichenor.   "Come along, Katy, I've things laid out for you to do."

I wanted to go close to Mrs. Tichenor, to shake her hand, tell her I thought she was beautiful, and I was sure she just had to be good.   But nobody I ever knew did anything like that, make such a show of themselves.   So I just bobbed my head and mumbled, "Pleased to meet you, Ma'am."   I didn't realize until I was on the front porch that I had backed out of the room.

Mama whirled on me and whispered, "Don't look so dauncey, girl.   You look like that and Papa will know for sure we've been up to something."

Once we were outside the yard I said, "Oh, Mama, she's so beautiful, she's got to be good inside.   You think she's good too—that's why you take things to her every day."

"Hush!   Not every day."

"And God shouldn't let her die!"   To my horror I began to fight back tears.

"Katy Prendergast, stop that!   I should never have taken you along.   If your father hears about it—"   Mama's voice trailed off and her face crinkled with worry as she looked at me. "Now don't fret about it. She may get better—folks do sometimes, even with consumption. Just put your mind on helping me get Papa's supper."

I wasn't much help though, because my mind was still up the street with Mrs. Tichenor. Mama fussed, saying I was dreaming over the radishes and onions, she might better have done everything herself. But when Papa came home for supper he was in a good mood for once and pulled on my long heavy braid as he came into the dining room. I yanked away and said sharply, "Don't!"

He looked surprised, because if Papa pulled on your braid it was considered a compliment. "Humph!" he grunted. He walked on into the kitchen and I heard him ask, "What's the matter with that girl of yours, Mattie? Kind of sassed me."

"Sassed you! Oh, I don't think she meant anything, Mr. Prendergast. It's just her age, growing up, you know, that's all."

He didn't mention it again, but at the supper table he kept looking at me over his glasses, like he was expecting me to say, "Excuse me, Papa." I didn't say anything out loud. But inside I was saying, *I hate you, I hate you for being mean about Mrs. Tichenor.*

Suddenly I thought of the one person I knew who really loved Mrs. Tichenor, no matter what anyone said. Jim Gibbs.

Next afternoon I hurried home from school, looked up the street toward the Tichenor house, and didn't see Big Ben hitched outside or the doctor's buggy. So I made it my business to hang around in the front yard by the picket fence to see when Jim came. After a while I heard hooves plopping on the road. It was Big Ben, his shiny red neck arched, and Jim on his back with his big hat tilted to one side of his red hair. I tell you, they were a sight. Both handsome, red-haired, Big Ben proud-stepping, Jim sitting easy but proud too. Jim tipped his hat to me, just like I was grown up. I smiled and said, "How-de-do."

He tied Big Ben to the iron hitching post beside Mrs. Tichenor's front gate, then clicked his high-heeled boots up her walk, his steps light and quick as though he were in a hurry to get there. He didn't knock, just opened the screen door and went in as though it was his house. The door shut softly and I felt lonely, left out. I wanted to go see Mrs. Tichenor too.

Why couldn't I? Why couldn't I take something, like a present, and go too?

But what did I have that was all mine, that would really be a gift from me? Funny. My papa was one of the richest men in the county, and I had nothing of my own to give away except—Quickly, before I got too scared, I hurried onto our porch, softly opened the front screen, tiptoed upstairs to my room, and opened the red velvet box that held my lavaliere with the pearl in it. Mama's younger sister who lived out in California had sent it to me. We didn't see her once in a blue moon, so she wouldn't know if I gave it away. Besides, she didn't like Papa and Papa didn't like her. He didn't like the lavaliere either so I never wore it.

I took it, velvet box and all, tiptoed back downstairs, out the front door, and ran up the street, my heart pounding. Big Ben snorted as I passed him and I jumped a foot. Then slowly, like a lady making a neighborly call, I went up the steps and knocked timidly on Mrs. Tichenor's front door.

The knock must have been too light.   Anyway, no one answered.   Voices came from beyond the back parlor in words I couldn't make out—spaces of silence, then words again.   I turned to leave.   But across the road there was Mrs. Dilson, our neighbor, walking up from town.   If she saw me, she would be sure to ask Mama what I was doing there by myself—or worse, ask my father when she went to the bank.   I opened the screen door and slipped inside.

A few steps across the rug and I reached the archway into the back parlor.   No one was there, but the voices were plainer.   Now I could make out what they were saying.

"Jim, it would be wicked."   Mrs. Tichenor's voice was sad, not crying, but like an echo of crying done long ago.   "The doctor won't say, but I know.   I am dying, Jim.   So don't talk about marriage.   I don't intend to be a bride who may turn into a corpse in days or weeks.   And I'll not let you be burdened with a child not your own."

"Melissa, hush!   I'll help you get well.   If we're married I can be with you day and night, looking after you.   And your child would be my child.   Besides, the old biddies would stop clucking their stories and making you miserable."

"No!   If I die, I don't want it on my soul—"

"Good God, what about my soul!   Think how I'd blame myself if I didn't do everything I could for you!   Melissa, Melissa, I want you for my wife, no matter what."

I walked backwards, very softly, towards the porch.   Stopped, because the voices were quiet and I was afraid the floor might creak.

"Please!   You said you love me.   Prove it," Jim implored.

"But I am!"   Her voice was desperate.   "I am—"

Something smothered her voice, and there was another silence before she spoke again uncertainly, "Oh, Jim, I don't know—"

"I know.   Please!"

"It isn't right, not fair."

"I'm going now.   To the courthouse to get the license, the papers, whatever you need to sign.   I'll bring the preacher here and we'll be married tonight."

"It's wrong, it isn't the way to start a marriage."

"It is!   Because it's the way we'll start ours.   Melissa, I'm going for the papers now.   Before you change your mind."

"But I didn't—"

I heard his feet move across the floor of the unseen room and I looked around frantically for a hiding place.   A settee sat crosswise in a corner of the sitting room.   I scooted under it, deep into the corner, and doubled up.   With my face pressed into the rug I watched his boots stride across the room, heard the screen door creak open, then slap against the wooden frame of the doorway.

For what seemed forever I kept my breathing shallow, listening, and heard no movement, no sound.   I crawled from beneath the settee and moved stealthily to the door.   As I touched the screen, my neck prickled a warning and I whirled around.   Mrs. Tichenor stood in the wide opening between the two parlors, her large black eyes startled, a hand at her breast.   "Oh!" she said, her voice soft and raspy, like a chapped hand rubbing on silk. "I didn't hear you come in."

"No, ma'am," I said. "I knocked but no one heard."

"Didn't—didn't Mr. Gibbs see you?"

"No, ma'am. I—well, I—I brought something for you. This." And I held out the red velvet box.

She took the box, looking at me uncertainly. Then she opened it and saw the lavaliere. "Oh, how lovely! It's so pretty and delicate. Katy—that is your name, isn't it?—Katy, it's so lovely that I mustn't take it from you. It looks like you, it belongs with you. You must keep it, Katy."

"Please—it's all I have to give you. I wanted to give you something because—" I choked, unable to tell her why.

"I'm so grateful," she whispered. "Truly. But when you wear it, it will be special for me. As though it belongs to both of us." She handed it back to me. "Now it does belong to both of us, because I've made it a present back to you."

As I took it she smiled so sweetly, looked so beautiful, I had to tell her the truth. Like, you wouldn't tell lies to an angel, would you? "I was really hiding under your settee. Because nobody answered the door when I knocked, I came in and—and heard what you and Mr. Gibbs said." The rest came out in an impassioned plea. "Oh, please marry Mr. Gibbs. He can take care of you!"

She took my hand, squeezed it gently. "Then if you heard, you know why I'm afraid to. A wife should help her man, not be a burden to him."

"But he takes care of you now. Wouldn't it be the same burden? Only you'd be married."

She looked into my eyes for what seemed a long time. Then she walked slowly to the settee and sat down. Her hands were trembling and she locked them together on her lap. "Trust a child to get at the truth," she said. "You're right. It is a burden now."

"But he *likes* taking care of you. Even better than riding Big Ben."

She stood up, moved unsteadily towards the back parlor. As she passed me she said, "Thank you, Katy. For everything." And went on, out of sight, into a room that I discovered later was her bedroom. I left too, running down the path, up onto our veranda.

Mama was in our kitchen, starting supper. "Set the table, Katy. It's lodge night for Papa—he'll be home soon."

Fried chicken, mashed potatoes, cream gravy, cole slaw, apple pie. Hot biscuits, of course, Papa wouldn't touch a meal that didn't have hot bread. Mostly Papa grunted at mealtimes and put his eyebrows together if anybody talked, but Mama's good food must have had a mellowing effect, or else the news was too much for him to hold back.

"What do you think Jim Gibbs did this afternoon, Mattie?" he asked, not expecting any answer. Papa never needed anyone's answer, least of all his family's.

"Why, I've no idea, Mr. Prendergast," Mama said, looking guilty at the mention of Jim Gibbs whom she saw more times than Papa knew about.

"Blame fool went for a wedding license at the courthouse. For him and that—

woman up the road. Said she was too sick to come with him, he'd take any paper needed back to her and return it after she signed it. Girl in the office started to give it to him but Joe Miller''—Mr. Miller was the County Clerk—''came in just then, so Jim told him what he wanted. Well, Joe's known Jim since he was born and naturally like a good friend of the Gibbses, he warned Jim to take second thought—could be the woman wasn't actually divorced, could get himself in a pack of trouble with bigamy. But Jim's got a temper like his hair. Hauled off, slammed Joe against the wall right in the county office.''

Mama's eyes were big as saucers. "Hurt Joe?"

"Lump on the back of his head. Jim banged him good, then tore off like a wild stallion. So Joe called me and asked if anything ought to be done about it, because Jim needed to be saved from himself, getting mixed up with another man's leavings. I told Joe as Mayor of this town I'd have none of that carrying on. Went over, gathered up Joe, and we swore out a warrant with the sheriff on Jim. Had it served right off. Like I told you, Mattie, when you wanted to traipse up there carrying victuals to that trashy woman. Fool around trash, you end up trash.'' He fixed his bleak harsh gaze on me. "Hear that, young lady? Keep that in mind.''

Except abstractly, simply because he was my father, I never really liked my father. That night I hated him. Mama's food knotted in my stomach and before I could do anything about it, there it was. All back in my plate with my father leaping from his chair, eyes blazing in a dead-white face.

My timid, self-effacing mother sprang up and set herself squarely between me and him. "Shame on you, Mr. Prendergast! Frightening the child, saying such things. Now leave this instant before you make her worse!''

Papa's mouth dropped open and his eyes took on the surprised, hurt look of a spoiled child who for the first time has been refused something. Without another word he stalked out of the room and out of the house, just as I was sick again.

As Mama tucked me in bed, I asked, "Will they put Mr. Gibbs in jail?" It was a terrible thought. Who would take care of Mrs. Tichenor if they did?

"I doubt that," she said. "Not with Jim Gibbs being who he is. Besides, likely he didn't hurt Joe Miller much. Now stop fretting over what your Papa said.''

"Do you think they'll still get married? Even if—" I started to say, *even if Mrs. Tichenor said she wouldn't.*

"Hush!" Mama said, trying to look stern. "You're working yourself up for nothing. Jim's not going to jail and whether they get married or not is none of your business.''

Silence dropped between us, singing in my ears in that soft lonely way like crickets singing in the grass when you're all alone except for them and yourself. Finally I broke it. "Do you think—she'll really die? Maybe she wouldn't if she got married. If she was happy she'd want to keep living.''

"Maybe. Now shut your eyes and go to sleep. I'll just run up the street a bit to see if I can do anything for the poor soul, take her a little something to eat.''

She blew out the lamp and went downstairs. I could hear her moving around the kitchen. At last the front screen creaked shut and I jumped out of bed, ran to the window, and watched the pale moth look of Mama's light dress move up the path until the night swallowed it. I dressed fast, hurried down the dark stairway, out of the house, and up to Mrs. Tichenor's.

I avoided the front porch for fear I might meet Mama coming out, and slipped around the side of the house. All the blinds were up and I saw no one in the back parlor window, so I kept on around the house, past another corner, and came to an open lighted window. Through it I saw Mrs. Tichenor in a big brass bed, her face as white as the sheet drawn up to her neck. At the foot of the bed Mama and Jim Gibbs were looking at each other, Mama big-eyed and solemn, Jim's face hard.

"She says she won't sign the paper for the license," Jim was saying. "Not here, or anywhere. I've been begging her to let me bundle her up and take her to the next county. We'll get married there. But she won't! Not after that damn—"

"Jim! Please!" Mrs. Tichenor's voice was thin and raspy.

"After that damn Joe Miller hiked over to your husband—begging your pardon, Mrs. Prendergast, but Bill's a damn prig and he egged on Joe. So the pair of them got the sheriff to send his deputy right here—right in front of Melissa, serving the paper on me. Now Melissa says no wedding. Ever. Says she's brought nothing but trouble on me."

He faced Mrs. Tichenor. "God, honey, can't you see it's trouble for me if you *don't* marry me? I care about *you*, not Bill Prendergast and Joe Miller, they can burn in hell! Don't let 'em have the satisfaction of stopping our marriage."

He turned back to Mama. "I hate saying this, Mrs. Prendergast, because you're as fine a lady as I know. It's nothing to do with you except to show you what happened. But outside the house, as the deputy left here, he told me it was your husband who insisted on the warrant being served. Said he'd have no such marriage on his street. And Melissa standing at the door, hearing that!"

"Quiet down, Mr. Gibbs," Mama said softly but firmly. "We're upsetting Mrs. Tichenor. But if this will be any help to you, I want you both to know I'd consider it an honor to be your witness if this lady does decide to marry you."

Jim touched Mama's hand, just for a moment, then walked around the bed, sat on its edge, and gently held the sheet-covered shoulders. "Hear that, Melissa? Please, Melissa."

Her head moved slowly from side to side on the pillow, her profiled features like those of a marble face. They were all so quiet that I feared they would hear my breathing, so I stepped deeper into the shadows. "I need to be alone," she said finally. "I need to think—things out. By myself."

He just sat there, as though he couldn't bear to move.

"I'll let you know soon, Jim. It's—I'm so tired."

"Tomorrow? Early?"

"Soon."

He leaned down and kissed her full on the mouth, right in front of Mama. Then he followed Mama into the next room. Mrs. Tichenor called, "Jim, will you close the door?''   He turned back, went to the lamp, leaned over to blow it out. ''No, leave the light on.   I don't like the dark.''   She tried to laugh.   ''The boogeyman, you know.''

Jim gave her a sickly smile, like the way I felt.   All of a sudden I was thinking how dark being dead must be.   He went over to the bed, kissed her again, and went out.

I tiptoed back around the house, figuring it was better to leave before Mama started home.   I passed the back-parlor window, saw Mama and Jim sitting beside a marble-topped table, Mama looking sympathetic, Jim talking and rubbing his forehead as though to rid it of an ache.   Since Mama wasn't leaving yet, I turned back to Mrs. Tichenor's window.

She had thrown the sheet aside and was sitting on the side of the bed, her hand on her chest like she had to hold it together.   After a little, maybe a minute, maybe longer, she stood up and walked unsteadily to a tall chest of drawers with a mirror on its top.   As she stared into the mirror I could see her full face, see her lips moving without sound.   Her eyes closed, her head bowed, and her lips kept moving.

It made me ashamed to spy on her prayer, when it belonged just to her and God, so I moved away, swallowing tears.   At the corner of the house I stopped, held my hand over my mouth to muffle a sob, then moved on again, past the back-parlor window, and turned toward the front of the house.

I knew what it was immediately.   Guns aren't strange in Texas.   It was a shot coming from the other side of the house.

I whirled back, oblivious of the noise I made, and reached the bedroom window as Jim, then Mama, ran through the bedroom door.   Jim bent to the floor, took the whiteclad figure in his arms, his face as white as Mrs. Tichenor's gown.   ''Get Doc Williams!   Quick!'' he yelled at Mama.

But I was already on the way, screaming as I ran, ''I'll fetch him, I'll fetch him!''

The screen door slammed behind me as someone came out on the porch, but I didn't turn to see who it was.   I ran, ran, my legs weightless, seeming not a part of me.   Once I fell as my toe stubbed on a tree root, but I felt no pain.   All the time screaming.   ''Dr. Williams, Dr. Williams, Dr. Williams!''

He was already on his veranda when I reached his house and I gasped, ''Mrs. Tichenor!   She shot herself!''

He dashed inside, came out with his satchel, ran beside me, then ahead as I clutched a pain in my side and stopped to catch my breath.

But running did no good.   Because Mrs. Tichenor was dead.   Someone—the house seemed filled with people—told me so as I came in.   When I reached the bedroom, Jim was sitting on the side of the bed, holding her in his arms, rocking her back and forth as though she was a child he had to comfort.

Suddenly my father was in the bedroom too.   News travels fast in a town like ours.   A lot of people, not just neighbors, were in the room too, seeming sucked there as though disaster had created a vacuum.   My father's face was yellow-white, his eyes fierce, his thin lips drawn against his teeth.   He said, ''Mattie, get yourself and that girl out of this house!''

Jim turned, stared at my father.   Then in a swift muscular movement he lifted the frail dead body and carried it to my father.   Jim's face looked as dead as Mrs. Tichenor's—not angry, just dead.

"Take a good look, Bill," he said.   "Fill your eyes.   So you'll remember forever how she looked the night you murdered her.   I'd like to send you on your way tonight too.   But that would be sacrilege, going along with her.   I hope you live a long, long time.   So you'll have plenty of time to remember you killed my girl.   And I swear, Bill, I'm going to stick close so every time you see me you'll remember you're a murderer."

He turned back to the bed, put the limp body on it, then sat, not moving, looking at her.

My father grabbed Mama's shoulder, shoved her through the door, and jerked his head at me to follow.

The three of us walked silently through the house, out to the porch, down the path, Papa and Mama ahead, me following.

I lifted my hand, held it stiffly with finger pointed, as Mrs. Tichenor must have held her revolver.   But not aimed at me.   At my father.   Pulled an imaginary trigger, gloated as an unseen bullet pierced his head and splayed through those fierce eyes.   I imagined him falling to the ground, lying in a dreadful dark pool.   And I strode forward, stamping across a body that had no substance, whispering softly, "Murderer!   Murderer!"

Now Jim's dead too.   I buried him last week after forty years of marriage.   I suppose that's why all this comes back to mind.   Jim was a good husband.   Kind.   Treated me fine, me and our children.   But I never remember him saying he loved me.

But I remember right enough the promise he made to Papa.   Everybody said how nice it was I got me a man who was so fond of my parents.   Especially of my father.   Jim dropping in every day at the bank, spending every Sunday with Papa on the front porch while I visited with Mama, inside, or helping him garden.   Even joined the same lodge.   Then, after my father had his stroke, sitting hour after hour with him in the bedroom.   Folks never seemed to notice that Jim never talked with Papa, just looked at him, with a kind of twisted half smile on his face.

Once I almost told Jim.   About how I shot my father the night Mrs. Tichenor died.   But I figured it wouldn't have changed him.   Towards me, I mean.   I never held any grudge about it though.   I loved her too.   Besides, in a way she gave Jim to me.

JACK RITCHIE

The Seed Caper

I studied the item I'd clipped from the newspaper last week. "Regan, we are going to kidnap five hundred pounds of tomato seeds."

He looked at me. "Tomato seeds?"

I nodded. "Regan, ours is a precarious profession, is it not? We have had our hairy moments, haven't we? Remember the A & C Supermarket? Here we dash out of the store with thirty-five hundred dollars only to find that we can't get our damn car started."

The memory of it pained Regan too. "The worse lemon I ever stole. Lucky for us that truck happened to pull up next to us."

"Yes. Nevertheless, fleeing in a Grandma's Homemade Doughnuts truck still rankles as one of the more embarrassing moments of my life. And there have been other incidents, have there not? The point I'm making, Regan, is that eventually our luck will run out if we continue our present line of operations."

Regan agreed. "But still what else is there? Supermarkets are just about the best thing going for us these days."

"Listen," I said, and began reading the clipping. " 'The J. C. Swenson Seed Company announces that its experimental farm has produced a new hybrid tomato, the Red Intrepid, which it claims is completely superior to anything yet developed in the field. It is a medium-sized fleshy fruit, smooth and of bright red color, with a unique sweet flavor. It is not subject to cracking and uneven ripening at the shoulders, and is completely resistant to fusarium wilt.

" 'Mr. Swenson, president of the company, reveals that the Red Intrepid is the result of ten years of experimentation. Only five hundred pounds of Red Intrepid seeds will be available for sale this year. The Red Intrepid will be listed in the J. C. Swenson spring catalogue. The seeds are expected to sell for seventy-five cents per packet, or $5.00 per one-half ounce.' "

Regan was impressed. "That's a lot of money for half an ounce of tomato seeds."

"Exactly. And extending that, one ounce should sell for ten dollars, and one pound for one hundred and sixty dollars, and five hundred pounds for *eighty thousand dollars*. Of course, that figure is retail and does not allow for probable discounts for purchases of more than one-half of an ounce. Nevertheless, I do think that it would not be at all unreasonable if we demanded $10,000 for the return of the seeds—especially considering that they are the result of ten years of work and apparently, at the moment, the world's entire supply of the Red Intrepid.''

Regan scratched his neck.   ''If the seeds are worth so much, why kidnap? Couldn't we just plain steal?''

''There would remain the problem of converting them to cash.   We could not dispose of them in bulk—certainly all seed houses and commercial growers would be alerted—and I simply cannot picture myself sorting tiny seeds into thousands of packets and peddling them from door to door.   No, we will kidnap the seeds.''

''Wouldn't the seeds be pretty well guarded?''

I smiled.   ''Regan, who in the world would be crazy enough to kidnap tomato seeds?''

We went to our car, and I drove Regan out to a hill overlooking highway 57 and its junction with county trunk C.

I parked on the shoulder of the road.   ''There it is, Regan.   The J. C. Swenson Seed Company.   Like most seed houses, it is located in a rural area.''

Regan studied the layout.   ''There are about twenty cars parked in the lot.''

I nodded.   ''The automobiles of the employees.   However, they need not concern us.   We will strike after closing hours.   I've driven by here a number of times in the last few days and I've noticed that after five o'clock the only car down there is a battered sedan and I imagine that it belongs to the night watchman.''

''How do you know they still got the seeds?   Maybe they're sold out.''

''Yesterday I dropped into the company's office to ask for their spring catalogue. I learned that the edition had not yet been mailed to prospective customers, but I was given a copy.   And while I was there, I asked one of the office girls if I could buy a packet of Red Intrepid seeds and she informed me that the seeds were still in their bulk containers.   They had not yet been packaged.''

''All right,'' Regan said.   ''So the seeds are still there.   Now how do we work the caper?''

''Late tonight we will enter the rear of the building.   We will tie up the watchman and transfer the seeds to our car.   After we get away, we will contact Mr. J. C. Swenson and make arrangements for the transfer of $10,000 from him to us.   It is as simple as that.''

It was nearly one o'clock the next morning when Regan and I drove back to the J. C. Swenson Seed Company.   The battered sedan was the only car in the lot.

We parked and slipped on our masks.   Regan got to work on the rear door of the warehouse and in a matter of minutes we were inside.   We found ourselves among numerous stacks of bags, some of them reaching to the ceiling.

Regan whistled softly.   ''Are all of them tomato seeds?''

''I doubt it.   Probably peas and beans and corn and so on.''

The huge warehouse was dimly lit by single bulbs here and there.   Regan and I proceeded cautiously down the aisles.

We came upon a young man seated at a battered desk, eating a sandwich and poring over one of the several thick books before him.

Regan stepped forward with his drawn gun.   ''Take it easy and nobody gets hurt.''

The night watchman put down his sandwich and raised his hands.   ''You're wasting your time. The company deposits all its cash at the bank daily. The safe is empty."

"I am not interested in the safe," I said. "Lead me to your tomato seeds."

He blinked. "Why?"

"Never mind why. Just show us."

He shrugged and led us back through the aisles to another section of the building. We entered a medium-sized room containing bins, boxes, and more stacked bags.

"There they are," he said. "Tomato seeds."

"Which are the Red Intrepids?"

"I don't know, but the bags have labels."

Regan and I found the Red Intrepids after a five-minute search. The seeds were in twenty-pound cloth bags.

"You don't mind me asking what you're doing?" the watchman asked.

"Not at all," I said. "As a matter of fact, I would like you to pass the information on to Mr. Swenson. We are kidnaping the Red Intrepid seeds and we demand $10,000 for their safe return."

The night watchman stared at us for some moments. "Suppose Mr. Swenson won't pay the ten thousand dollars?"

I put menace into my chuckle. "In that case we will charter an airplane and scatter Red Intrepid seeds to the four winds. Come autumn, there will be a bootleg harvesting of field-sown Red Intrepids from one corner of this state to the other."

We utilized the services of the watchman to carry the bags out to our car. When we were through, we took the watchman back to his desk. Regan produced a rope and began tying him to a chair.

"One other thing," I said. "Swenson is not to bring the police into this. If he does, we will immediately dispose of the seeds."

I picked up the open volume on the desk. It appeared to be a textbook. "Ah," I said. "A college student? Working your way through school? What is your major?"

"Botany," he said, "with emphasis on horticulture. How will Mr. Swenson get in touch with you?"

"We will phone him sometime during the day."

"Mr. Swenson is in the hospital," the night watchman said. "I don't know which one, but he got banged up in an auto accident. Both legs broken."

I thought that over. An obstacle, but a minor one. "What is your name?"

"Ingram. Joseph Ingram."

"Are you in the telephone book?"

"No. But I live with my parents. The William Ingrams. They have a phone."

"Good enough. We will use you as our intermediary. You find Swenson and talk to him and then we'll talk to you."

Regan and I drove back to our motel and got some sleep. In the morning we explored some country back roads until we found an abandoned barn, where we unloaded our bags of seeds in a dry corner.

In the afternoon I went to a public phone booth, looked up the Ingram number, and dialed. Young Ingram answered the call.

"Have you passed on our information to Swenson?" I asked.

"Yes sir."

"Very well.   Tomorrow morning I want you to put ten thousand dollars into a plain paper bag.   You will drive the East-West freeway for approximately twenty miles and take the Amesville off-ramp.   You will deposit the package in the tall grass at the first arterial stop sign you see."

"Yes, sir.   And where will I find the seeds?"

"I'll phone you about that later.   And remember, only one of us will pick up the money.   The other will be watching from a safe distance.   If anything, *anything*, goes wrong, he will immediately dispose of the seeds.   Do you understand?"

"Yes, sir."

The next morning, Regan and I flipped a coin and I lost.

I drove our car to the pickup point and found the package.   As I drove back toward the city, I glanced frequently at my rear-view mirror, but as far as I could tell I wasn't being followed.

After a while I turned into a motel and rented a room.   I phoned Ingram and told him where to find the seeds.   Then I sat down and waited.

If the police had been watching me, they would be closing in soon.   In the event they did, I would not, of course, betray Regan to them.   And neither would he have betrayed me if he had lost the toss of the coin.

But the time passed and the police did not come.

At noon I drove to our motel and rejoined Regan.

We divided the money equally and Regan kissed his share.   "I'm going out and pick up that sports coat I saw at the shopping center."

While he was gone, I packed our suitcases.   The job seemed to have gone perfectly, but I always prefer to put distance between us and the site of the latest caper.   I thought the West Coast would be fine this time of the year.

When I finished, I made a drink and switched on the TV set.   I caught the middle of a news broadcast and soon I found a TV reporter interviewing J. C. Swenson.   I recognized him from his picture on the catalogue.   And he was standing.   On two perfectly good legs.

I frowned.

"Yes," Swenson said, "the thieves—or kidnapers—definitely knew what they were doing."

I smiled.

"Did you recover the seeds?"

"Yes," Swenson said.   "We found them in two places—an abandoned barn and under a tree in Kaminski ravine."

Under a tree?   Kaminski ravine?

"How much was the ransom money?" the reporter asked.

"$100,000."

I sat up. $100,000?

Swenson continued.   "They were extremely selective in the flower seeds they took.   Our entire stock of North Ainu Vinca.   Some seven pounds.   That particular species is on the endangered list, you know.   And all six pounds of our Bangladesh Gypsophilia.   Extremely rare.   It has the distinctive fragrance of mashed bananas.   And all eighteen ounces of our Romanian Terre-verte Dictamnus. A collector's item.   And three pounds of—''

The reporter interrupted him.   "All together, how much was stolen?''

"Some ninety-two pounds of almost irreplaceable flower seeds.''   Swenson seemed puzzled.   "They also took five hundred pounds of Red Intrepid tomato seeds.   I just can't figure that out.   So bulky, I mean.   Proportionately not nearly as valuable as its same weight in flower seeds.''

I realized that my mouth was open and closed it.

Swenson answered another of the reporter's questions.

"Well, they just burst into the warehouse, locked my night watchman in a storeroom, and kidnaped the seeds.''

Locked him in a room?   Hell, no, we had tied him to—

I closed my eyes.   I saw it all now.   We had tied Ingram to the chair.   He had, of course, managed to free himself after we left.   Perhaps in a matter of minutes.   Then that horticulture freak had loaded his car with those damn exotic seeds and taken them off to some safe hiding place.   That done, he returned to the warehouse, locked himself in a storeroom, secreted the key, and waited until the firm's employees arrived for work in the morning.

I picked up the phone and dialed Ingram.   He answered.

I had difficulty speaking.   "I respect honor among thieves, but in this case I will make an exception.   I am going to send an anonymous note to the police.''

"I wouldn't do that if I were you,'' Ingram said.   "I'll tell the police that you were my accomplice.''

"Ha,'' I said, "you don't even know my identity.''

"True,'' he said.   "But I have your fingerprints.   I would turn those over to the police.''

I sneered.   "I am very careful about where I leave my fingerprints.   The only surface I remember touching is the rear doorknob and I wiped that clean before we left.''

His voice sounded as though he were smiling.   "Do you remember picking up my botany textbook?   You left fingerprints on that loud and clear.''

I hung up and doubled the bourbon in my second drink.

Regan came back, pleased with his new sports coat.   "Yes, sir,'' he said happily. "That was the smoothest, neatest job we ever pulled.''

I stared at him.   Should I tell him?

Hell, no.

We got into our car and headed for the West Coast.

PETE HAMILL

The Men in Black Raincoats

It was close to midnight on a Friday evening at Rattigan's Bar and Grill. There were no ball games on the television, old movies only made the clientele feel more ancient, and the jukebox was still broken from the afternoon of Red Cioffi's daughter's wedding. So it was time for Brendan Malachy McCone to take center stage. He motioned for a fresh beer, put his right foot on the brass rail, breathed in deeply, and started to sing.

> *Oh, the Garden of Eden has vanished, they say,*
> *But I know the lie of it still,*
> *Just turn to the left at the bridge of Finaghy,*
> *And meet me halfway to Coote Hill . . .*

The song was very Irish, sly and funny, the choruses full of the names of long-forgotten places, and the regulars loved Brendan for the quick jaunty singing of it. They loved the roguish glitter in his eyes, his energy, his good-natured boasting. He was, after all, a man in his fifties now, and yet here he was, still singing the bold songs of his youth. And on this night, as on so many nights, they joined him in the verses.

> *The boy is a man now,*
> *He's toil-worn, he's tough,* ·
> *He whispers, "Come over the sea"*
> *Come back, Patty Reilly, to Bally James Duff,*
> *Ah, come back, Patty Reilly, to me . . .*

Outside, rain had begun to fall, a cold Brooklyn rain, driven by the wind off the harbor, and it made the noises and the singing and the laughter seem even better. Sardines and crackers joined the glasses on the bar. George the bartender filled the empties. And Brendan shifted from jauntiness to sorrow.

> *If you ever go across the sea to Ireland,*
> *Then maybe at the closing of your day . . .*

The mood of the regulars hushed now, as Brendan gave them the song as if it were a hymn.   The bar was charged with the feeling they all had for Brendan, knowing that he had been an IRA man long ago, that he had left Ireland a step ahead of the British police who wanted him for the killing of a British soldier in the Border Campaign.   This was their Brendan: the Transit Authority clerk who had once stood in the doorways of Belfast, with the cloth cap pulled tight on his brow, the pistol deep in the pockets of the trenchcoat, ready to kill or to die for Ireland.

> *Oh, the strangers came and tried to teach us their ways,*
> *And scorned us just for being what we are . . .*

The voice was a healthy baritone, a wealth of passion overwhelming a poverty of skill, and it touched all of them, making the younger ones imagine the streets of Belfast today, where their cousins were still fighting, reminding the older ones of peat fires, black creamy stout, buttermilk in the morning.   The song was about a vanished time, before rock and roll and women's liberation, before they took Latin out of the Mass, before the blacks and the Puerto Ricans had begun to move in and the children of the Irish had begun to move out.   The neighborhood was changing, all right.   But Brendan Malachy McCone was still with them, still in the neighborhood.

A little after midnight two strangers came in, dressed in black raincoats.   They were wet with rain.   They ordered whiskey.   Brendan kept singing.   Nobody noticed that his voice faltered on the last lines of *Galway Bay*, as he took the applause, glanced at the strangers, and again shifted the mood.

> *Oh, Mister Patrick McGinty,*
> *An Irishman of note,*
> *He fell into a fortune—and*
> *He bought himself a goat . . .*

The strangers drank in silence.

At closing time the rain was still pelting down.   Brendan stood in the open doorway of the bar with Charlie the Pole and Scotch Eddie, while George the bartender counted the receipts.   Everyone else had gone home.

"We'll have to make a run for it," Charlie said.

"Dammit," Scotch Eddie said.

"Yiz might as well run, cause yiz'll drown anyway," George said.   He was finished counting and looked small and tired.

"I'll see you gents," Charlie said, and rushed into the rain, running lumpily down the darkened slope of 11th Street to his home.   Eddie followed, cutting sharply to his left.   But Brendan did not move.   He had seen the strangers in the black raincoats, watched them in the mirror for a while as he moved through the songs, saw them leave an hour later.

And now he was afraid.

He looked up and down the avenue. The streetlamp scalloped a halo of light on the corner. Beyond the light there was nothing but the luminous darkness and the rain.

"Well, I've got to lock it up, Brendan."

"Right, George. Good night."

"God bless."

Brendan hurried up the street, head down, lashed by the rain, eyes searching the interiors of parked cars. He saw nothing. The cars were locked. He looked up at the apartments and there were no lights anywhere and he knew the lights would be out at home too, where Sarah and the kids would all be sleeping. Even the firehouse was dimly lit, its great red door closed, the firemen stretched out on their bunks in the upstairs loft.

Despite the drink and the rain, Brendan's mouth was dry. Once he thought he saw something move in the darkness of an areaway and his stomach lifted and fell. But again it was nothing. Shadows. Imagination. Get hold of yourself, Brendan.

He crossed the avenue. A half block to go. Away off he saw the twin red taillights of a city bus, groaning slowly toward Flatbush Avenue. Hurry. Another half block and he could enter the yard, hurry up the stairs, unlock the door, close it behind him, undress quickly in the darkened kitchen, dry off the rain with a warm rough towel, brush the beer off his teeth, and fall into the great deep warmth of bed with Sarah. And he would be safe again for another night. Hurry. Get the key out. Don't get caught naked on the stairs.

He turned into his yard, stepped over a spreading puddle at the base of the stoop, and hurried up the eight worn sandstone steps. He had the key out in the vestibule and quickly opened the inside door.

They were waiting for him in the hall.

The one in the front seat on the right was clearly the boss. The driver was only a chauffeur and did his work in proper silence. The strangers in the raincoats sat on either side of Brendan in the back seat and said nothing as te car moved through the wet darkness, down off the slope, into the Puerto Rican neighborhood near Williamsburg. They all clearly deferred to the one in the front seat right. All wore gloves. Except the boss.

"I'm telling you, this has to be some kind of mistake," Brendan said.

"Shut up," said the boss, without turning. His skin was pink in the light of the streetlamps, and dark hair curled over the edge of his collar. The accent was not New York. Maybe Boston. Maybe somewhere else. Not New York.

"I don't owe anybody money," Brendan said, choking back the dry panic. "I'm not into the bloody loan sharks. I'm telling you, this is—"

The boss said, "Is your name Brendan Malachy McCone?"

"Well, uh, yes, but—"

"Then we've made no mistake."

Williamsburg was behind them now and they were following the route of the

Brooklyn-Queens Expressway while avoiding its brightly lit ramp. Brendan sat back. From that angle he could see more of the man in the front seat right—the velvet collar of his coat, the high protruding cheekbones, the longish nose, the pinkie ring glittering on his left hand when he lit a cigarette with a thin gold lighter. He could not see the man's eyes but he was certain he had never seen the man before tonight.

"Where are you taking me?"

The boss said calmly, "I told you to shut up. Shut up."

Brendan took a deep breath, and then let it out slowly. He looked to the men on either side of him, smiling his most innocent smile, as if hoping they would think well of him, believe in his innocence, intervene with the boss, plead his case. He wanted to tell them about his kids, explain that he had done nothing bad. Not for thirty years.

The men looked away from him, their nostrils seeming to quiver, as if he had already begun to stink of death. Brendan tried to remember the words of the Act of Contrition.

The men beside him stared out past the little rivers of rain on the windows, as if he were not even in the car. They watched the city turn into country, Queens into Nassau County, all the sleeping suburbs transform into the darker emptier reaches of Suffolk County, as the driver pushed on, driving farther away, out to Long Island, to the country of forests and frozen summer beaches. Far from Brooklyn. Far from the Friday nights at Rattigan's. Far from his children. Far from Sarah.

Until they pulled off the expressway at Southampton, moved down back roads for another fifteen minutes, and came to a marshy cove. A few summer houses were sealed for the winter. Rain spattered the still water of the cove. Patches of dirty snow clung to the shoreline, resisting the steady cold rain.

"This is fine," the boss said.

The driver pulled over, turned out the car lights, and turned off the engine. They all sat in the dark.

The boss said, "Did you ever hear of a man named Peter Devlin?"

Oh, my God, Brendan thought.

"Well?"

"Vaguely. The name sounds familiar."

"Just familiar?"

"Well, there was a Devlin where I came from. There were a lot of Devlins in the North. It's hard to remember. It was a long time ago."

"Yeah, it was. It was a long time ago."

"Aye."

"And you don't remember him more than just vaguely? Well, isn't that nice? I mean, you *were* best man at his wedding."

Brendan's lips moved, but no words came out.

"What else do you vaguely remember, McCone?"

There was a long pause. Then: "He died."

"No, not *died*. He was killed, wasn't he?"

"Aye."

"Who killed him, McCone?"

"He died for Ireland."

"Who *killed* him, McCone?"

"The Special Branch. The British Special Branch."

The boss took out his cigarettes and lit one with the gold lighter. He took a long drag. Brendan saw the muscles working tensely in his jaw. The rain drummed on the roof of the car.

"Tell me some more about him."

"They buried him with full military honors. They draped his coffin with the Tricolor and sang *The Soldier's Song* over his grave. The whole town wore the Easter Lily. The B-Specials made a lot of arrests."

"You saw all this?"

"I was told."

"But you weren't there?"

"No, but—"

"What happened to his wife?"

"Katey?"

"Some people called her Katey," the boss said.

"She died too, soon after—the flu, was it?"

"Well, there was another version. That she died of a broken heart."

The boss stared straight ahead, watching the rain trickle down the windshield. He tapped an ash into the ashtray, took another deep drag, and said, "What did they pay you to set him up, Brendan?"

He called me Brendan. He's softening. Even a gunman can understand it was all long ago.

"What do you mean?"

"Don't play games, Brendan. Everyone in the North knew you set him up. The British told them."

"It was a long time ago, Mister. There were a lot of lies told. You can't believe every . . . "

The boss wasn't really listening. He took out his pack of cigarettes, flipped one higher than the others, gripped its filter in his teeth, and lit it with the butt of the other. Then he tamped out the first cigarette in the ashtray. He looked out past the rain to the darkness of the cove.

"Shoot him," he said.

The man on Brendan's left opened the door a foot.

"Oh, sweet sufferin' Jesus, Mister," Brendan said. "I've got five kids. They're all at home. One of them is making her first Communion. Please. For the love of God. If Dublin Command has told you to get me, just tell them you couldn't find me. Tell them I'm dead. I can get you a piece of paper. From one of the politicians. Sayin' I'm dead. Yes. That's a way. And I'll just vanish. Just disappear. Please. I'm an old man now, I won't live much bloody longer. But the weans. The weans, Mister. And it was all thirty years ago. Christ knows I've paid for it. Please. Please."

The tears were blurring his vision now. He could hear the hard spatter of the rain through the open car door. He felt the man on his right move slightly and remove something from inside his coat.

The boss said, "You left out a few things, Brendan."

"I can send all my earnings to the lads. God knows they can use it in the North now. I've sent money already, I have, to the Provisionals. I never stopped being for them. For a United Ireland. Never stopped. I can have the weans work for the cause. I'll get a second job. My Sarah can go out and work too. Please, Mister. Jesus, Mister . . ."

"Katey Devlin didn't die of the flu," the boss said. "And she didn't die of a broken heart. Did she, Brendan?"

"I don't—"

"Katey Devlin killed herself. Didn't she?"

Brendan felt his stomach turn over.

The boss said, very quietly, "She loved Peter Devlin more than life itself. She didn't want him to die."

"But neither does Sarah want *me* to die. She's got the weans, the feedin' of them, and the clothin' of them, and the schoolin' of them to think of. Good God, man, have ye no mercy? I was a boy then. My own people were starvin'. We had no land, we were renters, we were city people, not farmers, and the war was on, and . . . They told me they would only arrest him. Intern him for the duration and let him out when the fightin' stopped, and they told me the IRA would take care of Kate while he was inside. Please, Mister, I've got five kids. Peter Devlin only had *two*."

"I know," said the man in the front seat right. "I was one of them."

For the first time he turned completely around. His eyes were a cold blue under the shock of curly dark hair. Kate's eyes in Peter's face. He stared at Brendan for a moment. He took another drag on the cigarette and let the smoke drift through his nose, creating lazy trails of gray in the crowded car.

"Shoot him," he said.

The man on his left touched Brendan's hand and opened the door wide.

Dead Ringer

Detective:
ELLERY QUEEN

The hush-hush man's name was Storke, and Ellery had once before worked with him on a case involving the security of the United States. So when Storke showed up out of nowhere and said, "Scene of the crime first, the rundown later," Ellery dropped what he was doing and reached for his hat without a question.

Storke drove him downtown, chatting pleasantly, parked on one of the meandering side streets below Park Row in a space that was magically unoccupied, and strolled Ellery over to a thin shop-front with a dusty window bearing the crabbed legend: *M. Merrilees Monk, Tobacconist, Est. 1897.*

Two young men who looked like Wall Street clerks on their dinner hour lounged outside, puffing on pipes. There was no sign of a police uniform.

"This must be a big one," murmured Ellery; and he preceded Storke into the shop.

It was as aged-looking inside as out, narrow and poorly lighted, with walls of some musty dark wood, Victorian fixtures, and a gas-jet for lighting cigarettes and cigars. Everything was pungent with tobacco.

In the deeps of the little shop, near the curtained doorway to a rear room, stood a venerable wooden Indian, his original splendor bedraggled to a sprinkle of color here and there; most of him was naked pitted wood.

The Indian appeared forlorn, whereas the dead man who lay jammed between the counter and the shelves looked outraged, for he had suffered cruelly at the hands not of time but of an assassin. His head and face resembled a jellied mash.

Curiously, his dead arms embraced a large squarish canister apparently used for the storage of pipe tobacco, for it was labeled MIX C and obviously came from a row of similar canisters on one of the upper shelves behind the cluttered counter.

"He was attacked from behind at this point," Ellery said to Storke, indicating a stiffening puddle at the feet of the wooden Indian, "probably as he was going into the back room for something. The killer must have left him for dead; but he wasn't dead, because this blood trail goes from the Indian all the way around and behind the counter to where he's lying now.

"The picture is unmistakable: When the killer left, this man somehow—don't ask me how!—managed to drag himself to that particular spot, and in spite of his frightful injuries reached up to that tobacco can and took it down from that empty space on the shelf before he died."

"That's the way I read it, too," said Storke.

"May I handle the canister?"

"Everything's been processed."

Ellery took the canister from the dead man, who seemed disposed to resist, and pried off the lid. The canister was empty. He borrowed a powerful magnifier from the hush-hush man. After a moment he put the lens down.

"This canister never contained tobacco, Storke. Not a shred or speck is visible under the glass, even at the seams."

Storke said nothing; and Ellery turned to the shelves. Nine canisters remained on the shelf from which the dead man had taken the MIX C can. They were labeled MONK'S SPECIAL, BARTLEBY MIXTURE, SUPERBA BLEND, MIX A, MIX B (and here was the space where the MIX C can must have stood), KENTUCKY LONG CUT, VIRGINIA CRIMP, LORD CAVENDISH, and MANHATTAN MIX.

"Those nine are *not* empty," said Storke, reading Ellery's mind. "Each contains what it's labeled."

Ellery squatted by the corpse. It was enveloped in a knee-length tobacconist's gown in the British fashion—a rather surprisingly muscular body of a man in his early forties with what must once have been a sandy-fringed bald pate and sharp Anglican features.

"This, I take it, was M. Merrilees Monk," Ellery said. "Or his lineal descendant."

"Wrong on both counts," Storke replied bitterly. "He was one of our topflight operatives, and don't mention him in the same breath with Monk. As far as we know, Monk's grandfather and father were respectable tobacconists, but the incumbent is a turncoat who ran this shop as a drop for foreign agents to pick up and pass along messages, stolen material, and so on.

"We got onto Monk only recently. We put the shop under round-the-clock surveillance, but we weren't able to spot any known enemy agent entering or leaving.

"Then we got what we thought was a break. One of our Seattle men, Hartman, turned out to be a dead ringer for this Monk rat. So we brought Hartman on from the Coast, put him through an intensive training course on Monk, then took Monk into custody in the middle of one night, substituted Hartman, and called off our outside men to leave Hartman a clear field in the shop. He knew the risk he was running."

"And it caught up with him. Dead ringer is right." Ellery brooded over the battered U.S. agent's remains. "How long had he been playing the part of Monk?"

"Fifteen days. And no one turned up, Hartman was positive. He spent his spare time in the stockroom out back, microfilming the shop's ledger, which lists the names of hundreds of Monk's customers, each with an account number and address. Good thing he did, too, because the killer's made off with the ledger.

"Just this morning," Storke went on somberly, "Hartman phoned in that he'd found out two of the listed customers were foreign agents—exactly how we'll probably never know, because he didn't get a chance to explain. A customer walked in at that moment and he had to hang up. By the time we felt it safe to make contact with him tonight, he'd been murdered. One or both of the agents must have paid a visit to the shop as Hartman was closing up and spotted him as a ringer."

"They probably had a signal Hartman missed." Ellery stared at the empty tobacco canister. "Storke, why have you called me in on this?"

"You're looking at the reason."

"The MIX C can? It was almost certainly Monk's repository for whatever was delivered to him to be passed along. But if it contained any spy material at the time Hartman was assaulted, Storke, his killer or killers took it and blew."

"Exactly," said the hush-hush man. "That means Hartman made that super-human effort in order to take down an *empty* can. Why was his last act to call our attention to the can?"

"Obviously he was trying to tell you something."

"Of course," said Storke impatiently. "But what? That's what we can't figure out, Ellery, and that's why I called you in. Any notions?"

"Yes," said Ellery. "He was telling you who the foreign agents are."

Storke was not given to displays of emotion, but on this occasion astonishment slackened his jaw and widened his shrewd eyes.

"Well, he hasn't told me a damned thing," the hush-hush man growled. "Now I suppose you'll say he's told you?"

"Well," said Ellery, "yes."

"Told you *what?*"

"Who the two foreign agents are."

CHALLENGE TO THE READER

*How did Ellery know the identity of
the two foreign agents?*

Ellery explained to Storke: "Two of the facts you gave me were: first, that the foreign agents are listed in Monk's customer ledger; second, that each customer's name in the ledger is assigned an account number.

"Hartman made his extraordinary dying effort to call your attention to the otherwise empty can labeled MIX C. MIX C—two word-elements. And there are two agents. This could be a coincidence, but it could also mean that each of the word-elements identifies one of the agents.

"Pursuing this theory, I noticed something unusual about the letters composing the words MIX C that is not true about any of the phrases on the nine other labels on the shelf: *every letter in MIX C is also a Roman numeral.*

"You take MIX. M equals 1000; IX equals 10 minus 1, or 9. MIX therefore becomes the Roman numerology for 1009. I'm sure you will find, Storke, that the customer's name listed in the ledger microfilms opposite Number 1009 is that of one of the two foreign agents.

"C is simply the Roman numeral for 100, and I think you'll find Number 100 in the ledger is the name of the other agent."

Under the Skin

In the opulent lobby lounge of the St. Francis Hotel, where he and Tom Olivet had gone for a drink after the A.C.T. dramatic production was over, Walter Carpenter sipped his second Scotch-and-water and thought that he was a pretty lucky man.   Good job, happy marriage, kids of whom he could be proud, and a best friend who had a similar temperament, similar attitudes, aspirations, likes and dislikes.   Most people went through life claiming lots of casual friends and a few close ones, but seldom did a perfectly compatible relationship develop as it had between Tom and him.   He knew brothers who were not nearly as close.   Walter smiled.   That's just what the two of us are like, he thought.   Brothers.

Across the table Tom said, "Why the sudden smile?"

"Oh, just thinking that we're a hell of a team," Walter said.

"Sure," Tom said.   "Carpenter and Olivet, the Gold Dust Twins."

Walter laughed.   "No, I mean it.   Did you ever stop to think how few friends get along as well as we do?   I mean, we like to do the same things, go to the same places.   The play tonight, for example.   I couldn't get Cynthia to go, but as soon as I mentioned it to you, you were all set for it."

"Well, we've known each other for twenty years," Tom said.   "Two people spend as much time together as we have, they get to thinking alike and acting alike. I guess we're one head on just about everything, all right."

"A couple of carbon copies," Walter said.   "Here's to friendship."

They raised their glasses and drank and when Walter put his down on the table he noticed the hands on his wristwatch.   "Hey," he said.   "It's almost eleven thirty.   We'd better hustle if we're going to catch the train.   Last one for Daly City leaves at midnight."

"Right," Tom said.

They split the check down the middle, then left the hotel and walked down Powell Street to the Bay Area Rapid Transit station at Market.   Ordinarily one of them would have driven in that morning from the Monterey Heights area where they lived two blocks apart; but Tom's car was in the garage for minor repairs, and Walter's wife Cynthia had needed their car for errands.   So they had ridden a BART train in, and after work they'd had dinner in a restaurant near Union Square before going on to the play.

Inside the Powell station Walter called Cynthia from a pay phone and told her they were taking the next train out; she said she would pick them up at Glen Park. Then he and Tom rode the escalator down to the train platform.   Some twenty people stood or sat there waiting for trains, half a dozen of them drunks and other unsavory-looking types.   Subway crime had not been much of a problem since BART, which connected several San Francisco points with a number of East Bay cities, opened two years earlier.   Still, there were isolated incidents.   Walter began to feel vaguely nervous; it was the first time he had gone anywhere this late by train.

The nervousness eased when a westbound pulled in almost immediately and none of the unsavory-looking types followed them into a nearly empty car.   They sat together, Walter next to the window.   Once the train had pulled out he could see their reflections in the window glass.   Hell, he thought, the two of us even *looked* alike sometimes.   Carbon copies, for a fact.   Brothers of the spirit.

A young man in workman's garb got off at the 24th and Mission stop, leaving them alone in the car.   Walter's ears popped as the train picked up speed for the run to Glen Park.   He said, "These new babies really move, don't they?"

"That's for sure," Tom said.

"You ever ride a fast-express passenger train?"

"No," Tom said.   "You?"

"No.   Say, you know what would be fun?"

"What?"

"Taking a train trip across Canada," Walter said.   "They've still got these crack expresses up there—they run across the whole of Canada from Vancouver to Montreal."

"Yeah, I've heard about those," Tom said.

"Maybe we could take the families up there and ride one of them next summer," Walter said.   "You know, fly to Vancouver and then fly home from Montreal."

"Sounds great to me."

"Think the wives would go for it?"

"I don't see why not."

For a couple of minutes the tunnel lights flashed by in a yellow blur; then the train began to slow and the globes steadied into a widening chain.   When they slid out of the tunnel into the Glen Park station, Tom stood up and Walter followed him to the doors.   They stepped out.   No one was waiting to get on, and the doors hissed closed again almost immediately.   The westbound rumbled ahead into the tunnel that led to Daly City.

The platform was empty except for a man in an overcoat and a baseball cap lounging against the tiled wall that sided the escalators; Walter and Tom had been the only passengers to get off.   The nearest of the two electronic clock-and-message boards suspended above the platform read 12:02.

The sound of the train faded into silence as they walked toward the escalators, and their steps echoed hollowly.   Midnight-empty this way, the fluorescent-lit station had an eerie quality.   Walter felt the faint uneasiness return and impulsively quickened his pace.

They were ten yards from the escalators when the man in the overcoat moved away from the wall and came toward them.   He had the collar pulled up around his face and his chin tucked down into it; the bill of the baseball cap hid his forehead, so that his features were shadowy.   His right hand was inside a coat pocket.

The hair prickled on Walter's neck, and he glanced at Tom to keep from staring at the approaching man, but Tom did not seem to have noticed him at all.

Just before they reached the escalators the man in the overcoat stepped across in front of them, blocking their way, and planted his feet.   They pulled up short. Tom said, "Hey," and Walter thought in sudden alarm: Oh, my God!

The man took his hand out of his pocket and showed them the long thin blade of a knife.   "Wallets," he said flatly.   "Hurry it up, don't make me use this."

Walter's breath seemed to clog in his lungs; he tasted the brassiness of fear. There was a moment of tense inactivity, the three of them as motionless as wax statues in a museum exhibit.   Then, jerkily, his hand trembling, Walter reached into his jacket pocket and fumbled his wallet out.

But Tom just stood staring, first at the knife and then at the man's shadowed face.   He did not seem to be afraid.   His lips were pinched instead with anger. "A damned mugger," he said.

Walter said, "Tom, for God's sake!" and extended his wallet.   The man grabbed it out of his hand, shoved it into the other slash pocket.   He moved the knife slightly in front of Tom.

"Get it out," he said.

"No," Tom said, "I'll be damned if I will."

Walter knew then, instantly, what was going to happen next.   Close as the two of them were, he was sensitive to Tom's moods.   He opened his mouth to shout at him, tell him not to do it; he tried to make himself grab onto Tom and stop him physically.   But the muscles in his body seemed paralyzed.

Then it was too late.   Tom struck the man's wrist, knocked it and the knife to one side, and lunged forward.

Walter stood there, unable to move, and watched the mugger sidestep awkwardly, pulling the knife back.   The coat collar fell away, the baseball cap flew off as Tom's fist grazed the side of the man's head—and Walter could see the mugger's face clearly: beard-stubbled, jutting chin, flattened nose, wild blazing eyes.

The knife, glinting light from the overhead fluorescents, flashed between the mugger and Tom, and Tom stiffened and made a grunting, gasping noise.   Walter looked on in horror as the man stepped back with the knife, blood on the blade now, blood on his hand.   Tom turned and clutched at his stomach, eyes glazing, and then his knees buckled and he toppled over and lay still.

He killed him, Walter thought, he killed Tom—but he did not feel anything yet. Shock had given the whole thing a terrible dreamlike aspect.   The mugger turned toward him, looked at him out of those burning eyes.   Walter wanted to run, but there was nowhere to go with the tracks on both sides of the platform, the electrified rails down there, and the mugger blocking the escalators.   And he could not make himself move now any more than he had been able to move when he realized Tom intended to fight.

The man in the overcoat took a step toward him, and in that moment, from inside the eastbound tunnel, there was the faint rumble of an approaching train.   The suspended message board flashed CONCORD, and the mugger looked up there, looked back at Walter.   The eyes burned into him an instant longer, holding him transfixed.   Then the man turned sharply, scooped up his baseball cap, and ran up the escalator.

Seconds later he was gone, and the train was there instead, filling the station with a rush of sound that Walter could barely hear for the thunder of his heart.

The policeman was a short thickset man with a black mustache, and when Walter finished speaking he looked up gravely from his notebook.   "And that's everything that happened, Mr. Carpenter?"

"Yes," Walter said, "that's everything."

He was sitting on one of the round tile-and-concrete benches in the center of the platform.   He had been sitting there ever since it happened.   When the eastbound train had braked to a halt, one of its disembarking passengers had been a BART security officer.   One train too late, Walter remembered thinking dully at the time; he's one train too late.   The security officer had asked a couple of terse questions, then had draped his coat over Tom and gone upstairs to call the police.

"What can you tell me about the man who did it?" the policeman asked. "Can you give me a description of him?"

Walter's eyes were wet; he took out his handkerchief and wiped them, shielding his face with the cloth, then closing his eyes behind it.   When he did that he could see the face of the mugger: the stubbled cheeks, the jutting chin, the flat nose— and the eyes, above all those terribly malignant eyes that had said as clearly as though the man had spoken the words aloud: *I've got your wallet, I know where you live.   If you say anything to the cops I'll come after you and give you what I gave your friend.*

Walter shuddered, opened his eyes, lowered the handkerchief, and looked over to where the group of police and laboratory personnel were working around the body.   Tom Olivet's body.   Tom Olivet, lying there dead.

We were like brothers, Walter thought.   We were just like brothers.

"I can't tell you anything about the mugger," he said to the policeman.   "I didn't get a good look at him.   I can't tell you anything at all."